D0057493

Three Heroes

Jo Beverley

The Demon's Mistress
The Dragon's Bride
The Devil's Heiress

NEW AMERICAN LIBRARY

New American Library
Published by New American Library, a division of
Penguin Group (USA) Inc., 375 Hudson Street,
New York, New York 10014, U.S.A.
Penguin Books Ltd, 80 Strand,
London WC2R 0RL, England
Penguin Books Australia Ltd, 250 Camberwell Road,
Camberwell, Victoria 3124, Australia
Penguin Books Canada Ltd, 10 Alcorn Avenue,
Toronto, Ontario, Canada M4V 3B2
Penguin Books (NZ) cnr Rosedale and Airborne Roads,
Albany, Auckland 1310, New Zealand

Penguin Books Ltd, Registered Offices:
80 Strand, London WC2R 0RL, England

First published by New American Library,
a division of Penguin Group (USA) Inc.

First Printing, June 2004
10 9 8 7 6 5 4 3 2 1

 REGISTERED TRADEMARK—MARCA REGISTRADA

LIBRARY OF CONGRESS CATALOGING-IN-PUBLICATION DATA:

Beverley, Jo.
  Three heroes / Jo Beverley.
    p. cm.
  Contents: The demon's mistress—The dragon's mistress—The devil's heiress.
  ISBN 0-451-21200-2
    1. England—Fiction. 2. Love stories, Canadian. 3. Historical fiction, Canadian. I. Title.

PR9199.3.B424A6 2004
813'.54—dc22   2003070636

Set in Cochin
Designed by Ginger Legato

Printed in the United States of America

Dear Reader,

Welcome to *Three Heroes*.

I'm so pleased that my publisher has brought together these stories about three friends who are as close as brothers, but who are separated by the suffering of war. As I began to think about these men, I became absorbed by the effects of war on those who survive without serious wounds. I was also focused on what home means to people, especially those who have been away for a long time. And of course, as each man's love story is told in this book, home takes on a new meaning with a special woman to help him build it anew, and hopes for future generations. The stories are also about friendship, courage, and the capacity to trust and love, even after betrayals. In other words, about heroism in ordinary life as well as in military action.

I hope you enjoy *Three Heroes* and will want to read more about Nicholas, Lucien, and the rest of the Rogues. The Rogues appear in the following books: *An Arranged Marriage* (Nicholas and Eleanor); *An Unwilling Bride* (Lucien and Beth); *Christmas Angel* (Leander and Judith), *Forbidden* (Francis and Serena); *Dangerous Joy* (Miles and Felicity); and the newest Rogue story, *Skylark* (Stephen and Laura.). They are all still available except *Dangerous Joy*, which will be reissued in December 2004.

I recently explored the subject of heroes in a different way in a novella in a science fiction romance collection called *Irresistible Forces* (February 2004) as you can tell from the title, "The Trouble With Heroes". . . .

You can find a list of all my books at www.jobev.com/booklist.html. Or you can receive one by writing to me, care of the Rotrosen Agency, 318 East 51st Street, New York, NY 10022. I enjoy hearing from readers. You can e-mail me at jo@jobev.com, or write to me at the above address. May there always be heroes—male and female

Jo Beverley

Chapter One

Glorious spring sunshine beamed through the open curtains, and the raised window let in courting birdsong. Nearby, people chattered amid their busy lives, and wheels rattled as a horse and cart hurried down the back lane.

The golden light danced on the disheveled hair and ravaged classic features of a young man lolling in the faded armchair beside the window. It glinted off half-lowered lashes and golden stubble that suggested a night without sleep or orderly waking, and dug deep into a jagged scar down one cheek that told of more dangerous adventures in the past.

His legs, in breeches and well-worn boots, stretched before him, and a half-full wineglass tilted in his lax, long-fingered hand.

On a round table by his elbow stood a decanter with an inch or so of pale amber wine, and a plain, practical pistol.

He raised the glass and sipped, seeming intent on the garden outside the window, but in fact Lord Vandeimen's gaze was directed at nothing close or visible. He looked at the past, both recent and far, and with increasing, slightly fretful curiosity, at the future.

Switching the glass to his left hand, he placed two fingers on the cold metal of the pistol barrel. His father's pistol, used for the same purpose nearly a year before.

So easy.

So quick.

So why was he waiting?

Hamlet had had something to say about that.

In his case, he decided, he was pausing to enjoy this particularly fine wine.

After all, he'd spent nearly all his last coins on it. He must be careful not to drift away under its influence and waste this moment of resolution. One bottle hadn't put him under the table since he was a lad, though.

So long ago, those days of wicked youthful adventures. Was it really less than ten years since he'd been a carefree youth, running wild on the Sussex Downs with Con and Hawk?

No, not carefree. Even children and youths have cares. But blessedly free of the weightier burdens of life.

The three Georges. The triumvirate.

His drifting mind settled on the day they'd tired of having the same patriotic name and rechristened themselves. Hawk Hawkinville. Van Vandeimen. It should have been Somer Somerford, but Con had balked at such a effete name. He'd taken a variation of his second name, Connaught. Con.

Con, Hawk, and Van. They'd grown up like brothers, almost like triplets. Back in those days they'd not imagined a time when they'd be so apart, but Van was glad the other two weren't here now, With luck, they'd hear of his death when it was history, the pain of it numbed. They hadn't seen each other since Waterloo.

Con had returned home directly after the battle, but Hawk and Van had lingered awhile. Hawk was still with the army now, tidying up Europe. Van had been in England for four months, but he'd carefully avoided his home and old friends.

He drained the glass and refilled it, his hand reassuringly steady. It was strange that Con hadn't hunted him down. Any other time, that would have worried him, but not now. If Con didn't care, that was good.

No friends. No family.

Once, in another life, there had been so much more. When he'd left at sixteen to join his regiment, mother, father, and two sisters had waved farewell. Ten years later, all were shades. Did they watch him now? If so, what did their ghostly voices cry? Wouldn't they want him to join them?

"Don't protest to me, old man," he said to his ghostly father. "You took the same way out when you were left alone. And what have I—? Oh, devil take it!" he snapped, slamming down the glass and seizing the pistol. "When I start talking to ghosts, it's time."

Impelled by some mythical urge, he picked up the glass and poured the remaining wine to stream and puddle on the waxed floor. "An offering to the gods," he said. "May they be merciful."

Then he put the long barrel cold into his mouth and with a final breath and a prayer squeezed the trigger.

The click was loud, but a click didn't kill. He pulled the gun out and stared at it with wild exasperation. A flick showed him the problem. The flint of the old-fashioned pistol had worn and slipped sideways.

"Shoddy work, Van," he muttered, desperately trying to think whether he had a fresh flint anywhere in his rooms, his hands trembling now. If he had to go out and find one, the moment might pass. He might try again to pull his life out of the pit.

He knew he didn't have a fresh flint, so he poked out the old one, sweat chilling his brow and his nape, and tried to fix it so it would work. He'd drunk enough to make himself clumsy. "Plague and tarnation, and hell, and damnation, and—"

"*Stop!*"

He looked up, dazed, to see a figure standing in his doorway, draped in white, crowned in white, hand outstretched, looking like a stern Byzantine angel . . .

Smooth oval face, long nose, firm lips.

A woman.

She swept forward to grip the pistol barrel. "You must not!"

He kept a hand tight on the butt. "What the devil business is it of yours, madam?"

An elegant woman in high fashion, including a turban-style hat with a tall feather. Where the pox had she come from, and what business was he of hers?

Her steady eyes held his. "I need you, Lord Vandeimen. You can kill yourself later."

He dragged the pistol out of her gloved hands. "I can kill myself anytime I damn well please, and take you with me!"

She straightened, looking down her long nose. "Not with only one pistol ball."

"There are many ways of killing, and I'll save the pistol for myself."

He saw her pale and suck in breath, but when she spoke it was steadily. "Give me a few minutes of your time, my lord. Then, on my word, if you still wish it, I will leave you to your purpose."

Such scorn. Such judgment in those blue-gray eyes. If the pistol had been working, he might have shot her to wipe away that scorn. He immediately put the weapon down.

She snatched it and retreated a few wise steps, pistol clutched to her creamy gown. Then she looked down at it, shuddered, and placed it on his open desk by the papers he'd carefully prepared.

Curiosity suddenly wiped out anger and urgency.

This woman knew him, but he had no idea who she was. Not surprising, since he hadn't been moving in fashionable circles.

Her gown was in the height of fashion, as was the long, pale cashmere shawl that looped over both elbows and almost trailed the ground. He knew enough of women's furbelows to price that shawl at a sum that would reroof Steynings.

It wouldn't fix the damaged plaster or the rotting wood, but the roof would be a start.

"Well?" he asked, linking his hands, ready to enjoy this interlude at the gates of hell.

She subsided into the chair that matched his, then jumped when it sagged down beneath her.

"It hasn't collapsed under anyone yet," he remarked. "Am I to know your name, or is this all cloaked in hoary mystery?"

Color blossomed in her creamy skin, making her look less like a plaster saint, and much more interesting in a fleshy way. He suddenly wondered what she'd look like far gone in sex, which was another thought he'd not expected to have again.

"My name is Maria Celestin."

His brows rose. The Golden Lily. The wealthy widow who had just emerged from mourning, causing every red-blooded fortune hunter to seethe with desire. Someone had suggested that he pursue the woman as the solution to his woes.

She'd have to be insane to marry him, however, and he'd no mind to marry a madwoman.

He knew the age of the Golden Lily. Thirty-three. That explained her composure and steady eyes. He knew her bloodlines. She'd been born a Dunpott-Ffyfe and married down to some upstart foreign merchant.

"And your purpose here, Mrs. Celestin? If you are seeking consolation of the flesh, I regret that I am neither in the mood nor the state to oblige."

"Then it is as well that I am not, my lord."

She didn't blush. Perhaps she'd heard the same too often. Distressing to be cliché.

She too had linked her hands in front of her, and now she'd grown accustomed to the chair she was trying to be elegant and composed. She wasn't, though. She was wound tight as a watch spring like a raw recruit on the brink of battle.

Gad, he hoped she wasn't here to fight for his immortal soul.

"You lost ten thousand at Brooks' last night, my lord."

It stung, but he hoped that didn't show. "And how did you find out about that, Mrs. Celestin?"

"There were many people there. Word is out. You cannot possibly pay."

He looked down at his hands before gathering enough will to meet her eyes coolly. "My estates, decrepit though they are, will probably settle the bill."

"I will pay that debt in return for your services for six weeks."

He hadn't expected to feel shock again. "You *do* want consolation of the flesh."

Now she did blush, though her tone was chilly. "It seems an obsession of yours, my lord. Unfortunately for you, I am not at all interested." She even dared to look him over, briefly, with patent lack of interest. "What I require is an escort and a bodyguard."

"Hire a dragoon, madam."

He began to rise, ready to throw her out, but something in her steady gaze pushed him back into his chair. Whatever this was about, she was deadly serious.

"A dragoon would not serve, my lord. To be precise, I wish you to pose as my affianced husband for the next six weeks, in payment for which I will give you ten thousand pounds. What is more, if you fulfill our agreement to the letter, I will give you a further ten thousand pounds at the end. You can drink it, game it, or use it to rescue your estates. That will be up to you."

The little beat of excitement that started in his chest was a betrayal. He was as good as dead, dammit. He didn't want this now.

He was lying.

It was the chance, the new beginning he'd been hunting for months. He wouldn't show hope or excitement. He wouldn't reveal his need to this mad-woman.

"Tempting," he drawled. "I have learned, however, that if a bargain appears too good to be true, it probably is."

Her neatly arched brows rose. "What trap do you foresee? That I hold you to our mock betrothal? Do you object to marrying a fortune?"

"Not at all. Why don't we simplify everything by marrying now?"

"Because you drink too much, and game too wildly, and, it would seem, choose the easy way out."

He knew he was turning red. "I see. So, what benefit do you find in your strange arrangement that is worth twenty thousand pounds?"

She rose with admirable smoothness, rearranging her fabulous shawl so it didn't drag on the floor. He was suddenly aware of full breasts and round hips beneath the elegant vertical flow of her ivory gown. Inappropriate for an almost-dead man to note such things but she was, in a chilly way, a very attractive woman.

"My purposes are none of your concern, my lord," she said in a voice one might use to a greengrocer. "I merely require you to engage yourself to marry me, and to act for the next six weeks as if that were true. This does mean," she added pointedly, "that you will have to act like a man I might wish to marry."

"Ah," he said, belatedly rising. The room wavered slightly, and he hadn't drunk enough for that. He wondered if the pistol had worked, if this was some heavenly illusion.

"What dreams may come. . . ."

The smell of spilled wine soured the air, however. Surely heaven could do better than that. "You will expect me to resist excessive drink and gaming, madam? Gad, will I have to squire you to Almack's? They'd never let me in."

"Almack's is boring. Balls, routs, breakfasts, masquerades . . ." She gestured vaguely with a hand covered by fine cream kid in color remarkably like her fine cream skin. "I will require you to escort me to most events I attend, to stay by my side for the usual amount of time, and to be well mannered and sober. When not by my side, you will do nothing to shame my choice."

"Alas. I must avoid my favorite opium dens and wild wenches?"

"You must avoid anyone hearing about them." She looked him in the eye, despite being six inches shorter. "You are in love with me, Lord Vandeimen. For six weeks, and a payment of twenty thousand pounds, in the eyes of the world, you adore me."

"Do I get to kiss you, then?" he asked, advancing on her, suddenly furious at this demanding woman who thought she could buy him, body and soul.

And probably could.

He found himself looking down the barrel of his pistol, held in her steady, but tense, hands. "You will never, ever, touch me without my permission."

He smiled at the pointless threat. "Why not pull the trigger?" he drawled. "That will achieve my end, and save me from the sin of self-destruction."

Her eyes widened, and for the first time he saw overt fear. She'd put herself in a situation she didn't understand and couldn't control, and had the wit to know it.

It was about time she learned some other lessons.

Glancing to one side to distract her, he snatched the pistol. She gasped and stepped back, pale becoming pallid.

He was tempted to seize her, press the useless pistol to her lush breasts, and claim the kiss he'd threatened. Disgusted by that, he snapped, "Leave."

She looked at him, breathing rapidly. "You are rejecting my offer?"

He wanted to say yes, but the same impulse that had sent him to the tables ruled him here. "No. You've bought six weeks of my life, Mrs. Celestin. I accept your terms. However, I'll need an advance on the second ten thousand if I'm to put on a show worthy of you. I am literally penniless."

Now that she had what she wanted, she attempted her former manner, but she couldn't hide her fear. Not a foolish woman, at least.

"I'll deposit eleven thousand for you at Perry's Bank," she said, a touch of panic fluttering in her voice. "One thousand is advance on our final settlement. Arrange your affairs, my lord, and have a night's rest. We can meet formally tomorrow at the Duchess of Yeovil's ball. Do you have an invitation?"

He glanced at the messy pile of cards and envelopes on the desk. "Probably. Even a ruined lord is a lord."

She too looked at the pile, lips suddenly pursing. What was it? A powerful urge to organize? Was she a meddlesome, managing woman? He almost set limits on their bargain, especially that she keep her fingers out of his affairs, but why fool himself? He'd come this far and would go further if necessary.

He'd sell himself to her in any way she wanted for nine thousand clear and a fresh start. She didn't need to know that, however.

"Is that all, Mrs. Celestin?" he asked in a bored tone, pistol still in his hand.

She jerked slightly, nodded, and after a hesitation where she clearly felt there was more to be said, walking rapidly out of the room.

Maria paused for a moment on the landing, a faint shudder passing through her. Athena, but she'd almost been too late. A few more seconds . . . ! And then she'd pointed his pistol at him, threatening to kill him.

She pressed a gloved hand to her mouth. Was anything more absurd? She'd never held a pistol before in her life, and then he'd dared her to kill him as if he wanted it! He was so young, so full of promise. Was self-destruction too deeply rooted to be pulled out?

Then he'd taken the weapon from her. So easily. She should have expected that from a man known as Demon Vandeimen. She should have expected that uncivilized edge anyway. He'd survived a long and bloody war. Of course he wasn't safe!

She hurried out of the house. Her liveried footman leaped forward to open the carriage door and assist her in to sit beside her aunt.

Harriette Coombs, round in face and body, was merry by nature, but knew when to worry. Like Maria, she was a widow, but she had enjoyed thirty years of happy marriage instead of ten years of mixed blessings. She had three children set up in the world, whereas Maria had none.

Maria sometimes felt that except for wealth, she had nothing. No, not true. She had Aunt Harriette.

"Home," she said, and as soon as the footman shut the door, the coach began to roll away from the most difficult thing she had done in her life.

"Well?" asked Harriette.

"I was almost too late! He was . . . No one answered the door. Some instinct made me enter anyway, and he was . . . He had a pistol in his hand, ready to fire!"

"By my soul! You promised him the money, dear? He will be different now?"

"I did, but—" It had all been done in urgency and on impulse, and now reaction was setting in.

"He looked so terrible, Harriette. Haggard. Clothes all awry. The room stank of wine and he was drunk. I was going to pretend the money was an old informal debt, but I knew I couldn't do that. He'd probably have gamed it away tomorrow!"

"So what did you do?"

Maria bit her lip, unwilling to even put her ridiculous plan into words. "I . . . I bought him. For six weeks. For six weeks, Lord Vandeimen is to be my besotted, impeccably behaved, husband-to-be and escort."

Harriette's eyes widened, but she said, "Very clever, dear! If he has any honor at all, he will have to behave well, and it may give him a chance to change."

"Will it work?"

Harriette patted her hand. "You've done the best you can, dear. It will expose you to talk, though."

"Oh! I'll look like—"

"A widow after tender meat."

"A tender wastrel, even. People will think me a complete fool. Or a predatory harpy. Harriette, he's eight years younger than I am!"

"I was eight years younger than Cedric."

"It's not the same." Maria sucked in a deep breath. "I have to do it, though. Maurice swindled his father out of that money. Ruined him, and pushed him to suicide. I have to put it right, at any cost."

She leaned her head back against the satin squabs. "Did I mention that he is beautiful? Hair the color of primroses. Classic bones. Lips so perfect they could have been carved. A mess, of course, after the wild life he's led recently, and scarred. But still, Lord Vandeimen is the most beautiful young man I ever stood face to face with."

And the world would think her turned idiot because of it.

Harriette squeezed her hand. "Don't worry, dear. While you're pulling him back from the brink, I'll look around for a suitable young lady for him, one with a strength of character and a generous dowry."

Maria smiled. "Thank you. I don't know what I'd do without you."

She firmly ignored a betraying stir of dissatisfaction with that plan.

Chapter Two

Van woke when the clock persistently chimed. Damn it, he'd drifted into a daze or a doze. He sank his head into his hands. Wine and a sleepless night had given him a tantalizing dream. Twenty thousand pounds. If only it were true.

He suddenly looked around the room. Had it been a dream?

His pistol still lay on the table, but then, he'd taken it from her and put it there. She hadn't conveniently left her shawl, or a glass slipper.

The Golden Lily. Could his imagination really have conjured up a flesh-and-blood woman of such distinctive appearance? That long, sleekly curved elegance and smooth oval face. That creamy skin which flushed so delicately when another woman would have been beet red, and gone waxy with fear.

Hell. He'd deliberately frightened her!

But no one was mad enough to offer twenty thousand pounds for nothing. It must have been a dream.

But what if—?

He was trying to sift truth from fantasy when someone tapped tentatively on his door. His heart suddenly raced. Was she back, but more cautious now? "Yes?"

The door creaked open, and his valet, Noons, peered around it. His ex-valet.

Disappointment swept through him like a chill. "What the devil are you doing here?"

Wizened Noons smiled tentatively. "Begging your pardon, my lord, but I went as you ordered. But I got to thinking about how you'd manage alone. You know you're no hand with your clothes, my lord. I'd be more than happy to stay with you until things come right again. And then stay on," he added hastily. "Begging your lordship's pardon . . ."

Van closed his eyes. If his pistol had worked, poor Noons would have returned to find the body, and after he'd dismissed him specifically to avoid that.

Or no. Mrs. Celestin would have. Bad planning, Van. Very bad. You should at least have locked the door.

He opened his eyes to see that the weatherbeaten creases on Noon's face were crumpling even further. The man thought Van would dismiss him again.

Making an impulsive decision, he surged to his feet. "I was just going to set the Runners to find you, Noons! Our fortunes are reversed. I have hopes of a rich widow, but I can hardly go a-courting without you to turn me out well, can I?"

He'd go to Perry's Bank. If the money was there, he'd have a start. If it wasn't, he'd complete what Mrs. Celestin had interrupted. Somehow without hurting Noons more than he had to.

Misery switched to blinding joy in the valet's face. "My lord! My lord! Oh, this is such good news! I was so afraid . . . I won't tell you what I was afraid of—"

His eyes, glancing around, had found the pistol.

Van thought of lying about it, then shrugged. "It misfired. Faulty flint." Then he saw the look on the valet's face.

Noons retreated. "I'm sorry, my lord. No, I'm not sorry! I couldn't bear what you might do when I was out of sight. And see, I was right, wasn't I?"

For a moment, Van wanted to throttle him, but then he forced a smile. "Yes, by gad, you were right. For six weeks, at least."

"Six weeks, my lord?" Noons gingerly picked up the pistol and put it out of sight in a drawer.

"Never mind. First order of business is to tidy me up so I can visit my bank."

"Bank, my lord?" Noons glanced at the empty decanter in concern.

"A small loan to enable me to go fortune hunting. So, work your magic."

Three hours later, rested, shaved, and turned out to Noons's satisfaction, Van looked in a mirror. He wished the signs of dissipation could be polished away like the scuffs on his boots.

If the Golden Lily had been real, however, he'd polish up. Though he often felt like Methuselah, he was only twenty-five. His body must still have some repairing powers.

He rubbed a finger down the scar on his right cheek. That wouldn't go away, but that, at least, was honorable.

He put on his hat and went out to test whether his visitor had been an apparition or real. A strange mission, almost like a trial. If he returned with no money and no hope, he would have to execute himself.

With that in mind, he paused by a gunsmith's shop and counted his few coins. Yesterday, he'd paid Noons and his bills, then taken the rest of his money to Brooks'. He'd come home and bought that one bottle of good wine. Now he had just over a shilling.

He left the gunsmith with a flint, a sixpence, one penny, and a farthing. All he possessed in the world.

Oh, he could tease things out by selling bits and pieces, but after last night's disaster, that would be stealing. Despite his words to the real or imaginary Mrs. Celestin, his estates would not completely cover his debt. Everything he owned, even to the clothes on his back, belonged to the men holding his IOUs.

The only hope lay at the bank. With the careless acceptance of fate that had carried him to hell and back for nearly ten years, he walked on briskly.

As he approached Perry's, however, his steps slowed. Somehow, passing through busy streets, greeted by the occasional acquaintance, he had begun to slide back under the damnable seductiveness of life. It shouldn't be difficult to stroll into the bank and ask whether an account had been set up for him there, but it had become the moment that would dictate whether he would live or die.

He hovered, seeking alternatives, but he knew there were none.

He'd inherited neglected estates drowning in debt. He had no skills but soldiering, and the war was over. Even if it wasn't, he couldn't go back. He knew now how Con had felt. Con had sold out in 1814, then returned for Waterloo, but after the break, he'd lost the habit of war, the crusty, protective shell. He'd come through the battle without serious physical wounds, but damaged in other ways. Van had known that. He should have found Con and tried to help. He'd been too wrapped up in his own problems.

In some ways Van had enjoyed war, enjoyed the constant test by fire, but he'd never become hardened to death. Each death around him had spurred him to fight more wildly, as if picking up the banner of the fallen without caution or consequences.

A clear form of madness. He'd been aware of that, and yet it had gripped him. No question of stopping, of backing away, with all the ghosts cheering him on.

But that drug had gone, drained to the last, overdosing drop at Waterloo. Once gone, there was nothing left. He could not fight again. He could not help a friend.

Why did a person live? What was the point? He'd carried on only because of another set of ghosts, his family preaching his duty to continue the line, to repair Steynings and restore it to the home it had once been.

He'd turned to gambling. He had luck and he stayed sober, so he generally won. Paid his way, in fact. He'd never made enough to change anything, however, in part because he couldn't bring himself to fleece the innocent or those who couldn't afford it.

Tiring of it, he'd made a bargain with the devil. He'd gamble the night away without restraint or caution. If he emerged a winner, he would settle in the country and work at restoring his home. If he lost, he'd put an end to it.

He'd lost. True to his bargain, he'd stayed through the night, even though the debts had mounted, actually welcoming the growing total that would remove any ambiguity.

He mourned that moment when he had known exactly what he must do, so like the absolute of a forlorn-hope charge in battle. Then, with a muttered curse, he took up his last forlorn hope and walked into the bank.

It was oak-paneled and sober, looking respectable and solid, as a bank must. Was it her bank? If she was real, if she had deposited the money, would everyone here know his account had been set up by the rich Mrs. Celestin?

He had no reason for pride anymore, but it still stung.

A neatly dressed clerk came forward, bowing. "How may I assist you, sir?"

Van gathered generations of wealth and arrogance as armor. "Lord. Vandeimen. I have an account here, I believe."

For a wretched heartbeat he thought the clerk was staring at him in puzzlement, but then he smiled. "Yes indeed, my lord. Permit me to take you to Mr. Perry, my lord."

Van wondered if he staggered as he followed down a corridor and into the handsome office of the owner of the bank.

Reprieve.

He had six weeks more of life!

He still felt dazed as he emerged, guineas in his pocket, wealth established, debts paid. Poor Mr. Perry had been disappointed to find that most of the fortune trusted to his care was to promptly leave it. Van still had a thousand pounds in the account, and nine thousand more if he could satisfy his employer.

The Golden Lily.

He took a deep breath of spring air, appreciating it like a fine wine. He blessed the warmth of the sun on his face.

But as he strolled back to his rooms, wariness grew. For twenty thousand pounds Mrs. Celestin had to want more than his adoring escort. What? He'd swallowed the hook, so now he'd be reeled in.

Despite her rejection, perhaps she was after coupling. He fought back a laugh. If so, he'd be the most overpaid whore in London, no matter what her tastes!

In fact, he rather liked the idea. He'd like to warm that damnable, cool composure, see her flush and become disordered, unruly, wild . . .

Madness. She was probably all cool composure in bed, too.

When a ragged crossing-sweeper hurried to clear some horse droppings from his path, he dug out the sixpence, the penny, and the farthing, and dropped them into the lad's hand. With the boy's enthusiastic thanks loud in the air, he strolled on, a sparkle starting inside him.

With difficulty, he recognized mischief and challenge. How long was it since he had felt that way? Despite his employer's command that he not touch her without permission, surely in six weeks of adoring companionship, he could find out whether she was cool in bed.

Even a servant deserved amusement.

As he passed the gunsmith's on the way home, however, he remembered the flint, and fingered it in his pocket. It comforted him. If the strange Mrs. Celestin demanded anything intolerable, he had the easy way out.

The next night, Maria entered the Yeovil mansion in a state of unusual turmoil. Few would guess, for it was her nature to conceal her emotions, but she knew, and she knew why.

He'd paid his debts. Everyone gossiped about that as much as they'd gossiped about his ruinous night at the tables.

Where had the money come from? they'd asked.

Had he gone to the moneylenders? If so, poor man.

Would he lose again? Then what?

A sad case, both men and women agreed. Hero in the war. Fine old family. No hope, though. Father ruined the properties, and the son doesn't have the heart to start from scratch. Shame for such a promising young gentleman.

A promising young gentleman.

On hearing that, Maria had thought of the slack-lidded, stubbled man in the rumpled clothes, and the way he'd taken that pistol from her. Promising?

Of what? Perhaps it was the fact that he was still a gentleman that had prevented him from shooting her.

If he was a gentleman, he'd work off his debt to her. He'd be here tonight. That terrified her almost as much as him not being here. If he was here, she'd have to deal with him.

For six weeks.

He did terrify her, and only the smallest part was a fear that he'd attack her. Instead it was fear of the energy and intensity he'd given off. She'd wanted to back away. To be safe.

Worse, she'd wanted to press closer, to inhale that energy, to absorb it, surrender to it. She'd surrendered to her physical nature once before, and lived to regret it.

She would not make a fool of herself again.

Harriette knew how she felt. Harriette was the one person who knew everything, and now her aunt glanced sideways and smiled—the sort of chins-up! smile given to someone before a trying experience.

They greeted the duke and duchess—the duchess was Maria's cousin, twice removed—and their daughter, Lady Theodosia, who was being launched here. Then they moved into a reception room, and on into the glittering ballroom.

It was, of course, a most sought-after invitation, and therefore well on its way to being a "crush." It might be hard to find her quarry. Or for him to find her. Maria felt an absurd temptation to climb on one of the chairs set around the walls, both to see and be seen.

"I don't see him," said Harriette, who was indeed stretching on tiptoe.

"Don't make a fuss," Maria hissed as she smiled and obeyed the beckoning Lady Treves. A pleasant lady, but she had a handsome, hopeful son, and so was destined to be disappointed.

So many hunted her fortune. She hadn't lied to Vandeimen about that, or that she'd pay a fortune to be able to attend these events without a swarm of what she thought of as her wasps. She saw two of the more persistent ones buzzing toward her now.

Ten proposals she'd had so far. Ten. And she'd only been free of mourning for a few weeks.

Of course it wasn't just the money, she acknowledged as she greeted Lord Warren and Sir Burleigh Fox. She was a Dunpott-Ffyfe. Marrying Maurice had not done her credit any good, but he was, after all, dead, and had left her a very wealthy widow with excellent bloodlines. A jam pot for wasps.

She smiled and chatted, trying not to favor any particular man and parrying the more clumsy attempts to flirt or flatter. Where was Vandeimen? Why wasn't he here?

She froze in the middle of an idle comment to the duchess. What if he'd paid his debts and gone home to shoot himself?

"Maria?"

"Oh! So sorry, Sarah. Of course I'll be a patroness of your charity for wounded soldiers. The government should have done much more. And after all, Maurice made a great deal of money from supplying the army."

She'd be paying conscience money—to the soldiers who'd worn shoddy boots and uniforms, and to Lord Vandeimen who'd been ruined. Military charities were Sarah Yeovil's passion, however, because she had lost her younger son at Waterloo. She was dressed tonight in dark gray and black.

Maria remembered Lord Darius as a charming young rascal, always up to mischief, but her mind was presently fretting over another young man of about the same age. Was Lord Vandeimen lying in a puddle of blood?

She itched to invade his rooms again, to prevent disaster, but she stayed where she was and smiled. If he was dead, he was dead, and discovering it would not repair matters.

"Tattoos, Mama?" queried Lord Gravenham, the duchess's older son.

Maria paid attention and tried to guess what they were talking about.

"Sailors have them," Sarah said earnestly. "So if they drown, their bodies are more easily recognized. If soldiers had tattoos, it would serve the same purpose."

"It would do no harm," said Lord Gravenham, but Maria suspected he was thinking as she was. There'd been more than ten thousand corpses to deal with after Waterloo, most thrown into mass graves to prevent disease. One of them had been Dare's, but in a situation like that, who was going to note tattoos for identification?

"I had the idea from Lord Wyvern," Sarah was saying. "A friend of Dare's," she added to Maria. "One of this Company of Rogues they formed at Harrow, though of course he wasn't Wyvern then. Just plain Con Somerford. Such good friends, and such good men . . ." She pressed a black-edged handkerchief to her eyes and took a visible moment to collect herself. "He and two friends had tattoos done before going to war. On the chest. A G for George."

"That's a very common name, though, isn't it?" Maria said, trying to cover the moment and show an interest. "For true identification, it would need to be more distinctive. A full name?"

"They were all called George."

Maria flashed Lord Gravenham a look, wondering if Sarah had finally slipped over the edge.

"So of course they needed something else," Sarah went on. "Wyvern has a dragon. It fits the title he's inherited, though at the time he could not expect to. The other two men were a George Hawkinville—a hawk, and George Vandeimen, a demon. It goes with the sound of his title, of course, and it's the family name too. But not a wise choice." She shrugged. "But then, they were only sixteen. I'm so glad to hear better news of him."

"Vandeimen?" Maria asked, and it came out a little high. "The one who lost his fortune?" He had a *demon* on his chest?

"I was saying to the duke that we should do something. He and the others were so kind to Dare last year. Professional soldiers, you know. But Vandeimen's affairs seem to have sorted out. So, can you help me there, too, Maria? I will have to hire people who can do these tattoos, and obtain the cooperation of the Horse Guards . . ."

The orchestra struck a louder note, alerting all that the dancing was to begin. Sir Burleigh hovered. Maria promised support for the foolish tattoo fund and gave the persistent wasp her hand.

She loved to dance, though she knew she did it with grace rather than verve. They called her Lily because of her pale complexion and habit of wearing pale clothes, and Golden for her outrageous wealth. She knew they also called her the Languid Lily, and shared scurrilous jokes in the men's clubs about whether she was languid in bed.

She would love to be able to sparkle, and perhaps she had as a rompish sixteen. The years had taught her control and discretion, however, and they reigned even in the dance.

In the bed—well, that was a private matter.

Then as she turned in the dance pattern, she saw him.

She missed a step, and with a hasty apology she concentrated on the dance. When she glanced back across the room, Vandeimen was gone.

He was here, though. She couldn't have mistaken that tall lean grace and primrose hair, made more brilliant by dark evening clothes.

He was here.

Alive.

Ready to fulfill his bargain.

With a sudden beat of the heart she knew it had begun.

Chapter Three

When the set was over, Maria felt flushed, an unusual occurrence for her. She plied her fan as her wasps gathered, all seeking the next chance at the jam pot. Maria playfully put off choosing.

Where was Vandeimen?

Had she imagined him?

Then she saw him, in company with Gravenham. Beside the marquess's mousy solidity, Vandeimen seemed a wild spirit, despite his perfect, tidy appearance. His primrose hair shone in the candlelight, and his scar, doubtless honorably gained, suggested wickedness, especially with the lingering marks of dissipation.

"Mrs. Celestin," Gravenham said, "you have enraptured another of us poor males. Here's Vandeimen begging me for an introduction. Now mind," he added, "I wouldn't agree if you were a sweet young innocent, but I judge you well able to deal with rascals such as he."

Maria appreciated Gravenham's subtle warning. It showed that Vandeimen was in danger of losing his place in accepted circles.

"A rascal, my lord," she said to Vandeimen, offering her hand. "How intriguing."

She managed a cool manner, but was alarmed that she hadn't thought of this essential detail. Of course he couldn't just walk up to her. He had to find someone respectable to introduce him.

He bowed gracefully over her hand, perfectly judging the distance. A slight inclination would be cool. To actually touch his lips to her gloves would be scandalously bold. Just over halfway was within bounds, but hinted at interesting ardor.

She kept her light smile fixed and prayed not to shiver. This perfectly turned-out young man with deft social skills was not what she had expected.

"Then perhaps I might persuade you into the dance, Mrs. Celestin?" he said straightening but still holding her hand. "Some opportunity there to be rascally."

"Really? I was not aware of that."

"How dull your partners must have been." He tucked her hand into the crook of his arm. "Come, let me brighten your life."

He stole her from under the noses of her wasps, and she wasn't sure whether to be outraged or wildly amused.

"My partners have not been particularly dull," she said, as they joined a set.

"Good. Then you won't be shocked."

She wasn't sure about that. What did he plan?

She did know about rascally dancing. If she let her mind slide back to her folly with Maurice, she could remember times when he'd used the dance to full advantage. After all, where else could a slightly disreputable man get close enough to a lady to tempt her to folly?

The music started and they began the steps. For the moment it was just a dance, giving her room to think.

She hadn't anticipated him planning to kill himself.

She hadn't anticipated him being dangerous.

She hadn't anticipated the need for introduction.

She hadn't anticipated his perfect management of the situation, or how he matched the steps of society as skillfully as he matched the steps of the dance.

She should have expected all of it. Heavens, social duties were part of an officer's life. And yet, she had failed to anticipate his social skills.

What else had she neglected?

That he would be wary.

As she met his eyes in the dance, she recognized that. Of course her quixotic actions must appear suspicious. As they joined hands and passed, she wondered what he feared. What did he think she wanted for her twenty thousand pounds?

And what—even more fascinating—would he be willing to do for it?

She danced back toward him, wicked thoughts stirring despite every attempt to bury them deep in her mind. They linked arms in an allemande, and turned, eye to eye, bodies moving in harmony.

A sudden awareness rippled through her of exactly what she could demand from him in service—for six long weeks. She knew her rare color was building, and spun off to the next gentleman with relief.

She'd never thought of such a thing when she'd planned this. Never! She must immediately put it out of her mind. It would be both foolish and wicked. She was supposed to be rescuing him, not exploiting him, and he was eight years her junior.

She fiercely concentrated on the present, on the weaving steps of the dance. She couldn't help but watch, however, as he danced with other women in the set. She was not alone in her reaction. Each one, young or old, responded with a brightening of the eyes, a widening of the smile.

He was a flirt. A handsome, instinctive flirt whom women could not resist responding to. She'd not anticipated that, either. She'd known the world would assume she was buying youth, but not that she had been charmed out of her wits and money.

The idea was so repulsive that she wanted to cry halt now. He could have the money and go to hell or heaven—

Then he was back to partner her. As they stepped together, first one way then the other, he said softly, "Am I supposed to fall madly in love with you, or is this a more considered affair?"

Mouth dry, eyes locked with his, she said, "Madly in love. Why not?" If she was going to be thought a fool, she'd rather be thought a mad one.

His eyes held hers, and then, as the dance moved him on, they lingered for a speaking moment. Fascinated, she realized she was doing the same thing, and hastily looked at her new partner, Sir Watkins Dore, to see an understanding smile.

"A handsome rascal," the middle-aged man remarked, "but penniless and with a taste for the bottle and the tables, dear lady. A word to the wise."

From there on, Maria passed through the dance unable to block the mortifying awareness that everyone thought they were witnessing a powerful attraction between an older woman and a charming young rascal.

She couldn't blame Vandeimen. He was following her instructions to the letter. Though smiling and polite, he had somehow muted his effect on the other ladies, and turned it all on her. Often her eyes collided with his intent ones. It was hard for her not to believe that she had suddenly become the center of his universe.

When the dance ended and she curtsied as he bowed, she knew all eyes were on them. It was excruciatingly hard not to say something cutting, or behave in a chilly manner to show that she was not a gullible fool. As it was, she let him place her hand in the crook of his arm, and strolled with him.

"Everyone's watching," she said, though she knew she shouldn't. She was in control of this adventure, wasn't she?

"I'm sure you are watched anyway, the Golden Lily."

"I'm used to that, but not to this." How absurd to feel that she could talk honestly to him like this. Of course, apart from Harriette, he was the only one aware of their purpose. "I'm probably not looking as dazzled as I should."

"I'll be dazzled for both of us." When she glanced sideways at him, she saw how his smiling eyes were intent on her. "Some wariness on your part is doubtless realistic," he added. "You are too wise to actually marry me, after all."

She smiled at the joke, but it pressed on an old wound. Her feelings were too like the lunatic infatuations she'd succumbed to when young, culminating in Maurice. She had a weakness for dashing, handsome, dangerous men, but she was no longer young and silly. Had she learned nothing?

Cool air startled her back to the immediate, and she realized he had led her out onto a small balcony. They were still in view, but it gave some protection from being overheard. It also must cause more talk.

What point in balking, though? She was about to be society's favorite topic of amusement for six long weeks. It was a price she would pay to right a wrong.

"Thank you for coming," she said, wafting her fan and gazing out over the lamplit garden below.

"You thought I wouldn't pay my debt?"

A sudden chill in his voice made her turn to him. "I didn't mean it that way. You were . . . The need to—"

"Madam, you have bought me—body, mind, and most of my soul—for six weeks. I will go where you command, speak as you wish, act as you instruct, so long as it does not offend the part of my soul I have retained."

Oh dear. Pain and wounded pride. She must remember that though war had aged him in many ways, he could still be tender in others.

"Excellent," she said coolly, returning to the safe contemplation of the garden. "You are playing your part well, my lord, so please continue to act as if you were intent on winning me." She glanced back with a carefully calculated smile. "I doubt that will hazard your immortal soul."

They confronted each other for a moment in silence, and she nervously broke into chatter. "The lamps in the garden are pretty, are they not? I wonder if there is a way to explore there."

Her gloved right hand rested on the iron railing, and he covered it with his left. A hand brown from years of sun and weather, strong with sinews and veins, long-fingered, marked by many minor scars. A hand that looked older than he was. A fine hand perhaps meant by nature for softer ways, for music, for art, for gentle love . . .

"I would know that I had little hope," he said, curling his fingers around hers and lifting her hand from the railing, turning her toward him. "A penniless man with dilapidated estates, and eight years younger than you."

"True . . ."

He brought her hand between them, chest high, and in the process angled his body so that he shielded her from the crowded room. "The only reason you would consider my suit is for my looks and charm. Poor Mrs. Celestin," he added with a glint of edged humor, "you are going to have to succumb to looks and charm."

"I would hardly be the first widow to do so. I'm sure I can play the part." She returned exactly the same sort of edged look. "It's not as if I am actually going to place my person and my fortune in your hands, after all."

"Just the additional nine thousand pounds."

"*If* you behave yourself." She looked him up and down. "You do, at least, have both looks and charm, and conduct yourself well in society. It would be even more galling to make a fool of myself over an *unappealing* wastrel."

He stilled, his scar seeming to slash more darkly across his right cheek. She instantly recalled the man she had first met, the one who had disarmed her, and surely come close to hurting her.

He dropped her hand. "I can become unappealing anytime you want, Mrs. Celestin. I would advise you not to push me too far. A man ready to die is equally ready to consign nine thousand pounds to the devil."

The small balcony was suddenly confining, and he blocked the way out. She desperately wanted to look away, or to try to push out of this confined space. As with an animal, however, to show fear was to lose control. She met his angry eyes. "What of the eleven thousand, my lord? You owe me service for that."

His nostrils flared, and she suddenly saw in him a stallion. A young, magnificent, abused stallion on the edge of going bad. Dear heavens, who did she think she was, to try to keep together something so riven through with cracks?

"I'm sorry," she said quickly. "I spoke thoughtlessly. I chose you for this because you are a gentleman."

"But why did you choose anyone, Mrs. Celestin? What is the purpose of this extravagant charade?"

She'd hoped to put this off until she'd thought of a better rationale, but clearly she had to say something now. With great effort, she spoke lightly. "One person's extravagance is another's whim, Lord Vandeimen. I have a mind to enjoy this season, and I am pestered by fortune hunters. You are my guard against them, that is all."

She must have presented it correctly, for she saw his tension ease in scarcely perceptible, but significant, ways.

"You must be very, very rich."

"I am."

"Then of course, I am completely at your service. Command me, dear lady."

Shockingly, the requests that came to mind were all indecent. She sank back on what she had said before. "Do as you would if you were intent on sweeping me out of sanity and into your marital bed."

He looked at her for a moment, then raised his left hand and rested it on her naked shoulder. Warm. Roughened from the practice of war.

No, not practice. Real, deadly war. How many deaths had those intent blue eyes seen? How many had his elegant hands delivered? How much suffering, during battle and after? She had lost no one of importance to her except a baby brother, half remembered, and Maurice, who had died miles away on a hunting field, and by then not truly grieved.

They called this man Demon. A terrible label for a noble soldier and hero, but she could only think of how very familiar he must be with death. No wonder he'd seemed indifferent as to whether she shot him or not. He probably cared for nothing at all, and was wounded too deeply for that to change.

Was he going to kiss her, here in full view of everyone? She should prevent that, but for the moment, she was paralyzed.

With scarcely a pause, however, he brushed his hand across her bare shoulder, sending shivers down her spine, until his fingers moved into the loose curls at the edge of her hair. He could be tidying a curl or brushing away an insect. He played there for a moment, eyes holding hers, then lowered his hand to his side.

Fear still held her, but underneath surged something even worse. Lust.

Triumph glinted in his sudden smile.

Ah.

She sucked in a deep breath. He was going to do what she had paid for, but for pride's sake he was going to try to seduce her at the same time. Not surprising, though yet again, something she had not anticipated.

She certainly had never anticipated that it might be so terribly possible.

Already a part of her was crying, *Why not? Why not? You could lie together with him tonight!* Deep muscles clenched at the thought.

She often lay in the quiet night remembering a man's body on hers, in hers. She didn't wish Maurice back, but memory of hot intimacy always left her feeling aching and hollow.

She was staring at him. Carefully, slowly, she turned her head to look past, unfurling her fan. She couldn't afford to give him a weapon like that, and it would be wrong to use him. She must remember her purpose—to heal him and set him free with the money Maurice had stolen.

"The next dance is starting," he said. "Shall we be partners again? It will create just the storm you want."

Storm. An apt name for the tumult inside her, but she agreed. She had set her course and would pursue it, even through a storm of embarrassment, scandal, and yes—frustration.

She was no blushing ingenue. She could control herself and her demon. She went calmly with him to form an eight.

She completed the dance almost hectic with emotion. Beneath dissipation, dark memories, and that nasty scar, was a young man, a devastatingly attractive young man, who was doing his best to bewitch her.

And his best was very good.

She'd struggled to pin her mind to higher thoughts—to his experiences in the war and his need of gentle nurturing at home. Beneath that logical and noble mind, however, quivered a body that wanted to tear his clothes off, press to his heat, inhale and taste him, and bring him nurture and release of another kind entirely. His very youth, his pain, his sensitivity, his leashed resistance to her rule, were all exciting her more than she could have believed possible.

Before he even suggested an outrageous third dance, she accepted an invitation from another man. It didn't matter who, but it was Mr. Fanshawe, a pleasant gentleman who doubtless would like to marry her money, but who didn't make a nuisance of himself about it.

As they strolled, waiting for the next set to start, she made herself seriously consider Mr. Fanshawe as husband. She did want to marry again, and he was comfortable, undemanding, and her own age. He was the sort of man she had expected to choose, but now the prospect made her want to yawn.

She knew why, but that was only a temporary insanity.

The music started and she let the dance sweep her up, enjoying as always the neatness of fluid movements up and down the line. When she extended her hand to dance round and past the next gentleman, she almost faltered.

Vandeimen!

She recovered, smiled, and danced on. Idiot! Nothing to stop him joining the same line. If he was playing the part of ardent suitor, of course he would. Her hand still tingled from his touch, however.

It must not be.

She wove back down the line, approached him again, joined hands, stepped around, and onward.

That was how it would be. Swirled together by fate, six weeks of linked hands, and then onward and apart. He would have a new chance at life, and she would have a clear conscience.

She did wish it had been possible to do it impersonally, but while she'd been coming up with elaborate schemes, he'd plunged suddenly into darkness and she'd known she had to act. She'd been right, too. Frighteningly right. She still shuddered at the thought of being moments too late.

When it was his turn to dance down the middle of the long line with his partner she saw that he was partnering a flushed and dazzled young thing burdened by a pudding face and frizzy mousy hair. He'd either chosen or been dragooned into partnering a wallflower, but his smile for her was bright and warm, and he was creating a brief heaven for her.

Beneath the wastrel lay a good man. She shouldn't be surprised, and she certainly shouldn't feel a proprietary pride. He wasn't hers, and that was exactly where he should look for a bride. Among the innocent and fertile young.

Fertile. She grasped that painful thorn. In ten years of active marriage she had not conceived, and it hadn't been Maurice's fault. He had four bastards that she knew about.

Vandeimen needed children to rebuild his line.

What a betrayal that she even needed to remind herself of that! Beneath the dark and the scars, however, Vandeimen was a good man, and she was glad of it.

Women teasingly divided potential husbands into three groups—heaven, purgatory, and hell. Maurice had promised heaven but turned out to be pur-

gatory, which she gathered was all too common. Vandeimen, she suspected,
was a purgatory who would turn out to be heaven for the right woman.

But not for her.

For supper partner, she chose Lord Warren. He was a widower with two
sons, so the fact that she was unlikely to have children didn't matter to him.
He was sensible, honest, and persistent in pursuit, but would make an excellent husband. He held a minor position in the government. Perhaps being a
political hostess would amuse her.

She concentrated on his interesting conversation, and that of the other
people at her table, but then a burst of laughter made her glance across the
room. Vandeimen was at a table with a group that glittered with youth, life,
and high spirits.

His natural milieu.

"Noisy, aren't they?" Lord Warren said.

Maria turned back to him, pulling a slight face, grateful that she hadn't revealed a touch of wistfulness. "They're young."

"Indeed. My eldest is not much younger, and he and the rest can destroy
tranquility in a moment."

She sipped her wine to hide another reaction.

If she married Lord Warren, she would become stepmother to sons not a
great deal younger than Lord Vandeimen. Only eight years divided them, but
the way the world worked they were almost different generations.

She conversed with Lord Warren and the other older people at her table,
trying to block the sounds of lively chatter and bursts of laughter from across
the room.

It was a relief to rise to return to the ballroom. As she strolled out with
Lord Warren she decided she would leave the ball soon. She'd done enough
for one night. Vandeimen could come up with other modes of pursuit tomorrow.

Then he rose fluidly from his table to put himself in her way, smiling,
seemingly relaxed. Gorgeous.

"Mrs. Celestin, you expressed an interest in exploring the gardens. Miss
Harrowby had just suggested a stroll out there. Would you care to come?" He
gestured to the French doors that stood open to the warm night.

She froze for a moment. It was bold. It was almost impolite, though Warren would expect to hand her over to a new partner soon. If she accepted, it
would be a clear sign to all that she was encouraging him.

Everyone was watching.

She smiled at her escort. "If you don't mind, my lord . . ." then moved her hand from his arm to Vandeimen's.

Glances shot around the young people carrying many messages, and whispering began behind her in the room, but in moments she and a number of other couples were heading into the lamplit dark.

Chapter Four

"A m I a chaperon?" she asked as they walked outside and a breeze touched her skin. That surely explained the slight shiver.

"I do hope not."

The next shiver was not due to the breeze.

The other couples melted into the shadows, so only the ghostly pale of the ladies' dresses, soft talk, and laughter revealed their presence.

"I feel like a chaperon," she said, trying to remind him of her advanced age. "Who is partnered with whom, and are the pairings acceptable?"

"Don't fuss. I doubt anyone is going to be ravished." He turned to her and added, "Who doesn't want to be, that is."

"Who would want to be?"

"All the men."

It startled a laugh from her, and he grinned, looking much younger. *Oh, Maria, do you know what you're doing?* When he guided her farther from the house, however, she did not resist.

Though the garden was not large, paths wound around bushes and trellises, creating illusions of privacy. Illusions only, as giggles, conversation, and the occasional squeal could be heard all around.

It was a sleeping garden, but someone had planted nicotiana and stock that perfumed the air, and the paths were studded with creeping herbs that released scents as they walked. The sultry air increased her awareness of folly. This was not necessary for her plan, though it fit neatly with his.

He was going to try to kiss her, perhaps even to ravish her, to prove that he was master. One of these matters of male pride that she recognized without understanding them at all.

The question was, what was she going to permit, and why?

He paused beneath a tree. "Would this be too early for me to beg for your hand in marriage?"

Ridiculously, her pulse began to race. "It would seem impetuous."

"So. Be a wild, impetuous woman for once."

The tone stung, and an overhead amber lantern laid harsh lines on his face, deepening the jagged scar.

"I eloped with Celestin," she said, and relished startling him.

"Your family didn't approve?"

"He was foreign and self-made."

"You must have loved him very much."

After a heartbeat, she said, "Yes, yes I did."

It wasn't a lie. Wild, impetuous love had driven her into Maurice's arms— carefully created wild impetuous love as unreal as this mock devotion.

"Then have another adventure." He took her hands. "Agree now to marry me. We'll put the notice in the papers tomorrow and shock all London."

She realized that he was speaking as if they might be overheard, and they might. She was vaguely aware of a couple nearby talking softly but earnestly about the meaning of freedom and love.

Ah, youth.

"Well?" he asked.

No point in hesitation. "Very well."

He smiled. Even with the amber light it seemed warm. "You've made me very happy."

"Have I?"

"But of course. Now I get to kiss you. But not here," he said before she could protest. "That amber light is doing terrible things to your looks."

That disconcerting thought allowed him to tug her into deeper, untinted shadows. Then she got her wits back. "You do not have permission to kiss me."

"Are you going to scream?" He pulled her into his arms. "Wouldn't that rather spoil the show?"

She braced her hands against his chest. "Stop this!"

Shockingly, however, his strength and hard body weakened her, as such things always did. Maurice had not loved her, but he'd been a good lover when he'd bothered, and he'd given her what most excited her.

He would turn up in the middle of an ordinary day, seize her arm, and march her to the bedroom. She'd been practically in orgasm before he had her clothes off, and he'd made sure she whirled into that madness two or three more times before he went on with his busy day, leaving her languid.

Satiated.

Conquered by her flesh.

And it had been a conquest, a matter of pride to him to succeed in everything. She'd known it, but never had the strength to resist.

Zeus, she didn't need those memories now. Despite hot skin and aching thighs, she said, "Force a kiss on me, Lord Vandeimen, and our arrangement will be at an end. It will make you a thief of the money you've already spent, and I assure you, you won't see a penny more."

She couldn't see his expression, but his arms neither tightened nor slackened. "You threatened me once before, Maria. Didn't you learn that I don't care enough? Send me to hell if you want. I'll have my kiss."

He knocked up her bracing arms and cinched her close, then captured her head and kissed her.

Ravished her.

Shock and remembered hungers opened her mouth and pressed her closer, betraying her utterly. It had been so long, so long, since a man had held her, kissed her like this. She'd told herself she was glad to be free of it, and known that she lied.

She found she'd thrust her hands beneath his jacket, and was clawing at his long, tight back through silk and linen. She stopped that at least, but her heart thundered and that betraying ache had become throbbing demand.

His lips released hers and slid down her neck.

She should stop him now. She should. Instead, she was fighting not to fall to the ground and tear his clothes off.

He pushed his thigh between hers. She heard her own sound of need, and finally dragged herself out of his arms. "St—"

His hand came hard over her mouth.

He was right. She'd been about to scream.

"Hush," he said softly, "hush."

No apology, just soothing sounds he might make to a frantic animal.

Animal.

Oh, God.

She closed her eyes, excruciatingly mortified to have reacted like that to the cynical attentions of a man more suited to be her son than her lover.

Then she was in his arms again, being held quite gently, her face pressed to his shoulder, however, just in case.

Oh, to wipe out those foolish moments! To take frosty leave of him and never see him again.

You can, whispered a voice. *Just give him the money and cut free.*

She couldn't. He needed more than money. He needed a clean break from corruption, and a helping hand back to ordinary, sane ways. The fact that he'd stolen that dishonorable kiss showed he was still deep in the pit. She suspected that soon he'd be ready to shoot himself over it.

She moved her head slightly to take a clearer breath, and he let her. His head rested against hers, however, and his arms were no longer imprisoning. Despairingly, she sensed that he was relishing this embrace. How often had he simply been in someone's arms?

His mother and two sisters might possibly have held him if he needed it. Mother and younger sister had died of influenza. His older sister had died in childbirth round about the time of Waterloo. His father had shot himself not long after, and perhaps the other deaths had been part of it. It had mostly been the debts, though, and they had been Maurice's fault.

There must have been women abroad, but had they been the sort to just hold him when he needed holding? The sort to whom he could confess fear and doubt? The sort to let him weep?

Did he ever allow himself to weep?

Her own eyes were blurring, tears ached in her throat, and she realized her hands were making stroking movements on his back. Motherly, she told herself. He probably could do with a mother substitute.

She wanted to burst into wild laughter.

She fought for composure and looked up. "I believe we are engaged to be married, Lord Vandeimen."

She couldn't really see his features, but that meant he couldn't see hers either. The silence stretched too long, however, before he asked, "I should send the notice to the papers?"

She heard surprise. "Yes."

After another silence he asked, "And then what? Do we go through the form of drawing up marriage settlements?"

"Why not? They will make a model for when I truly commit to marriage."

He moved slowly away, then linked her arm with his and drew her back to the path and the amber light.

"I apologize for what happened," he said, looking fixedly ahead. "You are being nothing but kind, and I attacked you, frightened you. Since you are kind enough to continue with this arrangement, I give you my word it will not happen again."

Maria stopped herself from protesting. This was how it must be, and if he hadn't recognized her reaction for what it had been, that was a blessing.

"Then we have everything settled. Now I would like to go home. You will escort me and my aunt?"

"Of course."

But he paused beneath a bright lamp and deftly tidied her appearance, straightening her pearl necklace, adjusting her sleeve, and tucking a curl back into a pin. Every brushing touch was flaming temptation, but she concentrated fiercely on the fact that he was being clever again. There'd be enough talk without them reentering the house in disarray.

Presumably tidying up after garden embraces was part of the skills of a military officer.

"Were there many social events in the Peninsula?" she asked, and to keep the balance, reached up to adjust his cravat, thankful for her gloves. Even so, the sense of his skin, sleek over his firm chin, or the muscles and tendons of his neck, could drive her wild.

Heavens, but she wanted him. Rawly and demandingly wanted him.

"Sometimes," he said, raising his chin for her. "In Lisbon, mostly. And Paris. And Brussels."

The Duchess of Richmond's ball, from which the officers had slipped away, many not to be seen alive again. Yes, doubtless he had experience at partnering respectable young ladies at balls, and occasionally slipping out for a kiss—or even more—in a garden.

Neglected wives and hungry widows. She knew how men saw these things. Maurice had told her that men, too, thought of women as heaven, purgatory, or hell, but in two different ways. They assessed brides that way, but they also used the terms to assess lovers.

In a potential lover, hell was diseased, or married to a suspicious, vengeful man, or tainted in some other way. No wise man chose such a lover, but she could hear Maurice laugh as he quoted that the way to hell was often paved with good intentions.

Purgatory was what most men had to put up with to get sex they neither had to pay for nor marry for.

Heaven was an attractive married woman with a strong sexual appetite

and a safe husband. Some widows fit into that category if they emphatically
did not want marriage.

She realized that in some ways she was heaven. She was even barren. A distinct advantage.

She gave the starched cloth a final twitch, then they linked arms to reen-
ter the house. She knew the people lingering in the supper room were watching, as were those they met as they went in search of Harriette. Probably
everyone knew by now that the Golden Lily had gone into the garden with
wild young Lord Vandeimen who desperately needed money.

She caught a few disappointed grimaces from the wasps and their families,
and a few looks of concern, or even pity from others.

It was hard not to shout out an explanation.

*Of course I'm not bewitched by this young fool! I'm saving him. In weeks I'll
be free, and so will he!*

Thank God for Harriette. Maria found herself blank of conversation, but
Harriette chattered to Vandeimen without any inhibition at all.

By the time they climbed into their carriage, Harriette had opened the
subject of his family and offered condolences on his losses. Along the way,
she uncovered the fact that he'd had little contact with the remnants of his
family, and hinted that he really should change that.

Maria watched anxiously for signs that his patience with this interference
was snapping, but he seemed, if anything, bemused.

Harriette progressed next through the war, gaining a brief account of his
career before moving on to her favorite subject, the Duke of Wellington.

Vandeimen seemed indulgent. "If you want stories of the great man,
Mrs. Coombs, you'll have to hope my friend Major Hawkinville returns to
England soon. He was on his staff."

"Really! Then I do hope to meet him."

"My aunt has a *tendre* for the duke," Maria teased, both pleased and disconcerted by the way Harriette could deal with Vandeimen while she could not. Of
course Harriette was over fifty and had sons older than this dangerous creature.

She noted his casual mention of Major Hawkinville, who must be the
friend the duchess had mentioned. Who was the other? Lord Wyvern. Ah,
yes. She'd heard gossip about the recent death of the mad Earl of Wyvern,
and the passing of the title to the sane, Sussex branch of the family. Vandeimen needed friends. Perhaps she could find them for him.

At last the carriage drew up in front of her house, and the first battle was
over. "Norton can take you on to your place, my lord," she said.

He had climbed out to help them down. "No need. And it's somewhat out of the way."

"All the more need," said Harriette firmly. "Your place is too much out of the way, young man, and did not look at all comfortable." She turned to Maria. "I think he should move in with us."

"Harriette, that's impossible!"

"Why? We have one unused bedroom, and I and the others can be chaperon if anyone thinks it's needed. Well, my lord?"

He looked between them. "Others?"

After half an hour of Harriette, the poor man looked like someone swallowed by the ocean and spat out drenched and exhausted.

"Other guests," Maria said, unable to help a sympathetic smile. "My late husband's aunt and uncle have lived here for years. They are somewhat invalid, but still present in the house. There is also my young niece Natalie, and my aunt, of course."

As she spoke, she realized that having him in her house would make it hugely easier to control his way of life. With him off in Holborn she'd be in a constant fret as to whether he was drinking, gaming, or priming his pistol.

"It would be an economy, and my poor valet would be ecstatic to return to civilization . . . If you are sure you don't mind. It will cause talk."

"We will cause talk anyway, and it will be a great deal more convenient to have you nearby. Please, let Norton take you to your rooms, and tomorrow, move in here with us."

He bowed. "Your wish is my command, as always, O ruler of my heart." There was a distinct edge to the last part, and she wondered if he understood her purpose.

Not a stupid man. Why had she assumed he would be?

Because, she thought, as the coach carried him away, so many of the cavalry officers she'd met had been. Dashing, courageous, but not of sparkling intellect. She rather gathered that those who were clever found themselves seconded to other duties.

"Well done," said Harriette as they entered the hall. "Everything set."

"I think him moving here is a bit extreme."

"Truly?"

Maria shrugged. "There's a lot of work to be done. But he has friends. That's a hopeful sign." She explained what the duchess had said.

"Tattoos?" said Harriette with a grimace. "What were their mothers thinking? But it will certainly be easier for Lord Vandeimen to meet his friends here."

Maria looked around at pale walls, marble pillars, and discreetly tasteful classical statues—or copies of them, to be precise. Maurice had made every effort to impress, and this house had been his principal point of impression. She had been another. Sadly, all his impressions had been imitation. Even the pillars were faux marble.

He'd taught her many lessons, including that most people had two or even more faces. She'd already seen a number of faces to Lord Vandeimen, but she suspected there were more.

The six weeks loomed in front of her and she hurried to the peaceful sanctuary of her bedroom, but even there uncomfortable memories stirred. She'd enjoyed Maurice's demanding visits to her bed. Once she'd realized the truth, however—that she was merely part of his strategy for entering and using English society—her hunger had shamed her.

As her maid stripped off her finery, she remembered the many lonely nights when she'd longed for him to come to her. She'd often thought of going to him, but never found the courage. How could she? His care for her sprang at best from mild affection, and at worst from a need to keep her pacified so she wouldn't crack his illusion of perfect success.

Begging for more had been unthinkable.

Though he'd been discreet, she'd known about his mistresses. They had all been lively, colorful women. Not like her.

She knew about his bastards, too, because he'd told her about each one, and the provision he was making. The allowances had been specified in his will. Another inherited burden.

And then there was Natalie.

Natalie's mother had been Maurice's aristocratic Belgian cousin, Clarette, but she was also Maurice's child. When her official parents had died, she had come to live with him. The truth was never spoken, but Tante Louise and Oncle Charles knew that Maurice and Clarette had been in love since their teens.

Natalie was a delightful girl, but Maria had resented having a reproach at her infertility under her roof. Now she'd invited a demon there.

She smiled wryly as she dried her hands and applied cream. No danger in that. If she hadn't been able to go to her husband demanding sex, she certainly could not invade her hired escort's rooms with that in mind.

Chapter Five

The next morning, Maria sat at the desk in her boudoir trying to pretend that she was working on her accounts, but with every sense alert for his arrival. She'd sent the coach and had no reason to believe that he wouldn't come as arranged. Still, she felt she would not have a moment's peace until he was here.

Safe.

Oh, what nonsense, but that's how she felt.

A laugh escaped, and she rested her head on her hand. She wanted to wrap the man in flannel cloth and protect him, like a mother with a delicate child. Was anything more ridiculous?

And yet, it wasn't ridiculous to see him as delicate, if by that she meant fragile. It was her task to make him robust again—without giving in to other, baser, desires.

A carriage? She shot to her feet and peered out of the window. It was. Her carriage. At last!

Heart suddenly racing, she made herself stand still and take a deep breath. *You make him strong again, Maria, and then you let him go. You mustn't permit anything to happen that might entangle him with you.*

Her throat actually ached, which was an alarming warning.

If he even shows interest in you it will simply be a game, a game to prove he's your master rather than your debtor. Have some pride!

That worked better to bring her to her senses. She glanced in the mirror to be sure she was her usual cool and elegant self. Her simple morning gown was white with a narrow, pale blue stripe. A fichu ensured modesty, and matched the white cotton cap tied beneath her chin with pale blue ribbon.

She looked a perfect, respectable widow, and thus armored, went down to greet her guest.

She almost collided with Natalie rushing toward the stairs.

"I just wanted to see," the girl whispered, flashing her dimples. "I looked him up in the library this morning. He was mentioned in dispatches *four times*! He must be very brave."

"Yes, I believe so." Instinct made Maria speak coolly even though she knew she should be acting besotted. She looked her sixteen-year-old "niece" over and reset a hairpin to hold up escaping curls. "Since you're presentable, why not come down and be properly introduced?"

Excited delight lit up Natalie's face. She was not one to hide emotions. Every one showed, and usually at twice normal intensity.

Being short with mousy hair, Natalie couldn't claim beauty, but she had enough vivacity and character to become a raging success when Maria let her loose on the world. She was sixteen now. Next year there would be no putting it off. Such a daunting responsibility.

She heard the door below open, and voices, and continued down, aware of Natalie by her side as if excitement gave off noise. Pray heaven she wasn't as audible. At the bend in the stairs, where the hall came into view, she paused.

He was wearing a brown jacket and buff breeches that could be the same ones he'd worn two days ago, but now they were neat. He looked so perfectly comfortable in them that she felt she was seeing him for the first time. She was caught by the fluid grace in the way he moved, and the effortlessly genuine smile he tossed as reward to the footman who had carried in his trunk.

Such a beautiful young man . . .

She collected herself and moved on, reaching the bottom of the stairs, then crossing the hall, hand extended. "Lord Vandeimen, welcome to my home."

He turned, still smiling, and bowed over it. "It was kind of you to invite me, Mrs. Celestin."

His eyes flickered to her side, and she said, "My niece, my lord. Natalie Florence."

He bowed, and Natalie dropped a curtsy, dimples deep with excitement. Oh Lord, Maria thought, don't let her fall into an infatuation with him. I can't cope with that on top of everything else.

Then she realized he was chatting with Natalie in a very easy way, and if he had dimples they might be showing too.

Oh Lord, don't let him fall in love with Natalie!

But then, like a cold wind, she realized it was all too likely. They were going to bump into one another all the time. And what would be wrong with it? In a year Natalie would be ready for her season, and if Lord Vandeimen courted her then, it would be completely appropriate.

It would make her his secret stepmother!

See it that way, she sternly directed.

He turned back to her. "The notices have gone to the papers, my dear. I should perhaps seek a private moment for this, but why shouldn't the world witness our happiness?" He produced a ring from his pocket and held out his hand.

A quick glance showed Natalie standing there, hands clasped in vicarious ecstasy, showing no sign of jealousy. Yet.

Maria hadn't anticipated this. She hastily twisted off the rings Maurice had given her, and held out her hand. He pushed the new ring onto her finger—with a little difficulty.

He gave her a rueful glance. "I estimated it for the jeweler, but I think it will have to be stretched a little."

"Easy enough." She looked at the ring, which was surprisingly modest. The small diamond in the center was surrounded by pearls. She didn't mind the simplicity, but she'd expected a pretentious statement. Perhaps she'd been remembering Maurice. The ring she'd just taken off held a very large blue diamond.

"The smaller stones were rubies but I had them changed," Vandeimen said. "Since you have a taste for pale colors."

She hadn't liked Maurice's ring, which had been tastelessly ostentatious, but she didn't much care for this one either. Not because of the value, but because it was insipid. Was that how he saw her?

She looked at him in buff and brown, and at Natalie in a boldly striped dress with a sky-blue sash.

Perhaps it was time to change. But not for the next six weeks. For this business, insipid was good. Very good.

"It's lovely," she said. "Now, let me show you the house and your room, my lord."

She shooed Natalie back to her lessons—she wanted no fledgling love affair for the next six weeks, at least—and led him upstairs.

When Van was eventually alone in his bedchamber, he shook his head. When had he last been in such elegantly opulent surroundings? Had he ever?

Steynings in his youth had been a fine country house, but it had been a country house, a home. The houses of his best friends had been even more so. Hawkinville Manor was an ancient, rambling place, Somerford Court a rather ugly Restoration construction, but wonderfully welcoming. Army living had thrown him into everything from pigstys to palaces, but they'd all been the worse for wear.

This house must be less than twenty years old, and appointed with great wealth and fairly good taste. He didn't exactly like it—he'd never been in a place before where everything seemed so shiny new—but it was an extraordinary setting.

"Good reminder that it isn't your setting, Van," he muttered, exploring his new quarters.

Noons had already put his scant belongings in the drawers, and a table held glasses, a number of full decanters, and bowls of fruit and nuts. A richly marqueteried breakfront desk contained heavy writing paper, and everything else needed. The glass-front shelves above held a selection of books that seemed to be chosen with care to meet every possible taste.

By her?

It hadn't been wise to agree to move in here, but last night he'd not been able to resist. Comfortable living tempted him, but he also wanted to get to know Maria Celestin, to come to understand what was going on here, and the way he felt.

Hades, he'd almost ravished her! It hadn't felt like that at the time, but it was obvious from her reaction that he'd completely misjudged it. Of course he had. He was a hired servant, nothing more, and he'd attacked her.

He'd gone over and over it in the night.

There'd been pride involved, yes. He'd wanted to master her. Revolting thought. It had spun out of control, though.

Something about her drove him wild. It wasn't just her coolness, either. Today, when she'd come down the stairs, the way she moved had practically rendered him breathless, even if she had been in a shapeless pale dress and a concealing cap.

Last night she'd worn an elaborate turban. At their first meeting she'd been in a toque. He felt almost rage that she hid her hair so much. Soft, dark blond curls had ruffled out around her cap, and when she'd turned to her niece he'd seen escaping tendrils against her long, pale neck.

Did it curl all over? How was it arranged? How long was it? Naked in bed, would it flow long, loose, and pale around her?

Stop it, Van.

He pressed his fist to his mouth.

Stop being an animal. She's a mature, respectable widow who would not even let you touch her except for this eccentric plan of hers.

He was rough from war. Broken in fortune. Broken in spirit. What was he doing now, after all, but marching to duty's drum, left foot, right foot, like the most wretched dullard in the infantry?

In six weeks he'd have enough money to continue the march, that was all, and doubtless he'd never see Maria Celestin again.

They attended two routs and a soirée that night. Maria wanted first reaction over with. She had to endure some sly comments about his youth and good looks, and about his moving into her house, but people mostly seemed to accept the situation, though with amusement.

She left Vandeimen to decide how to behave, and he managed to project a kind of reverent adoration that made her want to scream. Bad enough to be thought an older woman made foolish by lust. Even worse to be treated like a revered saint.

But then, partway through the evening she began to wonder if he was doing it deliberately to try to counteract the more sordid aspects.

If so, it didn't work.

"My dear," said Emily Galman, a thin, predatory woman Maria had known since her first season, "a tiger on your leash! I shall study you for teeth marks."

Her quick dark eyes already were.

"Divinely handsome," said Cissy Embleborough, who'd also made her curtsy at the same time, but who was a friend. "I'm not sure I'd find him comfortable, though."

"Comfort isn't everything." Maria immediately wished the words unsaid.

Cissy laughed. "True. And it may come in time."

It was three days later that she encountered Sarah Yeovil at a private exhibition of medieval art. "Maria," Sarah said, drawing her into a quiet corner, "are you sure this is wise?"

"Wise?" Despite the mild words, there was something ferocious in Sarah's manner.

"He's such a disturbed young man. Are you being fair?"

"It isn't—"

"A woman of your age should be wise for both, not . . . not *use* someone!"

Maria knew she was coloring. "I'm not using him, Sarah," she said, praying there wouldn't be a scene. "I'm *marrying* him. And if you think he doesn't want to—"

"Of course he wants to," Sarah hissed. "You're rich as Croesus. But what else can you offer him? You're old and barren."

It was so cruel that Maria froze. But then she realized that Sarah was thinking of her lost son, a man of the same age. She was reacting as if Maria had trapped Dare. She hadn't trapped anyone, but the thought of herself and Dare, whom she'd known when he was a gap-toothed child, made her shrivel with shame.

She longed to explain, but she didn't want to reveal Maurice's sin to anyone. Perhaps she was more like him than she'd thought, always trying to keep the facade in place.

"We suit," she said rigidly. "He's excellent company."

Sarah was hectically red. "You met him less than a week ago! Gravenham should never have introduced you."

Maria had to stifle laughter at this reversal of Gravenham's discreet warning, but she ached for her cousin's pain.

"You must release him," Sarah said. "You know he cannot draw back."

Nor can I. "But we suit very well."

Sarah stared at her as if she were a worm, and walked away.

Maria let out a breath, praying that her cousin not make this a public estrangement.

Vandeimen came over. "You look upset."

She forced a smile. "The duchess still mourns her son. She sometimes says things she doesn't mean."

"We all mourned Lord Darius. He had the gift of merriment."

She looked at him. "She said you and your friends were kind to him."

"A despairing sort of kindness, though his *joie de vivre* was a gift just then, before Waterloo. But you don't want to speak of war. Come, the abbey choir is about to sing 'Palestrina.' "

She went, mainly because it would remove any need to talk for a while. She suspected that was his idea, too.

To her, it was as if something pleasant had suddenly been spoiled. It surprised her that it had been pleasant, but she had begun to enjoy the season in the past few days. Her wasps had flown after other jam pots, but the true magic was that she'd enjoyed Vandeimen's company.

He was unfailingly courteous and an excellent, efficient escort. He wasn't a wit, but he held up his end of a conversation. He knew how to acceptably flirt with the ladies and joke with the gentlemen. People were slowly looking past the shocking match and his reputation, and beginning to accept him as simply a gentleman, which he clearly was.

Now, however, the thought of Dare rose up to corrode everything. Her family had regularly visited Long Chart, the Duke of Yeovil's seat, and she could remember Dare still in a toddler's skirts. She'd only been eleven, but that picture stuck because he'd managed to escape his nurse and climb a tree, causing pandemonium.

He must have been eight when he'd recruited most of the children in the area to dig a moat around the castle folly in the grounds. The duke had been impressed enough to complete the job, but at sixteen and on her dignity, Maria had thought him a grubby menace.

She'd last met him when he was a lanky, grinning youth passing through London on his way to Cambridge.

She'd been married a few years by then, a matron and mistress of her own home. She'd also been a veteran of awareness that she'd been duped by an imaginary love, and suspicion that she was barren. She had faced a difficult, dutiful life, whereas he had been practically bouncing with anticipation of a limitless future. She'd felt old then, and she felt old now.

Listening to the angelic voices of the choir—she'd probably been dancing at a ball when Dare's voice broke, when Vandeimen's voice broke—she reminded herself that this engagement was completely imaginary.

She glanced sideways at her youthful responsibility, at the strong, clear lines of his profile, and the vibrant health of his skin. In only days, the marks of dissipation had disappeared, but it would take longer for the inner wounds to heal.

She'd begun to let him choose where they went, and he seemed to prefer the more cultural events. He'd chosen this one and was enjoying it. He'd been at war for so long that much of society's routine pleasures must be fresh to him.

Her personal reaction to him was her problem—hers to control and hers to conceal.

As the days turned to weeks, control never became easy, but she managed it, helped by the fact that he kept his word. He never again tried to kiss her, or to touch her in any way other than courteously.

The worst times were those spent quietly together—lingering over breakfast, or sitting in the Chinese room, or strolling in the summer garden. Sometimes they talked, but often they were each involved in reading or even thought.

It was too much like husband and wife, and she liked it very much. She told herself that he was on best behavior for the six weeks, and she knew it was true, but she still thought that they rubbed together surprisingly well.

Vandeimen could listen as well as talk. Maurice's breakfast table conversations had mostly been monologues on whatever issue of the day interested him. She had been his attentive audience.

He could endure a silence. Maurice had seemed to feel obliged to throw words at any lingering silence as if it were a rabid dog.

He liked to read. They did not have a great deal of time for reading, but he appeared to enjoy it. He picked seemingly at random from her excellent library—again chosen by Maurice for effect.

Oh yes, he had become a pleasant part of her life.

Thank heavens Harriette was their buffer. She went nearly everywhere with them, treating Vandeimen like another son, and gave off relaxing warmth like a good fire. The healing was all Harriette's work.

But then, one day, Maria realized that her aunt's healing powers were not working.

They were chatting before dinner when Harriette said something about Vandeimen's home. He snapped at her and left the room.

As the door clicked shut, Harriette pulled a face. "I shouldn't have pressed him for his plans, but—"

"But why not?" Maria asked. "We have spent four of our six weeks. It's time he made plans to restore Steynings."

"My dear, have you not noticed that he never speaks of the future?"

Maria sat there, hands in lap, searching back over four weeks. "Never of the future, and rarely of the past. He talks easily of the present."

"Because the present offers no threat."

"Threat? I thought it was going well."

"Oh, he seems whole," said Harriette with a sigh. "He is healthy, polite, even charming. But it's like a lovely shell around . . . around nothing."

Nothing? Maria suddenly felt as if she were trying to inhale nothing, as if there was no air. "But I can't hold him beyond the six weeks."

"No, you probably can't. So you must find a way to get beneath that shell."

"If there's nothing there?" It was a protest of sorts. She'd fought so hard to keep apart.

"Something must be *put* there. What about those friends of his?"

"Con and Hawk? He seems willing to talk of their boyhood pranks."

"Precisely. Where are they? He needs old friends, friends who will make him face the difficult past and plan the difficult future."

"You think he's avoiding them? Oh, heavens. He never goes to manly places such as Tattersall's, or Cribb's, does he? Or to clubs or coffeehouses. I've been pleased, thinking it safer. But it keeps him from his friends."

"Or his friends are avoiding him," said Harriette. "Find out. Find them."

A footman announced dinner and Maria rose, flinching under those instructions. She didn't want to get involved like that. She feared getting too close.

As she left the drawing room she wondered what to do about the theater party she had planned for the evening. She had invited guests to her box at Drury Lane to see Mrs. Blanche Hardcastle play Titania. There was no reason not to go, except that she and Vandeimen had never been apart in an evening, and she worried what he might do.

What did he do when alone in his room?

He wasn't drowning his sorrows. Though she hated to, she'd questioned the butler, and the decanters in his room were being used sparingly. She knew, however, that he wouldn't need to be drunk to kill himself, and he probably still had his pistol.

She'd have to stay home tonight, though if he lurked in his room and shot himself, she couldn't see how to stop him.

He appeared however as they crossed the hall, ready to escort both of them into dinner. Of course, she thought as she placed her hand upon his arm. He would always punctiliously give the service for which he had been paid.

She ate a dinner for which she had no appetite, wondering if she could use his powerful sense of duty and honor to save him.

Harriette, bless her, picked up conversation as if nothing had happened, and talked about plans for the garden.

The play was doubtless excellent, and ethereal Mrs. Hardcastle with her long silver hair was perfect as the fairy queen, but Maria paid little attention. She sat in her box seeking ways to put Vandeimen in contact with his past, his future, and his friends.

As Sarah had said, they had been born neighbors in Sussex and all called George. A patriotic gesture, he'd explained, in response to the actions of the French sansculottes against their own monarch.

"We were lucky, I suppose," he'd said. "We could have all been called

Louis. That would have been too much for our staunchly English fathers to stomach, thank God."

They'd been christened on the same day, in the same church, and been playmates in the nursery years. As lads they'd been inseparable, and in the end, they had all joined the army at the same time. Their talents and inclinations had differed, however, and their military careers had swept them apart. Con had chosen the infantry, Van and Hawk cavalry. But then Hawk had been seconded to the Quartermaster's Division.

They hadn't seen a great deal of each other during their army years, but he didn't talk about them as if they were estranged. So why weren't they in touch, at least by letter?

Lord Wyvern was probably busily involved with his new estate in Devon, but he could still write.

Hawk was Major George Hawkinville, heir to a manor that went back to the Domeday Book. His father, Squire John Hawkinville, was still alive, living at Hawkinville Manor. Her gazetteer had described it as "an ancient, though not notable house in the village of Hawk in the Vale, Sussex."

The same gazetteer had described Vandeimen's home as "a handsome house in the Palladian manner," and Somerford Court as "Jacobean, adapted and adorned, not entirely felicitously, in the following centuries."

The main word used to describe Crag Wyvern in Sussex was "peculiar."

Wyvern had been a second son, but Vandeimen and the major were both only sons. Strange that they had joined the army.

Major Hawkinville was still at his duties abroad, apparently, but Wyvern must know of the heavy losses Vandeimen had suffered—mother, two sisters, then father—so why was he doing nothing to help? If only one of these friends was here to help hold Vandeimen together . . .

The curtain fell, signaling an intermission, and she must leave her thoughts to smile and talk as her footman served refreshments. Everyone was enchanted by the play and delighted with the Titania.

"Mrs. Hardcastle's hair is naturally white, they say," said Cissy Embleborough, "though she's still under thirty. And she always dresses in white." Cissy leaned closer and whispered, "They say she was mistress to the Marquess of Arden until he married last year. So not quite as pure as the white suggests."

Maria had never imagined it.

Her guests were the Embleboroughs, including Cissy's son and daughter. Natalie was here, too, and Harriette, of course. Maria was mostly able to let talk flow around her. She noted Vandeimen doing the same thing. Did he generally do so, or was this part of his dark mood? She suspected she had been very unperceptive these past weeks.

There was a knock on the door. Her footman opened it and turned to announce, "Major Hawkinville, ma'am."

Maria stared at the tall man in uniform, feeling as if she'd performed a conjuring trick. Then she thought to look at Vandeimen. He was already on his feet. "Hawk!"

There was joy there, but a great many other things too.

Chapter Six

He was smiling, and it was a heartaching flash of boyishness she'd never seen before.

Now he was grasping his friend's hand, and she had the feeling that he'd like to embrace him. They weren't estranged, and whatever magic had brought the major here, it was good magic.

Everyone was watching them, doubtless sensing an important moment, then Vandeimen turned to her. "Maria, I've spoken of Major Hawkinville, an old friend and neighbor. Hawk, my lovely bride to be, Mrs. Celestin."

She held out her hand. "I'm very pleased to meet you, Major."

He was hawkish, though a second later she wasn't sure why. No hooked nose, no yellow eyes. His face was lean, his hair a soft brown, and worn a little long with a wave in it. He was, above all, elegant, making even Van look a little rough around the edges.

He took her hand and actually raised it to his lips. She felt their pressure through her glove. "How unfair of Van to steal you before I had a chance, Mrs. Celestin."

She started to smile, amused by his flirtation, but then she caught a hard glint in his deeply blue eyes. Hawkish indeed. But why was he turning a predatory eye on her?

"You are still in the army, Major?" she asked, to fill the silence, though it was inane, given his scarlet and braid.

"Easing my way out, Mrs. Celestin."

"They'll be reluctant to let him go." Vandeimen's smile said that if there'd been any ambivalence, it had gone. "We chargers and marchers are two-a-penny, but organizers like Hawk are treasured more than gold. Quartermaster Division," he added in explanation to everyone. "Got the armies to the field, with weapons and supplies intact. To the right field at the right time, even, if they were really good."

The teasing look between the two men suggested it was an old joke.

"And tidied up afterward," said the major, "which is why I get home a year late and find all the loveliest ladies taken."

He flashed Maria another look, but then turned to Natalie and to Cissy's blushing, seventeen-year-old daughter to express relief that some lovely ladies were still available.

Maria picked up conversation, but she was puzzling over the man's animosity. Was it Maurice? He'd made a great deal of money supplying the army with clothes and equipment. Perhaps he'd clashed with Major Hawkinville at some point.

Was it the age difference? She wouldn't have expected another young man to be outraged.

Or perhaps she was misreading a dark mood that had nothing to do with her.

The bell rang to warn of the end of the intermission, so Maria invited the major to stay. He accepted, and she settled to the next act plotting how to keep him by Vandeimen's side as long as possible. She could bear his antagonism if she must.

At the next intermission, they all strolled in the corridor. Maria wasn't sure how, but she ended up partnered with the major, while Vandeimen escorted Louisa Embleborough, a young miss suitable for either of these handsome heroes.

"Jealousy? Already?"

She looked up into those very blue, very chilly eyes. There was no doubt. He was antagonistic toward her. She'd like to confront him directly about it, but that might drive him away. She made herself answer lightly. "Not at all, Major. I know how devoted Lord Vandeimen is to me, and *I* trust his sense of honor."

His eyes narrowed, but then changed, so that she couldn't be sure what she'd seen. "Perhaps it is I who am jealous, Mrs. Celestin. You are exceptionally beautiful."

Ah. Blatant fortune hunters she could deal with. Smiling, she said, "No, I'm not."

"You must allow me to know my own mind, ma'am. Beauty is not the same in every eye."

"Strange, then, that some people become acknowledged beauties."

He looked around and discreetly indicated a young brunette surrounded by men. "I don't know who she is, but I assume she is a toast."

"Miss Regis? Yes, she is much admired."

"I'm sure she is perfect to many, but I cannot admire a turned-up nose, and her smile is far too wide." He looked back at her. "Your mouth, however, is perfect."

Her not-too-wide smile was making her cheeks ache. Did he know she didn't want to send him off with a flea in his ear?

"Perfect," she echoed. "How lovely. What else about me is perfect, Major? I'm thirty-three years old and must hoard any compliments that still come my way."

"You're barren," he said. "And that is not a compliment."

Her breath caught. "And you are an uncouth swine, but you probably can't help that either."

They were both smiling, hiding their battle from those around.

'Van's marrying you for your money. If he needs money, I'll find a way to get it for him."

"Are you Midas, then? He lost ten thousand in one night." She watched in satisfaction as his smile disappeared. "Now, escort me back to my box."

At the door he halted, smile absent, hostility unmasked. "He deserves better than to marry for money, Mrs. Celestin. And he needs a family."

She agreed with him, but she couldn't let that show. "I want his happiness, Major Hawkinville. For that reason, you are welcome to call at my house. You will understand, I'm sure, if I try to avoid you."

She went into the box alone.

Van was finding shy Miss Embleborough hard work, but he kept an eye on Maria and Hawk at the same time. He might not have seen a great deal of his friend over the past ten years, but he could still read him. He was in a hawkish mood.

Doubtless he thought Maria a heartless harpy and was riding to the rescue. As the bell sounded and people flowed back into their boxes, he managed to pass Miss Embleborough on to her brother, and paused with Hawk outside the box.

He closed the door, leaving them alone in the corridor. "You can't fight with Mrs. Celestin without picking a fight with me, you know. And I always win."

He said it lightly, but Hawk would understand that he was serious.

"Only because you've always been a madman." The tense look eased, however. "I probably did go a bit beyond the line."

"Why?"

"She said you lost ten thousand in one night. What the devil have you been up to?"

Van hadn't wanted any of his friends burdened with his problems. "My father left debts."

"And you decided to add to them?"

"I was trying to recoup them. You know I've always been lucky. Hawk, why were you picking a fight with Maria?"

After a moment, Hawk said, "I suppose it's mostly because of her husband."

"Celestin? You knew him?"

"Only as a name. He was one of the worst suppliers of shoddy goods and short measure, but we could never pin anything on him. Very clever use of middlemen. It galls me to think of all that money on a woman's back."

"Will it help to think of me benefiting from his ill-gotten gains?"

Hawk laughed. "Zeus, yes! Can't think of a better use at this point." After a moment, he added, "Look, don't throw a punch, but is it worth the money to marry a woman so much older?"

Van thought of explaining. He didn't mind revealing his follies to Hawk, but he didn't want to put Maria in a worse light. Then he recalled an amber light, and a ravishing kiss that hadn't been repeated . . .

"So," Hawk said, smoothing over the silence, "at least you'll be able to restore Steynings to all its former glory."

If Hawk thought this was a love affair, all the better. "That's the idea. Look, I'd better go back in. Come 'round tomorrow and we'll have more time to catch up. Have you seen Con yet?"

"I'm fresh off the boat. Heard about your engagement and set off—"

"—to save me, like George and the dragon? I don't think poor Maria should be seen as a dragon."

Hawk grinned. "And you're no trembling maiden. As for tomorrow, perhaps you'd better come to me. I'm staying at Beadle's Hotel in Prince's Street."

Clearly the disagreement between Hawk and Maria had been unpleasantly sharp. "Very well. Have you heard from Con at all?"

"No. Haven't you?"

"No."

"Have you tried?"

Van shrugged. "I didn't want to clutter his life with my problems. Since Waterloo, since Lord Darius died, he has enough."

"Perhaps your clutter would have been a distraction."

It was a reproof, and perhaps warranted, but Van said, "He'd have felt obliged to lend me money, and his family's never been wealthy."

"What about the earldom?"

"I still wouldn't want to dun off him. Forget it. Perhaps you should have come home sooner instead of playing around Europe."

"Playing around—?" Hawk sucked in a breath.

Van knew he should apologize. Hawk had been cleaning up the bloody mess left by the battle, by mounds of corpses, by destroyed property, by allies turned to arguing among themselves over responsibility and reparation and even what to call the battle.

The apology stuck, though, and after a moment Hawk said, "Come over and we'll talk tomorrow." He strode off, never looking back.

Van leaned against the wall and closed his eyes, the sweet image of a pistol floating in front of him. He'd trained himself into a demon of destruction. Perhaps there came a point of no return.

He'd thought some things endured, particularly his lifelong friendships with Hawk and Con. But if Con needed his friends, he'd not found one in him, and now he'd lashed out at Hawk.

Perhaps there was no going back. He could reroof Steynings and bring the land into good heart again, but he doubted he could re-create past happiness in a house empty except for ghosts.

He might be able to do it with Maria's help.

He couldn't tell if this feeling was love, frustrated lust, or an insane kind of dependency, but he realized that his bleak mood, his bitterness, his attack on Hawk all grew out of the rapidly approaching end of his service to Maria.

And she insisted that he not touch her in any intimate way.

He knew what he ought to do. He ought to prepare to bid her a courteous farewell, leave to restore his home, then pick a young lady like Miss Embleborough to marry and have children with.

He'd rather shoot himself.

Maria entered her house on Vandeimen's arm as usual, and as usual they all took a light supper and chatted. She thought he looked strained, and hoped desperately that he hadn't fought with his friend over her. She silently berated herself for letting Major Hawkinville goad her, though how else she could have reacted, she didn't know.

Perhaps she should write an apology, though she'd done nothing wrong. It galled her that he, too, saw her as an aging harpy prepared to suck the blood from a younger man. Did everyone? Sarah Yeovil hadn't spoken more than the briefest word to her since that medieval affair.

And in a couple of weeks it would all be over.

If she were a weaker woman, she'd sink into tears.

Persistent Harriette was using Major Hawkinville's appearance as a lever to open up discussion of Vandeimen's friends and his home. He looked strained, but he was still in the room and talking, though saying little to the point.

She found herself watching him through a prism of his friend's eyes. Major Hawkinville hadn't seen Vandeimen for nearly a year, she assumed, and he had been disturbed. That was why he had attacked her.

She remembered the incident before dinner, and Harriette's words. A glossy shell with nothing inside.

That was not true. There was a lot inside, all of it tangled, dark, and dangerous. And now, for some reason, he was pushed to a brink.

When they separated to go to their bedrooms she tried to persuade herself that her concerns were only tiredness—hers or his. As her maid undressed her, however, and combed out her long hair then wove it in a plait, she worried.

When she climbed into bed, she knew that tomorrow she must insist that they travel to Steynings.

It was duty that drove her. She must correct the terrible wrong that Maurice had done to his family. By now, however, it was more than duty. She had to rescue him. She could bear to let him go, but she could not bear to let him fall back into the pit.

It was as if she saw a wonderful person through crazed glass. His honor showed in the damnable fact that he'd never again tried to kiss her. His cleverness showed in the way he managed to exhibit devotion and passion in public without ever doing anything improper.

His natural kindness showed in many ways. He never made fun of anyone. He would dance with clumsy shyness as if with a beauty, talk with a bore as if with a wit, smooth over rudeness so it was almost unrecognized.

He even spent time with Tante Louise and Oncle Charles, and no one would deny that they were a sour old couple who constantly carped at each other and the world.

She began to see, however, lying there in the dark, that all his kindnesses came from dogged duty, the same sense of duty that had driven him into the next battle, and the next, and the next.

Dogged? He had been a madman, an enthusiast, hadn't he?

Now she wondered, wondered if it had been more a case of never doing things by half measures, and whether that was what he was doing now, bleakness still in his heart.

And what exactly was he doing now, this very minute?

She tried to tell herself that he too had gone to bed, but something was screaming that he hadn't. That he might have his pistol in hand again. After a struggle, she climbed out of bed and reached for her wrap.

Oh no. Definitely not. She was not going to look for him in her nightgown!

Feeling more foolish by the moment, she put on a shift, dug through her drawers for one of her light corsets that hooked up the front, then for her simplest round gown. She wound her plait around her head and pinned it in place.

When she looked at herself in the mirror, she saw a woman blatantly well past the blush of youth in a plain gown, with plain hair and no ornament. She turned toward her jewel box, but then stopped herself. To decorate herself would put a wicked twist on this errand.

Grabbing her candlestick, she went out to make sure that her demon was not bent on something hellish.

The house was still. Surely everyone except herself was sensibly asleep. She knew she couldn't sleep until she had made a thorough check, however.

The ground floor was peaceful. She went back upstairs and checked the drawing room. Nothing.

She paused in the corridor, accepting what she'd always known. Whatever Vandeimen was up to, he was in the privacy of his bedroom, and she could not invade there.

Yet she could not let this rest.

She allowed herself to creep down to his door and listen.

Silence.

There, see. He was asleep.

Then she heard something. A movement, no more, but it suggested that he wasn't asleep.

He could be ready for bed.

Even naked.

She stood there, watching candlelight play red and black on the gleaming mahogany of the door panels, hearing only silence. Then, with a sigh and a wince, she gave a tiny tap on the door.

A voice. She couldn't tell what he'd said, but she turned the knob and peeped in.

He was sprawled on the floor in breeches and open-necked shirt, head and shoulders supported by the chaise near the empty fireplace. The room had been in darkness, and he raised a hand to shield his eyes for a moment.

"Devil take it, it's the angel again," he muttered, lowering his hand and staring at her. An empty glass was almost falling out of his other hand, and a half-empty brandy decanter sat on the floor nearby.

She almost berated him, but stopped herself. That would do no good. She closed the door behind her, thinking, thinking.

It had all been illusion these past weeks. He was still the half-drunk man who'd been about to kill himself, and she still had to save him.

Chapter Seven

W hat's the matter?" he said in a voice turned lazy by drink. "No one's going to know except Noons, so I'm not breaking the rules."

A chair sat opposite the chaise on the other side of the fireplace. She went cautiously toward it, but then at the last moment she turned to the table of decanters. She put her candlestick there, took a glass and the decanter of claret, and sat on the floor in front of the chair, facing him.

She filled the glass, then placed her decanter on the floor in mirror image of his and took a drink. "There are certainly times when getting drunk seems like an excellent idea."

Guarded eyes rested on her as he sipped. "You mean there are times when it doesn't?"

The bleakness hit her, but she tried not to show it. She didn't know what she was doing here, but she knew she mustn't fall into emotion. "Did you get drunk before battle?"

"Not on purpose." He shifted slightly, relaxing. He was, at least, willing to talk. "Some did. They tended to die. Perhaps happier than the ones who died sober. Or even the ones who lived . . . I was caught in the bottle once or twice . . ."

He eyed his almost empty glass and the decanter, and then went about filling it with notable care.

Maria sipped her wine. This was the first time he'd mentioned the darker side of war. Was that good, or bad? Was it war memories that chained him in the dungeons, or the loss of his family, or both? She couldn't wipe one away, or bring the other back. She had to try to give him reason to live.

"Why did you join the army?" she asked, as if making idle conversation. "You were an only son."

"Still am. Last of the line as well. All the hopes and expectations of the Vandeimens rest upon these paltry shoulders." He toasted her and drank. "You have a lot of hair."

Instinctively, she touched the tight knot of plait, but she stuck to her purpose. "So, why did you join the army?"

The eyes half-glimpsed beneath lazy lids suddenly shot wickedness. "Let down your hair and I'll tell you."

Perhaps she should rise and leave now, but she knew she couldn't abandon him here like this. She could call his bluff, but she suspected that Demon Vandeimen never bluffed.

She raised her hands and pulled out the pins, letting the braid fall heavily down her back. "Don't think to play your games with me, sir. You'll neither win nor escape by pretending to desire me."

"Pretending? You can come over here and feel if you want."

Her breath caught and she couldn't help glancing at his crotch. She hastily looked up. "So, why did you join the army?"

"That isn't really down," he complained, but then said, "The others were. Why not?"

"The others?" Her mind was stuck on his earlier words, however. He was aroused? Now? By her? A responsive beat began between her thighs.

"Con. Hawk." He knocked back an irreverent amount of her very good cognac. "Con was a second son and willing to do his duty. Defeat the Corsican Monster. Save the women and children of England from invasion, rape, and pillage. Hawk saw a way to escape his family. As for me . . . what more could a sixteen-year-old who fed on excitement and challenge desire?" Those dangerous eyes met hers again. "I feed off excitement like a vampire feeds off blood, dear lady. Do you want to come over here and let me drink your pale, angelic blood?"

"No," she lied, beginning to burn with raw lust. She should leave . . . "And my blood is as red as yours, I assure you."

"All the better." He put down his glass and shifted to begin crawling over to her. In another man it might have been clumsy, but she immediately thought of a wolf, a lithe and lethal wolf. She wanted to flee, but she knew that would be disastrous. And part of her wanted to stay, even to bleed . . .

He knelt beside her on all fours and raised a hand to her neck. "So pale, so pure . . ."

"I'm a widow." Despite fingers stroking her neck, she used a cool tone, trying to deny all this, trying to summon the strength to flee.

His eyes were close now, intense, pupils large in the dim light. "You shouldn't have chained me, dear widow, if you didn't need me."

Need. She did need him. It had been so long, and here was that danger that always drove her wild.

It was real danger now. Not her husband, who had only pretended because it excited her, and that excited him. It was this wild and wounded young man with heat and sex rising off him like steam.

A wise woman would get up and run.

A decent woman would save him from himself.

Mouth dry with fear and longing, she whispered, "Do you need a woman, Vandeimen?"

"I need you."

"Then take me."

He kissed her with brandy-soaked heat and greedy passion, and she kissed him back as fiercely, sprawled against the seat of the big chair. It had been so long, too long, and he tasted like hell and heaven combined.

Then she was flat on her back, her legs up over his shoulders and him in her, deeply, fully, in her. He reared up, hands on the floor on either side of her head, eyes triumphantly on hers.

Magnificent. Beautiful. Virile.

Lethal—and she loved it.

She clutched his arms, moving, then firing off into her own particular hellfire heaven.

When she opened her eyes, swooningly pleasured, she was still locked in position with him, wishing she could see behind his closed eyes and set face.

Was he in heaven or in hell?

He shifted, sliding out of her and away, letting her legs come down, head turning from her.

"Don't," she said quickly, "say you're sorry."

He knelt between her legs, sweaty, rumpled, troubled, but he looked up at her. "You liked that?"

"Is it unladylike? In these things, I am not a lady."

She saw that he was hunting for evasion, for polite lies. She had no way to convince him with words, so she simply waited, lewdly disheveled, on the floor.

"What else do you like, then?" The unvarnished hunger in his voice made her want to smile, but she was afraid a smile might be misunderstood.

"A bed for a start. I'm too old for carpets all night." She put in the reminder of her age deliberately. She wanted this, but honestly.

She stretched out a hand to be helped up, but he went to his haunches, put his arms under her, and rose to his feet. His raw strength started the thunder of excitement again. Oh, she was a wicked woman to like this so, but she did.

He staggered slightly as he carried her to the bed, but it was drink not weakness.

Was she taking advantage of a drunken man?

He wasn't that drunk, and he was getting as much from this as she.

He placed her on the bed carefully enough. "Will you undress for me?" he asked. "As I watch?"

It stirred a little qualm. "If you'll remember that I'm gone thirty, and can't rival a sweet young thing of eighteen."

"Does it matter?" He leaned against a bedpost, prepared to watch.

His comment could be taken many ways. She chose to ignore it. Even this was exciting her—the demand that she do something a little difficult and daring.

Did he understand her all too well?

Eyes on him, she loosened the drawstrings of her gown and pulled it off over her head. He was still watching. She had nothing on now but her shift and corset. Heart seeming to beat in her throat, she undid the front hooks of her corset, one by one.

He suddenly moved to brush her fingers away, to undo the last hooks and peel it open, almost reverently. She didn't want reverence. She pulled his shirt out of his unfastened pantaloons. "Strip."

With a laugh, he obeyed. She thought she moaned at the sheer beauty of his body. An anatomist could study muscles from him without dissection, but they were all sweetly smoothed by flesh—ands scars. Dozens of slashes, some puckered from rough healing.

For every one, she suspected, there was an internal scar. Scars, once formed, were permanent, though time did soften them. What of the scars that marked his heart and his soul?

She saw the dark stain of a tattoo on his chest, and remembered the duchess's comment.

"Rumor says that's a demon," she said.

"Rumor tells the truth, for once."

He came toward her and she saw that it was a demon, pitchfork in hand, amid red flames.

What was she doing here in a bed with a mad young demon?

He stripped off her corset and tossed it aside, then pushed her down on the bed in her shift. With a sudden grin, he ripped the garment open down the front.

Mad. Demon. And he understood her. It frightened her that, but thrilled her at the same time.

While her heart still raced, he spread the garment wide so she lay on it and leaned down to suckle her left breast, deep and firm.

"I love that," she breathed, even though her body's surge must have told him. "I love it. Teeth too, if you don't draw blood."

He looked up, bright-eyed. Whatever else, he was alive now, alive in this moment. Every inch of him. "And what if I do draw blood?" he asked, sending another mad shiver through her.

"You'll spoil this." Deep in her mind, however, an imp stirred with curiosity. No. She couldn't want that.

He kissed her breast softly—both a tease and a promise. "You're a remarkable woman, Maria."

"I'm a hungry one, too."

He laughed and returned to the ravishing of her breasts while she used nails to torment his skin. Without drawing blood.

Then he spread her legs and pushed into her again, and she rose eagerly, hungrily, nearly in orgasm already.

He moved in and out once with tortuous slowness. "It'll be longer this time." He made it into a thrilling warning.

She opened her eyes. "Will it?"

His wolfish smile was answer. "Do you like it long?"

Her head was buzzing, and the world swirled. "I don't know," she whispered. "My husband never went very long. He was over thirty when he married me."

"You've had no one else?"

She could protest the implication, but just said, "No."

"Am I better then?"

She laughed because it was only part tease. Deliberately, she challenged the demon. "I don't know yet."

He shifted and put one hand firmly over her mouth, while beginning deep, even strokes. She looked up, excited by that mild restraint. It implied that she had no right to object. That he could do anything with her, even draw blood.

And perhaps he could.

As she'd thought, Maurice's demanding sex had been a very safe game. Now she might be in the jungle with the animals. It excited her as nothing before.

She moved to wrap her legs around his waist, but he said, "No. Keep them down."

It could be a request. It sounded like a command.

Then he stilled and lowered his head to her breasts again, sucking painfully strongly, arching her, breaking a muffled cry from her. His teeth. She felt his teeth, pressing so carefully, but so lethally.

Her heart pounded with sudden terror and violent lust. His silencing hand felt like a gag, but when she tried to fight it off, it tightened. He raised his head and looked at her, a glint of triumph in his eyes before he lowered again to her breasts. Mercy on her, it was that contest again. What might it drive him to do?

Instead of biting, he licked. Slowly, lazily, he licked all around her breasts when she wanted to scream at him for more.

She lay there, pinned to the bed, resentfully enduring this meaningless tonguing, resenting even more that he'd assessed the game as a whole and was winning a Pyrrhic victory simply by being gentle. She was full with the burning hardness of him, and apart from an occasional twitch, he wasn't moving at all.

He looked up again, claiming the mystery. She could hate him, but she didn't. She realized that she was hot, hot all over, boiling with need, excited by being entirely in his power and that she'd never before had time to know what this felt like.

Desperately intolerable.

He took his hand from her mouth and began to thrust. Deep rhythmical thrusts that truly did feel as if they could go on forever. He was watching her as if she was more interesting than his own pleasure. She watched back, desperately fighting dissolution under those competitive eyes.

Losing.

"Bastard!" she hissed, and surrendered.

When she swam out of the hot darkness he was still thrusting.

"Zeus, no," she muttered, but he didn't stop. Why did she think she could say no to this? And did she want to? Soon her body ripped off into madness again.

It happened one more time but that time he was with her, or far, far away from her. When he collapsed on her, she had to fight the urge to push him off and run away.

No more.

She couldn't take any more.

But of course, there would be no more. It was not physically possible. Was it? What did she really know of this?

Maurice's lovemaking had been strong, and when he demanded that daytime sex she'd been excited before he'd entered her, and exploded quickly. He'd always stroked her to more pleasure afterward as if in a kind of payment. She didn't know why, and had never asked. He'd seemed to enjoy watching her fall into pleasure.

She'd never experienced anything like this, however. Ravished expressed it perfectly. Ravished, razed, and conquered. Aching, burning, and drained, and ashamed about how much she was already grieving the loss of it.

There was no doubt. Lord Warren would never do this to her . . .

She woke exhausted, parts of her body still sore. She gently touched her nipples and almost flinched. When she tried to move away from him, however, she found he was lying on her hair.

When had it been freed of her plait?

During that other ravishing sometime in the night, as hot, as fierce, as strong as before. Could she walk?

She had to.

The light through the partially open curtains suggested very early morning, but she must be back in her room when her maid came.

She looked back at him and saw his eyes open, watching her. Blank eyes. Guarded eyes. With a suppressed groan she knew she couldn't let him feel the slightest regret about what had happened. And there wasn't any. She just didn't want more at the moment.

Or most of her didn't want more.

Parts of her were shameless hussies.

"Good morning," she said softly.

"Is it? Good?"

"It promises to be a lovely day." But she realized they were going to have to talk about sex. It was not something she had ever imagined doing. She reached up to touch his stubbled cheek. "I fear you must have a low opinion of me this morning."

By a sudden release of tension, she knew she had found the right words. He moved his rough chin against her hand. "You really enjoyed that?"

"Oh yes. But," she added quickly, "I couldn't take more now."

Too late she realized that the "now" promised things she wasn't sure about, but she couldn't retract it.

"I liked it, too," he said.

She tapped his cheek in playful rebuke. "You like challenge, Lord Vandeimen. How silly that sounds. May I call you Van?"

"Of course. Or," he added with a grin, "Demon. You called me that a time or two."

She knew she was coloring. "I'm sorry."

"Don't be. It's one of my names. I'd rather you not call me George." But his lids had lowered over his eyes.

"What is it?" she asked. "Better to be honest."

He looked at her. "Was this what you wanted all along? What you're paying for?"

"No!" Then she calmed herself. "No. I promise."

But it reminded her why she'd started this, and that he didn't know the truth. She didn't want to tell him now, to spoil this strangely beautiful night, but she must. For the sake of the fragile connection between them, she must.

She eased her hair free of him, then laid her hand on his shoulder. "Van, I have to tell you something. I don't want to, but I must."

She felt the tension, even though her eyes could not detect it. "Yes?"

"I know your father lost most of his money and shot himself . . ."

His brows twitched, but he didn't say anything.

"The money was lost in an investment involving rubber production."

"You do know a lot. Why?"

That was a more dire question than he suspected. She tried to find words to soften it, but there were none. "My husband was the principal in that scheme."

She left it there, not trying to explain or excuse because there was no explanation or excuse, searching his still features, braced even for violence.

He moved slightly, freeing himself of her touch, lids lowered so she could no longer read his eyes. "And your part in this?"

"None! I knew nothing about it until after Maurice's death. I found it in his papers, his accounts . . ."

She noticed his chest rise and fall with his breaths wondering what else she could say to hold off disaster. But then he looked at her. "Is that why you sought me out? Why?"

Panick gripped her. If she told him, he'd know he didn't owe her anything. He'd leave!

So be it.

She licked her dry lips. "When I realized what Maurice had done, I knew I had to put it right. From pride, however, I didn't want anyone to know what a scoundrel my husband had been. I tried to think of cunning schemes. I followed your doings anxiously, and even thought of finding someone to deliberately lose a fortune to you at cards."

"Why didn't you?" But he was looking lighter, if rather dazed.

"I didn't know how. That's how I heard about your disastrous loss, though. It was so unlike you. I'd heard that you nearly always won. I knew I had to act." She reached out again to touch him, and he didn't move away. "Thank God I did."

He collapsed down on his back. It broke contact again, but she didn't mind. He was staring at the ceiling. "I wish your husband was alive to be killed," he said, almost idly. "But it wasn't entirely his fault, you know. There were too many deaths in the family. They broke my father's spirit. In the end, he was probably glad of an excuse to go. I should have dragged myself away from war to help him."

She took a risk and lay down beside him, close to him. He moved his arm and gathered her in, and she almost melted with relief. She'd told him, and it hadn't destroyed everything.

"You were doing your duty," she said.

"Doesn't duty to family come first?"

"If it did, there'd be no more wars."

"And that would be a good thing."

She rolled closer, put her arm across him. "Speak of war if you wish, Van, but don't torment yourself. Sometimes there are dragons, and they have to be fought. Doubtless Saint George left family behind to worry."

"Saint George. We all wanted to be Saint George the dragon killer, so none of us could be. And Con ended up getting a tattoo of a dragon. I never did understand why."

"So much worse than a demon?" she teased, licking over his grimacing devil, then blowing.

He rolled over her, smiling. "To us it was. To us the dragon was everything bad, from the head gamekeeper to the French. But he insisted."

"It links in to the title he has now."

"But he never expected to inherit that . . ." He took a handful of her hair. "This is beautiful."

"It's mousy brown."

"Not at all. It makes me think of young deer and the soft mystery of the forests. It's very English hair." He buried his head in it for a moment, then looked at her again. "If we couple again it will be on my terms. Gently."

"You don't like it like that?"

"I like it. But I want to cherish you gently to heaven one day, my lady."

"This is only for the six weeks!" It came out harsher, blunter than she meant, but she meant the warning. To herself as much as to him. "In fact, as you now know, you owe me nothing."

"Are you saying that I owed you this?"

She colored fiercely. "No. But the money is yours. You don't have to pretend to be engaged to marry me."

"I keep my word. I am still yours to command, my lady."

A number of lewd suggestions flashed through her mind, but the saner parts of her body protested, and anyway, she still needed to help him heal. That had been the main purpose all along, and now she knew what must happen next.

"Then we visit your home for a few days," she said. "Just us."

He stared at her. "Why?"

"Why not? If I were really to be your bride I would want to."

"But this is mere pretense."

She tried not to show that the flat words stung. "Why not?" she asked again.

"It's been virtually uninhabited for a year and before that it hadn't been kept up too well."

"Then it's time you assessed what needs to be done."

He rolled away to lie on his back again, but this time it was hostile. "I know what needs to be done."

Her mouth dried, but she had to continue. His fierce resistance showed that it was important. "You will soon have the money to care for it. You need to start making plans."

He did turn back to look at her then. "Is this a command, O ruler of my heart?"

At the biting edge, she wanted to say no, to let him escape, but she said, "Yes."

He rolled away from her, out of his side of the bed, shocking her with his beauty because her mind had not been in that place. Every muscle, every bone, was angry.

He turned. "Didn't you want to get back to your room?"

She was tempted to clutch things around her and scuttle, but this was another of the demon's damned battles. She climbed out of her side of the bed stark naked. Not trying to cover herself, but glad of her curtain of hair, she asked, "When can you be ready to leave?"

"In moments if necessary. How do we travel? Horseback?"

She winced at the mere thought, and knew he'd said that deliberately. "Curricle?"

"I don't have one."

"I do. You can drive if you want."

"I don't know how." At her look of surprise he said, "It's not something you do in the army in wartime. I can ride twelve hours at a stretch, though, if I have to."

She wondered if it was only her lustful side that caught an ambiguity there, and leaped toward it even as most of herself recoiled. She turned to look for clothing, even if it did lose her points. Her shoes. Her corset. Her dress . . . Where was her shift?

Still in the bed. She turned and he had found it. He tossed it to her. She realized she was going to have to hide it and hope her maid didn't notice the loss. She looked at him again. He was slightly erect.

She scrambled into her dress over nothing, and tugged the laces tight beneath her breasts. Without her corset she had to push them up first, and she glanced anxiously at him.

Anger had been replaced with a hint of a smile.

"What are you laughing at?"

"You're beautiful, even if you're not eighteen. And that comes free of charge. And I like to make you turn from a lily to a blush-pink rose. The journey will take four to five hours. Can you drive that long?"

It astonished her that he asked instead of stating it. Warmed her. "Probably not. We'll travel post."

"Where will we stay?"

Even thawed, he was making this trip entirely her concern, dissociating himself while being obedient to her commands. She would not be weakened by that.

"There must be an inn."

"The Peregrine, where I am known. We are engaged to wed, but an unchaperoned journey is still slightly shocking."

"Only slightly. I'm not a delicate young miss, and we'll have separate rooms. I'll order the post chaise and a hasty breakfast, and we'll set out in an hour."

She left with that, creeping back to her room feeling like a naughty child. No, like a wicked woman.

She was wicked to have let it go this far when it could never go further, but at least she had told him the truth. She felt lighter for that, happier, cleansed of deceptions and sins.

As reward, she'd steal the two remaining weeks for herself before saying farewell forever.

Chapter Eight

They sped out of London as true daylight broke, alone. She'd announced that they did not need their personal servants. She very much wanted to be alone with him, and it wasn't for lustful reasons. She hungered to know him better.

"You never really explained how you joined the army," she said as they passed through Camberwell Toll Gate. "Didn't your parents object?"

"Somewhat. I think they recognized the madman in me, though."

"You're not mad."

He smiled. "I feed off excitement as a vampire feeds off blood," he said again, making her instantly hot and needy. The glint in his eyes sent off warning signals, but it was so much part of him that she rejoiced.

"I can't cure you," she said calmly.

"I don't want to be cured. I think you're something of a madwoman yourself."

Oh no. She was not going to talk about sex in broad daylight. "So your parents let you go."

His smile acknowledged her retreat. "Bought me a commission in the regiment of my choice. Waved me farewell." The smile faded. "And I more or less forgot about them."

He leaned back into his corner and stared into nothing. "It was all so exciting, so new. New friends, new places, new challenges. Then when it ceased to be new, ceased to be pleasant, it had swallowed me whole. I always assumed they'd be there, frozen like waxworks, when I was ready to return."

Maria inhaled a careful breath, thinking carefully about what to say. "Did you never return home?"

"Not in the last five years. I could have. I should have . . ."

"Your family understood, I'm sure. They must have been proud of you. And later, their spirits guided you to safety."

He turned sharply at that. "Pap. Good men with adoring families died all the time."

Shame flooded her for speaking such an empty platitude, but all she could think to say was another. "They must want you to be happy."

"I am attempting to live, and live well."

It was like trying to read a foreign script. "Why is it so hard, Van? Do you not want a good life?"

"Do I deserve one? For some reason you see me as something worth saving. I'm not so sure." But then he turned to look out of the window, and she knew he wanted to be left in peace.

She granted him that, for now. She felt as if she were cracking open the cage of a seething demon, here in a confined space. She remembered, an eon ago, feeling inadequate and unprepared. Back then, she'd had no idea of the true challenge. Back then, however, she hadn't cared as she cared now.

After the first change of horses, she broke the silence. "Tell me about getting a tattoo."

His brows rose, but he answered. "It hurts."

"I suppose it must. Does it take a long time?"

"Ours did."

"Do you ever regret having a devil engraved on your chest?"

It was meant to be a light question, but he said, "I have wondered if I was inviting a dark fate."

"That's not possible!"

"It's surprising what's possible."

"Did your friends' designs have any mysterious power?"

"Hawk was always hawkish, but he's become more so. Con . . . It was strange that he chose a dragon. I've never been sure what it meant to him."

"A taste for sacrificial virgins?" she suggested.

He laughed, fully, eyes bright. "I have no idea. We've been out of touch too long."

She risked a probing question. "I gather he came home after Waterloo. Why haven't you seen him?"

That killed the laughter, but he shrugged. "I came home in January, and he was hunting in the Shires. When I visited Steynings he wasn't in the area."

"You could have written, arranged a meeting."

"Perhaps I didn't want him involved in my mess."

That made her heart ache, but it was hopeful that he was speaking of these things. Perhaps the physical act of moving toward home was moving his mind. Had their passionate night had any part in this? She'd like to think so.

Over the hours they chatted about childhood, and families—but only the sunnier aspects—and about the easier parts of their adult lives. It was clear that his childhood had been happy, his family loved, and that one of his greatest problems since returning to England might have been loneliness.

At the fourth change she suggested that they stop for refreshments, but he looked around almost like a dog sniffing the air, and said, "No. Not long now."

She'd been noting the mileposts to Brighton, forgetting that his home was not in the town. They were six miles away and must be close to Steynings.

He spoke to the postboys, giving instructions, and not far from the inn they took a side road. She read the signpost. Mayfield, Barkholme, and Hawk in the Vale.

"Hawk in the Vale?" she guessed.

"That's the nearest village, yes. It's pronounced Hawk'nvale."

"Like your friend's name."

"Almost. The family's been there about as long as the village."

He was looking out of the window, but it was no longer a means to escape conversation. She knew he was seeking signs of home. They reached the top of a rise, and he pointed to the left across rolling hills to a white house on a hillside. "That's Steynings."

She relaxed. Perhaps he'd just needed to come here to embrace his home and his purpose. Perhaps their talk along the way had helped as well, and their night of passion. Whatever had worked the miracle she sensed that he was finally, truly, coming home.

Her face suddenly ached with unshed tears, but she made herself be happy. Soon her task would be over, and she could go on with her life with an easy conscience.

"How long until we get there?" she asked.

"An hour, likely. It's not far, but we're off the good roads."

"It's a handsome house."

The house had disappeared behind trees now, and he turned to her. "Built new by my Dutch ancestor who came across with William of Orange and married into the English. Then fancied up in the Palladian style by my grandfather." He flashed her a slight smile. "Around here, we're the *nouveau riche*."

"The Hawkinville name was in the Domesday Book, I assume."

"Lord yes."

"And Lord Wyvern?"

"That title's only a couple of hundred years old, and it belongs to Devon, not Sussex. But the Somerfords have been here for five hundred years or so. Typical English blue blood. Saxon, Norman, Dane, and a bit of everything else that's come by in the last thousand years. Like the Dunpott-Ffyfes."

"True."

They shared a smile that might be the most honest one ever.

Eventually the coach slowed to turn into a village. "Hawk'nvale," he said with soft satisfaction.

It lay in a gentle valley, with a broken row of old cottages set along the river. Each had a narrow garden running down to the water. That style marked a truly ancient settlement dating back to the times when rivers were more important than roads.

The large church set on a rise across the village green had a square Anglo-Saxon tower that marked it as at least eight hundred years old. To either side, like curved arms, lay newer buildings, so that the whole village embraced the green.

Surely it stood ready to embrace a returning son.

They drew up on the modern side of the village, in front of the stuccoed Peregrine Inn and climbed down.

"This is New Hawk," Van said, looking around. "Down by the river is Old Hawk."

"Where does Major Hawkinville live?"

"Wherever he puts his hat. But his father's house is in Old Hawk, of course. The walled place with the tower inside."

It was so much part of the older section of the village that her eye had ignored it. Now she saw a walled conglomeration of buildings surely going back in parts to the days of the ancient church. "Ancient, but not handsome," she remembered.

"Did it actually hold against the Normans?" she asked in fascination.

"The wall's not that old, but the tower probably saw William the Conqueror go past. It's a fascinating old place, but getting impossible to live in comfortably."

A tall, cheerful man strode out of the main doors to greet them. He seemed glowingly happy to see Van. Van, smiling, introduced him as Smithers, the innkeeper.

The healing was happening, she was sure.

Mr. Smithers regaled her with stories of the Young Georges' impish youth as he led her to her room. It proved to be as up to date as her own at home. A maid brought water and she freshened herself. When she went down, she was directed to a private parlor where Van had arranged a meal.

She was glad of it, but would have been as happy to go directly to his home. To complete this healing journey. He wasn't in the room yet, so she looked out of the window at the green, watching people cross, sometimes stop to chat. This had the feel of a good place.

She heard laughter, and returned to the door of the parlor to look out. Van stood in the middle of a group of men of all ages and types, a few maidservants hovering as well. It was clear they all were delighted to see him home again, and were at ease with him. He looked more relaxed than ever.

And younger. Much younger.

He was home.

She'd done her job.

All that remained now was to set him free.

After the meal they hired the inn's gig and drove to Steynings Park. Though she was sure he could manage a gig, he insisted that she drive.

The neglect soon became obvious. The road worsened, the hedges were untrimmed, the ditches at the sides of the road appeared clogged. All the kinds of things that didn't get done without someone in charge.

"Have you not been here at all?" she asked.

"Once. There was nothing I could do."

She could have pursued that, but let it go.

When they came to the walls of the estate it was as well the iron gates stood open because the gatekeeper's cottage was deserted. From a slight sag, she suspected the gates couldn't be moved without a mighty struggle.

"That isn't a recent problem," he said as if she'd remarked on it. "My father felt it was unseemly to have closed gates, as if the local people weren't welcome."

"I like that."

"He was a very likable man. Very generous and trusting."

And thus used by Maurice. Thank heavens Van didn't hold that against her.

Weeds tufted the long drive, evidence not just of neglect but that little traffic had passed this way. The drive took them straight up to the square house with the two curving Palladian wings on either side.

The windows were dirty, and a sad air of neglect hung over the place, but there was no sign of serious decay. He directed her down the side of the house to a separate stableyard at the back. A middle-aged man came out lethargically to take the horse.

Van greeted the man as Lumley, but there seemed little fondness there. Probably the few staff remaining in the house were short on wages and tired of neglect.

Van assisted her down. "Let's do the guided tour, but even at its best, Steynings wasn't a jewel. I suppose some architects must be better than others."

As they toured the house, she saw what he meant. In places the proportions were not quite right, and some doors were inconveniently placed. All the same, it was a pleasant home, and ghosts of happier times lingered in pictures on the walls and arrangements of cloth-shrouded furniture.

She looked at one excellent portrait of his Dutch ancestor. "You never thought of selling this?"

"All or nothing."

Victory or death, even in financial matters. Infuriating in one way, but she couldn't help admiring it.

They ended up in a small drawing room, where the cloths had been removed and tea set out. She sat to pour. "I don't see that much needs to be done here other than cleaning."

He roamed the room restlessly. "There's some leakage from the roof. Brickwork needing pointing. Possibly dry rot in one section of the basement. Not obvious things, but if neglected the place will crumble about somebody's ears one day."

She passed him a cup. "The nine thousand will cover it?"

"Oh yes. And the servants etcetera."

It seemed invasive to quiz him on his affairs, but he needed to focus on them. "And the estate? Is it profitable?"

A look suggested that he thought it was invasive, too, but he answered. "Slightly. Times are hard now the war's over, but we'll make do once some money's been plowed in. Drainage, fencing, marling. All the things tenants put off. I should have been here helping, shouldn't I? I should have sold the damn pictures and plowed in the money."

She sipped, deliberately calm. "Why didn't you?"

She thought he wasn't going to answer, but then he said, "Now, I'm not sure." He looked around the room as if it represented the whole house. "I couldn't bear to peck away here like a crow pecking out the eyes of the dead—"

He stopped, and she could find no words to invade that silence.

He suddenly put down his cup and saucer and said, "Come upstairs. There's something I want to show you."

They'd toured all the main rooms, but she rose and went with him up the wide stairs and along a short corridor. He opened a door and invited her in. She entered and looked around curiously at what was probably the master bedchamber, shrouded in white cloths.

Then she saw his expression. "No, Van."

It was instinctive and she didn't entirely mean it, but she knew she must.

He came close to rest warm fingers on either side of her face. "Why not?"

Her wretched body was already shimmering with excitement but she knew she had to do what was best for him. He was running away into something simple. "The servants . . ."

"Aren't likely to come up here unless ordered to." He unfastened her bonnet ribbons and tossed it aside, then her cap, then began on her hairpins.

She whipped herself out of his hands and retreated clutching her wanton hair. "No!"

He simply stood there, temptation incarnate, by his need as much as his beauty. "Why not?"

She struggled to push back loosened pins, to re-create order. "We didn't come here for this."

"We didn't come for tea, either. We've just had tea."

"Is that what it is for you? Like tea?" It was nonsensical, but she threw it as a weapon.

"I don't much like tea." Then he sobered. "Is this one of the games you like, or do you really not want to?"

It made her feel ashamed, and confused, and uncertain, and she wanted to soothe him in the one way that seemed to work . . .

"Marry me, Maria."

At the shocking words, she retreated another step, shaking her head. "No, Van. No. That was never part of this."

He became still. "So. It was just an amusement for you."

"No!"

"Then what? Why not? Am I wrong in feeling there's something special between us?"

She lowered her hands and felt a heavy hank of hair tumble down her back. "Not wrong, but not right either. I'm eight years older than you."

"Well then," he said, "will you mind if I marry Natalie?"

She just stared. Eventually she managed to say, "If she's willing—"

"She's nine years younger than I am."

She could have slapped him. "That's not the same thing!" Then she braced herself to say the words that always hurt. "More importantly, I'm barren."

She saw it hit him, shaking him. "Are you sure?"

"Of course I'm sure." She snared the fallen hair, coiled it, and fixed it in place. "I've never shown any sign of conceiving." She fired a fatal arrow. "And it wasn't Maurice's fault. Natalie is his daughter."

His sudden pallor made his eyes an even more brilliant blue. He bent abruptly to pick up the hairpins that had fallen from her hair, and when he rose, he was merely sober. "What if I don't care?"

"You have to care. It's your duty to care."

"Maria, I love you."

She shook her head. "No. You can't."

He came over to her, pins in his extended, beautiful, scarred hand. "I thought that too. That I couldn't love. I thought I was dead except for an inconveniently beating heart. Then you burst into my room that day and brought me back to life."

She took the pins trying not to show how the mere brush of her fingers against his warm palm shuddered her. "I don't regret it, but I will if you persist with this."

Red flushed his cheeks, but he didn't look away. "Are you denying what burns between us? Can you say it means nothing, that it's on my side only?"

He'd put the blade in her hand, and all she had to do was wield it—deny her love, agree that it meant nothing . . .

She tried, but the sacrilegious lie stuck in her throat. Her lips moved, but no sound came out, and heaven only knows what he read in her face.

She turned sharply to the mirror, stabbing pins into her hair, striving for courage to cut him free.

She heard the door close and turned to find that he'd gone.

Van went downstairs in that state of shivering lightheadedness that had always swept over him after battle, when he'd realized that yet again he was miraculously alive and intact. But this battle had only just begun.

She hadn't said that the fire burned on his side only.

Was it willful folly to believe she'd stuck on a lie rather than a hurtful truth? All he knew was that this was demon Vandeimen's most crucial battle and he'd fight, fight to the end.

He stood in the silent, slightly musty hall stirring again the dreams that had built here for him this afternoon.

He'd begun to dream of a freshly-painted hall, the plaster cornice repaired in that corner, the parquet floor perfumed and gleaming with wax. Now his mind put flowers in the vase on the table, and potpourri in the china jar. Then laughter trickled from upstairs and children ran down and out, out into the grounds to explore as the triumvirate had, to be Robin Hood in the woods and pirates on the river—

The vision shattered and he sucked in a deep breath.

Yes, his idyll had contained children and it would hurt to let that part of the picture go, but children weren't as important as Maria. Anyway, they could bring children into their lives as she had Natalie. Heaven knows, there was no shortage of orphans in the world.

Natalie. Oncle Charles and Tante Louise had gossiped maliciously about Natalie, so that had been no surprise. He hadn't made that other connection.

He burned with the need to act, to charge wildly into battle, but where was the enemy here?

He went over to the china potpourri pot his mother had loved and lifted the lid to find that it still contained dusky petals, doubtless put there by her own hands. Having been covered for so long, a faint perfume stirred like a ghost of summers past.

Tears stabbed, and he looked up, swallowing, fighting, until the danger passed. There could be summers here again, and children even if they were not of his blood. There could also be Maria.

There had to be.

It wouldn't be the first time he'd led a forlorn hope.

He heard a sound and turned to see her coming down the stairs, gloved and hatted, composed except for something bruised in her eyes. He would cut off his arm rather than cause her pain, but he could not let her run away without a fight.

He met her at the bottom of the stairs, blocking her way.

He saw her flinch, but she met his eyes. "We should return to London. We can make it before dark."

"Of course, but let me say something first. We can have children." He overrode her protest. "We can give a home to orphans as you have to Natalie."

"You have bastards you need to house, Lord Vandeimen?"

It was harsh as a swung saber, but attack had never daunted him. "Not that I know of. Fight with me, Maria, instead of against me."

She met his eyes, lily-pale, steel-cold. "We are not on the same side in this."

"Maria—"

"No!" She sidestepped to walk around him and he grabbed her arm.

She whirled, furious—and afraid.

Instinctively his fingers loosened, but then he tightened them again. "All I want to make clear is that if you are barren it is not an insurmountable obstacle."

"Your title would die."

"So, it would die. It's an upstart Dutch transplant only five generations old. It's not worthy of human sacrifice."

Her lips tightened and she suddenly looked older, older than her years. All he wanted was to cherish her and he was bruising her in mind and spirit.

She opened one gloved hand and he saw his ring in it. "I'm sorry, Lord Vandeimen," she said, looking at some vague point behind him, "I find we would not suit."

"Dammit, Maria"—he sucked in a breath—"We have a contract and it has nearly two weeks to run."

Her eyes clashed with his. "I'm ending it now. As soon as we return to town I'll have your nine thousand pounds transferred to Perry's."

"A contract has two parties. I say it will hold until the end."

"Hold to it if you want. I will not wear your ring, and you will not live in my house. I will not see you again, Lord Vandeimen. In fact, if you have any honor at all you will stay here and get on with restoring your home!"

It hurt, like blows, like blades raining down on him, but he kept hold of her arm and spoke steadily. "And leave you to return unescorted? I think not. But you're right, we should leave."

He let her go then, and stalked out of the house before he gave into temptation to shake her, kiss her, or ravish her.

He suspected she'd succumb to angry ravishment, and that would be the cruelest blow of all.

Chapter Nine

Maria sank down onto the lowest steps, shaking with fury and pain. It was like trying to hack off one of her own limbs, and he was making it harder and harder. Why wouldn't he simply take the money and go?

The last thing she wanted to do was to follow him, to travel with him back to the village and then on the four-hour journey to London, but what choice did she have? Like so many other wounds, it could be endured and survived. She pulled herself to her feet and gathered strength to walk out to the stables.

When she arrived there the gig was ready and he was sitting with the reins in his hands. She climbed up beside him in silence and they set off.

"Maria—"

"Van, don't. Please." She gripped her hands together and realized that she still had his ring clutched in one. It would be a grand gesture to toss it away, but she couldn't do that. She couldn't do that any more than she'd been able to cut him free cleanly with cruel words.

He steered around a deep dip in the drive then picked up speed again. "I amputated one of my men's arms once," he said, eyes ahead. "It was mostly off anyway, but he was bleeding to death and we were stuck in the remains of a village in the sierra. I tied it, hacked off the remains, and cauterized it with my saber heated in the cooking fire." He turned to look at her. "He begged, too, but he's alive today and home on his family's farm in Lincolnshire. He married a childhood sweetheart and has a baby now."

She didn't know what to say other than to beg again, and she believed what he was saying. He wouldn't stop because she begged, because he believed that what he was doing was right.

They turned out of the generously open gates onto the country road. "Are you sure about Maurice?" he asked quietly. "About Natalie?"

She could weep for clung-to hopes, but answered flatly. "Yes. He had four other bastards that I know of, currently aged two to ten. I can list their names if you want. He never concealed them from me, and he left provision for them in his will."

"List their names."

"What?" She stared at him.

He glanced at her, seeming almost calm, almost as if none of this mattered at all. "You said you could list their names. I asked you to."

Feeling as if they'd slipped into a land where nothing made sense, she said, "Tommy Grimes, Mary Ann Notts, Alice Jones, and Benjamin Mumford."

He nodded, but said nothing. The children should have been a winning blow, and yet Maria felt uneasily as if she had put a sharp weapon into his hands. She needed a shield. She would marry Lord Warren. He wouldn't expect a passionate heart, and marriage would distract her. After all, she'd have the care and guidance of his sons, not much younger than Van.

But she'd never again burn in the fire of her demon's passion.

Human sacrifice.

Oh yes, he had the right of it there, and was it right to sacrifice Lord Warren in her cause?

When they arrived back at the inn, she hurried up to the privacy of her room, leaving him to arrange for the coach to be ready. As she waited her mind circled that incident he had mentioned, the amputation.

How old had he been then? He'd said sierra, so in Spain. At least two years ago, perhaps longer, and he was only twenty-five now. She could imagine the inner terror, the sweating hands, the threatening vomit. She was also sure of the courage and willpower that had kept his hands steady, had done what had to be done as quickly and deftly as possible.

Love poured through her again, carried on respect and admiration. She wanted him in so many, many ways. But she loved him enough to cut him free and cauterize the wound despite his protests. Then perhaps one day she would be able to speak calmly of his happy life along with a sweetheart and a baby.

Van made the arrangements, and considered four hours in the coach with Maria. He couldn't. He couldn't trust himself not to argue, or worse, try to persuade by force or seduction. The demon was writhing inside him, calling for the fight to the death, for all or nothing.

He asked the innkeeper about a horse to hire and found that a Mr. Slade kept three fine horses at the inn and rarely rode them. Slade, apparently, was a wealthy iron founder who'd retired to the village and built the overlarge, stuccoed house that stood out in the village like a tombstone in a garden. Van was surprised Squire Hawkinville had permitted it.

Slade was a convenience for him, however. At the price of a few moments being oozed over by Slade he had the use of a bay gelding for the journey to London. It would cost more later. The iron founder was clearly delighted to put a local lord under an obligation. It was worth the price. He'd pay any price for Maria's comfort—except to let her go.

By the time they arrived back, the light was going and a misty drizzle completed a miserable day. Maria had spent the journey planning ways to force Van to accept that their arrangement was at an end, but she'd been constantly distracted by the sight of him on horseback.

He rode superbly of course, one with the fine horse, and completely in control. He mostly rode alongside, but occasionally he raced ahead then circled back exhilarated, smiling. Until his eyes met hers and settled again to cool purpose.

He was going to fight, and she shivered at the thought.

She was drowning in guilt, too. He was a cavalry officer, and she'd never thought to offer him a horse. She put that aside as a minor sin past redemption, and focused on amputation.

As soon as she was out of the coach and he was off the horse, she said, "Your indentured servitude is at an end as of now, my lord."

He paled so the scar stood out starkly on his cheek, but said, "Not here, Maria," and turned to tip the postboys and to arrange for one to ride his horse to the livery stables.

She was left burning with embarrassment. She'd spilled her words in the open street. She hurried into her house feeling not like a resolute matron, but like a guilty child. She almost fled up to her room, but he'd follow her there. She knew he would. She couldn't deal with this in such an intimate setting.

Surely she had the right to throw him from her house!

Harriette came down the stairs. "Maria? What are you doing home? Is something the matter?"

"I've decided my arrangement with Lord Vandeimen is at an end. He will be leaving."

"Will I?" he said behind her, and she turned. Her footman was hovering, looking uncertain. If necessary, John would throw him out. If he could, that is. A brawl in the entrance hall of her house? How had matters come to this?

"Maria." It was Harriette, and she had the door to the reception room open. "We need to talk."

Maria wanted to refuse, but if she did, Harriette would speak her mind in front of the servants. She stalked into the room and shut the door. "Don't interfere, Harriette."

"You cannot be so impossibly inhospitable."

"There's no longer any need for him to be here."

"He's healed?"

Maria was struck by uncertainty. It was only last night that he'd taken to deep drinking. So much had happened since that it seemed an age ago, but it had only been last night.

"He's ready to begin restoring his home," she said. "That's what you wanted, isn't it?"

Harriette eyed her. "I think he's making you uncomfortable, and that's why you're trying to cast him out. What's he done?"

Maria circled the room then admitted it. "He proposed to me."

"Ah. And you said?"

"No, of course. It will not do."

"Why not?"

"Put aside age and the fact that I bribed him into this, I'm barren."

Harriette's face sagged. "Oh my dear, I had forgotten. It would have been wonderful."

"No it wouldn't. I'm too old for him. He's too . . . demanding. Controlling."

"Oh no. You're made for each other. I've thought it almost from the first. You laugh with him, and blush with him. He makes you young again. He's steady with you, at ease with you. You anchor him. Be that as it may," she added briskly, "you are not throwing him out of here so suddenly, especially if you've just hurt him—"

"I haven't hurt him."

"Any rejected proposal is hurtful. He's staying for the remaining days."

"Whose house is this?"

"Yours, but you'll do as you're told. You don't want to have to wonder whether he's digging out his pistol again, do you?"

"He wouldn't . . ." Maria glared at her aunt. "You're a conniving old woman."

"I'm not so old as that. In fact," she said with a naughty grin, "if you don't want him, perhaps I'll set my cap at him. I don't mind a bit of control in the right places."

She walked out of the room leaving Maria gaping. She sank into a chair and leaned her head against the back.

Twelve days. Only twelve days. That could be endured.

And twelve nights, every one of them temptation.

Maria retreated to her room that first night, but she could hardly hide forever. She emerged after breakfast the next day braced for persuasion, even seduction.

He had gone out.

Feeling deflated instead of relieved she set out to have a normal day, the sort of day she'd enjoyed before meeting Demon Vandeimen, the sort of day that would fill the rest of her life.

His absence crept with her like a gray ghost.

When she visited Crown and Mitchell to consider one of the new kitchen stoves, she turned to him for an opinion. When she found that a book she'd been waiting for was available, she anticipated sharing it with him. When she flipped through her pile of invitations, she thought of which would most please him.

She didn't want to attend social events. People would notice the absent ring. After a moment she pulled it out of her pocket and slid it on her finger again. It was still small and pale, but precious. She was entitled to keep it, and she would.

She would never wear it again, but she slid it off and put it back in her pocket. A guilty weakness, but it would be something to remember him by through the rest of her life.

Van went to Beadle's Hotel, and was taken up to Hawk's rooms.

Hawk closed the door on the nosy maid. "Trouble?"

Trust Hawk to see that instantly. This was his private parlor, comfortably if plainly decorated. Van had the irrelevant thought that it would have been luxury during their campaigning years. And that, despite danger and death, life had been simpler then.

He'd come here to get Hawk's help, but putting the situation into words felt like sealing it in reality. "Maria's decided she doesn't want to marry me."

"Ah. I'll be honest and say that I'm not sorry."

"Why?" Van could have said other, more bitter words, could have thrown a blow even, but restrained himself. "You met her once, and spoke a few words. What the devil reason do you have to try to come between us?"

So much for restraint.

Hawk stayed calm, but Van saw him shift slightly, balancing to be ready for attack. He couldn't believe this. Was everything in his life going to fall apart?

"I haven't tried to come between you," Hawk said calmly. "Though I could. I wasn't going to speak of this, but perhaps it will help you accept your lucky escape. I said that her husband engaged in shady dealings. I had other suspicions, which I confirmed by making some inquiries yesterday."

"You've been making inquiries about Maria?" Van could feel the words in his mouth like ice, like fire. "How dare you?"

"Of course I dare. I couldn't let you marry a woman like that without—"

"A woman like that?"

Hawk stepped back, raising a hand, his eyes fixed on Van as on a predatory animal. "Hear me out before you hit me."

Van sucked in a deep breath. "Speak."

"Celestin had his fingers in many rotten pies, including highly speculative investments. He was leading partner in the investment that ruined your father. He got out intact—he generally did—leaving your father to bear the loss. He as good as put the pistol to your father's head, Van. I don't know what game his widow is playing, but—"

"Is that it?"

"What?"

"Is that your evidence?"

For once, Hawk looked unsettled. "Yes."

Van felt muscles unbunch, sinews release. "She told me. Why should she be blamed for her husband's dishonor?"

"She obviously knew about it."

"She found out after Celestin's death, from his papers and accounts. And I believe her on that, Hawk."

Hawk didn't look relieved, but he said, "Then for your sake, I'm glad. Except that apparently she has cast you off."

With matters so on edge between them, Van didn't want to expose Maria any further, but it wouldn't make sense otherwise, and he needed Hawk's help. "The engagement is a pretense. Maria hired me to play her husband-to-be for six weeks. She said it was for protection from fortune hunters, but as I discovered, it was to return the money my father lost in that investment."

"So it was all pretense anyway," Hawk was saying, looking brighter. "Your six weeks must be nearly up and you'll be able to restore Steynings. All's well that ends well."

"Except for the fact that I love her. I took her to Steynings yesterday and realized that the place will mean nothing to me without her by my side. I asked her to marry me, and she said no. I'm not willing to accept that answer."

"I'd say you don't have any choice."

"I can fight. That at least I can do well."

"Perdition, Van, if the woman doesn't want you, she doesn't want you!"

"I love her, and I think she loves me too, though she won't admit it."

"Will you try to throttle me if I say that we are easily misled about such things? If she loved you she would marry you."

"She thinks the age difference matters. But more important, she thinks she's barren."

"Ah. She has no children. More honor to her, then. The line dies with you."

"So it dies! What the devil difference will that make to the world? But I'll never persuade her to marry me as long as she believes it true." He collapsed into a chair. "Thing is, Hawk, I'm not sure it's true. I don't want to raise false hopes, but I want you to put your inquisitive talents to some use, for once."

Hawk stayed standing. "You're being damn rude for someone wanting a favor."

The sudden chill shocked Van back into his sense. "Gad, so I am." He looked up at his friend. "Have you ever been in love?"

"I don't think so."

"It can blast away common sense as well as manners. That's why I need a cool head to look into Maurice Celestin's intimate affairs and bastards." He tried a smile. "For old times' sake?"

Hawk pulled him out of the chair and into a brief hug. "For past, present, and future, you idiot. But I warn you," he added, eyes steady, "I'll tell you everything I find—good or bad."

Van met his eyes. "Can you not see how wonderful she is?"

"I see a handsome woman with strength of character. She claimed to have saved your life, and it's probably true. But that means you were vulnerable to her maturity and strength of character. Van, when she first came to London to flirt at Almack's, we were pretending your gamekeeper was the Sheriff of Nottingham, and that Con's father's bull was the Minotaur."

Van laughed. "Zeus, that poor bull! But you're as bad as she is, Hawk. It doesn't matter. Trust me on that—it doesn't matter. Just find out the truth about Celestin's bastards."

"And if she really is barren?"

Van smiled. "Then I'll try to win her anyway."

Maria found she lacked the courage to go out. She had no taste for gossipy company or idle pleasures, and no courage to face questions about her missing ring and missing fiancé. She would have to one day, but not yet, especially not with him still in her house.

Every day Van took an early breakfast then left the house, returning in time for the evening meal. She joined him for that meal because it would be petty to leave him and Harriette to eat alone. And anyway, she hungered for the last few scraps of the feast—the sight of him, the sound of his voice, his expression whenever their eyes met, the ache in every muscle, every bone at the memory of their lovemaking.

When she and Harriette left the dining table he did not linger, but nor did he join them for tea in the drawing room. He retired to his room for the night, but always with a look that said as clearly as words, "If you join me again, you will be welcome."

Every night, it was another Waterloo not to take up that invitation.

She counted the days till this torture would be over, and counted the nights as the beginning of an eternity without him.

Then the last night came, the last good night, the last look across the dining table. He'd announced that tomorrow he would to return to Steynings and begin his work there.

She rose, but lingered, one hand on the back of her chair as if glued there. The final cut. She couldn't bear it. She must.

From courtesy, he was standing too, separated from her by the wide table and a tasteful arrangement of spring flowers. She'd had plenty of time for flower arranging.

"I hoped you would change your mind," he said quietly. "I have been tempted to force you. Perhaps I would have failed anyway, but I managed to stop myself trying. But I have words I could say, things I could show you that might make a difference."

Maria glanced to the side and realized that Harriette had already left. Her heart rose up, beating fast. "I don't see how." It was weak, but it was all she could manage. Now the absolute end was here, she couldn't quite face it.

"Things and words might not matter," he said. "It all comes down to love.

I love you, Maria, in the deepest truest way. I am sure of that. But I don't know whether you love me enough to take the chance."

A breaking heart was proof, wasn't it? A breaking heart clearly wasn't visible. "What words, what things?" she whispered from a dry mouth.

"Misty words and butterfly things. It's the love that counts. Come to me, Maria, and speak of love, and perhaps we can fight side by side. If not, there really is no point, is there? And whatever happens, I will leave tomorrow unless you ask me to stay."

He walked from the room then, lean, lithe, beautiful. Her beautiful, beloved young demon, whom she shouldn't want at all, but wanted more than breath itself. She stood staring at the flowers choking back a scream of, *What words? What things?*

She gripped the chair harder. She mustn't weaken now. Truths were truths. Words couldn't wipe away the years between them. No *thing* could make her womb fertile.

But then she turned and ran upstairs. Ignoring Harriette waiting in the drawing room she ran down the corridor and flung open the door to his room. "What words? What things?" she cried. "Why are you doing this? There is no way to change what is!"

He quickly shut the door, then stood barring it. "Why? Because I'm Demon Vandeimen, of course, and you are my last forlorn hope. Do you love me, Maria? Or does the fire only burn on my side?"

She stood looking at him, fighting, fighting . . . "I love you, Van. But don't you see that—"

He swept her into his arms and carried her to the bed. She melted even as she cried, 'No, Van. This won't change my mind!'

All the same, she was ready, ready to be taken in a violent storm that would sweep away reality for a brief while.

But he laid her down gently and sat beside her on the bed. "This isn't part of the battle. Let me love you, Maria, one last time. Tell me what you want tonight."

You, now—hot, hard, and fast. But this would be the last time, so she said, "Show me the gentle love you promised once, Van. And pay no attention if I weep."

He smiled and began to undress her, cherishing each revelation with touch and kiss so that every inch of her body felt worshiped. The lust stirred and the fire burned, but the gentleness encircled it so she could only lie and watch as he stripped off his clothes to join her, skin to skin in the bed.

She was afraid that it wouldn't work this way, that she'd be left softly quivering with need, that she'd disappoint, but he swept her up with tenderness, with worship, up into a slow, sweet crescendo of heaven that she'd never even known existed . . .

She did weep, though she did not mean to, wept deeply in his arms, against the devil on his naked chest, because gentleness, she found, went deeper into the soul than hard passion, and the thought of its loss was like ripping roots from her heart.

He stroked her hair, seeming to know these were tears that should be allowed to fall. "Say again that you love me, Maria. Please."

Impossible to deny it now. She swallowed. "I love you, Van. But it doesn't change anything."

He pushed her back and smiled at her, a blissful smile that made her want to weep again, but bitterly. "Don't try to deny facts, please," she begged. "When I married Celestin, already somewhat on the shelf, you were a scrubby schoolboy!"

He shook his head. "Let's look at things first."

Chapter Ten

H
e slid out of the bed, picked up a leather folder from the table, and came back to sit up beside her.

Puzzled and wary, she eased up by his side. "What is it?"

"My drawings." He undid a tie and opened the portfolio. "Are you a connoisseur? I hope not." He began to turn sheets of paper to show rough sketches of army camps and assorted buildings. Tolerable, but nothing special.

What had this to do with their age difference?

Then as he turned the sheets, she reached out to stop him. "That's Major Hawkinville."

It was a quick sketch of a man in shirtsleeves at a desk laden with papers, but it captured him perfectly.

"Before Waterloo. That was an organizational nightmare." He flicked through a few more sheets. "That's Con."

She saw a man with strong features and short dark hair standing in classic soldier pose staring into the distance, a long cloak concealing most of his uniform. He almost looked like a statue.

"He looks tired," she said. "After battle?"

"Before Waterloo. He didn't want to be there. None of us did, of course, but he especially. He left the army in 1814, so he'd been away for nearly a year. He'd grown used to living in sunlight, and came back to join us in the shadows. I think he's still in the shadows, and I haven't tried to help."

He moved on and showed her a series of drawings of boys and men. Some were quick sketches, others highly worked pencil portraits. All were of distinct individuals. Not a professional standard, no, but drawn by a skilled amateur who had captured his comrades-in-arms in many moods.

She stopped him so she could read the names, and found that the writing wasn't complete names. *Ger, Badajoz,* she read. *Don, Talavera.* With a chill, she knew that he'd recorded the battles where they had died.

Then one drawing said only, *Hilyard.*

"He didn't die?"

"The bloody flux in a muddy village. We didn't even know the name. We lost more men to disease than to battle."

She took the folder and flicked through it quickly, seeing name and location on every one. "You only drew dead men?"

"They were alive at the time." Before she could ask, he said, "I generally gave the pictures to the sitters. These are men who died before I had a chance. I've wondered if the relatives would like them. They're not very good."

"Good enough," she said, staring at one near the end.

Dare, Waterloo.

There were a great many Waterloo ones, but this sketch had leaped out at her because she recognized the long face and merry smile. "He looks ready for a great adventure," she said, touching the paper. "I think his mother would like this. They don't have a recent likeness."

"You knew him?"

"He's a distant cousin." She traced his smile. "He looks so happy."

He picked up the paper and studied it. "Drove us crazy. We all knew it was going to be hell, but Dare saw it as an adventure. He was Con's friend. Part of a bunch of Harrow men who call themselves the Company of Rogues. He was one of the enthusiastic volunteers that we scoffed at, but you couldn't scoff at Dare. At least he knew he didn't know."

All the pictures disturbed her, but Dare's in particular. He and Van were of an age. Van could so easily be dead. Was that why he was showing them to her? "Why did you want me to see these? They don't change anything."

"Don't they?" He flipped through the pages and pulled another one out, one not obviously different from the others except in being a little more clumsy. A picture of a sinewy, grizzled man who looked cynical but kind.

"Sergeant Fletcher. He taught me how to survive. When you were marrying Celestin, the scrubby schoolboy was drawing his first picture of a walking corpse."

The clock on his mantel tinkled the hour.

He gave her the picture. "Don't think that I'm a child, Maria, not knowing what I want and need. You are my heart's blood. Perhaps we all know when we meet that one person who is the perfect match." He took another sheet out of the folder, the very last sheet, and gave her a picture of herself. "Not drawn from life, of course."

It was just head and shoulders. Her hair was loose, as she never wore it, tendriling down the front of a simple gown. She looked serious, but not unhappy, and unlike any self she had seen in a mirror.

"You have a gift, but this isn't really me."

"It's the Maria I see." He began to tidy the papers. "I will leave tomorrow if you insist, but my feelings will not change." He tied the strings and looked up. "You do not have to protect me from myself."

She caressed his scarred cheek. "How can I not? Love does that to us."

"I'm not your child, Maria. I'm your lover." He kissed her then, proving it, and loved her in the wild-fire way.

She lay there afterward, sweaty and sticky, stroking the lean length of his powerful body.

I'm not your child, Maria. I'm your lover.

When you were marrying Celestin, the scrubby schoolboy was drawing his first picture of a walking corpse.

He was a man, mature enough to be fair mate for her. He was more than her lover, though. He was the man she loved as she had never thought to love. She would marry him quickly, joyfully if she could give him at least hope of a child.

Could she be his mistress? Let him marry a suitable young woman who would bear him children?

No. Never. If he married someone else she could never corrode his marriage like that, and she didn't think he would consider it.

So . . . As he'd said, they could be happy without children of their own. The title would die, but if he didn't mind . . .

Was she being weak or strong?

Would he—and this was the crucial question—would he come to regret it?

She turned and looked at her mate, her destiny. He was sleeping, lashes long on his cheeks, looking at ease. Perhaps he had not slept much these past nights.

She had the sudden realization that her life had flowed to make this moment possible.

When she had entered society at sixteen—shy, proud, and rather awkward—Van had truly been a scrubby schoolboy. They would never have found each other. The years since had been necessary to bridge the gap of years and experiences.

Without the army, Van might not have become her match. With his wild nature, he might have become one of the callow, irresponsible young men of the *ton*.

If she'd not married Celestin, she would now be settled with some other man, not free to love. Without the pleasures and pains of that marriage, she would never have been able to deal with Van's complexities.

Fate had shaped them and finally tossed them together for this brief trial. This was her golden moment. Her only chance. She brushed silky hair from his forehead, tussling with courage and honor in her mind . . .

His lashes rose and he smiled, confused for a moment, then warm. "Marry me, Maria."

She was struck dumb again, but surrendered in a whisper. "If you're sure . . ."

His eyes shut, then opened, and she saw the gloss of tears. "I'm sure. Maria!" He gathered her in for a hug that made her squeak. They broke apart, laughing.

"I feel wicked," she protested. "Wrong."

He grinned. "Of course you do. You are lying ravished in an unblessed bed. But marriage will fix that."

"I'm not sure our sort of ravishment is right even with a blessing."

"Oh it is, it is," he murmured, nuzzling at her breasts.

She suddenly held him there, held him close, stabbed by the thought that no child would ever suckle at her breast. And that she was binding him to her barren fate. She was a greedy, wicked woman.

"Promise me you won't regret, Van."

It was a whisper because he could not promise that, but he said, "I promise."

They lay for a moment, but then he stirred, pulled apart, and sat shamelessly naked facing her. "I've shown you the things. I still have the words."

She sat up, too, suddenly wary. "Words? What more is left to say?"

He looked down for a moment, then met her eyes. "I don't want to raise false hopes. It's still in the hands of fate. But you may not be barren."

The pain of tears swept through her. "Van, don't! We have to accept the truth."

"Then accept it. Listen." It was an officer's command and she stilled.

"I've spent time with Oncle Charles and Tante Louise, and things they said didn't entirely match Natalie being your husband's daughter. For a start, the idea only stirred about six years ago."

"That was when Natalie's parents died and she came here. The truth came out because her mother was beyond scandal. And why else would she come to live with Maurice? Van—"

"She came here because there was nowhere else" he interrupted. "The wars wreaked havoc with Celestin's family in Europe. She also came here, I believe, because it suited him." He took her hand, her ringless left hand. "I set Hawk to making inquiries, Maria. It's his forte. Celestin was almost certainly not in the right place at the right time."

She looked at him, her brain feeling fogged. "What? Why would he lie? It doesn't make sense. It doesn't matter anyway, Van. There are four others!"

"All definitely false."

She stared at him. "They can't be."

"They are. It can't have been hard to find women unfortunately with child willing to call a man the father in return for an income."

She pulled her hand free, moved back, back against the headboard. "Such women would say anything for money, too. Did you arrange this to try to persuade me into marriage?"

She was suddenly reminded of the man she had first met, the one who'd threatened and disarmed her. He neither attacked, however, nor shrank from her. "I knew you might think that. That's why I wanted our feelings settled first. The matter of children doesn't matter that much to me, Maria. I'm sure that's undutiful of me, but you matter more than the damned title. I set Hawk to finding out the truth to remove the last barrier in your mind. That's all. Talk to the women if you want. I think you'll be convinced."

His leashed anger stung, but a trace of doubt lingered. "Why would Maurice do such a thing, construct such a painful, complex lie?"

"Because he was a self-made man who cared about appearances. He doubtless wanted to found a dynasty, and when it didn't happen, he couldn't bear to have people think it was his fault."

That rang with the clarity of absolute truth.

"So he constructed another facade!" she exclaimed. "The swine. The worm. The toad! I felt so *guilty*. So *flawed*." She launched herself toward him. "Oh, Van, please forgive me! I should never have even thought you might have made it up."

He pulled her into his lap. "Of course you should have thought it. I was desperate enough." He brushed hair off her face and looked into her eyes. "It might still not happen. There might not be children."

She smiled up into his eyes through tears. "But there might be. That's enough. And you are more important to me, too, than children of our bodies." All the same, she ran a hand down her belly. "But think, there might be a child growing now!"

He covered her hand with his. "And we'll certainly be willing to work hard at putting one there. I've always been lucky, you know." He rolled her down beneath him on the bed and reached out to take a silver box off the table.

She could hardly think for hot muscles weighting her, but she focused on it. "What now?"

He opened the box to show her a ring, and a piece of sharp stone. The ring held a fine, flashing ruby in a circle of diamonds.

"A new ring?" she said. "I still have the other."

"My Maria needs a ring with fire in the heart." Still over her, his erection pressing between her thighs, he slid the ring onto her finger. "A new ring for a new beginning."

She looked at it. "You were very sure of me."

"I wasn't sure at all. But the only way to fight is to convince yourself that you'll sweep all before you."

"Thank God you always did." She brought the ring to her lips, tears escaping. "I'll always cherish the other one, too." She looked back at the box. "And the stone? A flint . . . ?"

He put the box aside, but kept the flint in his fingers. "When you burst into my room that day I'd already pulled the trigger—"

"Van!"

"—but the flint failed. This flint. Sheer demon's luck, but mostly luck in having a valet who loves me more than I deserve, and finding a woman willing to fight my devils with me."

He tossed it on the table. "Marry me in Hawk in the Vale, Maria, soon?"

She traced the demon on his chest, and knew they could make it little more than a memory of darker times. "Can we share our happiness with everyone there? A grand party for all? Your friends will attend?"

"Hawk and Con? I'm sure of it."

She hoped he was right. She suspected that Major Hawkinville still disapproved, and the Earl of Wyvern seemed to be a dark mystery. If his friends failed him she would fill any void, but if she could, she'd heal the connections to them, too.

With love so strong, and happiness burning in them like a winter fire, how could they fail?

"A wedding, my lord. In four weeks. In Hawk in the Vale. A celebration to show that sometimes we poor mortals can find heaven here on earth."

The Dragon's
Bride

The Dragon's Bride is dedicated to
Romantic Times reviewer Melinda Helfer,
who sadly died in 2000. Melinda was a
steadfast friend of the romance genre, but she
was especially supportive of new writers. On
my first novel in 1988, she wrote in her review,
"The sky's the limit for this extraordinary talent."
I was stunned and moved to tears, and also
inspired to try to reach those heights.
For you, Melinda.

Chapter One

May 1816
The south coast of England

The moon flickered briefly between windblown clouds, but such a thread-fine moon did no harm. It barely lit the men creeping down the steep headland toward the beach, or the smuggling master controlling everything from above.

It lightened not at all the looming house that ruled the cliffs of this part of Devon—Crag Wyvern, the fortresslike seat of the blessedly absent Earl of Wyvern.

Absent like the riding officer charged with preventing smuggling in this area. Animal sounds—an owl, a gull, a barking fox—carried across the scrubby landscape, constantly reporting that all was clear.

At sea, a brief flash of light announced the arrival of the smuggling ship. On the rocky headland, the smuggling master—Captain Drake, as he was called—unshielded a lantern in a flashing pattern that meant "all clear."

All clear to land brandy, gin, tea, and lace. Delicacies for Englishmen who didn't care to pay extortionate taxes. Profit for smugglers, with tea sixpence a pound abroad and selling for twenty times that in England if all the taxes were paid.

In the nearby fishing village of Dragon's Cove, men pushed boats into the waves and began the urgent race to unload the vessel.

"Captain Drake" pulled out a spyglass to scan the English Channel for other lights, other vessels. Now that the war against Napoleon was over, navy ships were patrolling the coast, better equipped and manned than the customs boats had ever been. A navy cutter had intercepted the last major run, seizing the whole cargo and twenty local men, including the previous Captain Drake.

A figure slipped to sit close to him, one dressed as he was all in dark colors, a hood covering both hair and the upper face, soot muting the pallor of the rest.

Captain Drake glanced to the side. "What are you doing here?"

"You're shorthanded." The reply was as sotto voce as the question.

"We've enough. Get back up to Crag Wyvern and see to the cellars."

"No."

"Susan—"

"No, David. Maisie can handle matters from inside the house, and Diddy has the watch. I need to be out here."

Susan Kerslake meant it. This run had to succeed or heaven knew what would become of them all, so she needed to be out here with her younger brother, even if there was nothing much she could do.

For generations this area had flourished, with smuggling the main enterprise under a series of strong, capable Captain Drakes, all from the Clyst family. With Mel Clyst captured, tried, and transported to Botany Bay, however, chaos threatened. Other, rougher gangs were trying to move in.

The only person in a position to be the unquestioned new Captain Drake was her brother. Though he and she went by their mother's name of Kerslake, they were Mel Clyst's children and everyone knew it. It was for David to seize control of the Dragon's Horde gang and make a profit, or this area would become a battleground.

He'd had to take on the role, and Susan had urged him to it, but she shivered with fear for him. He was her younger brother, after all, and even though he was a man of twenty-four, she couldn't help trying to protect him.

The black-sailed ship on the black ocean was barely visible, but a light flashed again, brief as a falling star, to say that the anchor had dropped. No sign of other ships out there, but the dark that protected the Freetraders could protect a navy ship as well.

She knew Captain de Root of the *Anna Kasterlee* was an experienced smuggler. He'd worked with the Horde for over a decade and had never made a slip yet. But smuggling was a chancy business. Mel Clyst's capture had shown that, so she kept every sense alert.

At last her straining eyes glimpsed the boats surging out to be loaded with packages and half-ankers of spirits. She could just detect movement on the sloping headland, which rolled like the waves of the sea as local men flowed down to the beach to unload those small boats.

They'd haul the goods up the cliff to hiding places and packhorses. Men

would carry the goods inland on their backs to secure places and to the middlemen who'd send the cargo on to Bath, London, and other cities. A week's
wages for a night's work and a bit of 'baccy and tea to take home. Many
would have scraped together a coin or two to invest in the profits.

To invest in Captain Drake.

Some of the goods, as always, would be hidden in the cellars of Crag
Wyvern. No Preventive officer would try to search the home of the Earl of
Wyvern, even if the mad earl was dead and his successor had not yet arrived
to take charge.

His successor.

Susan was temporary housekeeper up at Crag Wyvern, but as soon as the
new earl sent word of his arrival she'd be out of there. Away from here entirely. She had no intention of meeting Con Somerford again.

The sweetest man she'd ever known, the truest friend.

The person she'd hurt most cruelly.

Eleven years ago.

She'd only been fifteen, but it was no excuse. He'd only been fifteen, too,
and without defenses. He'd been in the army for ten of the eleven years since,
however, so she supposed he'd have defenses now.

And attacks.

She shivered in the cool night air and turned her anxieties on the scene before her. If this run was successful, she could leave.

"Come on, come on," she muttered under her breath, straining to see the
first goods land on the beach. She could imagine the powerful thrust of the
oarsmen, racing to bring the contraband in, could almost hear the muttering
excitement of the waiting men, though it was probably just the wind and sea.

She and David had watched runs before. From a height like this everything seemed so slow. She wanted to leap up and help, as if the run were a
huge cart that she could push to make it go faster. Instead she stayed still and
silent beside her brother, like him watchful for any sign of problems.

Being in command was a lonely business.

How was she going to be able to leave David to his lonely task? He didn't
need her—it was disconcerting how quickly he'd taken to smuggling and
leadership—but could she bear to go away, to not be here beside him on a
dark night, to not know immediately if anything went wrong?

And yet, once Con sent word he was coming, she must.

Despite treasured summer days eleven years ago, and sweet pleasures. And
wicked ones . . .

She realized she was sliding again under the seductive pull of might-have-beens, and fought clear to focus on the business of the moment.

At last the first of the cargo was landing, the first goods were being carried up the rough slope. It was going well. David had done it.

With a blown-out breath, she relaxed on the rocky ground, arms around her knees, permitting herself to enjoy the rough music of waves on shingle, and the other rough music of hundreds of busy men. She breathed in the wind, fresh off the English Channel, and the tense activity all around.

Heady stuff, the Freetrade, but perilous.

"Do you know where the Preventive officer is?" she asked in a quiet voice that wouldn't carry.

"Gifford?" David sent one of the nearby men off with a quiet command, and she saw some trouble on the cliff. A man fallen, probably. "There's a dummy ship offshore five miles west, and with luck he and the boatmen are watching it, ready to fish up the goods it drops into the water."

Luck. She hated to depend on luck.

"Poor man," she said.

David turned his head toward her. "He'll get to confiscate a small cargo like Perch did under Mel. It'll look good to his superiors, and he'll get his cut of the value."

Lieutenant Perch had been riding officer here for years, with an agreeable working relationship with the Dragon's Horde gang. He'd recently died from falling down a cliff—or being pushed—and now they had young, keen Lieutenant Gifford to deal with.

"Let's hope that satisfies him," Susan said.

He gave a kind of grunt. "If Gifford were a more flexible man we could come to a permanent arrangement."

"He's honest."

"Damn nuisance. Can't you use your wiles on him? I think he's sweet on you."

"I don't have any wiles. I'm a starchy housekeeper."

"You'd have wiles in sackcloth." He reached out and took her hand, his so solid and warm in the chilly night. "Isn't it time you stopped working there, love? There'll be money aplenty after this, and we can find someone else who's friendly to the trade to be housekeeper."

She knew it bothered him for her to be a domestic servant. "Probably. But I want to find that gold."

"It'd be nice, but after this, we don't need it."

So careless, so confident. She wished she had David's comfort with whatever happened. She wished she weren't the sort to be always looking ahead, planning, worrying, trying to force fate. . . .

Oh yes, she desperately wished that.

She was as she was, however, and David didn't seem to accept that she had a strange unladylike need for employment. For independence.

And there was the gold. The Horde under Mel Clyst had paid the late Earl of Wyvern for protection. Since he hadn't provided it, they wanted their money back. She wanted that money back, but mainly to keep David safe. It would pay off the debts caused by the failed run and provide a buffer so he wouldn't have to take so many risks.

She frowned down at the dark sea. Things wouldn't have been so difficult if her mother hadn't set off to follow Mel to Australia, taking all the Horde's available money with her. Isabelle Kerslake. Lady Belle, as she liked to be known. A smuggler's mistress, without a scrap of shame as far as anyone could tell, and without a scrap of feeling for her two children.

Susan shook off that pointless pain and thought about the gold. She glanced behind at the solid mass of Crag Wyvern as if that would spark a new idea about where the mad earl had hidden his loot. The trouble with madmen, however, was that their doings made no sense.

Automatically she scanned the upper slit windows for lights. Crag Wyvern served as a useful messaging post visible for miles, and as a viewing post where miles of coast could be scanned for other warning lights. Apart from that, however, it had no redeeming features.

The house was only two hundred years old, but had been built to look like a medieval fortress with only arrow-slit windows on the outside. Thank heavens there was an inner courtyard garden, and the rooms had proper windows that looked into that, but from the outside the place was grim.

As she turned back to the sea, the thin moon floated out from behind clouds again, silvering the boats on the water, lifting and bobbing with the waves. Then the clouds swept across the moon like a curtain, and a wash of light drizzle blew by on the wind. She hunched, grimacing, but the rain was a blessing because it obscured the view even more. The sea and shore below her could have been deserted.

If Gifford had spotted the dummy run for what it was, and was seeking the real one, he'd need the devil's own luck to find them tonight. Let it stay that way. He was a pleasant enough young man, and she didn't want to see him smashed at the bottom of a cliff.

Lord, but she wished she had no part of this.

Smuggling was in her blood, and she was used to loving these smooth runs that flowed with hot excitement through the darkest nights. But it wasn't a distant adventure anymore.

It was need now, and danger to the person she loved most in the world—

Was that a noise behind her?

She and David swiveled together to look back toward Crag Wyvern. She knew he too held his breath, the better to hear a warning sound.

Nothing.

She began to relax, but then, in one high, narrow window, a candle flared into light.

"Trouble," he murmured.

She put a hand on his suddenly tense arm. "Only a stranger, that candle says. Not Gifford or the military. I'll deal with it. One squeal for danger. Two if it's clear."

That was the smuggler's call—the squeal of an animal caught in the fox's jaws or the owl's talons—and if the cry was cut off quickly, it still signaled danger.

With a squeeze to his arm for reassurance, she slid to the side, carefully, slowly, so that when she straightened she wouldn't be close to Captain Drake. Then she began to climb the rough slope, soft boots gripping the treacherous ground, heart thumping, but not in a bad way.

Perhaps she was more like her brother than she cared to admit. She enjoyed being skilled and strong. She enjoyed adventure. She liked having a pistol in her belt and knowing how to use it.

As well that she had no dreams of becoming a fine lady.

Or not anymore, at least.

Once, she'd been caught up in a mad, destructive desire to marry the future Earl of Wyvern—Con Somerford, she'd thought—and ended up naked with him on a beach. . . .

She physically shook the memory away. It was too painful to think about, especially now, when she needed a clear mind.

Heart beating faster and blood sizzling through her veins, she went up the tricky hill in a crouch, fingers to the ground to stay low. She stretched hearing and sight in search of the stranger.

Whoever the stranger was, she'd expect him to have entered the house. Maisie might have signaled for that too. But Susan had heard something up here on the headland, and so had David.

She slowed to give her senses greater chance to find the intruder, and then she saw him. Her straining eyes saw a cloaked figure a little darker than the dark night sky. He stood still as a statue. She could almost imagine someone had put a statue there, on the headland between the house and the cliff.

A statue with a distinct military air. Was it Lieutenant Gifford after all?

She shivered, suddenly feeling the cold, damp wind against her neck. Gifford would have soldiers with him, already spreading out along the headland. The men bringing in the cargo would be met with a round of fire, but the smugglers had their armed men too. It would turn into a bloody battle, and if David survived, the military would be down on the area like a plague looking for someone to hang for it.

Looking for Captain Drake.

Her heart was racing with panic and she stayed there, breathing as slowly as she could, forcing herself back to control. Panic served no one.

If Gifford was here with troops, wouldn't he have acted by now? She stretched every quivering sense to detect soldiers concealed in the gorse, muskets trained toward the beach.

After long moments she found nothing.

Soldiers weren't that good at staying quiet in the night.

So who was it, and what was he planning to do?

Heartbeat still fast, but not with panic now, she eased forward, trying not to present a silhouette against the sea and sky behind her. The land flattened as she reached the top, however, making it hard to crouch, making her clumsy, so some earth skittered away from beneath her feet.

She sensed rather than saw the man turn toward her.

Time to show herself and pray.

She pulled off her hood and used it to wipe the soot around so it would appear to be general grubbiness. She tucked the cloth into a pocket, then stood. Eccentric to be wandering about at night in men's clothing, but a woman could be eccentric if she wanted to, especially a twenty-six-year-old spinster of shady antecedents.

She drew her pistol out of her belt and put it into the big pocket of her old-fashioned frock coat. She kept her hand on it as she walked up to the still and silent figure, and it was pointed forward, ready to fire.

She'd never shot anyone, but she hoped she could if it was necessary to save David.

"Who are you?" she said at normal volume. "What is your business here?"

She was within three feet of him, and in the deep dark she could not make out any detail except that he was a couple of inches taller than she was, which made him about six feet. He was hatless and his hair must be very short, since the brisk wind created no visible movement around his head.

She had to capture a strand of her own hair with her free hand to stop it blowing into her eyes.

She stared at him, wondering why he wasn't answering, wondering what to do next. But then he said, "I am the Earl of Wyvern, so everything here is my business." In the subsequent silence, he added, "Hello, Susan."

Her heart stopped, then raced so impossibly fast that stars danced around her vision.

Oh, Lord. Con. Here. Now.

In the middle of a run!

He'd thought smuggling exciting eleven years ago, but people changed. He'd spent most of those years as a soldier, part of the mighty fist of the king's law.

Dazed shock spiraled down to something numb, and then she could breathe again. "How did you know it was me?"

"What other lady would be walking the clifftop at the time of a smugglers' run?"

She thought of denying it, but saw no point. "What are you going to do?"

She made herself draw the pistol, though she didn't cock it. Heaven knew she wouldn't be able to fire it. Not at Con. "It would be awkward to have to shoot you," she said as firmly as she could.

Without warning, he threw himself at her. She landed hard, winded by the fall and his weight, pistol gone, his hand covering her mouth. "No squealing."

He remembered. Did he remember everything? Did he remember lying on top of her like this in pleasure? Was his body remembering . . . ?

He'd been so charming, so easygoing, so dear, but now he was dark and dangerous, showing not a shred of concern for the lady he was squashing into hard, unforgiving earth.

"Answer me," he said.

She nodded, and he eased his hand away, but stayed over her, pressing her down.

"There's a stone digging into my back."

For a moment he didn't respond, but then he moved back and off her, grasping her wrist and pulling her to her feet before she had time to object. His hand was harder than she remembered, his strength greater. How could she remember so much from a summer fortnight eleven years ago?

How could she not? He'd been her first lover, and she his, and she'd denied every scrap of feeling when she'd sent him away.

Life was full of ironies. She'd rejected Con Somerford because he hadn't been the man she'd thought he was—the heir to the earldom. And here he was, earl, a dark nemesis probably ready to destroy everything because of what she'd done eleven years ago.

What could she do to stop him?

She remembered David's comment about feminine wiles and had to fight down wild laughter. That was one weapon that would never work on the new Earl of Wyvern.

"I heard Captain Drake was caught and transported," he said, as if nothing of importance lay between them. "Who's master smuggler now?"

"Captain Drake."

"Mel Clyst escaped?"

"The smuggling master here is always called Captain Drake."

"Ah, I didn't know that."

"How could you?" she pointed out with deliberate harshness, in direct reaction to a weakness that threatened to crumple her down onto the dark earth. "You were here for only two weeks." As coldly as possible, she added, "As an outsider."

"I got inside you, Susan."

The deliberate crudeness stole her breath.

"Where are the Preventives?" he asked.

She swallowed and managed an answer. "Decoyed up the coast a bit."

He turned to look out at the water. The sickle moon shone clear for a moment, showing a clean, strong profile and, at sea, the armada of small boats heading out for another load.

"Looks like a smooth run, then. Come back to the house with me." He turned as if his word were law.

"I'd rather not." Overriding her weakness was fear, as sharp as winter ice. Irrational fear, she hoped, but frantic.

He looked back at her. "Come back to the house with me, Susan."

He made no threat. She had no idea what he might be threatening, but a breath escaped her that was close to a sigh, and she followed him across the scrubby heathland.

After eleven years, Con Somerford was back, lord and master of all that surrounded them.

Chapter Two

Susan felt dazed, almost drunk with shock. How could it feel as if eleven full years had disappeared like melting snow? And yet it did. Despite the physical changes in both of them, and a virtual lifetime of experiences, he was Con, who for that brief time had been the friend of the heart she had never found since.

Who for an even briefer time had been the lover she could never imagine finding again.

Con. Con, short for Connaught, his second name, because his first name was George and his two friends were called George, and they'd all agreed to choose other names. . . .

Her mind was dancing crazily, flinching off memories and feelings, then ricocheting back to them again.

He'd simply been Con when she'd known him.

She bit her lip on nervous laughter. In the biblical sense. The sweetest, steadiest young man she'd ever known in any sense. She'd teased him about being her Saint George, who'd save her from any dragon.

He'd promised to be her hero, always.

In almost the next breath she'd told him she never wanted to see him again.

The house loomed ahead with only the one candlelit window to break the blackness. Con was back, but he wasn't Saint George anymore. He was Wyvern. He was the dragon.

"There's a door on this side, isn't there?" he asked.

"Yes." She stepped past him, but even she had to feel for the door in the dark. When her unsteady hands found the iron latch, the door opened silently into light, for she'd left a lamp burning for her return. Once inside she quickly closed the door, then turned, afraid of what she might see.

She saw lines and angles that had not been there before, and two white slashes up near his hairline that hinted at danger narrowly missed. He'd been a soldier for ten years.

And yet, he was still Con.

His rebellious, overlong hair was now trimmed severely short. She'd run fingers through that long hair, sticky with sweat. . . .

His eyes were the same steady gray. She'd thought they were as changeable as the sea, but she'd never dreamed of seeing them so stormily cold.

He was earl. In theory at least, he ruled this part of England. In practice, the smugglers took the *free* in Freetraders very seriously. He looked like the sort of man who might try to stop the smuggling, and that could get him killed.

She was suddenly as afraid *for* him as *of* him. Lieutenant Perch had come to a bloody "accidental" end. That could happen to anyone who got in the way of the Freetrade. She didn't think David would kill to save himself and his men, but these days she wasn't sure.

David would kill to save her. She was sure of that.

"What are you going to do?" she asked, not even sure if she meant about the smuggling, herself, or everything.

Con was looking at her with an unnervingly steady gaze. He probably didn't approve of the jacket and breeches, but was there something more personal in his scrutiny? Was he contrasting her with the fifteen-year-old, as she was him?

"What am I going to do?" he echoed softly, silver eyes still resting on her. "Having ridden hard for far too long, I plan to eat, have a bath, then go to bed. The servants seem to be in short supply, however, and my housekeeper is also missing."

There was no choice but to admit it. "I am your housekeeper."

His eyes widened and it was wryly pleasant to shock him. "I was told my new housekeeper was a *Mrs.* Kerslake."

"Told? Told by who?"

"Don't pretend to be stupid, Susan. It won't wash. Swann has been sending me regular reports ever since I inherited."

Of course. Of course. She felt stupid. Not a spy, but Swann, the earldom's lawyer, who rode out from Honiton every fortnight to check his client's property.

"I am Mrs. Kerslake," she said.

He shook his head. "One day when I'm less tired and hungry, you must tell me how this all came about."

"People change." Belatedly she added, "My lord," desperate for distance and protection. "And a housekeeper doesn't actually scrub the grates and bake the cakes, you know. You will find everything in order."

She seized the lamp to lead the way out of the constricting room.

"But I didn't find everything in order."

She turned back sharply, alerted by his tone.

He was still angry. After all these years he was still angry. Fear surged through her in a sickening wave. This was a man to fear when he was angry.

He frowned. "Are you all right?"

She'd probably gone sheet white. "Like you, I am tired. If you expected a better reception, my lord, you should have sent warning. Come along and I will see to your needs."

She opened the door, wishing she hadn't used quite those words. What was she going to do if he wanted her in his bed? She didn't want to kill him. She didn't want anyone else to kill him. She didn't want to stir anymore trouble around here than they already had.

She didn't want to bed him.

A slight but deep ache said that perhaps she lied. . . .

Aware of stillness behind, she turned.

He was giving that excellent impression of a stone statue. "If I choose to act on impulse, Mrs. Kerslake, it is for my household, my servants, to accommodate me."

"You inherited the earldom two months ago and haven't seen fit to visit here until today. Were we to stand in readiness, just in case?"

"Since I am paying you, yes."

She raised her chin. "Then you should have made it clear that you wanted to waste money. I would have had a banquet prepared every night!"

His eyes narrowed and danger prickled through the room. From fear as much as anything, she whirled and marched out into the corridor. "This way, my lord. We can produce simple food quickly, and a bath for you within the hour."

She kept on walking. If he chose not to follow, so be it. Better so. She needed time away from him to regroup.

Alas, she heard his footsteps behind.

"Are you alone, my lord, or have you brought servants with you?"

"Of course I've brought servants. My valet, my secretary, and two manservants."

She grimaced. She must be sounding like an idiot. But she kept thinking of him as Con, the ordinary young man she'd met on the headland and on the beach, exploring, teasing, and talking, talking, talking as if they'd make a world out of words and hide in it forever. They'd crawled into caves and waded tidal pools without stockings. Then one day they'd gone swimming in scanty clothing, and that had been their undoing.

He's the earl now, she told herself. *Remember it. Earl of Wyvern, with all the strange things that implies.*

"You have two footmen?" she asked to fill the silence as she began to climb the stairs. "That will be useful. The old earl didn't like male household servants, and I haven't engaged any since."

"They're not footmen, no. Consider them grooms."

Consider them? Then what were they? Soldiers? Spies? She wished she could slip away to warn David, but it would be pointless. There was nothing to be done tonight. Was there anything to be done at all? They couldn't attack an earl without bringing the wrath of the nation down on them.

But someone could push him off a cliff. . . .

She realized that she'd thoughtlessly chosen one of the simple servants' staircases that riddled the house. So be it. If it was beneath his dignity, then he could go the longer way to find steps more suited to his noble feet. Her soft boots made no sound on the plain wood, but his riding boots rapped hard with each step.

Having him behind her began to unnerve her. She didn't really think he'd attack her, but her neck prickled. He'd thrown her down and unarmed her so easily.

She was a tall, strong woman, and she'd fooled herself that she was a match for most men. Perhaps she was, but more likely no man had ever seriously attacked her before.

Born Captain Drake's daughter. Now Captain Drake's sister. She was close to untouchable on this stretch of coast, but she understood the message of that attack. Anyone who threatened the new earl would be instantly and effectively contested, no matter who they were.

She opened the door into the south corridor, her lamp glowing on walls painted to look like rough stone.

He spoke behind her. "The dear old place hasn't changed, I see."

She turned and some trick of the lamplight made his eyes seem paler and more intense. "Oh, it has. You probably didn't notice the gargoyles outside in the dark. We have a torture chamber now, too."

She answered his unspoken, startled question. "No, he didn't use it, except to scare the occasional guest. But he commissioned waxworks of victims from Madame Tussaud."

"Good God." She expected some comment, perhaps an instruction to rip the place apart, but he merely said, "Food and a bath, Mrs. Kerslake?"

She turned, stung by his indifference. What had she expected?

So much time had passed, and he must have known many women. She'd given her body to two other men, but they hadn't erased a moment of the memory of Con, clumsy and imperfect as it had been.

She'd wanted them to, but they hadn't.

As they walked along the gloomy corridor she said, "You won't want to use the earl's chambers, my lord. The Chinese rooms are the next grandest. Everything is tolerably well maintained, though I cannot guarantee that the mattress will not be damp. Not having been given notice to prepare."

"I've endured worse than a damp mattress. Why don't I want to use the earl's chambers?"

"Trust me, Con, you don't."

She froze. She'd called him Con, and he was probably laughing at the idea of trusting her. She couldn't help it. She turned.

He looked more weary than amused, but like a man who could fight and even kill when weary.

She was suddenly aware of the sweeping curve of his dark brows above his dark-lashed pale eyes. She'd always thought his eyes the most beautiful she'd ever seen.

"Who is your husband?" he asked.

She blinked, puzzled for a moment. "I'm not married."

"*Mrs.* Kerslake?"

Absurdly, she felt her cheeks heat, as if she were caught in a lie. "It's convention for a housekeeper to be addressed that way."

"Ah, so it is. But I find your domestic incarnation surprising. How did it come about?"

"I thought you were hungry, my lord."

"I've known hunger before. Well? How?"

Buffeted by his will, she explained. "When the old earl died, Mrs. Lane wanted to retire. No one else suitable wanted the job, so I offered to take care of things for a while. Despite tonight, my lord, I am well trained in domestic economy."

"And your brother, David? Is he my butler?"

Susan suppressed a twitch, as if the truth would flare out. "Don't you know he's your estate manager?"

"Swann must have neglected to mention it. How very cozy, to be sure." He gestured. "Lead on to the Chinese rooms, Mrs. Kerslake. I remember them as being all barbaric splendor, but I suppose I will become accustomed."

The Chinese rooms were on the far side of the house, and since Crag Wyvern was built like a monastery around a large central courtyard, the walk there was long. A continuous narrow corridor ran along the outside walls, leaving the rooms facing inward, overlooking the courtyard garden. The only windows into the corridor were the narrow glazed arrow slits.

The effect was gloomy on a sunny day. At past midnight it was cavernous, especially with the trompe l'oeil stone walls and floor and the ornamental weaponry hanging on them. Susan was accustomed to it. She was not accustomed to a dark presence at her back.

The weaponry was not, in fact, completely ornamental, and he could seize a sword or ax and decapitate her. She knew he wouldn't, but she walked between shining blades, nerves twitching.

"Old Yorrick's still here," he remarked as they turned the corner that held a skeleton hanging in chains.

He touched the chains, setting the whole thing clattering and clanging. Susan did the same childish thing herself sometimes, but now the lingering rattle behind them raised the hairs on her neck.

Dear God, but she'd thought she was accustomed to this place, but tonight it seemed newly horrid—an outward sign of the traditional madness of the earls of Wyvern. The last one had certainly been insane. Thank heavens Con came from a different branch of the family.

The walk seemed endless, and she flung open the door of the bedroom of the Chinese suite with relief. Golden dragons snarled in the lamplight, fangs bared against bright red walls framed in black-lacquered woodwork.

"Zeus," he said with a short laugh. "My memory had faded somewhat. I remember wishing I had this room. It's obviously wise to be careful what you wish for."

He swung his heavy riding cloak off and spread it over a chair. Beneath, he was neatly dressed in brown and buff. "Are there servants' rooms attached?"

"There's a dressing room, which includes a bed for a valet."

"The Norse rooms are next door, aren't they? I remember that my father had this room and Fred and I were in the Norse suite. To begin with."

A memory sparked like a falling star. She ignored it. "Yes."

"Put my secretary in there. His name is Racecombe de Vere and he's a rascal. My valet is Diego Sarmiento. His English is excellent and he will use it to complain about the climate and to try to seduce the maids. My other two servants, Pearce and White, are down in the stables in the village. The stables that are strangely lacking grooms and horses."

She didn't respond. He had to know that the Crag's horses were on loan to the smugglers tonight, along with most other horses in the area. What would he do when he discovered that Crag Wyvern had supported ten horses for years when the old earl never left the place? It would be an inconvenience to the Horde not to have those excellent, sturdy horses available.

Perhaps he sighed. "Light the candle and go about your housekeeping duties, Mrs. Kerslake. Any sustenance will do, but I want that bath within the hour, regardless of any other business taking place."

For some reason, Susan found herself reluctant to leave, and seeking words to bridge the gap that lay deep and wide between them. Did the words exist to make sense of their situation, past and present?

Probably not. She lit the solitary candle by his bed and left, closing the door on all the dragons within.

Chapter Three

Con sucked in what felt like his first clear breath since that figure had walked up to him on the headland and he'd realized who it was.

Eleven years.

It shouldn't be hitting him so hard. There'd been other women.

They lay in his mind like ghosts, however, when Susan had always lived there in vibrant flesh.

Being rejected in the cruelest, harshest way was like a brand, it would seem. Something a man never got rid of.

Like a tattoo. He rubbed absentmindedly at his right chest. Another permanent mark.

He wandered the room, idly opening drawers that were, of course, empty. Everywhere he looked, the dragons writhed and snarled. He glared at one and snarled back.

Damn the mad Earl of Wyvern. Damn the whole line of them, and the last one for dying far too soon. If not for that, he would be in the peace of Somerford Court in Sussex.

The curtains and bed hangings were a glorious black silk with more dragons embroidered on them. The frame of the bed was black lacquer, as was all the furniture. The carpet covered nearly the whole floor with thick silk in paler, gentle shades, but still containing a picture of a coiled dragon. He hated to be walking on it in his boots, but he couldn't get them off without a jack or Diego.

His army boots had been more practical, but he'd thought he should be fashionable now he was done with all that. Thus, he'd ended up with boots too snug to drag off himself.

He crossed the carpet to one of the long windows and looked down at the dark courtyard garden. Two lamps cast pale circles of light on paths and touched the edges of branches and leaves. He remembered it as a pleasant spot in the middle of the peculiar house.

Through a youth's eyes, Crag Wyvern had seemed a prime adventure, the crazy earl a figure of fun. Now he wasn't so sure. A torture chamber. He shook his head. The Devonish Somerfords had been mad since the first earl, who'd liked to be called Dragonkiller. He'd claimed to have killed a dragon here two hundred years ago.

Rumor said they dabbled in witchcraft. They'd certainly been blessed by good fortune enough to indulge their mad whims. Disappointing, then, to find the coffers almost empty now.

He wondered what was so peculiar about the earl's traditional chambers and felt a natural curiosity to go and look. He smiled. The boy never left the man entirely. He'd be happy to surrender to the boy again if he could, but life seemed to conspire against it.

His boyhood had ended when Susan Kerslake had ruthlessly destroyed it, and he'd taken the next step himself by joining the army. He didn't entirely regret it. As a second son he'd needed employment, and neither the navy nor the church had appealed. Men were needed to fight Napoleon, and he had decided that he might as well be one of them.

He'd served eight years and felt proud to have done his duty, but he'd also been damned glad when Napoleon had abdicated and it was over. He'd been needed at home anyway, with his father dead, and then his brother drowned in a silly boating accident. He'd become Lord Amleigh, and though he mourned his father and Fred, he had felt blessed to have lived through the war to become owner of his lovely Sussex home.

Those brief golden days had ended a year ago when Napoleon had left Elba to snatch back his power and his crown. Wellington's victorious, experienced army had been dispersed, so of course any seasoned officer had to return for the final battle.

Waterloo, it had ended up being called.

It had been a bloodbath, as he'd expected. Leaving England for Belgium, he'd known that neither general would be able to ride away to fight another day. It would be to the death, and somewhere in the months of peace and happiness in England he'd lost the calluses that made a soldier able to kill and kill, to wade through blood and mud, and climb over corpses, some of them of friends, to the only goal—victory.

No, he'd not lost the ability to do that. He'd lost the ability to celebrate afterward.

And somewhere in the mud and blood he'd lost himself.

His life before the army was a myth to him now, the memories of his life up till sixteen all invention. Perhaps he'd never been a happy child in Hawk in the Vale, a venturesome schoolboy at Harrow, an innocent youth on the rocks and beaches of Devon.

A precipitously impetuous lover . . .

He shook that away and looked around the extravagant room, catching sight of himself in a gilded mirror.

Dark, harsh, and somber—scoured down to the man that war and killing and constant, encircling death had made, a man who smiled only with conscious effort.

He still had purpose, at least—duty. And the earldom of Wyvern, including this house, was part of it. He'd avoided coming here for far too long. He must make sure that the place was being properly run, that his people here were being taken care of.

It would be nice to make some sense of the finances, too, so there was money to take care of Crag Wyvern without draining Somerford Court.

He'd come here knowing that he might meet Susan Kerslake. He'd never imagined meeting her so swiftly and directly.

And now? He was perfectly aware of all the irrational reactions sweeping through him, but he was not a boy anymore.

The important question was, What was she up to? Why was she here, playing at being housekeeper? The smuggling didn't surprise him—it was in her blood—but the domestic work was as ridiculous as setting a thoroughbred to work a mine pump.

She was up to something.

He caught his breath. Could she be crazy enough to think she could try again to whore her way into the rank of countess?

A laugh escaped. She'd have to be as crazy as the crazy earl to think it possible.

And yet . . . and yet the panicked reactions swirling inside him said that it might be entirely too possible if he let his guard down. She was not the coltish girl he remembered, but she was more.

She was the same person grown devastatingly womanly.

Despite rough men's garments and a sooty face, she'd still had the clean-cut features he remembered, and the beautiful hazel eyes. She was tall and lithe and moved like a woman who could still climb cliffs like a mountain sheep and swim like a fish.

He took a deep breath and stood straight. He was an officer, and a damn good one. He'd faced many dangerous enemies and survived. He could face, and survive, Susan Kerslake.

Susan hurried down the corridor, fighting panic to try to think which servants could best be spared from the cellars to prepare food and heat bathwater for Con.

No, the earl. She had to think of him as the earl to remind herself that he wasn't the sweet-natured youth of the past, and that he held the livelihood of everyone here in his hands.

She'd left spine-twisted Maisie in charge of the main part of the house, never thinking she'd have to climb up to tell Diddy to light that candle signaling guests.

Who else could take care of Con? Middle-aged Jane and young Ellen.

Con, Con. What had he thought of her?

She knew what he thought of her! What else could he think after what she'd done all those years ago?

He was her employer now, that was all, and he wanted food and a bath.

She thoughtlessly started down the wide stairs that ran straight into the great hall, and hastily swung back out of sight—so hastily that her lamp tilted. *Get a grip on yourself, my girl, or you'll be up in flames!*

There were people down there waiting—two men—and here she was in men's clothing with dirt smeared over her face. Where were her wits? She might as well announce that she was part of the smuggling gang.

She knew where her wits were, and she didn't seem able to do anything about it.

She let herself lean against the wall for a moment, steadying herself as the white-gold flame steadied, taking the moment to come to terms with the situation.

So Con was here. Clearly he felt nothing for her now except old anger. If they kept in their proper stations, they need hardly meet. They were both adults now, and that insane youthful passion was a thing of the far past. He wasn't the same person, and neither was she.

Deep inside she didn't believe that, but she must. It was stark truth.

She took servants' stairs to the kitchens. Only Maisie was in there.

"Did I do right, ma'am? Took me a while to get up there."

"You did perfectly, Maisie. Don't worry. Everything's all right. It's just that the new earl arrived at last."

"He looked right frightening, though, ma'am."

"He's just tired. He wants food and a bath, so build the fire under the big kettle while I go get Ellen and Jane. And boil the small kettle for tea."

Tea! Wild laughter threatened. Would Con demand to know where the tea and brandy he drank came from? Most of England used smuggled goods if they could get them, but there were always those who stuck on principle.

Perhaps Con would follow the pattern of past generations and come to a gentleman's agreement with the Horde, but it didn't seem likely. He was a soldier, used to obeying orders and enforcing the law. He wouldn't find smuggling romantic anymore.

If he insisted, she'd buy everything, taxes paid, at ten times the price. She'd be the laughingstock of south Devon, though.

But most people couldn't afford those prices. Why wouldn't the government come to its senses and accept that there'd be more money in taxes if taxes were lower?

Of course if they did, that'd be the end of smuggling, and then where would the south coast be?

It was coming to a point where she didn't know what to pray for.

Maisie was moving burning coals under the big water kettle, and adding fresh so they crackled and flared.

"When you've finished there, Maisie, put together a soup of some sort."

Susan gathered herself, feeling slightly breathless, as if the world were whirling around her.

What now? What should she do now?

Go down to get Ellen and Jane, or change? She should go down first, but what if Con decided to pursue her here? She wanted to be safe in her severe housekeeper clothes when she had to face him again.

She hurried into her rooms, a bedchamber and small parlor that the previous housekeeper, bless her, had fitted out in a cozy modern style with pale green painted walls. Susan had added some of her framed insect drawings and a lot of books. Unexpectedly, she'd come to love these rooms, the only private space she'd ever owned.

She'd been raised at Kerslake Manor with love and kindness, but love and kindness couldn't produce enough rooms for everyone to have their own. That was why she'd spent so much time outdoors.

That was why she'd met Con. Why they'd—

A glance in the mirror showed her a pale face streaked with black, her hair simply tied back. Oh, Lord. This was not how she would have chosen to meet Con again.

The *earl!*

The Earl of Wyvern, who was no longer any personal business of hers.

She tore off her jacket, then shed the rest of her clothes. She washed off the soot, then slipped into a fresh shift, a light corset, and one of her plain gray dresses. She pinned a crisp white apron on top.

This wasn't how she wanted to look for Con either, but it was better. Much better. It was armor.

She twisted her brown hair up on top of her head and pinned it in place, then covered it with a cap, tying the strings under her chin. Not quite armored enough, she added a fichu of starched cotton around her shoulders.

Deep inside, like a tolling alarm bell, pounded the need to escape, to run before she had to see Con again. Counterpoint to it beat the desperate rhythm of need.

To see him, to hear him, the man the youth had become . . .

She swallowed, and as ready as she was likely to be, went out again into the kitchen. On the big hearth, steam was already rising from three pots, and Maisie was finely chopping vegetables. Susan praised her, picked up the lamp, and plunged down into the chilly depths of Crag Wyvern to summon the other maids.

It was only a temporary escape, however.

Above, the dragon still waited to be faced.

Con wondered if an earl in his noble home was supposed to stay in his grand chambers until service arrived. He wasn't in the earl's grand chambers, however—the Wyvern rooms, he remembered they were called—and the service was likely to be snail-slow.

The bed tempted him like a siren song. He'd been on horseback since early morning, pushing on as the light faded because of a need to get here, to get the first part over.

Or the need to escape.

Despite the call of duty, he probably wouldn't have left Somerford Court to come here if one of his oldest friends had not returned to his neighboring estate. Instead of riding across the valley to meet Van for the first time in a year, however, he'd lurked at home. When work had started on Steynings, indicating that Van might be returning for good, he'd discovered an urgent need to inspect this property in Devon and set off with no preparation at all.

He rubbed his hands over his weary face. Mad. Perhaps he was as mad as the Demented Devonish Somerfords.

Van had lost all his immediate family in recent years. And yet, knowing he probably needed a friend, Con had fled like a coward fleeing a battle.

Because Van might want to help him—

God! Con grabbed the candle and plunged back out into the corridor. *Dammit.* Which way did he go in this crazy place? It was full of staircases, he remembered. Circular ones at the corners. A straight one down into the hall. Servants' narrow stairs.

Right or left, he'd come to a circular one. Left, why not? He was left-handed.

He found the arch and headed down, remembering that his left-handed-ness gave him an advantage here.

In castles, these staircases always curled counter-clockwise so that defend-ers from above would have their right arm—their sword arm—free, while at-tackers from below would be cramped by the inner wall. The Crag Wyvern stairs curled clockwise because left-handedness ran in the blood of the De-vonish Somerfords.

The old earl had been left-handed, and apparently so had most before him. Con was left-handed. Was that a bad omen? He could feel the pressure of madness in the very walls of this place.

He certainly wished he had a lamp or lantern rather than the candle he was holding in his right hand, instinctively leaving his left hand free, even though he carried no weapon. He wished he had a weapon, but the greatest danger he faced was that the wildly flaring candle might blow out, leaving him to feel his way down the stairs in the pitch dark.

He stepped out into a corner of the huge medieval-style hall with relief, pausing to let his hammering heart settle. The room was as peculiar as the rest of the place, the walls encrusted with weaponry, but it contained two rel-atively sane human beings.

"Ah, a human!" declared Racecombe de Vere, lounging on an oaken settle with deceptive languor, golden curls framing a fine-boned face, smoky-blue eyes cynically amused at the world.

"If an Earl of Wyvern is ever human," Con replied.

"No? At least they seem to have been warlike." Race gestured at the walls.

"Not a bit of it. This stuff must have been bought by the yard."

"Alas. I was hoping some of the muskets and pistols might work. There's a distinct feeling here of imminent battle."

Race would know. He was an army man, but he'd missed Waterloo. He'd been part of the men rushed back from Canada who'd arrived too late. At which point he'd sold his commission in disgust.

Con put his candle with a stand of three others on the massive dark oak refectory table in the middle of the room. "The only likely battle would be against ghosts."

"Then why did you disappear for a solitary midnight stroll?"

Con met Race's mischievous eyes. "To stretch my legs. Servants are being roused."

"Roused from sleep on the heathy headland?"

Con merely gave him a look.

Race had been his subaltern for a while in Spain, and they'd met again in Melton Mowbray in February. Con had just heard of his mad relative's death. Race had decided he needed a secretary and appointed himself.

At the time it had seemed rather farcical, but Con hadn't cared enough to object. Race, however, had turned out to have a gift for administration. He still could be an imp from hell at times.

"You are tired, my lord." The soft, Spanish-inflected voice snapped his eyes open. He'd almost gone to sleep on his feet.

He shuddered and turned to Diego, a weather-beaten man nearly twice Con's age. He had dark Spanish eyes, but light brown hair touched with gray. Con knew Diego was here only to look after him. Once Diego was sure he was all right, he would return to his beloved, sunny Spain.

"We're all tired," Con said, rubbing scratchy eyes. "I can tell you where to bed down now if you want, but there should be food soon, and a bath."

There'd only be hot water enough for one bath at a time. It was a fact of being an earl that he would enjoy it first, a fact of life that Race and then Diego would use it after him if they wanted to. A tub of water could go through ten before it was cold and exhausted. Tenth in line for a tub had often been a dreamed-of luxury during the war. . . .

"I would be happy to oversee the servants and encourage them to greater speed, sir," said Diego.

The notion of Diego hounding Susan was vaguely alarming—vaguely because of invading sleep. "No." Con battled fatigue. "No need. The housekeeper has the matter in hand."

"The Mrs. Kerslake? What is she like, sir?"

"Young," he said, walking about to keep the blood flowing to limbs and brain. "And despite the Mrs., unmarried,"

"Pretty?" asked Race, sitting up.

"Depending on taste." Con suppressed an urge to growl a warning. "If you're interested, treat her as a lady, because she is one. She's niece to the local squire."

No need now to get into the more complicated matters of Susan's parentage.

To both of the men, he added, "If she asks any questions about me, don't tell her anything."

Diego's brows quirked, and Con saw mischievous curiosity flit across Race's face.

Damnation. But there was no point hiding all of it. "I knew her years ago and she might be nosy. The important fact is that everyone here is involved in smuggling, and for the moment we're going to pretend that it isn't happening."

"Which it is, of course," Race said, coming to full alert. "Hence the lack of servants in the house or horses in the stables. Fascinating."

"Remember, Race, we are for the moment blind, deaf, and very, very stupid."

Race subsided, giving Con a very ironic salute. "Sir!"

"My lord."

Con turned sharply to see Susan walking toward him. He couldn't help but stare. He'd not been surprised to see her in men's clothing, even though he'd never seen her dressed like that before. He was shocked to see her in dull housekeeper's garb.

Affronted even. He wanted to tear off the ugly cap and starched fichu. To command her not to wear dark gray that stole the color from her face. The outfit almost did the impossible and made her ugly.

He recovered and performed the introductions. He noted Race attempting to flirt and being frostily discouraged.

Good.

Zeus, could he sink so low as jealousy?

She turned back to him. "We have simple food ready for you all, my lord. Where do you want everyone to eat?"

Diego would normally eat with the servants, but Con didn't want him where he might see smuggling activity. Smugglers tended to keep their secrets with a knife. "In the breakfast room on this occasion, if you please."

She nodded. "If you remember the way, my lord, perhaps you could take your party there and I will have the food served within moments."

She disappeared again, and that was the last Con saw of her for the night. Two maids brought soup, bread, cheese, and a currant pie into the breakfast room. On request they returned with tankards of ale to go with it. One was past first youth and plain, the other young, thin, and bucktoothed. Con wondered whether Susan saw him and his men as a bunch of seducers and had chosen the plainest servants.

When they'd finished, he led Race and Diego upstairs, and found a steaming bath ready for him. By then he was almost too tired to care, but since coming home from Waterloo, he had tried never again to go filthy to sleep. He stripped, sat in the wooden tub, scrubbed briskly, and staggered off to fall into bed, asleep almost as soon as he was horizontal.

Chapter Four

Daylight awoke him. He'd neglected to draw the curtains.

Daybreak and birdsong—a very English awakening that he still savored every single day. He loved England with a passion built through all the days when loss of life and loss of England had rushed upon him. Perhaps if he could get enough of the true England he could heal.

The England he loved, however, was the England of the gentle Sussex downs, of tranquil Somerford Court and pastoral Hawk in the Vale. It wasn't this aberrant house on a heathy headland, haunted by madmen and criminals.

He climbed out of bed, snarled back at the dragons, and walked naked to the small-paned window to look into the garden. At Somerford his room looked out into the garden, but beyond that lay the valley and a view for miles. Here, the garden was enclosed by dark stone walls. At least the walls were covered with ivy and other growing plants, and the courtyard even contained two trees. They were stunted, however, and a sense of enclosure, of limits, pressed on him.

Such enclosure had doubtless been deliberate in a monastery or convent, but he had not renounced the world. Or perhaps he had. Perhaps riding away from Hawk in the Vale and his friend had been a renunciation of the deepest kind.

At least there were birds. He'd not imagined the birdsong, and he saw a sparrow fly across from tree to ivy, and swifts swooping up near the roof. He could pick out a thrush's trill and a robin's happy song. Maybe the birds were singing that there was a lot to be said for an artificial garden surrounded by high walls.

He began to see a pattern in the courtyard paths. Pentangles. An occult symbol. He shook his head. In the center stood a statue fountain that had not been here eleven years ago. There seemed to be a woman and a dragon. He assumed it was bizarre.

A torture chamber, too.

Deeply, truly, he wanted no part of this place, safe or not.

A movement caught his eye, and he saw Susan come out of one side of the house and walk briskly across a diagonal of the courtyard. She was still in the dull gray and white that offended him, with that cap covering almost all her hair, but her walk was free and graceful.

Her clothes eleven years ago had been schoolroom wear, but more lively and becoming than this. Come to think of it, they'd been almost entirely pale colors, and she'd always been grimacing about mud, sand, and grass stains from their adventures.

What was his free spirit doing in gray playing housekeeper here?

Clearly not seeking to seduce him. She'd dress more becomingly for that.

She paused to study some tall, plumy flowers. He suspected that there was some interesting insect on them.

She had always loved insects.

What do you mean, always? You knew her for two weeks.

But it hadn't simply been a fortnight. It had been a lifetime in fourteen days. She'd loved to watch insects, often lying down on the ground or in the sand to study and wonder, to analyze their quirks of behavior. She'd carried a sketching pad and drawn them, showing real talent. That had been her key to freedom, the fact that she went out to study and draw insects, but it hadn't been pretense.

He watched her watch. Then she straightened, stretching her head back to take a deep, relished breath.

He inhaled with her, and carefully, quietly, opened the casement window to let in the same perfumed air that she was breathing.

Not quietly enough. With the window only half open, she started and looked up at him.

He conquered the urge to step back. The sill hit him at hip level, so he was essentially decent, though naked.

Their eyes held for what seemed to be far too long. He saw her lips part, as if she might speak, or perhaps just to catch air.

Then she broke the contact and turned to walk briskly, more briskly, across the courtyard and away.

He stayed there, arms braced on the sill, breathing as if breathing were difficult. For so long he'd told himself that their time here had been a minor thing, a passing moment, that her agonizing dismissal of him had wiped away any warm feelings and—paradoxically—hadn't hurt a bit.

He'd always known it was a lie.

Fifteen. He'd been fifteen, bedazzled, scared, eager. . . .

It had been a strange progression from sitting on the headland talking about everyday things, to lying side by side on their bellies talking about personal matters, to holding hands as they walked along the beach, to sitting in one another's arms sharing dreams and fears.

The moon had become full during that second week, and twice they'd sneaked out at night to sit on the beach surrounded by the magic music of the sea, to talk of anything and everything. He'd wanted to build a fire but she'd told him it was illegal. It could be a signal fire for smugglers, so it was illegal.

She'd known a lot about smugglers and shared it all, and he'd been romantically thrilled by stories of the Freetraders. Then she'd admitted her personal connection—that she wasn't a daughter of Sir Nathaniel and Lady Kerslake at the manor, but of Sir Nathaniel's sister Isabelle and the keeper of the George and Dragon tavern in the village of Dragon's Cove.

And then that her father, Melchisedeck Clyst, was Captain Drake, leader of the local smuggling gang.

She clearly didn't know whether to be proud or ashamed of her parentage. Though "Lady Belle" lived openly with Melchisedeck Clyst in Dragon's Cove, they'd never married.

Con was delightfully scandalized by this blatant sinfulness—things like that never happened in Hawk in the Vale. Overall, however, he thought it a grand connection, and it made Susan even more exceptional in his eyes.

He and his brother Fred spent time in Dragon's Cove, and he started to look out for Captain Drake. He didn't see him, and had no reason to go into the George and Dragon.

They had a grand time in the village anyway. The fishermen were mostly willing to talk as they cleaned their catch or mended nets. They picked up fishing lore and tall stories as they tried to spot which were smugglers and which weren't.

The truth was, of course, that they all were.

Sometimes the fishermen took them out in their boats and even let them have the huge treat of hauling in nets for them. Fred liked being on the boats more than Con, so he'd had time alone to wander the village straining to hear smuggling secrets.

Stupid boy.

He'd finally spotted Mel Clyst, a sinewy man of only moderate height, with a square jaw and Susan's hazel eyes. He wasn't exactly handsome—his bones were heavy and his nose had been broken a time or two—but it was easy to see him as a leader of men. He'd been dressed like the prosperous businessman he was in a cutaway coat and stylish beaver hat.

Another time he saw him with Lady Belle, who was dressed as a fine lady, though with a flamboyant touch that Lady Kerslake would never attempt. A wicked woman, and Susan's mother, although he gathered she had nothing at all to do with her children.

Lady Belle fascinated him, but Captain Drake fascinated him more. It became his dearest ambition to have a chat with his hero.

He got his wish, but it was not a chat he would have wanted.

He'd been sitting on the pebbly beach listening to old Sim Lowstock telling his version of the killing of the dragon by the first earl when they were interrupted. He was politely but firmly escorted into the George and Dragon. Not into the taproom at the front, but into a back room fitted out more like a gentleman's sitting room.

Mel Clyst was sitting on a sofa in gentleman's dress, Lady Belle beside him. It was the first time Con had seen her up close, and he noted plump, clear skin and large blue eyes, but above all he recognized her lush, carnal appeal. Her bodice was very low, and her wide hat held a sweeping, glorious plume dyed scarlet.

Captain Drake and Lady Belle sat on the sofa like a king and queen, and Mel Clyst had chatted about Con and Susan.

Now a man—and a man tested by fire—Con could still feel the sick nervousness and embarrassment of that interview. Or trial, even.

Clyst had not been cruel, but Con had felt all Captain Drake's power that day—the power of a natural leader, but also the power of a man who held the allegiance of most of the population of the coast. If he ordered one of the fishermen to take Con out and throw him into the deeps, it would be done.

In later years, developing his own authority, and using the power of the direct warning and the unspoken threat, Captain Drake had been one of Con's prime models.

All it had been, however, was a conversation, one in which Mel Clyst acknowledged that Susan Kerslake was his daughter, that she enjoyed great freedom to wander the area because surely no one would do her any harm. That a promising young man like Con Somerford had an interesting life ahead of him, one away from here, in the army perhaps, or the law.

It had been a silent but clear warning, man to man, not to do what he and Susan had done the very next day.

Had the warning put the idea into his head, sown some sort of seed? There was no way to know. His affection, his boyish adoration, had been essentially pure, but his body had been young, healthy, and lusty.

Mel Clyst had given one blunt order—no more nighttime meetings. Without a word of threat, Con had known that he, and probably Susan, would suffer sharply if they disobeyed.

So they had met in the afternoon the next day, in Irish Cove, a mile or more along the coast from both the fishing village and Crag Wyvern. It was not easily reached, since an old road there had been cut off by a landslip, and the way down to the beach was steep and treacherous. A smuggler's path, Susan told him, intended to be difficult. They'd scrambled down in search of privacy, aware now of being observed.

They hadn't been planning anything.

At least, he hadn't been.

They'd shared their grievance about interfering adults who didn't understand a friendship, and laughed at the suspicions.

Then they'd kissed to test it out, to prove that it wasn't . . .

Except that it was.

He had kissed a girl or two before. It had been mildly intriguing, but not something he particularly wanted to do again.

When he'd kissed Susan, it had been different. He closed his eyes now and could almost feel it again, taste it again, that soft, uncertain innocence that had left him hot and breathless.

He could still smell her—something subtle and flowery over the heat of her body in the sun. He could relive the hesitancy, the growing enthusiasm, the absorption. Then the breaking apart in shock, fear—and intense, burning speculation.

He'd had an erection. Astonishing, alarming, demanding. He'd had many erections before, but never one with such direct and present purpose.

She knew. She looked at his breeches and smiled, blushing. He was fiery-faced too.

"Cold water will cure that, they say," she said, and stood to strip off her dress. She hadn't even been wearing a corset on her firm, lightly curved body, only a shift, stockings, and shoes. She'd shed shoes and stockings, then said, "Come on!" and run down into the water.

Slim, lanky, but oh, so feminine in those subtle curves hinted at beneath her sturdy shift.

They were in view of anyone on the clifftop! But the road there went nowhere, so unless they were being closely watched, no one would pass by to see by accident.

If they were being watched he'd be married or dead come morning. Susan would likely receive the whipping of her life. Even so, he fought out of entangling clothes down to his breeches and ran to join her in the cool water.

Since she hadn't hesitated, he didn't, and plunged in to swim. She could swim too, better than he could, and they swirled back and forth in the salt water, her shift molded to her body now. It was a kind of dance, but as with other dances, awareness swam with them, heightened by brushing touch and glimpse of shape. Knowledge sat deep in eyes that rarely parted.

Then she stood, water lapping at her small, high breasts, hiding then revealing her nipples beneath opaque cloth. He couldn't stop looking at those flickering buds.

"You can touch them if you want," she said.

And he did, after one frantic glance at the deserted headland. He was dead—dead—if Captain Drake found out he'd touched his daughter's breasts.

Death seemed worth it.

Her breasts were cold from the water, and rough with the covering of cloth, but soft and firm, and sweetly unlike any part of his own body. They were womanly mystery in form, and he kissed them by instinct alone, wishing desperately that he were brave enough to uncover them, to feel silky warm skin instead of rough, cold cotton—

A squawk jerked him out of the past.

A red-faced maid stood in his doorway, a huge jug clutched to her chest. "I knocked, milord! Mrs. Kerslake said you were up—" She bit her lip, going puce at what she'd said.

He was stark naked and didn't need to look to know he had a full erection.

They both stood frozen for a moment. Then the maid scuttled over to his washstand, eyes averted, then out again. Except that she hesitated at the door, her color merely rosy. Her eyes slid to him, down, then back up to his face. "Unless there's anything else you need, milord."

He caught his breath as base temptation sank its teeth. She was willing, and though she was plain, with a heavy face and thick neck, it didn't seem to matter.

"No," he managed to say, "that's all."

The door closed, and so did his eyes as he struggled for control. It would be the last bloody straw to start using the servants as convenients.

He knew that wasn't the real reason he'd turned down the offer, though. The absolute barrier had been the thought of Susan's reaction when she found out.

Susan was in the kitchen supervising little Ellen in the making of toast when Diddy Howlock rushed in. "He were naked. Stark, staring naked! And ready to go, too!"

Laughter and exclamations ran round the five women in the room, young and old.

"And you just left him like that, Diddy," said Mrs. Gorland, the middle-aged cook who came in daily. "That's a turn up."

Diddy giggled. "I did offer. I'd not mind an earl's bastard. Likely set me up for life, and this one'd be able to, I reckon."

Susan bit back cold, angry words, knowing they'd be far too revealing. With a bit of prompting some of the local people might remember that she and Con had been . . . well, whatever they had been.

Friends. They'd been friends.

People would remember that meeting between Con and Captain Drake in the George and Dragon. No one knew what had been said, but enough guessed. Most thought it had been a youthful love affair, though no one seemed to think they'd gone as far as they had.

Who would think it? A young lady of the manor, even if a bastard, and a young gentleman of Crag Wyvern. Simple people persisted in thinking that the higher orders had less fleshy desires than they, even in the face of evidence to the contrary such as Lady Belle and Mel Clyst. And the old earl taking any youngish woman who was willing to his bed.

People would soon realize that the new earl was Con Somerford, that likable lad who'd hung around the village soaking up any story a body wanted to tell, and who'd spent dunamany hours on the cliffs with Miss Susan. He'd made a good impression, and thus haunted her for years after with the villagers' talk about "that young man of yours, Miss Susan."

It would start again. *Fancy the earl being that young man of yours, Miss Susan.*

How was she to bear it?

All around her, the women chattered and giggled about the naked earl, while she remembered the sight of him in the window earlier. She'd assumed he was wearing drawers, but now she knew he must have been stark naked. Despite logic it made that moment freshly embarrassing.

Or freshly stirring.

"Lovely body on him," Diddy was saying, relishing being the center of attention. "Good hard muscles, and no really bad scars . . ."

Yes, thought Susan. The sleek youthful body had grown and hardened to perfection. Wide shoulders, just enough muscle.

No really bad scars? There were scars?

Of course there were.

"Got a tattoo on his chest, though," Diddy said. "Can't say as I like that on a man."

So it hadn't been a freak shadow of the half-open window.

"A dragon it is. Not like the Chinese ones. I rather like those ones. . . . I know!" Diddy exclaimed. "It's like the one in the Saint George bedroom! Nasty old beast. Could be taken right off the walls there, it could. Coiled all around his . . ." Diddy circled her own large right breast.

Susan smelled burning and turned sharply. Ellen was watching Diddy, slack-mouthed.

"The toast's burning," Susan snapped, giving the girl a slap to the head, which she regretted immediately.

Ellen started to cry as she pulled the charred bread off the fork and grabbed a fresh slice. "I'm sorry, ma'am!"

Oh, Lord. She'd had little sleep last night, what with having to be sure the contraband was well settled down below, and then Con rattling in her mind like a spiked ball. But she shouldn't be taking it out on poor Ellen.

Susan rubbed the girl's cap for a moment. "I'm sorry. But watch the toast, not Diddy's boobies." She turned to the rest of the room. "Enough of this shameful talk. This is a decent house now. There'll be no goings-on, do you hear?"

Everyone hurried back to work, but Diddy said, "He be Earl of Wyvern, b'ain't he? And he thought about my offer. I saw him. So there."

Susan was sure he had. Diddy was plain, but she had a ripe body, a huge, generous curving of breasts and hips. She had plenty of suitors, and the only reason she wasn't married already was that she had an eye to bettering herself.

Diddy's ways weren't responsible for the churning inside Susan, however, or for her surge of bad temper. Nor was tiredness. "Heaven knows why the earl is awake so early," she said, "but we'll have a good breakfast ready for him. Get to work. Whatever he might desire."

Diddy chuckled.

Susan swallowed a retort and retreated to her rooms. There she sat, hugging herself.

It wasn't Diddy.

It wasn't even the thought of Con and Diddy.

It was the dragon.

If Con Somerford had a dragon tattooed on his chest, a dragon like the one in the big picture of George and the dragon in the Saint George rooms, it was all her fault.

Chapter Five

They'd talked about his name, George, and why he didn't use it. She'd heard about the other two Georges—Van and Hawk—and how they'd chosen their names.

All three had been born within weeks around the time the French were imprisoning their king, and so all three boys had patriotically been christened George. They'd been born into neighboring families, too, and grown up as close friends, so the name became a constant confusion.

Eventually they'd sat down to sort it out. They'd all wanted to be George, not for the king but for the saint who slew the dragon. To them the dragon represented all the evil in the world, and Saint George was the perfect hero. They'd discussed drawing lots, but in the end they'd decided that if they couldn't all be George, none of them could. Instead they'd take names from their surnames.

George Vandeimen had become Van, George Hawkinville had become Hawk, but George Somerford had balked at the sissy name Somer. Instead he'd taken Con from his middle name, Connaught.

She remembered how she'd drunk in the stories of his close friends. Growing up at Kerslake Manor, she'd had her cousins for friends, but there were no other suitable young ladies nearby, and her cousins, though very sweet, were not mates for her adventurous soul. David was more in tune with her, but he was a brother, and two years younger.

Con had been the first true friend she had known, the only friend of instant, perfect connection. In her imagination, his friends were her friends.

The Georges, as Con had called them. Or, sometimes, the triumvirate. Con, Van, and Hawk.

He also had friends in the Company of Rogues, a group of friends at Harrow School. Twelve new boys gathered by a boy called Nicholas Delaney and formed into a band for protection from bullies—and for creative mayhem.

Fourteen good friends in all.

Riches beyond her imagination.

Yet all that happiness was now shadowed by that tattoo.

Con had loved the story of Saint George and the dragon, and all the dragon stories at Crag Wyvern. Though he had no high opinion of the Devonish Somerfords, he was thrilled to share the blood of a possible dragon slayer. He and his brother had been put in the Norse rooms together, but once he'd found the Saint George rooms he'd asked to move.

One day he'd sneaked her into Crag Wyvern and up to his room, to study the picture on the wall. Strangely, there had been no trace of awareness that they were together in his bedroom. That had been on the seventh day, before things changed.

"The George looks like me, don't you think?" he'd said, eager expectation in his eyes.

She looked at the saint, so covered in Roman armor, swirling red cloak, and huge crested helmet that it was hard to see him at all. She knew what friendship demanded, though. "Yes, he does. He has your square chin. And your cheekbones."

"I might be Con," he said, "but in my heart I'm George, defender of the weak and innocent. I'll defend you, Susan, if ever you are threatened."

"I'm not weak and innocent!" she'd protested, with a disgust that made the older Susan wryly smile.

He'd been so flustered, apologizing and protesting at the same time, that they'd fled outdoors again, where everything seemed so much simpler.

She remembered thinking that he might like her to call him George, but it hadn't seemed to fit him. He was Con, steady, fun-loving, beautiful Con. But in the aftermath of lovemaking, she'd said, "My George," and he'd kissed her and said, "Forever."

She could still remember that moment, perfect as a diamond set in gold. Lying in his arms in the warm shade of the cliff, seabirds calling, waves chuckling around nearby rocks.

It wasn't what they had just done. It was that she'd found her person, the one she would be with all her life, the one from whom she would never want to part.

She'd known they'd have to separate for a while. They were young. People would make them wait. But they were joined for all eternity. And the perfect final detail was that her Saint George, her hero, her friend, would also one day be Earl of Wyvern.

She would be Lady Wyvern, queen of all she knew.

It had never crossed her mind that Con wasn't the older son. He had been as tall as his brother, and both stronger and more vigorous. Fred Somerford had even been painfully shy, and only at ease when talking about boats.

So, all through those magical days as she had fallen in love with Con, she'd fallen in love with a vision of the future.

She wouldn't be Lady Belle's bastard daughter, always being told how kind it was of Sir Nathaniel and Lady Kerslake to treat her and David as part of the family.

She wouldn't be a person who didn't really belong.

She would be Countess of Wyvern.

It would be perfect retribution for all those people who treated her and David as not quite members of local society, who discouraged their children from spending time with them, who watched constantly for misbehavior.

She would be Countess of Wyvern. She would belong without question, and everyone—everyone!—would have to curtsy and smile to her. And she'd take David into respectability too, so he could go anywhere, do anything. Marry an heiress. Become a grand lord himself if he wanted.

No one would be able to look down on them again.

So she had lain there in his arms, sure of complete perfection.

"I don't know when I'll be back," he said, stroking her, looking at her body as if it was a wondrous mystery to him.

She was looking at him the same way. What they'd done had hurt a bit, and she was sure there was more to it, but still, it had been the most magical thing she could ever imagine, and she wanted to do it again.

There was the danger of catching a baby from him, but if it happened it might not be so bad. They'd have to marry immediately then, wouldn't they?

"Don't be long," she said, tracing a pattern in the dusting of sand on his chest.

They'd had enough thought to spread their clothes beneath them, but some sand had still stuck on their skin.

"It might not be for a year. I don't see how I can bear it."

"A year?" She shifted so she could look at him. "You could ask to come back sooner than that."

"With what reason?"

She'd kissed him. "To see me?"

He smiled. "I don't think anyone would be impressed by that. They'll say we're too young."

"Say you want to learn more about your future estate then."

He blinked at her, lashes clumped, dark hair stuck to his temples by sweat. "It's not my future estate. It's Fred's."

She could remember, even now, the sick, aching coldness that had swept through her. "He's younger than you," she'd protested, already knowing it was stupid, that he wouldn't lie about such a thing.

"Perhaps he looks it, but he's thirteen months older. Sorry I'm not the heir?" He said it lightly, teasingly confident of a laughing denial.

But she'd been shivering as if they'd been tossed from August to November. It wasn't just that he wouldn't have Crag Wyvern, that he was a younger son who'd never be a lord. He didn't belong here. He didn't belong back in Sussex at Somerford Court. He didn't belong *anywhere* any more than she did!

If she married him she'd have to go wherever he went, rootlessly with the army, or moving from parish to parish as a curate's wife, when all she'd ever wanted, above all other things, was to belong.

Here.

She'd given her maidenhead to Con to seal him to her. She'd seduced him. He hadn't been unwilling, but he'd never have done it if she hadn't taken the first steps. She'd done it to claim her place here at last, and instead she'd thrown her fate upon the waters, to be swept wherever the wind blew.

What if she was with child!

Looking back, she couldn't understand that girl. Why hadn't she seen that Con would have been her place, her security, her stability in the world? Perhaps she'd been misled by his gentle nature, his ability to simply enjoy life, and not thought him dependable.

If so, she'd badly misjudged what lay beneath.

She'd only been fifteen, though. What fifteen-year-old made subtle judgments about these things? Few sealed their lives with their folly, however.

No wonder parents protected their young from their very youth.

The light, the confidence, had faded from his face, and she had wanted to kiss him, to say that of course she didn't mind that he wasn't the heir. She could remember that. Remember feeling sliced into two parts, the part that loved Con Somerford, and the part that had gambled all to be Countess of Wyvern.

The lightness had gone entirely, and he said, "Susan?"

She'd wanted him so much, ached for him, the friend of her heart, that she'd only been able to leave harshly. She'd pushed away from him, grabbing her shift to cover her nakedness, to fight off the chill.

"Yes, I'm sorry you're not the older brother. I want to be countess. Nothing less will do."

Perhaps she'd hoped saying it like that would make it make sense. She had tried to add an apology, but eleven years later she still winced at its inadequacy: "I'm sorry."

He had simply sat there, naked, beautiful, the shock of betrayal stamped in every line of his face, so she'd tried once more. "You'll be glad when you think about it. You don't want to be tied to the bastard child of a smuggler and a whore."

It had been a mistake. She'd seen the spark of hope, the beginning of argument, so she'd clutched her clothes to her and fled, but not before shouting, "I don't want to see you again! Never speak to me again!"

And he'd obeyed.

If he'd come after her then, or sought her out in the remaining few days, if he'd argued with her, perhaps she would have seen sense. But being Con, he'd taken her at her word, and she'd not seen him or heard him speak again until last night.

Her heart had been shattered, but in a twisted way that had strengthened her will. Her mother had followed her heart and her desires into a shameful union, causing all Susan's problems. Lady Belle could have married well. She'd been courted by half the county, including the earl himself.

Instead she'd followed her stupid heart to a tavern in a fishing village, and even if Mel Clyst was Captain Drake, that didn't coat her shame with glory in the eyes of most of the world.

Susan would *not* be the prisoner of her desires like her mother. She would not run up to the Crag to sneak into the Saint George rooms to find her own George and beg him to forgive her. She would not send the letters she wrote to him after he left.

Looking back, she was awed by the steely will of that fifteen-year-old, able to crush every instinct in order to pursue a goal of being a grand lady instead of a charity case.

Hand over her mouth, she swallowed tears. She thought she'd forgotten better than this.

The fifteen-year-old had ruthlessly tried to scrub Con from her mind.

With age had come wisdom, and then regret, but she had still worked at forgetting. It was done and couldn't be undone, and she'd felt at times that she might bleed to death if she let herself think of it.

She should have known it hadn't worked. For eleven years, every rock and plant and insect had reminded her. Irish Cove was intolerable. She'd never been there since.

But she'd thought she'd buried it all deeper than this.

She'd let two men seduce her solely to drive the memory of Con from her flesh. That hadn't worked either, not even Lord Rivenham, a skilled rake, who'd given her all the pleasure she'd expected, and still failed to dissolve the sweetness of that clumsy time with Con.

Fixed on her goal, she'd even tried to attract the attention of Con's older brother, Fred. After all, she'd given up heaven for Crag Wyvern, so she had to have it or her sacrifice would have been for nothing.

She could look back now and thank God that Fred Somerford had not been looking for a wife. Imagine meeting Con again after all these years as his sister-in-law.

She'd realized eventually that the prize was worthless tinsel, but it had been far too late. She'd dreamed sometimes of finding Con and trying to heal the wounds, but amiable Fred had visited a few times a year and brought news, so she'd known that Con had gone abroad with the army not long after leaving her, and was rarely home.

For some reason, his being out of England had made him even more lost to her. Even so, she'd written letters over the years to Ensign, then Lieutenant, then Captain George Connaught Somerford, letters she'd torn up and burned.

She'd known all about Con's career because Aunt Miriam had encouraged his brother, Fred, to visit the manor as often as he wished. It was partly true kindness, but also because she had two daughters and a niece, and why shouldn't they end up as Countess of Wyvern as well as any other young woman?

She remembered the time, at a family dinner, when Fred had produced a miniature that Con had sent him, done in his new captain's uniform. It had passed from hand to hand. Susan had watched it circling toward her with a mix of unbearable anticipation and terror.

Once in her hands it had stolen her breath. She'd had to pass it on before she'd had nearly enough time to absorb it.

She'd desperately longed to snatch it, hide it, steal it.

He'd been twenty-two when the picture had been done, the square chin stronger, leanness making the high cheekbones more pronounced. Following regulation, his hair had been powdered, seeming to emphasize his dark-lashed silvery eyes. He'd been smiling, however, and she'd genuinely rejoiced that he might be happy, might have forgotten her entirely.

But he had still been at war. Weakly, she'd checked the obituaries and casualty lists, praying never to see his name.

Through too many sleepless nights she'd relived the moment of decision, imagining what might have happened if she'd followed her weak heart instead of her strong will. They'd only been fifteen. No question of marriage unless she'd caught a child which, thank the Lord, she had not.

As a younger son Con would have needed a profession, but perhaps he would have chosen differently for her sake. Been safer. At the least she would have been with him, even following the drum.

It had been a pointless, painful circling that she'd tried to block, but which had often sucked her down, especially if she woke in the gray middle of the night. Over the years, however, it had become almost a fantasy, the people no longer quite real—people she knew rather than a person she had been. That had drawn its fangs.

Until now. Until here, with Con back marked in ways she would never have wanted him marked, but still Con. If she'd not been so willful, if she'd let herself love and be loved, might he still be the gentle, laughing person she'd once known?

He'd seen himself as Saint George, warrior against evil, but at some point he'd had a dragon tattooed on his chest.

She stood, and planning a route that would avoid any possibility of bumping into him, she hurried to the Saint George rooms.

Chapter Six

The Saint George rooms were decorated in a vaguely Roman style, with a mock mosaic floor and classical white linen draperies. The picture of George and the dragon was a fresco that took up most of one wall in the bedroom. This wasn't the first time that she'd come to look at it.

Saint George did look a little like Con, but now the saint looked softly unformed in comparison to the hardened warrior. He held his upright lance in an elegantly curved hand that seemed incapable of strength and violence. Con had touched her once last night, to pull her to her feet, and his hand had been hard and strong. The saint's cocked-hip stance seemed more feminine than masculine. There had always been a grace to Con's movements, but they were strong and direct, and now they were devastatingly, completely masculine.

The dragon was not dead. It reared up behind the saint, its head horned like a devil, the fainting virgin sacrifice chained to the rock behind it. Fangs and forked tongue were visible at the slightly open mouth. It was truly an evil dragon, and she wanted to shout to the stupid Saint George to look behind him—

The door opened, and she whirled to look behind.

Con stopped as if frozen, and perhaps a hint of color touched his brown cheeks. "I'm sorry. Are you using these rooms now?"

She knew she was red, and her mouth felt sealed by dryness. She made herself speak. "No. I have the housekeeper's rooms below. I . . . I was—"

"Don't lie." It was said flatly. "There was something special between us, wasn't there?" He came over to look at the picture, but carefully distanced from her. "I was an arrogant young ass to see a resemblance, though."

"No! No, you weren't." It was pointless to think she could soothe his pride after all these years, but she couldn't help it. "The first earl stood as a model for it, you know."

"I suppose that might account for it then." He turned to her, and there was even a hint of humor in him. "Though I'm not sure I want a resemblance to the Demented Devonish Somerfords."

A hint of humor only, like the promise of sun on a heavily overcast day.

She wanted to ask why he was here, but she knew. For the same reason she was—a pilgrimage to the past.

She wanted to ask why he'd had this evil dragon etched into his skin.

But she knew—because of what she'd done to him in the past.

Most of all, she wanted to ask if there was any way to undo the hurt at this late date.

But no. The wounds she had inflicted must have healed and scarred over long since. Scars, like tattoos, could not be rubbed away. There was no bridge back to sweet yesterdays.

And anyway, she realized, she was here to find the mad earl's stash of gold for David and the Horde. It was by rights the Horde's money, and desperately needed, but Con wouldn't see it that way. He'd see only a new, fresh betrayal.

Unless the run had gone smoothly.

It was a glimmer of brightness. If the run had gone as perfectly as she thought, then the Horde wouldn't truly need the money. She wouldn't have to betray Con again. . . .

There'd been too long a silence between them, and she was in danger of saying all the wrong things. To break the moment, she moved to open a nearby door in the wall. "There's been an innovation since you used these rooms."

Seeming calm, he strolled over and looked into the room. "A Roman bath?"

"Yes." She led the way across the short stretch of tiled floor and up the steps so they could look down into the huge mosaic bath. She hadn't thought about the picture, just about getting away from that other one.

Now she was blushing because the picture on the bottom showed a hugely endowed Saint George, identified by his helmet, which was all he wore, about to impale a woman who was presumably the rescued princess.

Rescued? She was still bound to the rock with iron chains and obviously struggling to escape her fate.

"Physically impossible," Con remarked, "or a bizarre form of murder. I'm not sure this bath is possible either. Are the taps functional?"

"Of course." She walked around the wide rim to put the width of it between them. "There's a cistern in the attics with a furnace below it. It takes time to heat the water, but the bath can be filled."

"Ah, I see the drain too. What an interesting anatomical position for it."

A laugh escaped her before she caught it, and their eyes met for a moment across a space both physical and temporal.

He looked away. "Where does it drain to?"

The tiled walls gave the room a slight resonance, and she felt that her pounding heart should be audible too. When he wasn't looking at her, she was drinking in the details of him, of his manly beauty so unlike—so like—the youth.

"Out of a gargoyle's mouth," she said, "and down on anyone who happens to be below." She pointed to a gilded chain. "It's polite to ring that bell first."

He looked around at the mosaic walls, where even the stylized trees were subtly phallic and gave tantalizing glimpses of other lewd activities. "Did my dear departed relative use this facility much?"

"Now and then, I gather."

"Alone?"

"I don't think so. It is rather large for one."

He looked at her, completely the earl. "I wish to move into these rooms, Mrs. Kerslake. I'm very fond of baths. See to it, if you please."

She almost protested. Having him in the Saint George rooms was too close to the past, and she hated to think that he'd changed so much that he liked this lewd display.

But she said, "Of course, my lord."

Whoever he was now, however, she didn't want him sharing this bath. With Diddy, for example. As they left the room she tried to establish some rules. "I run this house in a respectable manner, my lord. I hope you will not use that bath in any lewd way."

"Are you trying to dictate my conduct, Mrs. Kerslake?"

"I believe I have a right to concern myself with the welfare of the servants, my lord."

"Ah, I see. But if I were to bring in ladies—or others—from outside to share my bath, you would have no objection?"

She met his eyes. "You would be exposing the servants to impropriety."

"And they have not been so exposed before?"

"Times have changed."

"Have they?" He let it linger, then added, "And if I do not obey your dictates, Susan, you will do what?"

It was a neatly decisive blow.

The only possible retaliation was her resignation, but she couldn't leave Crag Wyvern just yet.

At her silence, one brow rose. There was a hint of humor, a lot of triumph, but also speculation. She didn't want him thinking about why she needed to stay.

She headed for the door. "I believe your breakfast will be waiting, my lord."

"I believe my breakfast will wait for me. There have to be some privileges of rank. Show me the late earl's rooms."

She wanted so desperately to escape, but she wouldn't simply be running from time spent with Con. She'd be fleeing the dream-memory friend of her heart. Her first clumsily wonderful lover. The youth she'd deliberately hurt. The man he had become.

More urgently, she'd be fleeing the dragon, coiled, patient, and the embodiment of silver-eyed peril. With a horrified glance back at the huge picture she saw that though the color of the saint's eyes was impossible to tell, the dragon's eyes were silver-gray.

"Mrs. Kerslake?" he prompted with a hint of authority.

She gathered her wits. "As you wish, my lord. They are next door so the earl had easy access to the bath."

She had to control her wretched reaction to him. If he felt anything at all for her it was anger. And yet . . . and yet he'd admitted he'd come here for the same reason as she, and that there had been sweetness between them once. . . .

She realized she'd almost walked past the first door to the Wyvern rooms, and stopped to unlock it. The key seemed to fight her about going into the lock, probably because Con was standing close beside her. She could swear she felt the heat of his body. She could certainly detect a faint but recognizable smell.

She'd not thought people had such a powerful individual smell, but even though he'd bathed, there was something, something in the air that carried her straight back to a naked tangle on a hot beach, and a youthful, muscular chest she had nuzzled and kissed again and again.

Stop it!

The key jerked home and she turned it, then thrust the door open, blessing the stale, pungent air that swamped sweeter memories. These smells— herbal, chemical, and the lingering hint of vomit—were all of the old earl. She walked briskly to fling open the window.

"He died here?" Con asked, as if he could smell death. Perhaps a soldier could.

She turned to face him, safer now that the large desk and wide worktable lay between them. "Yes. The room's been cleaned, of course, but otherwise left untouched. Some of these scrolls and books are valuable. Some of the ingredients, too."

The walls were covered by mismatched shelves stuffed higgledy-piggledy with texts, jars, bottles, and pots.

"Only to another of his kind." Con strolled over to inspect a shelf of glass bottles. "Was he pursuing alchemy or chemistry?"

"Alchemy, with a touch of sorcery thrown in."

He turned to look at her. "Trying to turn lead into gold?"

"Trying to turn age into youth. He was seeking the secret of eternal life."

"And he died at fifty from drinking his own nostrum. How ironic. We are generally a long-lived family, barring accidents. My father succumbed to influenza, my brother to a careless moment on the water. My grandfather was thrown from his horse at seventy, and had the misfortune to land on his head."

For some reason she was clutching the windowsill behind her as if needing a tether to sanity. "He was afraid of death, and afraid of meeting his ancestor, the first earl."

"Why?"

"He had no heir. He was the one to let the Dragonkiller's line die out."

"He should have married."

She didn't explain the mad earl's ways. She couldn't talk about things like that with Con.

He settled his hips against the desk, long, lean, hard, and still dueling with her. "How do you know so much about him? You only came here after Mrs. Lane left, didn't you?"

She was reluctant to admit the truth, but it was common knowledge. "I was the earl's assistant for three years before that."

"Assistant?" he queried, and she could see he was thinking the worst.

"I copied old documents, did research, and found sources for his ingredients. I was a kind of secretary."

"My, my, you were keen to become countess, weren't you?"

She gripped the sill behind her more tightly. "I was his secretary, and I took the job because I wanted employment."

"The manor threw you out?"

"Of course not. I preferred not to live on charity anymore."

"And this was the only employment available?"

Why was she even trying to explain? But burdened by so many things she couldn't explain away, she would try to avoid guilt over this.

"It was the only employment locally for someone like me. A Miss Kerslake of Kerslake Manor could hardly be hired for menial work, and the offspring of a smuggler and a whore is not desirable for polite occupation. The earl offered me the position, and I took it."

"Did he offer your brother the position of estate manager, too?"

"Yes."

"Why?"

She hadn't considered the question. "I assume my father suggested it."

"And the earl did as Mel Clyst suggested?" A slight smile of disbelief touched his lips.

"They had an agreement." After a moment, she added, "Smuggling, Con."

"Ah." He pushed off from the desk. "You can tell Captain Drake—I assume you know the current Captain Drake—that there will be no agreement."

"Con—"

His sharp, angry look silenced her, but then the moment was broken by an outsider.

"Good Lord, what is this?"

Con's secretary sauntered in like a spring breeze into a stale cavern. Lissome, she thought, with his light, lithe body and soft blond hair. But no angel. Every inch of him denied angel.

Snatched from an entirely different existence, for a moment she couldn't remember his name. He smiled—a speculative, knowing smile. "Racecombe de Vere, ma'am, at your service. My friends call me Race."

Susan dropped a curtsy. "Mr. de Vere."

She realized then that she had never once curtsied to Con.

De Vere's lips twitched and charming humor glinted in his eyes. He was a lady-killer, but he was having no effect on her except a slight irritation—and huge relief that he had interrupted.

"What is this weighty atmosphere I sense?" de Vere asked.

"Equal parts witchcraft and exasperation," Con said. "This was the old earl's lair. He was completely barmy, and killed himself with some brew that was supposed to give him eternal life."

"Does he haunt the house?" de Vere asked, clearly thinking this a treat.

Con looked at Susan, so she said, "Not that anyone has noticed. Surprisingly, Crag Wyvern has no ghosts at all."

"That's because the torture chamber victims are made of wax."

"Torture chamber!" declared de Vere, eyes bright. "Con, you best of good fellows. Let us go there immediately."

"If you want to be stretched on the rack, we can do that later." Con seized the younger man's elbow and marched him to the door. "For the moment, I gather that breakfast is waiting."

At the door, however, he looked back. "After breakfast I want a complete tour, Mrs. Kerslake, and most of your time throughout the day. Also, make sure your brother is available with the estate records."

He didn't wait for a response, which was as well, as she didn't have one except a shiver that made her fold her arms and rub herself. Even when fighting, even when a third person had been present, they'd talked to each other in a ghostly reminiscence of past intimacy. As if they alone were real in an unreal world.

It was the other way around. The world was real and Susan Kerslake and Con Somerford were phantasms, ghosts of two young people from a summer so long ago, two people who no longer existed except in memory.

But ghosts could carry a potent aura. His friend had sensed it, and he was the sort to make trouble.

She had to get away.

How long would it take to hire a new housekeeper and make a dignified exit? Too long. Yet to flee was impossibly weak, and there still was the gold. She'd organized a complete cleaning of Crag Wyvern over the past few months and found nothing. The old earl's hiding place must be obscure.

She left the room, locking it carefully, and went to her room to write a message to David. When he came up to see Con he could confirm that the run had been smooth. Then she would find a new housekeeper and make her escape, dignified or not.

Of course, where to go and what to do was another question entirely. Perhaps she should set off after her errant parents and head for the Antipodes!

As they went down a circular staircase, Race said, "I gather the lovely lady is out of bounds."

Con hoped he hadn't twitched. "Not particularly. As I said last night, you are free to woo her if it's honorable wooing you have in mind."

"Unlikely, but I might attempt an honorable flirtation if I'm not likely to feel your fist over it. She is the only good-looking woman in the place. The maid who brought my water was only one step more substantial than the skeleton in the corridor. This is a decidedly strange house."

"I hadn't noticed," Con said dryly, and crossed the courtyard to the break-fast room. He paused to look at the fountain statue. The dragon, as overen-dowed as Saint George, was about to have its way with the clearly unwilling, naked sacrifice. Around the rim of the basin was carved *The Dragon and His Bride.*

"I've never seen a dragon doing that with the traditional maiden before," Race remarked. "Throws a whole new light on the story, doesn't it?"

"I always thought Saint George's lance was pretty suggestive, myself."

"Especially the way pictures show him fondling it."

Con laughed as he led the way through the open glass-paneled doors into the breakfast room. The furniture was the usual dark oak, but white walls lightened it, and the open doors to the garden were pleasant.

And he was laughing. He was suddenly grateful to Race for attaching him-self to him and bringing laughter here.

"Remind me to show you the bath in my new rooms," Con said as he sat down.

"The Chinese dragons too much for you?"

"The Saint George rooms have a very large, very interesting bath."

"Ah. You and your baths. So what's so special about this one?"

Con described it, and Race shook his head. "I've often wondered how those poor maidens felt about the price of rescue. I can think of a lot of he-roes I'd not want to have to be grateful to. And what if the lady liked the dragon, and didn't want to be rescued by a boring saint?"

The thin maid bustled in with a coffeepot in one hand and a chocolate pot in the other. "The rest won't be long now, milord," she gasped, and rushed out.

"Why would the lady choose the dragon?" Con poured himself coffee. "A hoard of jewels wouldn't make up for being married to a monster."

"Some women lust after monsters."

"Then they deserve the monsters they get."

Race's eyes glinted with humor. "And those who choose saints deserve that fate, too?"

"Cynic."

"I ask you, would you like to be married to a saint?"

For some reason, the image of Lady Anne Peckworth rose in Con's mind.

Saint was too strong a word, but she was gentle, kind, good, and devoted to practical charities to do with the education of children and the care of the old.

She was the woman he was probably going to marry. He'd certainly paid her enough attention in the past two months to give her reason to hope. . . .

Two maids came in this time, blessedly interrupting his thoughts.

They unloaded laden trays onto the table. Neither maid was the one who'd come upon him naked. One was the skeleton, poor thing; the other was the older one from last night.

"Anything else, my lord?" the older one asked.

Con looked at the enormous amount of food on the table. "No, thank you. I think we can make do with this."

The maids left and Con and Race shared a grin. "We could feed the regiment on this lot," Race remarked, helping himself to a number of eggs and half the plate of ham.

Con speared a slice of beef on his fork and put it on his plate. "Trying to make a good impression, I suppose."

"They're succeeding." Race spread butter lavishly on a roll. "So, who should a wise woman marry?"

"A good and boring man. Why are we stuck on the subject of women?"

"Something to do with the angelic Susan, I assume."

Con looked at him sharply. "Why?"

"My dear fellow, tell me to button it if you want, but don't pretend there's nothing."

Con evaded the question. "She's the least angelic woman imaginable. She was out with the smugglers last night."

"How splendid," Race said, mopping up egg yolk with his bread. "As for angel, have you not realized she has the look of one of those Renaissance angels? Too beautiful to be a man. Too strongly featured to be a beautiful woman. Perfect, however, for angels, which are neither male nor female, but pure spirit."

"I assure you, Susan Kerslake is entirely female and flesh."

Con regretted it immediately, and wondered if he was going to have to kill Race to stop him from talking.

But after a moment Race said, "So, what orders for the day?"

Con grasped the change of subject with relief. "I plan a physical inspection of the place. Your mission is the old earl's papers. The sooner I'm sure everything is in order here, the sooner I can leave, but it would be pleasant to pinpoint the leakage of funds as well."

"What about the smugglers?"

"I'm curious about the earldom's relationship with them, but otherwise we ignore them." He saw Race's mild surprise. "Race, smuggling is as much part of life here as the sea. If I put a stop to it people would starve. If I shipped every smuggler off to Australia, the coast would be empty. If there's murder, extortion, that sort of thing going on, I might have to act. Otherwise we might as well try to rid the world of ants."

"Right," Race said, but looked surprised. Of course he was from Derbyshire, far from any coast. Con had grown up in Sussex. Not on the coast, to be sure, but close enough to understand smuggling ways.

"Start in the office, which is next to the library. The estate manager should turn up soon to fill in the details. I want a complete report of matters here over the past year. Make sure the accounts are sound."

Race groaned, but Con said, "You can't wait. Admit it."

"You steal my little pleasures. I enjoy appearing to suffer."

"Then I'll make you spend your days squiring ladies around the shops, and your nights gaming."

Race laughed. "Tortures of the damned. Dashed peculiar, though. If I'd suspected I had such a taste for paperwork, I'd have taken a nice safe job in London instead of marching around in mud and dust for years."

"Heaven help London." Con watched Race absorb another plateful of food, wondering where he put it. "How long am I likely to benefit from your peculiar tastes?"

"Until you bore me."

"And I haven't done that yet? I'm a pretty boring man."

Race laughed, grabbing his serviette to cover his mouth. "Lord, don't say things like that. You'll kill me!"

Con leaned back in his chair. "I stick you in a quiet part of Sussex overhauling the antiquated administrative system of a minor estate, then drag you to this prisonlike place."

Race took a clear breath. "Torture chamber, remember. And all those lovely papers."

Con studied the curved handle of his coffee cup for a moment. "You aren't by any chance playing the angel yourself, are you?" He looked up. "Guardian angel?"

Race looked back at him with perfect innocence. "Guarding you against what?"

Con almost answered, but then shook his head. "Clever, but no. I am not going to list possible answers."

Race dropped his serviette on the table, seeming to drop his playful manner with it. "You were an officer I admired, Con, and you are a man I admire. But you were a different officer and a different man in the Peninsula than you are now. If I can help you find that man, I will."

Con wasn't quite sure what to do with this. "And here I thought I was giving you needful employment."

"Employment is always nice."

"There you go again. . . ." But he might at least try to match honesty with honesty. "I'm not sure whether the Captain Somerford in the Peninsula was a better man, but whatever he was, he doesn't exist anymore. If you start chipping at this dry shell you may find only dust."

"Or a butterfly."

Con burst out laughing. "A *butterfly*!"

Race smiled. "There, see. I've made you laugh."

"I laugh."

"There's laughter and laughter. Remember the pigs?"

Con couldn't help but smile. "Piglets, Race. Piglets. What were there? Twelve? All tucked into the packs and jackets of men on the march. The company looked like a set of weavilly biscuits." He straightened his face and frowned at his secretary. "If your aim is to turn me into the sort of man who's always telling knee-slapping stories about army life, it's a forlorn hope."

"Talking of forlorn hopes," Race said. "Remember Santa Magdalena?"

Con stood, pushing his chair back roughly. "Enough. Sometimes war knocks the heart out of a man. But it seems possible to live without a heart."

Race stayed where he was. "Lord Darius is dead, Con."

Dear God, in what maudlin moment had he given Race even a sniff of Dare?

"Isn't that the problem?" Con said. "He's dead. I feel grief over it. Grief and laughter do not go well together."

"Sometimes they do. Is it grief, though? Or guilt?"

"I have nothing to feel guilty about. Dare played his part at Waterloo, and like so many others, he died."

"Quite."

"For God's sake. What the devil are you up to? Why are you acting as clumsy surgeon?"

Race frowned slightly. "I have no idea. I think it's this house. It worries me."

"It damn well worries me, too. That's why I'm going to do my conscientious duty by it, then put it into good hands and ride back to the sanity of Sussex. Can I possibly persuade you to do your part?"

Race grimaced, but without a sign of repentance, and rose. "Persuasion is hardly necessary."

Wanting to argue with Race, or throttle him, or both, Con led him to the estate office, where most of the administrative papers should be housed.

Guilt.

Dare had been an old friend, one of the Company of Rogues, and a complete civilian. Con felt that he should have found a way to stop Dare from volunteering. When Dare's ducal connections had won him a role as a courier, he should have prepared him better. He should at least have kept an eye on him, though the devil alone knew how when Con was fixed in his regimental position and Dare was hurtling around all over.

He should definitely, however, have done the final duty of a friend and found Dare's body for decent burial.

In the cool part of his mind Con knew none of it was his fault, but most of his mind was not cool. Dare had come to represent all the death and suffering that had been Waterloo, and it hung over everything still.

He flung the door open. The estate office was a relatively normal room for Crag Wyvern, walled with orderly shelves and drawers, with only a solid oaken desk in the middle. The carvings on the desk didn't bear close inspection—though Race, of course, sank to his haunches to inspect them, and laughed—and the ceiling was painted with a vision of hell, complete with imaginative tortures of the damned.

Race looked up at it. "Clearly whoever ordered that did not enjoy paperwork. But it does remind me that you haven't shown me the torture chamber yet."

"I'm holding the treat back as a reward for work well done."

"Very well, what is my work?"

Con looked around the room, which would be a torture chamber to him. "Go through everything. Make sense of what's happened here. Find any shady goings-on or anomalies."

To him it sounded like ordering a troop to wade through a torrent, crawl through a swamp, and take a hill crowned with army guns, but Race smiled and said, "Right!"

By the time Con left, Race had already shed his jacket and begun to go through the desk drawers.

Con shook his head and returned to the breakfast room.

Damn Race. Perhaps he and Diego huddled in the evenings to share nurse-maid reports!

So Waterloo had left him bleak. It hardly seemed an irrational reaction to monstrous slaughter including the deaths of many friends and colleagues.

And now he had scheduled an interview with Susan.

He felt as if he'd been ordered to wade through a torrent, crawl through a swamp, and take a hill crowned with army guns. . . .

He rang the bell.

When the skeleton maid responded—he found out that her name was Ada Splint, which seemed somewhat unfortunate—he asked her to tell Mrs. Kerslake that he was ready.

As he waited, he poured himself more of the excellent tea, sure that it had carried no tax, and planned the best line of attack.

First, he would treat her as housekeeper. That was the role she'd chosen for herself. She'd doubtless intended to be gone before he made his announced arrival, but now that she was caught she could damn well live with it.

Next, he must find out what she was up to.

Unfortunately she wasn't intending to seduce her way into the countess's bed. Being housekeeper was no route to that, especially with the clothes she was wearing. Or at least, she would think that way. In truth, he suspected that she could seduce him in rags. . . .

Ah, no. He forbade his mind to go in that direction.

Third, he would never, ever, call her Susan.

He drank some of the cooling tea and made himself consider why she was playing housekeeper.

Something to do with smuggling, he was sure. The Crag's horses were used by the Dragon's Horde, of course, and doubtless somewhere below were caves or chambers used for storage. Was that it? Was she simply guarding the Dragon's Horde's territory?

Susan came in from the corridor then, encased in her gray and white, blankly unreadable.

Hiding things.

Her chin went up slightly as she curtsied, and her eyes met his in a very unservile way.

Chapter Seven

Con saw immediately that Race was right. Her straight nose, square chin, and perfectly bowed lips did have that classical angelic look to them, especially with those clear eyes with smooth, arching brows. If Race had seen her at fifteen with her golden brown hair waving loose around her, he'd have thought he was seeing a heavenly vision. . . .

"My lord?"

Dammit. Keep this businesslike. He indicated the seat to his right. "Please sit down, Mrs. Kerslake. We have a great deal to discuss."

She obeyed stiffly, clearly wary.

"Now, Mrs. Kerslake, explain to me how things have been managed here since the late earl's death."

He saw the slight relaxation. She'd been braced for something else. What?

"The sixth earl died suddenly, my lord, as you know—"

"Was there any inquiry about it?"

She stared at him, and her surprise seemed genuine. "Do you think it suspicious? He was constantly trying new ingredients."

"Someone could have added a noxious herb if they had wished to."

"But who? He entertained few guests, and never took them to his sanctum, as he called it. And," she added with a direct look, "no one gained by his death but you, my lord."

"Gain? This place, and a property peopled entirely by smugglers?"

"And the title."

"I had a title. Many of us do not set such store on high rank."

It was a jab and he instantly regretted it. Not because she flinched, but because it showed he remembered. Perhaps cared.

If it stung, she hid it well. "Ah yes, Viscount Amleigh, was it not, my lord?"

"And I assure you I was content with it. As for other suspects, people sometimes have concealed desires and angers."

Her brows twitched, but it could be puzzlement as much as guilt. "His valet was with him when he prepared the potion, and when he drank it, and Fordham had been with him for thirty years. It is possible that some ingredient was not what it seemed, but the suppliers had no reason for mischief. They have lost an excellent and generous customer."

She sounded completely honest about this. He didn't even know why he'd taken that tack. He had enough problems without trying to create a murder out of nothing. "Very well. What happened after the death, Mrs. Kerslake? You had been acting as his assistant?"

She sat with a stillness that seemed all wrong for her—hands loosely linked in her dark lap, everything muted by white and gray until she seemed colorless. He had to concentrate to see that yes, her lips were slightly pink, her eyes hazel, her few visible curls that rich, complex brown. He'd always remembered her as vibrant, and despite the dark last night and dark clothes, she'd seemed so then.

Oh, yes. Susan was up to something.

"Yes, my lord."

Yes, what, dammit?

His mind was full of other things, but he pulled it back into order. Her employment here. That was what they'd been discussing.

"And you became housekeeper after the earl's death?"

"Yes, my lord."

"Why?"

She didn't flinch. "The earl left Mrs. Lane an annuity in his will, and she wished to retire. She was over seventy, my lord, and suffered in her joints, but she would not go until there was a replacement to care for Crag Wyvern. So I took the position on a temporary basis. It is expected that you will hire a housekeeper to your taste now."

"Did your aunt and uncle not object to your taking such employment?"

Her brows rose slightly. "I am past my girlhood, my lord. Since I haven't married, I need occupation. I also need an income. My aunt and uncle are generous, but I cannot live forever on their charity."

"Ah, yes, I remember that you were always ambitious."

Another unworthy jab, and when she paled he almost apologized. But at the same time, the dark part of him wanted to see her flinch.

"Did your father not provide for you?"

She raised her eyes, but only as far as the silver teapot. He noted the delicate skin of her eyelids, the faint veins visible there, the dark line of her lashes. Her tense jaw. Did she want to let out honest, angry words?

He wished she would. He felt long overdue for a raging fight with Susan Kerslake.

"He purchased some property for me, my lord. It provides a small income."

"Yet you felt obliged to work here?"

"I need occupation, my lord."

"You should have married."

"I have not received an offer that tempted me, my lord."

"Held out for the Earl of Wyvern, did you?"

Look at me, Susan. I want to feed off every expression in your eyes.

As if he'd spoken, she did raise her eyes then, to fire a pointed, rather impatient look at him.

Ah, of course. Focusing on his own turmoil, he'd ignored the larger picture. Bringing an outsider here would be very inconvenient for the smugglers. Putting someone local in charge, someone in sympathy with the Dragon's Horde, had been the sensible action.

Why Susan, though? He couldn't believe that the area lacked women able to give basic care to a house, even a grand one like Crag Wyvern.

Perhaps, he thought, controlling every reaction, the question was, Who was the new Captain Drake? Susan had been out with the smugglers last night, but being the daughter of the old Captain Drake wouldn't entitle her to be there.

Being the lover of the new one might.

Hardly surprising if she'd followed in her mother's footsteps and taken up with the smuggling master. Hardly surprising if she was playing housekeeper for his sake.

It was the most reasonable explanation he'd come up with thus far, and without knowing the man he wanted him dead. Or at least captured and transported to join Melchisedeck Clyst in Botany Bay. He'd see to it.

No, dammit, he would not. He would not become the sort of man to harm weaker rivals over a woman.

He took a moment to clear his head, then asked, "Are you willing to stay on until I make decisions about Crag Wyvern, Mrs. Kerslake?"

He thought she would refuse, but then she said, "For a little while, my lord. I thought to begin the search for a replacement."

"Very well, but there is no need to seek a highly qualified woman. I do not intend to live here. I have a home elsewhere, and a family well suited there."

"A family?" The words were followed by a flush of color, and a quick, mortified lowering of her startled eyes.

He could have crowed with triumph. That had stung her.

By God, *did* she have hopes of entrancing him after all? He'd like to see her try.

Oh, yes, he'd very much like to see her try.

He'd also love to claim a wife and children and make her wounds bleed. If he'd a hope of maintaining the lie he might have done it, but it wouldn't stick.

"My mother and two sisters," he said. "They would not like to move here." But then he realized he had one blade that might cut deeply. "Also, I am to marry. Lady Anne would not be comfortable here."

You have a rival, Susan.

A serious rival.

What are you going to do about that?

He had met Lady Anne only a few times in London, then spent four days at her father's home, Lea Park. Nothing was settled, but he was thinking of making an offer of marriage. It wasn't an outright lie, and Lady Anne was too good a weapon to leave in the scabbard.

Susan was guarded now, however, and little showed, though her widened eyes gave him a bit of satisfaction.

"It is not good for a house to stand empty, my lord."

"I hardly think Crag Wyvern will appeal to many tenants."

"Some people have unusual tastes, my lord," she said with a slight, cool smile. "The earl had guests who liked Crag Wyvern very much indeed."

The smile was an act of pure bravery that made him want to salute her.

Damnation, Susan. Why?

"Then please supply Mr. de Vere with their names, ma'am. They may have first refusal. I know that leaving the chief house empty is always an economic hardship to an area."

Her brows rose, and her lips tightened, but it was a suppressed smile rather than annoyance, and it danced in her eyes.

"You're thinking of smuggling," he said. "Yes, at the moment the area is prospering from the Freetrade, but the end of the war is bringing hard times everywhere. On top of that, the army and navy have men to spare to patrol the coasts. That, I assume, is how your father was caught."

Her smile fled. "Yes, though if the earl had raised a finger to help him, he'd not have been transported."

"Remarkable that the mad earl for once did the right thing. The law is the law, and must be upheld."

There, that was a clear enough message for her.

"If there's any sanity in Parliament," he went on, "duties will be reduced and smuggling will cease to be profitable enough to justify the risks. The change won't come today or tomorrow, but it's on the horizon, Susan. People hereabouts need to remember that they once lived by farming, and by fishing for something other than barrels and bales."

"We know," she said softly.

"We?"

"The people hereabouts."

That was not what she'd meant. She'd meant herself and the new Captain Drake, damn his black soul.

And somewhere in that he'd called her by her name, which he'd resolved not to do.

Con stood abruptly. "The tour of the house, Mrs. Kerslake."

She rose with controlled grace and led the way back into the faux-stone corridor, heading toward the kitchen area first.

There weren't many surprises. He'd roamed this house as a youth and discovered most of its nooks and crannies. One startling new feature was a kind of drawing room off the great hall, plastered and painted in the modern style, furnished with spindle-legged chairs and tables.

"I persuaded the earl to have one room where conventional guests might feel more at ease," Susan said, standing composedly beside him, smelling faintly of lavender soap. Not the right perfume for her at all. She should smell of wildflowers—and sweat, and sand.

"Did he have any conventional guests?"

"Occasionally, my lord. People will drop by."

"How alarming. Perhaps that's why he constructed a torture chamber. I've known drop-by guests I'd like to hang in chains."

He intended it to be a joke but had forgotten whom he was with. When her eyes flickered to his, alight with startled laughter, he instinctively stepped away.

"Now I suppose we must tackle the upper floors," he said. "Including a more thorough check of the late earl's chambers."

Her face was carefully blank as she turned to lead the way. "They are not particularly alarming, my lord, but in some disorder. . . ." From the back he saw her slight shrug, which drew his attention to her square shoulders and then to her straight back.

Which he could remember naked . . .

Breathe, dammit, breathe. And listen. She'd said something about disorder.

"I remember he didn't like to leave Crag Wyvern," he said as she led the way up the wide central stairs. Her long back seemed to point down, down to the full curve of her bottom, which was bewitchingly at eye level. He sped up to climb the stairs alongside her, housekeeper or not.

He ached for her now as if she were a fire on a freezing night in the sierra. But fire burned. Fire destroyed. Even a safe fire, built within stones, could harm. He'd seen frozen men ruin their hands and feet by trying to warm them too close to a hot fire.

"He never left here," she was saying. "Certainly not as long as I've been aware of his movements."

"Why not?"

"He suffered from a fear of the outside."

"What did he fear out there?"

For Con, the danger was all within.

Could even fear enable him to resist the flaming power of Susan, especially if she was to stop, turn, approach, press, kiss, begin to shed her clothing . . . ?

She stopped, turned. . . .

"He had nothing real to fear as far as I could tell. He simply feared being outside these walls. He was insane, Con. It was mostly in subtle ways, but he was insane."

As insane as he was to imagine that Susan planned seduction! He gestured her to lead on and soon they reached the earl's rooms. She unlocked a different door this time and they entered the bedroom, though it did not seem a precise term for the room he saw.

The bed was there, huge, hung with faded red hangings that were actually moth-eaten to holes in places. It sat in a jumble of other furniture, however, as if the earl had tried to make this one room into a house.

The red window curtains were drawn against the courtyard light, but the holes let in some light. As his eyes adjusted, he saw a large dining table with just one chair, an armchair, a sofa, a breakfront desk, and bookcases everywhere.

There were more bookcases than would fit around the walls, so many were the freestanding, rotating sort. All were full, with surplus books staggering on top. Con hesitated to try to move through the room, and for other reasons as well. The smell of musty books and vaguely noxious things hung heavily in the gloomy air.

Every surface was scattered with objects from riding crops to strange glass vials to stuffed animals. Con saw two human skulls, and not the neat, clean skulls found in anatomists' collections. There were other bones, too, which he hoped were from animals. Some were small enough to even be leftovers from the earl's dinners.

Presumably the crazy earl hadn't eaten the body of the crocodile, however, leaving only the glassy-eyed head, or the rest of whatever had owned the black and leathery claw hanging from the cobwebbed lamp near the desk. The upper rail of the bed boasted a fringe of other dark and shriveled things.

Curiosity made him work his way through the room to have a closer look.

"Dried phalluses," she said. "From as many species as he could obtain them. His most prized collection."

Con stopped, then pushed his way to the window to drag open the heavy curtains. The right one tore in his hand, spewing dust and other things over him so that he coughed, and had to brush off his face.

Through sunlight swarmed with motes he faced her. "Did you really think of joining him in that bed?"

She stared at him like a marble statue, and for a moment he thought she'd say a cold yes. But then she said, "No. I never came here before becoming housekeeper."

It was damnably ambiguous. "Then why spend so many of your years here?"

"I told you. I needed employment, and it wasn't easy to find. What's more, this was interesting employment. The earl was mad, but his madness was fascinating at times. After all," she added with a wry twist of her lips, "how many women in England have such an extensive knowledge of phalluses?"

It almost broke a laugh from him, and he looked away, at one of the two adjoining doors, the one that didn't lead into the sanctum. "What's through there?"

"His dressing room. Theoretically."

Susan worked her way carefully through the clutter to open that door, feeling as if she were constantly working her way through chaotic and often rotten obstacles to try to reach some sort of understanding with Con.

She could not recapture the past, but did they have to clash like enemies? Wasn't there at least neutral ground?

She stepped into the dressing room and stood aside for him. This room was blessedly clear of furniture other than two large armoires and the tin bathtub hung with draft-excluding curtains. The window curtains were open here, so the light was good.

She watched his reaction.

He stopped, staring at the figure hanging from the ceiling. But then he stepped forward and poked a finger into one of the flock-spilling gashes in the dummy.

A smile fought to show on her lips. Against logic she was deeply proud of the cool nerves formed in him by war. Against logic, a deep ache near her heart told her love still lingered in her. Love like a smoldering fire, threatening to burst into flame again.

Despite a growing longing to stay, she had to escape this place before she did something she would regret even more than she regretted the past.

He turned to a frame on the wall holding a number of swords and touched the blade of one with a careful finger. "Not ornaments," he remarked.

"He told me he'd been a skilled fencer in his youth, but along with his fear of the outdoors, he feared anyone near him with a weapon. So he fenced with that." She indicated the swaying figure that was suspended so that its feet almost touched the floor.

"Hanged by the neck?" Con asked.

She just shrugged.

"What a way to spend a life. There's that Roman bath, however. How does that fit in?"

"He developed an obsession about physical cleanliness, and would spend hours in the tub. Then he had the idea of the larger one. He decided physical cleanliness was the key to a long life and good health, and also to fertility."

"Zeus, that's enough to give a bachelor a distaste for bathing."

Their eyes met for a startled moment. She knew he too was thinking of the risk they'd so thoughtlessly taken eleven years ago.

Chapter Eight

I was young and foolish," he said, "and never gave the matter a thought. I hope . . ."

She wished she weren't blushing. "Of course not. There would have been hell to pay."

It was a delicate subject, but the wash of heat running through her skin was not only from that. Finally they were really talking about the past.

"That's what I supposed." He looked at her a moment longer and she held her breath, hoping for something that might weave a thread of connection, but then he looked around again. "Why haven't these rooms been put into better order, Mrs. Kerslake?"

She suppressed a sigh and regrouped. "Anything likely to turn to slime has been thrown away, my lord. And of course they were inventoried. But apart from that, the earl stated in his will that everything was to be left for your disposal."

"I hadn't realized quite what that meant. Very well, dispose of that figure for a start." He strode to the armoires and threw open the doors to reveal a collection of long robes. The drawers, she knew, contained a few suits of clothing, none younger than ten years.

"And get rid of this lot," he said. "Give them to the vicar for the poor if they're any use." He walked back into the bedroom. "Have the extra furniture moved out of here. Is there still empty space in the floor above?"

"Yes, my lord."

"Then put it up there." He looked at the bed. "Get rid of that. Burn that stuff hanging around it. And where the devil did he get those skulls from?"

"I don't know, my lord."

"I'll talk to the vicar about decent interment. And about whether any graves have been disturbed around here. All these books can go to the library, though de Vere had better check to see whether there's anything extraordinary about them." But then he frowned. "He has enough to do. Is there someone else in the area who could organize and evaluate those texts?"

"The curate is a scholar and would welcome the extra income," she said, enjoying seeing Con take command and issue crisp orders.

She might have enjoyed seeing him in battle except that it would have killed her, moment by moment, to watch him in danger. Bad enough to have known he was at war, to pick up each newspaper fearing to see his name.

She hadn't been able to help following Con's career through Fred Somerford. He'd entered the infantry. He'd made lieutenant, then captain, and once been mentioned in dispatches. He'd been at Talavera and wounded at the taking of San Sebastian—

Wounded!

—but not seriously.

He'd changed regiments three times to see more action.

Trying to pretend only polite interest, Susan had wanted to scream, "Why? Why not stay safe, you stupid creature?"

Her Con, her laughing gentle Con, had no place in fields of cannon fire and slaughter.

Yet it had made him the man she saw today. . . .

He was opening and closing drawers in the desk, glancing at the contents. "The curate had better go through everything," he said. "In fact, perhaps you shouldn't get rid of the bed. Just the hangings and mattress. There's a dearth of money in the coffers, so I can't afford the grand gesture of throwing away solid furniture."

Susan worked at keeping a bland expression but was jabbed by guilt. She remembered Con saying years ago that his branch of the family was the poor one. It had sprung from the first earl's younger son, and what modest wealth the Sussex Somerfords had accumulated had been wiped out by royalist sympathies during the Civil War. Since then they'd lived comfortably enough, but more as titled gentlemen farmers than as members of the aristocracy.

Times were hard for farmers now, however, even gentlemen farmers, and the old earl had run the earldom's coffers almost dry with his crazy pursuits. And she must try to take what little coin might be left. . . .

One idea stirred. "What of the contents of his sanctum, my lord? The . . .

specimens and ingredients. I believe some of them are valuable. Certainly the earl paid a great deal for them."

He looked at her. "So I shouldn't consign them to the fire? Hell. Is there an expert nearby who might be willing to organize the sale of them?"

"The late earl dealt with a Mr. Traynor in Exeter. A dealer in antiquarian curiosities."

"Is that what they call them? Well, waste not, want not. Give the details to de Vere and he'll summon Traynor. And the various peculiar objects in this room might as well be put in the sanctum for his assessment. Perhaps crocodile heads have mystic powers. We wouldn't want to deprive the world of such valuable artifacts, would we?"

A smile was fighting at her lips as she glanced at the withered objects hanging around the bed. "And those?"

"By all means."

But then he worked his way over to a sideboard and gingerly extracted something from under a pile of old magazines. It was a pistol. He carefully checked it, then tipped something out. The powder in the firing pan, she assumed.

He turned to her. "He feared invaders?"

"I don't know, but he liked to keep in practice."

"What did he practice shooting on if he never went out?"

"The birds in the courtyard. He was quite good."

He turned to look out at the courtyard. No birds were flying now, but the busy chirping and twittering was audible. "Not so safe after all," he murmured, and she wondered what he meant.

He put down the pistol and headed so quickly for the door that he bumped into a set of rotating shelves, sending it spinning and books tumbling.

"Hell!" He stopped to rub his thigh.

She hurried over to pick up the books, but he said, "Leave them," and continued out into the gloomy corridor.

She followed, wondering what was suddenly so wrong.

"How many keys are there?" he demanded.

"Just two. Mine and the earl's, which should have been sent to you."

"A large bunch of keys, yes. I thought they were symbolic." He pulled the door shut. "Lock it. We'll let this Traynor loose on all of it before touching anything."

As she turned the key in the lock, he spoke again, however. "Are there anymore firearms in there, do you think?"

"I believe he had a pair."

She saw him brace to return to the room, and then give up the idea. "Before Traynor arrives, I'll have Pearce check the room for danger. No need to accompany him, Mrs. Kerslake. You can trust him with the key."

They were back to formality, when for a moment back there it had slipped. "Very well, my lord."

Then he said, "You'd have married him to become Lady Wyvern?"

"No."

"It never crossed your mind?"

Ah.

"I was a girl, Con." All she seemed to have to offer him was honesty, tarnished though it was. "Yes, I thought of it, but I'd never met him. I'd hardly seen him. He was as mythological to me as a dragon. I sought the position as his assistant with the idea in the back of my mind. But then I learned that he wouldn't marry anyone until he was sure they were carrying his child, and I could not do that. Which made me see that I could not be intimate with the mad earl before or after marriage. And that was before I saw that bed."

"He demanded a trial marriage? Did he think to get a local lady to marry him that way?"

"The local *un*-ladies were willing enough."

"He would have married *any* woman carrying his child?"

"Apparently."

"And no one fooled him?"

"He was mad, Con, not stupid. Any woman had to come here during her courses—and he checked to be sure it was real—and then stay here until she bled again. As you know, there are no male servants other than his valet, who was fanatically devoted."

"The old goat."

"They came willingly enough, and he gave them twenty guineas when they left. A handsome amount for simple folk. In fact," she added with a distinct flare of mischief, "some may come up here hoping you'll be interested, too."

"Hell's hounds! I'll pay them twenty guineas to go away."

"Don't let word of that out in public."

She thought he might laugh, but then he shook his head. "We should progress to the dungeon, I suppose, and get this over with, but I promised de Vere the treat."

* * *

Con set off down the corridor, hoping it looked like a steady, well-ordered retreat, not the panicked flight it was. He believed her. She'd not seriously contemplated joining the mad earl in that bed, and yet the image haunted him.

She'd thought of marrying the old earl.

She was behind him. He sensed her even though she made no sound in her soft slippers—like a memory, or the ghost of a memory.

She'd only thought of it.

He'd thought of doing a good many things he was blessed not to have done. Suicide once, even. Only the thought of it.

He'd contemplated desertion once, too. In the early days before he became hardened to men and animals in agony, to causing men and animals to be in agony. For a few days it had seemed the only sane choice, and he'd planned how to go about it.

But then they'd come suddenly under attack and he'd fought to survive and to help his comrades survive. Somewhere in the process he'd committed himself to the fight against Napoleon and been able to carry on.

He'd almost raped a woman once.

He'd been with a group of officers drinking in a taverna in a Spanish village. It had been not long after battle, though he was damned if he could remember which one or anything else about the place. Blood had been running hot still, and they all wanted a woman.

Some of the women were willing, but a few were not, and their protests and attempts to escape had seemed amusing. Exciting, even.

He could look back at it now as if from the outside and wonder how he could have behaved like that, but he also remembered feeling a godlike ecstasy. That the women were his warrior's due.

Pressing the struggling, sobbing woman down on a table with the cheers of the men and the wild Spanish music still playing . . .

His cock had been throbbing, jumping with eagerness and he'd had his flap half undone. Other hands had been helping hold her down.

But something in his mind had clicked. Some shard of sanity had shot icy reality through him.

He'd grabbed her up off the table and pushed out of the room saying something about doing this properly. Some had tried to stop him, but he'd fought free into the hot Spanish air and a touch of sanity, the woman still writhing and sobbing in his grasp.

He'd kept her in his tent all night and sent her off at dawn with some coins. Pausing before leaving, she'd asked, "Do you wish me to say that you can do it, Capitan?"

She'd thought the rescue was to cover up impotence. He'd managed to hold back wild laughter, and simply said, "Say whatever is easiest for you, señora."

He heard days later that she'd spread tales of heroic virility. He supposed she'd meant well, but it had made life damned difficult at times. He'd never spent a whole night with a woman since in case she expected a heroic performance.

So he could understand that sometimes people did things in a kind of temporary madness, or thought of them. And that consequences, even of well-intentioned acts, were unpredictable.

And that people were often not what they seemed.

As they approached the office door he turned to her. "What do you think of Mr. de Vere as secretary?"

Her brows rose. "It is not for me to make such judgments, my lord."

"Drop the servant act, Susan. Do you think he'll be snoozing, or sitting with his feet up enjoying a book of questionable pictures?"

"I did, but now I assume not."

He opened the door to reveal Race, as expected, at the desk surrounded by stacks of paper and an aura of intense activity. He looked up impatiently and Con could almost see the words *Go away* coming out of his mouth, as in a satirical cartoon.

After a moment, however, he put his pen in the standish and stood.

"The records are in fairly good shape, my lord," he said, even giving Con the tribute of his title in front of Susan. "But you know, there's a great deal of money unaccounted for."

Ah-ha! Con turned to Susan. "Any idea where it might have gone, Mrs. Kerslake?"

"No," said Race. "I mean there's a lot of money that's appeared on the books out of nowhere."

Con turned back to him with a look. "Smuggling."

Race pushed hair off his forehead. "Oh, I suppose so. As I'm from Derbyshire, it doesn't come first to mind." He picked up a piece of paper to review it. "It must be a very profitable business."

"It is." Con glanced back at Susan. She had a rather fixed look on her face, as if she'd rather deny that such a thing as smuggling existed. "As the earl's secretary in the past," he prompted, "I'm sure you know something about his involvement."

The look she flashed at him was almost a glare. "The earl invested in cargoes, yes, my lord. Most people hereabouts do."

"And how much profit does a run make?"

With another irritated glance, she said, "About five times the investment, if all goes smoothly. There are always some runs that fail, of course, creating a total loss."

Con saw Race's eyes widen and said, "Remember this is illegal."

"So are a great many interesting things," Race replied. "Mrs. Kerslake, do you know the amount invested and raised on a good run? I ask only out of fascinated interest, of course."

Susan suddenly relaxed and smiled—at Race. A relaxed, friendly smile that made Con grit his teeth.

She moved toward the desk. "It's said that a cargo came in down the coast last year with a thousand gallons each of brandy, rum, and gin, and a quarter ton of tobacco. I hear that tobacco can be bought abroad for sixpence a pound and sold here for five times that. Spirits might be a shilling a gallon and six shillings here."

Race bent to make quick calculations on paper. "Almost a thousand pounds from an investment of about a hundred and sixty. Lord above."

She moved closer to look at his figures. "There are expenses, of course. The ship and captain, payment to the landers, tubmen, batmen, and for use of horses and carts. Everyone will expect a little of the goods to take home, too. On the other hand," she added, "tea is even more profitable. Ten to one."

Race was looking decidedly dazzled. It was the profit, not the person, but Con's jaw was aching with the need to drag her away from his side.

"You know a surprising amount about it, Mrs. Kerslake," he said, and saw her remember discretion with a start.

"Everyone does in these parts." She moved away from Race, however, which was an improvement.

Race looked up from his papers. "No wonder the earldom seems to have taken in at least two thousand pounds on top of rents each year."

"Has it, by gad?" Con strode to the desk to look at the papers Race had spread in front of him. "Yet according to the records Swann's sent me, there's only a couple of thousand in the earldom's bank." He looked across the desk. "Any explanation of that, Mrs. Kerslake?"

"The sixth earl spent a great deal on what interested him, my lord. His antiquities." She was hiding behind her servant's manner, but he wasn't fooled. She was tense with knowledge.

"'Eye of newt and tail of frog' being very expensive these days?" Con turned back to Race. "Any idea if there's any squirreled away?"

"It's 'Eye of newt and toe of frog,' actually," Susan interjected. He looked at her and was hard-pressed not to smile at the touch of mischief there—an adult mischief based on wit and wisdom rather than girlish high spirits.

"Tails may make more sense," she pointed out, "but toes must bring more profit, frogs having more than one."

"Tails would have rarity value, however, since they do not have one once they're fully grown."

Her eyes sparkled. "That would make them a symbol of eternal youth . . . !"

He picked up her thought. "And if the earl were still alive, I could make a fortune selling him frog's tails."

Con thought they both came to a shocked awareness of relaxation, of memory of past times, simultaneously. She certainly sobered and turned to Race at the same time Con did.

"Hidden profits?" Con prompted, aware of his secretary's intrigued interest, damn him.

"I've found none yet, my lord. Not all his incomes and expenditures are clearly itemized, however, and he clearly often dealt in cash. It is possible he spent it all."

Surely after being the earl's secretary for so many years, Susan would know. He challenged her directly. "I presume you don't know where the extra money is, Mrs. Kerslake?"

She looked him straight in the eye. "No, my lord."

That was the truth.

"Keep up the search," he ordered Race. "It will enliven your dull days. And note any records of the purchase price of his peculiarities. That might be the key to my fortune."

Susan's expression turned so perfectly blank he knew she was hiding something. He really must stop thinking her an honest woman. She was beautiful, fascinating, deadly.

But not honest.

She'd had years to play with the books here, diverting money at will. She was up against Race now, however, whose chief delight was finding the truths and secrets hidden in records and ledgers.

Raw from that moment of friendly banter, he had to escape. "I am going to inspect the estate."

Then he realized this would leave Susan free to get up to all sorts of mischief. "Mrs. Kerslake, I wish you to work with Mr. de Vere. You are familiar with the earldom's management."

"The torture chamber, my lord?" she reminded him.

"A thoroughly superfluous addition." He saw her puzzlement, but wasn't about to explain. Crag Wyvern was one huge torture chamber when Susan Kerslake was in it, and a trap, too.

Race was showing absolutely no interest in rack and pincers, so Con left, shutting the door on them.

Then he turned to go back. Susan and Race, alone together? After a moment he made himself walk away from the door. Perhaps Race could save him from himself.

A few more days of this new Susan and he might be rolling in the sand with her again, and this time there was nothing to prevent him offering marriage and being caught for life.

Except, he suddenly thought, a prior commitment.

Last week he'd been drifting toward offering marriage to Anne Peckworth. Nothing had changed. She was well-bred, well dowered, kind, and gentle. His mother and sisters liked her. She was the perfect wife for him.

She had another advantage—the reason, in fact, that he'd sought her out. Earlier in the year, a fellow Rogue, Lord Middlethorpe, had been about to offer for Lady Anne when he'd met and married his beautiful wife, Serena. Lady Anne had been led to expect that offer, and been hurt, but she'd behaved beautifully.

He'd decided that since he seemed to lack the ability to fall in love, he might as well take Francis's place with Anne, who had a crippled foot and thus didn't find it easy to attend social events.

It was rational, reasonable, and yet here, with Susan, he was in danger of losing his grip on that sane decision.

He went to his room and opened his traveling desk to take out a sheet of paper. After fighting an instinct to hesitate, he wrote a swift letter to Anne Peckworth.

A gentleman writing to an unmarried lady was tantamount to commitment anyway, but to make all safe he stated clearly that he intended to speak to her father as soon as he returned to Sussex, which he hoped would be in a week or so.

He did not sand the ink but watched it dry, knowing he was burning his bridges. He was burning bridges between himself and the enemy, however, which was an excellent military tactic.

Attraction, even love, was not always good. He'd seen men bewitched and entangled by unworthy women, often to their destruction. He would not be one.

The ink was dry.

He folded the letter, sealed it, addressed it and scrawled *Wyvern* across the top to cover the postage. Then he gave it to Diego. "Take this down to Pearce. He's to get it into the mail immediately. If he has to ride to Honiton or Exeter, so be it. I want it on its way."

So that I can't weaken and snatch it back.

He saw Diego's brows rise, but the valet only said, "Yes, my lord."

He sat back and considered his defensive position. It was perfect. Now he could resist any weapons Susan brought to bear.

Chapter Nine

Susan tried to pay attention to de Vere and the paperwork, but her mind and heart were still with Con. That brief moment of fun had been like a drop of water on parched earth.

Tantalizing rather than refreshing.

She could not endure more such encounters. They made her feel like the most fragile shell on the seashore, being worn thinner and thinner with every wave of interaction. She'd be transparent soon, and shatterable with the slightest pressure. She'd end up as sand, swept away with the next tide. . . .

"Mrs. Kerslake?" De Vere's voice broke into her thoughts.

She turned to him and saw his expression—intrigued, but not unkind.

"Perhaps you could explain how the earl recorded his investment interests. It seems somewhat unclear."

She concentrated on simple matters. "He was secretive by nature, Mr. de Vere."

He had brought over a chair so she could sit by him, and now asked a series of focused, intelligent questions. She was impressed by how quickly he'd grasped the arcane aspects of the records and by how clearly he understood what was contained in them, including what was implied.

She was also impressed and worried by his systematic approach. She had been efficient, but not so meticulous. Though de Vere was working with remarkable speed, he was stripping every sheet of paper of its information and organizing it for future reference.

She was almost sure that there were no details here about smuggling matters, but things might be learned between the lines. Payments were made to the George and Dragon tavern for wine and spirits, for example, which were disguised investments in smuggling. Would de Vere, from Derbyshire, realize that?

Large sums of money were entered under loan repayments without any record of the loan.

Also the earl had been inclined to scribble notes to himself on all kinds of matters on the edge of papers, or on scraps that often ended up mixed in with other things.

What might de Vere learn that way?

Might he learn that David was the new Captain Drake? If he did, what might he do with that, as an outsider and a soldier?

She needed to speak to David, to warn him, even though she knew such a warning was useless. There was nothing he could change, nothing he could do, except perhaps lie low.

And where was he? She'd sent the message saying he was wanted here. She needed to know the run had gone smoothly, that she could put aside the matter of finding the hidden money.

She gazed sightlessly at a row of figures. What if it hadn't gone well? What if David was wounded somewhere and that was why he wasn't here?

She made herself be sensible. She'd have received word. Someone would have told her.

What if no one knew? If her aunt and uncle thought he was staying with friends . . . ?

She realized that de Vere had asked her the same thing twice. He must think her an addlepated female.

Trying to speak calmly, she said, "You know, I think my brother would be able to help you more on these matters, Mr. de Vere. I wonder where he is."

"Until he comes, perhaps—"

She rose. "I will go and make sure the message was sent." Before he could object, she escaped.

She went to the kitchen and put Mrs. Gorland in charge. She almost ran out as she was, but she disciplined herself and put on her plain, wide hat. She must be Mrs. Kerslake, respectable housekeeper, not Susan Kerslake, who'd tramped free on the hills.

Who'd gone adventuring with Con Somerford.

As soon as she was outside Crag Wyvern, her panic faded and she took a deep breath. She'd never liked the Crag, but until today she'd not felt its full constrictive power.

David was doubtless fine. Merely tired from last night and careless about responding to commands. But she was outside now, and she'd make the most of it.

The most of her freedom.

She'd never felt quite like this before, but then, Con Somerford had not been inside Crag Wyvern before. Or not for eleven years.

She set off down the hill to the inland village of Church Wyvern. For a blessing, the sun was shining from an almost cloudless sky. It had been a dreadful summer, apparently because of the eruption of a volcano last year half a world away. Sweet summer days were scarce, and after last night they could have expected overcast and even rainy weather, but heaven had sent sunshine when she needed it so badly.

She prayed that the run had been successful. Then she could quickly find a new housekeeper and be out of Con's orbit before she did something to destroy him, or herself. It would break her heart to separate herself from him again, but she knew she must.

Destroy, she thought, glancing back at the gloomy house. So strong a word, and yet she felt that kind of power swirling in the house between them.

He was so dark, so unlike the Con she remembered, even though her sweet, magical Con was there, too. Trapped, perhaps? If he was trapped inside that dark shell, she didn't know how to free him. Even if it was all her fault, if she'd started the encrustation all those years ago in Irish Cove, she didn't know how to break him free now.

But she could avoid making things worse.

Going down the hill, the pretty village was spread before her, with cottages clustered around the church spire. She saw Diddy's mother hanging out the wash in her back garden, little children running around her. Grandchildren, probably, though Diddy's youngest brother was still an infant. One little girl was solemnly handing Mrs. Howlock the pegs, and Susan thought wistfully of such simple pleasures. A home, children, daily tasks that didn't require much thought or anxiety.

She knew it was nonsense, that worry lived in the cottages as well as in the manor and at the Crag, but most people didn't deliberately entangle themselves with madness and hanging crimes.

Could she get David to forget about all of this? They could move far from the coast and live ordinary lives. . . .

She shook her head. The blood of a wanton and a smuggling master mingled in them both. David had been reluctant to become Captain Drake, but he'd taken to it like a cat to mousing, and she knew he wouldn't give it up now.

Anyway, it was his duty, and he knew that. The people here needed smuggling, and needed an orderly leadership. He couldn't walk away from his inherited responsibility any more than Con could.

She could go anywhere, however.

But where?

She was completely unsuited to be a governess or a companion, and her birth made her unattractive for that or as a bride to a gentleman. She wasn't sure she had the temperament to make a good wife anyway, and of course, she wasn't a virgin.

Where could she go?

What could she do?

She had enjoyed being the earl's secretary, but such a position normally belonged to a man. And she didn't want to leave here, the one place on earth where she belonged.

Jack Croker was working in his garden, ready to plant his beans by the looks of the long stakes he was setting, as he had for thirty years or more. A tumble of very young piglets was all over a sow in Fumleigh's farmyard. Apple blossom carpeted the manor's orchard, promising autumn fruit.

There was no way to belong to a village like this without being born to it. Everyone else, no matter how pleasant, was an outsider. She belonged, but she was and would always be the daughter of Mel Clyst and Lady Belle, a couple who hadn't even bothered to put the gloss of marriage on the scandal of their union.

If she'd been willing, or able, to live like a young lady of the manor, she would have been accepted better. But no, she'd had to spend all the time she could outdoors, exploring, questioning, learning to swim and sail, so that soon people had begun to whisper that she was as wild as her mother and would come to the same end.

Which perhaps she had, though less happily.

She turned into the lane that circled around the village, noting the faint cart tracks in the soft earth. Last night's drizzle had softened the ground enough to leave the trace, but no more than a trace. The Dragon's Horde was skillful, and men always followed the cart with a roller, smoothing out the tracks a bit to make them look older, then superimposing footprints, even those of children. Everyone hereabouts was involved in the smuggling trade.

There were hoofprints too. The manor's horses would have been borrowed for the run, and returned around dawn. Farmers grumbled sometimes about tired beasts and men, but most accepted the payment in kegs and bales found among the straw.

She'd never been sure what Uncle Nathaniel and Aunt Miriam thought about smuggling. It was rarely mentioned at the manor, and only then as something that went on elsewhere. From being the earl's secretary and now helping David with the Horde's accounts, she knew they didn't invest.

Probably like most of the gentry along the coast, they were neutral, not noticing when their horses were borrowed, nor looking too closely at things hidden on their land, and not asking questions about kegs of spirits, packages of tea, or twists of lace that appeared—

"Mistress Kerslake!"

She turned with a start to see a horseman waving from a nearby rise. For a heart-jumping moment she thought it was Con. But of course not. Only one person used the old-fashioned term of address "mistress." Lieutenant Gifford, the riding officer.

He set his horse to a canter then jumped the low wall down the path a bit before trotting to join her.

She tried not to show her sudden burst of panic. He didn't suspect anything. He was new to the area and had not even realized yet that she and David were not Sir Nathaniel's children. But the ghostly cart tracks seemed suddenly deep and obvious beneath her feet.

He dismounted to stand beside her, such a pleasant young man with a slightly round face and soft brown curls, but also with a firmness to his mouth and chin that reminded her a bit of Con. Gifford, too, had fought at Waterloo. She liked him, and he was only trying to do his conscientious duty, and yet he was their enemy.

"A lovely day, is it not?" he said with an unshadowed smile.

She smiled back, and hoped it looked natural. "It is indeed, sir, and we deserve it after the dull ones we've had."

"That dashed volcano. And we're doing better here than on the continent and in America. You are walking to the manor house, Mistress Kerslake? May I walk beside you?"

"Of course." What else could she say?

The man was courting her, however, and it embarrassed her when it was so impossible. She cared nothing for him, and he would not wish to pursue it when he learned about her irregular birth. More than that, however, no riding officer could marry a smuggler's daughter without ruining his career.

She'd like to tell him, but could not point the way to David like that. Perhaps she could at least use this moment to find out about last night. "And how goes your business, Lieutenant Gifford?"

He pulled a face. "Now, Mistress Kerslake, don't play me for a fool. Everyone in the area knows when there's been a run, and there was one last night. Two, damn them. One I was allowed to stop, whilst another went on elsewhere along the coast."

Such a pity he was intelligent.

"I've been stuck up at Crag Wyvern all morning, Lieutenant, so I haven't heard any gossip. The new earl has arrived."

"Has he?" His eyes sharpened. "A military man, I understand."

She knew where his thoughts were turning. "I believe he was a captain in the infantry, yes."

"Then perhaps I'll have an ally in these parts."

She felt some sympathy for him, but had to say, "The earl doesn't intend to live here, Lieutenant. He has a family home in Sussex and prefers it."

He glanced up at the dark house. "Hardly surprising, but a shame. The Earl of Wyvern can make or break smuggling in this area. I heard talk that the old earl helped bring down Melchisedeck Clyst."

"What?" She collected herself, hoping her shock hadn't shown. "You must be mistaken. The earl was known to support the smugglers."

"A falling-out, perhaps. There's no honor among thieves, you know, ma'am."

Susan's head was spinning with the idea that the mad earl had not just failed to intervene, but had actively caused her father's arrest and the loss of a whole cargo.

Why on earth would he do that?

"I've heard rumors that last night's cargo came in near here," Gifford was saying, "but I can find no trace of it. I don't suppose you heard anything, Mistress Kerslake."

It sounded like a statement of fact rather than a question. He knew that no one around here would give him information.

"I'm afraid not, Lieutenant."

"There was a battle up near Pott's Hill with a couple of men left badly wounded. Doubtless a quarrel over the spoils, so the cargo must have been brought in near here."

Her heart skipped a beat. "A battle?" she said, thankful that shock would seem natural. "Whatever do you mean, sir?"

"One gang trying to steal from another. Happens all the time, my dear lady. These smugglers are not the noble adventurers some would have you think."

Lord above, did he really think anyone born and raised here had any illusions about smugglers? But what had happened? Had David truly been hurt? Had the cargo been stolen?

She tried her best to put on a look of innocence—or stupidity, maybe. "But then, can you not arrest the injured men?"

"Not without evidence, Mistress Kerslake," he said kindly. "They claim to have fought over a woman and will not be moved from that. Unfortunately, before we arrived, any contraband had disappeared."

She waited for a moment. If David was one of the injured he must surely mention it. When he didn't, she felt she could breathe again.

"Surely a fight over a woman is not so very unusual, Lieutenant."

"On the night of a run, Mistress Kerslake, even women are of lesser interest." But then he smiled. "That is, to lowborn wretches. To a gentleman, a lady is always first in his mind."

She could say something scathing about duty, but she managed not to. Thank heavens the gate into the manor orchard was only yards away.

"I see all too little of you, Mistress Kerslake. There was an assembly at Honiton last week that was blighted by your absence."

Susan managed not to roll her eyes. "I am employed, Lieutenant, and not free to attend such events."

"Come, come. Before the earl's arrival your duties cannot have been burdensome."

"On the contrary, sir. The late earl's eccentricities left the place in disorder. I have been attempting to set everything to rights."

"Indeed?" For some reason he seemed to disbelieve her. "But I'm sure you must be enjoying entertainment in some quarter or other. If you were to let me know, dear lady, I would make such places my special haunts."

This struck her as a very peculiar thing to say, as if he expected her to be spending her nights in taverns, but she had no time or patience for this now.

"I live a very quiet, boring life, Lieutenant," she said, opening the gate.

"You are funning! Very well, you pose a mystery for me to solve. For the moment, I am on my way to Dragon's Cove to solve another mystery, though I doubt there'll be anything to learn among that secretive lot."

He mounted his horse. "With that scoundrel Melchisedeck Clyst gone, they're doubtless in too much disorder to attempt a large run here, but I'll take a close look at the new tavernkeeper, and keep my eyes open for cart tracks."

Susan did not look down at the tracks beneath his horse's hooves, but she was hard-pressed not to laugh. The new tavernkeeper at the George and Dragon was Mel's cousin Rachel Clyst, a jolly middle-aged woman as wide as she was tall. She was certainly in league with the Horde, but a less likely Captain Drake was hard to imagine. She wheezed going up a few steps, never mind up a cliff.

Her humor faded as she watched Gifford ride away, however. He wouldn't find anything at Dragon's Cove, but he was clever enough and dutiful enough to find things eventually.

She went into the orchard worrying about that battle. When it came to smuggling, *battle* was an accurate word. Hundreds of men could be involved, some of them carrying guns. Deaths could occur.

What had happened?

Was David lying bleeding somewhere?

She cut through the kitchen garden past a sleepy-looking lad who was pretending to hoe between some cabbages. Nearly everyone along the coast would have gone short of sleep last night.

The lad called a cheery greeting, however, and her flurry of anxiety calmed. No one would be smiling if Captain Drake had been wounded or captured. And everyone would know.

She walked more calmly through a honeysuckle arch onto the lawn that ran up to the lovely house. It was as neatly rectangular as the Crag, but the dull stone was whitewashed. Set amid wholesome land and pleasant gardens and filled with warmhearted people, the manor was another world.

She paused to study it, thinking that she must be mad not to feel completely at home here. Her family here were good people and she loved them dearly, but she didn't think she'd ever truly felt she belonged, even as a young child. Once she'd learned the truth about her parents, she'd understood why. . . .

"Susan!"

She started, and saw her cousin Amelia running across the lawn waving. Amelia was twenty, plump, and excited, and typically her wide villager hat was sliding off her brown curls to hang down her back. "I hear the earl's turned up!" she gasped as soon as she was close.

"Yes, late last night."

"What's he like? Is he handsome?"

"He has been here before."

"Once, and I was nine years old! I do remember the father and two sons in the Wyvern pew at church, but it's a faint memory. This one was darker and steadier, wasn't he? I thought he was the older brother."

"Yes," Susan said, walking on toward the house, "so did I."

"I knew Fred Somerford, of course," Amelia chattered, falling into step. "Since Mother was always encouraging him to treat the manor as his home." She giggled. "Do you remember Father muttering about mad Somerfords, and Mother arguing that he was a perfectly sane young man? She had such hopes that one of us would snare him. I wonder what she'll do about the new one."

Susan could have groaned at the thought of Aunt Miriam matchmaking again.

"Shame he drowned," Amelia said. "Fred, I mean. But it's not really surprising. I always thought of him as Fred the Unready, like Ethelred the Unready."

Susan laughed, then stopped it with a hand. "Oh, dear. That isn't very kind."

"I suppose not. But is the new one more ready?"

Ready for what? Susan suddenly remembered Diddy describing him as "ready to go," and blushed at the vivid image that sprung to mind.

"I couldn't say," she said.

"I remember him as dark. Is he still dark? I like dark men."

"He could hardly be paler, unless he'd turned gray."

"Well, some people do, don't they? With stress, or fright. And Michael Paulet came back from the Peninsula with his light brown hair turned blond by the sun."

"I don't think dark brown hair does that." She wished Amelia would stop asking all these questions.

"There was that miniature Fred Somerford brought," Amelia said as they stepped onto the stone path that led to the back door. "I quite lost my heart to that dashing captain. Is he as handsome now?"

Susan fought not to react. Amelia and Con? She couldn't bear it.

"Are you going to toss your cap at him?" she asked as lightly as she could.

Amelia grinned, showing deep dimples. "It can't hurt to try."

"Even if he's not to your taste?"

"I won't know without trying, will I? And an earl to my taste would be very nice indeed."

"Even if you had to live at Crag Wyvern?"

Amelia glanced back at the house with a grimace. "A hit, I confess. But it could be changed. Windows on the outside, for a start. And white paint. Or stucco."

It astonished Susan that her cousin could be so lighthearted about all this, as if life presented only sunny options. This was the Kerslake way, though, and why she always felt like an outsider. An envious outsider.

"The earl has a very pretty secretary," she offered, knowing she was trying to deflect Amelia's interest. "A Mr. Racecombe de Vere, who has all the air of a fine gentleman despite his lowly status. In fact, I doubt his status is particularly low. You should look him up in one of Uncle Nathaniel's books."

Amelia's dimples deepened. "Two handsome strangers! It's about time something interesting happened here."

Susan glanced at her cousin. Surely Amelia knew.

"What's the matter?" her cousin asked. "Is it the new earl? Is he truly mad?"

"No. No, of course not. But he'll bring changes, and it's hard to tell what they might be."

"It has to be better than what's gone on before. He's young, he's eligible, he's handsome with a handsome friend. Will he be giving balls?"

Susan laughed. "At Crag Wyvern?"

"Why not? From what you say, it would be wonderful for a masquerade."

It was as if Amelia had turned everything to show a new aspect. "You're right, it would. And it might chase away some of the shadows. For the good of the area the place needs to become somewhere normal people might live and entertain their neighbors."

Not one of the crazy earl's crazy friends. Solid, normal tenants. She wondered how much it would cost to cover the walls with fashionable stucco. Perhaps those faux stone corridors could be painted cheerful colors, too. And windows cut . . .

Astonishing possibilities.

Chapter Ten

They entered the manor, finding Aunt Miriam working in the steamy kitchen alongside the cook and maid baking bread. Her round face tended to red anyway, and in the steam was puce, but her eyes lit. "Susan, love, how nice to see you. Give me a moment, and we'll have a cup of tea."

"I need to speak to David first, aunt."

The warmth of her aunt's smile was easing her, and stirring guilt. She knew Aunt Miriam thought of her as a daughter, and loved her like a daughter, and yet she could never be quite the daughter her aunt wanted her to be.

Conventional, happy, and married by now.

"He's probably still in the breakfast parlor," Aunt Miriam said, kneading away at a mound of dough. "I don't know what hour he returned home last night, or what he'd been up to. Young men will burn the candles, won't they?" she added with a wink.

Susan resisted an urge to state unwelcome truths, and went toward the front of the house hoping for a word in private with her brother. Aunt Miriam snared Amelia to help in the kitchen, which got rid of one problem, but when she entered the sun-filled breakfast room she found their cousin Henry keeping David company.

All the true Kerslakes tended to a comfortable roundness, and at twenty-eight Henry was developing a prosperous stomach. He had his hands clasped over it now as he watched David finish his breakfast and lectured him about the importance of the Corn Laws.

At the sight of Susan, however, he stood, beaming. "Now this is a treat!" He came around the table to take her hands and kiss her cheek. "We don't see enough of you, cousin."

Truly, everyone here was impossibly kind. She always felt like a thistle in a flower bed. David, despite being so like her, bloomed carelessly along with the rest.

She sat at the table, looking at the evidence of his hearty breakfast. "Anyone would think you actually worked for your living, love."

She saw evidence of tiredness, but none of fighting. He seemed his usual lighthearted self, thank the Lord. Everything was all right.

He flashed her a look from subtle blue-gray eyes. Apart from the eyes they'd been very alike when young, with their father's square chin and their mother's golden brown hair. By now, however, he'd grown heavier bones and six more inches of height, and a great deal of muscle.

She had the disconcerting concern of how it would go if he and Con got into a fight. David had inches and breadth on Con, but something warned her that Con might win.

"Aren't you supposed to be working, too?" he asked, forking the last piece of fried bread into his mouth.

"I am. I'm playing sheepdog. A message was sent commanding your presence up at the Crag."

"And you've come to nip me up there? Is the earl in such a hurry?"

"It's almost noon. And I don't know about hurry, but he's thorough. Or rather, his very efficient secretary is. He's going through everything like a miser hunting for a penny."

It was a warning. There shouldn't be anything in the Wyvern papers about smuggling operations, but it was possible.

"Right and proper thing to do," Henry said. "Take over the reins. See what's what. It's about time there was some order and decorum up there. He'll want your records and advice, Davy, and if you're ordered up there, up there you should be!"

David poured himself another cup of coffee and leaned back, mischief in his eyes. "If he wanted instant service, he should have sent warning of his arrival."

As he sipped from his cup, those smiling eyes slid to Susan carrying a question. *Trouble?*

She smiled a little to show that there wasn't. Which was true. Con wasn't throwing a fit over the smuggling run, which was all David would care about. She needed to talk to him, though, and Henry was stuck in his chair like a burr in a long-haired dog.

So she gossiped about the earl, and entered into aimless speculation with

Henry on the effect on the neighborhood. Again, she passed on Con's message that he wasn't going to make this his principal residence.

"Shame, that," Henry said. "Perhaps he'll change his mind if we show him what a pleasant little community we have here."

David's brows and lips twitched in a humorous wince. There was nothing he wanted less than an earl in residence at the Crag. Even a friendly one had to be constantly thought of and pacified. "You'll have to see if Amelia can steal his heart, Henry. That would tie him here."

Henry reddened. "Marry her off to a mad Earl of Wyvern? I'll know the man a great deal better before I'll countenance that, and I'll go odds Father will feel the same way."

"Then if he's a handsome devil, perhaps we shouldn't encourage him to hang around."

Henry looked at Susan. "Is he a handsome devil?"

It wasn't hard to play her part. "I'm afraid so."

He pushed to his feet. "I need to talk to Father about this."

He paused however, to lecture David. "Obey orders and get up there, Davy. It's a nice little post you have, and if the earl isn't going to be in residence, an easy job with local influence. You don't want to lose it."

"How true." David was still lounging, however.

"You may think now that you do well enough as you are," Henry said with exasperation, "but one day you'll want to marry and set up your own establishment. That takes money. You need your employment."

"You're completely right, Henry," David said, eyes twinkling. "I'll just finish my coffee and be off."

Henry sighed and left to consult with Sir Nathaniel. Susan looked at her brother and suppressed laughter. She wouldn't hurt Henry by letting him hear them laughing at him, but David's prospects in life no longer depended on his post, and anyone aware of what was going on around them would know it.

The tendency to laughter faded. She'd rather David was simply an earl's estate manager.

"Everything went smoothly last night?" she asked quietly. As usual, there was no certain privacy here.

"Not exactly," he said, abruptly sober. "I'll tell you later."

Her stomach clenched. She chose her words carefully. "I met Lieutenant Gifford on the way here. He was on his way to Dragon's Cove looking for evidence of a run coming in there last night."

David drank the rest of his coffee. "I doubt he'll find anything."

So that wasn't the problem. She began to imagine different kinds of disasters.

"So what's the new earl really like?" he asked.

"Not mad." He needed a warning about the sort of man Con was now. "Strong," she said. "He was a captain in the army. He fought at Waterloo." Reluctantly, the word escaped. "Unforgiving."

Her brother became thoughtful. "You knew him when he was here, didn't you? In 1805."

She hastily picked up a piece of bread and nibbled it. What had David heard? The last thing she needed was antagonism between David and Con over her, but she equally didn't want to confess to David how badly she'd behaved.

"Yes, I knew him," she said. "We're the same age."

"Tom Bridgelow said something last night. About Mel thinking you two were getting too close, and warning him off."

"There was nothing to it," she said, trying to make it sound absurd. "We met here and there and were friends of a sort. He was only here two weeks."

"According to Tom once Mel had said his piece you and he weren't seen together again."

"Not surprising. No one would want Mel angry with them. A rare example of paternal concern."

"He kept an eye on us." Before Susan could ask what he meant, he added, "Shame there was nothing between you. It would be useful now if you were on close terms."

"It was eleven years ago, David, and we've not so much as exchanged a letter!"

He shrugged. "Just a thought." He pushed back from the table and stood, sober and thoughtful enough to please Henry, if he'd been here to see it. Susan suddenly saw a similarity between David and Con, an aura that came of being a leader, of carrying the lives and welfare of many on his shoulders.

It made her shiver. That way lay glory, but that way lay death, too. Then she saw him wince and favor a leg as he moved from the table.

"What's the matter?" she whispered.

"Got into a fight," he said in a normal voice. "Lots of bruises, but no real damage, so don't fuss. I'll get my record books and we can be off up to prostrate ourselves before the demanding earl." He stopped to yawn, wincing again as he stretched. "I hope his questions aren't too deep or difficult, though. I've only had four hours' sleep."

Susan waited for him in the kitchen, smothering her anxiety with a hot bun running with butter, and chatting with her aunt about Con.

"A lovely lad," Aunt Miriam said. "Full of energy but kind with it. George," she added, pouring cups of tea all around. "But he preferred to be called something else. Ah yes, Con."

She passed Susan a cup and saucer, a twinkle in her eye. "I suspect he's grown into a handsome man."

Susan hadn't asked for the tea, but she took a fortifying gulp. "Yes, he has." As a defense against that hopeful twinkle, she added, "He's betrothed to a nobleman's daughter."

Aunt Miriam pulled a face. "Ah, well. I remembered that you met him here and there when you were studying your insects. A shared interest is always nice."

"I doubt he's much interested in entomology anymore." Susan finished her tea, astonished by the complete lack of suspicion in her aunt's manner. Had she never thought it dubious that her almost-daughter was out with a young man, no chaperon in sight?

Sometimes it seemed to her that her manor family lived inside a soap bubble, disconnected from the reality of the Crag, Dragon's Cove, smuggling, or anything less than idyllic.

It must be lovely.

But she knew the notion of cozy complacency was an illusion. Four children had died in this house, three of Aunt Miriam's and one of Lady Belle's, and many members of previous generations. Aunt Miriam knew all about the less pleasant aspects of life.

Susan had been ten when her second brother had arrived at the manor. She'd been too young to question David's birth, but little Sammy had required explanation.

The truth had driven her to help take care of the frail baby, but had also stirred dreams and longings. She only vaguely knew Mel Clyst and Lady Belle, since none of the children of the manor were encouraged to go over to the village of Dragon's Cove.

But once she knew that Mel and Belle were her parents, her real parents, they fascinated her.

She'd fought to keep Sammy alive for his own sake, but perhaps as well she'd hoped to prove worthy of her parents' attention. She'd been heartbroken when the baby gave up the fight at six weeks, and guilt-struck as well.

She vividly remembered Lady Belle and Mel Clyst coming to the manor to look at the waxen body. Though she'd hovered nearby, Lady Belle—lush, queenly, and richly dressed—had paid her no attention. She'd looked at the baby as if he were an exhibit in a glass case.

Melchisedeck Clyst, who despite being a tavernkeeper had been dressed as well as Uncle Nathaniel, had seemed to feel something. He'd touched the swaddled child, and glanced at Susan in a way that might have been an acknowledgment. But no more than that.

They'd gone with the coffin to the church for the service, and then to the graveyard to see the small box settled in the Kerslake plot. To Susan, weeping, it had seemed that Lady Belle was profoundly bored.

From that day on she had put aside all hope that her true parents would clasp her to their bosoms. She didn't know why she had wanted it when she'd had the love of Aunt Miriam, Sir Nathaniel, her brother, and her cousins.

But from that day on she'd also longed to belong.

Sometimes she wondered if she'd simply needed to be in a position where Lady Belle would be forced to acknowledge her existence.

When David came into the kitchen and snitched a bun despite just having finished that huge breakfast, Susan rose and impulsively gave her aunt a hug. Her aunt hugged her back, but with a question in her eyes. Susan could see that she was touched, though, and was glad she'd done it. Had she ever shown her aunt and uncle how grateful she was for what they'd done for them?

"Is everything all right, Susan?" Aunt Miriam asked, holding on to her hand for a moment.

Susan felt a brief urge to burst into wild laughter and tears, but she said, "Yes, of course. Though the earl being at the Crag is going to bring changes. I don't think I want to stay there as housekeeper much longer."

"It always was a temporary thing, love, and it'll be grand to have you back here again."

Susan smiled, but she knew she couldn't do it. She'd taken a fork in the road, and she couldn't return to this coziness any more than she could explore the cliffs with Con again. She didn't say that, though, merely squeezed her aunt's hand and went on her way.

As soon as they were out of earshot of the house, David asked, "Is the earl going to make trouble?"

Trouble? What was trouble? Perhaps she should tell David the whole story so he would be warned. She was very afraid that if Con discovered that her brother was the new Captain Drake he'd turn against the Dragon's Horde for that reason.

"I don't think he'll fight the smuggling," she said, hoping it was true. "As things are at the moment. I suspect he won't invest, though, and he might not cooperate about the cellars and the horses."

"Inconvenient. Are you sure you can't persuade him to play a part? Smuggling has to continue, or I wouldn't be doing it."

"Truly?" She looked at him.

"Truly. I confess, I enjoy it in part, but I'm all too aware of the dangers. If you can, persuade the earl to be on our side."

Susan suppressed a shudder at the thought. "I think Gifford is more likely to persuade him into complete opposition. They're both army men."

"But isn't Gifford sweet on you?"

"I am not encouraging the poor man, not even for you."

"Ah, well," he said as they passed through the arch into the orchard, "Mel always said we had to play the hand we were dealt."

"Mel," Susan said, remembering. "David, Gifford suggested that the old earl helped bring about Mel's arrest."

He stopped to stare at her. "What? That's nonsense. They had an agreement."

"Might they have had a falling-out?"

"I'd have thought you'd know that better than I."

"I didn't see anything. . . ." They walked on. "But he might have hidden it from me. He wasn't stupid, and he'd know that I'd probably warn Mel of danger."

"Only probably?"

"We've no reason to feel kindly toward our parents."

He glanced at her. "I used to go down to the George and Dragon sometimes. I suppose it was easier, us being men. . . ."

For some reason it hurt. "Were you friends, then, you and Mel?"

"I don't know what you'd call it. Not father and son. Not friends either. I'm no happier than you about the way they ignored us, but I came to like him. He told me I'd have to take over if anything happened without giving him time to prepare. That's why he talked to me about the business."

She realized she was hurt by this connection, and by the fact that David had kept it secret.

But then, she had secrets, and now she didn't feel so responsible for pushing David into being Captain Drake.

"And Lady Belle?" she asked. "Were you friends with her too?" She heard the sour note in her voice but couldn't seem to help it.

His look said he heard it too. "She liked the company of handsome young men."

"Handsome, are you?"

"Stupid to say no. Susan, look, some women just aren't made to be mothers. I think Mel would have liked to be closer to us, but he wouldn't cross her for it. And he liked his children being raised at the manor as gentry. He didn't want us living in Dragon's Cove, part of his class. He kept an eye on us, and everyone around here knew better than to harm us."

Kept an eye. As Mel had by talking to Con. And she'd always felt safe roaming the coast. Perhaps her aunt and uncle had known she was under Captain Drake's protection, and that was why they'd given her so much freedom.

Her world had twisted again.

"How do you think he'll do in Australia?" she asked.

"Mel? If he's survived the voyage he'll probably thrive. I gather that after a while they can set up businesses."

"And Lady Belle?" But then she burst out, "I don't even *like* her, so why am I concerned?"

He laughed. "Blood will out? She'll be queen of Australia."

"On gold that doesn't belong to her."

"In a way, it did. Mel kept a handsome sum to back up the Horde in difficult times. He even paid people for sitting idle so they wouldn't get up to trouble. But it was his money. His profits."

Susan was bouncing from one shock to another. "The earl's gold is the Horde's though, isn't it? The earl didn't keep his part of the bargain."

"Assuredly."

So it was right to take it. She still didn't want to take it from Con. Or, to be more precise, she didn't want Con to know if she took it.

She shifted to something firmer. "What happened last night. How bad is it?"

"Half bad. We have half the cargo secure, though we won't be able to move it for a while with Gifford and his men poking around everywhere. The fight last night has them all over this part of the coast, dammit."

"What happened? How badly are you hurt?"

"Don't fuss. A line of tubmen was attacked. I think it was the Blackstock Gang, but I'm not sure. I arrived before they'd snatched all the tubs, but they got some and left a lot of men bruised and battered."

"Gifford said he knows of some of the injured. Were they ours?"

"Yes. I let him find them, since there was nothing to prove the cause of the fight—we had the cargo away by then. They'd get better doctoring that way. The others carried away their wounded."

She was afraid he might go after the Blackstocks to teach them a lesson, afraid he'd get more badly hurt, but she knew she had no say in such things. He wasn't her little brother anymore.

But there was an area where she could speak. "How much did we lose? What's our situation now?"

"About half the profit, but I've kept that quiet. I'll forgo my share, and if you do the same—"

"Of course." It would leave her with no money to finance an escape, however. Unless they found the money hidden at the Crag. "But the Horde will have no reserves."

They were out in the lane, and they stepped aside to let a man with a barrow pass, exchanging pleasant greetings. The man winked as he went past. "Grand night last night, weren't it, Cap'n?"

Susan took a deep breath. "Clearly he doesn't know of the loss. But I wish everyone didn't know about you."

"Don't be silly. How could it work if everyone didn't know? No one's going to say anything."

"It has to get out. Perch knew who Captain Drake was, but he accepted money not to know. Gifford won't do that." She said what she knew she shouldn't say. "David, I don't want him hurt."

He stopped to look at her. "Gifford? Perhaps you do fancy him."

She felt the color rush into her cheeks. "Of course not. But he's a good man simply trying to do his duty. It would be evil to kill him."

"You do think I've turned into a monster, don't you?"

"No. But when it comes to you or him. To your men or him . . ."

"I won't kill him or order him killed. It's not the Dragon's Horde way, Susan. You know that."

"But I don't want you hanged or transported, either!"

"Make up your mind, love." But then he linked his arm with hers and urged her onward. "Don't borrow trouble. But I have to say, it would be useful if you could get your hands on that gold soon. Once we move last night's cargo, we'll be able to pay the investors. But as you say, no reserves. We'll have to do another run. Soon."

"How soon?"

His glance said, *Too soon.* "Captain Vavasour has a tea cargo he couldn't get in farther up the coast."

"You can't bring it in here! And the moon's fuller every night."

"We're having such dull weather, the chances are it'll be overcast—"

"Chances!"

"Susan, smuggling's a chancy business."

"That's why I want no part of it."

"No, that's why you don't want me part of it. Stop it."

The firm command took her breath away. But he was right. Her panic was more likely to get him killed than help him.

"Of course we'd not bring it in here, but tea's a lighter cargo, so we can use somewhere tricky. Irish Cove, perhaps. That's not been used for years."

Her breath caught, even as she knew it shouldn't matter. It was just another bay along the coast. But in some twisted way it seemed another betrayal of Con to use that special place for a smuggling run when he was nearby.

"It's a hard climb up with the goods," she said.

"We could drop lines and hoist the tea up. It's equally hard for the Preventives to get at. Or get Vavasour to sink the bales with markers. Then pick them up by boat . . ."

He was lost in his plans, but Susan knew Gifford would be hawkeyed here. "David, if I find the gold, would you be able to wait?"

He looked at her. "It's a hard opportunity to pass up, a nice cargo just waiting. . . . But all right, if you find the money we can lie low for a month or even two. Isn't it going to be hard now the earl's in residence?"

"I don't think it makes much difference unless it's hidden under his bed, and it isn't. I've checked all such places already under cover of the inventory and spring cleaning. I confess, I expected finding it to be much easier. He had to be able to get at it, to add to it and take from it."

"Perhaps he spent it all on potions and dried diddlers," he said with a grin. She'd shown him the earl's bedchamber, and he'd nearly died laughing.

She swatted at him. "Remember, I was his secretary. I know what he spent. From what he received from the Horde, even just in recent years, there should be over two thousand in gold coin somewhere. That's not exactly easy to hide, even in small caches around the place, and if there were small caches, I should have found at least one."

"Perhaps a secret room, or secret chamber in the walls," David said.

"I know, but that could be anywhere. At least there's very little paneling."

"I need to let Vavasour know in two days."

"Two days! Very well, I'll buckle down to a ruthless search—for cunning hidey-holes in particular. Which reminds me. Con's brought a secretary with him."

"Con?" he said with interest.

She prayed not to blush. "I knew him as Con once. It slips out. Listen, his secretary—"

"Of course he has a secretary."

They were beginning the steeper climb up to the Crag, and perhaps that was why her heart beat harder. "Well, he's set him to going through all the records and papers. What if there's something there about smuggling?"

"Don't you know?"

"The earl was as crazy about his administration as about everything else. He scribbled notes to himself and pushed them in odd places. He did the same with letters he received."

"I very much doubt that Mel wrote him letters."

"I know, but I feel as if de Vere is bound to uncover something."

He smiled at her. "We'll play that hand when we're dealt it. It's not like you to be in such a fidget."

Again she longed to tell him the truth, but she'd hide her past—all her past, if she could.

"It is time for you to give up your job there, though," he said. "It's not suitable."

"If I can't tell you how to manage your affairs, you can't tell me." She stopped to catch her breath, something she couldn't remember having to do before. "You work for him," she added.

"I'm his estate manager," he said, not breathless at all. "That's suitable employment for a gentleman. Housekeeper is different. Are you all right?"

No, no, I'm not. I'm afraid, and confused, and both longing to see Con again and terrified of him.

"I'm just tired. I didn't get much sleep last night either."

He put his arm around her and hoisted her up the last bit of hill before the flatter land around Crag Wyvern. "I won't try to order you around, Susan, but I'd like you out of that place and not worrying about me."

She rolled her eyes. "I do intend to find a replacement, but I have to have a last try for that gold first. As for not worrying about you—how?"

"Perhaps you need to get away from here."

She stopped in the chilly shadow of the great house. "Away? You want me to go away?"

"I don't want you to, but I don't want you constantly worrying, either. I can't promise to live safely for you. You know that."

"Yes, I know. I'm sorry. I'm just out of sorts today."

"Ah, that time of the month, is it?"

It wasn't, but she smiled and said, "You know too much about women."

He laughed and they carried on toward the gargoyle-crowned arch that led into the house of the demented earls of Wyvern.

Chapter Eleven

Con had fled Crag Wyvern. His official excuse was to inspect his estate and tenants, but he'd taken young Jonny White and fled to the normal world, which was so easily forgotten inside the Crag's fortress walls.

After an hour or so he was soothed by the normality and good health of this part of Devon. He noted the strange quietness at first, and the absence of people other than the old and young. As the day advanced more people inhabited the scenery, all pleasant enough, and eager to talk to the new earl. All smugglers the night before.

He accepted the hospitality of one cottage to share a hearty midday meal, chatting about farming matters as if that were what put the food on the table.

He sensed all around him the unspoken question: What was his attitude to smuggling? He gave his answer as best he could without talking about it—he didn't intend to change anything.

It was true. Any attempt at sudden change would be disastrous. However, it was his duty to try to put a stop to the Freetrade eventually, and to prepare the people here for the change that would inevitably come.

He mentioned the naval cutters now patrolling the coast, and the number of army officers and men looking for peacetime employment. When an elderly woman blessed the fact that the war was over, he commented that they were also blessed that the government should need less money and could reduce the iniquitous duties on things like tea.

She agreed wholeheartedly, showing that none of the simple folk understood the implications—low taxes would reduce prices, and that would take away the profit in smuggling. No one was going to take on the risk and the work for a ten-percent return.

The burden of it pressed on him. This place needed a lifetime's care, and he didn't want to give it his life. He could leave the simpler part of it to his estate manager, but he needed to either give Kerslake more powers or hire a steward. That could wait until he had the measure of Susan's brother. He vaguely remembered a rapscallion with a toothy grin.

Zeus! He couldn't leave everything here in the hands of her and her brother!

The property seemed to be in good heart, at least, with crops growing and animals healthy. The sorry summer had not had too serious an effect in these parts. The cottages and farms were in good repair, and the people looked well fed. There was even a school in Church Wyvern run by the curate's wife with assistance from Miss Amelia Kerslake. He was invited to admire the large room furnished with benches, slates, a globe, and a good selection of books.

All paid for, he was sure, from smuggling, but there was much to be said for prosperity, no matter where the money came from.

He managed a word with the curate, who expressed himself delighted to help sort through the earl's private collection of books. The hearty young man confessed to great curiosity about them.

"Have an interest in the dark arts, do you, Mr. Rufflestowe?"

"Know thine enemy, my lord," said the curate, but a twinkle in his eye admitted to simple human curiosity.

Since he seemed an admirably down-to-earth man, Con asked, "What's the correct procedure for a skull, Rufflestowe?"

"Procedure, my lord?"

"There are two human skulls in the earl's rooms, and they look to me as if they were disinterred in the not-too-distant past. Have there been any disturbed graves?"

"Good heavens. Not as far as I know, my lord. But there are some ancient burial sites around here. Most interesting . . ." He caught himself up. "A little interest of mine, my lord. Perhaps it would be best to leave the matter of the skulls until I can inspect them. Tomorrow, perhaps?"

Another enthusiastic worker, thought Con. "By all means, sir."

He found Jonny sitting at a desk in the schoolroom, working his way carefully through the words on a hornbook. The lad had been a London orphan before taking the king's shilling just before Waterloo. He'd doubtless had little education. Con made a mental note to arrange reading lessons for him, but dragged him off on the rest of the circuit of the estate.

As the Church Wyvern clock struck four, he turned his horse back toward

Crag Wyvern, as reluctant to return to the house as he had been to enter it the day before. The feeling reminded him of Waterloo. He hadn't wanted to go there either, but duty had left him no choice. Then, however, he'd known he was riding into hell. Now, he only felt like it.

He left the horses and Jonny at the stables in the village and walked up to the house. At the great arch into Crag Wyvern, he hesitated, tempted to linger outside.

He could walk across the headland. . . .

With a bitter laugh, he realized that he was dreaming of encountering a friend there, of exploring rock pools and caves, of lying in the sun talking, talking, talking. . . .

He squared his shoulders and walked through the gargoyle-crested arch into the shadows of Crag Wyvern.

He crossed the echoing great hall, heading toward the office, aware of being on the alert for Susan, both warily and eagerly. She didn't appear, but she might still be with Race.

When he opened the door to the office, however, he found someone else in the room with Race—a young man rising from an extra chair at the desk.

It could only be Susan's brother. The resemblance was remarkable, though no one would ever mistake one for the other. She might look like a Renaissance angel, but her brother, despite sensible country clothes, was all Renaissance warrior.

"Mr. Kerslake," Con said.

The man bowed. "My lord."

He was tall and strong, with an aura the officer in Con recognized. Things fell into place. This was Captain Drake. Of course he was. He was Mel Clyst's son. It was hard not to grin. Susan was certainly not the mistress of the new local leader. On the other hand, he thought, sobering, she was certainly neck-deep in smuggling.

"So," he asked Race, "how has the estate done in recent times?"

"Very well, my lord. Of course, it's suffering as everywhere with the end of the war and the fall in prices. . . ."

Con picked up a chair from by the wall and sat at the desk so the others could sit as they went through an efficient review.

Kerslake might be carrying two jobs, but he seemed to be doing this one well. If Race hadn't found any problems in the estate records, there weren't any to be found. Con asked a few questions and received sensible answers.

When Kerslake had to look up some figures he seemed to know exactly where to find them.

After a while, Con held up his hand. "Enough. Everything seems to be in order, and de Vere will filter this all down to simplicity for me. Will you stay to dinner, Kerslake?"

There was a hesitation. "With pleasure, my lord. But you do know that my sister is your housekeeper?"

"Does that make a difference?"

"Some might think it would create awkwardness."

Con realized that the young man disapproved of Susan's being here, and was sending a subtle warning. It reminded him sharply of Mel Clyst's all those years ago.

That warning in the past had sparked trouble. What would this one ignite?

A touch of mischief.

"Then I invite her to dine with us, Kerslake," Con said. "She is hardly the common run of housekeeper, and she assures me that her duties don't include actually cooking." He was sure that Susan wouldn't like this move. And of course, it meant she couldn't hide from him, if that was what she planned. "Why don't you carry the message to her?"

Kerslake rose, but his eyes were steady. "Is this an invitation, my lord, or a command?"

"I'm an army man, Kerslake. If I give a command, you will be in no doubt about it."

When David Kerslake left, Con turned to Race and raised a brow.

"Honest, competent, thorough, and severely underemployed," Race said. "I'm not sure why he's still at the job."

Con sighed. "Smuggling, Race. Smuggling."

"It's that attractive to a man of such ability?"

"The best of games, and he's captain of the team. I'm sure of it. He is the old one's son, after all."

"What?"

Con realized that Race didn't know. "Both Susan Kerslake and her brother are the bastard children of Melchisedeck Clyst, tavernkeeper and the former Captain Drake—"

"Captain Drake?"

"The name taken by the smuggling master in these parts."

Race's brows rose. "But the manor?"

"Their mother is Miss Isabelle Kerslake of Kerslake Manor."

"The deuce you say. And they never even married?"

"It seemed unimportant to them. Their children were raised by the mother's relatives at the manor. Having the Kerslake name is useful, since everyone will look for Captain Drake to be a Clyst. I gather the Preventive officer is new. He might not even realize yet that David Kerslake is not a true son of the manor."

"What happened to the old Preventive officer?"

Con smiled. "You're beginning to get the feel of the place. Fell down a cliff one night. I gather the general belief is that he was pushed, and by one of the rival smuggling gangs hoping to make life difficult for the new Captain Drake."

"I'd think it would make life difficult for all of them, unless the old one was sharp and the new one blunt."

"Ah, but the key word there, Race, is *think*. Many smugglers don't often think. And no, Lieutenant Perch was middle-aged and obliging. Lieutenant Gifford is apparently young, clever, and ambitious."

"Idiots." He glanced at Con. "Kerslake doesn't like his sister being your housekeeper, does he? Strange that he permitted it."

"Do you think she is a woman who is allowed or not allowed?"

"I see you've found more amusement for me." Race tidied his papers and closed the ledgers. "First the anticipation. Will the lady attend the dinner or not? If she does, will she still hide in gray? Then the thrill of watching the by-play between you all . . . Does the formidable brother know about the past?"

"What past?" Con asked, but it was useless.

Race grinned. "Does the lady still desire? Does the lord? Will they speak their hearts? Will they be forbidden? It'll be as good as Drury Lane!"

Con swiped at him, and Race ducked, laughing like an imp from hell.

Susan was checking the preparations for the evening meal and preparing wines. As the Crag lacked a butler, the old earl's valet had done that job, and as she'd often dined with her employer she'd learned something about his cellars. She hoped the wines she'd chosen would be suitable. They were all French. All smuggled, of course, but she didn't think Con would raise the subject.

When arms snared her from behind, she almost dropped a bottle. For a startled, insane moment, she thought, *Con!* But then she turned to glare at her brother. "What do you think you're doing?"

"Scaring you."

She put down the bottle. "You do that all the time. Well, did you pass muster?"

"Of course. I'm a very good estate manager, and there isn't a great deal to do. For an earldom the property's quite small."

"So what are you doing now?"

"Playing messenger. You're commanded to dine with the lord and master." Alarm shot through her. "Alone?"

His brows went up. "Of course not. Is he bothering you?"

"No." She tried to make it believable, which should be easy because he wasn't. Yet still she was bothered.

"I'm to eat with the earl and Mr. de Vere?" she asked, wondering what was behind the order.

"And me. Sorry if you don't like it, love. I probably caused it by saying it might be awkward to eat at the earl's table while my sister acted the servant. Come on. You used to dine with the old earl and me sometimes."

"I know, but I wore ordinary clothes when I was secretary. . . ." She gestured at her plain clothes.

"You must have something suitable up here."

Dress in a pretty gown for Con? A shiver of alarm collided with a stab of eagerness. The invitation was as good as a command. Or perhaps even a challenge.

So she would take it up boldly. Con had only seen her in schoolroom dresses, in men's clothing, and in housekeeper gray. Perhaps it was time to remind him that she was a lady.

"I do have a couple of finer dresses here," she said, adding with a smile, "mainly to stop Amelia from borrowing them."

"She's six inches shorter."

"But the same size around. She stitches up the hems but the gowns are never quite the same afterward."

"Can't you stop her?"

"Not when I'm up here and the gowns are down there. I brought my favorites to preserve them." She smiled. "She's welcome to borrow the rest."

She looked at the wine. "Would you help out by decanting the wine and spirits and taking them to the dining room?"

"Get him to hire a butler," he said rather haughtily, and she reflected again on how comfortable he was in his role as gentleman. Why couldn't she be the same?

He set to work, however, and Susan hurried off to her rooms, calling for Ada to help her.

She needed the maid's assistance with her fashionable corset. She could get into her working ones on her own, but the one she needed for her best dresses required back lacing. Once the corset was snug and supporting her breasts at a fashionable height, she had Ada help her on with her ivory muslin dress.

It had been through a number of changes over the years, but it was still her favorite. The upper layer, embroidered with white and just a touch of golden brown, veiled an underskirt which she had recently retrimmed with deep, pointed Vandyke lace—smuggled, of course. Since she'd cut eight inches off the underskirt to allow for the lace, it had created a delightful veiled effect around her ankles.

Was it too risqué? Too suggestive? Her only alternative other than her working clothes was a deep pink silk, which was much too grand, and a blue day dress with long sleeves and a high neck. Was there time to send down to the manor for her peach cambric? It was an altogether better choice for an informal dinner. . . .

But no, there wasn't time.

She plucked anxiously at the low front. It revealed a considerable amount of her breasts, which were thrust up by the corset. She'd worn the retrimmed dress a few months ago without a quiver of alarm—but then she hadn't been about to face Con.

As Ada worked on the pearl buttons Susan fought panic and pure excitement. The dress became her, she knew that.

It was suitable armor for a coming battle.

Had Con felt like this before battle—afraid, afire, eager?

Eager for what?

Her goal should be simple. Find the gold and leave. But another goal was stirring.

She couldn't recapture what they'd had all those years ago, and Con had found happiness with another woman. She didn't want to leave Crag Wyvern, however, leave this area, without trying to get to know him a little, the man he had become.

And she ached to heal him. Whatever the causes of the darkness around him now, some were her fault. They had been friends once. Could she reach out now to help a friend?

She looked in the mirror and grimaced at herself. She might think noble thoughts, but in truth she was excited to be looking her best, to be able to show him that she was a woman able to attract men.

Attract men?

By the stars, she'd worn this dress six years ago when she'd let Lord Rivenham seduce her! It had been higher-necked then, sans lace, and with a trim of golden ribbons, but she'd been wearing this dress.

The next day, when he'd taken her for a drive to a conveniently private place, she'd been in pink jaconet, but the day before at the Bath assembly, it had been this dress.

Oh, what folly that had been.

Ada finished with the tiny buttons, and Susan sat so the maid could brush out her hair. She couldn't stop dwelling on past follies.

She'd been in Bath with her aunt and cousins. Her aunt had been advised to take the waters, and she'd taken her two oldest girls, as she always called them, along to enjoy society there. Cecilia, at twenty-one, had met her husband in Bath. Susan, at twenty, had seized an opportunity to try to drive Con Somerford from her mind and heart.

It hadn't been frightening or unpleasant. Lord Rivenham had been some years older, married, and a known rake. He was not an honorable man, but skilled. He'd even brought a sponge soaked in vinegar and shown her how to insert it.

It had all been very interesting, especially the contrast between Con's ignorant enthusiasm and Rivenham's expertise. It hadn't been an improvement, however, except in the simplest mechanical sense.

When they were leaving the rooms, strangely back to normal after that brief tumult, he'd asked, "Get what you wanted, pet?"

She could remember the moment as if someone had pinned it in a frame for eternity. Her face had burned, but she'd met his curious, cynical eyes and said, "Yes, thank you."

He'd laughed. "I don't suppose I'll ever know what brought you here today, but I hope you find the man you want for more than an afternoon."

She hadn't exactly lied to him. She'd wanted to wipe Con from her mind, from her skin, and she'd failed at that. But she had gained in knowledge, and not just about preventing babies.

This matter between men and women could simply be an act, but it wasn't always. What had happened between her and Con had been both less and more. It had been different because of the feelings involved. It hadn't caused the feelings; the feelings had caused the effect.

Therefore, she had set herself to fall in love. Cecilia and even young Amelia and most of the young women she knew seemed to find it easy to fall into love with handsome gentlemen and dashing soldiers. And just as easy to fall out again.

So she stirred herself into tremulous excitement about Captain Jermyn Lavalle in his dashing Hussar uniform. When she'd let him make fumbling, hasty, unsatisfying love to her in the gazebo of his colonel's country villa, however, she'd been used without care or even appreciation.

Too proud to protest, or scream, or weep, she'd known she was a mere physical convenience to him, and a trophy as well. She'd parted from him, chin high, terrified that he'd boast of it to his fellow officers, and knowing she was on a course to insane disaster.

At least Con wasn't a Hussar. She remembered thinking that, as if it were the crucial point.

The encounter with Lavalle had not made a scrap of difference to the secrets of her heart, but it had changed her behavior. She'd recognized at last that life would not be forced into the channels of her choosing, but must be lived with honor as it came.

Play the hand that was dealt her, as apparently Mel Clyst had put it. She wished she'd known her father better.

She'd spitefully wished Captain Lavalle dead in his first battle, but she'd overcome that too, and even managed to be glad when she saw notice later of his making major. She'd prayed, however, that their paths would never cross again, and that he would keep their assignation secret.

As Ada began to sweep her hair up, Susan adjusted the low bodice of her gown. At least she hadn't been wearing this dress with Lavalle. He'd thrown up the skirts of a pink dress trimmed with rosebuds. Immediately afterward she'd spilled blackberry cordial down it so it would have to be thrown out.

Ada screwed the hair up into a knot and jabbed in pins. Susan winced. Ada was no lady's maid, and Mrs. Gorland would be fuming that she wasn't out in the kitchen. In this gown, however, Susan couldn't reach up to arrange her hair for herself. In truth, fashion for women could be a kind of prison, but then, some men's tight jackets and high shirt points trapped them, too.

Not Con, unless he dressed very differently for fashionable affairs.

Finished at last, Ada added a slender bandeau decorated with golden brown ribbon and tiny silk rosebuds. Susan thanked her and sent her back to her work, then put on her pearl earrings and necklace.

The pearls had been a gift from her father. She'd forgotten that. They'd been sent to her just before she was to make that trip to Bath. David had received a handsome set of pistols on his twenty-first birthday.

She touched the large pearl that hung in the center of a cluster in the front, thinking of David's words about Mel Clyst. Bitter because of her mother, she'd made no attempt to know her father. Maybe he had kept his distance because he'd seen his children bettering themselves through his wife's family.

But why in heaven's name hadn't he married Lady Belle? The union would still have been a scandal, but not so much of one if it had been blessed. Had it simply been so that his children would be Kerslakes rather than Clysts?

She sighed and put the matter aside. If he'd meant well, it was far too late to acknowledge it now. It was probably too late for everything. The past happened. It set like concrete and must be lived with.

She stood and slipped on the silk slippers that went with the gown, raising her foot to the chair to tie the golden brown ribbons, thinking again of veiled ankles.

Would Con notice? Would he care?

She pulled on long gloves, draped a gauzy scarf over her arms, then reviewed herself again.

Elegant and ladylike. Not a bit like the housekeeper, or like the young girl scampering over the rocks and shore. Shorter tendrils of hair were already escaping around her face, however. She reached to repin them and found she couldn't. After a moment she decided the effect was becoming—in a wanton kind of way.

So be it. In fact, she'd go further.

She took a pot of rouge out of a drawer and subtly deepened the color of her lips, then added a touch on her cheeks. There. That completed the effect. With a laugh she thought of the warrior tribes of Africa and America who went into battle with their faces painted. Apparently it was supposed to frighten the enemy.

She hoped it made her dragon shake in his shoes.

Chapter Twelve

David was waiting for her in the kitchen, chatting to the servants. "Lovely, but a little grand, isn't it?"

"I don't have anything in between," she said, linking her arm with his.

As they walked along the corridor he said, "You're not thinking of trying to marry him, are you?"

She wondered whether rouge hid or enhanced a blush. "Of course not. Why would you think that?"

"I can't imagine," he said dryly. "What are you up to? I always thought you might have fallen a little in love with him that time. You were strange for a while afterward."

"I didn't think you noticed."

"Of course I noticed. I don't want you hurt, love."

She tried to find a joke, to find any response that made sense, but then said, "I don't want to talk about it."

"As bad as that, is it?"

They'd taken the outer corridor toward the dining room. She stopped and faced him. "Perhaps there was a bit of love, but it was a long time ago and we were very young. We didn't part on good terms, though, and this invitation is a kind of challenge."

"What caused the falling-out?"

"None of your business."

"In other words, you were in the wrong. Would it be asking too much for you to say you're sorry?"

The idea appalled her. "After eleven years? What is all this to you anyway?

Not still hoping I can turn him to your cause? Believe me, David, I can't apologize. It wouldn't help."

"As bad as that, is it?" He tucked her arm back through his. "Why do I feel you're ready for battle? Honey would serve the cause better than vinegar."

It was almost a command, and she narrowed her eyes. "Being Captain Drake is going to your head."

"Being Captain Drake is a real and demanding responsibility. I don't want things snarled by some petty disagreement between you and the earl."

"Petty!"

"You admit there's a disagreement."

"I admitted that we parted on bad terms. I will be civil as long as he is."

"I'm sure he will be," he said with confidence that made her want to throw something at him. "Come on, then. Let's advance together."

Con and de Vere were in the drawing room, and to Susan, walking into that conventional room seemed shockingly like walking into another world. The two men had both changed, but not into formal evening wear, probably because David would still be in day clothes. She was slightly overdressed, but she'd known she would be.

She noted Con's sharp attention before he looked away, however, and it was reward enough.

One glance at Susan was almost enough to knock Con off his feet. This was a Susan he'd never seen before——the beautiful, elegant lady. But at the same time it was the Susan he'd expected to see here. There was no clear connection to the coltish girl in rumpled schoolroom clothes, and yet the essence was the same, and it ignited the same urgent response.

He'd wondered if she planned to seduce him again, and now he saw that she did. He tried to be outraged, but something inside growled like a hungry tiger.

He managed a calm smile as he greeted her. "Mrs. Kerslake, I'm pleased you could join us." He gave thanks for the *Mrs.*, which reminded him of the Susan in gray and white, and set her slightly among the married.

However, Kerslake said, "I think my sister should be Miss Kerslake for this occasion, my lord."

Susan seemed as startled as he was. "David, that's not necessary."

"I think it is."

It was as if Kerslake had read his thoughts. Or perhaps he was an ally in the planned seduction. Con's sense and senses steadied. He would regard their hopeless efforts as an amusing show.

"Of course. Miss Kerslake, may I offer you sherry?"

There were no servants in attendance in the room, so he poured the wine himself. As he passed it over, their fingers brushed, and it took all his discipline not to start. It was like touching hot iron.

Even with control, he'd come close to knocking her wine down her lovely dress. Her lovely dress that revealed far too much of her round breasts, much fuller now than they'd been back then . . .

He snared his wits and stepped back. "If I am to be here for any length of time, it will be necessary to hire a footman. To serve wine, among other things."

He saw her eyes flicker to his with understanding, and her cheeks color. But then he suspected a touch of the rouge pot on those cheeks. She'd definitely come here all guns to the ready.

"And a butler, my lord," Kerslake said. "My sister had to recruit me to wine duty."

"My apologies," Con said dryly. "But in the chaos left by my predecessor, we all have to make do. It would seem excessive to engage a butler when I will rarely be here."

"I think the ladies of the area hope to persuade you to stay, my lord."

"Really?" Con shot Susan a look.

Her color deepened, but she was otherwise composed as she said, "Everyone hopes you will stay, my lord."

"Even the smugglers?" he asked.

He hoped Kerslake would have to answer, but Susan's brother looked admirably as if smuggling were a matter of scant interest. It was Susan who said, "That rather depends on your attitude to the Freetrade, my lord."

"And what is your attitude, Miss Kerslake?"

Her look told him that she thought that an unfair blow. "I cannot approve of any illegality, my lord, but in truth, the taxes levied by London are criminal themselves. And of course, I am the daughter of a man transported for smuggling."

A bold attack. A warmth that was almost tenderness spread through him. She was as brave and direct as she'd always been.

He turned to Kerslake. "And you are his son, Kerslake. Does the association cause you much trouble?"

"Very little, my lord. And of course he is no longer here."

There was a spark of mischievous humor in the young man's eyes that he'd do well to conquer. It cracked his otherwise excellent act.

"So there must be a new Captain Drake, I assume," Con said.

But Race joined the conversation then. "Captain Drake. Called after Sir Francis Drake?" Eyes bright and alert, he was, as he'd promised, acting like an audience at an enjoyable play.

No, he'd said *farce.*

Con let the silence ride, and it was Kerslake in the end who said, "Yes, but also from the associations with dragons here. A drake is another name for dragon, of course, as is wyvern."

"A two-legged winged dragon who eats children," Con contributed. "The earls of Wyvern do seem to have sealed their fate, don't they?"

"We can only hope it is not unfixably attached to the title, my lord," Kerslake said smoothly, then added to Race, "Have you visited Dragon's Cove yet? A guide to the area described it as a quaint fishing village. . . ."

Con watched with admiration as Susan's brother steered the conversation to local points of interest and other innocuous subjects. A young man of remarkable talents.

Susan smiled at David's comment, but her mind was buzzing with the effect of Con. That one, sizzling look had speeded her pulse, had alerted her to him in a way she'd not experienced before.

She watched him turn, and her breath shortened. It was such an elegantly powerful movement. He was by the fireplace, and his strong hand was framed for a moment, brown against white marble, stunningly beautiful despite the white slashes of minor scars.

When he'd smiled at David's comment, it had been a frank, open smile unlike any he'd given her here, though it recalled smiles of the past. If only he would smile like that for her again.

This was no good. She joined in the talk of local points of interest, and didn't let herself look at Con at all, but he still dominated her mind.

Her reaction was simply physical, but she'd felt nothing like it for eleven years. It had its own power, its own imperative. She was struggling to converse coherently.

Could she bear to part from Con without tasting this desire between two mature people with time and freedom to explore it . . . ?

A sip of wine almost went astray because of her unsteady hand. Was she thinking of trying to wipe away Lord Rivenham and Captain Lavalle in Con's bed?

Oh, no. There be dragons, indeed.

* * *

When Race and Kerslake fell into hunting talk, Con seized the opportunity to talk to Susan. "Your brother seems to be an excellent young man. De Vere is impressed with his administrative capabilities."

"He's very clever, yes." She was sipping her wine and looking at her brother, not at him.

"Is he moving with a limp now and then? A permanent affliction?"

She hesitated a second too long, but that was the only betrayal. "I gather he was involved in some sort of fight last night. Over a woman."

"Did he win?"

"I have no idea."

"I suppose it's not the sort of thing a brother tells his older sister. Do you mind him being protective of you?"

Her eyes met his then, a little startled. That he'd understand her impatience with it?

"It is the way of the world, my lord. But it's one reason I prefer to have employment."

"How very American." At her questioning look, he said, "The lure of independence. So, what will you do when you leave your position here, Miss Kerslake?"

"I have not yet decided, my lord." She met his eyes. "What is your opinion of the American states, my lord? Do you think they can continue to prosper?"

Thus she steered talk firmly toward different forms of government, leaving Con puzzled. He'd given her an opening and there'd been not a trace of flirtation in her.

Did she think her lovely and arousing appearance would do the work for her? Again?

Ah, no. He had to have learned better than that.

When Diddy came to announce that dinner was ready, Susan gave earnest thanks and took Con's arm to lead the way to the dining room. It had been rarely used in recent years, however, and despite polish and flowers had that strange aridity of an abandoned place.

The massive, dark oak furniture gave it a somber atmosphere even though she'd ordered the table reduced to its smallest size, and candles lit. Even the chairs were huge and carved, and upholstered on arms and seats with red velvet.

As they all sat, she felt as if they were a body of judges gathered to consider the case of the meal. As with all the other ground-floor rooms, glass-paned doors opened into the courtyard, but they were closed. It wasn't yet dark outside, but the two branches of candles created intimate ovals of light, intensifying the sense of a secret meeting.

She almost expected Con on her left to bang a gavel and launch an accusation against David for being Captain Drake.

Instead, Jane came in with the soups and placed them on the table. Susan was distracted for a moment by watching to see that the service was correct, and then by tasting her soup to see that it was good. Then she made herself put that aside. She was Miss Kerslake tonight, not the housekeeper, and she had other need of her wits.

David had adroitly engaged Con in talk about his home in Sussex, and Susan listened as best she could, remembering the fondness he'd shared for it in the past. She was pleased that affection lived on. He had a home he loved, and a woman he loved too. It gave her genuine pleasure.

Courtesy, however, demanded that she pay attention to de Vere on her right. "I hope you are enjoying your visit to Crag Wyvern, sir."

"Now, now, dear lady. You are Miss Kerslake, a guest here."

It was a mild rebuke, or perhaps just a reminder. More likely mischief, in fact.

She sipped some more soup. "Then I am two people in one, Mr. de Vere. I don't think anyone can put aside a part of themselves at their convenience."

"Can't we? Sometimes there are parts we'd like to put aside."

And that was true. "Then perhaps it can be done with strict effort." She looked at him. "You, Mr. de Vere, are also a Janus. One face is the idle, laughing man, but when it comes to paperwork you show a more serious aspect."

"Not a bit of it. Paperwork has me giggling with glee. There is something fascinating about it, don't you think? Especially confused accounts. Each item provides a piece of a mysterious picture."

"A picture of Crag Wyvern? Hardly worth your effort."

"A picture is a picture, and sometimes we piece one together for amusement. Have you seen such things? Pointless in a way to cut a picture up so that someone else can put it together, but engaging all the same. This picture is part of Wyvern's life, and that interests me. As do you, Miss Kerslake."

"I?" she asked, a sudden tension in her belly.

"You. You are a striking woman. I pointed out to Wyvern that you resemble a Renaissance angel."

She looked at him, tempted to laugh. "And what did he say to that?"

"He recognized the truth, of course. Too beautiful to be a man. Too strongly featured to be a beautiful woman . . ."

Jane came to remove her soup plate, which gave her time to think. "I could take that as an insult, Mr. de Vere."

"Now, would I be foolish enough to insult you with two ardent defenders to hand? Your looks are very attractive."

His words gave her an excuse to look away, at Con and David talking together as if they were just two gentlemen. "*Two* ardent defenders?"

"Definitely. So I suspect it would not be wise to set up a flirtation with you."

She looked back. "But why be wise, sir? I don't have much opportunity for flirtation these days." She leaned her elbow on the table and put her chin on her hand to gaze at him. "And you know, you have much of the look of an angel yourself."

A genuine smile fought to be free. It was so long since she'd played this game.

"Too beautiful to be a man?" he murmured, both wariness and amusement sparking in his blue eyes.

"But very attractive, even so."

His lips twitched. "And what, I wonder, do two fine angels do together in private moments? Shall we find out, Miss Kerslake?"

Slowly she lowered her arm and sat straight. She could not afford even the most playful entanglement. "It would doubtless not be worth the bother, sir. I assume angels pray."

"Or dance on the head of a pin. Easy to fall, wouldn't you say?"

She turned aside in an instinctive retreat, and found herself looking at Con, who had probably heard every word. The conversation switched so that she was talking to him.

"De Vere isn't the earl, you know," he said pleasantly, but with cool eyes.

"Goodness, I must have been confused for a moment."

His smile widened as his eyes chilled. "He is heir to a pleasant estate in Derbyshire, however, unless his disapproving father disinherits him. Worth your effort, perhaps, if you're not absolutely set on Wyvern."

Now she was smiling as falsely as he was, and praying that the other two men weren't listening. "Do I have a chance at Wyvern?"

He froze, looking at her, not smiling at all, and she wondered why she'd fallen into such a destructive exchange.

"Play your hand, Susan, and find out."

It was a challenge. A challenge to seduce him again in case he could be swayed? Surely he knew she would not do that.

No, perhaps he didn't . . .

She wanted desperately to speak to him directly, to talk about the past, to try to recapture the friendship and trust they'd once had. He was still angry and distrustful, however, and with reason, and she couldn't imagine how to change that.

Not with words, that was sure.

"And you, my lord," she said, directing most of her attention to her plate, "what ambitions do you have?"

"Ambitions," he repeated, in the same polite tone. "I am ambitious for peace, Miss Kerslake. International peace, and personal peace. For simple country days, and comfort for those I love."

She looked back at him, relieved that they'd found a safe subject. "Your mother and sisters."

"And Lady Anne."

Her throat tightened. She was trying to accept the idea of his chosen beloved, but it was hard. She prayed that the hesitation of her fork had not been visible, but the delicious lobster became like clay in her mouth, heavy and liable to choke her.

She chewed slowly to steal time, then made herself swallow. There was nothing between them anymore, so why did the reminder that he was engaged to marry create a painful lump in her chest?

She took a sip of wine. "Will your future wife like Crag Wyvern?" It sounded reasonably normal to her ears.

"No. We are remarkably in tune, Lady Anne and I."

"I see now why you do not plan to live here, my lord." She felt as if she'd reached solid ground again after wallowing in a swamp. It was not ground she'd have chosen, but it was solid.

"Remember, I do not want to live here either."

He was hammering the fact home, and she realized why. He was telling her that even if she somehow inveigled him into marriage she would still not catch the prize he thought she wanted.

Oh, Con, can we not do better than this?

She tried. "I do not like Crag Wyvern either, my lord," she said plainly. "Perhaps Lady Anne and I will find ourselves in tune, if she ever does visit here."

"Unlikely."

She raised a brow.

"You are the housekeeper, Mrs. Kerslake. You and my wife would be unlikely to discuss such matters."

It was so deliberately discourteous that Susan simply stared at him, and after a moment he looked away. That gave her a chance to squeeze her lips together to fight back tears.

Only pain would make Con into this hurtful man, and some of the pain—most of it?—was her fault.

She caught de Vere's all too perceptive eye on her, but that at least gave her an excuse to address a remark to him and switch the pattern of the conversation. She managed to force a bit more of her dinner down.

She had never expected this meal to be enjoyable; but she hadn't expected torture. Despite David and a stranger as safeguards, she felt as if she were being forced to walk on broken glass.

It was David who found a topic for four-sided conversation—a discussion of the role the newspapers should play in the setting of public policy. None of them had strong political leanings, so they could debate it warmly without friction. She could have kissed him. She didn't know whether he'd been aware of what was going on or not, but she was certainly coming to appreciate that he was a person well able to deal with the world, and not her troublesome little brother anymore.

Another end. A good one, but an end. Except possibly in the matter of the gold, David didn't need her anymore. It hurt a little, but it freed her. She could leave, and if Con was going to bring his bride here, even for the briefest visit, she would make sure to be elsewhere by then.

She'd never thought Con's marriage would hurt so much. She'd never realized how deeply she still cared.

Was there anything she could do to try to reclaim the treasure she had carelessly thrown away?

No. She must not think that way.

Though she was the only lady, she assumed she should behave in the conventional way and was glad of the chance to escape. At the earliest excusable moment she rose to leave the gentlemen.

All the men rose too, but Con said, "I don't think any of us wishes the freedom to get drunk and tell risqué stories, Miss Kerslake. I plan to move into the courtyard to enjoy port and brandy in the evening air. Please join us."

There was a distinct edge of command to it.

So she was not to escape so easily. Very well. She would advance with bravado. "With pleasure, my lord. I enjoy a good brandy."

"And I'm sure the brandy here is very good."

He flicked a glance at David, who responded with a bland smile, but she was suddenly sure that Con had guessed. He knew David was Mel Clyst's son, after all.

Would he move against David as a form of revenge? Though it seemed alien to the Con in her heart, she sensed that this man held darkness enough to do it.

Con turned toward the doors into the garden, putting a hand on his chair back for a moment. Perhaps he had drunk a little more than he should have. How many bottles of wine had been served? She couldn't be sure, nor how much of it he had drunk, but she prayed he wasn't intoxicated. That tipped many a man—or woman—into doing and saying things they otherwise would not.

He flung open the doors into the courtyard. The enclosing walls cast shadows, but it was not yet dark. "Bring the decanters and glasses," he said to no one in particular, and strolled out along one of the stone paths toward the central fountain.

Susan noted that someone had turned on the water, probably trying to do their best for the new earl. Despite the unpleasant design of the fountain, the gentle splashing was soothing. She felt a desperate need for something soothing.

Susan looked back, but David said, "Go on. De Vere and I will play servant this time. Would you rather have tea?"

She made a lightning calculation. Tea would be so blessedly normal, but she knew she'd feel absurd attempting to preside over a tea table out beside the lewd fountain.

"I will drink brandy with the rest of you," she said, and followed, but slowly. She had no intention of having a tête-à-tête with Con by the fountain.

She also had no intention of showing how uneasy all this was making her. She'd drink her brandy, which she did enjoy, and then she'd politely say good night. And nothing short of a direct order would stop her from finding her rooms and staying in them.

Tomorrow, she resolved, pausing to inhale the perfume of some hyacinth, she would begin her retreat. There was nothing here for her or Con but pain. He was tied here for life, so it was for her to leave.

It wouldn't be hard to find someone to fill in as housekeeper, and in her remaining days she would conduct a thorough, clearheaded search for secret rooms, compartments, or other hidey-holes for the gold. If only she'd done that sooner, but she'd been so sure that the earl would have stashed the gold carelessly, and for safety's sake, she hadn't wanted even the servants to know when she took it. Now, with Con here, it was more dangerous, but she would do it. Even if she didn't find the money, she needed to know that she had done her best.

"Another insect?"

She started, and looked up to see that Con had walked back to her side.

Chapter Thirteen

Insect?" Susan asked.

"Wasn't that what you paused to study this morning?" Perhaps she, too, had drunk too much. It took her a moment to realize what he meant, and then she became freshly aware of him studying her from his bedroom window, of him being naked from the hips up—and invisibly, from the hips down.

Despite his clothes, her mind filled with the image of his splendid torso, and the dragon that apparently marred it.

She gathered her wits. "Oh, yes. But not now. Now I am simply enjoying the scent of the wallflowers."

She saw him inhale. "So English. Spain and Portugal are full of smells, and some of them are even pleasant. But not like the scents of an English garden."

It was so honest, so ordinary, so tender even, that she breathed it in as she had the perfume, holding on to the moment as if she could stop time. She didn't even dare to look back to see what had happened to David and de Vere.

Then she realized she had to say something. The only thing that occurred to her was prosaic. "The garden needs a gardener. It was Mrs. Lane's pride and joy. I've done my best, but I do not particularly have the gift for it."

"You're not a gardener?"

"No."

Did he feel it as meaningfully as she did, that he didn't know, and that he'd asked?

"Are you?" she asked.

"God, no. Though I appreciate a wholesome garden when I find one. Imagine Crag Wyvern without this."

He turned to look around, and she did too, seeing it with different eyes.

It was quiet in the failing light, but during the day the garden buzzed with insects for which this was their entire world. Even the birds didn't seem to leave it. A world, a wholesome world, within the Crag. Without it, the place would truly be dead and rotten.

There was even the musical splash of the fountain to add to the magic.

He walked toward it and she followed, not so nervous now. A glance showed David and de Vere coming, decanters and glasses in hand, talking animatedly about something.

Almost a normal moment.

In Crag Wyvern.

Astonishing.

Then she almost bumped into Con because he'd stopped dead.

"I want this removed," he said.

She followed his gaze. "The fountain?"

"I want the figures out of here. Tomorrow." His eyes turned savagely to hers. "If you don't see why, Susan, you have been eaten whole by the dragon."

Shaking under that attack, she looked at the fountain, really looked at it. The maiden writhed beneath the dragon as always. The beast pinned her arms with its claws and spread her legs with its lower body.

She thought it horrid, but she'd learned to ignore it. The water was rarely turned on, however, because then the cistern in the roof had to be refilled. When it had been gushing water she hadn't looked at it clearly.

Now, however, she did.

The dragon's huge phallus spewed over the captive bride, some liquid filling her screaming mouth, more pouring off her outstretched, piteous hands.

After a horrified moment, she turned away. "Yes. Yes, of course."

She still heard the music of the water, but now the image made it foul.

He was right. The garden was the healing heart of Crag Wyvern, but by creating the dragon's bride fountain, the mad earl had introduced a blight.

"I don't know how it's constructed," she said, "but I'll find out what needs to be done to remove it. Tomorrow."

"I'm sorry," he said in very different voice.

She looked and saw a different man, less dark, less hard, closer surely to the Con she remembered.

"Sorry?" she asked, wondering if he was going to apologize for some of the darts he'd thrown at her tonight.

"You aren't my housekeeper at the moment, are you? I shouldn't be giving you orders."

She suppressed a sigh. "It doesn't matter, my lord. It should be done."

Her brother and de Vere were close, but Con moved away from the fountain. "There are benches beneath the lime tree, I think. We'll sit there."

David flashed her a look that suggested that he thought this earl was as mad as the rest of them, but Susan understood. Having been alerted to the abhorrence of that fountain, she didn't want to sit near it either.

There were two benches, and she ended up sitting beside David, while Con and de Vere sat on the other. She rather thought David had engaged in some clever maneuvering to achieve that, and she wondered what he was seeing here. As she warmed her cognac, the finest that the Freetrade had to offer, she wished this were a more wholesome evening.

The idea of sitting in a tranquil evening garden with Con and friends was something she had never dreamed of, and even in this flawed state it was sweet enough for tears.

"Miss Kerslake," de Vere said, "do you know what was here before this garden?"

She took a small sip of her brandy. "I'm not sure, sir. The original plans for Crag Wyvern show a garden here, but I've heard that before Mrs. Lane took care of it, it was in sorry shape. At one point it was all grassed to make a tennis court."

De Vere looked around. "And the windows survived?"

"I don't think so. Originally the lower windows were stained glass. There's a painting in one of the corridors."

De Vere shook his head. "Mad. And through the ages, too."

"No one's denying it, Race," Con said.

"If I were you, I'd disown the lot of them."

Con took a mouthful of the brandy. "Ah, but that's the burden of the aristocracy. We can't disown our ancestors and keep the spoils." He turned to Susan. "Are there records of the first earl, Miss Kerslake? I would be interested to know more about the story of the dragon."

"I don't know, my lord. There's a room in the cellars full of boxes of ledgers and documents."

De Vere gave a faint moan, and surprisingly, Con laughed in seemingly true humor. "You are not getting a sniff of them until you've dealt with current matters. And in fact, I have engaged the curate to deal with the books. He might be willing to include archives."

"Unfair. Unfair."

"We'll probably not be here long enough to make any order of them anyway."

"I could stay," de Vere said, and flickered a smiling look at Susan.

That was unwise. She felt Con's cold disapproval like a lance. It seared through his words as he said, "You are my secretary, Race. Where I go, you go."

"Sounds more like a damn wife to me."

"For that, you lack certain essential qualifications."

De Vere didn't seem daunted by the sharp edge in his employer's voice. In fact he smiled in a deliberately winsome way. "Miss Kerslake said I was angelic."

Con looked across the gathering shadows at Susan. "Don't forget, Miss Kerslake, Lucifer is an angel, too."

They were both speaking laconically, lounging at either end of the bench, but Susan wanted to scream at them to stop it, to stop sliding knife-edged comments through the conversation.

She drained her glass of brandy and stood. "I believe it is time I retired, my lord, gentlemen."

David stood too. "And I must return to the manor. Thank you, my lord, for an excellent dinner."

They went through the courtesies, but all the time Susan felt weighed down by Con's attention, quivering with the fear that he would command her to stay. There surely was nothing to fear, but here in the darkening garden at the heart of Crag Wyvern, she was afraid.

He didn't stop her, and she walked away with David, making herself not rush. They reentered the house through the dining room, and Susan was pleased to see that the servants had quietly cleared the table while they were outside. They had even restored the table to the usual seating for eight, which better suited the proportions of the room.

As they entered the corridor, David said, "De Vere is a damn strange secretary."

"I think he's more of a friend."

"A damn strange friend, too. Are you all right up here with them?"

She knew that if he suspected any awkwardness he would want her to leave immediately. She could deal with awkwardness, and it would become nothing more than that.

"Of course I'm all right." But she added, "The earl is troubled. I think it's something from the war, which is not surprising. Perhaps de Vere suffers in the same way but handles it by creating mischief. It's not likely to affect me, however."

"If you're sure. But if you ask me, the mad blood runs in both sides of the family."

"That could be true. . . ." Yet she'd seen no sign of imbalance in Con all those years ago. He'd been the sanest, most even-tempered person she'd ever known.

They parted with a kiss in the great hall, and Susan went to the kitchen area to compliment the staff. She was still there when the bell rang. She told Diddy to go and see what the earl wanted. "Probably more brandy," Susan muttered, but she'd be happy enough if he drank himself into a stupor.

Diddy came back. "He wants to speak to you, Mrs. Kerslake. He's in the dining room."

Susan was strongly tempted not to go, but how would that look before the servants? The rest of the servants. And it wasn't as if this were a medieval castle and the earl had droit du seigneur or anything so absurd. Nor was she an unprotected waif. If she couldn't defend herself, she had a family of men ready to do so, or to avenge any wrong.

He must know that.

If he was sane.

If he wasn't dangerously drunk.

She hesitated, wondering if there was time to change into the defense of her housekeeper's clothes, but there wasn't.

She left the kitchen, but as she did so she said, "If I scream, come and rescue me."

She made it light, but she knew the women would do it. They'd lived with one mad Earl of Wyvern already.

She entered the garden a different way. With darkness almost complete the lamps created pools of light and shadowed corners. In the heart of the shadows the fountain still played.

The bride still drowned.

She detoured to the concealed wheel valve, and switched the water off.

Splash diminished into trickles, and then to peaceful silence. Susan walked through it toward the shining rectangle of the dining room doors, where Con stood waiting. Alone.

She hesitated out in the dark, but she would not be afraid. To be truly afraid of Con would be the final denial of all that had once existed between them.

She stepped into the room. "My lord? You needed something?"

He was blank, impossible to read. She wished the wide table stood between them, but he had waited for her near the doors. She wished she'd come in from the corridor.

She edged a little farther into the room to put more distance between them, trying not to make it look like a retreat. She was stopped by the table. To work her way around it would be ridiculous.

"In Spain, I almost raped a woman," he said.

She looked at him, seeking the meaning beneath the words and finding it. "That's why the fountain offends you?"

"That's probably why I am more sensitive to it than you. I regret implying that you are uncaring."

A flutter of something started within. Not hope, no. That would be foolish. But . . . pleasure. Pleasure that he could say that to her. That he wanted to and felt free to.

"Not uncaring, no. But I am callused," she said. "Crag Wyvern does that. The constant abrasion of the wicked and the bizarre makes us insensitive after a while."

"Like war. The constant abrasion of violence, suffering, and death. I tried once to peel away the calluses. It was a mistake."

She wasn't sure what had caused this moment of openness, but it was a treasure to savor. She leaned back slightly against the table between two chairs. "Why was it a mistake?"

As if mirroring her, he leaned back too, against the doorjamb. "Because I had to go back to war. Waterloo. Good calluses take time to build. Or restore."

Clearly he needed to talk and he'd chosen her to talk to. Privately, she gave thanks, but she simply said, "What happened?"

He shrugged. "We won. We lost. I mean, we lost too many good men. Ten thousand of them. I suppose it was worth it, but sometimes it's hard to see why. If they'd dealt with Napoleon properly the first time . . ."

He shrugged again.

"You must have lost many friends there." She hesitated, wondering whether mentioning his closest friends, something shared in the past, would be a mistake. But she did it. "The other two Georges? The Rogues?"

He did look startled—perhaps it was a flinch—but he answered. "One of the Rogues. Lord Darius Debenham."

She ached for him, but treasured the moment. "One of the Duke of Yeovil's sons. I heard of his loss. I'm sorry."

He said nothing more, and she sensed that this connection, whatever it had been, was fading. She'd recapture it if she could, but had no idea how. They stood in silence for a moment or two, and then he said, "What happened eleven years ago, Susan?"

The suddenness of it stole words. Eventually she said, "You know what happened, Con."

Did he think she would deny it? Try to claim it had been some huge mistake?

"I suppose I do. You made your ambitions clear enough. Did you try to marry Fred?"

She was poised on a razor edge. Did she admit that she'd never felt the same way toward any other man, that she'd bitterly regretted what she had done? Did she protect her pride with lies?

She could summon the courage to go only halfway. "Aunt Miriam had hopes. I suppose we all tried a bit, but my heart wasn't in it."

Do you hear what I'm saying Con? Do you care?

His eyes were steady, his face without any readable expression. "And your heart was in it with me?"

In the face of that daunting blankness, she could not make the ultimate surrender.

And of course he didn't care.

He had Lady Anne.

"Why do you ask, Con? It was a long time ago, and you are to marry soon."

His long lashes blinked over silvery eyes. "Ah, yes. Lady Anne. She has nothing to do with the past."

"She makes the past irrelevant."

He pushed off from the doorjamb and moved a step closer. "The past is never irrelevant, even if we wish it were. I wonder why you haven't married. If you are telling the truth and don't want the Crag anymore."

Through a tightening throat she said, "I am telling the truth."

The atmosphere had changed. He was still unreadable, but danger swirled with the candle smoke in the air. She'd told David she was in no danger here, and she'd thought it was true. Perhaps there were things men could sense that women couldn't.

"So," he asked, "why haven't you married?"

He was demanding surrender and offering her nothing in exchange. "The bastard child of a tavernkeeper does not receive many worthy offers."

"You said Mel Clyst provided you with a dowry."

"I have no intention of being married for my money."

"Just as I have no intention of being married for my earldom. But you do have money?"

She hesitated. Mel had bought property for her, but she'd poured all her recent income from it into supporting the Horde. She didn't want to tell Con that, however, and she would be repaid.

"Yes," she said. "I have money."

"Then why are you playing housekeeper?"

She realized too late that he'd come closer and closer until she was trapped against the table between two solid oak chairs with no way to escape short of pushing him out of the way.

Would he move if she pushed?

She didn't think so.

Heart pounding, she stood up straight. "I'm not playing. I work for my wages."

He put a hand on the back of each imprisoning chair, caging her. She gripped the table behind for strength. She didn't fear that he would hurt her. She feared that he would kiss her, and by kissing her, conquer her entirely. . . .

"What happened eleven years ago?" he asked again, his eyes dark now, the gray only a rim around his pupils. At least one of the candles behind her must be guttering, because it played erratic light over his somber face, creating saints and devils in turn.

"What do you mean? What do you want to know?"

He leaned a little closer. "When we kissed that day in Irish Cove, was it as much a miracle to you as it was to me? Or was it simply an opportunity?"

She couldn't deny him this. "It was a miracle," she whispered.

"Ah." He lowered his lips and she didn't try to escape, but it wasn't the fierce, experienced kiss she'd expected. It was the same tentative tasting she remembered. As hesitant. As wary.

As miraculous.

She sank her hips back against the table for support, clutching it for dear life as his lips pressed innocently against hers.

He licked her cheek and her eyes flew open.

She realized that tears were leaking. He straightened, and so did she. She brushed away the other betraying tears with her hands.

"Memories?" he asked. "Or regrets? Whichever, Susan, it's a damned shame you did what you did in Irish Cove."

He turned and walked out of the room, out into the silent garden. After a moment, Susan found the strength in her legs to leave by the corridor door and make it to the sanctuary of her rooms.

Tears welled up.

She never cried!

But the tears broke free and she collapsed into a chair to weep for what she had done to a fifteen-year-old boy in love, and for the living pain it had created. She wept for the man he had become and the loss of the man he could have been.

But she also wept for the loss of the man he was, a loss stated by those flat words. *It's a damned shame you did what you did.*

Because it said clearly: *Abandon hope. The damage done is irreparable.*

Con paused by the evil fountain, glad at least that the water was turned off, though it left the enclosed garden eerily quiet. The faint light of the two distant lamps still glimmered on the splayed legs and arms of the woman pinned by pitiless claws. Her dark mouth looked like a scream.

If he thought it possible, he'd tear it apart now with his bare hands. It would be gone tommorow. If Susan didn't see to it, he would. He couldn't believe that he'd tolerated it even for a day.

His mind had been fogged by Susan, but perhaps he was numb. Numbness was welcome sometimes, but mostly it was dangerous. He didn't feel numb right now.

He walked on, aching with the need to kiss Susan as he'd wanted to kiss her. That was the road to agonizing folly, however. That private discussion had been insane, but he'd wanted her to know. He'd not wanted her to think—

God, stop it. Put this place in order, then leave. Return once a year for an inspection. Next time bring armor. Bring Lady Anne, a wife.

He tried to summon a clear image of Anne, and could only assemble facts—slender, blond, a slight limp. That didn't do her justice, but it was all his struggling mind could come up with.

That was all right. They hadn't met that many times as yet, so it wasn't surprising that he couldn't summon a clear picture.

He knew she would make a perfect, tranquil wife.

Chapter Fourteen

Susan arose the next morning and set to work on her escape. She'd dreamed of being back in Irish Cove, of not saying those dreadful words, but a dragon had surged up out of the water. Con had tried to fight it, but been seared by flaming breath.

She'd lain awake after that, going over and over everything Con had said, seeking hope.

That was enough to tell her that she had to escape.

Over her breakfast, brought by Ellen, she drew up a list of three local women who could be housekeeper at Crag Wyvern. They weren't really of the caliber to run an earl's household, but this was not a normal earl's household, and Con did not intend to live here. If he managed to lease it, the new residents would hire their own principal staff.

She wrote letters to them, asking if they were interested in the position. At some point she'd have to ask Con if he wanted to interview them, or to leave it to her judgment. For the moment, however, she intended to avoid him.

Then, armored in her housekeeper's clothes, she emerged to send off her letters and to organize the day. She unlocked the store-cupboards to distribute necessary supplies, noting everything in the record books. She noted what supplies were running low and sent off orders to local merchants. She allocated tasks for the day as fairly as possible, then went to supervise the breakfast preparations.

Con's Spanish valet was in the kitchen, and he inquired about laundry facilities. She explained that washing was sent down to some women in Church Wyvern.

He seemed a quiet and proper man, but he was creating quite a flutter among the maids with his Spanish ways and his wicked smiles. Thank heavens the two other men Con had brought were living at the stables in the village.

Sarmiento had clearly been with Con for many years, and seemed both devoted to his master and proud of him. He was certainly ready to talk about him whenever one of the maids asked. Susan couldn't resist lingering in the kitchen to listen.

Then the valet turned to her again. "Mistress Kerslake, is the water for the big bath always available?"

"Yes, Señor Sarmiento. I have ordered the cistern to be kept full, and the fire fed with charcoal. Has the earl not used it yet?"

"Last night he was perhaps a little overtired. He asked only for the small tub. I will remind him tonight. He seems weighed down by his new responsibilities here, and would benefit from the luxury."

She couldn't resist. "What do you think of Crag Wyvern, señor?"

He rolled his eyes. "In my native land, dear lady, we often build with the forbidding outside and the sensual garden within, but we have the strong sun that must be hidden from and protected against. Here . . . here where the sun is like skim milk and scarcely warms the earth . . . ?" He shrugged and shook his head.

But then he said, "Now, Lord Wyvern's other home, Somerford Court, that is a suitable English home. There the gardens are outside and the rooms look out over distant vistas of the beautiful, green English countryside. People here say that this is not a good summer, that it rains too much. But I . . . I see the green the rain brings, and it is sweet to my eyes and heart."

Surely this was safe to talk of. "Somerford Court is on a hill?"

"On a hill overlooking the valley of a river called Eden. Paradise. In the valley is the village of Hawk in the Vale. An old place, and friendly in the way of old places." His dark eyes twinkled. "That is to say, they look at a foreigner like me with suspicion, but do not actually throw stones. It is the same in my own village back home. The earl's close friend, Major Hawkinville, is son of the squire there. A great hero is Major Hawkinville, though he rarely raised a weapon. A warrior of the mind."

Susan wasn't quite sure what that meant, but she thirsted for more of this information.

"Major George Hawkinville, I assume," she said. "And the other George? George Vandeimen?"

His look was startled, and quickly hidden. "Ah. You know about the Georges, Mrs. Kerslake! He is Lord Vandeimen now. In that one, the family name and title is the same, which is not often the case, I understand. His family is all dead. It is a great tragedy. But now he is to marry a very rich woman. That is good, yes? He and my master have not met since Lord Vandeimen left the army, so I only know what I hear in the village."

"They haven't met?" She knew immediately that she'd stepped over the line she'd drawn for herself, but she had to know. "Lord Vandeimen has been out of the country?"

"No, señora. He returned to England in February, but has spent his time in London."

"What of Major Hawkinville?"

"He is with the army still. Even after battle and victory there remains a great deal for the Quartermaster-General's Department to do."

"It would be better if he were in England, though, would it not?"

Susan knew she was showing more personal interest than was wise, but she fretted about Con. If there was some problem with Lord Vandeimen, then this other friend would help. The Rogues did not seem to have penetrated the shell, and the Georges—the triumvirate—were lifelong friends.

"Lord Vandeimen visited his estate just before we left, señora," Sarmiento said. "He was in the company of the rich woman who is to be his wife. He will now be able to restore Steynings to its former state. But alas, we had to come here before there was chance of a meeting."

Susan realized that she was being told these things deliberately. Lord Vandeimen returned to his home and Con moved to Devon? There'd been no particular reason for him to come here now. And he'd sent no word.

It had been an impulse? A sudden need to escape?

She didn't need more concerns, more twists in the tangle, but she couldn't not care.

"And the Rogues?" she asked.

The valet's eyes lit. "Ah, the Rogues! *¡Qué hombres más admirables!* We spent much time with some of them in the winter." He shivered dramatically, but still smiled. "The hunting. In what they called the Shires. They chase around all day after a fox. Why a fox, I ask? It cannot be eaten. But the English, they spend a fortune on horses to chase a fox. They spend another fortune protecting the fox so it can be chased. They are mad, the English, but the Rogues, they are magnificent. And after that we went to London, also with the Rogues. My master, he seemed happy then, but underneath is still the sadness."

"Lord Darius?"

She'd startled him again. "He has told you of Lord Dare?"

Did Con speak so little of something that obviously mattered so much to him?

Sarmiento said, "A happy soul, Lord Dare, and worth mourning, but the darkness is not really Lord Dare, señora. It is war. War, she is like a fire that men walk through. As long as they do not see how hot it is, it does not burn. But then," he added with an eloquent gesture, "if that changes . . ."

Susan swallowed. She didn't want to know this. She didn't want to know that Con was suffering when there was nothing she could do. "And Lady Anne?"

"Lady Anne?" He seemed confused for a moment, but then said, "Ah. So kind and pretty."

What she wanted to know was whether Lady Anne was helping Con deal with his devils, but to ask would be to go too far. She excused herself and went to deal with a question about peas, knowing she should force all she'd learned out of her mind.

It was impossible.

Con was at outs with the Georges? Because they were both connected to the war?

He was still close to the Rogues, but they didn't seem to be helping him.

It particularly worried her that he appeared to have come here expressly to avoid Lord Vandeimen.

She went into the pantry to check that the silver had been polished properly. "Stop it!" she muttered, pushing a drawer closed. She was powerless, and going around and around these things was likely to drive her mad.

Diddy came in. "The curate's here, ma'am."

Susan turned to go, but Diddy added, "The earl's got him. Taken him up to the Wyvern rooms. Wish I could see Mr. Rufflestowe's face when he sees that lot!"

So did Susan, but it reminded her of the fountain. She sent for Con's men, Pearce and White, and asked them to look at it to see how it could be taken apart. White was a mere child, pale and nervy, but Pearce was a substantial man who might be able to do the job. She told him to hire more hands from the villages if needed.

Then she set out to search Crag Wyvern for clever hiding places. Con, as far as she knew, was still upstairs with Mr. Rufflestowe, and de Vere was in the office, presumably engrossed. If the gold was hidden in there it would be difficult to find. The man seemed unlikely to leave the room!

That had been one of the places she'd searched thoroughly, however, and it was hard to imagine a large concealed compartment that she hadn't found.

Thought of de Vere made her be systematic in her search rather than using her usual method—depending on inspiration. She considered where to start.

The great hall was an unlikely spot, since it was frequently used as a passageway. The kitchens and servants' areas could never reliably be private, and she'd never known the earl to go there.

Very well, on the ground floor that left the dining room, breakfast room, drawing room, and library.

She went first to the dining room, pushing aside all memory of the previous night. She had searched this room—she had searched everywhere—but now she tried to find clever, concealed hiding places.

The plain painted walls made this easier. It was impossible that there was a secret compartment behind them that could be accessed at will. She checked the dark oak floor and the plain ceiling and reached the same conclusion. There was an ornate plaster cornice but no other decoration, and she couldn't see how the cornice could disguise any useful opening.

Determined to be meticulous, she made her eyes travel the room again, seeking out anything suspicious. She didn't find it, but when her eyes passed over the glass-paned doors into the garden she wondered if the gold was hidden out there.

But no. She'd rarely seen the earl go there, either. He'd preferred to move around the house using the outer corridors. She'd never thought of it before, but it had been as if even the enclosed openness of the garden had been too much for his irrational fear.

Even if he'd been in the habit of sneaking out to dig and bury at night, the garden had been under Mrs. Lane's assiduous care. She would surely have noticed the ground being disturbed.

Through a bush she could see Pearce over by the fountain. She resisted the distraction of going to see what he thought.

She moved on to the breakfast room, which with its monastic simplicity was easy to cross off the list. When she went back into the corridor, she realized that she had to consider the corridors themselves. But the outer walls were not of medieval thickness, and the inner walls were even thinner unless there was some very skillful disguise work somewhere.

She'd leave them for last.

She followed the corridors to the great hall, however, scrutinizing the surfaces all around, and then went on to the drawing room. Having been carved out of one end of the hall, it alone did not have doors into the garden. There was only one window, and the room was poorly lit during the day.

With paneled walls set with silk wallpaper, and elaborate plasterwork in the ceiling, it was a promising site for a hiding place, but it was only five years old, and she had been involved in some of its design.

She was almost certain that no hiding place of any substance could have been built in. She made her eye seek for any thickening, any unusual crack or line. . . .

"Looking for something?"

She spun around to see Con standing in the doorway watching her.

"Cobwebs," she said hastily. "It's one of my housekeeperly duties."

"Poor spiders. Mr. Rufflestowe is suitably shocked by the books and manuscripts, and thoroughly enjoying himself. I've left him to it. How are we doing with the fountain?"

We.

She put that aside. "I've set your men to the task. You could go and discuss it with them."

"Why don't we go together?"

Oh, no. She glanced at the fob watch dangling from her high belt, though there was no duty hovering. "I am needed in the kitchens, my lord."

She expected some further argument but he merely said, "Very well," and walked out.

She blew out a breath, accepting that there was regret in her as well as relief. She wanted to spend time with Con, but she was determined to be sensible, which meant she must avoid him whenever possible.

Since the drawing room had only the one door out into the great hall, she waited a few minutes before cautiously leaving.

Con wasn't lurking.

She was a little disappointed about that, too.

Truly, she was in a perilous state of mind, and the sooner she was away from here the better.

Having said she was needed in the kitchens, she felt obliged to go there. As she crossed the hall, however, she glanced out of a window, and saw Con in the garden down to his shirtsleeves, helping his men raise the dragon off its unwilling bride.

It would appear that the parts of the fountain were separate, but it did look strangely as if they were forcing the monster off the woman. Rescuing her.

She changed direction and ran up the circular stairs and along the corridor to the nearest room. She sneaked up to the window to watch.

The dragon was lying on the ground now, on a path, thank heavens, not on a bed of plants, but the woman still sprawled there. Free of water and rapist, she looked embarrassingly rapturous.

Were fear and rapture so close? Was rapture from the same root as rape? She must look that up. It certainly would cast a strange light on things.

Con leaped agilely onto the stone rim of the fountain and extended a hand for some tool. He'd unfastened his cuffs and rolled up the sleeves of his shirt. He'd taken off his cravat too, so his shirt was open at the neck.

He looked stunningly loosened, vulnerable, powerful, approachable. . . .

She breathed deeply as she watched him begin to work on something, a bolt probably, to release the figure.

Susan realized her hand was tight on the silk curtains—black silk embroidered with dragons. She was in the Chinese bedroom—the room where Con had slept the first night. This was the same window from which Con had watched her that first morning.

Yesterday morning. A lifetime in a day.

She should go. She shouldn't expose herself to this, and she certainly shouldn't let him see her here, watching him as he had watched her.

But she only eased back slightly. He seemed unlikely to look up. He was intent on his task, as if freeing the bronze figure was crucial to him.

Of course. In Spain he had almost raped a woman. Now he was freeing one. She ached for his obvious anguish, but rejoiced over it too. It must be easy for soldiers to grow numb to violence, but he hadn't.

Of course he hadn't. He was Con.

She realized she was crushing the precious curtain and carefully unclenched her hand, then smoothed it out. These Chinese dragons were a symbol of spirit and joy, but Con didn't have a Chinese dragon on his chest. He'd chosen a Saint George dragon, the evil oppressor who demanded the innocent as tribute. The dragon like the one in the fountain that violated all that was pure and good.

Why?

Why, when he'd always wanted to be Saint George?

She watched him toss the tool back to young White, then begin to lever the figure up off the base, legs braced, forearms taut with muscle. He wasn't a heavy man, but he was all muscle.

She realized she was licking her dry lips.

The big man, Pearce, used a thick stick to help, and then grabbed the woman's spread ankles so that she could be lifted over the side and onto the ground beside her slain tormentor.

Con threw his jacket over her.

Susan stepped back, taking what seemed to be her first deep breath in minutes. Even if Con had a dragon on his chest, he was still the heroic George. He could never be anything else.

And she must wish him happy with his chosen bride.

She couldn't resist one last temptation, however.

She left the room and went back downstairs to the library, hoping that neither Rufflestowe nor de Vere was there. She had every right to enter, but guilty conscience makes an innocuous task suspect, and she planned to check on Con's beloved.

The place was somnolently empty. Almost dormant, in fact.

Though full of books the library had been little used. The earl had kept his favorite books in his room like a squirrel hoarding nuts. The library had been given a thorough cleaning recently, but it had a sad air of neglect.

It contained a reasonably recent *Peerage*, however, and she took it down and opened it on the table.

Lady Anne Peckworth . . .

She soon had the entry. Middle of three daughters of the Duke of Arran. She was twenty-one years old, and both her younger and older sisters were married when this book was compiled two years before.

She frowned slightly, wondering why Lady Anne was still on the shelf. Idiotic to fret whether she was worthy of Con—he'd made his choice—but Susan did. He must have the best, a sterling woman who adored him. The prosaic details on the page revealed nothing about Lady Anne's qualities, however, or about her feelings.

How could she not adore Con?

Was it a long-standing engagement, delayed by the war? But in that case they would surely have married as soon as possible, not still be unwed nearly a year after Waterloo.

No matter how long she looked at the closely printed page, it offered no more enlightenment. She closed the heavy book, creating a flurry of paper dust, and tried to close her pointless and intrusive curiosity. All the same, she was thinking that if she left Crag Wyvern and went a-traveling, she could go to Lea Park and investigate Lady Anne. If she wasn't worthy of Con, she could . . .

What? Murder her?

With a wry laugh, she placed the book back on the shelf. This was no more her business than was the good government of India.

She turned to leave the room, then realized that she might as well search for the gold.

She'd recently supervised the spring cleaning, and every book had been taken out and wiped over; every shelf had been dusted. She had surreptitiously checked at the time for false compartments behind the books.

She went over to the window seat and opened it to check it again. Of course, the space inside was still the right size for the external dimensions.

She straightened, hands on hips and frustrated. Where the devil would the demented earl have hidden his gold? Probably closer to the Wyvern rooms, but that meant the whole upper floor, including the corridors, and the hidey-hole could have been built before she was born, perhaps even into the very fabric of the Crag.

Searching for it was beginning to look like a labor of Hercules.

She glanced out into the garden again, wondering how the fountain project was going. And yes, she admitted, hoping for another glimpse of Con. From the ground level she didn't have a clear view, but it looked as if Con and the men had gone.

Curious, she opened the doors into the courtyard and went out.

Yes, they'd definitely gone. She walked to the center and found that the dragon and the maiden had been taken away, but the chain remained, still connected to the rock at one end, the other end trailing limply into the dry basin. She wondered idly what Con would do with the two bronze figures. She almost felt the bride should have a decent burial.

All that remained was the rock in the middle upon which the bride had lain, and a simple metal pipe sticking up at one side where it had fed into the dragon. She wondered if they could still have the music of the fountain without the figures. The water would just splash onto the rock.

She went to the valve and began to turn the wheel.

It took about three complete turns before the water passed through, and it had to be fully open for the fountain to operate properly. She turned it quickly.

A spout of water exploded up. It pulsed roof-high then rained down again to hit the rock and splash out in a crazy pattern all around. Thoroughly soaked, she danced back, but she couldn't help laughing with childish delight. She looked up at the tall spout, then down at the diamond-sparkling water shooting erratically around, spraying grateful flowers and bushes.

And then she saw Con watching from the other side of the courtyard.

He was still in shirtsleeves, and suddenly, he smiled.

At her, probably, at her being wet and laughing at the water, but she didn't mind. He was smiling a smile she remembered with joy.

It was silly, it was nothing, but she couldn't help the laughter bubbling up and bursting free like the fountain water. She put her hand over her mouth, but couldn't stop.

It could only have been a moment, but her stomach was beginning to ache when she heard him say, "Don't you think you should shut it off?"

Gasping, she saw that he'd come close, over to the other side of the basin, but carefully in a spot between two arms of spray.

"It seems a shame," she managed to say.

"Such untrammeled pleasure in Crag Wyvern?"

The mad hilarity was simmering down. She wanted to say something about untrammeled pleasure, but had sense enough not to. She turned toward the wheel, but paused.

The deflected jet that had first caught her was still spraying the wheel, as if to prevent anyone putting an end to its freedom. She looked back at Con but he merely raised his brows, still grinning at her. She took a deep breath, prepared, and ran for the wheel, turning it despite the drenching spray.

The water stopped hitting her, but she heard a yell.

She turned and saw that the pattern of spray had changed now that the pressure was lower, and Con had been completely drenched.

Laughter won again, but then turned into a smile of simple delight. His hair was flattened to his head, water ran all down him, but he was standing there as if welcoming it, arms spread.

Shirt plastered to him. Breeches plastered to him . . .

She grabbed the wheel, but her hands seemed slippery and somehow weaker. Perhaps the water was truly fighting to be free. Suddenly hands were there to help her—strong hands, brown hands, hands marked with scars. Together they turned the wheel, shutting off the water completely.

In the last splashes and into silence, she looked up at Con.

He was no longer smiling, though something of it lingered in his eyes.

"Revenge of the water?" he said.

"I think it hated being forced through that fountain."

"Perhaps it just hated being forced."

His shirt showed every contour of his chest, and was almost transparent. It showed a dark shadow on the right side.

It could not be ignored.

She wanted to touch it but did not dare. She had to speak of it, however. "A dragon, I understand."

He seemed puzzled, but then his faced cleared. "Ah, the lusty maid saw it. Diddy, yes? We all had tattoos done—Van, Hawk, and I. The idea was that if we were searching for one another's mangled bodies, we'd find the task easier. Not a bad notion, as it turned out."

The sudden bleakness was not because of Crag Wyvern or herself.

"Who could you not find? Lord Darius?"

"There were so many dead and dying," he said, looking away again, but not in a way that broke the magic, "and some had been stripped, or trampled, or blown apart." He shook his head. "You don't want to talk about such things." He turned to the fountain. "What do you think we should put in place of the dragon?"

She wouldn't let the connection break without a fight. There would be only brief moments like this, when once they might have been eternal. "He was a Rogue, you said. I remember you speaking of them."

He looked back at her, dark, but not because of her, not directed at her, thank heaven. "You remember a great deal."

She hesitated a moment, then said, "I remember everything, Con."

His lips twisted. "So do I." But then he inhaled. "Yes, he was a Rogue. He wasn't a soldier, though. He shouldn't have been there. I should have stopped him."

"Perhaps he didn't want to be stopped."

"I should have stopped him anyway. Or prepared him better. Or—" He suddenly looked her over, and she knew, with clarity, that he'd remembered everything, and firmly closed a door. "That gray stuff would hide a tattoo, but it isn't hiding much, you know."

She looked down and saw that of course her dress was molded to her body as much as his shirt was to him. Her corset shielded her upper body, but her belly, her thighs, the indentation between her thighs . . .

Face flaming, she pulled the cloth away, flapping it to try to make it not adhere. She glanced at him and couldn't help a shiver of excitement at the look in his eyes, even though it wasn't proper, or respectful, or even particularly kind.

"You're not hiding much either," she said, and let her eyes look at his breeches.

"I know."

Her heart started to pound.

"Are you as curious as I am, Susan? To know what it would be like? Now."

Curious and more than curious. A warm heaviness grew inside her, an ache. . . .

After a moment she managed to say, "What of Lady Anne?"

"She isn't here, is she?"

Ah. Her throat tightened. She made herself swallow.

Curiosity. That was all it was for him.

For her it was a longing which went much deeper, but she wouldn't do this. She wouldn't be a convenient release and she wouldn't offend against the woman he had chosen, even if she wasn't here. She wouldn't reduce herself to a whore, not even for Con. It would destroy them both.

"She is here in spirit," she said, and stepped back. "I must go and change, my lord." She looked at the fountain behind him, however.

"I think it should be a Saint George," she said. "Crag Wyvern needs a hero to vanquish the dark."

Then she walked briskly into the house.

Chapter Fifteen

Con turned and leaned his hands against the rough, cold rim of the basin, looking down at the inches of water glimmering there.

Saint George.

A hero.

Where had that youthful idealist gone?

Susan had hurt him deeply but she hadn't killed the hero. The war had done that. Oh, officially it had made him a kind of hero. He hadn't been the dashing sort to attract a lot of notice, but he knew he'd done his job well for the benefit of his men, his general, and his king. Hawk had told him that Wellington had referred to him once as a "damned fine officer," which was praise enough for any man.

But the endless years, though full of excitement, triumph, and even pleasure among the bleaker times, had killed the saint. He didn't fear what the future would do to him, but what he might do to others in his soulless state.

Some fortune-tellers claimed to be able to reveal the future from reflections in water. What would anyone make of his?

He'd summoned Lady Anne as his defense, and now she was a barrier. Susan wouldn't come to his bed because of Lady Anne.

That was what he wanted, wasn't it?

What he wanted, ferociously, was Susan.

The sight of her laughing uncontrollably at the unpredictable spray had cracked something and carried him straight back to the sun-shimmered past. Then the sight of her body, lusher, more womanly in its mysteries, but still Susan, had undone him.

He couldn't let himself be used again, and despite the soulless need throbbing in him, he wouldn't use her. But could he bear to leave here without experiencing Susan as she was now?

He could always tell her that Lady Anne was a possibility rather than a commitment. Tempt her with the chance of winning Crag Wyvern for herself. She'd claimed she didn't want it anymore, but it must be a lie. Why else was she here?

He suddenly had a wicked vision of Susan—womanly, experienced Susan—setting her mind to seducing him. . . .

But Lady Anne was more than a possibility. He'd sent that letter.

And she was the perfect, ideal wife for him.

If Susan married him, it would be for Crag Wyvern. Since he had no intention of spending more than a duty week or so a year here she would be miserable.

No, Susan would never wallow in misery. She'd fight for what she wanted. He'd seen men married to women determined to change them and their circumstances to suit. Seen them nagged into joining the army, leaving the army, changing regiments, spending beyond their means, saving beyond sanity.

No peace in those homes. He'd told Susan the truth about his ambitions. What he longed for above all was peace. Peace and gentle pleasures in Somerford Court, where he thought he might eventually rediscover his soul, and perhaps even his youthful ideals.

He leaned down, scooped some of the water, and splashed it over his face. It was warm from the sun by now, however, and did no good.

He pushed away from the fountain and walked back into the house. He'd change and ride out again. It was the only safe thing to do.

Susan was shivering by the time she stripped off her wet dress, and it wasn't entirely from the cold. She'd never expected to feel such urgent, physical need for a man. She hadn't known it existed!

With Con all those years ago it had been an unknown, a mystery. With Rivenham it had been a plan. He'd brought her to desire, but it had been a deliberate path for both of them.

With Captain Lavalle it had been a plan again, but a huge mistake. Physically it had been nothing.

Worse than nothing.

It had been disgusting.

Now, without even touching Con, she ached, she burned for him. Out there in the garden, she'd longed to touch him, to press against the hard muscles his wet shirt had so tantalizingly revealed, to embrace him, to comfort him, to be comforted and healed. . . .

She thumped down on the edge of her bed, still in her damp corset and shift, trying to understand this unexpected force.

She knew she *loved*. That was a force of its own, but it was one she could rule with willpower. She loved, and because she loved it was possible not to show it, not to distress him with it, and to let him go to the woman he had chosen.

But this . . . this was more elemental. Part of the ache, she was sure, was from struggling not to act, as if battling a fierce wind, or the pull of a stormy sea. It seemed all too likely that the force could overwhelm her, sweeping her into disaster.

Disaster for them both.

She shuddered, then stood to strip off the rest of her clothes, to rub herself sternly with a towel until her skin burned and the ache subsided.

She had to leave. Immediately. She had no explanation she could give anyone, but Con would understand. She'd return to the manor, and then go elsewhere—

She stilled, seeing many problems.

She had no money until the Horde was prosperous again.

She had nowhere to go, and no easy chance of employment. . . .

It didn't matter. For both their sakes, she had to at least leave Crag Wyvern. Mrs. Gorland could manage the household until a new housekeeper was hired.

She'd claim she was ill.

At the moment she felt almost ill.

She pulled on a dry shift and added another working corset. She took out her second gray dress and put it on. If she was leaving she could dress in ordinary clothes—but this was armor.

Yet it hadn't protected her from Con. . . .

She thrust away memory and added a starched fichu. She redid her hair, pinning it up tightly, and put on a cap, tying the laces.

It wasn't enough.

There could never be enough.

There was no protection except distance.

She looked at her possessions—books, needlework, ornaments. What could she carry them in?

She couldn't delay to pack them. She had to go now.

She walked out into the kitchen.

"We're almost out of butter, ma'am," Mrs. Gorland said. "And I could do with a nice sirloin."

Susan longed to rush by but duty made her pause. "Send down to Ripford for the beef, and buy as much butter as you need from the village."

"Very well, ma'am." Then the cook looked at her. "Are you all right, dear?"

The switch from business to personal was almost too much for Susan, but she found a smile. "Yes, of course, but I need to go down to the manor again."

"That's all right. We can manage fine."

"I know. Thank you." Susan left, wishing she could take a proper farewell of them all.

She felt she should sneak out by one of the small doors, but the main entrance was closest, so she headed there via the great hall. When she walked into that space a man was waiting.

Con!

No, not Con, thank heavens. Just Lieutenant Gifford. But he was someone else to talk to before she was free.

"Lieutenant. May I help you?"

He looked at her and blushed. She'd swear it was a blush. She looked down at her hastily put on clothes, but she couldn't see anything embarrassingly amiss.

He reached up and tugged at his military stock. "I came to speak to the earl, Mistress Kerslake. A maid is looking for him. For me . . ."

Speak to Con? About smuggling? And Con probably knew David was Captain Drake and might say something. Surely he wouldn't . . .

She couldn't deal with this now.

Dear heaven. Con would be coming here at any moment!

"Then if you'll excuse me, sir, I have an errand to run."

She moved to one side to go around him, but he blocked her way.

"I . . . I would prefer you kept me company for a while."

She looked up at him, trying to focus her mind on this. "I beg your pardon?"

"I would prefer your company," he said more firmly, looking a little alarmed, but also a great deal determined.

Insane humor tried to bubble up.

Was he going to propose to her?

Here?

Now?

She stepped to the side again. "My errand is urgent, Lieutenant—"

He blocked her again. "So is mine. Please, you will want to hear what I have to say."

Devil spit. Con could be here at any moment, or the maid returning to take Gifford to him! She pushed him hard on the chest with both hands, prepared to run if necessary. But he only fell back a step before grasping her wrists.

"Release me!" she hissed, wishing she dared scream for help. "Lord Wyvern will be here directly. He will not like to see you holding me prisoner like this."

"Got to you already, has he? That'll have to stop."

"What?" Either she was mad or he was.

He looked around wildly, clearly checking to see if anyone could see them. He was flushed again, but this time with excitement. It glittered in his eyes.

"I couldn't quite believe it," he said rapidly, quietly, as if they shared a secret. "But I saw you and the earl out in the courtyard. Only lovers look at one another like that, Susan. And to think I was advancing on your defenses so politely."

"Lieutenant—"

"Giles, Susan. Giles."

"Lieutenant . . ."

The flash of fury in his eye stole words for a moment. She made herself relax in his grip and look at him calmly. "Lieutenant, I'm very sorry but I could not possibly marry you—"

His eyes widened, and then he laughed. "Dear lady, I'm not after marriage. I want what Captain Lavalle enjoyed."

Heavenly mercies. Her legs threatened to betray her. She'd always feared this, that the cad would talk of it to other officers. It had been so many years, though. . . .

Too late, she tried to bluff. "I don't know what you're talking about."

"Oh yes you do. Keen for it, Lavalle said, and now I see how right he was. The earl's only been here two nights and he's clearly had you. So now it's my turn. You're a fine looking woman, Susan. I find you a real cock-stirrer, especially in your starchy gray and white, your hair all tucked up under that cap. . . ."

He was pushing her backward and she went, unable to think what to do.

Her hips hit the center table and he trapped her there, licking his lips as he did so, pressing himself against her, trying to part her thighs.

"Are you mad?" she said in a frantic whisper. "Release me immediately!"

"A mere lieutenant not good enough for you after an earl?" He pressed harder so the table dug into her.

"Stop or I'll scream," she hissed, meaning it, though then he'd tell Con about Lavalle. *Oh, God. Oh, God . . .*

"No, you won't. Or I'll arrest your brother as Captain Drake."

Her throat seized up.

He knew.

No, she realized, her wits sharpening—he guessed.

She made herself meet his eyes and look astonished. "David? A smuggler? You *are* mad."

"David, son of Mel Clyst, Susan, just as you're daughter of Mel Clyst."

He stepped back and let her free, clearly confident now that she wouldn't run. Should she run to prove David's innocence?

Before she could decide, he said, "I wondered why you weren't respectably married by now, but you're not Miss Kerslake of Kerslake Manor, are you? You're the bastard daughter of a smuggler and a whore, and truly your mother's daughter, by what I heard from Lavalle."

"Whatever he told you, he lied. I assume men often boast of these things if they think they can get away with it. He tried to seduce me, yes. Five years ago, I think. He did not take my rejection well."

She saw a flicker of uncertainty and pushed her advantage. "I'd thought better of you, Lieutenant, than to believe such doubtless boozy talk."

Uncertainty disappeared. "He wasn't drunk, Susan, he was dying. We shared a mat on the ground in the crowded surgeon's tent after Albuera. I survived, and he didn't. But we talked of home, and one of the things he talked about was you. A beautiful, well-bred lady who'd just about begged him to tumble her. But he'd found out later she wasn't really a well-bred lady, and her mother was a whore, so it hadn't been such a miracle after all."

Susan couldn't think what to say, but relief was washing over her in a dizzying wave. It was possible that Lavalle hadn't talked of her in every mess tent in the Peninsula.

But she still had Gifford to deal with.

"Be my whore, *Mistress* Kerslake, and your brother will be safe."

Lord, and she'd thought Gifford a good man! Surrender? Or fight.

Fight, of course.

"My brother is the earl's estate manager," she said flatly, "and you, sir, are a cad."

He paled, but his lips tightened. "But you won't be telling the earl what I've done, will you?"

"He'd probably think that I'm as mad as you are. I doubt you're brave enough to admit your words to him."

"So he is your lover, is he?"

She met his eyes. "No. If I try to continue on my way, Lieutenant, are you going to manhandle me again?"

She had him rattled. He even bit his lower lip.

But then he stood straighter. "A week from now," he said. "When the moon is too full for the plaguey smugglers. Come to my rooms at the Crown and Anchor." His grim smile showed that he had his nerve back.

"The local smugglers have been trying for months to find a way to pay me off," he added. "Well, now they have it. For as long as you please me, Susan, you can be the payment."

Footsteps saved her from having to find a response. Both she and Gifford turned as Con walked in.

He paused.

What did they look like, standing so close together?

Con's face was expressionless as he came forward. "Lieutenant Gifford."

Gifford bowed. "My lord."

He sounded half strangled by sudden nerves, and Susan felt a bubble of laughter threatening. She kept forgetting that Con was an earl, that he was supposed to be regarded with awe and trembling.

Ah, no. She could do the awe and trembling very well indeed.

She knew that if she told him what Gifford had threatened, showed him the marks that had to be on her wrists, he would destroy Gifford for her. Doubtless here and now.

But she couldn't, because she'd have to tell him why.

And she didn't want to bring about Gifford's destruction. He'd been led astray by Lavalle's story, which had been essentially true. As with her other sorrows, she had brought this on herself.

Now, however, flight to the manor seemed pointless. The enemies were outside as well as in.

Con and Gifford had been speaking together, and now Con indicated that Gifford should accompany him. "Mrs. Kerslake," he said to her with chilly formality, "please have refreshments sent to the library."

She pulled on the manner of the perfect housekeeper, and curtsied. "Yes, my lord."

Con led Gifford across the garden to the library, wishing he had an excuse to plant the man a facer. Gifford and Susan? Damnation, why would a Preventive man take up with a smuggler's daughter?

Perhaps he didn't know.

Gifford made some inane remark about the garden, and Con replied. He could drop the information into conversation. He assumed they were about to talk about smuggling.

They were passing the fountain basin and he remembered what had been there. He could not betray Susan. He was a dragon, but not a dragon of the foulest sort. Gifford was bound to find out soon, and if Con was any judge, that would be the end of any chance of a marriage, but it wouldn't come at his hands.

But then he wondered, if Susan was encouraging Gifford, did she truly not want Crag Wyvern anymore?

Or was she encouraging Gifford in the Dragon's Horde's cause?

The momentary hope faded.

Of course she was.

Poor Gifford.

Victim of the dragon in another way.

Susan gave the order for the refreshments, then scurried off to hide in her room.

What in the name of heaven did she do now?

She circled her haven, clutching her useless cap. She needed to warn David, but she didn't want to tell him about Gifford's threat. David always seemed levelheaded, but no man was going to stay levelheaded if told about his sister being blackmailed into whoredom!

He might challenge Gifford to a duel.

As Captain Drake, he might order Gifford killed out of hand.

That would be so wrong, and it would be disastrous to have yet another riding officer die on this stretch of coast. They'd end up with troops every few feet, and once the local smuggling master was caught, they'd find a way to hang him. If not, he too would doubtless fall off a cliff.

Gifford's threat was hollow. He couldn't arrest David. He had no proof. But now he'd be watching David and this area like a hawk.

She dropped her hands and sighed. She couldn't tell David any more than she could tell Con, because she'd have to tell them about Lavalle. Of all the things she had done of which she was ashamed, Captain Lavalle was the worst.

She wanted *no one* to know, and now it appeared that Lavalle had talked of it.

While she'd been speaking with Gifford she'd felt sure that Lavalle had only spoken about her when he'd been dying, but what if he'd shared the story with dozens? Or what if Gifford had spread it about since? No, no, he wouldn't do that. It was his weapon. But what if . . . ?

She recognized the ache of weak tears and fought them. But they broke free and she collapsed in a chair, trying not to sob out loud, trying to keep the storm quiet with her hand. That seemed to force the misery back painfully into her chest, into her bruised and aching heart. . . .

She managed to control it in the end, but Lord, she hurt. Her chest ached, and her throat, and her eyes burned. She couldn't imagine where the term "a good cry" came from.

But slowly she did begin to feel better.

Not good. But better.

She'd learned in the past that some things couldn't be changed and that the world did not crash to its end because of one person's anguish. She'd learned that life must be dealt with as it was, not as she wished it to be. She'd learned that she could not take life in her hands like wet clay and mold it.

This was simply another bruising lesson.

She stood and blew her nose. Her mirror showed her red and swollen eyes. How could she face anyone like this?

She ripped off her scratchy fichu, however, and her confining cap. Clearly they were not armor at all. In fact, she remembered with a shudder, Gifford had said they excited him!

With a shock of laughter she wondered if she was going about this in the wrong way. Perhaps if she flitted around the place half-dressed Con would not be affected, and men like Gifford would shy away!

But no. Her low bodice last night had not been safe either.

Gifford had given her a week.

A week to decide what to do.

A week to find the gold.

Which meant a week here, with Con, and already in two days things were getting out of hand. That force, that power that had driven her to run was still swirling through Crag Wyvern.

But the gold was the answer.

With the gold, David could lie low for months. Gifford could watch him until his eyes dried to raisins and not find a thing.

And with the gold, David could pay back the loans she had made. She could move far away. In fact, she thought, excited by the idea, she'd ask David to come with her to help her settle.

Bath perhaps. No, too close.

London.

Scotland?

Could she get him to take her to Italy?

The farther the better.

Perhaps she could keep him away for weeks, a month, even more. He'd have to return, of course. He'd have to be in danger in the future, but the critical danger would be past.

Gifford would surely forget about her once she was far away. He'd still suspect David, but the Preventives had more than suspected Mel. They'd simply not been able to catch him at it or prove anything.

Until helped by the old earl, apparently, damn his black heart.

Yes, that was a plan. For now, however, this was an excellent time to search for the gold.

Con was with Gifford in the library, and de Vere was presumably in the office engaged in his love affair with accounts. The bedrooms upstairs should be deserted.

She slipped out of the kitchen area without attracting attention and headed for the circular stairs. As she passed a window into the garden, however, she saw movement.

It was de Vere, out of the office, for once. It was one of the rooms she knew best, and had searched most carefully. She was almost sure that the money could not be hidden there, but she had better check one last time.

Chapter Sixteen

As soon as Susan entered she saw the effects of a new hand. The standish and pens were arranged differently. Piles of papers stood around the desk, each with a note on top. She glanced at them and saw one note saying, *Further investigation.*

What had de Vere found?

She flicked through that short pile but found nothing about smuggling. It contained mostly bills, and she supposed there was no record of payment.

It only took moments to assure herself that there was no hiding place she'd overlooked. However, she saw a small wooden box on the desk that had been tucked in a drawer for years. She opened it and found it half-full of scraps of paper, even chunks torn out of printed books.

She recognized the old earl's scribbled notes. De Vere must be collecting them as he found them. She took them out and flicked through them.

Some were nonsense. Some were clear. *Look up nao cha.* Some were cryptic. *Bats or cats? That is the question.* Two pieces made her frown, though.

One said: *Mel and Belle. Belle and Mel. Who should tell? Toll the bell.*

Another said: *Mel and Belle, Belle and Mel. Go to hell. To demon's land, in fact! Ha! Ha!*

"Ha! Ha!"? What a childish form of madness that illustrated, but what had impelled him to write these notes?

Gifford had hinted that the earl had played some part in Mel's capture, and the notes certainly showed animosity.

Why? Why would the earl have planned trouble for Mel and Lady Belle? Smuggling had provided the money he'd used to indulge in his mad pursuit of an heir. Until the end he'd seemed an enthusiastic supporter.

Did a madman need reasons?

She shrugged and put the notes back in the box. Whatever had stirred in his deranged mind, it was history now. He was dead, and Mel and Belle were at the other side of the world. She went to the globe that stood on its stand beside the courtyard window, turning it to look at Australia, so very far away.

She still couldn't forgive Lady Belle for taking all the money without regard to her son's safety, but perhaps she understood a little better now. Con's return had taught her something of the power of love, and now she knew the power of desire.

Her experiences with Rivenham and Lavalle had made her shut off that part of herself, made her deny that it existed. Easy enough when she hadn't met a man who tempted her.

She suspected now that she was beyond temptation. Eleven years ago, in two weeks of sunshine and friendship and one day of sinful exploration, she had been captured for all time.

She spun the globe idly.

Con had not been as trapped as she, thank heavens. He had escaped the shadows of that day to find love elsewhere, and it was proof that sometimes life was just. He'd done nothing wrong.

Her eyes were looking at the globe without seeing it, but something alerted her brain.

South of Australia. An island.

Van Deimen's Land . . .

To demon's land.

Dragon spit! The mad earl *had* planned to send Mel to the penal colonies of Australia! It sounded as if he'd planned for Lady Belle to go there too, but that was impossible unless he'd guessed that she'd do something so outrageous.

Did he know her well enough to be able to predict what she'd do? Susan wasn't aware of the earl and Lady Belle knowing one another at all, except, she supposed, as members of local society growing up together.

But even if he had planned to send them both off to "demon's land," why?

His madness had been a cunning sort, not completely wild. He'd always had reason for the things he did.

Why?

She was staring out of the doors into the garden as she thought, and she suddenly drew back. De Vere had come out of the library doors, and was heading this way.

She turned and walked quickly out of the room. The mad earl was history and she had an urgent present to deal with.

For the rest of the afternoon, between dealing with routine matters, she checked all the bedrooms for secret spaces. Nothing. To take care of the corridors she set Ellen, Diddy, and Ada to sweeping and dusting them, telling them to check as they went for cracks in the walls.

After a visit to the kitchen to check that all was in order for dinner, she climbed to the top floor, which would be the attics in a normal house. Here most of the space was taken by two large water cisterns.

The big one on the west side held water for the house, including the fountain, and was original to the house. Because the house sat on the cliff, the water was pumped up from the village by a clever screw design worked by horses. The smaller one on the north, above the Saint George rooms, held and heated the water for the Roman bath. That drew water from the main cistern by a gravity feed. Beneath it a stone hearth held charcoal to heat the water.

She noted that her orders were being followed. The fire was steady, and four buckets of charcoal stood nearby. If Con took it into his head to use the big bath, it would be ready for him. She was aware of a stupid tenderness about arranging such comforts for him. She was his housekeeper, for heaven's sake. She was paid to arrange every detail of his comfort.

Even so, it pleased her.

For the first time she wondered if the gold could be hidden in one of the cisterns.

She carefully opened the hatch and peered through warm steam. It would have been quite a cunning hiding place for something indestructible like gold, but there was no sign of a box or bag, or a line to anything submerged.

She went to the other, bigger cistern, and checked that. Nothing, though running the fountain so much had left the water low. She'd send a message to the village to get it filled.

She stood there smiling sadly at the memory of that encounter by the wildly spraying fountain.

Precious, but painful. A clear demonstration of what she had thrown away.

She moved on briskly to check the rest of the floor. She'd never known the old earl to come up here, but he might have sneaked up in the night. She had previously checked every box and piece of discarded furniture here. Now, she looked for more cunning places, but poke around as she might, she found nothing.

As she prepared to leave, dusting off her hands, she noted the ladder that led up to the roof. She was sure the old earl would not have gone up there—into the open, by gad!—but she might as well be thorough. She kirtled up her skirts and climbed up, unlatching and pushing open the heavy trapdoor. It stopped just past the vertical, thank heavens, or she would have had to let it fall with a shocking bang. When she climbed out, she saw that it rested against a chimney.

She'd never been up here and she found herself on a wide walkway between the slope of the roof and the chest-high battlements. She gave thanks they were chest high—it was a long way down.

Up so high, however, the breeze was a brisk wind, cool and fresh off the sea. Enjoying it, she began a circuit, noting that the roof was shallow enough not to show from outside, and that it sloped from the courtyard side to the battlements. A groove ran around the walkway, and she finally came to a hole and realized that the groove collected the rain and funneled it here, which surely led down to the water cistern.

An efficient design. It made the recently added gargoyles particularly ridiculous, however. She leaned carefully out between two merlons to look at the one on the nearest corner. On true medieval buildings they were usually waterspouts. This one snarled uselessly into nowhere.

An image of something, that. She preferred not to look at it too closely.

She was on the sea side now, and she leaned her elbows on the rough stone to look out across the Channel. On this overcast day, the distance was misty, but up close the waves rippled silver on the steel gray sea, and fishing boats bobbed industriously on it. Shrunk small by distance, a sailing ship swooped along, heading west toward the Atlantic, perhaps to Canada, or south to Spain, to Africa or India.

Or to Australia.

Gulls swirled and cried, and the sea air whipped past her skin, brisk and unbearably clean. To right or left she could see misty miles down the coast.

Other places, other people.

Places she would have to go to, people she would have to live among. The old fear of not belonging cramped in her, but she made it release. She would do what she had to do.

She continued on her way, looking out all the time, dazzled by this new view of her commonplace world. Patchwork fields spread green or brown, the new grass dotted with animals. She had an angel's view of coppices and stands of evergreens, and the occasional majestic solitary tree. Of hills and valleys and silvery hints of water.

She looked down on the cottages, farms, and church spires of her familiar life—and out at distances containing secrets, and even adventures.

When she arrived back at the trapdoor, she almost could not bear to go down.

Trap. Indeed.

She'd thought she'd evaded the trap of Crag Wyvern, but she had come here, first by day, and then to live. And she was still here when she wanted to be elsewhere. . . .

Just a little while longer.

She quickly climbed down the ladder, managing the tricky business of bringing the heavy trapdoor down behind her, then latching it, sealing out the light and air.

The upper floor felt stale and suffocating now, and she hurried away and down the circular stairs to the floor beneath. Even there she was in one of the narrow dark corridors, and she hastened on, down and down, around and around, and out at last into the fresh air of the courtyard.

She inhaled, but it wasn't the same as the air she'd breathed above.

Once again she hurried to escape Crag Wyvern, but this time she wanted only freedom and fresh air. She burst through the great entrance arch and took a deep breath.

She was in the shadow of the house, however, and she picked up her skirts and ran, ran out of shadow into light, down to the cliff edge where the wind blew off the sea, swirling her skirts and tugging her hair loose from confining pins.

The sailing ship still billowed on its way, the fishing boats still danced on closer waves, the men on board letting down nets or hauling them in. The calls of the gulls were louder here, and the vegetation was alive with insects and small birds. Delirious with delight at everything, she sat, arms around her knees, to soak it in.

How long was it since she'd done this? Simply enjoyed the air and the world around. Too long. She rolled to lie on her stomach like a child, to look down at Wyvern Cove tucked below, to watch the people coming and going, the old men working on boats, or sitting mending nets.

The salt tang of sea and seaweed mixed with the smell of fish here, but she loved it. It was part of her world. Not for much longer. But there must be other places as sweet, and she would learn to belong.

She rolled away from the view onto her back, looking up at the misty sky. She felt small, but whole, or more whole than she had for a while.

She lay there a long time, knowing she should move. She was not a child anymore, but an adult with employment and responsibilities. She should be in the house doing something. . . .

She couldn't think of anything in particular needing her attention and so she stayed where she was, feeling rested for the first time in days.

Since Con had arrived.

It was more than that, though. It was the pull of the earth.

She'd used to do this all the time, to connect to the earth with as much of her body as possible, but somewhere along the way she had forgotten.

Had it been as long ago as eleven years?

Surely she'd done this since then. But she couldn't remember when. After Con, the appeal of the open headlands and the beaches had faded. No, not faded, but become shadowed by memories and regrets.

To Aunt Miriam's delight, she'd then spent more time with her cousins doing the things young ladies were supposed to do. Young ladies were certainly not supposed to sprawl on cliff tops.

Housekeepers were not supposed to, either.

She really must get up and return to Crag Wyvern. . . .

It was as if the earth held her down with gentle hooks, however, or as if her hungry need of the earth pressed her there. She closed her eyes and let her other senses drink deeply.

Clean breeze over her skin, tugging at her hair, playing with her skirt.

Cries of gulls and curlews, faint calls from people below in the village. Children laughing. A dog barking. The ever-present rumble of waves on shingle.

All the wonderful mixed smells from plants and sea that she'd breathed in all her life.

A shadow fell across her lids. She opened her eyes, but she knew before regaining her sight who it would be.

He towered over her and she supposed she should be afraid, but all she could think was how wonderful it would be if he fell on top of her, if he kissed her. . . .

"You still like the cliffs," he said.

The sun was behind him, hiding any expression.

"Of course."

She should get up, curtsy even, but she refused to scramble to her feet like a guilty child, and the earth still hugged.

Of course, she was a very guilty housekeeper. It made her want to smile.

He suddenly sat by her feet, legs crossed, and she could see his thoughtful face. "Gifford knows your brother is Captain Drake."

She thought for a moment of denying it, but this was Con. "I know. He told me, too." She sat up. She could meet him halfway.

"Why?" he asked.

She froze, unready for the question. But then here, outside in the sunshine on the cliffs, she had someone she could tell.

"He wants to be my lover."

"What?" His gray eyes seemed suddenly to become paler, silver.

"He has an excuse," she said quickly, then realized that pushed her farther than she wanted to go.

"You have been encouraging him?" Though he hadn't moved, she felt as if he were putting space between them. Telling him everything would probably drive him from her entirely, but wise or foolish, she had to be honest.

She looked away, though, away to the side at the wandering cliffs and the ruffled edge of the sea. "Some years ago, I made a mistake with a man. I . . . I thought I wanted to make love with him. But it was a mistake." *Dear Lord. How did anyone put these things in words?*

Say it simply.

She looked him in the eye. "I encouraged a military officer to make love— No, it wasn't love. I barely knew him. Whatever you want to call it. It was my idea, though he didn't need much encouragement."

"I'm sure he didn't." She could tell nothing from his tone.

She sucked in a breath and went on. "Apparently he spoke of it to Gifford as he lay dying, so Gifford thinks I do that sort of thing all the time." She managed a shrug. "Thus, he wishes me to do it with him. In return, he'll turn a blind eye to Captain Drake and the Dragon's Horde."

She watched him, fearful of his response, but immensely lightened by depriving Gifford of the power the secret would have held. She was lightened, too, by having someone she could tell about that painful event.

But Con?

Had the wild air gone to her head that she thought she could confide her most perilous secrets to this new Con?

"I'll destroy him." It was said with cool certainty.

She grasped his arm. "No!"

Silver eyes. Dragon eyes. "I see. You are not unwilling, then?"

"Of course I am." She was still holding him, through heavy cloth, but holding him. Was this the first time she'd touched him? "Don't duel him, Con. I couldn't bear to see you hurt."

He laughed and pulled free. "You don't have much faith in me, do you?"

Oh, Lord! "In a duel anyone can be hurt! And I don't want him killed either. I detest him now, but he does not deserve death."

He closed his eyes briefly, then looked at her. "Susan, I'm an earl. I don't need to call Gifford out to deal with him. If I want him posted to the tip of Cornwall, I can do it. I can send him to India, or to the hell pits of the West Indies, or to guard Mel Clyst in Botany Bay. If I want him thrown out of the service, I can do that too."

"But that would be unjust."

Too late, she realized it sounded like a criticism rather than a protest.

"It's an unjust world. What do you want me to do?" After a moment, he added, "I think I can still act Saint George on occasion."

He said it without expression, but it carried her back.

This wasn't Irish Cove, and they were both fully dressed, but she knew he, like she, was instantly back in another lifetime, before. . . .

"I'm not a maiden." What an idiotic thing to say.

It stirred the hint of a smile. "I believe I'm aware of that."

"I mean . . ." Suddenly it seemed essential that they have truth on this. "There have been others."

"You just told me that, didn't you?"

Now she wanted to clarify that there'd been only two others, and only two other times.

"There have been others for me too," he said, quite gently. "Rather more, I assume."

"Of course. And I'm glad of it."

But this was all going wrong. Her words weren't forming into the right meanings. She struggled to her feet.

He rose beside her. "Why are you glad?"

She tried again. "I don't want you to have suffered because of what I did that day. I am sorry, Con."

Oh, how inadequate that sounded.

He looked away, turning to face the vista of sea. "It's all so long ago, Susan. And it's impossible to imagine that anything could have come of it, isn't it? Two fifteen-year-olds. Me a younger son with my way to make in the world. You a young lady not considered ready for the world at all."

He was speaking so lightly that she wanted to protest, to insist that it was more than that. But perhaps for him it had been a simpler matter. Horribly embarrassing and painful at the time, but now a thing of the distant past.

And there had been many other women.

"That's true," she said, brushing off her skirts. "Even if I had ended up in a compromised condition they would likely not have made us marry. A visit to a relative, a family paid to take care of the child . . ."

She would never have allowed that, so like her birth and upbringing except that there had never been any attempt at secrecy. But he did not need to know that.

He turned back to her. "I'll warn Gifford off. If he has any sense, he'll heed it."

"He thinks we're lovers."

He raised his brow as a query, but a blanket of . . . comfort was growing around them. He wasn't assuming she'd told Gifford they were lovers.

"He saw us by the fountain," she explained.

"We never touched by the fountain."

"Even so."

He grimaced. "Perceptive of him."

She remembered then that Con had propositioned her by the fountain—out of curiosity's sake.

"Let him think what he wants," he said flatly.

"He may think you sympathize with the smugglers, too."

He shook his head. "Susan, I'd expect you to be quicker-witted than this. I'm the *earl*, remember. He'd have to find me hauling tubs up the cliff to even think of touching me, and even then he'd be a damned fool. The whole power system of Britain would rise up in rage at the thought of one of their own being dragged into the courts over such a petty matter. I'm damn near untouchable."

She hesitated for a moment because she wasn't sure what was happening between them, what it meant, but she asked anyway. "Will you protect David, then?"

His mouth tightened, but he said, "For your sake, yes."

"For his sake, too." She put her hand on Con's arm again, deliberately this time. "He didn't choose this path. He's Mel's son. Rival gangs were threatening to invade and no one else had the authority."

"I see. Very well. But I won't be here much. You know that."

It seemed to encompass more than the issue of smuggling.

"I know." She faced it squarely. "You'll be marrying Lady Anne soon, and living in Sussex."

The wind caught a hank of her hair, blowing it wildly around her face. She realized it had lost most of its pins and she must look a mess. She moved her hand off his arm to control the hair, but he was there first.

He caught it and tucked it off her face, behind her ear. "A plait was more practical," he said with a smile.

"It escaped from that too." She couldn't help but smile back.

"I remember." His hand lingered, but then he lowered it. "We were friends once, I think."

Her heart was rapid and high. "Yes."

"And again, I hope."

She sucked in a deep breath. "So do I."

"A man can never have too many friends. On the other hand," he added lightly, "an earl seems to have only one housekeeper. Shouldn't you be keeping house?"

She laughed and stepped beside him to walk back to Crag Wyvern, feeling suddenly as if she had found the only gold that mattered. By implication he had forgiven her for the past. She'd told him the worst about herself. And they were friends.

Certainly a person could never have too many friends.

By the time they went through the door into the cool of the house, however, delight was sliding into melancholy.

They were only friends.

He'd made it clear that friendship was all that could exist between them. She could weep over that for she didn't think she could bear to be only friends with Con. It would have to spin off into more dangerous waters, and that she could not allow. Despite temptation, she would not be the cause of Con breaking his wedding vows.

Any meetings between them in the future must be few and far between, and she would see that they were well chaperoned.

Con parted from Susan without a backward look and went directly to the office. Race was at a shelf, some sort of ledger in his hands, and as usual he looked up impatiently.

"Put that away," Con said. "We're going riding."

"How do you expect me to get this straight if you keep dragging me away?"

"Is it not straight?"

"Mostly, but there are some wonderfully arcane and tantalizing aspects."

Con propped his hips against the desk. "What do you think of Lady Anne?"

Race rolled his eyes and put the ledger back on the shelf. "I think you're more interested in Susan Kerslake."

Con straightened. "Who gave you the right to use her first name?" A fight might be just what he needed.

"No one. I'm tired of trying to decide if she's Miss or Mrs. Kerslake."

The inclination to violence dissolved into laughter. "The thing I like about you, Race, is that you don't give a damn that I'm the blasted earl."

Race leaned back against the bookcase, arms folded. "As I understand it, you have plenty of friends who wouldn't give a damn either."

Con eyed him. "The other thing I like about you—liked about you—is that you don't think you're entitled to dig into my personal affairs."

"Unlike the Georges or the Rogues." Race raised a brow. "Going to run?"

"I'm more likely to throttle you."

Race smiled as if offered a treat.

"Damn it to Hades." Con pushed off from the desk and paced the room. "I thought employees were supposed to do as they're told."

"Friends aren't."

Con looked at Race, remembering that civilized little exchange with Susan.

Friends.

God!

"Nicholas Delaney lives a couple of hours' ride from here," he said, then realized that Race wouldn't know what he meant. He'd mentioned the Rogues, but not in any detail. "He founded the Rogues. Sometimes we call him King Rogue."

"You want to visit him? Sounds like a good idea, but not this late in the day with an overcast sickle-moon night to come."

"That's as well. Nick's an interfering bastard."

Race's eyes twinkled wickedly. "Sounds like just the potion."

"Don't say potion in a place like this."

"Think a demon will rise?"

"If it's one of the old earl's potions, it'll be something else that'll rise!"

Race laughed. "If I find that one, it'll make my fortune." He straightened from the bookshelves and picked up his jacket from the back of a chair. "Let's go riding, then."

Con was aware of the strength of the pull to visit Nick, to talk to him about Susan, and Anne, and smuggling, and the Georges.

And Dare.

Perhaps more than anything he wanted to talk to Nicholas Delaney about Dare. He had something of a magic touch with tricky matters.

Not today though. As Race had said, it would be a wildly impractical thing to do.

So was riding around the countryside with no purpose.

He was simply running. He'd run from Hawk in the Vale to here, and now he was running from Crag Wyvern and from Susan. But he'd have to come back here. Like a hound on a long leash, he was tethered to the thing he most feared and longed for.

He'd agreed to be friends with Susan.

He wanted to howl.

Chapter Seventeen

S usan heard that Con and de Vere had left Crag Wyvern, and she breathed a sigh of relief. It was like a pressure off her chest, though absurdly, she hated the thought of Con being any distance away.

Friends.

At least she had his protection for David.

Because she and he were friends.

It was more than she'd dreamed possible this morning.

It wasn't enough.

She made sure the dinner Con returned to would be perfect, and once again selected and prepared suitable wines. Then she checked that the table was perfectly arranged. Again, she took pathetic pleasure in doing these little things for him.

For her friend.

She could not stay here, could not be near, but perhaps there could be letters. . . .

Ah, no. She could control her feelings in letters, write and rewrite them until they said only what she wanted to say, but his letters back would kill her slowly. . . .

"Hello." David strolled in and pinched a grape from the bowl on the table. "What's the matter?"

She looked at him blankly for a moment, then said, "Oh! I asked you to come up."

"Right. *Is* something the matter? Is it Wyvern?"

"No," she said, probably too quickly. "But I do need to talk to you. Come." She led the way to the privacy of her rooms.

Once there, she said, "Gifford knows you're Captain Drake. Or at least, he has the strongest suspicions."

"The devil you say. What does he know?"

"That you and I are Mel's children."

"That's all?"

"That's enough."

He shrugged. "It was bound to come out, though I'd hoped for a little while longer."

"This means that you can't have another run anywhere near here for a long time. He'll be watching—"

"Susan, when is he going to *stop* watching me? Probably never. I'll think of something."

"David!" But then she stopped herself from lecturing him like an older sister. She wouldn't tell him about Con's protection, however. Not yet. He was overconfident as it was.

"Wait for a few months at least."

"A few months." He laughed. "You know that's not possible. Unless you've found the gold."

She shook her head. "I've spent most of the day looking for cunning hiding places, and I'm running out of places to search." She paced the room in frustration. "It has to be somewhere the earl went, at least now and then, and he spent nearly all his time in his rooms. He used the dining room occasionally when he had guests, and the drawing room once or twice. . . ."

"What about the storerooms and cellars below?"

She considered, but then said, "I can't imagine it. He thought it beneath an earl's dignity to go into such places. I don't think he even visited the kitchens." She looked at him. "I can't stay much longer, and I don't think I'm going to find that money. I do wish you were just the earl's estate manager."

"Well you know," he said with a smile, "if I was I'd be dashed bored. Probably into all sorts of other trouble."

"Alas, how true." She took his hands. "For my sake, love, try to be at least careful."

He gave a comforting squeeze. "I am careful—because I have the welfare of everyone around here in my hands."

He might not have intended it as a gentle rebuke, but it was. He was her younger brother, but he was past her control and a commander of men. All she could cling to was that Con had promised to try to keep him safe. Unlike the old earl, he would keep his word.

She pulled free with a light smile for him, and told him about the notes she'd found. "It was as if he hated Mel and Lady Belle."

"Mel said a couple of things that suggested that he and the earl were at odds. He kept him sweet with money, but also with things for his collection." He grinned. "Some of it is even more bogus than it's supposed to be."

"Perhaps the earl found out about that."

"Possible, I suppose."

Susan frowned. "But why include Lady Belle in his animosity?"

"Jealousy? I did hear that the earl courted her when she was young. Before Mel."

Susan remembered that. "They must both have been very young. She was eighteen, wasn't she, when she took up with Mel? She could have been countess and she chose to live in sin with a smuggler instead? A wise choice, but extraordinary."

And so different from her own choice. For the first time in her life Susan wished she'd been more like her mother.

"And he held a grudge for nearly thirty years? Truly insane." David shook his head. "But by God, I'll bet he did bring about Mel's capture. I wish he were still alive to pay for that betrayal, but he's beyond my reach."

He was all Captain Drake, and suddenly she shivered.

He turned suddenly watchful eyes on her. "How did you find out that Gifford knows?"

She had to do rapid assessments. She'd confessed her past to Con, but she couldn't bear to tell David. "He told the earl, and the earl told me."

"So the earl's on our side?"

"To a moderate degree. I think I persuaded him of how important smuggling is here."

He nodded. "Good. I'd better go. I'm engaged for the evening."

"Not—"

"Dammit, Susan, I do have interests other than smuggling, you know. It's a cricket match over at Paston Harby."

She laughed with relief. "To be followed by a drinking match at the Black Bull. Do try not to get into another fight, love."

He kissed her on the cheek. "You too. Try to keep on the right side of Wyvern."

With a carefree smile he was gone, and she tried to begin as she meant to go on by not fretting about what he might do next.

She ate her meal in her rooms, served by a maid, as was proper for a housekeeper. As she ate she read a novel—*Guy Mannering* by Sir Walter Scott. The high emotions had appealed to her a few days ago, but now the book seemed ridiculous in comparison to the real, feverish emotions swirling through her life.

She exchanged the novel for a book about beetles and made herself concentrate on it and not think about smuggling, friends . . . or lovers.

At a knock on the door, she said, "Enter."

Maisie popped her head around the door. "The earl wishes to speak to you, Mrs. Kerslake. They're still in the dining room."

Again? Instead of fear, silly hope leaped inside her.

Idiot. They were friends.

Only friends.

Yet there was that matter of curiosity. . . .

"They?" she asked.

"The earl and Mr. de Vere, ma'am," Maisie said, as if it were a nonsensical question. As indeed it was. But Susan had the information she needed. He wasn't alone.

She hardly thought de Vere a pattern card of respectability, but she trusted Con not to do anything embarrassing in front of a third party.

"Thank you, Maisie."

She checked herself in the mirror, tempted to reach for her cap and fichu again, but there was no need for that. They were friends.

She was tempted to change into a pretty dress, rearrange her hair. . . .

They were *only* friends.

She settled her mind about that, straightened her spine, and went briskly to the dining room by the corridor route.

Con was relaxed at the table, fingers cradling a mostly empty brandy glass. He smiled slightly at her, but it was a deep, thoughtful smile. The decanter was over half empty and there was no way to tell how much of it de Vere had drunk. De Vere was on his feet waiting for her, looking bright-eyed. She wondered what was going on in his mischievous mind.

They must have decided that there was no point to formality, for neither man was wearing a cravat, leaving their shirts wickedly loose at the neck.

Con raised his glass and sipped from it.

"Yes, my lord?" She tried to make it crisp. Crisp as the starched cravat he so obviously was not wearing.

Race de Vere spoke, however. "We would like to see this torture chamber, Mrs. Kerslake."

Con raised his brows, suggesting that he thought it folly, too, but he didn't contradict his secretary.

"Now?" She glanced between them. "It would be better left until the morning."

"Did the late earl visit it in daylight?" Con asked.

After a moment she said, "No. But—"

"Then we probably should see it in the appropriate manner." He pushed back from the table and rose, steadily, it seemed. "Don't worry. We expect it to be suitably horrid. In fact, de Vere is depending on it."

She gave Race de Vere an unfriendly look, but he showed no effect of it.

Con said, "If it frightens you, give us directions and we'll go by ourselves."

"Frightens me?" she said, turning to him. "No, it doesn't frighten me." Then she saw the glint of humor in his eyes and knew he'd tossed out a deliberate challenge. The trouble with friends was that they knew you all too well.

Even across a bridge of eleven years.

She swept up the candelabrum from the table. "It's more ridiculous than horrid. But if you want to see it, come along."

She led the way down the dark corridor, but paused by the arch above the stairs that spiraled downward. These particular stairs had been made with true medieval narrowness, and were tricky, especially with the candles in her right hand. She transferred them to the left, then held her skirts up with her right.

Someone touched her arm, and she started.

It was Con. She'd known it was Con. She'd known his touch, like ice, like fire.

He took the candles from her and stepped in front. "I'm sure it's the noble hero's part to lead the way down stairs like this, and after all, I am suitably left-handed. Race, I trust you to fight off any demons or dragons that attack us from behind."

She entered the downward spiral, therefore, between the two men, encased in their fragile bubble of light and protection. She was truly relieved to have one hand free to trace the wall as they went. She didn't like these tight stairs. She always felt trapped, as if the air would go.

When they stepped out into a small, plain chamber she sucked in a relieved breath. She especially hated the stairs in the dark. She should have remembered that.

Only one narrow corridor led off the room.

"Down there, I assume," Con said.

"Yes. It was made narrow to increase the spine-chilling effect. It is all done. for effect. Shall I lead the way, or do you wish to?"

He passed her the candles. "'Lead on, Macduff,'" he quoted. "If there's a trap, I assume you know how to avoid it."

"No trap. It is completely harmless, I assure you, though designed to stir fear."

She spoke calmly, but the narrow corridor pressed in on her, even three candles seeming feeble in the dark. The iron-bound door with a small barred opening seemed to waver in the flickering light.

She pressed down the cold iron latch, and pushed the heavy door open. It gave a long, eerie squeal. Prosaically, she said, "It was apparently quite difficult to make the door produce just the right noise."

"The miracles of modern engineering."

A hint of laughter in his voice warmed her and swept away fear.

Friends. Coming here with a friend was so different from coming here with the earl, as in the past. He'd insisted in showing it off to her three times.

She placed the candelabrum on a table among assorted strange implements, and stood back to watch the men's reactions.

"The room is not entirely below ground," she said as if giving a guided tour, her voice resonating in the chamber. "You will note the high barred windows, gentlemen. By day they let in a little light. For expected night visits, the torches on the walls are lit, and the brazier, of course, for heating hot irons and such." She gestured to the implements on the table. She didn't know what most of them were, and she didn't want to.

"The torches produce a lot of smoke," she continued, "but if the wind is right, it escapes through the windows."

Con and Race were wandering through the unsteady chiaroscuro of the room, studying the tools of torture on walls, shelves, and tables, glancing at the wretched victims. Three hung in chains on the wall along with ancient weaponry. Another screamed silently as his foot was crushed by the iron boot. On the pièce de résistance, the rack, a woman stretched, arched in agony.

The waxwork figures were astonishingly realistic, and the first time she'd come here she had been shocked. She looked at the two men, but couldn't read their thoughts.

"No waxworks of the torturers?" Con asked, flipping a cat-o'-nine-tails on the wall without expression. Of course, they were used in the army and navy on real flesh. They were used in the streets on thieves and whores, too.

"The earl or his guests liked to play those parts."

Susan looked at de Vere, expecting to see him reveling in his treat, but he was looking around with a slight frown. "Why?" he asked.

She found herself sharing a look with Con. It was an excellent question, but to those familiar with Crag Wyvern and the Demented Devonish earls, it hadn't occurred.

"Because he was stark, staring mad, of course," Con said. He looked at Susan. "Does any of this actually work?"

She knew what he was asking: Had it ever been used? "Of course not, but it's designed to be played with." She went to one of the haggard wretches hanging on the wall, scarred, bruised, and burned. "The burns aren't wax, but painted metal over wood, so a hot iron can be put against them. They can be covered with mutton fat to create smell and smoke. There are bladders of red fluid in various places that can be pierced to bleed."

Con shook his head. "He could have joined the army surgeons and had so much more fun."

Susan was hit by a sudden feeling of associated shame. This place had nothing to do with her, but she had thought it merely ridiculous when she should have been deeply horrified.

Like the dragon's bride fountain.

She glanced at the rack, struck by a similarity between the arched figure there and the arched "bride" bound to the rock. What a foul and twisted mind it had been to think up such things.

She should have seen them for what they were. She should have avoided contact with the mad earl entirely. Instead she had chosen to work here, and thus had let Crag Wyvern coarsen her.

She had almost been snared by the dragon.

Thank God for de Vere and Con, who'd seen real horror and suffering, the suffering of friends and heroes in battle and under the surgeon's knife, while the demented earl and his idiot guests played mad games here.

She longed to leave now, but Con had walked over to the rack. "And this?"

"It is operational to a degree. Do you want to see?"

"Oh, by all means."

"Dammit, Con, it's a woman," de Vere protested.

"It's wax and a wig, and should we feel less pity for the tortured man than for the tortured woman?"

Susan went over and grasped the handle on the large, ratcheted wheel. It took all her strength, but she turned the mechanism another notch. The taut figure stretched another impossible inch. Its back bowed, and a high-pitched shriek of agony bounced around the stone walls.

"Christ Almighty!" Con leaped forward and pulled the locking pin, letting the wheel spin backward and the ropes go loose. The figure sagged, its waxen arms flopping bonelessly. A long wheeze told of the bellows mechanism relaxing somewhere inside.

For a moment they all stood like waxworks themselves, then Con seized a hangman's ax off the wall and severed the ropes at the victim's hands. The next blows cut through the ones at her feet and into the wood beneath. Then he swung again, to dig deep into the wooden wheel, splitting it.

De Vere hauled the victim out of harm's way, but then he shed his jacket and grabbed a mace. He smashed the heavy iron ball into the bed of the machine, sending splinters flying. Con laughed, ripped off his jacket, and swung the ax.

Stunned, Susan retreated from swinging weapons and flying wood and two maniacs who had moments before seemed to be civilized gentlemen. But her hand over her mouth was holding back laughter as much as anything— at the wildness of it, and the rightness. It was past time parts of Crag Wyvern were smashed to bits.

Perhaps she was dazzled, too, at the sight of Con in destructive fever, swinging that mighty ax. It should frighten her, but he was so magnificently physical that she felt dizzy. His back was to her now, and through waistcoat and shirt she could see the muscle and power in ferocious action.

From the first blow, there'd been nothing tentative about him. Her gentle, fun-loving Con was used to wielding weapons to destroy, used to swinging them to cut through to the marrow, to kill before he was killed.

It appalled her.

It made her prickle with raw lust.

She tore her eyes away to look at de Vere, equally masculine, equally ferocious. More so. His face was toward her, and there was something terrifying about the fury and passion with which he destroyed, as if he'd reduce wood and metal to splinters, to dust, to nothing.

His violent certainty, however, stirred nothing in her, while she wanted to rip Con's clothes off.

She looked back at him, wondering what his face would show. He suddenly stopped to stand looking at the destruction, leaning on the ax and sucking in breaths. His shirt was plastered to his skin again, this time with sweat.

De Vere was still smashing the mace down on the shattered machine. Would Con try to stop him? She thought he might be killed and braced herself to run forward, to interfere.

Instead he turned to face her.

No madness in his face, but a deep and dangerous fire that made her instinctively retreat. He walked toward her, his eyes dark, and she would have retreated further, but her back was already against the great door, cold iron bolts digging into her flesh.

She didn't know what his face showed, but she was nothing but instinct now. Instinct to flee. Melting instinct to surrender to the dragon.

He collapsed over her, hands and strong arms catching him but caging her, and lowered his head to claim a ruthless kiss.

She could, perhaps, have escaped. She didn't know what he would have done if she'd ducked away. She could have turned her head. Instead, she surrendered.

With the clang and crash of continued destruction filling the stone chamber and violence in the very air she breathed, she surrendered to a kiss that had nothing to do with the sweet explorations of eleven years ago.

Did she remember a taste? She thought so, but that could be illusion. She remembered his smell, though, strong now with maturity and heat, spicy and deep, and branded in her senses.

Lady Anne. The thought came from somewhere far away in the distant sanity of her mind.

For Lady Anne's sake she would not reach, or touch, or curl her arms around his wide shoulders. But she let herself stay to be consumed by the dragon's hot mouth and potent smell so that her nipples ached and her legs shook.

They betrayed her in the end and she began to slide down, the bands and bumps of the unforgiving door scraping along her back. He came with her, mouth still on hers until he straddled her and captured her head to demolish her entirely.

Hands clenched, she still would not touch, but tears leaked, perhaps *because* she would not touch. . . .

Silence.

There was silence.

Still ravaged by his hungry mouth, she forced her eyes open to the flickering room. She couldn't see de Vere, but he must be watching them.

She touched then, pushing at Con's shoulders and arms, fighting free to gasp, "Stop it!"

Silly thing to say, and far too late. He'd stopped anyway, eyes closed. Too late for other reasons, as well.

That kiss had kindled deeper, stronger fires. . . .

She could see de Vere now over Con's lowered head, apparently sane, watching them with knowing interest. Con still had her pinned to the floor with his weight and his legs. Her back was bruised and stinging, her legs cramping.

What was he thinking? Was he thinking as she was of fire, of greater fires? Or was he bowed by regret?

She made herself speak with quiet firmness. "Con, let me up."

He shuddered, looked at her, then quickly pushed away and rose, grasping her hand to pull her to her feet as he had that first day on the headland. Her legs failed her for a moment and she leaned back against the door. He was still holding her hand, looking at her as if seeking something to say.

What was there to say, particularly with a witness?

What would have happened if there hadn't been a witness?

For a moment, unworthily, she thought of it, the pleasure of it. She thought how it might have broken his commitment to another.

Then he shuddered—like a horse, with every inch of his body—and let her go. He turned to his friend. "Destroyed enough for your liking?" It sounded a little hoarse, but it was probably more than she could manage just yet.

"Sorry about that," de Vere said, like someone who'd knocked a cheap vase off a table. Or was he apologizing for watching?

"Perhaps it's a useful release." Con walked over to pick his jacket up off the floor and shake it free of wood chips. "I'm sure Crag Wyvern can provide plenty of things to smash."

They were both ignoring her. Was it a type of courtesy? If they didn't look, it hadn't happened?

Or was it an insult? *Ignore the convenient drab.*

Had she just been assaulted, or had they exposed a deep, forbidden passion?

Curiosity or passion, she wanted him. With a shivering ache and a hollow need, she wanted Con. If it weren't for Lady Anne she'd shed all pride and restraint and beg him to take her to his bed, even if it was only to be once. Like him she wanted to do what they had done eleven years ago, and do it this time with adult bodies, with knowledge, strength, and will.

And heart. And heart. But that was her secret to keep.

"I was sobered by something indestructible, actually," de Vere said.

His tone shocked her back to sanity. She focused to see him step back and gesture at the heap of broken wood and twisted metal. She pushed off from the door to stagger to the wreckage to see what was there.

A body?

Some new bizarre device?

She saw the glint of gold at the same time de Vere said, "Your missing money, I assume, my lord earl."

She halted and looked down at twisted metal and splinters of wood and the gold coins spilling beneath them. Some of the splinters were parts of the shattered chests that had contained the gold.

Oh, God. No chance now of claiming it for David. She'd not be able to stop him risking another run, and Gifford would be watching and waiting. . . .

But Con had promised protection.

She remembered to breathe. Con had promised protection. But could even the Earl of Wyvern stop the law if David was caught red-handed?

Chapter Eighteen

"We were lovers when we were fifteen." Con was lounging in the enormous, steaming Roman bath, Race nearby. They both had their heads resting on the curved edge, looking up at the domed ceiling that contained yet another picture of a dragon claiming a bound woman.

It looked like the same bound woman. Same model for everything, including the waxwork on the rack. A beautiful young woman with a lush body. Generous thighs. Big breasts. Long, tawny hair. He wouldn't mind lying here enjoying her charms, but not while she was screaming for help and being impaled by a dragon.

A shame to ruin a piece of art, but it was going to have to be painted over.

Susan wasn't that lush sort of woman. She had all the right curves now, but she wouldn't be as soft. He was sure of it. Too much time spent climbing cliffs and swimming.

Did she ride? He didn't know. . . .

He'd wanted a bath for the past hour, but they'd had to deal with the gold first. He'd thought it best not to spread the word, so he'd summoned only Diego to help carry it up and cram it into the safe in the office. It hadn't all fit, so he had a bundle wrapped in a towel, and stashed in one of his drawers here.

Susan had disappeared and it was doubtless just as well. What was there to say about that kiss?

There was a great deal to think about it, but he couldn't bear to. Not yet.

When they'd finally finished, he'd remembered the Roman bath and told Diego to see if it could be used. So here they were, soaking together like warriors of old after battle.

It was heaven marred only by the persistent image of Susan in the water with him instead of Race.

And, of course, by the complete insanity of that kiss.

That damnable, betraying, annihilating kiss.

Race hadn't said a word about it, so in the end Con had felt he had to say something.

"I guessed," Race said. "Pretty good going at that age, especially for her."

Con wanted to defend Susan's virtue, but it had happened. And happened again since with other men, apparently. He hadn't forgotten that. He was trying to pretend it didn't matter. He remembered Nicholas saying something a couple of years back about the unfairness of holding women to a tighter virtue than a man was willing to accept.

There seemed to be an instinct to it, though.

He wondered if she were quietly raging at the thought of him in the arms of other women. In other women. It had mostly been a utilitarian use of whores.

It doubtless didn't bother her.

They were just friends, after all.

He laughed and it bounced around the tiled room.

"Life is damned funny at times, isn't it?" Race said idly. His eyes were shut and he looked blissfully relaxed.

Race was a friend, but more in the manner of brothers-in-arms than friends who shared intimate matters. In better times he could imagine talking about Susan with Van or Hawk, and even with a Rogue, but he'd not expected to be doing it with Race.

The Roman leaders had shared baths like this. Had it loosened their tongues? He amused himself by contemplating the effect on British politics if the powerful in London met naked in hot, communal water.

"She always was an unusual female," he said. "She was raised by her aunt and uncle at the manor house, but she's actually the daughter of the squire's wayward sister and the local smuggling master, Melchisedeck Clyst."

"Wonderful name."

"It's not uncommon hereabouts. He was transported a few months ago and apparently his lady went after him."

"Wild blood on both sides," Race remarked. "With a tendency to abnormal constancy."

"Lady Belle? She's certainly constant. Constant to the exclusion of her children."

"Children? How many did she have?"

"Three, apparently. Susan, David, and one who died young. Lady Belle treated Susan as just another girl, not even as a niece. Mel Clyst took a sort of interest."

He found himself telling Race about the time Mel Clyst had warned him off his daughter.

"I suppose she never told him then," Race said.

Con lapsed into silence, studying the fact that he'd never imagined that Susan would tell anyone, never mind Mel Clyst. Despite her behavior and her motives, he'd taken for granted that the friendship between them had been real, and therefore she wouldn't spitefully get him into trouble.

Of course, if she had, it might have ended with them married, which would not have fit with her plans.

She'd apologized today.

And meant it, he thought.

As he'd already accepted, most people came close to doing regrettable things in their lives. And the difference between *did* and *almost did* was often accident, or even weakness and cowardice.

Something inside him was cracking painfully open. He wanted to hold it closed with his bare hands, as he'd seen dying men trying to hold their innards in.

"Lucky you didn't get her with child," Race said.

"Very, though I was too callow to give it thought then. Astonishing to think about, having a ten-year-old child."

Children.

He'd never thought of children, though he'd assumed they would follow marriage. Now, however, he could almost picture them. Sons at Somerford, playing in the woods and valley as he, Van, and Hawk had played. Daughters too, perhaps, enjoying the freedom Susan had enjoyed . . .

He realized the children in his mind were his and Susan's, the daughters slim, agile, and adventurous.

Friendship.

What mad fool had talked about friendship?

"A ten-year-old," he said again, grieving a little for that nonexistent child.

"And a half dozen others by now, no doubt," Race teased.

Con splashed him, too lazy to have even a playful fight over it.

How strange life was, though. Paths taken, often for little reason, and others left behind.

He'd joined the army at Hawk's suggestion. Hawk had wanted to escape his unhappy family. He'd suggested that Van and Con join with him. Still raw from Susan, Con had agreed. He had been a second son who needed a profession, and one that would keep him far away from Crag Wyvern and Susan Kerslake seemed ideal.

Van had been an only son like Hawk, but with a loving family. He'd had more of a struggle, but he'd always been wild, and eventually his parents had let him go.

So they'd made plans to buy commissions in the same cavalry regiment, but in the end, Con had chosen the infantry. If he was going to do this, he was going to do it properly, and the infantry were the meat of the British army, where steadiness and discipline were key.

He'd served his country, mostly in ways he could be proud of, but all the same, his reasons for joining the army had been rooted in cowardice. It had been a way to avoid future visits to Crag Wyvern.

Over the years he'd come to see that as stupid, to think that there had been nothing to fear.

Now he knew otherwise.

Three days, and they'd exploded into that kiss.

It was more a sizzling blur now than a memory. It had overtaken him like a fever or a storm, and if it hadn't been for Race he'd have claimed her there on the stone-flagged floor.

If she'd let him.

Would she have been able to stop him?

Yes, he had to believe that, or he had indeed become the dragon.

He looked up at the damn rapacious dragon, then down at the one on his chest. At least it was just coiled there breathing fire.

"Dammit," he said. "Tattooing should be illegal."

Race opened his eyes, rolling his head sideways to look.

"It's rather a fine specimen."

"But permanent."

"Quite a few men in the regiment got a tattoo after seeing yours."

"Damned fools."

"Thought of it myself, but could never decide what would be most suitable."

"An angel, according to Susan."

A deep bracket dug into Race's cheek as he smiled. "Then I should have a contrast."

"A devil?"

"Doesn't appeal." He looked like a beautiful, decadent angel, his blond hair curling around his face. "Are you jealous of me and the angelic Susan?"

"Not if you're both behaving like angels," Con said.

"Angels being pure spirits, without carnal inclinations?"

"Precisely."

"I don't think either of us is an angel, then."

"Precisely."

Race laughed softly. "What are you going to do?"

"I don't know."

Had he acted the dragon in the dungeon? Con wondered. Had he forced that kiss on her?

She hadn't struggled until the end, but she hadn't touched him, either. Even in the fever he'd noticed that. He hadn't touched her at first except for his lips, as if that would keep him safe, though in the end he hadn't been able to resist.

But she had.

Burning inside him like a twisted blade was uncertainty—had she hated every minute? Had she submitted out of fear?

Or worse, had she submitted because his first suspicions had been right and she still wanted above all to be Countess of Wyvern?

Out on the cliffs he'd been sure that wasn't the case.

Back inside Crag Wyvern suspicion stirred.

Race waved his arms, creating sinuous snakes in the water. "Did you see Miss Kerslake's face when she saw the gold?" he asked.

Con looked at him. "No."

Race's slight smile was angelic—if one remembered that the devil was a fallen angel. "She was devastated. She wanted that money."

It hit Con as a new betrayal. He could think back and see Susan staggering forward from the door to look down at the gold. Race was right. She'd been sallow with shock.

"Have you seen any evidence of her searching this place?" Race asked.

"Yes," Con said flatly, refusing to show how much it hurt. "Of course, that's why she's here playing housekeeper. It's hardly her calling in life."

Friends.

Friends did not steal from each other.

Criminal on her father's side. Whore on her mother's.

He stood, and water streamed back into the bath. "Blood will out." He forced himself to speak lightly. "It should be interesting to see what she'll do now."

"Try to seduce you, perhaps," Race said with a beatific grin. "Yet more theatrical entertainment!"

In preference to bloody murder, Con climbed out of the bath and wrapped one of the huge linen towels around himself. Normally he emerged from a bath feeling relaxed and soothed, but not this one.

He stalked into the bedchamber, where Diego awaited, politely bland, a clean nightshirt in hand. Con kept the towel. Despite everything, the thought of Susan seducing him had him hard.

Lady Anne.

He pulled Lady Anne up in his mind like a shield. Her sweet smile, her gentle blue eyes, her easy conversation about light topics, or more earnest talk of serious causes—education and the plight of the elderly poor.

What charitable causes did Susan support? All her efforts were lavished on a bunch of thieves and murderers.

Even for her elderly poor, Lady Anne wouldn't steal. She wouldn't involve herself in smuggling, not even to fund a hundred schools. She certainly wouldn't invite a worthless officer to her bed on a whim.

Race emerged from the bathroom, also wrapped in a towel, looking very like an effete angel.

A dangerous misapprehension.

How extraordinarily difficult it was to know what people were really like.

"That bath disgorges through a gargoyle?" Race said.

"Apparently."

"Let's go out to watch."

"Watch water? The deadly tedium of Crag Wyvern has struck already, has it?"

"Perhaps I simply want to get outside."

Race's words hit home, but Con said, "It's dark."

"Not entirely. The sun's down, but there's still light."

Yes. In this case, Race's instincts were sound. "Clothes," he said to Diego, flinging off the towel. Race grinned and went off to dress. Con wondered what would happen if he met a maid on his way.

He suspected Race would be delayed.

Sensible Diego brought just drawers, breeches, and a shirt. Con dressed quickly, then pulled on his boots. "Watch from one of the arrow slits and I'll wave when we're in position. Then pull the plug. And ring the bell, I suppose."

"*Sí, señor.*"

Con smiled as he left. Diego lapsed into Spanish when Con did something boyish. It seemed to indicate that he was pleased.

Boyish. How long since he'd felt a touch of the boy?

Mere hours. In the garden, pelted by cool spray. Susan laughing . . .

Damn her.

He collected Race, obviously uninterrupted by rapacious females, and led the way outside.

The sun was down, but pink streaks still shot through a vast shell of pearly gray sky, and light danced on the water, turning it into a blushing opal. The fishing boats were in now, but a mass of screaming gulls circled Dragon's Cove. Doubtless some fishermen were gutting their catch and tossing the scraps to the birds.

It was deeply beautiful and wholesome. And Crag Wyvern deliberately shut this kind of vision off. The garden was lovely, but it was inside and, in a way, artificial. The outer world was blocked off and could begin to disappear even from memory. The old earl had had a fear of the outdoors. No wonder he'd gone mad.

Yet Susan had chosen the Crag for many years, first as secretary, then as housekeeper. No wonder she'd become a conscienceless thief.

A breeze danced up, chilly in his still-damp hair, but alive and free. Even the scrubby headland had its charms, scattered with wildflowers. When he looked away from the sea, the Devon countryside spread in shades of green and brown from woodlands, hedges, and fields, dotted with church spires, each marking a village, a community.

"A sweet place," Race said. "Shame about the house."

"You think I should have it torn down?"

"It's a tempting notion."

"Indeed. But then I'd have to build something else, and even with that gold, I can't afford it."

"You could invest in smuggling."

"No. Come on." He led the way around to the north of the house.

This was the bleakest face of Crag Wyvern. All four walls of the house were the same flat stone broken only by the arrow-slit windows, but the north always looked grimmest. Perhaps it was the almost perpetual lack of sun. Could dark gather in stones like damp and moss?

"It does look remarkably like a stark fortress from out here," Race said. "Has it ever withstood an attack?"

"Yes, as it happens. During the Civil War. The earls of Wyvern were staunch royalists, and a Parliamentary force marched here but failed to take the place. It was halfhearted, though, in part because my direct ancestor, the then Sir John Somerford, was high in the ranks of Parliament. We've tended to take opposite sides all along."

"Don't tell me. The Devon Somerfords for Stuart, the Sussex Somerfords for Hanover."

"And the Devon Somerfords for James the Second, while my branch welcomed William of Orange."

"They must all be rolling in their graves to see a Sussex Somerford here at last."

"Quite. Which is why the old earl was obsessed with trying to get an heir."

"Ah. But I thought he never married."

"One of the many mysteries of Crag Wyvern. Rumor says that he wanted to try the ladies out first."

"Don't we all?"

Con laughed. "This one apparently took the testing seriously." He told Race the system that Susan had described.

"You do have an interesting family. Did many women accept his invitation?"

"Some, I gather. Doubtless not from the upper classes."

Race suddenly laughed. "You know, it's rather like the mythic dragon demanding maidens in tribute!"

"Except that they didn't have to be maidens, and he paid. The girls were sent home with twenty guineas for their service. Quite a nice dowry in a farming family."

"Droit du seigneur as well. What a splendid place!"

Con buffeted him and waved to where Diego was presumably watching.

The bath gargoyle snarled out at them from the middle of the wall, a crested dragon with a long forked tongue. In a moment the bell chimed, and the dragon spouted water. It arced down, silver, but touched with pink by the blushing light, to form glimmering pools and rivulets on the rough ground.

Race applauded, and Con said, "You are easily amused."

"Probably as well in this place."

"What? Three days here and you've had smuggling, a torture chamber, an energetic piece of destruction, and a treasure trove. Not to mention all those lovely papers to play with. What do you expect for an encore?"

"Some concupiscent nuns at midnight would be nice."

Con laughed. "You could probably have Diddy if you tried." Then he winced at the callous words, and remembered Susan's warning. "Leave the maids alone."

"I could take offense at that," Race said quietly.

"I know. I'm sorry. Look, go in, will you? I'm going to stay out here for a while."

Race—perceptive Race—touched him lightly on the shoulder, and went away.

Con looked again over the land, his land, settling softly into the subtle comforts of evening. Inside Crag Wyvern, it was easy to forget, to become wrapped up in his own twisted problems. Outside, he knew that these farms and villages deserved better than an absentee landlord.

That was all he could offer, however. He truly believed Crag Wyvern could drive him mad, but above all, he couldn't live near Susan.

She might be a thief. No. She was.

Despite appearances and his instincts, she might be a whore.

She was still the woman who'd lurked in his heart for over a decade, and who could now ignite him with a glance.

And here he was, afraid to return to his own house.

His mind was full of Susan and that kiss, and he wasn't sure he'd ever be able to think straight again.

He could hardly stay out here, however, and dark was deepening around him, stealing color from sky and land. He retraced his steps and entered the Crag, but not without a shudder.

He went directly to the garden, thinking it would be a haven of sorts, but all he could think of was Susan laughing in the spray. Susan, her damp dress clinging to every delectable curve.

His Susan then.

His Susan on the cliff.

His Susan . . .

A maid bustled out of a door, then froze and turned to go back.

"Stop."

She turned back, eyes wide.

No wonder. He was still in just breeches and an unbuttoned shirt and doubtless looked wild. He walked over to her. "What's your name?"

She dipped a curtsy. "Ellen, milord."

She was slight, young, and looked frightened. Perhaps she was a lowly maid who shouldn't be here. Or perhaps she'd been taught to be afraid of any Earl of Wyvern, especially one who was acting in a strange way.

"Ellen, take a message to Mrs. Kerslake. Tell her I wish to see her in my room." She wouldn't come. He knew she wouldn't. She had to. "Tell her it's urgent."

The maid's eyes widened even more, but without suspicion. "Yes, milord." She hurried away almost at a run.

What the hell did he think he was doing?

He knew, though. He was in the grip of that mad force again, but he couldn't resist it.

She wanted gold, did she?

He'd give her gold.

He went up to his room and dismissed Diego. Then he glared at the picture of Saint George, pushing his hands through his hair in search of sanity. He should pray that she wouldn't come.

He begged heaven that she would.

She had to. He had to know her. He had to *know.*

How could he possibly marry another woman with this madness burning within?

How could he marry Susan, thief and whore?

Perhaps if she came tonight this obsession would burn out, leave him free. If she came . . .

There was a rap on the door and he whirled to face it.

Susan walked in.

Chapter Nineteen

S he was still in her modest, long-sleeved gray gown, but her hair was loosely tied back. She must have been preparing for bed.

Bed.

"Take it off," he said.

She stared at him, lips parted, pink flushing her cheeks.

"The dress. It's ugly. Take it off."

His mouth was working apart from his brain, but parts of him were in control that had nothing to do with brain.

She flushed.

Quickly, before she could refuse, he said, "You wanted that gold. I'll give you half for a night."

All the pretty pink drained away, leaving her ivory-pale. "You would make me into your whore?"

He wanted to deny it, to fall on his knees before her, but need raged over conscience. He found a shrug. "You clearly want the gold. I thought to offer you a chance to deserve it."

Fury flashed in her eyes, but she didn't leave. "A remarkably well-paid whore," she remarked, simply looking at him—mysterious, unreadable—for what felt like an eon. Then, as his knees weakened at the sight, she lifted her hands to unfasten the buttons on the front of her bodice.

He watched, a part of him disbelieving, as she reached behind to untie something. It all came loose, and she raised the gown up over her head, revealing by layers sturdy gray stockings, a simple shift, and a plain corset.

He stared at it. He'd never seen such a plain corset before. It was clearly something only working women wore, or only decent women wore. But

Susan, by her own admission, was not a decent woman. That's why they were here like this.

"What do you want the gold for?" he asked, hoping for some explanation that would make sense of it. Of her.

"That is none of your business, my lord."

"Con," he said firmly.

"Con," she submitted, chin still firm, eyes steady on him.

Ah Susan, magnificent Susan.

"But you don't deny you want it. That you've been searching for it?"

"No, I don't deny that."

She dropped the dress to the ground and stood there. She was wide-eyed, but not wide-eyed like little Ellen. Susan was no innocent, and she wasn't pretending to be. Nor was she reluctant. He saw—surely he saw—the same passions burning in her that were consuming him.

Battles could rage, kingdoms could fall, and he did not care. He wanted only this.

He walked toward her, looking at the corset, seeing hooks at the front. He put both unsteady hands there, at the top edge, between her breasts—the breasts that rose and fell against his fingers as he clumsily unfastened those hooks.

Susan wondered if she was visibly shaking, or if it was an insubstantial thing, this tremor in her heart, her soul. She'd come here with irrational hope, then been hit with cruel shock. But now . . . now all she could think was that she and Con were going to make love, that she would have this one night to remember.

I'm sorry, Lady Anne. But it is only the one night.

She knew she should have reacted to his offer with anger, with outrage, even. That, however, would have ended this. She knew Con. He would never allow himself to do this if he thought her honest and virtuous.

For that reason she would not tell him that the gold belonged to the Horde. If he believed her he might give her half the gold, or even all the gold, but he wouldn't give her what she ached and burned for.

Himself.

But now, with his hands upon her, she didn't know her part. What should she do? She'd been bolder eleven years ago, carried on the courage of ignorance and instinct. Now she stood passively as he parted the corset and let her tingling breasts free. He spread it, pushed the straps off her shoulders, and down her arms.

Let it drop to the floor.

She gazed at the open vee of his shirt as he untied the ribbon that gathered the neckline of her shift, loosening it. Such a strong neck he had now, such a square, firm jaw, darkened by the hint of a beard.

He pushed her shift off too, so that it slid down her unresisting arms. As it passed over her sensitive nipples, she shivered, shivering more as it rippled down over eager skin to pool around her feet.

Only her stockings remained.

She sucked in a deep breath, watching him, seeking the reassurance of passion, if not love.

His eyes lingered on her body, then rose to hers, darkened. "I'm not forcing you," he said.

She didn't know if it was a question or not, but she said, "No, you're not forcing me. Even for the gold I wouldn't do this if I didn't want you."

It was honest. Every part of her, inside and out, quivered for his touch. The heat gathered again, but not just between her thighs. Everywhere. If he touched her, she was sure he'd feel raw heat. *Please let him touch me!* Her legs felt quivery, as when he'd kissed her in the dungeon, and he wasn't kissing her. *Please let him kiss me!*

He seemed frozen there, inches away. Afraid of hesitation, she moved closer and put her hands on his chest.

He broke then, kissing her as he'd kissed her earlier, so they folded down irresistibly to the floor, mouths desperately melded. She'd have taken him there and then, but he picked her up and carried her to the bed, laid her there, and began to strip.

In seconds he was naked and she sat up. "Stop."

She saw his face and quickly said, "I want to look at you! That's all. I want to look at you, Con. You are so very beautiful."

He laughed and pushed her down again. "Look later. I am so very desperate."

Laughing with him—she hadn't expected laughter—she scrabbled the covers down beneath her so she could get to the sheets. With one mighty pull, he dragged them all off the bed, then flung himself beside her, one leg trapping her, there where she wanted to be.

"Better than a beach," he said, his chest rising and falling, his hunger swirling in the air.

"And no fear of being caught." She twisted onto her back and dragged him over her.

"Susan—"

"Hush," she said, adjusting her hips and guiding him into her with her hand. Shuddering with him as they slid together.

"Hush," she said softly again when he groaned, but she didn't mean it. She loved the sound of his need satisfied, of pleasure.

She loved its echo in herself.

He filled her, filled her beautifully, and it didn't matter that she had so little experience of this. A powerful surge of womanly knowledge swept her along.

He began to pump into her and she met him, trying not to surrender to the fever growing within, because she wanted to give him this and she wanted to watch, to watch Con, to drink in his pleasure to the last drop.

To remember it.

She was swirled away, however, into private heat and darkness and only dimly aware of his gasp, his force, then his full weight upon her. Silence fell, hot, deep-breathing, sweaty silence in which she lay, slightly sick and trembly.

She felt him slide out of her, leaving her throbbing, almost in pain. Was it going to be wrong with Con, too? She couldn't bear it.

She hadn't felt this way the first time, with him on the beach. She hadn't felt this way with Rivenham. She hadn't even felt so horribly unright with Captain Lavalle.

He stirred, moved off her slightly, hand sliding down her side, over her hip. His mouth brushed across her aching breasts, then found a nipple. He gently sucked.

Her whole body leaped. "Con!"

He raised his head to say, "Hush," a trace of laughter in it, then went to work again as his hand slid between her thighs. She flinched, she was so sensitive down there, and his touch immediately gentled. Became exactly what she wanted.

He used the flat of his fingers, gently circling, and a buzz started in her head, lifting her away from herself. With deep gratitude she recognized it, welcomed it, and surrendered.

She lay there afterward, flat on her back, his hand still cupped against her, amazed at how perfectly she felt. Perfectly what? She had no idea.

She rolled her head to study him. He looked thoughtful as much as anything, but with endearingly tranquil thoughts. His short hair was on end in places, and stuck to his forehead in others. His dark jaw made him very unlike her Con of the past, and yet she felt only moments had passed between now and the last time they had lain together in sweaty satisfaction.

She looked down and saw the dragon.

She pushed him onto his back and sat up to trace it. "It's beautifully done."

He was watching her from under lowered lids. "By sheer luck we came upon an expert. But it took a devil of a long time." After a moment he added, "I've grown, which has spoiled it a bit."

The dark dragon coiled, breathing flames toward the center of his chest. "Why the dragon, Con?" She had to ask. "Was it because of me?"

She looked up again. He was still watching her. She thought he wasn't going to answer, but then he said, "Yes."

She sucked in a breath, but it was mostly gratitude for his honesty. "I am so very sorry. I wish I could scratch it away."

He trapped her hand. "No, thank you."

She heard humor and looked up to his eyes.

He said, "It's done. It can't be undone. Like many things."

Heart breaking, she understood. She worked at keeping a slight smile on her face. "But we have a night?"

He raised her hand and kissed it. "We have a night. I wish I hadn't wasted the bath on Race."

She did smile then. "Your valet asked if it should be filled again and I said yes. It won't have had time to warm much. . . ."

He was already out of bed, candle in one hand, pulling her with him with the other. "How is it filled so quickly?"

"A gravity feed from the main tank."

"Wonderful design."

They were in the bathroom then, and he went to turn on the big taps. Water gushed out and he put a hand under it, then smiled at her. "Not as cold as the sea, at least."

Memories. Memories.

If she'd been a wiser woman then—if she'd been a woman at all—she could have claimed a treasure greater than gold.

But at least she had one night.

He put the candle on the edge, where it danced strange shadows around the pictures on the wall and left mysterious corners where wickedness doubtless lurked. Then he dropped down into the waist-high tub, the water already swirling around his ankles. He held his hands out to her, but she went to a shelf holding fine china pots.

"If those are some of the old earl's potions, I don't want anything to do with them."

She looked back, smiling. "No doubts about your virility, sir?"

He glanced down. "Not with you, Susan. Never with you."

She knew she was blushing as she turned back. "These are just perfumes."

"We don't need perfumes either."

She picked up a pot anyway, and returned to toss a handful of brown powder into the water. As she walked down the marble steps, the scent of sandalwood began to fill the room.

"If we let the cistern drain into here, will the bath overflow?" he asked, coming toward her.

"It's not supposed to. Why?"

"I might lose attention soon." He pulled her into his arms, then leaned her back against the smooth, cold side of the bath.

She rested there, nervousness stirring. That hot passion had been all very well, but she'd given him the impression she was vastly experienced, and now, like this, all faculties alert, she didn't know what to do.

She knew her supposedly vast experience was another reason he was doing this. He mustn't guess the truth.

He nuzzled at her neck and jaw. "What's the matter? Something in particular you want?"

What did that mean? "No," she said. Then, "Yes. Kiss me slowly, Con."

He moved one hand to cradle her neck, sliding behind to hold her for his lips, which settled firmly, hotly. She opened to him, feasting, her own hand going to his strong shoulder, his neck, his hair. . . .

The water thundered, creeping up her calves. Sandalwood created spicy mysteries.

He moved back. "Like that?" he asked, smiling.

She smiled back. "Just like that."

He kissed her again, and she kissed back, her body stirring with primal knowledge. Perhaps it was all instinct after all, which only emerged with the right partner.

He pressed against her, and the water swirled around her wobbly knees. Perhaps his wobbled too, for eventually he sank down, taking her with him into water that was now chest-high.

He smiled.

She looked down and saw that the water was lapping at her nipples.

She laughed up at him, knowing exactly what he was thinking.

"You can touch them if you want."

"Oh, I want." He put both hands under her breasts, raising them, flicking the nipples with his thumbs. "I remember thinking that I was a dead man if Mel Clyst ever found out I'd touched his daughter's breasts. And that it was worth it."

His touch and his words sparked sharp desire. Through clear water she could see his erection. With an unsteady hand, she dared to reach through the water to gently touch it.

He put his mouth to her raised breasts again, and because of the rising water she had to stand slightly, bracing herself on his shoulders.

He seemed completely intent on his play—licking, tugging, nipping. He suddenly nipped sharply, and she yelled and pushed backward. He let go and she went right under, emerging spitting water and pushing sodden hair off her face.

"You bit me!"

"Mmm." Laughing, he grabbed her by the waist and hoisted her out of the bath to sit on the edge, then spread her legs wide. He smiled at her as he'd smiled at her breasts, then put his mouth there.

"Con!" She tried to wriggle back, but he grabbed her hips, looking at her with surprise.

She knew then that this was something experienced lovers did. She stopped trying to escape, but didn't know what else to do, what to say.

"You don't like it?" he asked.

"Of course! You just surprised me." Did that sound convincing? "And you bit me," she added as a distraction. "I thought you were going to bite me there!"

"No teeth. I promise."

He put one hand on the rim and leaped with agility out of the bath. He went to the pile of linen towels on a shelf and came back to spread them lavishly on the tiles.

She sat there, drinking in the beauty of his strong body, trying to look as if she knew what he was doing. She'd just lied to him, and she hated that. She wouldn't tell the truth, however. She couldn't bear for this to stop now.

He picked her up and sat her on the towels, then dropped back into the water. It was certainly more comfortable than cold, hard tile.

"Now lie back."

She did so, but he kept his hands on her knees so she had to leave her feet dangling, up to the ankles in water. Then he began to draw her toward him, and hooked her legs over his shoulders.

She knew better than to cry a protest now, but she lay there on her back, quivering with ignorant uncertainty, staring at the lewd ceiling, but shockingly aware of being exposed to his very close eyes.

Then she felt his hands beneath her, thumbs brushing apart sensitive skin. She stared fixedly at the dragon about to impale the screaming maiden, water still thundering into the tub, echoing around the tiled chamber.

His thumbs entered her, opened her, shuddering her, making her want to squirm away—and to wriggle closer. Then it was only his mouth, stroking and sucking. She almost felt too sensitive to be touched there, and yet immediately her body responded, demanded.

His tongue swirled around her and she gasped for breath.

Her breasts ached, and she reached up to comfort them, squeezing and stroking. A mere touch at her nipples sent fire through her, and she pressed there, squeezed there. Hot pleasure swept down to meet his mouth, making her arch toward him, but the dragon had her lower body chained, completely in his power.

Her demanding dragon with the mouth of fire . . .

A moan escaped her to bounce around the room. She squeezed her breasts harder as he sucked harder and that blissful darkness circled in.

She was being ravished by her dragon, but raptured, not raped. This was the most perfect, the most blissful rapture she could ever imagine.

Then fiercely he was in her, wonderfully big, hard, and strong, driving the velvety darkness deep into her until it swallowed her whole.

She drifted back to hard tiles beneath damp towels, to sweat and sandalwood. To silence. The water had stopped.

Curious, she raised her head to look. It had stopped a hand's breadth from the rim.

"Have we created a flood?" he asked sleepily.

She let her head sink back. He was half over her, his head between her breasts, and she stroked him there. "No."

"Pity. I wouldn't mind the end of the world."

She knew what he meant.

She moved her hand down, exploring the firm strength of his muscled back beneath the smooth, wet skin, a worm of sadness stirring. Never to do this again. A bitter shame, but better than never to have known it.

The one candle gave little light, and the room, the house, was quiet. Even their breathing had calmed.

Then he stirred, pushing up off her to stand. He extended a hand and she put hers into it be pulled up. As she stood, she winced. She was tender, but her legs were protesting unusual exercise, too.

He smiled and pushed her into the water. She yelled as she splashed in, and it echoed around the room. Would it echo through corridors and court-yard to tell the world what they were doing here?

She didn't care.

He jumped in after her, and waves splashed over the edge, rippling down the steps.

"You'll bring the house down!" she protested, laughing.

"Good idea." He circled his arms to create waves, and she lunged at him to hold him still, his body slippery beneath her hands. They wrestled through and beneath the water, to emerge spluttering and collapse against the side.

"We could go out on the beach in the dark," he said, nibbling her ear. "Go swimming."

She shared his need to re-create the past, to make it whole and good, but she had to say, "There's not enough moon."

"Another time then." He said it lazily, but she knew from the tension of his body that he'd remembered that there wouldn't be another time.

Because there wouldn't be another time, every moment of the night be-came precious, and one thing she wanted was to know more about him.

She struggled up straight and embraced him in the water. "Tell me about the army."

"That's not something you want to hear."

"It's most of the years that divide us, Con. And there must have been some good times."

He moved back against the side, and she let him. When he leaned his head against the rim and let his body float, she floated beside him despite the dis-traction of his lovely body and soft, promising genitals.

"It seems barbaric," he said, "but it's true—there were some good times. Wild incidents. Insane acts of bravery and generosity. And pure farce, like the time the company tried to smuggle a bunch of piglets on a march . . ."

He began to talk, telling her stories, but leaving out so much. She wanted to ask: *Were you frightened? What was it like to kill? How often have you been wounded? How much did it hurt?*

They were stupid, invasive questions, but they made up a part of his life that she would never know.

She could tell from his body that he'd not been seriously wounded, but scars told of pain. She supposed everyone except an idiot was frightened sometimes. And certainly a soldier must kill.

Her sweet, gentle Con.

She turned to put an arm around him, to float against him. "I'm glad I was apart from you when all this happened."

He stroked her back. "But I was just telling you about the time Major Tippet made assignations with three Spanish women on the same night. That's not so terrible."

"I know," she said, without explanation, and he didn't ask for one.

"I checked the casualty lists," she confessed. "I knew that we'd hear the news eventually, but I couldn't bear not to check."

It was growing cold in the water, but she didn't want to move, didn't want to risk any change. "So many deaths. With each one, I thought what it would be like if it were you. I became intense about it. Uncle Nathaniel tried to forbid me to read the papers, but I always found ways. They couldn't understand, but of course, they didn't know about you."

"They had to know something."

She traced the coils of the dragon. "They knew we'd met. We'd been seen together often enough. But most of our time was out of sight. No one realized how much time we spent together. And of course, no one knew the whole of it."

"You never told anyone?"

She shifted to look up at him. "Did you?"

"No, of course not."

"Then why think I would?" It hurt, and she added, "It's not as if I wanted to be forced to marry you, after all."

They slid apart. "It was force you had in mind, was it?"

Appalled, she tried to repair the damage. "No! I thought you willing. You *were* willing! I simply encouraged you."

"But you'd have encouraged Fred if you'd realized he was the heir, wouldn't you? You did, in fact. I could tell from his letters that Miss Susan Kerslake was doing her best to be of interest to him."

She bit back tears. "I told you. Marrying the future earl had to be a worthy goal. I'd already sacrificed you on that altar."

"Any passionate little sessions on the beach with him? I doubt it. If you didn't have sails and a rudder, Fred would hardly notice you."

She sucked in a deep breath. "Don't do this, Con. It's so long ago now." Desperate for harmony again, she offered him a cautious bit of her heart. "He wasn't you."

He took it wrong. "That always was the problem, wasn't it?"

He yanked the plug out and water began to run away, taking her magical night with it.

She turned and climbed out by the stairs, grabbing a damp towel to wrap herself in, and drying herself as she hurried into the bedroom.

He followed, stark naked, watching her, silently.

"Are we finished?" she asked, knowing that too had come out all wrong.

"Oh, yes, I think we are."

She turned away to pull on her shift, to fasten her corset, to struggle into her dress. Her hair was still sodden, and she shivered at the water running down her back.

No, that wasn't why she shivered.

She'd constructed a time of lies here. She'd wanted him, and to get what she wanted she'd lied. As she'd feared, as she'd known, now she had only dust in her hands.

There was nothing for them now, but earlier there had been friendship, and tonight, together, they had thrown it away. What use was friendship, however, if they never met?

Once he left here, and she left here, they would never meet again.

She looked back at him still watching her, still naked.

The room smelled of sandalwood, and passion, and Con. She thought she'd remember it all her life.

What to say at such a moment?

In the end, she simply turned and left, in silence.

Chapter Twenty

Con could finally allow himself to collapse into a chair, to sink his head into his hands.

Susan. Susan.

A thief, and a whore, and a liar.

He stood and went to the table to pour himself a glassful of wine, knocking it back in one swallow. He finally really did understand those poor fools entangled with worthless women. He could feel the bonds winding around his limbs.

What did it matter? a voice was saying. As his wife she'd have no need to steal. He should be able to keep her satisfied and in line so she didn't whore around.

But could he ever trust a word she said?

She lied so well. So convincingly. She'd claimed lovers to overcome his resistance to surrendering to his needs.

But it had been his idea. He remembered that. His insane, overpowering idea. He'd bribed her with half the gold. . . .

Was he mistaken? Was she honest?

How could he twist the lens to see her as honest?

"Lady Anne. Lady Anne. Lady Anne." He spoke it aloud, an incantation against dark magic.

Thank God he'd sent that letter. It bound him. It protected him. But even so, he had to get away from here soon.

Swann was coming from Honiton tomorrow, and Race had sorted out the essentials of the earldom's affairs. Even after giving Susan half the treasure trove, there'd be enough to keep this place going for a while.

By tomorrow night he might be able to leave with a clear conscience and ride east.

To claim Lady Anne.

Sweet, kind, gentle, good—

He hurled the glass to shatter against Saint George's smug face.

Susan felt she could hardly breathe for suffocating sadness. She took refuge in the garden, but this was all too horribly like the past, without the brash certainties of youth to hide behind.

Then, for a while, she'd been able to think: *I made a brave sacrifice so I could continue to pursue my great goal.*

Now she could only think of might-have-beens.

They might at least still have been friends.

Where had she gone wrong?

Everywhere.

She should have reacted with outrage, as she'd wanted to, to being bought, and explained clearly why the Horde had the right to that money. He might not have agreed, but he'd have known she wasn't a greedy thief.

But then they would not have made love.

She circled the shadowy fountain, thinking of the dragon's bride splayed on her rock, screaming. Had she screamed in true terror, or because she was horrified at wanting to be ravished?

The chain still hung there, trailing limply into the stone basin. What had really chained the bride to the rock? What if she'd gone willingly, though shaking, to give herself to the dragon?

She leaned on the rough stone rim, shivering with loss, and with the prosaic chill of damp clothes and wet hair. What else should she have done differently?

She should have pretended more skillfully to be experienced.

No, no, she should have told him the truth.

But then they would not have made love.

Clearly she shouldn't have let her anger show at the end. Why not, though? Why not? Why shouldn't she be outraged at being thought of no honor? Was that how he'd thought of her all these years, as a person who would stir up trouble out of spite?

But if she'd held her tongue, perhaps they would even now be making love again.

She pushed herself straight and took a deep breath. Life goes on. Despite lost chances and broken hearts, life goes on and must be endured.

As she continued through the shadowy garden she tried to comfort herself with the fact that she'd earned half the gold. She didn't know how much half was, but it must surely enable David and the Horde to lie low for a month or two.

It didn't touch the pain eating deeply into her.

Susan was wakened the next morning as usual by Ellen with her breakfast tray. Tea, a fresh roll, butter, and jam.

Routine, blessed routine, except that she had no interest in food at all. She'd hardly slept, but she managed a smile for the girl, and thanks.

"Was it something terrible last night, ma'am?" the maid asked.

"What?" Susan froze, wondering what people knew, what they'd heard. . . .

"The earl, ma'am. He said it was urgent, and he looked ever so wild!"

Susan choked down a laugh. "No, no. It was a minor matter. Nothing to worry about."

"That's good, ma'am." Ellen smiled. "He's a lovely man, really, isn't he? It'll be all right here with him as earl."

Susan poured tea into her cup. *Life goes on.* "Yes, he's a lovely man, though he's not going to live here. But you're right, Ellen. Everything will be all right as long as he's earl."

The maid left, and Susan spread butter and jam on the roll, took a bite, chewed, and swallowed.

Life must go on.

A lovely man.

He was.

Beneath the dark and angry moments lived Con, the blessing of her youth. With Lady Anne he probably was that man. At Somerford Court he probably was that man.

That comforted her. She thought perhaps she could bear this loss if Con was living a good life somewhere in the world.

She rose and washed and dressed as usual, unable to escape memories of Con taking off the same clothes. So she faced the memories, embraced them. Most of them were to be treasured.

She almost felt the events of the night should have marked her, but the most careful scrutiny in the mirror showed not a sign. Last night her skin had been a little reddened, her lips a little swollen. Now no trace remained.

Just as it hadn't eleven years ago.

She'd returned to the manor sure that everyone would know what she'd done, that she was marked, changed. It appeared not to have been so. Con and his father and brother had left three days later, and after that Aunt Miriam had remarked once or twice that Susan was missing him. Perhaps there'd been a hint of sympathy for a young love that had come to naught. But no more than that.

Today, no one would notice anything either.

What secrets lay in the other hearts around her?

With a sigh, she went out to organize the day.

She was inspecting the laundry that had come up from the village when Amelia bounced in, bright-eyed and beaming. "Hello. Where's the dragon?"

"Not in these quarters," Susan said, waving the maids off to put the folded sheets and pillowcases away. "What on earth are you doing here?"

She was smiling, though. No one could help smiling at Amelia, and all the shadows suddenly seemed to shrink.

"I do have a reason," her cousin said, eyes twinkling with mischief, "but I won't tell you what it is unless you tell me something exciting about the earl."

"I'm a servant here," Susan said, deliberately being difficult. "It is not a servant's place to gossip about her employer."

"Susan! We've gossiped about the earl enough in the past. What I really want is to see him."

"I have to pick some flowers to refresh the arrangement in the dining room. You can come with me if you promise to behave."

"I'm not a servant here."

"Behave like a lady, I mean. And," she added, picking up a basket and some shears, "you're much more likely to see him there than here."

That made Amelia enthusiastic. Susan fought off a touch of guilt. If she was any judge, Amelia wouldn't catch a glimpse of Con while in her company.

When they entered the courtyard, Amelia looked around. "This isn't much of a garden. If I'd known you wanted flowers I could have brought some from the manor. We're awash with tulips."

"Two gentlemen don't require a lot of flowers." Susan snipped some wall-flowers and stocks.

Amelia was looking up. "All those windows. It's like being in a box, watched."

Susan looked up, realizing that Amelia was right—and that Con could be watching.

As if picking up the thought, Amelia asked, "Where is he? I do long to see him."

"I don't know."

It was true. He'd eaten breakfast but she knew no more. Mr. Rufflestowe was here again going through the curiosities. De Vere was presumably in the office. Con could be with either of them, or anywhere else. She didn't think he'd left Crag Wyvern, though. Mr. Swann was expected.

"How long are you going to stay here?" Amelia asked. "It must be pretty boring." But then said, "What does it mean? 'The Dragon and His Bride'?"

Susan looked over to see her cousin studying the words carved into the rim of the fountain.

"It used to have figures. A dragon and a woman."

Amelia turned to her. "What happened to them?"

Susan was remembering one of the problems she had with life at the manor. Everyone expected to know everything. The concept of private matters did not occur to them.

"The earl didn't like it, so he ordered it removed."

Amelia's eyes lit up. "Was it very improper?"

"Highly."

"I wish I'd seen it before it was destroyed. It really isn't fair. I never get to experience anything exciting."

Susan added some delicate rue to her basket. "You don't want to, either."

Amelia wandered back to her side. "Not if it was uncomfortable, no. But a naughty statue wouldn't be dangerous, would it?"

Susan suppressed a wry smile. "You'd be surprised."

Con was with Mr. Rufflestowe, unwillingly fascinated by the strange and occult items being entered into a meticulous catalogue.

"People really do use eye of newt?" he asked, looking into a glass vial of small, dry objects.

"So it would seem, my lord," said the round and polished young man. He rose to take down a heavy, leather-bound book from the section already recorded. He flicked through the pages carefully and then pointed to a recipe.

"I can hardly read that writing, never mind translate the Latin after all these years," Con said.

"It instructs the user to dissolve four eyes of newt in mercury and pig's urine."

"And what is that supposed to cure?"

Mr. Rufflestowe went pink. "Er . . . a female complaint, my lord."

"Should certainly stop all complaints dead, I'd think."

Con was mildly amused, and Rufflestowe was surprisingly entertaining company, but essentially he was in hiding, waiting for Swann to turn up so he could arrange his escape.

Susan was somewhere in the house, and he wasn't going to see her, or speak to her if he could help it.

He glanced out of the window, however, and one resolution crumbled. Susan was out there. A new aspect of Susan, smiling and chatting with a plump and pretty young lady in a sunshiny yellow dress that was all the brighter beside Susan's gray and white.

Dammit, as her employer could he order her to wear something different?

Unfair, and dangerous.

But he couldn't stop watching the two women. There was something so comfortable and familiar between them, and he realized that it reminded him of his sisters together.

That must be one of her Kerslake cousins.

He knew he should move back, turn away, as if from a spellbinder, but he continued to watch.

Then Race stepped into view.

"Good morning, ladies!"

Susan turned to see Race de Vere sauntering out of the office doors, smiling angelically. "Speaking of naughty and dangerous . . ." she murmured.

"Oh, lovely," Amelia murmured back, giving de Vere her best flirtatious look.

"Mrs. Kerslake, do we have a new maid?" he asked, eyes twinkling.

Susan heard a little squeak of outrage from her cousin and had to fight a smile. She'd thought she'd never smile again.

"Don't be mischievous, Mr. de Vere," she said. "This is my cousin, Miss Kerslake. Amelia, Mr. de Vere. Lord Wyvern's secretary."

"And friend," he said, stepping closer and bowing. "It must mean something to be an earl's friend."

Amelia dropped a curtsy, dimples showing that she'd overcome any outrage. "Have you been the earl's secretary long, Mr. de Vere?"

"Mere months, but it seems like an eon, Miss Kerslake. . . ."

Susan rolled her eyes and left them to their lighthearted flirtation as she looked around for suitable greenery. Amelia at least had what she'd come for here—an encounter with an interesting new gentleman. The selection in this area was limited and very familiar.

She wondered if Amelia had looked up de Vere in any books, and what she'd found. She was sure he was not a typical secretary with his way to make in the world. He was far too sure of himself for that.

As she worked her way around the garden, their voices and occasional laughter as background, she recalled Amelia's interrupted question. How long was she going to stay?

There was nothing to keep her here now.

Nothing.

A flutter of pain and panic told her how much she didn't want to leave. Not while Con was still here. It might be crumbs from the table, but if that was all there was she would stay for them.

And perhaps, just perhaps, he would summon her to his room again.

Wicked to even think of it, but she couldn't help it. And she didn't think she would be strong enough not to go.

Con felt unreasonable irritation that Race could stroll out there and flirt while he was pinned up here, a mere observer. Susan was now almost out of his sight unless he peered down from the window, and he wasn't about to do that. That left only the laughing, flirting couple.

How strange it was, however, to see such normal interaction within Crag Wyvern. He was sure it had been years, decades even, since two normal young people had enjoyed each other's company here.

Was it something to do with expectations? Could he and Susan get along better together if they weren't so aware of the poisonous nature of this place?

But then, it was their past, not their location, that had twisted everything into disaster.

A new person came onstage.

Susan's brother.

Ah, yes. Con remembered summoning him. If he was going to protect Captain Drake it might as well be an open matter between them.

For the first time, he wondered if he should warn Kerslake about Gifford's threat to Susan. She'd told him in confidence as a friend, he knew, and yet it was a matter that needed to be dealt with.

"Susan."

She turned to find David beside her.

"Good heavens. This is becoming a market square!" But then she said, "Trouble?"

"I don't think so. Wyvern summoned me."

"What?" But her sudden alarm subsided. "More poring over records with de Vere, I suppose."

He shrugged. "I was to report to him, not de Vere. Any idea where he is?"

David was Con's estate manager. It wasn't peculiar that Con wanted to speak to him. But prickles of alarm were running up and down Susan's spine.

Con couldn't want to talk about her. Of course he couldn't.

But men were so strange about these things.

He might want to talk about Gifford. Would he feel he had to tell David about Gifford's threat?

Would he want to talk about the gold?

What might he say about the gold?

She hadn't thought about how to explain the fact that she now had money for the Horde. . . .

"What's the matter?" David asked.

She found a smile for him. "Nothing. I didn't sleep well last night, that's all." That, at least, was true. "De Vere might know where he is. Otherwise we'll have to organize a search."

"A dragon hunt," David said lightly as they strolled over to the other couple.

Susan winced, but then she saw Maisie limping out of the great hall. "Mr. Swann's here to see the earl, Mrs. Kerslake."

"Market square indeed," she said, feeling as if the weight of three outsiders here—four if she included de Vere—was shifting something elemental about Crag Wyvern.

Or perhaps the change was all in herself.

"I'd forgotten," Susan said, going over to the others. "David, that's doubtless why the earl wants you here. Mr. de Vere, do you know where the earl is?"

"With Rufflestowe in the Wyvern rooms, I believe, ma'am."

How nicely formal they were all being.

"I'll go and talk to Swann," David said. "Someone else can dig Wyvern out of Wyvern."

With a grin he walked briskly off toward the hall. De Vere pulled a humorous face and said, "I'll go. I'm sure one day I'll be grateful for this exposure to fertility charms and auras."

"What?" asked Amelia as soon as de Vere was out of earshot.

After a moment's hesitation, Susan told her cousin about the earl's rooms.

Amelia was wide-eyed and laughing by the end. "Susan, I *have* to see that place!"

"It would be most improper."

"Foo. It would be no more improper for me to go there than for you, even though you are playing housekeeper here."

"I *work* here, Amelia. I earn my pay." It was appallingly tempting to tell Amelia exactly why they were different.

Amelia picked the shears out of Susan's basket and began to gather more blooms. "I've heard the rumors," she said. "About women coming up here hoping to get with child and become the countess. Strange they'd think it worth it."

"Very strange. But I talked to a couple of them and it was more a matter of getting a handsome dowry for nothing. I gather in recent years at least the earl was . . . incapable."

"Impotent?" Amelia asked, but then she pulled a face. "He'd still have wanted to touch and such, wouldn't he? Tom Marshwood tried to handle me in a most offensive manner at a picnic last week."

"The swine! What did you do?"

"Told him exactly what I thought of him, of course. He won't be so foolish again."

Such simple solutions among essentially decent people. Susan wondered if living in Crag Wyvern drove away all sense of proportion.

She recaptured the shears from her cousin. "This small garden can't afford such extravagance with flowers. Come to the kitchen and we'll have tea."

As they strolled there she chatted, but underneath her mind was fretting about the meeting between Con, David, and Swann. It should all be business, but it could turn to other things. . . .

Whatever was happening, she reminded herself, there was nothing she could do about it, and she had resolved to stop trying to force life into the channels of her choosing.

She settled to the haven of a session of light chatter and gossip with Amelia, wondering if there'd ever been a chance for her to be as straightforward as her cousin, or whether she'd been cursed from her irregular birth.

Con was glancing through a book about witchcraft when there was a rap on the door and Race walked in.

"Mr. Kerslake awaits below at your command, my lord," Race said like a bad actor in a poor play. His manner had become stranger over the past day, and Con wondered what the hell he was up to.

"But yet another waits below!" Race declared. "To be precise, in your great hall."

"Swann, I assume."

"So I am told, my lord, but it could be a mere goose, and the maid mistaken."

"A gander, at least, or the poor maid would be very much mistaken."

Race grinned. "Touché."

"And don't you forget it. Back to your den of archival iniquity, and prepare for invasion." Con realized Race's nonsense was infectious. "Are we ready to get everything straight?"

"Can a twisted tree branch ever be straight? We're ready to discuss matters as they are."

"That will have to do."

Con lingered a moment after Race had left and realized that he didn't want to set the earldom's affairs in order. Because then he would have no excuse not to leave.

Chapter Twenty-one

Tea and simple talk with Amelia seemed to bring some normality back into Susan's life. Perhaps it was helped by the awareness of other people in the house, though the kitchens had always been an oasis of sanity.

She and Amelia were sitting at the big table along with the other servants. With all the "betters" engaged in business, there would be no need of them in the other side of the house.

An aromatic soup simmered on the back of the modern stove Mrs. Lane had insisted be installed five years back, and fresh spice cakes sat cooling on a rack—those that weren't already on the table to be consumed.

She'd come to feel a sisterhood with the servants here. They were all, like her, at Crag Wyvern because in some way they didn't fit in elsewhere.

Ada and Diddy had come to try their luck with the earl and then stayed on. Diddy, at least, had tried her luck a number of times at twenty guineas a go. She was the one who'd told Susan that the earl was impotent.

"A lot of groping and complaining," she'd said, "but I can put up with that for a year's pay in a month. Pity, though. It would have been grand to be my lady, wouldn't it?"

When the earl had died, she'd said, "That's it, then. Time to start looking for a husband. With my nice little dowry, though, I'll be the one doing the choosing!"

Ada had spent only one month as a trial bride. Apparently the earl had been certain that a thin woman couldn't conceive. However, when Susan had realized that Ada had only a cruel father back home who had sent her up to the Crag, she'd added her to the staff and to the books, and if the earl had noticed, he hadn't cared.

That was four years ago, when she'd been secretary.

She'd employed Maisie and Ellen, too. Because of her twisted spine, Maisie couldn't find good employment, and Ellen had been scared out of her wits by her first position with the Monkcroft family over near Axminster. What she'd said about that violently argumentative family had been a revelation to Susan, and when Ellen had found Crag Wyvern a happy haven it had shown that everything depended on the point from which one viewed it.

Mrs. Gorland had been cook here for nearly twenty years, and with her skills could work anywhere. She was, however, of a somewhat republican disposition, and would find it hard to deal with a lady of the house who demanded deference.

Susan knew she would miss this assortment of women as much as she would miss her family at the manor.

Though Amelia hadn't been in Crag Wyvern's servants' dining room before, she was at ease with the servants, sharing tales of the local families, and absorbing stories of the old earl. Reasonably decent stories, Susan was pleased to note, though perhaps there was no need to protect Amelia. No country girl with all her wits was naive.

At fifteen, and never having kissed, she'd known enough to seduce Con.

She settled into a mellow contentment with the moment. Eventually, however, Amelia had to leave. Susan walked with her to the main entrance, feeling extraordinarily better. It was only at the door out of Crag Wyvern that she remembered Amelia's arrival. "Didn't you say you had an excuse for coming here?"

"Oh, yes!" Amelia dug in her pocket and produced a slightly battered letter. "This came for you. We think it might be from Lady Belle. Do you think she's reached Australia yet?"

"I doubt it. It's been only three months." Susan took the letter, which had been addressed to her at the manor, but showed nothing about the sender. "Why on earth would she write to me?"

"You are her daughter."

"Which fact she's ignored all my life."

She realized that she didn't know what her mother's handwriting looked like. That was strange, but then, her mother had given nothing to her in any practical way. So why a letter?

It had been roughly handled before it had come into Amelia's careless hand, and it was impossible to make out the smudged scribble that might have indicated where it had started its journey. It had come from abroad, however, and who else would write to her from abroad?

Despite a creeping reluctance, Susan snapped the seal on the thick package.

Perhaps one of her parents was dead.

There were three sheets of writing and a sealed enclosure, and at the end, the scrawled signature, *Lady Belle.*

Not *Mother.* Of course not. Did she really, after all these years, still harbor a hope that Lady Belle would turn into someone like Aunt Miriam?

Lady Belle. Not dead. And doubtless wanting something.

She returned to the first sheet. Lady Belle's writing was not an elegant hand. It was bold, splotchy, and sloped heavily to the right with big loops. Typically she had not tried to write small to save paper and postage. Instead she'd written extravagantly, and then turned the sheet to write crosswise over the first lines.

"What does it say?" Amelia asked, leaning closer. "Ugh. What a mess!"

"That sums up Lady Belle," Susan said dryly. "'My dear daughter,'" she read, and couldn't help rolling her eyes. But then she made out, "'I know the word *dear* has no real meaning between us, but how else could I open this letter?'"

Susan laughed. It was so typical. Lady Belle had never made any bones about her feelings or lack of them, nor made excuses. In a way Susan admired her for that.

Even more, however, she had a sense of foreboding about the letter. "I think I need to read this alone."

Amelia drew back from her shoulder, for once looking conscious of a need for privacy.

"I understand. How very strange it all is," she remarked, as if the peculiarities of Susan's parentage had never occurred to her before. "I should be going home anyway. Mother made me promise not to stay here too long. I'm not sure if she was worried what I would get up to, or that the wicked dragon would snatch me in his claws. And here I've not so much as set eyes on him. Remember that ball!"

With a cheery wave, she sauntered away.

Susan thought of retreating to her rooms to read the letter, but then instead she walked slowly to the headland, into open air and light, to the spot where she'd talked with Con yesterday.

Where for a brief moment they had found accord.

She'd known, she thought bitterly. She'd known that anything carnal would ruin it. But she hadn't been strong enough to resist.

Like mother, like daughter?

She sat down on the ground, smoothed out the paper, and began to pick out the words.

> *My dear daughter,*
>
> *I know the word* dear *has no real meaning between us, but how else could I open this letter?*
>
> *A sea voyage, I am discovering, offers a great deal of time for thought, and I have thought that my dearest Mel might disapprove of my taking the means to make this journey, though I have no doubt that he will be delighted to see me.*
>
> *I have found myself remembering that you said the Dragon's Horde could be in difficulty due to a lack of funds, and that my son might have to take over control and put himself at great risk. Of course, there is nothing to be done about that now, but . . .*

Susan had to turn the first sheet then and concentrate on the different layer of writing. What? Was there another cache of money somewhere?

> *. . . there is something which might be of assistance. Though you doubtless think me heartless, I am not completely uncaring about the safety of my only son.*
>
> *You threw up at me the fact that I never married Melchisedeck. I would have you know that this was not my fault, or Mel's either. Unfortunately, I had a prior marriage. I was wed to the Earl of Wyvern.*

Susan tilted the paper to make sure she hadn't read that amiss. No, that was definitely what it said.

Good Lord! Had her mother, too, run mad?

> *Wyvern courted me, and I confess that I was drawn to the idea of being a countess. He was not so strange in those days, though strange enough. He already had his obsession with producing an heir, and he actually made to me the proposition which became so infamous later.*

That ended the first page, and Susan flipped it over, having to turn it ninety degrees to get the next lines straight. Lady Belle must have realized that her letter would be long, for the writing became cramped and even harder to read.

Of course I refused, but he was so mad for me that he came up with another plan. We would marry secretly, and once I proved to be with child, it would be announced. He even offered me a normal wedding then. I was only seventeen, and I admit I was swayed by that. I have much regretted not being able to marry my dearest Mel in the church with all our friends around.

How was this arranged, you ask?

Yes, thought Susan. *I ask!* How could her mother, Miss Kerslake of Kerslake Manor, run off to Gretna Green and back and it never be noticed? Lady Belle had assuredly gone mad, or thought Susan a complete idiot to believe this farrago.

But irresistibly, she read on.

The means was so simple I wonder if it is not often done so. James Somerford was mad, but he was by no means stupid. He found a young whore who resembled me and went with her not to Gretna, but to Guernsey, just off the coast, where apparently the same convenience of marriage exists. Wasn't that clever? There the impostor declared herself to be me, and thus I was married without any inconvenience or discomfort at all!

When he returned with the marriage lines, we commenced our secret marriage, but without sullying your maiden's ears, daughter, it was not at all to my taste. In fact, it was quite shocking, and when I fled him in the night, I encountered Melchisedeck Clyst. It was a smuggling run, of course, and he kept me by him as he took care of business.

I am afraid, from what I know of you, Susan, that you lack the more sensitive emotions or a passionate heart . . .

"From what you know of me?" Susan muttered, switching to the next sheet. But she was totally caught up in this impossible tale. It was so impossible that she knew it must be true. And it did explain the great mystery of why her parents had not married.

. . . but to one such as myself, there comes a bond that cannot be denied, and that is for life, and such it was for me and Mel. I assure you, nothing short of an overpowering, tumultuous force could have impelled me into the arms of a mere tavernkeeper without the blessings of matrimony!

Susan laughed aloud at that. It was so completely Lady Belle.

Discovering that he was Captain Drake, and that smuggling was profitable, was some solace. It was also to my advantage that he was powerful enough to protect me from James, who could have claimed a husband's rights.

In brief, Susan, we all three agreed not to mention the marriage. That meant that James would be able to marry another if he managed to get a woman with child. In return for my discretion, James agreed not to interfere between Mel and I, and to protect the Dragon's Horde, for an outrageous tithe of ten percent of the takings. However, he vowed that if I attempted to go through a ceremony of marriage with Mel he would produce the marriage lines and exert his marital authority over me.

You can imagine that I prayed for a child at Crag Wyvern as ardently as James—except that he did not believe in holy prayer—for then I would have been free and able to openly plight my troth to my dearest Mel. I am a widow now, however, and thus I will do that as soon as I find him.

You see, of course, what this means for you.

"No," muttered Susan, almost dizzy from this strange story. Or perhaps it was just the strain of reading the crossed writing. She started the third sheet.

By the law, a child born of a marriage is legitimate unless there is evidence to the contrary. James never claimed David, of course, but nor did he deny him or you, and his clear evidence of insanity can doubtless be brought into play there.

For my son's sake, and to spite James, I admit, I have drawn up the enclosed sworn testimony that my children were fathered by the earl, but that in his insanity he threatened them, leaving me no choice but to give them into the care of relatives. That he then, in his madness, repudiated them.

You may not know, being a mere child at the time, but in the first years of my relationship with Mel, all was in secret. I continued to live at home, going on long visits for my confinements. My parents and older brother hoped I would come to my senses and make a good marriage, you see. Once I was twenty-one, not long after the birth of David, I left my home forever. You will see, however, how this too could support the idea that you and David are the children of my marriage to the mad earl.

If you are wondering about evidence of my whereabouts at the time of the marriage, I went with my old nurse to visit a friend near Lyme Regis. Nurse is long dead, and I doubt anyone can remember the name of the friend. I certainly cannot.

I have no idea if this can be done, but the marriage certificate is somewhere in Crag Wyvern. James would never have destroyed it when it gave him power over us. Perhaps you can use it to make David earl, which would take away the need for him to risk himself as Captain Drake. And you, of course, will be Lady Susan Somerford, and may at last find yourself a husband.

There, I have done my duty to make amends. Do with it as you will.

Lady Belle

Susan sat back half expecting the letter to crumble to dust in her fingers like some mysterious artifact in a gothic novel. But it sat there, presumably still carrying its bizarre message.

David. She shot to her feet. She must speak to David about this!

But then she realized that he would be with Con.

Con.

If she used this information, Con could lose the earldom.

But David as earl would be virtually untouchable. Leaving aside the benefits of rank and fortune, he wouldn't hang or be transported for smuggling. In fact, this whole area would probably enjoy decades of peace and illegal prosperity.

It wasn't right to use it. David wasn't the earl's son. But it was as tempting as the serpent's apple.

But Con.

They would be stealing title and fortune from Con.

She should destroy this letter and take the contents to the grave. She began to tear it, but after the tiniest beginning, she paused. Shredding it and burning it wouldn't scour the knowledge from her mind.

David or Con?

Lies or truth?

Chapter Twenty-two

Truth, she decided. Once settled, it was so clearly right that Susan could have wept with relief. She could see now that last night with Con had been a web of lies and untruths. Her intentions had not been bad, but all the same, it had been dishonest, and thus had fallen to pieces in her hands.

If she ventured into untruths again, her intentions would not be bad, but she would be back to her old ways, trying to manipulate life to suit her needs. She was through with that.

But then she realized that she really should put this in David's hands. It wasn't entirely hers to decide. Whatever David decided, however, she was going to tell Con the truth.

She returned to the house. If David hadn't left, she should be able to intercept him and talk to him alone.

In fact, she saw him coming out of the arch.

"David!"

As he turned, smiling, she found it easy to smile back. This was right, and it was good to be doing it outside the oppressive house.

"Believe it or not," she said as she joined him, "I have a letter from Lady Belle."

"What does she want?" he asked, and it made Susan laugh.

"Oh, she's all benevolence. Read it!"

He took it, but pulled a squint-eyed face at the writing. "I presume you've deciphered this. How about giving me the precis."

"No, I think you need to read it as given."

He sighed but then settled to it, complaining, but then falling silent as he reached the revelations. When he'd finished, he stayed silent.

She resisted the urge to demand his answer.

"She really is a most immoral woman," he said at last. "There's no trace of hesitation about perpetrating a deception, or making out false testimony."

"I know. It would be pleasant to discover that she wasn't our mother, but I'm afraid there's no hope of that."

"I'm proud to be Mel's son, especially now I know why they never married." He looked at the letter again. "She only sent this because she knew he'd disapprove. A sign of her love, I suppose, but still . . ."

She had to ask. "What are you going to do?"

"Do? Nothing. For heaven's sake, you didn't think I'd go along with this, did you? It's outright fraud!"

Susan was suddenly carried back to last night when she'd taken such fierce offense to Con's simple query as to whether she had told anyone about their lovemaking. Wrong again. Every step of the way, wrong, wrong, wrong.

She gathered her wits. "No, I didn't think you would. I hoped not. But I put it in your hands. I do think we need to tell Con, though. The documents might turn up, and I wouldn't put it past Lady Belle to stir the matter herself later. Now her husband the earl is dead there's no risk to her in asserting her right to be the countess."

"Except that letter," David pointed out. "It admits that we are Mel's children, and exposes her willingness to lie under oath."

Their eyes met. "So we have to give it to Con."

He folded it and gave it to her. "You do it." He hesitated a moment, then asked, "Can you tell me what lies between you two, Susan? Whatever it is, it isn't making you happy. I don't want to be unkind, but you are not looking your best."

With a sigh, she moved closer. "Give me a hug, David. I need a hug."

Susan appreciated his strong arms around her, and the certain knowledge that he would stand by her through life even if she continued to fall into follies. She thought soon she would be able to tell him the truth about some of the things she had done. But not yet.

She told him one truth as they parted. "I love him, David. I've loved him since I was fifteen years old. But he's going to marry Lady Anne Peckworth, who I am sure is a lovely lady and will make him very happy."

"Is it your birth? Is that what stands between you?"

She smiled. "No, of course not. He doesn't return my love. It happens all the time, I'm sure, and the world doesn't end."

"Eleven years, though. I wondered why you hadn't married. It would seem you share one thing with our mother. Eternal constancy."

"Hopefully not quite as obsessively. Go along. I'll give him this letter and tell you his reaction."

She watched him set off down the hill, then turned to enter the house. She supposed she needed to go dragon hunting. She crossed the courtyard, glancing in the window of the library, and saw Con still there with de Vere and Swann.

There was no great urgency about giving the letter to Con, and yet she felt it. Perhaps she was afraid that she'd weaken and try to persuade David to pursue safety through fraud. She wasn't entirely sure of her new skin yet.

Perhaps she simply wanted an excuse to be with Con again.

She took up a watching post in the breakfast room, from which she could see the library. She was soon rewarded when he emerged through the doors to the garden, leaving de Vere alone.

She hesitated for a last moment of thought, then hurried out. "Con!"

He turned sharply. She could almost see shields rising. "Susan."

"I have something I must show you, tell you."

He took the time to think, and it hurt, but then he said, "Very well."

She glanced up at all the watching windows. There were few people here now to watch, but all the same she said, "In the breakfast room would be better."

His look was both wary and suspicious, but he gestured for her to lead the way. Once inside, she shut the doors.

"This isn't something anyone should overhear," she said. At his expression, she quickly added, "This isn't some attack, Con. Please don't look like that. This is . . . a kindly act. At the least an honest one." She pulled out the letter from her pocket. "Amelia brought this. It's a letter from my mother. You can read it all if you want, though she writes in a terrible hand."

She glanced at the densely covered page. "I'd never seen her handwriting before. Isn't that strange?"

When she looked up, he was as blankly distant as if they were strangers. Why was she saying such irrelevant things?

"What does it say?" he asked.

She couldn't think where to start. "That she was married to the earl. I know, I know! But I believe her. It was a mad business, but he was mad."

She quickly related the details, seeing his distant coolness melt at least into bemusement.

She put the letter into his hands. "There. It's all there. The letter that you can use to stop her if she tries this again. The sworn false statement. Doubtless somewhere here are those marriage lines. If you find them, you can destroy them too, then she'll have no case at all."

"I believe records will have been kept in Guernsey as well."

"It doesn't matter. It's not true. Surely it can't be proved if it's not true."

"I wonder . . ." He looked at her. "You might have made it stick, then you'd have had Crag Wyvern at least through your brother."

"Dragon spit!" she exclaimed. "I do not want Crag Wyvern! I can't wait to escape this place."

"And yet you have just made sure that I keep it. And last night you proved I am vulnerable to you still."

She closed her eyes. "Con, please!" She opened them to look at him, to try one last time. "I know you have reason to distrust me, but in this I am completely honest. I, like you, will never stay in Crag Wyvern, no matter who owns it. I don't care about the title, any title. I'm deeply sorry to have given you reason to be so distrustful, but now, here, I am being starkly honest."

He was turning the letter in his hands as if it could reveal something extra from the outside. "Be honest then. How many lovers have you had?"

"Three," she said softly.

He looked at her, demanding more.

With a sigh she added, "On four occasions. I'm sorry for misleading you, but I thought that if you knew the truth you would not make love to me, and I was greedy for it. But it was wrong to lie, even by implication."

"Why only two other occasions? I have no right to ask, but I need to know."

She hesitated but continued on the honest path. "I was trying to wipe away the memory of you."

After a moment he put the letter in his pocket. "I need to think about this."

"There's nothing to think about. I told David about it, and he thinks as I do. It would be horribly wrong."

He continued to look darkly thoughtful.

"Con!" she protested. "Please. I will never do anything to hurt you again."

"I believe you," he said with a touch of a smile. "Don't leave here, Susan. I want to talk to you about this more."

"I am staying for a few more days at least."

He nodded, and left by the corridor door.

Con closed the door and paused to try to deal with the thoughts swirling in his head. It was no good. At this point, before making some crucial decisions, he needed an obviously sane head to help him.

He changed into riding clothes, then walked down to the Crag's stables and set off for the two-hour ride to Redoaks in Somerset, home of Nicholas Delaney.

He prayed Nicholas was at home.

As he rode it occurred to him that it was the first time he'd sought out any of his friends since he'd come home from Waterloo. He'd spent time with the Rogues in the Shires and then in London, but with masks and guards thoroughly in place. He'd been hiding within them rather than meeting them.

He'd last seen Nicholas in London a few months back when Francis had married his beautiful, scandalous wife. All the available Rogues had gathered to launch her into society. Being in hiding, he'd avoided Nicholas, who tended to notice such things.

The devil finds work for idle minds, so he'd kept his mind busy. He'd even gone to Ireland for another Rogue's wedding.

But in the end, the dark had crept in, and he'd begun to avoid those who knew him well. He'd sent chatty replies to letters from Hawk, who was abroad. He'd sent brief ones to various Rogues, who were busy with their own affairs. But he'd ignored Van's letters, because Van was too likely to seek him out.

He'd known Van had to be struggling with his own darkness, but he'd been too deep in his own hole to reach out to a friend.

Did he deserve to reach out to Nicholas?

He made good time and was soon looking at the brick house that was Nicholas's country home.

Redoaks was a simple place, but something about the proportions, the gardens, and the oak trees that gave it its name, all spoke of the kind of rightness that Nicholas would choose.

Quite a contrast to Crag Wyvern.

He turned his horse into the short drive, wondering what exactly he was going to say, but knowing that it didn't matter.

The door opened before he reached it, and Nicholas came out in an open-necked shirt and loose pantaloons, his dark blond hair obviously not cut for fashion. "Con! A surprise, but a delightful one."

He looked relaxed and welcome as a clear spring—which made Con aware that he was remarkably thirsty. He swung off the horse. "I'm at Crag Wyvern. You know I inherited the earldom?"

"Yes, of course. An interesting encumbrance, I'd think."

"That just about sums it up, yes." Con was smiling without any clear reason to, except that he was glad he'd made this journey.

A groom came running around from the back of the house and took the horse, and Nicholas led the way into a square hall painted a clear green and containing two pots of hyacinth. The sweet perfume of wax polish and blossoms made Con think of Somerford Court.

"It's what? About fifteen miles?" Nicholas asked.

"A little less, I think. This was an impulse, though if you'd ever visited Crag Wyvern, you'd know the impulse to go somewhere else is persistent."

Nicholas laughed. "I've known many places like that. I did look up a picture of it in a book. It was depicted suitably surrounded with dark clouds and stormy sea and looked rather like something dreamed up by Monk Lewis."

"Oh, a mere novelist could not do it justice. To create Crag Wyvern, you'd have to be completely mad. It runs in the blood."

He saw Nicholas give him a quick look as they went into a room that was probably called the drawing room, but which had a coziness that rejected such a formal term.

Of course there were books: books in bookcases, in small piles on tables, and three waiting on chairs. Sewing lay on one chair arm, and a chess table invited. Con wandered over, attracted by the unusual pieces, and saw they were some Indian design with elephants instead of horses.

"Metal," Nicholas said. "Very practical with little fingers around."

Con saw then that there were toys around the room, including a collection of dolls and carved animals set in a circle around a small lace cap.

"Guarding it, of course. It is currently Arabel's most precious possession. She and Eleanor are out, so you'll have to put up with crude masculine hospitality. What would you like?"

"Cider?"

"Of course." Nicholas went to the door and gave instructions.

Con put his hat, gloves, and crop on a table, feeling heavily overdressed. After a moment he stripped off his jacket and cravat and opened his shirt. When Nicholas returned, Con asked, "Why the devil do we men dress in so many clothes in May?"

"In recompense for demanding that women wear corsets."

"Do we demand that?"

"But surely they wouldn't ask that of themselves?" But Nicholas's smile pointed to most follies being self-imposed, which pretty well fit Con's thinking at the moment.

Nicholas would probably not ask any direct questions. It wasn't his way. Con, however, wasn't quite sure what he had come to talk to Nicholas about.

The Crag. Susan. Lady Anne. Dare. Gifford. Smuggling. Inheritance . . .

Inheritance was the blast that had blown him here, but it was all tangled with the rest of it.

The cider came in a sweating earthenware jug, accompanied by glass tankards. Nicholas filled both and gave one to Con.

At first taste, Con let out sigh of satisfaction. At second, he said, "This is strong stuff."

"Home brew," Nicholas said. "If you're not ready to tell me your secrets now, you will be in a while."

Con sat in a chair and took another deep draft. "I suppose I wouldn't just be dropping by."

Nicholas sat opposite with his distinctive lazy elegance. He never looked as if he thought about movement at all, and he doubtless didn't, but his body didn't seem able to arrange itself in awkward lines. "Dare?" he guessed.

Typical of Nicholas to hit the spot. Or one of them.

"It's like a nagging tooth," Con admitted. "Not quite bad enough to drive one to the dentist, but perpetually stealing comfort and rest. It makes no sense. It wasn't my fault. But I can't close the door on it. If only we'd found his body."

"His mother's the same way, poor woman. She has this obsession at the moment about having the whole British army tattooed to make identification of bodies easier. I gather you are to blame for that."

"God. I did mention our tattoos, that we'd had them done for that reason. Careless of me."

"You couldn't expect her to cling to it, and it gives her a purpose of sorts." Nicholas took another drink. "I don't suppose Crag Wyvern helps. I know you never wanted the earldom."

Con shrugged. "Once Fred died, it was bound to happen one day. I had reason to hope it would be a long time, though. The mad earl was only fifty. The damned man killed himself with a potion supposed to increase longevity."

Nicholas laughed and demanded details, so Con told him about the sanctum and bedroom—the dried phalluses were a big hit—and what he knew of the mad earl's eccentric ways.

"I wouldn't mind a look at those books and manuscripts, you know. I'm a collector."

"Of alchemical absurdities?"

"Of alchemical curiosities, among other things."

"You just want the dried phalluses. Slowing down in old age, are you?"

"Creaking and groaning. So, is that the worst of Crag Wyvern?"

Con thought of the fountain, and Susan, the gold, and Susan, and the bath, and Susan, but didn't know where to start, or even if he wanted Nicholas's clear eye on these matters at all. He'd come to talk about the inheritance.

"I'm presented with a dilemma," he said, and gave Nicholas the bare bones of Lady Belle's letter.

"What an interesting family you have, to be sure."

"She's hardly family."

"She's Countess of Wyvern, after a fashion. I suspect it would be quite hard to prove that she wasn't the woman in Guernsey if she stood firm about it."

Con groaned. "That's all I need—Lady Belle in residence in Crag Wyvern. Thank God she took it into her head to sail off in pursuit of Mel."

"You could probably pull some administrative strings to see that she and this Melchisedeck Clyst get good treatment in Australia. Wonderful name, by the way. I wonder if Eleanor would agree to naming our firstborn son that."

"Probably not."

Nicholas laughed. "True."

Con was thinking about what Nicholas had said, however. "If they were treated well, they might stay after Mel's seven years are up. I suspect there's scope for a man of his abilities in a raw land like that. But what do I do if she insists her son is the true earl?"

"You have that letter. It should blow her case sky-high. A foolish woman."

"Apart from the letter, however, it could stick."

"Ah," Nicholas said, and drained his tankard. Trust him to see the possibilities immediately. He rose to refill both tankards. "You dislike being Earl of Wyvern so much?"

"And more."

Nicholas sat down again. "What a very intriguing idea. Deliciously Roguish, in fact. It's a shame Stephen isn't here with his legal wisdom, but I can't see why it shouldn't prevail. It would create quite a storm in society, and a devil of a lot of talk."

"I believe I can handle that. It would be a falsehood, however. I may not feel strong allegiance to the Devonish Somerfords, but it goes against the code to put a complete cuckoo in the nest. The whole damn lot will probably come back to haunt me."

"Perhaps they can only haunt Crag Wyvern. Stay away, and you should be safe."

Con looked at his friend. "You really don't see anything wrong about it?"

"I like to look at consequences not conventions. Who suffers? The Demented Devonish Somerfords, perhaps, but they died out without force from you. Who gains? You. This David Kerslake. The local people who will have a resident lord. The smugglers who will have a great deal of security. Is he able to be a good Earl of Wyvern, do you think?"

Con considered it. "Yes. He's somewhat brash and overconfident, but then, he's only twenty-four and hasn't been knocked about enough to age quickly. I'd say he is sound. He's certainly bright and hardworking enough."

"Lord above, get on with it! How many peers of the realm could be described that way?"

Con shook his head. "You make it sound easy. It's possible he won't agree." He was going to have to mention Susan. "His sister is my housekeeper. That letter was sent to her. Before she gave it to me, she'd talked to him, and he wants no part of a fraud."

"To his credit, but he must be persuaded. We don't always get to do just as we like. How would it be if I return with you? I can't resist poking my fingers into such a delicious affair, and I truly would like first pick at the arcane collection."

"I'd like nothing more, but it's an oppressive place. I think it truly can turn people mad."

"If I was going to be driven mad by places, it would have happened long since. Ah," he added, and rose before Con had heard the footsteps and the childish babble.

A moment later, Eleanor Delaney entered wearing a sprigged gown and a wide, sun-shielding hat tied with emerald ribbons. As always, she looked ordinary, sensible, and very attractive. She was carrying her daughter in her arms, but she put her down as she said, "Con, how lovely. Nicholas said that you would probably ride over as soon as you visited Devon."

Con glanced at his friend, but Nicholas's attention was on his daughter.

Arabel, in a copy of her mother's outfit except trimmed with pink, had toddled rapidly to fling herself at her father, to be swept up and kissed. Then and only then did she look around and give Con a wide smile.

"Crag Wyvern," Nicholas said to Eleanor, "is apparently full of arcane books and manuscripts."

Eleanor groaned.

"You wouldn't want me to miss an opportunity like that, my love. You and Arabel can come too—"

"No!" It escaped Con, embarrassing him, but he went on, "Truly, Nick, it's an unhealthy place."

"The air?" Eleanor asked.

"The atmosphere."

Arabel wriggled to be put down, so Nicholas did, extracting her from her hat, which had fallen down her back and was threatening to strangle her with the ribbons. "Very well. I'll go over by myself."

"But not tonight," Eleanor said firmly. "We're promised to the Stottfords."

"So we are. Can you stay, Con? I'm sure they wouldn't mind an extra guest, especially a temporarily eligible earl."

"'Lo!"

Con looked down to see Arabel, now with the lace cap perched on her head, greeting him, he thought. "Hello."

She raised her arms, and somewhat hesitantly he picked her up. He wasn't sure he'd ever picked up a young child before. She seemed to be a professional, however, and settled herself, firm and wholesome, on his arm.

"Temporarily?" Eleanor asked. "Are you about to be married, Con? It's about time. It must be, oh, at least a month since we've had a Rogue wedding."

"Archness does not become you, my dear," Nicholas remarked. "It would be best to tie all the Rogues up before they wreak more havoc."

Con had suddenly remembered Lady Anne, however. He should tell Nicholas that he intended to marry there, to tidy up a bit of Roguish mess. But the words stuck. They stuck because he couldn't stop thinking of Susan.

But he'd sent that letter.

He looked at the pretty child with the chestnut curls who was exploring his shirt and skin with small, soft hands, and the idea of marriage, of children, became appealing in its own right.

Susan's children . . .

"Con? Can you stay the night?" Eleanor asked.

He walked over and returned her distracting daughter to her. "Tempting, but I'd better ride back. I made no arrangement to be away."

"We could send a groom with a message."

"If he can ride over, so can I." Con wasn't sure why he was so insistent on returning. In part, he knew, he wasn't quite ready for a full-blown exposure to normal people, but he was also anxious to return, and worried about what might happen in his absence.

Susan might disappear.

He had no right to chain her, but he could not bear to lose her yet.

He picked up his belongings, saying, "You'll come over tomorrow?"

"I won't be denied."

"Excellent. And stay as long as you want. It's just possible you will have an antidotal effect on the place. You can have the Chinese rooms. I'm sure rampaging, fire-breathing dragons have no effect on you."

"Chinese dragons? I don't fear them. The scales of the dragon, the Chinese say, are nine times nine in total, and thus the perfect lucky number. It brings storms, but also good spirits, health, and longevity."

"Does it, by gad? I wonder if my mad relative knew that? I'll go odds he didn't or he'd have used those rooms himself!"

Chapter Twenty-three

Con arrived home in the late afternoon, feeling better for time away from the Crag. Feeling better, too, for contact with Nicholas, Eleanor, and their child.

There was such an aura of sanity and good health around them, and yet both Nicholas and Eleanor had been through troubles. They'd not let the darkness drown them, however. They'd fought back, and fought for each other.

He rode into the Crag Wyvern stables at the bottom of the hill rather than riding up and letting a groom bring the horse back down. Delaying his return, he supposed.

He needed time to think.

He'd had hours of riding to think, but had let them wash his mind blank. Astonishingly, he felt better for it. A clean slate.

He chatted to the grooms, noting their watchful eyes. He was key to their lives, and what they really needed was a sane earl in more or less permanent residence. Guests would be especially nice, bringing their own servants for company, and paying generous vails for service.

He left the stables, but instead of heading straight up the hill he turned back to the village and walked to the church. It was not called Saint George's, but Saint Edmund's. Of course it had been here long before the first earl's supposed adventure with a dragon.

He walked up the short path and into the cool interior, which was blessedly deserted.

He'd remembered that there were monuments to the previous earls here. The first earl had a carved marble memorial in front of the altar. Typical grandiosity. And the man had started life as a simple country gentleman. Find favor with a king, then marry an heiress, and here he was in stone robes and lace, his adoring family depicted in miniature all around him.

"Remember, earl, that thou art dust," Con murmured, "and unto dust thou shalt return."

Perhaps it wasn't so outrageous that the earldom return into a bloodline of gentry and yeomen. He seemed to remember that back in Tudor times the Somerfords had been only farmers.

He found the various memorials to the next five earls, but had to go outside in search of the mad earl. The sixth earl had neglected to make provision for his burial, and when Con had been asked for instructions he'd simply told Swann to arrange a suitable grave.

The suitable grave was a box tomb with scriptures engraved on all sides. Reading them, Con thought that the vicar and various others might have gained considerable satisfaction from encasing the old madman inside them.

> *For we must needs die, and are as water spilt upon the ground. II Samuel 14:14*
> *And the great dragon was cast out. Revelation 12:9*
> *Be not deceived; God is not mocked: for whatsoever a man soweth, that shall he also reap. Galatians 6:7*
> *Thou hast shown thy people hard things: thou hast made us to drink the wine of astonishment. Psalms 60:3*
> *The fear of the Lord is the beginning of wisdom. Psalms 111:10*

On the top it recorded that James Burleigh Somerford, Earl of Wyvern, had lived from 1766 to 1816 and had passed into the next life dependent on the infinite mercy of the Lord.

Another clever turn of phrase.

Con looked around the pleasant graveyard, which was swept with spring flowers, and overhung by generous trees. A sweet resting place, but not his. Strange. Even in the dusty heat of Spain he'd not felt such homesickness for Hawk in the Vale and Somerford Court as he felt here in this equally wholesome place.

Was he contemplating chicanery simply to rid himself of a burden?

Yes, in part.

He knew he could cut through the graveyard to join the path up to the Crag, and so he took that route. As he went he found himself among the Kerslake graves. He stopped by one tiny stone recording the brief life of Samuel Kerslake, born in May 1799 and dead in June of that year. Susan's youngest brother, with no record of his parents given at all.

Was the infant to be re-created the Honorable Samuel Somerford, son of Isabelle, Countess of Wyvern and the Earl of Wyvern? Put like that, he could see that it would be just about irresistible to Lady Belle, no matter what David Kerslake thought.

He wandered through the other Kerslake graves, and found one very interesting.

The clock struck five as he let himself out through the small gate and walked the narrow path between green hedges full of noisy, nesting birds. Where the path joined the wider one he encountered a middle-aged countrywoman in broad hat and apron. It was her direct, shrewd look that alerted him to her being more than she seemed, and he wasn't surprised when a smile lit her face.

"Why, you must be the earl. I remember you now. I'm Lady Kerslake, Lord Wyvern. You and your family dined with us a couple of times many years ago. You've hardly changed at all."

Con felt as if no scrap of that innocent youth remained, but as he bowed he thought that such a positive statement doubtless came naturally to her. So this was the generous woman who had given a good home and unstinting love to her sister-in-law's carelessly discarded children.

"Lady Kerslake, I do remember. You were very kind."

"Oh, nonsense. A family of interesting strangers is an entertainment in these quiet parts. Are you walking up to the Crag, my lord? I'm going along that way a bit to see Will Cupper's grandmother at the stables."

They turned to walk together. "Susan says you don't plan to live at the Crag," she said.

"I know it will inconvenience the area, but I do have a home in Sussex. And," he added, "Crag Wyvern is Crag Wyvern."

"It is, isn't it? You know at various places along the coast the earth has given way now and then. I have thought it would be nice. But only if no one was injured, of course."

They shared a laughing glance that reminded him of Susan. So much of her must be from the family that had raised her—a good, solid family, all in all.

He was wondering what effect it would have on the Kerslakes if David established a claim to the earldom. He suspected that they were not the sort of family to enjoy the attention and speculation that would have to come.

At least the story was to their credit.

"I gather the Crag is built on a piece of reasonably solid ground," he said. "My relatives here have been peculiar, but not entirely crazy."

They had come to the stables and paused. "The first earl chose the building site, Lord Wyvern. I fear it has been all downhill since then. The lack of progeny could be seen as a sign of divine wisdom."

"I noticed in the churchyard that a Somerford woman married a Kerslake. Did that happen often?"

"Not to my knowledge. They've been peculiar all along. That would have been my husband's great-grandmother, I believe. A beauty, they say, but wild. The story goes that she danced herself to death by going to an assembly too soon after the birth of her third child."

Con sighed, looking up again at the house. "Do you think it's impossible? That anyone who lived there would be bound to go mad?"

Of course, David Kerslake wouldn't have to live there if he didn't wish to. He could build himself a house in the village here. But Crag Wyvern was still a burden any Earl of Wyvern had to bear.

"It's not a wholesome house," she said, "but it's the blood that is least wholesome, and that, thank heavens, has died out. Probably the place could benefit from some modern improvements and a lot of activity. My daughter Amelia has a great desire for you to hold a ball there."

"A ball! Would anyone come?"

"My dear Wyvern! Come to see the new mad earl? Most of the county would walk there in their bare feet."

He laughed. "A fashionable crush should certainly exorcise some ghosts."

"And if you need relief, come to dinner. You and your mischievous secretary. Take potluck. You will always be welcome."

"And Susan?" he asked, deliberately using her first name and watching for a reaction.

"She's always welcome, of course." She cocked her head, her eyes holding an appealing, practical wisdom. "You were good friends, I think, all those years ago. When we're young we tend to take such friendships for granted, thinking the world full of them. In time we see that they come rarely in life and should be treasured."

He noted the message. "Thank you. I do hope we can take up your invitation, Lady Kerslake, before we leave."

He opened the gate for her, closed it, and went on his way.

A rare and precious friendship. It was true, and he hadn't considered it that way, being generously provided with friends.

Or was he?

He, Van, and Hawk, being so close in age, and bound together by geography, had been destined to be friends. They were bound by time and proximity, but were in fact quite different in their natures. If they'd met elsewhere—at school or in the army, for example—they might not have formed such a close bond.

The same could be said for the Rogues. Nicholas had deliberately gathered a varied group. There were commoners and aristocrats, scholars and sportsmen, thinkers and men of action. They even had their republican rebel in Miles Cavendish, the Irishman.

There was a strong bond, but within the group other friendships had formed. During school terms Con's closest friend had been Roger Merryhew, who'd joined the navy and drowned within sight of England in a storm.

And then there had been Susan.

He and Susan could never be only friends and yet they could not be more. He'd sent that damned letter to Lady Anne. Though he'd love to wriggle off the hook now, he could not in honor do so.

Susan couldn't imagine where Con was. It wasn't the housekeeper's place to be fretting over her employer's whereabouts, and yet she couldn't help it. Had the letter so disturbed him that he'd ridden off a cliff?

Then she heard that he was back safely, and soon that he was sitting down to dinner with de Vere. She tried to put him out of her mind and, having made sure all was in order for the next day, retreated to her rooms.

Then Ada came to knock on the door and tell her that the earl required her presence in the library.

Oh, no. Not again. Tonight she would be strong. "Give him my regrets, Ada. Tell him I've retired with a headache."

"If you wish, ma'am, but your brother's there."

"David?" She stood and hastily pinned up her hair. "Very well."

She entered the library, wary of a trap. However, she found David there with Con. They were flipping through a portfolio of drawings they'd spread on the long table.

"Look at these," David said to her. "The original designs for the Crag."

He seemed completely unaware of any tensions or problems!

She went over, even though it brought her close to Con. A darkly thought-ful Con. Unease prickled through her. Why had he summoned David here? What did he intend to reveal?

"They were stained glass," she said, looking at a meticulous design for a set of glazed doors. "And one of the crazy earls had smashed them playing a ball game."

She caught a look from David that suggested that he wasn't completely unaware of tensions. Of course, she'd spilled the fact that she was in love with Con. She could only pray her brother wouldn't embarrass her.

Con firmly shut the portfolio. "I've asked you here for a reason, Kerslake. Take a seat, if you please, and you too, Susan." He sat on one of the library chairs, looking somber, and every inch the earl.

Susan and David sat on the opposite side of the table.

"Kerslake," Con said, "Susan showed you that letter from your mother."

"Yes. I hope you're not worried that I'll try to act on it."

It was all Captain Drake, and bloody arrogance.

"Not worried at all," Con said. "In fact, I hope you will."

Susan looked between them. David glanced at her.

"You want me to attempt to claim the earldom?" David asked. "Why?"

"Because," Con said, "I don't want it."

"You look sober."

"I am, and damned serious to boot. Listen. Even if the earldom was the wealthiest in England, and Crag Wyvern a place of beauty and refinement, I would not want it. I am foolishly attached to the place of my birth, and my father's title is good enough for me. I've accepted my duty, as we're all trained to do, but now I've been presented with an escape, and with your help, I in-tend to take it."

"And without my help?"

Susan realized that Con could use the papers without David's consent.

But after a moment Con said, "No. I won't force it on you."

David looked at Susan again, but she had no wisdom to offer. This had taken her completely by surprise.

"But I don't have a drop of Somerford blood in me," David said at last.

"That's not entirely true," Con said. "You probably don't pay attention to your familiar graveyard. The Kerslakes and Somerfords have intermarried at least once. Your great-grandmother was a Somerford."

"Lord, the one who danced herself to death? Mad blood, and it's a mere drop, thank heavens."

"Yet probably more than I share with this branch of the family. It's six gen-erations since the first earl's younger son left here and ended up in Sussex. Since then, there's been no mingling at all."

David leaned back in his chair. "Perhaps I don't want it."

"We could fight over it. Loser wins all." Only a hint of humor suggested Con was joking.

"Do I want that kind of attention? Notoriety?" David surged to his feet and paced the room. "Captain Drake should be a shadowy figure."

"Then be shadowy. But instead of seeking the protection of the earl, you can protect yourself." Con put a piece of paper on the table. "Here is Isabelle Kerslake's sworn, signed, and witnessed testimony that she married the Earl of Wyvern in Guernsey, and that her three children were all sired by him. I have already destroyed her letter."

David froze to stare at him. "You really do want to get rid of this, don't you?"

"With all my heart, but not casually. I wouldn't do this if I didn't think you would be a good ruler for this part of England."

David flushed slightly at that, with pride. The favorable judgment of a man like Con was an accolade.

"There'll be a horrendous amount of talk," Con added, "and it will touch all your family."

"My family," David said. "One reason I'm reluctant to do this is my fam-ily. Uncle Nathaniel and Aunt Miriam won't like the fuss, but . . . I don't like disowning Mel Clyst. I'm proud to be his son. And I certainly don't like claiming the mad earl's blood."

"Few things come without cost," Con said. "It's your choice. I won't force it on you."

Susan thought before speaking, but then said, "Mel would love to see his son the Earl of Wyvern, David. It would be the perfect revenge."

"Revenge?" Con queried.

She turned to him. "As you know from the letter, the earl and Mel had a pact. According to Gifford, the earl helped catch Mel. He betrayed him."

"But according to Swann, the old earl made him work very hard to make sure that Mel Clyst didn't hang."

"Really?" Susan thought about it. "But of course. Death would be too easy, and would free Lady Belle to do her unpredictable worst. She probably would have marched up and installed herself in Crag Wyvern as countess. I wouldn't be surprised if he egged her on to follow Mel. For some reason, he finally wanted to be rid of them. She did come up here after Mel's sentencing. Perhaps to ask for help. If so, she didn't get it, because then she took the Horde's hoard."

Thinking aloud, she didn't realize what she'd said until it was out. Perhaps it was time to tell Con why she'd wanted the earl's money, but he didn't seem to have noticed, and she had to remember that he was pledged to marry Lady Anne Peckworth. It would be embarrassing to be trying to gain his good opinion.

David suddenly said, "I need time to think about this." To Con, he said, "Even though you claim not to want any of this, I thank you for your generosity. And for your high regard."

He left, and Susan and Con looked at each other. Awareness of each other, of being alone together, shivered through the room. Yet neither of them moved closer, or farther apart.

"Would it work?" she asked.

"I don't see why not. In addition to Lady Belle's statement, there must be records on Guernsey. Note, however, that the foolish woman didn't give a date. You were born when?"

"August 1789."

"So sometime before November 1788—"

"You're not suggesting I really could be the mad earl's daughter?"

"Unlikely, but if the marriage was about then, you'll probably never know." A teasing light in his eyes made her want to throw something, but warmed her. It gave hope again of friendship.

"I pray it was in summer. Wouldn't it be more sensible to take a sea voyage to Guernsey in a gentle month?"

"Definitely, but we're talking about the mad earl and Lady Belle."

Susan groaned. "Let's send immediately to Guernsey to hunt those registers."

"It might be easier to find the marriage certificate here."

"You clearly haven't tried a treasure hunt here."

He looked at her, gray eyes warm. "You regard that gold as belonging to the Dragon's Horde, don't you?"

"Yes. I'm sorry, Con, but the earl broke his covenant with the Horde, so he didn't deserve that money. It wasn't the whole of Mel's payments. He used to bring in all kinds of expensive curiosities to keep the earl happy."

"And without the money?"

"David will have to run contraband dangerously often. There are debts, and on top of that people depend on their smuggling income. If there's no work here, they'll hire out to other gangs. Once allegiance slips . . ."

"I see. Have you told him yet that half that stash of coin is his?"

"I assumed you had."

She felt herself color at the memory of what she'd done to earn her half, and then she also remembered the way it had ended.

"I'm sorry for taking offense at a reasonable question, Con."

"Don't take all the blame. I wasn't rational either. I'm not . . ." He spread his hands. "I'm not myself, which is a strange concept when you think of it, since we are what we are. I have no idea what myself is anymore, but I was beginning to find out before Crag Wyvern came crashing down on me."

"And I have made your situation more difficult. Perhaps it would be better if I left immediately. . . ."

"No." But then he looked out into nothing, a shadowy nothing. In the end he simply said, "Don't go, Susan. Not yet."

He rose, and she could almost see him pulling on a calm shell with practiced ease. "Tomorrow we'll have a hunt for those papers. By the way, a friend of mine, Nicholas Delaney, will be visiting, and will stay at least one night. I promised him the Chinese rooms."

"King Rogue. Was that where you went today?"

It was intrusive, even between friends, but his retreat inside that shell seemed all wrong to her.

He looked at her, deeply thoughtful, "You do remember, don't you? He has a lovely home. I'd like to take you there—" After a halted breath he continued, "You'll like him, I think. Perhaps your brother and cousin would like to join in the paper hunt. Do you have any other cousins at home?"

"Only Henry, the oldest, and he's not one for games."

He'd thought of taking her to visit his friend, then remembered Lady Anne. She longed to go closer, to help him, but that way lay disaster.

He suddenly fixed her with his silvery eyes. "Come to my room again, Susan. For nothing this time. We'd be careful."

Her mouth dried. "No need to be careful if it's nothing."

He smiled. "For everything, then." But the smile didn't warm the shadow in his eyes.

"It wouldn't be right, Con."

"Oh, yes, it would."

She wavered, almost a physical wavering toward him, which she fought to resist. She wouldn't even mention Lady Anne, for that might make it seem like a contest between them. "You'd regret it later."

He began to come around the table to her. "Regrets are hard to judge ahead of time. Have you noticed that? I have deeply regretted not forcing you to see sense eleven years ago." He was on her side now, and coming close, and she couldn't make herself run.

"Do you regret last night?" he asked.

"Only the ending of it," she whispered. "But—"

He pulled her into his arms and kissed her. The first joining of open lips conquered her resolve and melded her to him. When their lips finally parted it took all her strength not to say the fatal words, *I love you.* She gazed at him, tempted almost beyond will. Who could resist a tempest . . . ?

Then she realized that someone was tapping on the door.

Eyes met in guilt, and then they stepped apart. He went to open the door. Jane stood there, eyeing them suspiciously. "You've a visitor, milord."

"Who?"

"Says his name's Hawkinville. Major Hawkinville."

Susan's first alarmed thought was that it was a new, higher-ranking Preventive man, but then Con said, "Hawk," and she remembered that this was one of the other Georges.

Here?

Now?

A blessed interruption, but she wasn't sure she could cope with any more shocks and surprises, not with her body still seething with forbidden passion for Con.

Chapter Twenty-four

Con looked back at Susan briefly, regretting yet not regretting the interruption. It would have been madness to have surrendered, and deeply wrong.

"Bring him here, please," he said to the maid. When she'd left, he said, "He's a good enough friend I could show him his room and ignore him, but . . ."

"But he'd guess, and we can't do this, Con. You know that." Before he could unwisely protest that, she added, "You must remember Lady Anne."

His self-imposed prison. But she was right. Strong, honorable, and right. "I must, mustn't I? Very well, what rooms do we have available for Hawk?"

"The Jason rooms, and the Ouroboros."

"Oh, yes, the circular one with the dragon eating its own tail. But the Jason rooms have mazes on the walls, don't they? Arrange for Hawk to sleep in there. He enjoys a puzzle."

She was looking at him with a slight frown. "You don't seem happy to see your friend."

He shrugged. "I wonder why he's here. It's either trouble or curiosity, or both."

She began to say something else, but then they heard footsteps, and in a moment Hawk walked in looking the same as always. An elegant devil, even in ordinary riding clothes and after a long journey.

He was suddenly damned glad that Hawk was here, and grinned. After a swift, assessing moment, Hawk grinned back, executed an elaborate, archaic bow, and declared, "My Lord Earl!"

Con dragged him into his arms for a back-thumping hug. He'd have been glad to see Hawk again in any circumstances after a year, but he felt as if sanity had just swooped into his chaotic life. For a start, Hawk had always had a gift for puzzles, and Crag Wyvern was full of them.

Hawk glanced to one side and Con saw Susan standing there, the perfect image of a housekeeper except for her good looks and the lack of a cap. He was faced with a sudden decision.

"Hawk, this is Miss Susan Kerslake of Kerslake Manor, who's been kind enough to fill in here as housekeeper. She's also an old friend. Susan, Major Hawkinville. You've heard me speak of him."

She gave him a quizzical look, but then offered her hand to Hawk rather than bobbing a servant's curtsy.

Hawk took it and bowed. "Charmed, Miss Kerslake."

Con had no doubt that he was making a hundred rapid assessments and calculations and coming to conclusions, many of them correct. But he didn't regret introducing Susan as she was.

She said, "The Jason rooms then?" and when he agreed, she left with a pleasant smile.

Hawk looked at Con, but all he said was, "An interesting house."

"Wait till you see the whole of it. Trouble?"

"I don't think so," Hawk said. "Van's probably getting married."

"Probably? I saw the notice in the paper."

"That was a pretense. Long story. But now it's become real if only he can persuade her. I provided him with some ammunition that should carry the day."

"That's good, isn't it?"

Hawk had always been hard to read, and his years in army administration, some of it secretive, had perfected his inscrutability. But Con knew he was concerned about something.

However, Hawk merely said, "Excellent," and wandered over to consider the books on the shelves. "A conventional selection. I thought you said your predecessor was mad."

Con certainly understood an inclination to keep secrets, so he let it go. "The interesting stuff's upstairs. Come along and I'll show you."

But Hawk stayed where he was. "Perhaps I am jealous of Maria. A lowering thought. One George married. You here in Devon."

"I've no intention of living here, but our lives can never be as they were when we were sixteen. We will doubtless all marry."

Con thought of three new families—Van's, his, and Hawk's—linked as closely as the old ones, their children growing up as friends.

But it was Susan's children he saw, not Anne's.

Perhaps it would become more real if he put it into words.

"I have more or less offered for Lady Anne Peckworth."

Despite having been out of the country for most of the past eleven years, and being a schoolboy when they joined the army, it took Hawk's encyclopedic mind only a moment. "Daughter of the Duke of Arran? A good match."

"Yes."

"More or less?" Hawk wouldn't miss a phrase like that.

"I've arranged to speak to her father when I return east."

"Ah."

Con could see questions in Hawk's eyes, but at least he didn't ask them. "What of you?" Con asked, "A lady in mind?"

God, such a stilted conversation. Was there no real friendship to recapture?

"Give me time. I've been in England for only a week. Besides, unlike my fellow Georges, I have neither title nor large estate to offer. Since I have no intention of living at Hawkinville Manor with my father, I don't even have a home."

Trouble there too. Despite Susan, despite a tentative healing, Con flinched back from probing it.

"How is your father? I heard he suffered a seizure of some kind."

"Recovering. I haven't been there yet."

Conversation dragged to a halt again. "Perhaps we should be taking a bath," Con said.

Hawk's brows rose in a question, and Con laughed. "Come and see."

At sight of the Roman bath, Hawk whistled. "Crazily extravagant, but I can't say I like the decor. He really didn't like women, did he?"

"I presume because they kept failing him. A man like that always blames the woman. But sharing hot water seems to encourage confidences."

"I must remember that next time I have a deceitful supplier to question. Though," he added, "considering the personal habits of most deceitful suppliers, perhaps not."

They strolled back into the bedroom, and Con looked at the fresco of Saint George and the dragon. "Apparently this was modeled after my ancestor, the first earl."

"Not a warrior, I assume. I wouldn't bet on this one against that dragon."

"Nor I. Notice there's no cross bar on that lance? The beast would keep running up it and eat him as it perished."

They fell into a humorous, professional analysis, then progressed to the Wyvern rooms, joking about various aspects of the corridors. Con felt the old ease unfurling between them tentatively, but with all the sure power of an unfurling leaf, and gave silent thanks.

When he saw the bed, Hawk burst out laughing. "After all this, he never showed signs of fathering a child?"

"Ah," Con said. "Now that is a most interesting question." He sketched in the details of Lady Belle's letter.

Hawk smiled. "What a splendid notion. You think you can persuade young Kerslake to go through with it?"

"I hope so. Can you see any problem?"

Hawk contemplated the blank wall facing the bed. "No serious ones. It's suspicious that he fathered no more children, but these things happen. And his habit of drinking strange brews might have had a negative effect. I wonder what happened to the young woman who played the part in Guernsey."

"She might come forward when it becomes common talk?"

"More likely demand money for her silence. That can be the new earl's problem. And you know, from my very brief exposure to your predecessor's nature, I wonder if she survived."

"He pushed her off the boat on the way home?"

"And kept that marriage certificate in these rooms. He'd want it close. Sewn into a book's binding. Or in a cavity cut into the walls . . ."

He walked forward and ran his fingers around a blank piece of wall opposite the bed. "Has anything been moved from here?"

"I don't think so. Why? You've found something?"

"I've found a blank piece of wall in a room otherwise completely cluttered, and a mark. . . . Ah." He dug his nails in and pulled, and part of the faux stone slid sideways.

Behind was not a secret compartment, however, but a drawing of a young woman. It was a highly worked professional piece clearly showing the delicate lace trimming of her dress, and the pearls around her neck. Her hair was simply gathered up in the manner of a girl just out in society. Nothing could be told from her face, however, because the paper had been slashed like a pie, and the triangular pieces hung away from the gaping hole.

"Isabelle Kerslake, I assume," Con said. He'd thought he was past being

shocked by his predecessor, but this was vile. "He lay in his bizarre bed looking at her, and hating her and Mel Clyst. I wonder why he suddenly decided
to act on it."

"Men break. The last straw, and all that." Hawk looked around at the cluttered room. "I admit, it will be interesting to take this place apart piece by
piece and find his other secrets along with that paper."

"We seek only to amuse," Con said. "Perhaps I should open this to the
masses and charge a penny a gawk. Nicholas Delaney will be turning up tomorrow too. He doesn't have your eye for solving mysteries, but he can be
perceptive in his own way."

"The founder of the Rogues? I look forward to meeting him."

Con shook his head. "Lord, but it feels strange to have people coming
here. Ordinary people. Perhaps we should invite up the Kerslakes. I only
worry that Crag Wyvern will split open and crumble away."

"Sorry if you're attached to it, but good riddance as long as no one's killed
in the collapse."

"Someone else said that. And neither she nor you have seen the torture
chamber yet."

"Thank the Lord. It wouldn't be surprising, you know, if this place had
loosened some of your screws."

"As obvious as that, is it?" Con asked, navigating a way out of the room
and back into the corridor.

"Is Diego still with you?" Hawk asked.

"Yes, why?"

"He'd only have come to England if he felt needed."

This was the astute assessment of someone who knew him well, the assessment he'd feared. Now it didn't seem intolerable.

"It's war sickness," he said as he locked the room. "I was getting over it."

"Dare?" Hawk asked, persistent as a surgeon after shrapnel.

In Brussels, before Waterloo, they'd all shared a billet—Van, Hawk, Dare,
and himself. Van and Hawk, professional soldiers like himself, had been
somewhat impatient with Dare's unshadowed enthusiasm, but they'd come
to like him. Cheerful, generous Dare was impossible to dislike.

"Dare's death didn't help," Con said, leading the way down the corridor.
"But it isn't insane to find the experience of death and agony unsettling."

"Of course not. But I gather you've been avoiding your friends."

"Not any longer," Con said, grateful to arrive at the Jason rooms. "Bring
'em all on. The more the merrier."

He left Hawk there, knowing it wasn't particularly friendly, but needing to be by himself. Friendship was unfurling, but he wasn't quite ready for the full power of it yet.

Where? In this fortress of rooms, where could he be sure to be undisturbed? In the Wyvern rooms, probably, but he wasn't going there.

The roof. He and Fred had found the way up to the roof and he thought he could remember it. He went up a circular staircase into the floor that contained the water cisterns. Then he found the trapdoor and climbed out.

Chill evening air hit him, blessedly welcome, and he leaned on a merlon to look at land and sea, at "outside."

Kerslake was reluctant to take this on for a number of reasons. Con wondered if it was pure selfishness to try to persuade him. But in holy truth he'd think himself blessed never to have to come here again.

Except that owning Crag Wyvern would offer the painful hope of at least seeing Susan again. If Kerslake did become earl, there would be no reason. No excuse . . .

He began to stroll around the parapet, but as he turned onto the south wall he stopped. Susan was there facing him, a knitted shawl wrapped around her for defense against the brisk sea air.

She looked like the simplest country woman.

She looked, as always to him, magnificent.

"I'm sorry," she said. "I was hoping you wouldn't notice I was here."

He didn't take it wrongly. He knew exactly what she meant.

He walked nearer. "Come to Irish Cove with me?"

She stared at him, but not with surprise. "It's a chilly evening."

"I wasn't thinking of going swimming."

She cocked her head, considering him, but then she said, "All right."

He led the way back to the trapdoor, but as he stood aside to let her go down first he said, "Would you change for me? Out of that gray gown."

She considered it again. "If you wish."

When they arrived at the garden level she said, "I won't be long," and walked off toward the kitchen area.

He'd like to go with her in case she changed her mind, but he made himself wait, hoping no one was going to interrupt this. Race was back in the office, but might pop out for some reason. Hawk . . .

He'd abandoned Hawk, and Hawk was doubtless drawing all kinds of conclusions. If he was drawing the right ones, he wouldn't interfere.

Though perhaps he should.

A gentleman engaged to marry one lady did not go for evening walks with another.

So why was he going with Susan to Irish Cove? To deal with shadows from the past. No more. It was certainly too chilly for a reenactment.

She appeared in a simple, high-necked blue cotton dress, her hair uncovered and in a plait, but with her shawl still wrapped around her for warmth. He'd rather she left off the shawl, but that would be asking her to suffer even more for him.

They walked out together and followed the path along the grassy headland for a while, contentedly in silence. He realized that this was a friendship he could accept in all its power, without reservation. If he hadn't built a wall between them.

Eventually they came to a slippage where they had to scramble over rough rocks. She laughed as she tried to hold up her skirts and cling to his hand. "This was much easier in a girl's shorter skirts!"

"Or in breeches."

She smiled at him. "Or in breeches. This is a mad enterprise, you know."

"Do you want to go back?"

"Not at all. Perhaps we'll be lunatic lovers, lost over the cliffs." Then she sobered with awareness of her words.

"We are lovers," he said, pulling her up to solid ground again. "Past, and almost present."

And future? almost escaped. But he didn't want to be Susan's lover. The carnal part would be wonderful, but it wasn't the essence of what he wanted. He wanted the golden friendship, the companion for life.

The wife.

He would not dishonor her by taking and giving less.

"Lovers are so often tragic, aren't they?" she said, wrapping her shawl more tightly around her and knotting it at the back. He helped, drinking in even this slight touch, his hands against her supple back.

"Because lovers are generally engaged in something illicit," he said.

"This isn't precisely licit, is it?"

Typical of Susan to insist on honesty. Could he live with anything less?

They walked on briskly, and gradually, out here where they'd roamed eleven years ago, they fell into the easy talk of the past, about plants and animals, and the sea and the sky. Then about the adventures of the years between.

First the light ones that carried no weight, but wove a fragile net between them. Then some of the more sober ones.

She told him more about working with the mad earl. He told her about army life.

He shared more about Waterloo and Dare, and she related with brief honesty her two times with other men.

The net they were building contained future pain as well as pleasure, but he was sure she was as willing as he to bear it.

Near an abandoned chapel, glassless windows showing a stark stone interior, they struck off across rough ground toward the cove. The route they followed was a faint smuggler's trail, mostly overgrown with weeds, and they had to watch the ground for unpredictable dips and bumps.

When they arrived at the steep path to the beach, Con hesitated. "Did we really go down there without a thought?"

"Too old to make it anymore?" With a teasing smile, she pulled the hem of her skirt up to her waist and produced pins to fasten it there, leaving her stockinged legs bare to the knees. Then she was off, finding handholds on roots, and on some rods conveniently driven in for the purpose.

With a laugh, he followed, not hesitating even when his boots slipped on the soft clay rock.

She jumped the last few feet to the pebbly beach and turned to watch him. He jumped too, and swept her into his arms. Just a hug, a friendly hug, but they clung in the salt air, and he knew she was absorbing him as he was absorbing her. Was she, too, feeling as if she was becoming a whole person here?

They drew apart in synchrony, perhaps both recognizing a point of no return, and looked around at the small cove.

"I think of it as bigger," he said.

"It hasn't shrunk, but there was more sand here. The sea changes. Like everything else."

She walked down toward the rippling waves, and he followed, admiring the elegant lines of her body, so different from those of a girl, but familiar, and not just from last night. A man knowing a young tree still recognizes it full-grown.

Last night. Had he been trying to prove something? To demonstrate his many lovers since her?

A smile fought through, and he said, "Susan?"

She turned, smiling, holding a strand of inevitably escaping hair off her face, her skirt still kirtled up to her knees at the front.

"Last night. I was trying to impress you."

A hint of a blush touched her cheeks. "You succeeded."

"I was fighting the memory of your many partners, all hugely endowed by nature, all possessed of the skills and experience of the world's greatest lovers."

She laughed. "Truly?"

"Truly."

"It wouldn't have mattered."

"I know." He had to speak the painful truth. "I'd welcome a chance to do better, but I have committed myself to Lady Anne, alas."

Her smile faded. "Alas?"

"Alas. Perhaps it would be better if I pretended otherwise, but I can only give you honesty. On my first day at Crag Wyvern I wrote to her and as good as offered marriage. I didn't come here with it settled in my mind, but I was drifting that way. It didn't seem to matter whom I married. She is a sweet young lady who deserves a husband. When I wrote the letter, however, I was using her—as a shield against you. Which she now is. Alas."

"And otherwise?" she asked.

Honesty, honesty. It could break his heart and hers. "Otherwise, I would have hope, at least, of winning you for my wife, my friend, my helpmeet all my days."

She turned suddenly away, hand still holding back her hair. From her stance he guessed she was fighting tears.

He walked up to her and put his arms around her from behind. "Once, you threw away what we had. Here, in Irish Cove. Three days ago I repeated the folly. It would seem we are tragic lovers after all."

He leaned down to kiss her wind-chilled neck. She lowered her arm slowly, letting her hair blow as it willed.

"All my life," she said, "I've been a fighter against fate. I've fought to make things be as I willed them to be, and what do I have?" She extended her open hands. "Wind between my fingers. But even so," she said, clenching those hands, "I am tempted again. Tempted to fight this."

He shook his head against hers. "I cannot draw back. A few months ago another Rogue, Lord Middlethorpe, courted Lady Anne. He didn't go so far as to offer marriage, but it was understood. She expected an offer, and he planned to make one. But then he met another. Soon the other woman was with child, and so one honorable necessity overrode the other."

She turned roughly in his hands. "I could be with child." But then she squeezed her eyes shut. "No, no! I don't want you that way, Con, with dishonor and regret around us."

He kissed her closed lids. "If you are with child, I must marry you, but I cannot in honor wish for it. And Lady Anne and her family will expect more from me before you can know. I told her I'd return in a week. I confess, I don't see how to handle any of this with decency, never mind elegance."

She leaned her head against his shoulder. "I'm praying not to be with child." He heard a soft laugh. "All my life, above anything, I have wanted to be normal. I wanted to be like my cousins, like David, who fits comfortably into the ordinary world. But a wildness beats in me. It drives me to disregard rules and conventions, to seek the open spaces and adventures, even as I long to be like others, to belong. I wanted a normal courtship and wedding, but my wild side threw me into your arms. Then made me tear us apart."

He held her tighter. "I don't want you to be anything other than as you are, Susan."

"But I seem to carry the seeds of destruction within me."

He deliberately chuckled. "I think you've been living too long in Crag Wyvern, love. Real life isn't so melodramatic."

"It feels it to me." She raised her head to look at him, and he saw tears glittering on the rims of her eyes. He didn't mention them. "Is there no chance that Lady Anne will refuse your suit?"

He felt her pain because it mirrored his own. "I don't know. It did occur to me that she might be less willing to marry Viscount Amleigh than to marry the Earl of Wyvern, but I don't think she is so petty. We got along together very comfortably, and I believe that is what she wants. It was what I wanted a week ago. Or thought I wanted."

Gulls gave their sobbing cries, swirling past on the winds.

He might as well tell her the rest of it. She'd find out one day. "Anne lives quietly because she was born with a twisted foot. It prevents her dancing, or walking long distances, so she doesn't have many opportunities for flirtation and courtship, but she wants marriage, I think."

He saw it register with her as it must. This was not an opponent she could with honor fight.

"It makes me think of breaking a leg and becoming crippled, too."

He laughed because it was a joke, and because it was so very much a part of her to express what many would keep shamefully secret.

Despite the chill he could stay here forever, but the sun was beyond the horizon, and the pink and pearly remnants of light were beginning to fade to gray.

"We must head back," he said. "We don't want to be out in the dark."

She moved apart from him and openly wiped her eyes with the back of her hand. He pulled out his handkerchief and she took it to dry her eyes and blow her nose. "I don't want to go back," she said.

"But we have no choice."

"I do. I'm going home to the manor."

After a moment, he nodded. "It is time. I won't ask you to persuade your brother. It isn't an easy burden to take up, and I understand all his scruples. Will you come up to Crag Wyvern tomorrow to join in the paper hunt? Whatever your brother decides, we need to find those papers and deal with them."

"Yes, of course." She took his hand and they walked back up the beach, soft pebbles shifting beneath their feet. "I don't know what I want him to do, either. I see all the advantages, but I wonder if there's a curse to being Earl of Wyvern."

"Curses can be broken. Perhaps one of those books says how." He looked up the narrow path. "Talking of curses, I think going up is worse than going down."

"The alternative is to drown, sir." With a saucy grin, she set off, agile as a cat. What could a man do but follow?

"Most battles are fought on fairly flat ground, you know," he called after her.

She only laughed.

There was still laughter, and that was a miracle.

At the top, however, looking down at the place that had been so crucial in their lives, she said, "Yours is the hardest part."

"Why?"

She looked at him. "Because you will do your best to be a good, loving, contented husband to Lady Anne, whereas I will be free to be a sour, eccentric spinster." She grabbed his hand and pulled him on, back toward the rest of their lives. "You can't imagine how relieved I am at the thought of not sleeping another night in Crag Wyvern."

"Oh, can't I?"

Though I'd sleep in hell itself, he thought, *to spend my nights with you.*

Chapter Twenty-five

He woke the next morning to a subtle awareness that Susan was not in the house, and that they had decided their future.

In harmony, but apart.

She'd spoken of the urge to fight, and it raged in him too. Fight to seize the treasure from the jaws of fate. Duty and discipline ruled, however. He had taken this course of his own free will, and since it involved another, he must follow it.

He got out of bed and managed to summon some enthusiasm for the day's paper hunt. On a simple level it could be amusing, and if David Kerslake accepted his part, it would pave the way to a kind of freedom, at least from Crag Wyvern.

Hawk was here, he remembered, and Nicholas had promised to come. Susan, too. It could, for a miracle, even be a day of lighthearted fun. In the presence of outsiders, so much about the mad earl now seemed ridiculous rather than horrific.

He pushed to the back of his mind all thoughts about the future, as he'd so often pushed away thoughts of death and maiming before battle.

He found Race in the breakfast room, consuming his usual enormous meal, and then Hawk walked in. Con performed the introductions.

Hawk sat, saying, "We met, I think, at Fuentes de Oñoro."

"Lord, yes," Race said, for once looking a little awed. "I was a cornet then. I'm surprised you remember."

Con smiled. "Don't flatter yourself. Hawk rarely forgets anything."

"It's a curse," Hawk agreed. "But in fact, de Vere was left in charge when his senior officers were wounded, and I had to leave the orderly retrieval of his troop in his hands. Did what he was told precisely and efficiently. That is truly rare."

"Obedient to a fault," Race said, seeming to have recovered his normal manner. "Which brings me to ask, my lord, if you have any particular duties for me today."

Con realized that Race didn't know what was going on. Once the maids had replenished the dishes, he explained.

"Beautiful," Race said, with all the glow of the cherubim looking on the face of the Lord. "I wish I had known this Lady Belle." .

"She'd have eaten you for dinner," Con said.

"Oh, no, I don't think so."

And on consideration, Con didn't either.

After another mouthful of thick ham, Race asked, "Did Lady Wyvern come up to Crag Wyvern shortly before she left?"

"I think Susan mentioned that, yes," Con said. "Why?"

Race smiled again. "She killed him, of course. Wonderful woman. He'd broken their pact and harmed the man she loved, so she came up here for vengeance. I assume he would let her into the sanctum, and while there, she slipped something deadly into one of his favorite ingredients."

"Because, of course," Hawk said with the same delight at the puzzle, "she could not have heard of his death on her travels, and yet according to your account, she assumed it in her letter to her daughter, yes?"

"Yes." Con absorbed it. "Of course she killed him. She is nothing if not consistent in her allegiances. She probably also calculated the advantages of having the influence of the Earl of Wyvern working for her—especially if it was her son. One wonders what will become of Australia—"

"Still at breakfast?"

Con turned to see Susan in the garden doorway in a becoming peach-colored dress and modish bonnet. Another Susan, and one he could become very used to seeing in the morning. Beside her was a shorter, pretty young woman with big, sparkling eyes.

"I'm Amelia Kerslake," she said, without waiting for an introduction, though she did drop a curtsy. "I'm sure you can use extra hands, Lord Wyvern."

As he rose with the other men, Con said, "We can use extra hands, if you're not easily shocked, Miss Kerslake." He looked a question at Susan, wondering if she'd told her cousin the details. She only smiled, which was somewhat hard to interpret, so he said, "But we poor paltry males have only just begun our breakfast and need our sustenance. Will you sit with us?"

Once everyone was seated, Con introduced Hawk, noting that young Amelia was eager to test her flirtatious teeth on anything male. He was sure Hawk and Race could cope.

To Susan, he said, "Is your brother coming?"

There were other things he'd rather say, but during a night short on sleep, he'd arrived at a point of calm and acceptance. It would seem that she had too.

"He had some business to do, but will come up later. He still hasn't decided."

"There's no hurry."

"No, but we ladies are impatient to begin the hunt," she said to everyone, "so do eat up."

All the men laughed and cleaned their plates with speed.

"Army training," said Race, standing first. "The call to battle means don't waste what's on the table."

"Only to someone who needs a deep trencher to support a reed-thin frame," Con said, finishing more slowly.

Susan was amazed at how possible it was to be with Con like this, to be friends. Almost sisterly, though very unsisterly hungers swirled beneath. It was as if life had layers.

Like living water under ice, though that wasn't a good analogy, since the top surface of her life was surprisingly warm and almost joyous.

Like a delicious crust on a pie?

Like cream on a cake?

Like manure spread on a fallow field?

"What are you smiling about?"

She looked sideways at Con and told him.

He laughed aloud. "Don't take up poetry."

"Perhaps there's a place in the world for earthy poetry."

He winced at her pun. "Like the stone around the hearth," he offered. "Warmed from what it contains."

Smiling, they followed the others into the courtyard. De Vere was protesting that he was a great deal more substantial than a reed. Amelia had plucked a tall ornamental grass and was considering him against it, pretending the matter was in doubt.

Susan laughed along with everyone else, feeling a powerful rightness in the world, which was strange when her heart was breaking. Stones around fires did sometimes crack from the heat.

There was something so steady and strong between her and Con, however, that it was precious. Once this was over, they might not meet again. She was sure they wouldn't seek meetings. But the knowledge that the bond still lasted would be sustaining.

She still wished for other things, even prayed for other things, but not at the expense of another woman's heart.

She did wonder if Lady Anne would want a husband who would rather marry another. In the night, she'd fought and won the temptation to write and tell her. She knew Con would do his best not to let his divided heart show, and his best would be very good. Perhaps, in time, his regard for his wife and the mother of his children would deepen into a true love.

She had to pray for that, too.

She had brought this upon herself. Con might try to take the blame for writing to Lady Anne, but he would never have reacted that way if she hadn't behaved so foolishly all those years ago.

She caught Major Hawkinville looking at her with far too keen an eye, and chose the bold approach. "The atmosphere of Crag Wyvern does incline to melancholy, doesn't it, Major?"

"Perhaps one has to be particularly susceptible, Miss Kerslake."

"And you are not of a melancholic disposition?"

"I'm far too practical. Why is this empty basin labeled 'The Dragon and His Bride'?"

She moved closer to it. "It had statues. The dragon and his bride."

"Ah. Having seen the Roman bath, I can imagine."

"Are you talking about the fountain?" asked Amelia, who had always been able to follow many conversations at once. "I'd like to see the figures."

"It's not suitable," Susan said.

"You've seen it, and you're as much of a maiden as I am."

Susan flashed Con a look, then knew it was a terrible mistake. She could feel her color rising and of course could do absolutely nothing to stop it. "I know it's shameful at twenty-six," she said in an attempt to cover it, "but there's no need to make such a point of it, Amelia."

"Susan!" Amelia exclaimed, going pale. "You know I never meant—"

"Yes, I know," Susan said, going over to hug her. "I was funning. But the statues are not at all pleasant."

She saw de Vere looking at her with raised, speculative brows and knew she might as well have shouted her sin from the rooftop.

"I think I should see it," Major Hawkinville said. "I need to see everything to do with the old earl if I'm to help solve this puzzle. But then," he added, with a slight smile, "I'm no maiden."

Susan thought he'd picked that up to cover the moment and said a prayer of thanks. As she expected, however, Amelia insisted that she should come too.

"Very well, but don't tell Aunt Miriam!"

She distinctly heard the major murmur, "I doubt she's a maiden, either."

Con led the way, since he knew where the figures had been placed—in a windowless alcove off the great hall.

"We couldn't face trying to get them up or down stairs," he said, "and they'd be leaving through the hall anyway. They're only about half size," he added, drawing back a heavy curtain, "but dashed difficult to manhandle."

Susan stood back to let Major Hawkinville go in, but when Amelia followed, she felt obliged to look.

Apart, the figures lost some of their unpleasantness. The dragon lay on its back, its legs in the air like a puppy, making its large organ ridiculous and its snarl rather like a silly grin. She bit her lip, and Amelia laughed outright. The woman, however, was still somewhat embarrassing, if only because she looked as if she was in a private ecstasy.

Con stayed outside, though when Amelia laughed, de Vere went in. Susan heard him say something, and Amelia laughed again.

"Doubtless highly improper," she said to Con, joining him outside.

"Almost certainly."

"What are you going to do with those figures?"

"If your brother takes up my offer, it can be his problem."

The others emerged then, Major Hawkinville steering Amelia and de Vere like a teacher with young pupils. He gave Con and Susan a wry smile, but even so, she thought he assessed them.

He was one of those men, she decided, who couldn't help puzzle out everything they came across. She gathered, from things Con had said on the way to Irish Cove, that puzzling out things had been part of "the Hawk's" work for the Quartermaster-General's Department. Mostly he'd been engaged in the usual QM work—moving the army around efficiently and making sure it had the necessary supplies to live and fight with. He'd also, however, shown a gift for sorting out problems and investigating crimes.

A man like that would be bound to detect the feelings between them, she supposed. All the more reason for these to be their last days.

Lady Anne could be perceptive and intelligent too, and even if she did not see them together, others would. Stories would weave from place to place and reach her eventually. They always did.

"Did inspiration strike?" Con asked his friend.

"No, but I didn't expect it to. My method is the tedious accumulation of details. Eventually a pattern emerges that points to the solution."

"You are assuming some sanity at work."

"True chaos is rare. Madmen have their logic and purposes, too."

"If you insist. I give you command of this, Hawk."

They all went up to the Wyvern rooms, Amelia exclaiming with delight at the gothic décor along the way. Yorrick the skeleton was a particular thrill.

At the sanctum door, Con took out his key, but it wasn't locked. They entered to find Mr. Rufflestowe busily cataloguing. He looked considerably startled at the invasion, and Susan at least was startled to find him there. She'd forgotten all about him.

"We're on a hunt, Rufflestowe," Con said. "A legal document that the earl misplaced, probably in these rooms."

"I have placed any papers I've found in the books on the desk, my lord, but none are legal documents. Most are scribbled notes, some are recipes."

Con went over and looked quickly through them. "As you say." He looked at the major. "What method do we use?"

"A systematic one," Hawkinville said, eyes already stripping the room of secrets. "We have six people and four walls, a desk, and the rest of the space. You take the desk, Con—"

But Mr. Rufflestowe interrupted. "If you will permit, my lord, I will begin work on the books in the other room."

Con's brows rose, but he said, "By all means, but keep an eye open for a legal document, or a place where one might be concealed."

The curate left, and Con laughed. "I wonder what devilment he thinks we're up to?"

"Here," Susan pointed out, "devilment is not a word to be laughed at."

"But laughter chases away the devil," de Vere said.

"Five," Hawkinville firmly interrupted. "Con, you should still take the desk, since there'll be papers there to do with the earldom. The rest of us will take a wall each."

Susan found herself with the door wall. That meant significantly fewer shelves to search, but even so, she was soon very weary of the painstaking business. She also wished she were back in her gray gown. Her hands and dress were covered with dust.

She glanced at Amelia and found her murmuring the odd comment to de Vere as she went through racks of scrolls, and laughing at his quiet replies. De Vere had the ingredients to explore, which he was thoroughly enjoying.

Con was sitting at the desk sorting papers into piles much as de Vere had done in the office, but when he looked up and caught her eye she knew it was not a task he enjoyed.

They shared a wry smile and returned to work.

Then the door beside her opened and Jane came in, her face disapproving as always. "A Mr. Delaney, milord," she said, looking around the room as if they were a bunch of children up to no good.

Con rose. "Nicholas. Good, you haven't missed the fun."

"As bad as that, is it?" said the man who must be Nicholas Delaney, leader of the Rogues.

As introductions were made, Susan studied him with interest. He was handsome in a casual style. Even his blond hair had a softer tone than de Vere's, and looked as if it was barbered only when he thought about it.

She remembered being intrigued by Con's stories of him. He had almost hero-worshiped him, though it hadn't been expressed as such. His name had simply come up a great deal, with many sprinklings of "Nicholas says."

Yesterday Con had mentioned visiting him. Though that had been about all he'd said on the subject, she felt the visit had helped him settle his mind about many things.

"Hawk's in charge," Con said. "I feel blessed to have the paperwork. Most of the rest of the stuff is foul in both physical and metaphysical ways."

"But remember," Delaney said, "I have an interest in these matters. Is that claiming to be mandragora?" he asked, going over to a jar on the shelves.

"Can you tell if it is or not?" Hawkinville asked.

"I was given an illustrated lecture on the subject once." Delaney opened the jar and extracted a withered, bifurcated root. "By all the sorcerers, I think it is." He popped it back in the jar. "You can sell that for a fair amount, Con."

"Excellent, but need I remind you that we're looking for a document?"

Nicholas laughed. "Aye-aye, sir!"

Hawkinville said, "If you have knowledge, Delaney, perhaps you could check for treasures while de Vere takes over my wall of books. I will search the spaces in between."

Susan saw Delaney nod as if this made perfect sense.

He caught her looking at him and smiled. She turned hastily back to her shelves of books, resenting another perceptive observer.

More than perceptive.

Knowing.

What had Con told him?

Nicholas Delaney worked quickly through the rest of the ingredients, then came over to study the books Susan had already opened and checked. "Did you see anything by the Count de Saint Germain here?"

"I haven't been looking at titles," she said. "But Mr. Rufflestowe has catalogued all these, I believe."

"He being interested in titles, but not in clever hiding places. I'll check his lists. Con has offered me first pick."

"You are a student of alchemy, sir?" She couldn't help but show her disapproval.

"I'm a student of everything," he replied with a smile, taking out a book, opening it, then returning it to the shelf. "You have lived in this area all your life, Miss Kerslake?"

"Yes."

"Probably you knew Con when he visited here years ago, then."

She grew belatedly wary, but wouldn't lie. "Yes. We are of an age."

"He clearly had interesting memories of his time here. Ah, excuse me." He reached in front of her to take a tall, leather-bound book off the shelf. "A *Physica et Mystica.* Con," he called across the room. "Your fortune is made. The last copy I heard about went for three hundred."

"The Earl of Wyvern's fortune is made," Con corrected. He looked at the desk and table. "I think I'm finished here. I suppose it was unlikely that the marriage certificate would be in such an open spot, and I can't see any secret compartments."

"No offense, Con," Hawkinville said, "but I'd like to check that." He pulled out all the drawers, checking for hidden compartments. Then he slid under the furniture on his back and they heard tapping and rattling, but when he worked his way out, he said, "You're right. Nothing."

He dusted himself off. "Nothing in the floor or ceiling. The shelves here are fixed very solidly to the walls, and there are no spaces between them. Windows, curtains, doors. All clear. The proportions of the room seem right."

So that was what he'd meant by the spaces in between. Susan thought of her haphazard search for the gold and knew they were in the hands of a professional.

She honestly wished she could leave it entirely in his hands.

"I think we should have a luncheon," she said, then realized that it was no longer her place to even think of such things. Even as housekeeper it had not been her place.

But Con said, "An excellent idea. We might as well invite Rufflestowe." He opened the door to the bedroom and Susan saw the curate bent over something on the cleared top of a bookcase.

"Found something?" Con asked.

The curate straightened, looking a little pink. "No, not really, my lord. I suppose this is not part of my ascribed duties, but the poor lady looked so . . ."

Con went in, and Susan followed. Rufflestowe had been bent over the slashed picture that had hung on the wall.

"I begged some egg white from the cook, my lord," the poor man said, looking as if he expected to be rebuked, "and used a sheet of thick paper on the back. It is not sticking down very well as yet."

All the same, the slashed scraps had been pulled together enough that a face existed.

Delaney demanded the story of the picture, and Con told it.

Amelia leaned closer. "She looks familiar. . . ."

"We think it's Lady Belle," Susan told her gently. "When she was younger than you."

"Oh, yes, there's a family portrait of her and Aunt Sarah hanging at the manor. This is probably a drawing for it. How horrid of him to cut it up like that and then keep it. If he disliked her so much, why not throw the picture away?"

"The ways of hatred," Con said thoughtfully. "I wonder if this can be picked up. . . ."

He did so, carefully, and it more or less stayed together. "Follow me."

He went out into the corridor and along to the Saint George rooms. Susan, realizing what he was thinking, hurried ahead to open the doors. They all ended up around the Roman bath with Amelia commenting wide-eyed on the pictures.

"It's the same," Susan said, whispering for some illogical reason, as if the woman on the ceiling, and on the floor of the bath, and in the portrait, might hear.

They were all the same person. All Lady Belle.

Her mother.

"And the fountain figure," Hawkinville said.

"By heaven, you're right." Con looked again at the slashed picture. "He had them all done in the image of Isabelle Kerslake, and doubtless saw himself as the dragon. God damn his black soul."

"Already done, I have no doubt, my lord," said Mr. Rufflestowe.

Con gave him the picture. "Take this back to the Wyvern rooms, Rufflestowe, then join us for luncheon."

The curate took the picture, but said, "I thank you most kindly, my lord, but I must return home. I am to preach tomorrow and must work on my sermon."

Con smiled wryly. "I think we must have provided much material for it."

The curate headed back to the old earl's rooms. The rest of them made their way thoughtfully down to the lower floor, coming to rest in the garden. Susan had no doubt they were all feeling in need of the relief provided by green and growing things.

They chatted about the strange items they'd encountered, and Susan wondered aloud where David was. Then she noticed Major Hawkinville still and silent. She glanced at Con, who was by her side as if it were the only place to be.

He said, "Thinking. He can become an island of calm in the middle of riotous disorder."

As if he'd heard, Hawkinville looked over at them. "Can I see those fountain figures again, Con?"

"Of course. You think there's a clue there?"

"Perhaps." There was something in the major's eyes that could almost be unease. When they paused outside the curtained alcove he said, "I'm not sure if decency requires that the ladies be excluded, or that only the ladies be permitted to search."

"Ladies should never be excluded," Delaney said. "Rogues' law."

"Really?" It was clear to Susan, at least, that Hawk Hawkinville thought this peculiar, but he said, "Come along then. Con, can we have a light?"

It was de Vere who went off to the kitchen to get a lighted candle. They all waited. Susan wanted to ask why Hawkinville thought they'd find the marriage certificate here.

"Because the fountain is labeled 'The Dragon and His Bride'?" she asked.

"It does seem somewhat pointed."

"And those figures are hollow," Con said. "But there are no openings to the inside. The pipe that fed water out of the dragon's er . . . shaft? Is that it?"

"It would be nice," Hawkinville said, but Susan didn't think he was optimistic.

De Vere returned with a candle guarded by a glass funnel, borne very obviously like an angel bearing a fiery torch. Con pulled back the curtain, de Vere marched in, and they all squeezed in after.

In the flickering candlelight, the dragon did not look so funny, and its mouth did seem to snarl. It was an opening of sorts, however, where not filled with the long forked tongue. There was also the water pipe.

Major Hawkinville said, "Con?" offering him the job.

"Please," Con said, gesturing for his friend to have the honor.

Hawkinville poked a finger into the mouth, but shook his head. He rolled the beast to peer down the pipe. "Anything hidden in here would have to be waterproof, securely attached, and quite flat. And fairly close to the opening." He produced a long, thin knife from somewhere and probed, then straightened. "I don't think so."

"You never did think so," Con said. "Where?"

Hawkinville turned to the figure of the woman. The raped or rapturous Lady Belle.

"Where," he asked, "do you think the demented earl would have hidden it?"

The bride's mouth was open, but it was obviously a shallow space.

Then Susan realized and looked down between the spread legs. It hadn't been obvious in the fountain with the dragon pressed against her, but the figure was anatomically correct. There still didn't seem to be a hiding place, but she went forward. "I'll do it."

Her tentative fingers found something that wasn't metal. Wax. "A knife, or something," she said, hearing her voice waver slightly in the silent room.

Con knelt beside her, offering his penknife. "Do you want me to do it?"

"No, it should be me."

Wincing slightly, she dug the knife into the wax and carved it away. It became easier. It became only wax. And when the final bit came free, she saw a slender roll. She pulled it out and gave it to Con, then picked up some wax and pushed it back into the space as best she could.

Nonsensical, but she had to do it.

She stood. "I want this statue melted down and made into something else. Something good."

"Saint George?" Con said. He took off his jacket and spread it over the statue, then led the way out of the alcove.

"No. Something free. A bird, perhaps. Perhaps it has never been easy being Isabelle Kerslake, fighting to be free."

Con gave her a smile that said he understood, then unwrapped the package and unrolled the document. "The record of the marriage of James Burleigh Somerford of Devon, and Isabelle Anne Kerslake of the same county, on July 24th, 1789. Nearly a year before you were born, Susan."

He'd understood the depth of her fear that she might be the daughter of the mad earl.

"He probably never could father a child," he added. "Now, however, it's all up to your brother. You can take these to him."

She met his eyes, but he had himself under control as well. "Keep them, please. If he declines the honor, they are for you to deal with."

"As you will."

It was farewell, and they both knew it. They were under the eyes of others, but it was, in its way, a blessing.

"Come along, Amelia."

Susan did not look back as they headed for the exit to Crag Wyvern, but they were stopped by a young lad hurtling breathlessly in.

"Miss Kerslake!" But then he broke off, looking wild-eyed at the people nearby.

Sudden fear gripping her, she took Kit Beetham's arm and pulled him aside. "What?"

"It's Captain Drake, ma'am! He's holed up in old Saint Patrick's Chapel with the Preventives around him. Maybe wounded, too!"

Chapter Twenty-six

W ounded? How badly?"

"Don't know, ma'am. They flashed a signal down and my dad saw it. Trouble. Three of them there, and one or more wounded. Dad reckons Gifford will have sent for reinforcements and is pinning them there until they come."

Susan's heart was thundering, making it hard to think. *Stupid, stupid!* was running through her head. How had David been so stupid as to try smuggling in broad daylight?

"What is it?" Con appeared beside her. "What's happened?"

She shared the boy's message. "I'll have to try to organize a rescue. There's probably no one else. . . ."

"Of course there is. There's me for a start, and Hawk Hawkinville, and King Rogue."

She looked up at him. "You don't want to be involved in this."

His gray eyes were rock steady. "If you're involved, I am. And where I'm involved, so are my friends." To the boy he said, "Wait here for instructions."

"Yes, sir!" the lad declared. Susan could see an instinctive response to command, and the comfort of it. Someone was in charge and all would be right with the world.

She felt it too, but beneath it lay terror. David was in dire danger, and Con could be too, earl or not.

He led her back into the great hall and said to the men, "Council of war. The office, I think." To Susan, he said quietly, "What of your cousin?"

But Amelia said, "It's David, isn't it? I knew he'd do something stupid!"

"It appears she's part of our merry band," Susan said, startled that Amelia clearly knew more than she'd thought.

In the office Con related the basic situation. He included Gifford's threat to Susan without giving the history behind it. "He'll lose leverage by this. A strange maneuver."

"Perhaps not," Susan said. "Catching David red-handed would put even more pressure on me."

"But then why send for more troops? He'll want a quiet settlement with you."

"That's speculation. He might not have sent for anyone. He'll have the local boatmen. . . ." Then Susan sucked in a breath. "Con, Saint Patrick's Chapel is that ruin near Irish Cove."

Their eyes met. If Gifford had seen them embrace, he might be acting out of rage and envy.

Unpredictably.

And David might be wounded.

"I don't know what to do," she said.

Con took her hand. "It will be all right. How many men could Gifford have with him?"

"There are six boatmen here, but they usually go in pairs on land."

"We'll assume just Gifford and two for now, then." Con described the chapel to the others. "Easy to hold out in there against a couple of local men who don't want to get killed, and probably don't much want to kill, either. The ground around is mostly open. I don't want this to be a pitched battle, but I want Kerslake and his men safely away. Suggestions?"

Delaney said, "Hawkinville and I are strangers here. That's a good card to play. If we happen upon the scene, we can't be blamed for getting in the way."

"Of a musket ball?"

"We take our chances. Meanwhile, you and de Vere can attempt your rescue."

"And me," Susan said. "I'll not be left behind."

"I want to help, too," Amelia said.

Before Susan could protest, Delaney said, "Of course. But like any inexperienced trooper, you'll follow orders. Yes?"

Amelia frowned, but then said, "Yes, sir!"

"I'm not military. I'm just a Rogue. Con, is there a map of the place here?"

De Vere produced one from a drawer, spreading it on the desk. He traced the coastline, then said, "I thought so. Here it is. Irish Cove, and the cross must mean the chapel. It seems to be not far from the road to Lewiscomb, but there's a break."

"There was a landslip there fifty years or so ago," Susan said, "cutting the road off. No one uses it anymore."

"Except smugglers," Con added.

"And people out for a stroll."

Their eyes met for a strangely peaceful moment.

"A road still suitable for riding?" Hawkinville asked.

"Up to the break," Susan said. "But if you ride out from here, you'll be cut off before you get to the chapel. Walkers can make their way over the rough patch, but not horses."

"We'll come around from the other way," Delaney said, tracing a path. "Even less connection to Crag Wyvern. As ignorant strangers, we don't know the road is a dead end. We ride along, see something to catch our interest, and approach the chapel."

"Gifford shouts to you to get out of the area. . . ." Con supplied.

"And we hang around asking what's the matter. That gives you some room to act. With such open ground, however, it's going to be hard for the trapped men to escape without being shot."

"I'll deal with Gifford," Con said, "but we may need another distraction."

"Children," offered Amelia. "I take the schoolchildren for nature walks up there sometimes. He wouldn't be able to shoot with children around, would he?"

"It puts them at risk," Hawkinville protested, and clearly the other men shared his objection.

"They're used to taking part in smuggling," Susan said, "and we'll keep them out of danger. Go, Amelia, and take Kit Beetham with you."

Amelia turned to leave, but Con said, "Wait. We might be able to get the men away in disguise. Have two other women go with you—the tallest women available—and have them wear an extra layer of clothes that they can slip out of easily."

Amelia grinned. "Clever idea! But what of David? He's too tall."

"I know. He's my estate manager, however, and I'm going to be haughtily furious with whoever threatened him on my land. Get word to him if you can, Amelia, that that's his role."

"Amelia," Susan said as her cousin turned to leave. "The message said he's wounded. Bring bandages and such as well."

"Right." Amelia had paled at the mention of wounds, but she hurried off.

Susan swallowed. She'd supported using the children, but even with the utmost care, there could be a disaster. She saw Major Hawkinville looking at her.

"The commander's burden," he said. "It's never easy."

"I'm not the commander here."

"You're doing very well. Forgive me, but your charming dress does not seem suitable unless you're going to ply your wiles as a card with the riding officer."

"Oh, no." Susan's protest was instinctive. She added, "I have a better idea."

She hurried off, glad that she hadn't had a chance to move her possessions out of the house. The more strangers involved, the better. Gifford might not recognize her dressed as a man.

In short order she was in her breeches, shirt, and jacket, a neckerchief making a rough cravat. She looked in the mirror, unable to dodge the thought that she'd last dressed like this on the night that Con had returned.

She screwed up her eyes to force back tears and concentrated on completing her disguise.

She didn't usually bother with a hat, but she had one, a wide-brimmed countryman's hat. She pinned up her hair and crammed the hat on top. As a subtle touch, she wiped some soot from the chimney with her finger and made a bit of a beard shadow on her jaw and over her lips.

She studied herself in the mirror and decided it would do. Shame she wasn't tall enough to pass for her brother.

She made sure to stride boldly back into the office. "Well?"

Only Con and de Vere were there, but both looked impressed.

"It's pretty convincing," de Vere said, "and I have another idea. Back to your rooms, quickly."

Con came with them, and when they arrived, de Vere began to strip. "I can probably fit in your gown."

They were of a height, Susan realized, though she wasn't sure the shoulders of her peach gown would hold. She helped him into it and didn't quite manage to fasten the buttons all the way up the back. She dug in a drawer and found a pretty shawl to drape around his wide shoulders.

"Shoes," he muttered, looking down at his boots. "Con, my dear fellow, I have evening shoes in my room."

Con went off to get them.

"Hat," Susan said and found her straw villager one. She fixed ribbons so it could be pulled down at either side to hide his short hair.

"Too strongly featured to be a beautiful woman," she said, "but too beautiful to be a man."

De Vere fluttered a smile. "Ambiguous creatures, aren't we?"

"Not if anyone looks too closely." She dug out her rouge and reddened his lips and cheeks. "You're not quite proper, dear, wearing so much paint, and keep your hands inside the shawl. You'll have to distract them." She pulled stockings out of a drawer. "Here. Stuff these to make a bosom."

While he did so, she found her watercolor paints and mixed a little dark brown. "I don't think this will hurt your eyes."

"Thank you," he said with some alarm, but stood still as she painted dark lines around his eyes.

"Definitely not proper, but it makes you look more feminine."

"You can't imagine how reassuring it is to know it's such a challenge."

They were chuckling when Con returned with the black kid slippers. De Vere put them on and Susan said, "It will do, I think. So we are to be a courting couple, are we? And you, Con?"

"I'm going to be the bloody arrogant Earl of Wyvern. Your job will mostly be to distract his men so they can't hear what I'm saying to Gifford. Much as I'd love to throttle the man, we have to leave him a way out of this with his honor, such as it is, intact. Let's go."

Susan strode at Con's side in a blend of excitement and fear she'd never experienced before. A good part of the excitement was Con by her side. If nothing else, they were partners in this adventure.

This was the end of their time together, but it was a glorious end. As long as David came away safe.

Con had ordered horses brought up by Pearce and White, so they rode part of the way, dismounting only when they'd be in sight. The two servants were left with the horses while they approached on foot.

When they neared the landslip, Con went forward cautiously. "I can see the chapel with someone in the window, and at least one person in a dip, watching. Why isn't he shooting? Whoever is in the window is a clear target."

Susan was close behind. "Gifford's waiting for reinforcements. Or for me."

"Then why hasn't your brother broken out?"

"Because then they'd shoot. David will be hoping his signal is bringing help. He'll want to get away without bloodshed. Dead Preventive men mean endless trouble, and anyway, it's not the Dragon's Horde way."

"I wish we could get a message inside the chapel."

"We can." She pulled out the small mirror she'd brought. "I know the signals. I'll go over behind those rocks so Gifford won't see."

Con gripped her arm to stop her. "Do it from here."

"Why?"

"I want Gifford to see, wherever he is. I don't think he's down there. I wouldn't be. There's Hawk and Nicholas approaching, and I think I hear the children."

"I don't have to hide," de Vere said, and stood to stroll a little way up the slope, holding his skirts against the breeze. "It is. About ten children and three women."

"Excellent. Start signaling, Susan."

She angled her mirror to the sunlight and began sending the code that meant *help coming*.

De Vere said, "Did I get dressed up like this for nothing?"

"That would be a shame," Con said. "Go and distract the boatmen."

"That's more like it." De Vere flashed them both a wicked smile, and scrambled over the rocks to the smooth ground leading to the chapel.

As the three distractions converged, Susan had the panicked feeling that everything was sliding out of control.

Con gripped her shoulder. "Keep signaling."

She did so, blowing out a breath. "This goes against everything I've been taught, you know. I feel like a rabbit saying, 'Come and eat me.'"

"Just follow orders," Con said, a smile in his voice.

"Yes, sir."

He kept his hand firmly on her shoulder, and she welcomed the beloved warmth. For a moment, just a moment, she let her free hand rise to cover his.

She heard the children singing, then saw them marching in pairs, Amelia at the head, two other women at the rear, carrying baskets.

The two riders swung toward the chapel.

A voice shouted from the bushes, warning the riders off. She didn't think it was Gifford.

Hawkinville and Delaney halted their horses neatly between the bushes and the chapel, circling as if confused.

A man in the blue and white Excise uniform rose up, waving a musket at them.

More shouting.

The children broke ranks to run down the slope to peer into the chapel.

The women rushed after, calling for order. Susan almost rose to scream for them to go back. They were in danger!

The trooper yelled louder.

"Someone's going to be killed," she said to Con. "We have to do something."

"Nick and Hawk will take care of them. Gifford's coming. In fact, it's time for you to be away from here, love."

"Then I'm going down to be closer to the children."

"Very well. Pursue your wanton maid."

She rose, but hesitated. "Will you be safe?"

"Just obey orders, lad."

She rolled her eyes at him, but then she heard hoofbeats approaching. Unable to resist, she pulled him to her for a rapid kiss, then hurried over the rocks.

Once clear of Con, she yelled in as deep a voice as she could. "Betsy, you damn whore. Get back here!"

De Vere looked behind, screeched, and hurtled toward the trooper. "Save me, sir! Save me!"

Con laughed and turned to look out at the sea as if he were merely admiring the view. When Gifford drew his horse to a rough halt beside him he turned. "Lieutenant! A pleasant day after the recent cool weather, is it not?"

"Damn your eyes, I'll see you in court for this, earl or no earl!"

"For what?"

"For signaling to smugglers, sir!"

"In broad daylight?"

Gifford looked down on the scene below, rose in his stirrups and screamed, "Shoot them, damn you. Shoot!"

Con launched himself and dragged him off his horse, knocking him half unconscious in the process. "Shoot women and children, sir?"

Gifford lay there, deep red with fury. "I'll see you hang."

"And I'll see you posted to Jamaica unless you do exactly as I instruct." He had the man pinned with a knee in the belly and a hand in his stock.

"I had smugglers trapped in that ruin, damn you!"

Con tightened his grip in the neckband. "If so, they're likely gone by now. Nothing to be done about that. But I take strong objection to your attempt to harm innocent bystanders. I also, of course, take violent objection"—he increased the pressure of his knee—"to your attempting to blackmail a lady into your bed. Don't say it," he interrupted, tightening the stock to the choking point when Gifford opened his mouth.

Gifford's red face began to purple.

"Miss Kerslake is a lady for whom I have the highest regard, Gifford, and if I hear of anyone suggesting anything to her discredit, anything at all, I will be forced to take action. Both as an earl and as a man. Are we reaching a point of understanding?"

Con took a gutteral noise as agreement and let him have more breath.

Gifford used it to curse at him. "You're hand in glove with the smugglers, are you? Just like the old earl."

"No." Con felt some sympathy for Gifford's attempt to do his job, if not for other things. "Gifford, there's little point in catching another Captain Drake, man. There'll be another, and another."

"It is my duty to catch smugglers, my lord, and you are a damned traitor for opposing me."

Con sighed. "Opposing you? I'm merely preventing a madman from firing on a group of children."

"You admitted—"

"What? I'm the Earl of Wyvern, man. I cannot possibly be a smuggler." Con rose, pulling Gifford to his feet. "Have sense."

Once free, Gifford grabbed for the pistol in a holster on his saddle.

"Ah," Con said to Hawk, who had climbed the rocks to this side. He'd seen him coming. "A witness."

He turned to face Gifford's pistol. "Shooting a peer of the realm in cold blood is looked upon very poorly, you know."

"What's going on here, Lieutenant?" Despite civilian clothes, Hawk's tone rang with military authority. "A trooper down there threatened my friend and I, then some children, then a young lady seeking his help. Are you his commanding officer, sir?"

Gifford's pistol drooped. "We are engaged in capturing some dangerous smugglers, sir."

"I'm Wyvern," Con said amiably to his friend, "and this is the local riding officer, Lieutenant Gifford."

Hawk bowed. "Major Hawkinville, my lord." To Gifford, he snapped a command. "Go and take charge of your men, Lieutenant."

Gifford stood to attention. "Am I to assume you are taking command here, Major?"

"Not at all, Lieutenant. I assume now your head is cool you see the way to go on."

Gifford glared at him in frustration, then thrust his pistol back in its holster. He stalked to the high point to look across the rocky slip at the chapel.

Con followed. Children were playing in and out of the church, watched over by Nicholas, while four women, Race, and Susan surrounded the bewildered boatmen. An earthenware bottle was passing around. Doubtless scrumpy cider, adding considerably to the men's bewilderment.

David Kerslake was sitting on the ground in a red-stained shirt, Amelia attending to him with bandages.

"By gad," Con said, "your demented trooper has shot my estate manager!"

"He's a damn smuggler."

"Kerslake?"

"Son of Melchisedeck Clyst, as you well know."

"I'm a relative of the late mad Earl of Wyvern, Gifford. Are you saying that makes me inevitably insane?" While Gifford attempted to come up with a retort, Con added, "Do you have any evidence against him?"

"I interrupted men bringing tea up from that cove, my lord, and Kerslake and some others held us up while it was carried away."

"Are you sure?" Con asked. "I told Kerslake to check this area to see if it would be practical to rebuild the road here."

"Then why did he hide in that ruin?"

"Zeus, if someone was shooting at me, I'd hide in whatever cover was available. I'm sure you've done the same many a time."

"But . . ." Gifford looked at Con, tears of fury in his eyes.

"You are not entirely wrong, Gifford," Con said softly, "though you lost my sympathy by your dishonorable behavior toward a woman who had shown you nothing but kindness. But be assured that you will have the complete enmity of the Earl of Wyvern if you disturb his people here."

"It is my job to disturb smugglers, my lord, and in these parts everyone is a damn smuggler! And Kerslake is that blackguard, Captain Drake!"

"Choose your targets, Gifford. Choose your targets. Captain Drake—whoever he may be—and the Dragon's Horde have the support and cooperation of everyone in these parts. It's been that way for generations. The Blackstock Gang to the west and Tom Merriwether's Boys to the east, however, are universally feared. They've both been known to flog men to death for crossing them, and rape women who get in their way. They flog and rape for amusement as well. One or the other murdered your predecessor, not the Dragon's Horde."

Gifford's lip curled. "Know that for a fact, do you?"

"I know their ways. Go after the other gangs and you'll get support. We learned in the Peninsula that a war can be won or lost on the goodwill of the local people."

Gifford whirled and marched over to his grazing horse. "I'll do you an ill turn if I can!" he declared as he mounted.

"Unwise to say something like that before witnesses," Hawk pointed out. "You'd better hope that Lord Wyvern doesn't suffer any kind of accident, hadn't you?"

Almost steaming, Gifford wrenched his horse's head around cruelly and spurred off.

Con pulled a face. "I feel somewhat sorry for him, but there's no place for personal vendettas in this."

They watched as Gifford raced inland until he could cross the slip, then hurtled down to berate his men and drag them away from temptation. He stopped his horse to look into the chapel, obviously hoping to find some contraband there, then glared around the area.

"Doesn't give up easily, does he?" Hawk said. "Shame, really. In wartime he'd probably be a hero."

Con noted that the two extra "women" had now slipped away, leaving the innocent intruders and David Kerslake. There also seemed to be a great deal of cider-fueled merriment.

"Let's go down and sort out our company."

When they arrived where Race and Susan were laughing together, he said, "Have you two made up?"

With a wicked smile, Race pulled her into his arms and kissed her. "My love! Forgive me."

In return, Susan bent Race backward for what seemed to be a ravishing kiss. When she straightened him, she said, "Only if you promise to behave."

"Sweetheart," Race fluttered, "I'm yours in all things."

Con felt a spurt of irrational jealousy. He knew neither of them was serious, but what if Susan did find another man to love? He had no right to mind, but it cut like a knife.

The thought of Lady Anne and him had to hurt her as grievously.

"How's David?" he asked deliberately, to turn her mind to other things.

She sobered and came over to him. "Not too bad. A ball in the shoulder, but not deep. What's Gifford going to do now?"

"Absolutely nothing, if he has any sense." He told her what had happened.

Her smile was brilliant. "Wickedly clever! As you say, now he'll have to be careful about any moves he makes around here. I do wish David would accept the idea of being the earl, though."

"Let's go and put it to him. This might have made it more attractive."

Nicholas and Hawk had gathered the children. Nicholas seemed to have confiscated the cider from the women as well. Con went over to where Amelia was finishing bandaging David Kerslake.

"Damn fool. Broad daylight?"

The younger man looked up, unabashed. "Creative thinking. Gifford's been all over this area with extra troops at night. I tried to bring the tea in here last night, but a navy ship came close. So I had it dropped as floaters. You know what that means?"

"Weighted so it rides just under the water with a marker on top. Seaweed or something like that."

"Right. We waited until Gifford was away from here, then brought 'round a couple of boats to haul them in and bring them to shore. Gifford and his men have been up all night the last few nights. They should have been fast asleep!"

"How did you get shot?"

"A boatman called for me to halt. I hoped he was bluffing."

"David!" Susan exclaimed. "You're lucky you're not dead."

"Lucky he was trying to kill me, you mean," Kerslake said with a grin. "The chance of Saul Cogley actually hitting his target is remote."

Con shook his head. "Have you had time to think about the earldom? It would make this sort of thing a great deal easier, I assure you."

Kerslake winced as Amelia tightened the bandage. She looked cross, too.

"It's not a burden a man of twenty-four wants," he said, pulling a face. "Since I would be living here, I'd have to host a plaguey number of events and take part in county affairs. Then there's London and Parliament, for heaven's sake."

"The price of leadership," Con said without sympathy.

"Damn you."

"And you didn't even mention the fact that you'll instantly become a prize trophy in the marriage hunt."

"Didn't you say you *wanted* me to accept it?" But Kerslake sighed. "I don't really have any choice, do I, if I'm going to do the best for my people here."

Con noted that "my people" with a slight smile. Yes, willing or not, David Kerslake would be good for this area.

"Help me up, will you?" Kerslake asked, and Con supported him. "I wrenched my knee as well, which was another reason I couldn't make a break for it. Very well, damn you," he added as soon as he was standing. "I'll try to prize the earldom from your clutching fingers. As you said, Susan, Mel will be cock-a-hoop over it if it works."

Susan came to hug him and for a moment Con could steal a hug, too. Then he pulled apart.

This truly was the end. He could leave Crag Wyvern immediately. Perhaps even ride over to stay at Nicholas's place today.

Never have reason to return.

So be it.

After one last shared look with Susan, he turned his mind to the logistics of getting Kerslake back to Church Wyvern. Carry him over the rocks, or use one of Nicholas's and Hawk's horses and go the long way around?

He chose the latter course, and helped Kerslake into the saddle. Hawk prepared to mount to go with him, but then Race spoke up, in the arch, feminine manner that went with his disguise.

"My dear sirs, I do hope I can depend upon you for protection."

"What?" Con asked, sharing a look with Nicholas and Hawk.

"I have a little sin to confess," Race said, digging flirtatiously in his plump bosom.

Chapter Twenty-seven

Con suppressed an urge toward minor violence. "Race, this is no time for idiocy."

"Well really, my lord! That is rather a case of the pot calling the kettle dirty. Here." He pulled out a rolled-up paper and offered it, limp-wristed.

It was a letter of some sort. Con took it impatiently, but then his heart stopped. It beat again, it thundered, as he broke the seal and scanned it. It was! It was the letter he'd written to Lady Anne a lifetime ago.

Three days ago.

"Devil take you!" He glared at Race, not sure whether to throttle him or kiss him. "What right have you to hold back my letters?"

"The right of a friend," Race said in a normal manner. "I didn't read it, but Diego and I decided it couldn't be urgent and might be unwise. Send it now if you want."

Con looked again at his fateful words, thinking for a moment of Lady Anne. He was certain there was no grand passion there, but he must have raised hopes. He was truly fond of her. Not fond enough, however, to sacrifice everything now he'had a second chance.

He looked at Susan who was staring at him as if afraid to believe. "I mentioned writing to a lady. . . ."

The last trace of color left her cheeks. "Con?"

Eyes on her, he ripped the letter into tiny shreds and let the breeze tumble them across the headland and into the endless sea.

"By a miracle," he said, "I have hope of winning you for my wife, Susan, for my friend, my helpmeet all my days."

Susan had so firmly sealed off hope that now she could not quite believe. "Con . . . ?" she asked again, reaching tentatively toward him.

He met her and took her hand, strong, firm, real. She wasn't dreaming.

"I'm not committed, Susan. I'm free. . . ." Then his eyes twinkled. "Oh dear, you've changed your mind. Race's luscious figure has—"

She threw herself into his arms to be swept up, to be swung around and around in the clean air and sunshine.

Then they kissed.

With scarcely a thought to their audience, they kissed as never before, because this time, after so long, it promised true eternity.

It was hard to stop kissing, to unseal their bodies for even a moment, but they slowly parted, smiling, blushing under the interested eyes of friends, family, and neighbors.

"Don't tell me you were sacrificing yourself for the honor of the Rogues, Con," Delaney said.

"It wouldn't have been a dire sacrifice." He turned to look at Susan, a look that made her breath catch and her toes curl. "Then."

She sensed his honorable concern and drew him close. "If Lady Anne is as good a person as you say, love, she'll find her true mate. Someone who loves her as we love."

Numbness, then delirium were turning into urgent purpose. "When can we marry?" she demanded.

His expression showed the same needs. "It is for you to name the day."

"Today?"

He laughed unsteadily. "I don't think even an earl can quite manage that." He brushed his lips close to her ear. "And though I desire you here and now, beloved, I want to celebrate our love with May blossoms, and ribbons, and grain thrown in promise of a bountiful future. . . ."

She turned her head to meet his lips in a kiss. "A *normal* wedding?" How had he known before she knew how much she wanted that? "How long will it take?"

"I have no idea. If we set Hawk to organizing it, it can doubtless be done in brisk military efficiency."

She laughed and turned to look at the major, but found that their audience was courteously moving away, leaving them blessedly alone.

Miraculously they had forever, but these first moments were a jewellike treasure.

Hands linked, they wandered to look down on Irish Cove, then sat together there in one another's arms, in silent wonder.

"I still can't quite believe it," she said at last, turning to him, unable to resist raising a hand to touch his face, to trace the beloved lines of his face. "I longed for a miniature of you once, you know." She told him about the one his brother had brought to Kerslake Manor.

He trapped her hand and kissed the palm, slowly, lids lowered. "I had no picture of you. I tried to tell myself that I didn't want one, but it was a lie."

"Con, I'm sorry. I'm so sorry."

"Hush," he whispered against her skin. "Hush, love. Right or wrong it's all in the past, and who can say if it will not be better now, from this beginning? What did those children know of life, of temptation, of faltering steps and brave recoveries?"

He looked at her, smiling. No, more than smiling, adoring. Her tears began to flow.

"I know women have this damnable habit of crying when they're happy," he said, "but please don't, love. Listen to my words. You, as you are, with all your past, both good and bad, are perfect to me now. That is the Susan I love beyond words to express it."

She did her best to swallow the tears. "I can't imagine better words." She took his hand and kissed it. "I have always loved you, but I adore the man you are now, tested and true. I feel drunk with it, as if I could leap off this cliff and fly!"

He pinned her to the ground. "No, you don't!"

So like that first night, but now everything was different. It turned into a kiss. It turned into more, sprawled there on the rough greenery above Irish Cove, but they did not make love. They drew apart in the end, though seething with hunger.

"Cold water," she said, glancing at the sea. "I hear it's a good cure for this."

He leaped to his feet and took her hand to pull her up. "There's no cure for this save death, love. Let's go to your home and see how quickly a decorous wedding can be arranged."

With a license and many willing hands, it took only days, and could likely have been quicker except for the time needed for Con's family to travel from Sussex.

Van escorted them, and brought along his bride-to-be, Mrs. Celestine, as well. Susan understood that the matter had been uncertain, but no one could doubt the love and veiled passion between them now.

"I confess," said Mrs. Celestine, on greeting her, "you make me regret my setting a date some weeks from now."

She was an elegant, composed woman—except when Lord Vandeimen made her blush. Susan sensed genuine warmth in her, however. It was pleasant to think of them as neighbors and friends.

"I wanted a grand celebration in Van's home," Mrs. Celestine said. "A homecoming. A new start. A way for me to begin to belong, I hope. Please say you will take part, even though your wedding is to be here."

Susan took her hands with true gratitude. "That is so generous of you, Mrs. Celestine. Are you sure you won't mind? I confess, the idea of going to live among strangers daunts me."

The older woman smiled. "Van and I are not strangers. Nor is Major Hawkinville. Nor is Lord Wyvern's family."

Susan had already been warmly accepted by Con's mother and sister, and knew the words were true. She would not be going to live among strangers. Venturing forth into the world did still make her a little nervous, but it was becoming a more anticipated adventure day by day.

On the eve of their wedding, however, as they strolled in the orchard, Con said, "Somerford Court is not by the sea."

Susan kissed him. "I'm not a fish, love. I can live away from the sea."

"It's five miles away."

She looked into his eyes seriously. "I can live anywhere with you, Con. You are my world. I should have realized that long ago."

"No dwelling on the past." He pulled her close and they rested in one another's arms, a lark filling the soft air with song. "If I am your world, then I will work to make your world as perfect as humanly possible. That is, and always will be, my main intent."

"And I yours," she replied. "We have a second chance at heaven, and will treasure it."

Susan felt as if they said their vows then, but the next day, in a gaily decorated church full of family, friends, and neighbors, they said the traditional vows, then ran out together to be showered with grain.

When the first person greeted her as Lady Wyvern, she shared a look with Con, one that smiled at the folly of the past. It was only for a little while, anyway, and then she would become Lady Amleigh, a title that held no dark shadows or memories.

They shared their joy with everyone, but then at last they were alone together, man and wife.

Susan looked at the big bed, its sage-green coverlet strewn with petals. "Con, I have to say that I feel very strange about doing this in my aunt and uncle's bed."

He embraced her from behind, laughing. "I, on the other hand, am exceedingly grateful to them. I certainly had no intention of sleeping again in Crag Wyvern."

Henry and David had moved up there to make room in the manor, and they were playing host to a number of the guests. The Delaneys were sleeping there, along with Lord Vandeimen and Mrs. Celestine, and Major Hawkinville. There were some other Rogues there, too—the Earl and Countess of Charrington, Mr. and Mrs. Miles Cavanagh, Major Beaumont, and Mr. Stephen Ball.

There had been warm messages and generous gifts from the Marquess and Marchioness of Arden and Lord and Lady Middlethorpe. Apparently both couples were awaiting a happy event.

Susan felt as if she were swimming in new and welcoming friends. It was terrifying in a way, but glorious, like swimming in the high waves.

Con nuzzled her neck. "However, if you truly don't think it right, we can wait. . . ."

She turned in his arms. "I could call your bluff."

"I'd win."

With a smile, she eased free the silk fichu that filled the low bodice of her gown. "Are you sure?" The bodice, by her design, was extremely low.

She saw his eyes darken and his lips part. Stepping back, she raised one foot on a chair and slid up her skirts to reveal a flesh-colored silk stocking embroidered with red roses. A red, rose-trimmed garter, held it up. Slowly, she undid it—

He fell to his knees beside her and took over the task. "You win."

"I thought so."

He looked up, laughing with her. "I am undoubtedly the happiest loser the world has ever known."

Later, lying limply in one another's arms, Con said, "Shame about that bath, though. There's no room for such a thing at home. When David's earl, we'll have to pay him a visit."

Susan rolled to face him. "Only when he's done considerable renovations." She traced the coiled dragon on his chest. "Shame about this too, but you are not the dragon, Con Somerford. You are Saint George. My Saint George."

She had to refer to the past, though it was a past no longer able to hurt them. "I said it once, and I mean it now. My George, forever and ever."

"Amen." He rubbed his head gently against hers. "And I'm pleased to see that I was right," he murmured.

"Right?"

His tongue traced slowly around the rim of her ear, making her shiver. "I always suspected that when Saint George rescued the dragon's bride, his true reward came later, more or less like this. . . ."

ACKNOWLEDGMENT

I had visited Brighton in the past, but I wanted up-to-date information about particular streets. On the Web I found Gail and Pete Robertson's Writers Information Registry at http://www.pacificpast.net/~gprobert/registry.html and put in a request for Brighton. Gary Crucifix replied with some help and his father took photographs and sent them to me over the Net. Isn't technology wonderful! Thanks to all.

Chapter One

ome.

It had been a word without much meaning, but today, with his village *en fête* for his friend's wedding, the contact, the bone-deep belonging, was like a cannonball for Major George Hawkinville—one slamming into earth far too close and knocking the wind out of him.

Following Van and Maria out of the church into the midst of the bouncing, cheering crowd, he felt almost dazed by the familiar—the ancient green ringed by buildings new and old, the row of ramshackle cottages down by the river, the walled and thatched house at the end of the row . . .

Hawkinville Manor, his personal hell, but now, it would seem, his essential heaven.

"Welcome home, sir!"

He pulled himself together and shook hands with beaming Aaron Hooker. And with the next man, and the next. Soon women were kissing him, not all decorously. Hawk grinned and accepted the kisses.

This was Van's wedding, but Con was introducing his bride, Susan, here, too. Clearly the villagers were making it into a return festivity for all three of them.

The Georges.

The plaguey imps.

The gallant soldiers.

The heroes.

It wasn't the time to be wry about that, so he kissed and shook hands and accepted backslaps from men used to slapping oxen. In the end, he caught up to the blushing new bride and the very recent bride, and claimed kisses of his own.

"Hawk," said Susan Amleigh, Con's wife, her eyes brilliant, "have I told you how much I love Hawk in the Vale?"

"Once or twice, I think."

She just laughed at his dry tone. "How lucky you all are to have grown up here. I don't know how you could bear to leave it."

Because a tubful of sweet posset could be soured by a spoonful of gall, but Hawk didn't let his smile twist. He'd been desperate to leave here at sixteen, and didn't regret it now, but he did regret dragging Van and Con along. Not that he'd have been able to stop them if their families couldn't. The Georges had always done nearly everything together.

What was done was done—wisdom, of a trite sort—and they'd all survived. Now, in part because of these wonderful women, Con and Van were even happy.

Happy. He rolled that in his mind like a foreign food, uncertain whether it was palatable or not. Whichever it was, it wasn't on his plate. He was hardly the type for sweethearts and orange blossoms, and he would bring no one he cared for to share Hawkinville Manor with himself and his father. He had only returned there because the squire was crippled by a seizure.

If only he'd died of it.

He put that aside and let a buxom woman drag him into a country dance. Astonishing to realize that it was shy Elsie Dadswell, Elsie Manktelow now, with three children, a boy and two girls, and no trace of shyness that he could see. She was also clearly well on the way to a new baby.

Somewhat alarmed, he asked if she should be dancing so vigorously, but she laughed, linked arms, and nearly swung him off his feet. He laughed too and ricocheted down the line off strong, working-women's arms.

His people. His to take care of, even if he had to fight his father to do it. Some of the cottages needed repairs and the riverbank needed work, but prizing money out of the squire's hands these days was like getting a corpse to release a sword.

A blushing girl missing two front teeth asked him to dance next, so he did, glad to escape mundane concerns. He'd dealt with mass army movements over mountainous terrain, through killing storms. Surely the squire and Hawk in the Vale couldn't defeat him. He flirted with the girl, disconcerted to discover that she was Will Ashbee's daughter. Will was only a year older than he was.

Will had spent his life here, growing children and working through the cycles of the seasons. Hawk had lived in the death cycle of war. Marching, waiting, squabbling, fighting, then dealing with the broken and burying the dead.

How many men had he known who were now dead? It was not a tally he wanted to make. God had been good, and he, Van, and Con were all home.

Home.

The fiddles and whistles came to the end of their piece, and he passed his partner to a red-faced lad not much older than she was.

Love. For some it seemed as natural as the birds in spring. Perhaps some birds never quite got the hang of it, either.

He saw that a cricket match had started on the quiet side of the green. That was much less likely to stir maudlin thoughts, so he strolled over to watch and applaud.

The batter said, "Want a go, Major?"

Hawk was about to say no, but then he saw the glow in many eyes. Damnable as it was, he was a hero to most of these people. He and Van and Con were all heroes. They were all veterans, but most important, they had all been at the great battle of Waterloo a year ago.

So he shrugged out of his jacket and gave it to Bill Ashbee—Will's father—to hold, then went to take the home-carved bat. It was part of his role here to take part. As son of the squire and the future squire himself, he was an important part of village life.

He wished he weren't their hero, however. Two years after taking up a cornetcy in the cavalry, he'd been seconded to the Quartermaster General's Department, and thus most of his war had been spent out of active fighting. The heroes were the men like Con and Van, who'd breathed the enemy's breath and waded through blood. Or even Lord Darius Debenham, Con's friend and an enthusiastic volunteer at Waterloo who'd died there.

But he was the major, while Con and Van had made only captain, and he knew the Duke of Wellington. Rather better than he'd wanted to at times. He took the bat and faced the bowler, who looked to be about fourteen and admirably determined to bowl him out if he could. Hawk hoped he could.

The first bowl went wide, but Hawk leaned forward and stopped it so it bumped across the rough grass into a fielder's hands. He'd played plenty of cricket during the lazy times in the army. Surely he could manage this so as to please everyone.

He hit another ball a bit harder to make one run, leaving the other batter up. The bowler bowled that man out. Disconcerting not to be able to put a name to him. After a little while, Hawk was facing the determined bowler again, and this time the ball hurtled straight for the wicket. A slight twist of the bat allowed the ball to knock the bails flying, raising a great cheer from the onlookers and a mighty whoop of triumph from the young bowler.

Hawk grinned and went over to slap him on the back, then retrieved his coat.

Ashbee helped him on with it, but then stepped back with him out of the group around the game. "How's the squire today, sir?"

"Improving. He's out watching the festivities from a chair near the manor."

Sitting in state, more likely, but Hawk kept his tone bland. The villagers didn't need to feel a spill of bile from the Hawkinville family's affairs.

"Good health to him, sir," said Ashbee, in the same tone. Folly to think that the villagers didn't know how things were, with the servants in the manor all village people except the squire's valet.

And after all, men like Bill Ashbee could remember when handsome Captain John Gaspard arrived in the village to woo Miss Sophronia Hawkinville, the old squire's only child, and wed her, agreeing to take the family name. They would also remember the lady's bitter disillusion when her father's death turned suitor into indifferent husband. After all, Hawk's mother had not suffered in silence. But she'd suffered. What choice did she have?

And now she was dead, dead more than a year ago of the influenza that had swept through this area. Hawk hoped she had found peace elsewhere, and he regretted that he could not truly grieve. She had been the wronged party, but she had also been so absorbed in her own ill-usage that she'd had no time for her one child except to occasionally fight his father over him.

He realized that Ashbee was hovering because he wanted to say something.

Ashbee cleared his throat. "I was wondering if you'd heard anything about changes down along the river, sir."

"You mean repairs." Damn the squire. "I know there's work needs doing—"

"No, sir, not that. But there was some men poking around the other day. When Granny Muggridge asked their business, they didn't seem to want to say, but she heard them mention foundations and water levels."

Hawk managed not to swear. What the devil was the squire up to now? He claimed there was no money to spare, which Hawk couldn't understand, and now he was planning some improvement to the manor?

"I don't know, Ashbee. I'll ask my father."

"Thank you, sir," the man said, but he did not look markedly satisfied.

"Thing is, sir, later on Jack Smithers from the Peregrine said he saw them talking to that Slade. The men had stabled horses at the Peregrine, you see, and Slade walked them from his house to the inn."

Slade. Josiah Slade was a Birmingham iron founder who'd made a fortune casting cannons for the war. For some devil-inspired reason he'd retired here in Hawk in the Vale a year ago and become a crony of the squire's. How, Hawk couldn't imagine. The squire came from an aristocratic family and despised trade.

But somehow Slade had persuaded the squire to permit him to build a stuccoed monstrosity of a house on the west side of the green. It would not have been so out of place on the Marine Parade in Brighton, but in Hawk in the Vale it was like a tombstone in a garden. The squire had brushed off questions rather shiftily.

All was not right in Hawk in the Vale. Hawk had come home hoping never to have to dig in the dirt again, but it seemed it wasn't to be so easy.

"I'll look into it," he said, adding, "Thank you."

Ashbee nodded, mission complete.

Hawk headed back into the crowd, looking for Slade. The trouble here was that he was damnably impotent. In the army he'd had rank, authority, and the backing of his department. Here, he could do nothing without his father's consent.

By his parents' marriage contract, his father had complete control over the Hawkinville estate for life. He'd heard that his mother had been mad to have dashing Captain Gaspard, and had been the indulged apple of her father's eye, but he wished they'd fought for better terms.

It was all a pointed lesson in the folly that could come from imagining oneself in love.

He saw Van and Maria dancing together, looking as if stars shone in each other's eyes. Perhaps sometimes, for some people, love was real. He smiled at Con and Susan too, but caught Con in a contemplative mood, a somberness marking him that would have been alien a year ago, before Waterloo.

No, he'd been changed before Waterloo, changed by months at home, out of the army, thinking peace had come. That change, that gentling, was why the battle had hit him so hard. That and Lord Darius's death. Amid so many deaths one more or less shouldn't matter, but it didn't work like that. He could remember weeping on and off for days over the loss of one friend at Badajoz.

He wished he could have found Dare's body for Con. He'd done his damnedest.

He saw Susan touch Con's arm, and could tell that the dark mood fled. Con would be all right.

He spotted Slade over by a beer barrel, holding court. There were always some willing to toady to a man of wealth, though Hawk was pleased to see that not many of the villagers fell into that category. Colonel Napier was there, and the new doctor, Scott. Outsiders.

Hawk had to admit that Slade was a trim man for his age, but he fit into the village as poorly as his house did. His clothes were perfect country clothes—today, a brown jacket, buff breeches, and gleaming top boots. The trouble was that they were too perfect, too new—as real as a masquerade shepherdess.

Hawk had heard Jack Smithers commenting on the horseflesh Slade kept stabled at the Peregrine. Top-class horses, but the man was afraid of them and when he went out riding he sat like a sack of potatoes. Slade clearly wanted to exchange his money for the life of a country gentleman, but why, in the name of heaven, here?

And what new monstrosity did he have planned?

Replace the old humpbacked bridge over the river with a copy in miniature of the Westminster one?

He strolled over and accepted a tankard, and a kiss, from Bill Ashbee's wife.

"A grand affair, Major," declared Slade, smiling, though Hawk had noted before that the man's smiles to him were false. He had no idea why. Van and Con had both complained of the way Slade beamed at them, obviously trying to insinuate himself with the two local peers. A mere Hawkinville wasn't worth toadying to?

"Perhaps we should have more such fêtes," Hawk said, simply to make conversation.

"That will be for the squire to say, will it not, sir?"

Hawk ran that through his mind, wondering what it meant. It clearly meant something more than the obvious.

"I doubt my father will object as long as he doesn't have to foot the bill."

"But he won't be squire forever," said Slade.

Hawk took a drink of ale, puzzled. And alert. He knew when people were running a subtext for their own amusement. "I won't object either, Slade, on the same terms."

"If that should arise, Major, you must apply to me for a loan. I assure you,

I will always be happy to support the innocent celebrations of my rustic neighbors."

Hawk glanced at the "rustic neighbors" nearby, and saw some rolled eyes and twitching lips. Slade was a figure of fun here, but Hawk's deep, dark, well-tuned instincts were registering a very different message.

He toasted Slade with his tankard. "We rustic neighbors will always be suitably appreciative, sir!" He drained the ale, hearing a few suppressed chuckles and seeing Slade's smile become fixed.

But not truly dimmed. No, the man still thought he had a winning hand. What the devil was the game, though?

Hawk turned to work his way through the crowd to where his father sat near the manor's gates, his valet hovering. A few other people had brought out chairs to keep him company—newer village residents who doubtless saw themselves as too good to romp with their "rustic neighbors," even for a lord's wedding.

Hawk put that thought out of mind. They were harmless people. The spinsterish Misses Weatherby, whose only weapon was gossiping tongues. The vicar and his wife, who probably would prefer to be in the merriment but perhaps felt obliged by charity to sit with the invalid. That Mrs. Rowland, who claimed her husband was a distant relative of the squire's. She was a sallow, dismal woman who dressed in drooping black, but he shouldn't be uncharitable. Her husband still suffered from a Waterloo injury and she was in desperate need of charity.

The squire had given her free tenancy of some rooms at the back part of the corn factor's, and freedom of produce from the home farm. In return, the woman was a frequent visitor, and she did seem to raise his father's spirits, heaven knows why. Perhaps they talked of past Gaspard glory.

Hawk remembered that he'd meant to look in on Lieutenant Rowland to see if anything could be done for his health. No one in the village had so much as seen him. Another duty on a long list.

At the moment he was more interested in Slade. There was something amiss there.

So badly amiss that Hawk changed his mind and turned back to the celebration. He didn't want to confront his father in public, but confront him he would, and squeeze the truth out of him if necessary. Whatever Slade was up to could be blocked. All the land in the village was owned by the manor.

He'd learned to put aside pending problems and grasp whatever pleasure the moment held, so he joined a laughing group of young men, who had once been lads of his own age to play with or fight with.

He kept an eye on the squire, however, and when his father was finally carried back into Hawkinville Manor, Hawk eased away from the revels and followed. He crossed the green and the road that circled it, and went through the tall gates that always stood open these days. Once those gates and the high encircling wall had been practical defenses. A tall stone tower still stood at one corner of the house, remnant of an even sterner medieval home of the Hawkinvilles. He was aware of a strange instinct to close the gates and man the walls.

Against Slade?

The door opened and Mrs. Rowland came out, a basket on her arm. "Good evening, Major Hawkinville," she said, as if good was an effort of optimism. She was a Belgian and spoke with an accent. "A pleasant wedding, was it not?"

"Delightful. How is your husband, Mrs. Rowland?"

She sighed. "Perhaps he grows a little stronger."

"I must come and visit him soon."

"How very kind. He has some days better than others. I hope it will be possible." She curtsied and left with a nunlike step that made him wonder how she'd produced two children.

A very strange woman.

He shook his head and crossed the courtyard, evening-full of rose perfume and bird twitter. The hounds greeted him at the door, still not entirely used to him. Only old Galahad dated from his boyhood. Hawk had named him, in fact, to his father's disgust at the romantical name.

The squire called him Gally.

Perhaps it was a miracle that his father's dogs didn't bite him on sight.

When he walked in through the oak door his boots rapped on the flag-stoned corridor. Strange the things that a person remembers. When he'd returned here two weeks ago, that sound—his boots on the floor along with the slight jingle of his spurs—had been a trigger for explosive memories, both good and bad.

There were other triggers. The smell of wax polish, which this close to the door blended with the roses in the courtyard. There had always been, as now, roses in the pottery bowl on the table near the door. In the winter, it was rose potpourri.

Hawkinville's roses had perhaps been his mother's savior. Over the years she had abandoned everything to her husband except her rose garden. Wryly, he could remember being jealous of roses.

When he was young. When he was very, very young.

He had always been practical, and had soon learned to do without family fondness. Anyway, he'd had the families of his friends to fill any void.

It would be different now. Perhaps that was what had tinged the day with slight melancholy. By some miracle, the close friendship of the Georges seemed to have survived, but it could never be the same, not now that Van and Con had another special person in their lives. Soon, no doubt, there would be children.

But it was still there, the rare and precious friendship. As close as brothers. As close as triplets, perhaps.

Perhaps that was the tug of Hawk in the Vale. It was the home of his closest friends. But here, in the entrance hall of the house in which he had been born, he knew it was more than that.

The Hawkinvilles had been here far longer than the house, but even so his family had worn tracks in these flagstones for four hundred years, and doubtless cursed the damp that rose from them when heavy rain soaked the earth beneath.

Perhaps his older ancestors hadn't needed to duck beneath some of the dark oak lintels, though at least one had held the nickname Longshanks. Hawkinvilles had made marks in the paneling and woodwork, sometimes by accident and sometimes on purpose. There was a pistol ball embedded in the parlor wainscoting from an unfortunate disagreement between brothers during the Civil War.

He'd thought he didn't care. Over the years in the army, he could not remember experiencing homesickness. A fierce desire at times to be away from war, a longing for peace and England, but not homesickness for this place.

It was a shock, therefore, to be falling in love like this. No, not falling. It was as if an unrecognized love had leaped from the shadows and sunk in fangs.

Hawk in the Vale. Hawkinville Manor. He reached out to lay his hand on the oak doorjamb around the front parlor door. The wood felt warm, almost alive, beneath his hand.

My God, he could be happy here.

If not for his father.

He pulled his hand away. Bad luck to wish for a death, and he didn't actively do so. But he couldn't escape the fact that his dreams depended on stepping into a dead man's shoes. There'd be no happiness for him here as long as the squire lived.

He went up the stairs—too narrow for a gentleman, his father had always grumbled—and rapped on his father's door.

The valet, Fellows, opened it. "The squire is preparing for bed, sir."

"Nevertheless, I must have a word with him."

With a long-suffering look, Fellows let him in. God knows what the squire told his man, but Fellows had no high opinion of him.

"What now?" the squire demanded, his slightly twisted mouth still making the words clearly enough. Perhaps it was the damaged mouth that made him seem to sneer. But no, he'd sneered at Hawk all his life.

The seizure had affected his right arm and leg, too, and he still had little strength in either, but at a glance he did not appear much touched. He was still a handsome man in his late fifties, with blond hair touched with silver and the fine-boned features he'd given to Hawk. He kept to the old style, and wore his hair tied back in a queue. On formal occasions he even powdered it. He was sitting in a chair in his shirtsleeves now, however, his feet in slippers. Not particularly elegant.

Hawk was blunt. "Is Slade planning more building here?"

His father twitched, then looked away. "Why?"

Guilt, for sure.

But then the squire looked back, arrogance in place. "What business is it of yours? I still rule here, boy."

Eleven years in the army teaches self-control. A number of those years spent working close to the Duke of Wellington perfects it. "It is my inheritance, sir," Hawk said, "and thus my business. What is Slade planning, and why are you permitting it?"

"How should I know what that man intends?"

" 'That man'? You had him to dinner two nights ago."

"A politeness to a neighbor." He didn't look away again, but Hawk had questioned more skillful deceivers than his father, and he could see the lie behind it.

"I was told that there were men here who sounded like surveyors studying the area along the river and that they later spoke to Slade. What interest could Slade have down here? There is no available land."

His father glared at him, then snapped, "Brandy!"

Fellows rushed to obey, protesting all the while that brandy was not allowed. The squire took a mouthful and said, "Very well. You might as well know. Slade's planning to tear down this place, and the cottages too, and build himself a grand riverside villa."

Hawk almost laughed. "That's absurd."

Into the silence, he added, "He does not have the power to do that."

Doubt and fear stirred. His father, for all his faults, was not a fool, nor had his illness turned him mad. "What have you done?"

The squire took a sip of brandy, managing to look down his long, straight nose, even in the chair. It was posing, though. Hawk could see that. "I have gained a peerage for us."

"From *Slade*?" Hawk couldn't remember ever feeling so at a loss.

"Of course not. You are supposed to be clever, George. Use your wits! It is a title from my own family. Viscount Deveril." He rolled it off his tongue. "It was thought to be extinct when the late Lord Deveril died last year, but I proved my descent from the original viscount."

"My congratulations," Hawk said with complete indifference, but then his notoriously infallible memory threw up facts. "Deveril! By God, Father, the name's a byword for all that is evil. Why the devil would you want a title like that?"

The squire reddened. "It's a *viscountcy*, you dolt. I'll take my place in Parliament! Attend court."

"There is no court anymore. The king is mad."

Like his father?

The squire shrugged. "I am reverting to my rightful family name as well, of course. I am now John Gaspard, soon to be Viscount Deveril."

"Are you also leaving here?" Hawk asked. He kept his tone flat, but it was hard. Unlikely sunshine was breaking in. My God, was all he wanted about to drop into his hands?

But then he remembered Slade.

"What has Slade to do with this? You can't—" Words actually failed him for a moment. "You aren't allowed to sell the estate, Father."

"Of course I have not sold it," his father declared haughtily. After a moment, however, he added, "It is merely pledged."

Hawk put out a hand to the back of a nearby chair to steady himself. He knew every word of the besotted marriage settlement that had given his father power here. His father could use the estate to raise money.

It wasn't an outrageous provision, since the administrator of an estate might have need to raise money for improvements or to cover a disastrous season. His grandfather had been sensible enough to have it worded so that

Hawkinville could not be staked in gambling, or used to pay off gaming debts. Not that that had ever been an issue. His father's flaws did not include gambling.

"Pledged against loans?" he asked.

"Precisely."

"I must admit, sir, that I am at a loss as to how you have sunk into debt. The estate is not rich, but it has always provided for the family adequately."

"It is quite simple, my boy," said his father almost jovially. It was a mask. "I needed money to gain the title! Research. Lawyers. You know how it is."

"Yes, I know how it is. So you borrowed from Slade. But surely if you have the title, you have property that comes with it to pay him off."

"That was my plan." The squire's face pinched. "Deveril—rot his black heart—willed most of his worth away."

"It wasn't entailed?"

"Only the estate."

"Well—"

"Which seems unproductive."

Hawk took a breath. "Let me get this clear. You have mortgaged this estate to Josiah Slade to get money to claim one that is valueless."

"It's a title! My family's title. I would have paid more."

"Borrowed more, you mean. How much?"

Over the first shock now, Hawk was beginning to arrange facts and make calculations. He had some money of his own. He could borrow elsewhere to pay off Slade.

"Twenty thousand pounds."

It was like being hit by a pistol ball. "*Twenty thousand pounds?* No one could possibly spend that much to claim a title."

The Hawkinville estate brought in only a few thousand a year.

"I have been pursuing Deveril's money as well, of course."

"Even so. Your lawyers would have to have been eating gold quills for breakfast."

"Investments," the squire muttered.

"Investments? In what?"

"All kinds of things. Slade does well off them. There was a foreigner here a while back—Celestin. He'd made a fortune at it. Then Slade turned up with some good ideas . . ."

Maria's dead husband, who had led Van's father to ruin this way. But Slade—Slade was the active villain here.

"So Slade lent you money and then lent you more to invest to earn it back?"
Twenty thousand pounds.

An impossible sum, and throttling Slade would not fix the disaster.

Hawk forced his mind to look for any possibility.

"How much did Deveril leave that was willed elsewhere?"

"Close to a hundred thousand. You see why I had to have it!"

"I see why we have to have it now. What reason do you have for thinking you can overturn the will?"

"Because it gave everything to a scheming chit he planned to marry, by a handwritten will that was certainly false."

"Then why don't you have the money?"

The squire knocked back his brandy and held the glass out to be refilled. "Because the poxy chit has all the Deveril money to pay for lawyers, that's why! And some plaguey high-flying supporters. Her guardian's the Duke of Belcraven, no less. The Marchioness of Arden, wife to the duke's heir, stands her friend. I wouldn't be surprised if the little whore has the damned Regent in her pocket."

"It would have to be a very large pocket," Hawk remarked, his mind whirling on many levels.

Twenty thousand pounds. It couldn't be borrowed, even from friends. Especially from friends. Even if they could raise it, it would take Hawkinville a generation to pay it off, and only by squeezing the tenants hard.

His father laughed at his comment. "I have to say, you're taking this better than I expected, George."

Hawk looked at his father. "I am taking this extremely badly, sir. I despise you for your folly and self-indulgence. Did you ever give a thought to the welfare of your people here?"

"They are not *my* people!"

"You've been pleased enough to call them such for over a quarter century. Families have lived in those cottages for centuries, Father. And do you care nothing for this house?"

"Less than nothing! It's a plaguey farmhouse, for all you like to call it a manor."

Hawk wished his father was well. Perhaps then he might feel justified in hitting him. "And Slade will be squire here, since the title goes with the property. You are selling everyone here for your own petty ends."

His father reddened, but raised his chin. "I do not care! What is this place to me?"

"So what is? The Deveril estate? It's going to be a damn chilly comfort with no money to go with it, isn't it?"

His father glared, but said, "You have a point. That is why I have come up with a solution. You are not a bad-looking man, and you have a certain address. Marry the heiress."

Hawk laughed. "Marry a 'poxy chit' to rescue you? I think not."

"To rescue Hawk in the Vale, George."

It hit home, and his father knew it.

All the same, every instinct revolted. He had made one vow, many years ago—that he would not repeat his parents' mistake. He would not marry unless he was sure of harmony. He'd accepted that it meant that he would likely never marry, but that would be better for everyone than more bitterness and bile.

"I have a better idea," he said. "Do you have any cogent reasons to believe the will is false? What arguments have your lawyers made in court?"

His father glowered, but he said, "It was handwritten, and it left all his money to this girl, to come under her complete control at twenty-one."

"Absurd."

"Quite. And the heiress is one Clarissa Greystone. You may not have heard of the Greystones. Drunkards and gamblers, every one."

"And yet you failed to break it. Why, apart from better lawyers and influence in high places? Our courts are not so corrupt, I hope, that they would overrule reason."

"Because the will was in Deveril's hand and found in his locked desk with no sign of a break-in."

"Witnesses?"

"Two men in his employ, but they went missing after his murder."

"Murder?" Hawk repeated. "How did he die?"

"Stabbed in a back slum in London. His body wasn't found for some days."

"Good God. So he was murdered and this Greystone chit has all his money and no one has been able to prove she did it?" He laughed. "And you think I will marry a woman like that?"

"That, or lose Hawkinville, dear boy."

Hawk gripped the back of the chair tightly. "You're finding a kind of satisfaction in this, aren't you? Does it give you so much pleasure to see me wriggling on this hook?"

The twisted smile was definitely a sneer now. "It gives me pleasure to see you taken down a peg or two. So superior you've been, especially since returning home. You've always despised me for marrying for money, haven't you? Well, what are you going to do now the shoe's on your foot, eh?"

"What am I going to do?" *Short of throttle you?* "I'm going to prove that damn will false, and if possible see the Greystone creature hang for murder. And then, I hope, I'll see you out of here, and begin to repair the lifetime's damage that you've done."

The sneer became somewhat fixed, but his father disdained to answer.

"When does the loan come due?" Hawk asked.

His father laughed. "The first of August."

"Two months!" *Control. Control.* Hawk carefully let go of the chair. "Then I had best get on with it, hadn't I?"

It was only as he left the stuffy room that another disastrous aspect hit him. Titles were hereditary. One day he would have to be Lord Deveril.

For the first time he sincerely wished his father a long, long life.

But away from here.

At his precious Deveril estates.

Instinctively he sought his mother's rose garden, even though this mess was her fault. He'd heard that there had been solid, reliable local men courting her.

He shook his head. That was all past history. For the present and the future, the Hawk had one more hunt to fly, and as reward, a golden future tantalized.

If he could prove the will a forgery and get the money for his father, the new Lord Deveril would move away from here. After paying off Slade, of course.

Twenty thousand pounds. It was a sum that staggered him, but he put it aside. Five times that much waited if he did his job right.

Then he would have Hawkinville. His father called it a farmhouse, and he was right. It was two stories and contained only four bedchambers. The ceilings were low, the fixtures practical, the "grounds" merely the courtyard and a garden at the back.

But it was his piece of heaven. He would not let it be torn down, nor would he let Slade rip the heart out of Hawk in the Vale village.

He walked back out onto the green. A few people called to him, waving, with no idea that their world was threatened. He waved back but turned to look at the manor house and the line of cottages.

Most of the front doors were open, with children running in and out. Old people, who had lived in their cottage for most or all of their lives, sat hunched on chairs, watching their generations enjoy themselves. Mothers, babies on hip or even at the breast, chatted together as they kept an eye on their families.

None of the cottages had a straight line, and most of the thatch needed work, but that was all the responsibility of the manor, not the tenants. No roses bloomed at the front because the cottages opened right onto the road around the green and faced north, but he knew that in the long gardens running down to the river roses bloomed among the well-tended vegetables that fed these families.

He watched Slade strolling around, beaming, clearly—in his own mind at least—already the master here. Perhaps he was envisioning a tidy clearing, a modern improvement.

A pure and simple urge to murder held Hawk rigid for a moment. But no. That would not serve.

What if he couldn't prove the will false?

Then he would prove the Greystone chit a murderess. That would work just as well to throw doubt on the will. It probably wouldn't even be hard for a man like him. His work in the war had included investigations, and he'd been very good at it.

He'd hoped never to unleash the Hawk again. Those investigations had left unpleasant memories, and sometimes pushed the borders of his honor.

But this, again, was war. He made a silent vow that greed and folly would not destroy Hawk in the Vale.

Chapter Two

Clarissa Greystone stared at Miss Mallory in shock. "You are saying I have to leave?"

Miss Mallory, neat and round, took her hand to pat it. "Now, now, dear. I am not throwing you out into the street. You have been welcome here for the past year, but that year is nearly over. And this is a school, not a home for stray ladies. I have been in communication with the duke, and with Beth Arden, and both agree that you must begin to take your place in the world."

They were in Miss Mallory's private parlor in the school, a cozy room warm with potpourri and lavender linen that had always held pleasant memories for Clarissa. Miss Mallory had an office, and that was where a girl went to be scolded for misbehavior. The parlor was for special teas and treats.

"But where am I to go? The school has been as good as a home to me since I was ten."

"That is what you must think about, dear. I'm sure Beth would be glad of your company in time."

In time, because Beth Arden was expecting her first child soon. But even in time, Clarissa didn't want to live with the Ardens. She was fond of Beth, who had been her favorite teacher here, and who had helped her last year in London, but she disliked Lord Arden. He was a terrifying brute.

"Or the duke has offered you a home at Belcraven Park."

Clarissa almost shuddered. She'd visited there once to meet the man who had taken over her guardianship from her father. The duke and duchess—especially the duchess—had been very kind, but they were strangers, and Belcraven was a place of such massive magnificence she could never imagine living there.

"I think I would prefer a small house with a companion. Perhaps here in Cheltenham."

"No." Miss Mallory's voice was the one that all girls in the school learned to heed. "Not here in Cheltenham. You must start afresh. But a house and a suitable companion is a possibility. In London, perhaps. You should rejoin society, my dear."

"Rejoin society!" Clarissa heard her voice climb too high. "Miss Mallory, I was never part of it. I was a Greystone, and Lord Deveril's betrothed. Believe me, few doors were open. No, I will live quietly. Perhaps in Bath."

It was a dismal prospect. She'd spent most of her school holidays with her grandmother in Bath. Lady Molson was dead now, but the place was doubtless as stuffy as ever.

But safe. Perhaps.

"Or in a little village," she added. That was better. There she'd be less likely to be recognized as what society called the Devil's Heiress.

A shudder passed through her at the memories the name brought back. She rose. "I will think about it, Miss Mallory. When must I leave?"

Miss Mallory rose too, and gave her a hug. "Oh, my dear, there is no great hurry. We simply want you to begin to think on it. But I advise you not to try to hide. You have your life before you, and your fortune can make it a good one. Not many young women have the choices you have. It would be a sin to waste them."

Miss Mallory was a follower of Mary Wollstonecraft, author of *The Rights of Woman,* and she judiciously shared those beliefs with the pupils in her school, so Clarissa knew what she meant. Beth Arden was also an adherent, and had discussed these matters in more detail last year. After Deveril's death.

She should be delighted to be free.

It was all very well in theory to rage against the shackles of masculine oppression, but as Clarissa left the parlor she couldn't help thinking that it might be nice to be taken care of now and then. First a father, and then a husband—if one had a good father, not one like Sir Peter Greystone.

As for a husband, she sighed. She had little faith in the notion of a good husband. A woman put her fate so completely in his hands, and he could be a tyrant.

Like Lord Arden.

Clarissa would never forget the awful argument she had overheard, and running into the room to find Beth on the floor, clearly having been driven there by Lord Arden's blow. The next day Beth had had an awful bruise.

She'd said it was over, was a problem that had been dealt with, but it had been a lesson to Clarissa. Handsome men could be whited sepulchers. On her twenty-first birthday she would have a hundred thousand pounds or more. Folly indeed to put it into the hands of a man, and herself totally in his power.

Up the stairs and along the familiar corridor, every corner of the school was familiar. She wouldn't exactly say precious. Last year she'd been desperate to leave here and take up her life. Even though she'd known her parents didn't care for her, she'd leaped at the chance to go to London. To have a season. To attend balls, routs, parties.

She'd known she was no beauty, and would have no dowry to speak of, but she'd dreamed of suitors, of handsome men courting her, flirting with her, kissing her, and eventually, even going on their knees, begging for her hand.

Instead, there'd been Lord Deveril.

She stopped and thrust him into the darkest depths of her mind. Loathsome Lord Deveril, his foul kiss, and his bloody death. At least he didn't wait for her out in the frightening world.

She knew everyone was right. She couldn't stay here forever.

She glanced down at her clothes, the beige-and-brown uniform all the girls wore here. She had nothing else to wear other than the London gowns that lay in trunks in the attic. She would never wear them again!

But she could hardly go on like this. She bit her lip on a laugh at the thought of herself—plump and fifty—trotting around Cheltenham in brown and beige, that eccentric Miss Greystone, with a fortune in hand and nowhere else to go.

But she had nowhere else to go. She would certainly never again live with her family.

She needed someone to talk to and knocked on the door of her friend Althea Trist. Althea was the junior mistress who had come last September to take Beth Arden's position.

The door opened. Clarissa said, "I'm going to have to—"

But then she stopped. "Thea, what's the matter?"

Her friend had clearly been crying.

Althea pressed a soggy handkerchief to her eyes and tried for a smile. "It's nothing. Did you want something?"

Clarissa pushed her into a chair and sat nearby. "Don't be silly. What is it? Is there bad news from home?"

"No." Althea grimaced, then said, "It's just the day. June eighteenth. The anniversary. Waterloo."

Realization dawned. "Oh, Thea! You must feel the pain all over again." Althea's beloved betrothed, Lieutenant Gareth Waterstone, had died at the battle of Waterloo.

"It's foolish," Althea said. "Why today rather than any other day? I do grieve every day. But today . . ." She shook her head and swallowed.

Clarissa squeezed her hands. "Of course. What can I do? Would you like some tea?"

Althea smiled, and this time it seemed steadier. "No, I'm all right. In fact, I am to take the girls out soon."

"If you're sure." But then it dawned on Clarissa. "Thea, you can't. You can't go to the parade! Miss Mallory would never have asked you if she'd thought."

"She didn't. Miss Risleigh was to do it, but she wished to attend a party. She is senior to me."

"How callous! I will go and speak to Miss Mallory immediately."

She was already up and out of the door as Althea was crying, "Clarissa! Stop!"

She hurtled down the familiar stairs, back to the parlor to knock upon the door. The parade was in honor and memory of the great victory at Waterloo. Althea could not possibly be expected to go there and cheer.

The knock received no response, however. She made so bold as to peep in and found the room deserted. She ran off to the kitchen, but there found that Miss Mallory had gone out for the afternoon. There were a great many parties taking place, and the better folk of Cheltenham had been invited to choice spots from which to watch the parade.

What now?

The school was closed for the summer, and only five girls lingered, awaiting their escorts home. There were only three teachers—Miss Mallory, Althea, and the odious Miss Risleigh.

What could be done?

The girls could do without their trip to the parade, but Clarissa knew that dutiful Althea would never permit that. There was only one solution. She ran back upstairs to her room, put on the brown school cloak and the matching bonnet, and returned to Althea's room.

Althea was already dressed to go out.

"Take that off," Clarissa said. "I am going to take the girls."

Althea stared. "Clarissa, you can't. You're not a teacher! In fact, you're a paying guest."

"I was a senior girl until last year. We often helped out."

"Not as escort on a trip like this."

"But," said Clarissa, "I'm not a senior girl anymore. I'm only a few months younger than you are." A lock of hair tumbled down, and she went to Althea's mirror to tuck it back in. If she was going to do this she had better try to look mature and stern. Or at least sensible.

She pushed some more hair in and tried to straighten the bonnet.

"It is my responsibility," Althea protested, appearing behind her in the mirror.

Clarissa couldn't help wishing she hadn't done that. Althea was a rare and stunning beauty, with glossy dark hair, a rose-petal complexion, and every feature neatly arranged to please.

She, on the other hand, had unalterably sallow skin and features that while tolerable in themselves were not quite arranged to please. Her straight nose was too long, her full lips too unformed, and even her excellent teeth were a little crossed at the front. Her eyes were the dullest blue, her hair the dullest brown.

It shouldn't matter when she had a hundred thousand pounds and no need of a husband, but vanity does not follow the path of logic.

She put that aside and turned to put an arm around her friend. "There are only five girls left, Thea. Hardly a dire task. And you cannot possibly attend the Waterloo Day parade and cheer. If Miss Mallory knew, she would say the same. Now, go and lie down and don't worry. All will be fine."

She rushed out before Althea could protest anymore, but only ten minutes later, she could have laughed aloud at that prediction.

One, two, three, four—she anxiously counted the plain brown bonnets around her—*five*. Five?

She whirled around. "Lucilla, keep up!"

The dreamy ten-year-old turned from peering at a gravestone in Saint Mary's churchyard and ambled over. Unaware, she caused one hurrying woman to stumble back to avoid running into her.

Clarissa rolled her eyes but reminded herself that a noble deed lost its luster if moaned over. "Hurry along," she said cheerfully. "We're almost there!"

At least the youngest girl was attached to her hand like a limpet. It would be nice, however, if Lady Ricarda wasn't already sniveling that she was scared of the graves, she was going to be sick, and she wanted to go back to the school, *now*.

"We can't possibly go back now," Clarissa said, towing the girl out into the street. "Listen—you can hear the band." She glanced back. "Horatia, *do* stop ogling every man who walks by!"

Horatia Peel was fifteen and could be expected to be some help, but she was more interested in casting out lures. She'd pushed her bonnet back on her head to reveal more of her vivid blond curls and had surely found some way to redden her lips.

At Clarissa's command, she turned sulkily from simpering at a bunch of aspiring dandies. She was not a hard-hearted girl, however, and took Lucilla's hand to make sure she didn't wander off again.

Clarissa's other two charges, Georgina and Jane, were devoted eleven-year-old friends, arm in arm and in deep conversation. They were no trouble except for their slow pace.

Afraid to speed ahead in case someone disappeared, Clarissa gathered her flock in front and nudged them forward like an inept sheepdog. It would be wonderful to be able to nip at some dawdling heels!

What would the world think if it could see her now? The infamous Devil's Heiress, with a dubious past and a fortune, dressed in drab and in charge of a bunch of wayward sheep.

"Walk a little faster, girls. We're going to miss the soldiers. Horatia, keep going! No, Ricarda, you are not going to be crushed. Lucilla, look ahead. You can see the regimental flag."

She blew a corkscrew curl out of her eyes, reminding herself that this was a good deed. It would be horrible for Althea to have to be here. For her part, she didn't mind some cheering and celebration. It was exactly one year ago today that loathsome Lord Deveril had died. One year since she'd been saved. Bring on the flags and drums!

She counted heads again. "Not long now. We'll find a good spot to watch our brave soldiers march by."

Her forced good cheer dried up when they popped out of the lane and into Clarence Street. People must have come in from the surrounding countryside for the festivities. The place was packed with a jostling, craning, chattering, pungent mob and all the hawkers and troublemakers that such a throng attracted.

A bump from an impatient couple behind them moved her on into the thick of the crowd with everyone around pushing for a good spot.

One, two, three, four, five.

"Let's go toward the Promenade, girls. The crowd may be thinner there."

"I want to go *home!*"

"Ricarda, you can't. Hold tight to my hand."

Hawk had a flock of schoolgirls in his sights.

After intensive investigations in London, he had come to Cheltenham in search of the heiress herself. She was clearly key, and she was being kept out of sight. He'd discovered that she wasn't living with her family, or with her guardian, the duke.

He had eventually learned that she was supposed to have spent the past year back at her very proper Cheltenham school. He had trouble imagining the Devil's Heiress at Miss Mallory's School for Ladies at any age—though he gathered her education there had been the work of her grandmother—but certainly not at nearly twenty. Surely it was a blind for some other, more lively, lodging, but it was where he had to start.

He had spent the day hovering, watching for someone willing to gossip about school matters. He'd had no luck, since the school was officially closed for the summer, though he had learned from a butcher's boy that there were some staff and a few girls still there.

Now, at last, he had possibilities. The pupils all wore a kind of uniform of beige dress, brown cloak, and plain brown bonnet, but two of the flock were within flirting age—a lively blonde and the plain young woman who seemed to be in charge.

He focused on the plain one. Plain ones were more susceptible. As he followed them into a churchyard, however, he began to think that the blonde would fall more ripely into his hand. On leaving the school, she'd begun to push her bonnet back on her head, gradually revealing more and more curls. Even with a plump child by the hand, she was lingering behind with the clear intent of flirting with any man who showed interest.

Could this actually be Miss Greystone? He'd not expected to find her in the school at all, never mind in schoolgirl clothes, but she seemed the type. Pretty, and a complete minx. She didn't look nineteen, but such things were often deceptive. Nor did she look evil, but in his experience, that meant nothing. He could certainly imagine Deveril drooling over such a tender morsel.

The girl slowed even more to dimple at a group of young would-be gallants.

Hawk moved in.

He was within five feet when the plain one turned. "Horatia, do stop ogling every man who walks by!"

"I wasn't *ogling,* Clarissa. You're so mean!" But the minx did rejoin the others.

Hawk fell back to regroup. The plain one was Clarissa Greystone? He'd had a clear look at her face when she turned, and she was definitely nothing special to look at.

As he discreetly followed, he realized that it had been an error to assume beauty. "Lord Devil" wouldn't have had much choice in brides. Few upper-class families would consider such a fate for a daughter. The Greystones were just the type that would.

They all gamed, and father and sons were drunks as well. Lady Greystone was a wanton. She was growing virtuous with age, but only because her raddled looks were ceasing to attract. When he'd struck up a conversation with her in the course of his investigations, the damn woman had propositioned him!

He'd assumed Clarissa Greystone would be like the rest of her family, but she seemed to be a cuckoo in that nest.

Or, more likely, she was brilliantly disguising her true nature.

That explained it, and it pointed right at guilt. Most people who stole gave themselves away by immediately enjoying their spoils. Not clever Miss Greystone. Perhaps she was even pretending to be in mourning.

The old excitement stirred. The excitement of challenge, of a worthy opponent. It was comforting, too. With a clever enemy, there was no need to feel squeamish about tactics.

Clever, but guilty as the devil. A week in London sifting fact from fallacy had proved his father right. That will—in fact, everything surrounding Deveril's death—stank to high heaven. Strings must have been pulled for it not to have been investigated more closely.

Lord Devil had not been accepted in society until nearly two years ago when he'd suddenly acquired a fortune. No one knew the source of it, but everyone assumed it was dirty money.

He'd been partner in a popular bordello run by a woman called Thérèse Bellaire, which was an interesting tangent. Hawk happened to know that Thérèse Bellaire had been part of Napoleon's inner circle—mainly pandering for his intimates and senior officials. She had been in England in 1814 as a French spy, working for the reinstatement of her master.

Madame Bellaire had fled before she could be arrested, presumably leaving the bordello to her partner, but its sale would not have produced a fortune. Deveril had been involved in other things, however. Gaming hells. Opium dens. White slavery.

Regardless of where the money had come from, it had gained him an entrée with the less discriminating members of fashionable society. He'd leased a handsome house in the best part of town, and not long afterward, his betrothal to Miss Greystone had been announced.

Soon after that, he'd been murdered.

It had all the marks of a cunning and cleverly executed plot, and far beyond the talents of the Greystones. He didn't yet know who was behind it, but he would.

In a mere week he had some threads in his fingers. The forger was probably too clever to reveal himself, but Hawk had found the names of the two missing witnesses on the records of a ship bound for Brazil. Strange destination for a couple of London roughs, but they'd presumably been paid off and told to make themselves scarce. It would be interesting to follow up on it, but he didn't have time now.

He'd dug up another of Deveril's henchmen. They could hardly be called servants. After a jug of gin, the gap-toothed man had remembered some prime whores Deveril had sent to the house while he'd been on duty there.

"Night of the big celebration, it was," the man had remembered. "When we heard about Waterloo and the whole of London set to celebrating. We were stuck there, and these prime titties came knocking, but then their men came and dragged 'em away. One of 'em knocked Tom Cross out with a skillet, she did! He called her Pepper, and she certainly made him sneeze."

Lazily, Hawk had asked, "Why did she do that, do you think?"

"He paddled her for being saucy. I bet her pimp paddled her harder. Seems as if they were off trying to do a bit of business of their own. Shame, though," he said, sagging lower over his drink. "Never so much as got a feel, I didn't."

"You didn't look them up later?"

"No names. Anyway, the next day they found bloody Deveril's body and that were the end of that. Duchess," he said. "Her sister called her Duchess because of her airs and graces. Wanted to drink out of a glass, she did."

For a wild moment, Hawk had thought of the Duchess of Belcraven, but she was an exquisite middle-aged Frenchwoman. He still wondered about the role of the Duke and Duchess of Belcraven in the Deveril affair. The duke was widely known as a man of dignity and principle.

Pieces that didn't fit always told a story, however, and that one would too, in time.

Time was so damnably short.

Those whores had been a distraction for the planting of the will, however.

He was sure of it. And it seemed likely that Clarissa Greystone had been one of them.

The one called Pepper and Duchess, who'd knocked a man out for daring to spank her for being saucy? It had fit.

Until now.

He contemplated the harried figure ahead of him, dragging one whining child along the crowded street, chivying the others in front of her like a demented sheepdog, rattails of hair escaping from her bonnet.

Could there be more than one Clarissa in Miss Mallory's School?

"I can't see!" Ricarda screeched, still clinging.

They were in the Promenade, a much wider street, but could still see only a solid line of backs. Clarissa was ready to admit defeat, but then the adults in front made way and a smiling countrywoman said, "Come on forward, luvs. We can see over your sweet heads."

With the music coming closer and the drums shaking the air, Ricarda transferred her clutch to Lucilla's hand and slipped forward. Georgina and Jane went too. Then the adult ranks closed between Clarissa and most of her charges.

Oh, no!

She went on tiptoe to watch the four girls. They were standing still with other children at the front, but Lucilla was capable of wandering off in any direction, and now she would probably take Ricarda with her.

Constantly checking the four brown bonnets, Clarissa was aware of the parade only as approaching drums. She glanced once and saw the lord mayor still some distance away, marching along in his robes and chain of office accompanied by his mace-bearer. Beyond, she saw the aldermen, a cart or two, and the magnificent scarlet of the local regiment.

The sight of the redcoats did catch her for a moment. So many brave men, and so many others, like Althea's Gareth, lost in the wars against the Corsican Monster. More than ten thousand dead at Waterloo alone.

How did one imagine ten thousand dead, all in one place?

She pulled her mind back to simple things, to counting her charges. *One, two, three, four—*

Five?

Horatia. Where was Horatia?

With a puff of relief, she saw her right beside her. Horatia couldn't have much of a view—she was shorter than Clarissa—but of course the minx was not interested in the mayor, or even the soldiers. She was dimpling at the handsome man by her side.

A handsome, dangerous man. Horatia was trying out her flirtatious techniques on a rake of the first stare. Clarissa was frozen, not knowing what to do.

Then the man glanced over Horatia's bonnet to meet Clarissa's eyes, his own shadowed by the tilted brim of his fashionable beaver hat. His slight smile deepened. It was an insolent, blatant challenge to her ability to protect her charges.

She seized Horatia's wrist and dragged her sideways, taking her place and then pointedly ignoring the scoundrel.

To Horatia she hissed, "Admire the soldiers. They're doubtless safer."

Much safer!

She would have liked to claim immunity to handsome rakes, but her nerves were jangling like a twanged harp. Who was he? Certainly no provincial dandy. Beautifully cut olive coat. Complex, snowy cravat. An indefinable but unignorable air. Her brief stay in London had taught her something about judging men of the *ton* and he was top of the trees.

Another quick glance confirmed her assessment. All the gloss and arrogance of a London beau, and a handsome face as well.

He suddenly looked sideways, catching her, and that amused challenge returned to his eyes.

She jerked her eyes away, away toward the approaching parade, grateful for once for the close bonnet that would hide her blushes. She remembered to go on tiptoe and check. *One, two, three, four.*

Horatia by her side, an older couple beyond her.

Safe for the moment.

All safe.

Apart from the *something* from the man on her other side. She'd met handsome beaux and wicked rakes in London and been able to laugh at the folly of other females. That was remarkably easy when neither beaux nor rakes paid her any attention.

This rakish beau should be the same, and yet she felt a prickling awareness—as if he was studying *her*.

She would *not* look to see.

Then the sway of the crowd suddenly pushed her against him, and he put his hand on her arm to steady her. She felt it. She felt his hand, felt his whole body—arm, hip, and leg—against her for a shocking moment before she pulled away.

She suddenly felt like Ricarda, panicked and longing for the safety of the school.

Which she had to leave soon.

Very well. She would soon have to leave the school, have to venture into a world full of handsome men. She must learn to cope. After all, she had a fortune. There would be fortune hunters.

She swallowed and focused on the passing parade, on a cart carrying a portly man dressed as Napoleon, looking beaten and downcast. On another containing men dressed as the Duke of Wellington, Nelson, Sir John Moore, and other heroic leaders.

A Saint George passed in front of her in Roman armor, spear in hand, foot on the neck of a vanquished dragon that wore the French tricolor. She rather thought Saint George was Mr. Pinkney, who ran a small circulating library and was the least martial man imaginable.

"No stop," said the man, who was still pressed by circumstances too closely beside her.

She had to turn her head. "I beg your pardon, sir?"

"His spear is a throwing spear, not a dragon-killing one. It has no cross-bar. A common mistake in art. If he managed to impale a dragon, the beast would run up it and eat him. Of course, the maiden might applaud."

"What?" Clarissa was beginning to fear that the man was mad as well as bad. But, Lord, he was handsome, especially with that twinkle in his eye!

He glanced at the white-robed woman at Saint George's side, presumably the rescued maiden, but also managing to look like Britannia. "If her rescuer died in the attempt, she would be free without having to be the victor's prize."

The maiden was the mayor's pretty daughter, and she certainly wouldn't want to have to be too grateful to Mr. Pinkney. Clarissa was unwillingly beguiled by the man's nonsense—and by the effect of teasing humor on already fine features—but she firmly turned her attention back to the parade.

All around her the crowd was booing Napoleon and applauding the heroes. Then it burst into huzzahs for the real heroes, the veterans of the great battle who marched to cheerful fife and the demanding, tummy-quivering thump of the drums.

She joined in, waving her plain handkerchief.

"Clarissa! Clarissa! Did you see that? He blew me a kiss! He did! Oh, wasn't he the most handsome man you have ever seen?"

Horatia was literally bouncing up and down, her curls dancing and her cheeks bright red. Clarissa smothered a laugh. The officer in question was quite ordinary, and much older than Horatia's usual practice ground, but he was in a moment of glory and he had noticed her, and so he was an Adonis.

But then a sudden squeal sent panic shooting through her. Ricarda! She stretched on tiptoe again, but the girl seemed all right. The scream had probably been caused by a horse dropping a steaming mound on the road in front of her.

"They are all quite safe," said the rake. "I can see them easily and will tell you if anything untoward occurs."

It was most improper for two strangers to be talking like this, and yet the situation made it impossible to object. She turned to him again. "Thank you, sir."

The angle of his head moved the shadow of his brim, and she was caught by startlingly blue eyes. Cornflower blue made brighter by skin that was browner than fashion approved. That, a silly detail like that, was probably what made him seem more dangerous than the general London beau.

Or perhaps not.

She seemed trapped, and then those intent eyes crinkled slightly with humor that she was invited to share.

She hastily turned her own boring gray-blue eyes forward, but she suddenly felt completely unlike herself.

As if she might do something outrageous.

With him.

By gemini! Was he *flirting* with her?

But men didn't. Even during her horrible time in London, men hadn't flirted with her.

So what was the rake up to?

Ah. Trying to get around her to Horatia, of course. Not while she had blood in her body.

Horatia, however, craned past Clarissa. "You're very kind, sir! Little Lucilla, the plump one, daydreams so. If she took it into her head to wander in front of the horses, she'd do it."

"No, she wouldn't," Clarissa said. "Ricarda would scream the heavens down."

"Ricarda is scared of horses, sir," said irrepressible Horatia, innocently smiling in a way designed to invite a man to her bed.

"Watch the parade, Horatia," Clarissa commanded. "It's nearly over."

Horatia pulled a face, but obeyed.

After a few moments Clarissa risked a glance at the rake. He was looking ahead, not at her.

Victory! He knew his evil plans were thwarted.

She smiled to herself at sounding like a character in an overly dramatic play, but she was feeling victorious. See, it wasn't so very difficult to deal with importunate men.

One skirmish won was enough for the day, however. Thank heavens this would soon be over and she could herd her flock back to the school.

As soon as the last marchers passed and the crowd began to break up, she pulled the four younger girls into a bunch around her, making sure that Horatia stayed close too. The rake moved on without a backward look.

Folly to feel disappointment at that.

"Come along," she said briskly. "It's all over now."

Anxious to be done with this, she nudged her group into the thinning crowd. It wasn't as easy going as she'd expected. The crowd had not truly thinned out. Instead, it swirled chaotically.

When they'd hurried here everyone had been streaming in one direction, but now people went all ways at once. It was market day and many were heading there, but others wanted to get to the taverns, to homes, or to the fairground that had been set up on the outskirts of town.

The mob pushed and pulled, like a monster with a hundred hands snagging at one child or another. Ricarda began to cry again. She let go of Lucilla and clutched Clarissa's skirts. Clarissa reached out to keep Jane and Georgina close.

Then a mighty voice rang out. The town crier. "*Oyez! Oyez!* Mr. Huxtable, landlord of the Duke of Wellington, is rolling out three casks of free ale so all can toast our noble heroes!"

Oh, no! As the crowd's mood changed, Clarissa was already gathering her flock close. Lucilla, her butterfly attention caught by something, swirled off between an enormous man and two elbowing lads. Clarissa just managed to seize the back of the girl's cloak and haul her close—at some risk to the poor child's neck!

She shed her own cloak, letting it fall to be trampled. "Hold tight to my skirt!" she commanded. "Jane, Georgina, do the same. Horatia, help me keep everyone together. We'll stay still for a moment to let the crowd pass."

She put every scrap of calm and confidence that she could muster into her words, and the girls did press close, but staying still was easier said than done. Most of the crowd seemed hell-bent on the free ale, and the rest were struggling to get free.

Rocked and buffeted, she was seized by blank panic.

Cries and screams all around flung her back to other screams, and blood.

To the thunder of a pistol.

Shattering glass.

Blood, so much blood . . .

And a woman quoting Lady Macbeth. *"Who would have thought the old man to have had so much blood in him?"*

Darkness crept in at the edge of her vision.

No. Stay in the present. The girls need you. You will not fall apart again in a crisis!

She pinched her left hand hard to get her wits back, then clutched terrified Ricarda close. She began to ease her little group sideways to a nearby brick wall where perhaps the mob would flow past them.

"Stay close!" she yelled. "Hold on!" Her voice seemed swallowed by the cacophony around, but the girls were all with her, clinging, dragging on her arms and gown.

The press of squirming, elbowing bodies had her sweating with heat and terror, but she would not weaken. Lose their footing here and they could be trampled. The stench turned her stomach. Her foot slid on something squishy, almost making her fall. She prayed it was as innocent as a piece of dropped fruit.

One, two, three, four, five.

Horatia—good girl—had wrapped an arm around her waist so they were locked into a huddled unit.

Then her bonnet was knocked forward over her right eye, so she couldn't see from that side at all. She didn't dare raise her hand to straighten it for fear of losing one of the children. The crush was so tight, she'd never get her arm down again.

All the younger girls were wailing now, and she wanted to wail herself. But she was the protector here. "It's all right," she said meaninglessly. "Hold tight. It will be all right."

When someone crushed into them from behind, she didn't hesitate to jab back with her elbow.

There was an *"Ooof!"*; then a strong arm came around them and a voice said, "Hold back, hold back, make way, make way there." He didn't shout—in the tumult there would be no point—but somehow his commanding tone seemed to cut through and create a moment's pause so they could slide sideways.

The crowd sealed tight behind them, but his voice opened the way until they landed entangled against the wall.

There was no indent here, however, no doorway to press back into. No barrier except a simple iron lamppost. Had they fallen out of the pot into the fire? They could be crushed. Terrified screams said that might be happening elsewhere in the maddened crowd.

But the man grasped the lamppost and made himself a barrier that the crowd must flow around, creating a tiny pocket of sanity.

Clarissa held her crying charges closer, trembling. "It's all right, dears," she said again. "Don't be afraid. This kind man is making sure we don't get hurt."

It was, of course, the wicked rake, to whom she'd been so cold. Horatia had better instincts. He was a true hero. He had rescued them and was now their protector.

Chapter Three

Clarissa could see only the man's back, for he was facing the throng. She could see the faces of the passing crowd, however—young, old, angry, fearful, excited, greedy, impatient. She watched them see him, see him as a barrier to the direction they wanted to take, then shift away as if he wore spikes.

She wondered what expression he was using to warn them off, but she could only be grateful. Now that she had a measure of safety her knees felt like limp lettuce. If not for the girls she might have sagged to the ground and given in to tears herself.

But she'd done it! She'd been terrified, the memories had tried to overwhelm her, but she hadn't collapsed. Instead, she'd surely helped save them all. Though still shaking and close to tears, she felt as if great weights had fallen away, leaving her light enough to fly.

She could face fear and survive.

A woman was suddenly pushed beside them. A desperate young countrywoman in coarse, disheveled clothes with a screaming baby in her arms. She did collapse, her legs giving way so that she sank down, back against the wall. Even Ricarda stopped wailing to stare at her.

Clarissa couldn't help thinking about fleas, but the mother needed help as much as she and the girls did. As the woman lowered her dirty shift and put the frantic baby to her big breast, Clarissa looked away, looked again at their savior and guardian.

She didn't generally allow herself to study men, but since his back was to her, she could indulge.

He was tall—her head barely came up to his shoulders. His olive coat lay smooth across broad shoulders and down his back, suggesting a lean, strong body. He stood with strong legs braced apart.

She ripped her gaze away. Studying a man like that was not only immodest, it was dangerous. Looks said nothing about a man's true qualities, but they could weaken a woman's mind.

Yet she couldn't resist sneaking another look. He'd lost his hat in the riot, revealing disordered honey-brown hair.

She remembered earlier assessing him as a London beau. She'd sensed that danger, but never imagined him the stuff of which effective heroes are made. Another lesson about judging by appearances.

She suddenly realized that the nature of the crowd had shifted like a change in the air, danger fading, shock lingering. Pressure eased as people began to mill around, many pale and dazed while others sharpened to bring order and assistance. Through wails, and the cries of parents trying to locate their children, she heard the beat of a drum, doubtless calling the soldiers to riot control.

She quickly counted, even though she knew they were all safe. *One, two, three, four, five.* She found a smile for Horatia, whose bonnet was down her back, revealing all her lovely curls, but who clearly was not thinking of that at all. "Thank you. You were magnificent."

The girl smiled back, proud but a bit wobbly.

Horatia, too, had probably learned in a test of fire that she was braver than she'd thought.

"Quite an adventure, girls," Clarissa said in as light a tone as she could manage. "Let go of me now and help one another to straighten bonnets and bodices."

They did so, and with Horatia's encouragement, even began to giggle a bit as they repaired one another's appearance. Clarissa made sure her own gown was straight, wondering what had happened to her cloak. She took off her crooked bonnet, using it to fan herself for a moment before putting it back on.

The man turned.

She was caught hatless and staring, because there was nothing grim and indomitable about him. Instead, he was all rake again, with a wicked glint in those blue eyes and a slight smile on his well-shaped lips.

And a wavery, warm feeling skimmed over her.

None of that! No amount of willpower, however, could halt her blush, so she turned away as she settled her bonnet back firmly on her head.

No amount of willpower could stop her from wishing she looked her inadequate best. She tried to at least tuck her hair away neatly, knowing it was a forlorn gesture. It was unruly by nature, and it had just been given an excellent opportunity to riot.

She firmly tied the ribbons, then looked at him. "I don't know how to thank you, sir. We might have been in terrible trouble without your assistance."

"I was pleased to be able to help."

She was braced to resist flirtation, but he hunkered down in front of the countrywoman. "Are you all right, ma'am?"

Well, of course.

Men didn't flirt with her.

All the same, a foolish part of her envied the mother, who was blooming under his attention. "Oh, yes, sir," she said in a country accent. "So kind, sir! I thought for sure I was to be crushed to death, or have poor Joanie here torn from my arms."

But then her eyes widened and she paled as she tried to push herself up one-handed.

He helped her, not seeming conscious of her half-exposed breast or the attached suckling infant.

"My littl'uns!" she gasped, her hand going up to push straggling brown hair off her face. "They're out there somewhere. I must go—"

"No, no," he said calmly. "Tell me what they look like and I'll find them for you. What of your man?"

"He's back tending the cows for Squire Bewsley, sir. There be three of 'em, sir. Three boys, and they do stay together if they can. Four, seven, and ten. All brown hair."

Clarissa wondered how anyone could find three urchins on that description, but the man didn't seem daunted.

"Names?" he asked, as Clarissa looked out at the street, hoping three young brown-haired lads were in sight.

"Matt, Mark, and Lukey," the woman said, and even produced a smile when she added, "Little Joanie was going to be John."

The man grinned. "Stay here, and I'll return soon to report. Hopefully with your little evangelists in tow."

His grin, Clarissa discovered, could shatter a lady's common sense. How fortunate that Horatia wasn't looking. She'd be in a swoon.

He turned to leave, but suddenly Clarissa couldn't bear for this strange encounter to end like that. "Sir, could I know the name of our rescuer?"

He turned back and bowed. "Major Hawkinville, ma'am." He raised his hand to his hat, then said, "The deuce. I wonder where it is."

"Wherever, I fear it will be sadly flattened."

Then she found herself sharing a smile that left her feeling positively light-headed.

"Better a hat than people," he said, those richly blue eyes on hers, making her heart race.

How rash she had been to come to names with a man she knew nothing about. Especially with one who seemed able to spin her out of common sense with a look.

It was done now, however, so she curtsied and gave him her name in return. Suddenly at a loss to describe her status, she added, "Of Miss Mallory's School here."

He turned to the wide-eyed girls. "As are you all, I suppose. All right?"

"Yes, sir," the girls chorused adoringly.

Oh, no. Horatia was gazing at him as if he were a god, and now the man could probably claim to have been introduced. Clarissa realized that she'd rashly created a very improper situation, and she winced at what Miss Mallory would think of this whole affair.

"Were you at Waterloo, Major Hawkinville?" Horatia asked breathlessly.

"Yes, I was."

"In the cavalry?" asked Jane.

"No."

Before anyone else could ask a question, however, he bowed farewell. "But now, ladies, I must be off to other battles."

And thus he was gone, striding away through the dazed stragglers, looking, to Clarissa's dazzled eyes, like a hero among lesser men. Finding three young strangers in the chaos seemed impossible, but if anyone could do it, Major Hawkinville could.

Definitely a hero, but judging by his swift departure, one who sought no glory in war.

Not cavalry, so infantry. He had shown great steadiness in the face of the crowd. She could imagine him leading his men to assault the walls of an impenetrable fortress, or keeping them steady in the face of a French cavalry charge.

"Wasn't he handsome, Clarissa?" Jane sighed. "And one of our noble soldiers!"

"A warrior angel," Georgina said. "I shall draw a picture of him as Saint George when we get back."

Clarissa didn't point out that Saint George was not one of the angels. This wasn't the right time for a lesson, and she wasn't a teacher, thank heavens.

"A major," sighed Horatia. "Mentioned in dispatches a dozen times. He must have met the Duke of Wellington."

"Doubtless." But Clarissa was shocked that her thoughts had been so like those of the younger girls. "Come," she said crisply. "We must return to school. If news of this crush has reached them, they'll be worried."

After their fright, the girls made no trouble on the return journey. Clarissa chose a roundabout route that should avoid any problems and determined to put any thought of handsome Major Hawkinville out of her mind.

That was hard to do when the others were determined to chatter about him. There was a great deal of romantic babble, despite their youth. Horatia was silent, probably drifting in a true hero-worshiping ecstasy.

Clarissa supposed that wouldn't hurt. She'd certainly done the same at times.

Florence Babbington's handsome brother had rendered half the school breathless when he'd come to take his sister out to tea. Clarissa remembered writing a poem in his honor, and she'd only been twelve at the time.

> *O noble man, tall, chaste, and bold.*
> *So like a gallant knight of old,*
> *Turn on me once, lest I expire,*
> *Those obsidian orbs full of manly fire.*

Her lips twitched at the memory. What nonsense people could create in the throes of romantic fervor.

Then there'd been the groom at Brownbutton's livery.

The stables were behind the school, separated by a high wall. From the attic windows, however, a person could see over the wall, and it was a wicked amusement for the senior girls. A stalwart young groom had been a special treat two years ago. He'd generally worked without his jacket, and with his sleeves rolled up, revealing wonderfully strong brown forearms.

One deliciously naughty day Maria Ffoulks had caught him working without his shirt. She'd run to gather as many of the senior girls as she could, and they'd pressed to every available window for about ten minutes until he'd gone into the stables and emerged covered again.

That hadn't been infatuation, however. It had been more like worship from afar. Worship of the male of the species, and of the mysterious, forbidden feelings he stirred in them all.

That sort of thing was probably why she'd been such a ninny as to hope when her parents had finally summoned her for a London season.

A ninny. She'd been in danger of being ninny over Major Hawkinville, too. "Come along, girls," she said briskly. "Cook was making Sally Lunns when we left." Mention of cakes removed any tendency to dawdle.

Hawk moved swiftly down the Promenade, following the flotsam of the crowd toward the Wellington Inn. The innkeeper deserved to be flogged for causing this mayhem.

He guessed the three boys would have gone along with the crowd, and as long as they kept their feet would have come out of it all right. He passed some people being attended to, but none of the injuries seemed serious. The only boy he saw among them was clearly being attended to by his mother.

A bunch of lads ran by, but they all seemed happy and purposeful, and none particularly fit the description of the evangelists. A wail caught his attention and he turned to look, but then a man scooped up the crying child and carried her away.

There were people scattered around, many of them disheveled or dazed, some on the ground. Since they were all being cared for, he followed the trail again, part of his mind scanning for the boys, part assessing the puzzle that was Clarissa Greystone.

A thief and a murderer?

Not a whore called Pepper, that was for sure, not even by deception.

The image of her face rose up, blushing, freckled, frankly thanking him for his help. No, she wasn't a beauty, but astonishingly, his heart had missed a beat there. One of these quirks that comes after battle, and she had been remarkably gallant.

Damnation, he must not let her under his guard! What was to say she hadn't played the whore, and wasn't playing a part now?

Because no one played a part in battle. In battle, the truth about a person spilled along with the blood and guts, and that riot had been a minor battle.

He paused to question two brown-haired lads hunkered down to play with ants in the road, but they said they lived in a nearby house. A blond urchin wandered by eating a plum, not seeming to be in distress other than the juice all over her hands and dress. Hands on hips, he looked over the untidy groups of people but didn't see any children who seemed likely.

He spotted a young brown-haired boy standing tearfully alone and went over to him. "What's your name, lad?"

The boy looked up, knuckling his eyes. "Sam, sir."

Hawk suppressed a sigh. "Who were you with, Sam?"

"Me dad, sir. I lost 'im, sir. He'll be cross."

This wasn't one of his targets, but he couldn't leave him here. Hawk held out a hand. "Why not come along with me? I'm going to check out the Wellington. Perhaps your father's having a drink there."

A damp, sticky hand wrapped trustingly around his, and they progressed down the street. Soon he gathered two frightened sisters, and another lad who was older but seemed slow-witted. Then stray children began to attach themselves like burrs collected during a march through rough country, and he eventually found the evangelists.

"Your mother's worried about you," he told them.

"We couldn't help it, sir," the wild-eyed eldest said. "And we stuck together."

Hawk ruffled his hair and looked around at his collection, all putting their absolute trust in him.

Clarissa Greystone would probably trust him too—if she was as honest as she seemed to be. The encounter had tangled all his threads, but she was still his only lead to the heart of the conspiracy, and he had to pursue her.

Once he dealt with his present duties.

He and his burrs turned a corner and faced the Duke of Wellington Inn. The Great Man would not be amused.

The place was jam-packed, with free-ale patrons spilling out into the street in all directions, many of them already drunk. He spotted the town crier leaning boozily against a horse trough, and guided his squadron there. He pulled out a notebook and began to take down names.

When he had them all, he ripped out the page and commanded the town crier's attention. "These children are lost. You are to go around town announcing their names, and that they are to be found here."

He used his military voice, and the rotund man stood straight. "Yes, sir."

"Good. Start with the Lord Wellington."

In moments, the man's mighty bellow was breaking through the din. Hawk turned to the children. "Stay here. Your parents will find you." He put the oldest boy in charge of making sure the little ones didn't wander, then took Matt, Mark, and Lukey back to their mother.

He was not surprised to find that the heiress and her charges had left. That was no problem. He now had an excellent excuse to call on the school.

Chapter Four

Clarissa settled the girls at their tea under the eye of the cook, then carried a tea tray upstairs. She hoped Althea was recovered enough to talk.

As she put down the tray on the small spindle-legged table by the window, she thought of how much she would miss this room. She'd once itched to be out of school and in the world. Now it and the walled garden were her comfort and safety.

But then she realized that the wall was the one around Brownbutton's livery stable. From this low level, however, she couldn't see into the yard. Muscular men could be wandering around there stark naked and she wouldn't know.

Safer so.

Safe. But she was going to be forced to leave.

Someone knocked at the door, and Clarissa opened it. "Come in, Thea. I was just going to invite you for tea." But then she realized that there was something different about her friend. "You've put off your mourning."

Althea was in a pretty gown of cream sprigged with pale blue flowers, and she looked lovely. Even more lovely. Suave Major Hawkinville would probably trip over his feet if he set eyes on Althea looking like this.

Clarissa didn't like to examine why that depressed her.

It was over. They would never meet again.

"It's been a year," Althea said, smoothing the soft fabric. "Gareth would not have wanted me to wear dull colors forever. He . . . he liked this dress." She pulled out a handkerchief and pressed it to her eyes, then blew her nose. "It will get easier."

"Yes, I'm sure," said Clarissa helplessly. "Come and have some tea."

Althea sat and Clarissa poured. "Today must be difficult for you." She offered the cake.

Althea took a piece, her eyes still glossed with tears. "For you, too."

Oh, lord.

Clarissa had let Althea think they shared a bond of mourning. It had just happened, and then she hadn't known how to set things right. It had been impressed upon her that no one must know the truth about Lord Deveril's death, and that it would be better if she didn't show her relief over it.

Now, suddenly, however, it was intolerable to be lying to Althea, and after all, who could think that she didn't loathe Lord Devil?

"An anniversary," she said, "but not a sad one."

Althea stared.

"I'm sorry for letting you think otherwise. I— I never wanted to marry Lord Deveril. He was my parents' choice. I have never grieved for him."

"Never?" Althea asked, eyes widening. "Not at all?"

"Never." Clarissa thought for a moment and then admitted a little more. "In fact, I was glad when he died. More than glad. Over the moon."

Althea just looked at her, and it was clear that her Christian soul was shocked.

"Lord Deveril was my father's age," Clarissa hurried on, beginning to wonder if she should have kept silent after all. "But age wasn't the problem. He was ugly. But that wasn't it either." She met her friend's eyes. "Put simply, Thea, he was evil. Despite his wealth and title, he was accepted hardly anywhere. Nobody spoke to me of such matters, but I couldn't help realizing that he indulged in all kinds of depravity."

She started at the touch of Althea's hand. "I'm sorry. I wish you'd told me sooner, but I'm glad you've told me now. It explains so much. Why you're here. The way you think about men." After a moment, she added, "Not all men are like that."

Clarissa laughed, her vision blurring a little. "It would be an impossible world if they were. Truly, Thea, I doubt you've ever met anyone as foul. The mere thought of him makes me feel sick."

Althea refilled Clarissa's teacup and put it into her hand. "Drink up. It'll steady you. Why did your parents permit such a match?"

Clarissa almost choked on a mouthful of tea. "Permit? They arranged it and forced me to agree. They sold me to him," she went on, hearing the acid bitterness in her voice, but unable to stop it. "Two thousand upon my betrothal in the papers, and two upon my wedding. Then five hundred a year as long as I lived with Deveril as a dutiful wife."

"*What?* But that's atrocious! It must be illegal."

"It's illegal, I think, to force someone into marriage, but it's not illegal for parents to beat a daughter, nor for them to mistreat one in all kinds of ways."

Instead of distress, Althea's eyes lit with outrage. "Though it may not be entirely in keeping with the Gospels, Clarissa, I, too, am delighted that Lord Deveril died."

Clarissa laughed with relief. "So am I. Glad he died, and glad I told you. It's been a burden to lie to you."

Althea cocked her head. "So why did you tell me now?"

Clarissa put down her cup. "I dislike dishonesty." She sighed. "Miss Mallory says I must leave, and my guardian agrees."

"What will you do?"

"That's the puzzle."

"What do you want to do?"

Clarissa rubbed her temples. "I've never quite thought of it like that. Last year I wanted balls, parties, and handsome gallants."

"There's nothing wrong with that."

"But now I'm a walking scandal. The Devil's Heiress. And a Greystone to boot. I don't think I'm going to receive many invitations. And of course, any gallants I do attract will be after my money."

"Not all of them, I'm sure," Althea said with a smile.

"Thea, please, be honest. No man has ever shown interest in my charms." Then she winced at Althea's distress. "I'm sorry. It's all right. I truly don't want to marry, and with money I don't need to."

"But you want the balls and parties."

"Not anymore," Clarissa said, aware that it was a lie. If it could be done without scandal, she still wanted what most young ladies wanted—a brief time of social frivolity.

Althea fiddled with her sprigged muslin skirts. "I might be leaving Miss Mallory's, too."

"But you've been here less than a year."

Delicate color enhanced Althea's beauty. "A gentleman from home has approached my father. A Mr. Verrall."

Though Clarissa had just talked about leaving, this felt like abandonment. "Approached your father? Isn't that a little cold-blooded?"

"Bucklestead St. Stephens is seventy miles from here, and Mr. Verrall has four children to care for."

Worse and worse. "A widower? How old?"

"Around forty, I suppose. His oldest daughter is fifteen. His wife died three years ago. He's a pleasant gentleman. Honorable and kind."

Clarissa knew it was a reasonable arrangement. Althea would live near her beloved family, and this Mr. Verrall would doubtless be a good husband. As Althea's father was a parson with a large family, she wouldn't have many desirable suitors. All the same, Mr. Verrall sounded like dry crumbs to her.

"Don't you think perhaps you should look around more before committing yourself to this man? You attract all the men."

Althea shook her head. "I will not love again."

"You should give yourself the chance, just in case."

Althea's eyes twinkled. "By all means. With whom? Mr. Dills, the clock mender? Colonel Dunn, who always raises his hat if we pass in the street? Reverend Whipple—but then, he has a wife."

Clarissa pulled a face. "It's true, isn't it? We don't meet many eligible men. At this time of year, there aren't even any handsome brothers passing through."

"And handsome brothers are usually dependent on their fathers, who would turn up starchy at the thought of marriage to a penniless schoolteacher."

"Surely not quite penniless," Clarissa protested.

"When it comes to eligible gentlemen, I am. My portion is less than five hundred pounds."

It was virtually nothing. Clarissa took another bite out of her bun and chewed it thoughtfully. If only she could give Althea some of her money— but her trustees were sticklers for not letting her be imposed upon. And it didn't sound as if Althea would wait until Clarissa was twenty-one.

"Beth Armitage married the heir to a dukedom," she pointed out, "and though I admire her a great deal, she has not a tenth of your beauty."

Althea laughed gently. "The sort of story to make idiots of us all. Such things cannot be relied on."

"True," said Clarissa, remembering the dark side of the fairy tale.

Althea was right. She had nothing but her beauty and good nature to recommend her. The world would say she should be grateful for any suitable offer, even that of an elderly widower with a daughter not many years her junior.

"I came to thank you again for taking the girls," Althea said, clearly changing the subject. "I'm so sorry you ended up in such trouble."

"It wasn't too bad."

"The girls seem to see it as a wonderfully perilous adventure, including rescue by Saint George, complete with halo."

Clarissa laughed. "Hardly, but Major Hawkinville did help us, yes." She gave her account of the event. "I wonder if he found the woman's lost evangelists. He seemed capable of it."

Althea cocked her head. "Heaven, purgatory, or hell?"

"I'm a nonbeliever, remember? No marriage for me."

"Nonsense. I'm sure Lord Deveril was as hellish as you say, but when you meet heaven you'll change your mind."

"I won't trust heaven." Major Hawkinville somehow merged in her mind with handsome Lord Arden, afire with rage. "Any man, if angered enough, can turn into hell."

"Not Gareth," Althea said firmly.

Clarissa couldn't hurt her by arguing. "Perhaps not, but how are we to know?"

"A decent period of courtship. Gareth and I had known each other for years, and been courting for two."

Clarissa pounced. "So you shouldn't consider marrying this widower without a decent period of courtship."

"But I've known Mr. Verrall for years too, and I like him."

Balked, Clarissa still protested, "You need to meet some other men first."

"Perhaps it's a shame I didn't take the girls to the parade and fall into an adventure with the handsome major."

Clarissa chuckled, but a plan stirred. Althea needed to meet eligible men, and, as she'd said, that was unlikely here in the school. Once the last girls went home, Althea would return to Bucklestead St. Stephens and marry her doddering widower.

What was needed was what the army called a preemptive strike.

"I wonder where I should go?" she mused. " 'The world's mine oyster . . .' "

" 'Which I with sword will open'?" Althea completed.

"With money, perhaps. It frightens me, Althea. Miss Mallory says I should not stay in the familiarity of Cheltenham, and Bath is so dreary."

"London, then."

"No." It came out rather abruptly, but then Althea would guess that London had bad memories for her. "Anyway, it's the end of the Season there. The place will soon be empty."

Clarissa still hadn't worked around to her true purpose—persuading Althea to accompany her for a few weeks and meet a suitable husband. "Where would you go if you were me?" she asked.

But Althea shook her head. "I'm a country mouse. I like life in a village."

"I think I might, too," Clarissa said, "though I've never tried it. My father sold his estate when I was in the cradle to pay debts and buy a London house."

A village, however, would be an unlikely place in which to find Althea a prime husband.

Her frustrated thoughts were interrupted by a knock on the door. Clarissa answered it and the school's upstairs maid said, "There's a gentleman inquiring for you, Miss Greystone." Her expression was a combination of disapproval and interest. "Miss Mallory isn't home yet . . ."

"A gentleman?"

"A Major Hawkinville, he says." Mary added with disapproval, "But he's not wearing a hat."

Clarissa actually squeaked with surprise, but managed to compose herself. The major. Here!

Then she saw Althea's smiling interest and realized that this was a chance to introduce her to at least one eligible man. He must be eligible, mustn't he, and Althea clearly favored a military man.

"Major Hawkinville lost his hat saving me and the girls, Mary. We cannot turn him away. Miss Trist and I will be down in a moment."

As soon as the maid left, Clarissa whirled to the mirror. She could hear one of Miss Mallory's favorite admonishments: *Only God can give beauty, girls, but anyone can be neat.* It had usually been accompanied by a pained look at Clarissa. God had neglected to give her tidiness, too.

She began pulling the pins out of her hair.

Althea came over and pushed her hands away. After a few moments with the brush and a few more with the pins, Clarissa's hair was pinned in an orderly, and even slightly becoming, knot.

"I don't know how you do it," she said somewhat grumpily.

Althea just laughed again. "Don't you have any ribbons?"

"No, and they'd look silly with this plain gown." Clarissa felt that she'd exposed enough folly for now. "Thank you for tidying me. Now let's go and thank the hero of the day."

"Don't you have any other clothes?" Althea asked, frowning at the beige dress.

Clarissa ignored the trunks in the attic. "No. Come along, Althea. It hardly matters what I look like."

"No?" Althea teased.

Certainly not as long as I'm with you, Clarissa thought without acrimony, leading the way downstairs. Despite that, her heart was racing on nervous little feet, and she tried to command her senses. The major was here out of courtesy. Despite his earlier behavior, there was no chance that he had been slain by her wondrous charms.

And, of course, she did not desire any man's serious interest.

He was just the sort of man, however, likely to shock Althea's heart out of the past and into thinking beyond the hoary ancient awaiting her back home.

They arrived in the neat front hall, and after a steadying breath, she led the way into the parents' parlor—so called because it was where parents were taken when they visited.

Oh, my. Speaking of wondrous charms . . .

The image in her mind had not been fanciful.

Even without a hat, he was strikingly elegant, not just in the quality of his clothes but in the way he wore them, and the way he moved. There was all the straight-shouldered authority of the military, but surprising grace as well.

He bowed—perfectly. "Miss Greystone. Excuse my intrusion, but I wished to be sure that you and the girls were not harmed in any way."

Clarissa dropped a curtsy, commanding her heart to settle so that she could think clearly. Her heart, however, was a rebel, as was her awestruck mind. "So kind, sir. We are all safe." She introduced Althea and then took a seat on the sofa, inviting him to take a chair.

They talked of the riot and the consequences—apparently two people were seriously injured, but most had merely been frightened. All the time, Clarissa was fighting her tendency to be dazzled, and observing Althea to see how she was reacting to this gem.

Althea was sparkling, which was a truly remarkable sight. Clarissa thought she was seeing the Althea that Gareth Waterstone had loved, and she was amazed that the major managed to pay herself any courteous interest at all.

Yet he did. He seemed to share his attention between them, and when he looked at her— Clarissa fought for reason, but his attentive eyes, his quick smiles seemed meant for her.

She didn't need a man.

She didn't want a man. And she must be mistaken. Such men were never interested in her.

But she wouldn't mind the company of one if, amazingly, he did find something about her to admire.

Perhaps it was her behavior during the riot. She had done well. Was it possible that he *admired* her?

Her heart scurried again. "Do you live in Cheltenham, Major?" she asked.

Those eyes. Those eyes that seemed to like looking at *her*. "No, Miss Greystone. I am passing through on my way to visit a family property. My home is in Sussex, not far from Brighton."

"Have you seen the Pavilion?" Althea asked with interest, drawing his attention.

"A number of times, Miss Trist, as a youth. I have been out of the country with the army for many years, however."

Clarissa saw thoughts of the army, and of Gareth, mute her friend's spirits, and spoke quickly, "Brighton is the most fashionable place to be in the summer, isn't it, Major?"

"Indeed it is, Miss Greystone. I recommend it to you."

She stared at him. "To me?"

"To anyone who would like a pleasant place in which to pass some summer months," he responded smoothly, but she didn't think that was quite what he had meant.

Was he a mind reader? Here she was, in her well-worn schoolgirl clothes, and he was suggesting a move to the most fashionable, and expensive, resort in England.

Some of the glow disappeared from the room.

"Cheltenham is delightful," he went on, "but it does not have the sea, never mind the Prince of Wales and most of the *haut ton*."

"How true." She met his smiling eyes, sorting through her tumbling thoughts.

Althea broke in. "Miss Greystone is to leave here soon, Major, and enter fashionable life."

Clarissa felt herself color, and knew it did nothing to improve her looks. Althea meant well, but Clarissa wished she hadn't said that.

The major smiled as if he'd received good news. "Then perhaps you and your family will visit Brighton, Miss Greystone."

Her family. Mustn't such a man-about-town know the Greystones? And know about the Devil's Heiress.

Hiding foolish hurt, Clarissa retreated behind a formal smile and a slightly cool manner. "I doubt it is possible to move there this late in the year, Major Hawkinville. Perhaps next year—"

She rose to hint that the visit was at an end.

He rose too, with admirable smoothness. "You are thinking of the difficulty of finding good houses to rent, Miss Greystone?" He took out a card and pencil and wrote something on the back. "If you should think of visiting Brighton, apply to Mr. Scotburn and mention my name. If there is a house to be had, he will doubtless find it for you."

Clarissa took the card, though she felt it would be safer to take nothing tangible from this encounter. How could she refuse, however, short of pure incivility?

Then he was gone, and that should have been the end of it, except that she had his card, and his even, flowing handwriting. She turned it and confirmed what she suspected.

She also had his address.

Major George Hawkinville, Hawkinville Manor, Sussex.

Major George Hawkinville, who almost certainly was a fortune hunter who knew exactly who she was and what she was worth. Whose admiration had been stirred by her money, not her charms.

But, she thought, looking at the card again, that admiration had been deliciously enjoyable. Why should a lady not play games too, and enjoy such company, especially if she was awake to all his tricks?

Hawk left the school and didn't allow himself a pause to savor success. People leaving were often watched.

His quarry had cooled for some reason, but he didn't think she was beyond reach. In fact, he'd be willing to bet that she was already thinking of a move to Brighton. If not, he could come up with some other ways to persuade her. It was the obvious resort for a wealthy young lady in search of social adventure in the summer, and he was sure that Miss Greystone was in search of social adventure.

In fact, she was ripe for trouble, and his pressing instinct was to protect her! Damnation, why couldn't she be the harpy he'd imagined?

He wasted a few moments seeking other ways to the Deveril money, but knew he'd worn that path bare. He simply didn't want to be doing what he was doing, playing on an innocent young woman's vulnerability.

Hawkinville, he reminded himself.

And no matter how innocent she was, that money was not hers by right.

He decided, however, to move on immediately to inspect Gaspard Hall. He knew how useful a strategic absence could be. Before seeing his father's new property he loathed it, but if there was something to be made of it, perhaps they could survive somehow without the Deveril money.

Twenty thousand pounds?

And, damnation, that will was a forgery. It galled him to think of anyone, even that lively young woman, benefiting from it!

For the first time in his life he was being deflected from battle by a pretty face. Not even pretty, but with power all the same.

Hawkinville, he reminded himself.

But even for Hawkinville, was he really willing to see Clarissa Greystone hang?

Clarissa retreated back to her room, card in hand. "Brighton," she announced.

"Clarissa! You can't. You hardly know the man."

Clarissa laughed. "I'm not going to *marry* him, Thea, but it is the obvious place to go. Think of it. I'm the Devil's Heiress and no matter where I go, sooner or later people will learn of it. I might as well be brazen and enjoy myself in a fashionable spot."

"But that doesn't mean the major—"

"Of course not. He merely put the idea into my mind. However," she added, twirling the card, "if we happen to meet it will not be unpleasant."

"What if he's a fortune hunter?"

Even though it put Clarissa's own thoughts into words, it stung. "Oh, he probably is," she said lightly. "As I said, I have no intention of marrying him. If he wants to play escort and charming companion, well, why not?"

"If he is a fortune hunter, I wish nothing more to do with him."

Althea had what Clarissa thought of as her Early Christian Martyr face on. Clarissa was trying to work around to the topic of Althea's accompanying her, and this was not the right direction. Unless she gave it a twist.

"I do have to leave and join the world, Thea," she said meekly, "but it will be hard. I did nothing wrong, but I am a Greystone, and I was engaged to marry Lord Deveril, and he did meet with a very unfortunate death—"

"He did?" Althea asked, disapproval thawing to curiosity.

"Stabbed in a very poor area of town."

"Stabbed!" Althea gasped.

Clarissa tried to stay focused on the part she was playing, and not let memories of the truth invade to overset her.

"Doubtless something to do with the company he kept," she said, "and well deserved. The point is, Thea, that I'm a little worried about being accepted by society."

Althea took her hand. "None of it was your fault."

"That is not how people will see it. What I am thinking," Clarissa plunged on, "is that I would feel easier with a companion. A friend." She looked at Althea, realizing that her words were true. "With you. If I go to Brighton, Thea, I ask most sincerely that you accompany me for a little while."

"Me?" Althea gasped, eyes wide. "Clarissa, I couldn't! I know nothing of fashionable circles."

Clarissa gripped her hand. "Your birth is respectable, and you have excellent manners, and unquestioned beauty."

Althea broke their handclasp. "I'm only twenty. I'm not old enough to be your chaperon in a place like Brighton."

"But I don't want you to be that. I want you to come as a friend, to enjoy Brighton with me. Do say you will."

Althea blushed and covered her cheeks with her hands. "It's still impossible, Clarissa. I don't have the sort of clothes that are needed in a place like Brighton, and I certainly can't afford to buy them."

Clarissa absorbed the truth of that. She knew her trustees would not allow her to buy Althea new clothes. She considered sharing, for she would have to buy a new, fashionable wardrobe herself. But she and Althea did not suit the same colors, and her friend was a good few inches shorter.

An idea burst upon her. She seized Althea's hand and dragged her out of the room.

"Where are we going?"

"To the attic!"

"Why?"

"To look at my London clothes!"

They clattered up the narrow stairs into the storage rooms. In the dusty gloom, Clarissa eyed the two hardly used trunks. She didn't want to open them and stir revolting memories, but she'd do it. For Althea.

At the very least Althea deserved a few weeks of pleasure in Brighton. At the best, with her beauty, virtue, and sweet nature, she might attract a wonderful husband.

A lord. A duke, even!

So she lifted one heavy lid and pushed back plain muslin to reveal a froth of pale blue trimmed with white lace.

"If you're going into society, you'll need these clothes," Althea protested.

Clarissa pulled out the blue and passed it over. "I'll never wear these again." She tossed aside that layer of muslin and unfurled the second. The pink.

She shuddered. She'd been wearing that when Deveril had kissed her. Her mother had screeched about the trouble of getting the vomit stains out of it, but it seemed someone had managed it.

"These were all chosen by Lord Deveril and paid for by him," she said, tossing the ruched and beribboned gown to Althea. "Anything connected to that man revolts me, and they don't even suit me. Imagine me in that shade of pink! If you don't take them, I'm giving them to the maids for whatever they can get for them."

Althea put down the blue and studied the pink. "The color would suit me, but it's a bit . . ."

"Overdone? In bad taste? Oh, definitely." Overcoming her distaste, Clarissa held the dress in front of her friend. "The shade is lovely on you, though."

"Won't it bother you to see me in these dresses?"

Foul memories were swirling with the attic dust, but Clarissa pushed them away. "Everything will have to be altered. You're slimmer and shorter. We can strip off the trimming at the same time." She gave Althea the dress. "A wardrobe is here for you, if you're brave enough to come adventuring with me."

"Adventuring?" echoed Althea, but her eyes were bright and her color high.

Heartbreaking that her Gareth wasn't here to enjoy the Thea he'd known and loved, but Clarissa resolved that she would find her friend someone almost as good. Not just an adequate husband, but another chance at heaven.

"Well?" Clarissa asked. "Will you do it?"

Althea stared into a distance, and perhaps for a moment she thought of Gareth, for she sobered. But then again, perhaps he spoke to her, for she smiled in a steadier, no less glorious way. "Yes. I'll do it."

The next day Hawk rode slowly down a driveway clumped with foot-high weeds, taking in his father's hard-won inheritance. One chimney of Gaspard Hall had crashed down onto the roof, partly accounting for the broken and missing tiles. A substantial crack ran up one wall, suggesting that the foundations had given way, and the wood around the broken windows flaked with rot.

He directed Centaur carefully around the side of the house, keeping to the grass rather than the drive. Less danger of potholes or falling debris.

A couple of years ago, with farming prices high and industry profitable, this place might have been worth something for the land alone. The end of the war had brought hard times, however. Trading routes were open to competition, and prices had fallen, sometimes to disastrous levels. In various parts of the country farms were even being abandoned.

Gaspard Hall in its present state was nothing but an extra burden. There must be tenants here still, and others dependent on the place, all hoping that the new Lord Deveril would help them.

At the back of the house he found the deserted stableyard. He swung off the horse and led it to a trough and pump. As expected, the pump was broken.

"Sorry, old boy," he said, patting Centaur's neck. "I'll find you water as soon as possible."

He looked around and called out, "Halloo!"

Some birds flew out of nearby eaves, but there was no other response.

A quick check of the stable buildings found only ancient, moldy straw and rat-chewed wood. From here, the back of the house was in as bad a state as the front.

It offended his orderly heart to see a place in such condition, but it would take a fortune to restore it. He wondered why the late Lord Deveril hadn't spent some of his money here. He assumed he simply hadn't cared.

Hawk could easily go back in his mind fifty years or so, however, and see a pleasant house in attractive gardens and set amid excellent farmland. A family had lived here and loved this place as he loved Hawkinville Manor. That raised the strange notion of there once being a pleasant, wholesome Lord Deveril. Lord Devil had likely been born here fifty years ago or so. Had he been a normal child? What had his parents been like? His grandparents?

He put aside idle speculation. The plain fact was that Gaspard Hall offered nothing. No money to pay off even part of the debt. No home for the squire without a fortune being poured into it. He was back to the duty he was trying to escape.

He led Centaur back the way they'd come. There'd be an inn in the nearby village where he could stay the night. Tomorrow . . .

Tomorrow he should return to Cheltenham and seduce the secrets out of Clarissa Greystone. But he turned and ran from that. He'd return to Hawk in the Vale and hope that she came to Brighton. It might be easier to hunt and destroy her amid that tinsel artificiality.

Chapter Five

Clarissa and Althea arrived in Brighton in a grand carriage with out-riders. Her guardian, the Duke of Belcraven, had sent his own trav-eling coach and servants to ensure her comfort and safety. Her trustees, Messrs. Euston, Layton, and Keele, whom she called the ELK, had arranged every other detail in magnificent style.

This was all rather unfortunate when she still didn't have any stylish cloth-ing, and Althea did. At every stop, innkeepers and servants had groveled be-fore Althea and assumed that Clarissa was the maid. She'd found it funny, and at one place had even slipped off to hobnob with the servants in the kitchen. Poor Althea, however, had been mortified.

The problem should be fixed soon. A stylish Brighton mantua-maker had all her measurements and should have a complete wardrobe, chosen by Clarissa herself, ready except for the final adjustments.

Despite a number of fears, she could hardly wait for any of this adventure. Now, looking out at the lively, fashionable company strolling along the Ma-rine Parade in the July sun, she felt like a bird taking its first terrified but ex-hilarating flight.

Or perhaps like a bird being pushed out of the nest and desperately flap-ping its wings!

From the first, impulsive decision, everything had been snatched from her control. Miss Mallory had completely approved. Althea had bubbled with ex-citement. The duke and the ELK had immediately put the idea into opera-tion. All that had been left for her to do was consult fashion magazines and samples of fabric and choose her new clothes.

Major Hawkinville's recommendation had not been necessary. The ELK had assured her that there were always houses available for people willing to pay handsomely for them, and they had engaged Number 8 Broad Street, which boasted a dining room, two parlors, and three best bedrooms.

It seemed a lavish amount of space for two people—but then there was also the lady hired to be chaperon and guide to society, a Miss Hurstman. Clarissa had been somewhat surprised that the lady was a spinster rather than a widow, but she had no doubt that the ELK would have chosen the very best. The lady had been described as "thoroughly cognizant of the ways of polite society and connected to all the best families."

The ELK had also arranged for a lady's maid and a footman in addition to the staff that came with the house. Clarissa had chuckled over this entourage, but in truth it made her nervous. In her parents' penny-pinched household, one overworked upstairs maid had had to attend to the house and play lady's maid as well.

In fact, she was still rather uncomfortable with all the lavish spending, especially when she didn't really feel she deserved Deveril's money. She'd loathed the man, and it was only a quirk in the wording of his will that had led to her inheriting it. At least there was no one else entitled. When she'd expressed her doubts, she'd been told that he'd died without an heir. Without the will, the money would all have gone to the Crown.

To provide more gilded onion domes, perhaps, she thought, catching a glimpse of the Prince Regent's astonishing Pavilion. She couldn't wait to visit it, but she couldn't regret not having funded it.

She couldn't regret any of this, and in part that was because of the secret anticipation of meeting Major Hawkinville again. She'd discouraged Althea from talking about him, pretending that he was of little interest, but now, as the carriage rolled along the Marine Parade, the sea on one side and tall stuccoed buildings on the other, she surreptitiously fingered the oblong card that she'd tucked into the pocket of her simple traveling dress.

Hawk in the Vale, Sussex. She'd looked it up in a gazetteer. It lay about six miles out of the town. Not far, but perhaps he didn't visit here very often.

Or perhaps he did.

Perhaps they wouldn't meet. Perhaps when they did she would find him less fascinating, or he would not be interested in her.

Or perhaps not.

After all, if he was a fortune hunter he would find her and pay her assiduous attentions.

She did hope so!

The gazetteer had mentioned his home, Hawkinville Manor, an ancient walled house with the remains of an earlier medieval defense. Picturesque, the author had sniffed, but of no particular architectural elegance.

Would she see it one day?

Then she noticed the attention they were attracting. A number of *ton*nish people were turning to watch the grand coach and outriders pass along the seafront, ladies and gentleman raising quizzing glasses to study it. Mischievously, Clarissa waved, and Althea pulled her back, laughing.

"Behave yourself!"

"Oh, very well. Did you see the bathing machines drawn into the water? I intend to sea-bathe."

"It looks horribly cold to me, and they say men watch, with telescopes."

"Do they? But then, men bathe too, don't they? I wonder where one buys a telescope."

Althea's eyes went wide with genuine shock. "Clarissa!"

Clarissa suppressed a grin. She loved Althea like the sister she had never had, but like sisters, they were different. Althea would never feel the wild curiosity and impatience that itched in Clarissa. She didn't understand.

But Clarissa knew she had to control that part of her. It would be hard enough to be accepted by society. For Althea's sake, there must be no hint of scandal.

The coach began to turn, and she looked up to see the words "Broad Street" painted on the wall. "At last. We're here."

"Oh, good. It's been a long journey, though it seems ungrateful to complain of such luxury."

"And not a highwayman to be seen."

"Praise heaven!" Althea exclaimed, and Clarissa hid her smile.

Despite its name, the street was not very wide, and the massive coach took up a great deal of it. The terraced houses on either side were three stories high, and with bay windows all the way up. All that stood between the house and the road, however, was a short flight of stairs and a railed enclosure around steps down to the basement servants' area.

Clarissa had glimpsed even narrower streets nearby, however, and knew this was indeed grand by Brighton standards.

The coach rocked to a stop outside number 8, an ELKishly perfect house, with sparkling windows, lace curtains, and bright yellow paint on the woodwork. The door opened to reveal an ELKish housekeeper, too. Plump and cherry-cheeked.

One of the outriders opened the door and let down the steps, then assisted them from the coach. Clarissa went toward the house feeling rather like a lost princess finally finding her palace.

"Good afternoon, ladies," said the housekeeper, curtsying. "Welcome to Brighton! I'm Mrs. Taddy, and I hope you will feel perfectly at home here."

Home.

Clarissa walked into a narrow but welcoming hall with a tile floor, white-painted woodwork, and a bowl of fresh flowers on a table. Home was a singularly elusive concept, but this would do for a while; indeed it would.

"This is lovely," she said to the woman, but then found that Mrs. Taddy was looking at Althea, also assuming that she was the heiress. What a powerful impression clothes made.

"I'm Miss Greystone," she said with a smile, as if merely introducing herself, "and this is my friend, Miss Trist."

She covered the housekeeper's fluster with some idle comments about Brighton's beauty, wondering where their chaperon was.

"Ah, you've arrived," a brusque voice barked. "Come into the front parlor. We'll have tea."

Clarissa turned to the woman standing in a doorway. It couldn't be!

She was middle-aged, with a weather-beaten face and sharp, dark eyes. Her graying hair was scraped back into a bun unsoftened by a cap, and her gown was even plainer than Clarissa's simple blue cambric.

"Don't gawk! I'm Arabella Hurstman, your guide to depravity."

The ELK must have run demented. This woman could never gain them entrée to fashionable Brighton!

"I'll bring tea, ma'am," said Mrs. Taddy to no one in particular and hurried away. Clarissa felt tempted to go with her, but Miss Hurstman commanded them into the room.

It was small but pretty, with pale walls and a flowered carpet, and Miss Hurstman looked completely out of place. This was ridiculous. There must have been a mistake.

The woman turned and looked them over. "Miss Greystone and Miss Trist, I assume. Though I can't tell which is which. You"—she pointed a bony finger at Althea—"look like the heiress. But you"—she pointed at Clarissa—"look like the simmering pot."

"I beg your pardon?"

"Don't starch up. You'll get used to me. I gave up trying to act pretty and pleasing thirty years ago. Someone described Miss Greystone as a simmering pot, and I see what he meant."

"Who?"

"Does it matter? Sit. We have to plan your husband hunt."

Clarissa and Althea obeyed dazedly.

"I gather you're a protégée of the Marchioness of Arden," Miss Hurstman said. Clarissa didn't know what to do with that statement.

"Lady Arden was a teacher at Miss Mallory's School," Althea said, filling the silence. "She was kind to Clarissa last year in London."

Clarissa supposed that summed up a very complex situation.

"That explains Belcraven, then," said Miss Hurstman. "He must be thanking heaven to see his heir married to a woman of sense."

Mrs. Taddy hurried in then with a laden tea tray and put it in front of Miss Hurstman.

"London," continued the lady, pouring. She handed Clarissa a cup. "Lasted all of two weeks there, and got yourself engaged to marry Lord Deveril. At least you ended up with his money, which shows some wit."

"He was hardly my choice," Clarissa stated, wondering what would happen if she ordered the woman out of the house. She had a burning question first. "Why would anyone describe me as a simmering pot?"

A touch of humor flashed in the dark eyes. "Because a simmering pot needs to be watched, gel, in case it bubbles over. 'Bubble, bubble, toil and trouble'? Oh, I expect trouble from you two." Miss Hurstman switched her gimlet gaze to Althea, who almost choked on a cake crumb. "You're a beauty. Here to catch a husband?"

"Oh, no—"

"Nothing wrong with that, if it's what you want. If you don't like your choices, I can find you a position. One where you won't be abused. Bear that in mind. There are worse things than being a spinster."

"Thank you," said Althea faintly.

"What about you?" Miss Hurstman demanded of Clarissa. "You want a husband too?"

"No."

"Why not?"

"Why should I? I'm rich."

"Sexual passion," said Miss Hurstman, causing Clarissa and Althea to gape. "Don't look like stuffed trout. The human race is driven by it, generally into disaster. If you wait long enough, it cools, but in youth, it simmers."

Clarissa felt her face flame. Surely whoever had said she was a simmering pot could never have meant *that*.

Who could it be? The duke? Hardly. Lord Arden? She didn't think so. Major Hawkinville?

That thought proved her mind was spinning beyond reason.

"There's all the romantic twaddle as well," the astonishing woman continued. "That alone can turn man or woman into an unwise marriage."

She surveyed the plate and chose a piece of seedy cake. "I was young once, and reasonably pretty, though I doubt you believe it, and I remember. I decided early not to marry, but I was still tempted a time or two. And *I* wasn't fool enough to visit Brighton in the summer, where romantic folly is carried on the breeze. What's worse," she added with a look at Clarissa, "you're an heiress. You'll have to fight 'em off."

Clarissa eyed the woman coldly. "Isn't that your job?"

Miss Hurstman gave a kind of snort. "If you really want me to. You probably won't. You'll probably scramble after the most rascally ones around. Young fools always do. I'll have no scandal, though. No being caught half naked in an anteroom. No mad dashes to Gretna Green. Understand? Now, you two go off and settle yourselves in. There's nothing we can do today."

Clarissa found herself on her feet, but regrouped. "Miss Hurstman, my trustees *employed* someone"—she emphasized the word—"to gain us entrée to the highest circles. I appreciate—"

"You think I can't? Don't judge by appearances. If there's a member of the *ton* here I'm not related to, they probably have shady antecedents. And though I don't spend much time in their silly circles, I know most of 'em, too. If you want to waltz with the Regent at the Pavilion, I can arrange it. Though why you'd want to is another matter."

"Even though I'm the Devil's Heiress?" Clarissa challenged.

"Stupid name. Concentrate on the heiress part. That'll open every door. A hundred thousand, I understand."

Clarissa heard Althea gasp. "More. It's been well invested, and I've been living simply."

"Obviously." Miss Hurstman looked her over. "With a fortune to hand, why are you dressed like that?"

"You are," Clarissa pointed out sweetly.

"I'm fifty-five. If you want to be a nun, enter a convent. If you want me to introduce you to Brighton society, dress appropriately."

Clarissa desperately wanted to state that she'd wear plain gowns forever, thank you, but she could see a pointless rebellion when it was about to cut off her nose. She admitted to the clothes waiting for her at Mrs. Howell's.

Miss Hurstman nodded. "Good. We'll go there first thing tomorrow and hope no one of importance sees you before you're properly dressed. You should have borrowed something from Miss Trist. Off you go."

Clarissa longed to sit down again and refuse to be removed, but that was pointless too. As she went upstairs with Althea she muttered, "Intolerable!"

"Perhaps she's able to do what she's supposed to do," Althea suggested.

"If so, she can stay. Otherwise, out she goes."

"You can't!"

Clarissa wasn't sure she could either. Moving Miss Arabella Hurstman might require the entire British army and the Duke of Wellington to lead it. But could she endure much more of Miss Hurstman? The woman was going to turn this delightful adventure into misery.

She went into the front bedroom that Mrs. Taddy indicated, finding their luggage already there and a sober-faced maid beginning to unpack.

"Who are you?" Clarissa demanded.

The woman dropped an alarmed curtsy. "Elsie John, ma'am. Hired to be maid to Miss Greystone and Miss Trist." She, too, was clearly having trouble deciding who was who.

"I'm Miss Greystone," said Clarissa, beginning to lose patience with this farce. "That is Miss Trist."

The maid rolled her eyes and turned back to her work. Clarissa sucked in a deep, steadying breath. She had failed to stand up to Miss Hurstman, so she was taking out her anger on the innocents.

Then Althea said, "Would you mind if I lie down, Clarissa? I have a headache."

"No, of course not. It's probably because of that dreadful woman."

Clarissa knew, however, that it was as much her fault as Miss Hurstman's. She reined in her temper, and even found a smile for the maid. "Elsie, you may go for now."

She helped Althea out of her gown and settled her in the bed with the curtains drawn, but then didn't know where to go. She couldn't stay here and be quiet. She didn't feel at all quiet. She needed to pace and rant.

She left the room, closing the door quietly. There were supposed to be three bedrooms, and there were three doors. What if the third was the housekeeper's? She crept downstairs, but she suspected the only rooms below were the front parlor and the dining room. She headed for the dining room.

"Ah, good!"

Clarissa jumped.

Miss Hurstman had emerged from the parlor like a spider from a hole. "Come back in here."

"Why?"

"We have things to discuss. Believe it or not, I'm your ally, not your enemy."

Clarissa found herself too fascinated to resist.

"You're strong," Miss Hurstman said, as Clarissa reentered the room. "A bit of brimstone, too. That's good. You'll need it."

"Why?"

"You're the Devil's Heiress. And you're a Greystone. Even under my aegis, you'll receive some snubs."

"I don't care, except if it hurts Althea."

"It'll hurt her if people are cruel to you. She can't take any fire at all, can she?"

"She doesn't like discord, but she can be strong in fighting for right and justice."

"Pity we don't have lions to throw her to. She might enjoy that."

Enough was enough. "Miss Hurstman, I'm not at all sure you will suit, but if you are to be caustic about Miss Trist, you certainly won't."

The woman's lips twitched. "Think of me as your personal lion. Now sit down. Let's talk without a delicate audience.

"I like you," Miss Hurstman said as she returned to her straight-backed posture in her chair. "Don't know what fires you've been through, but it's forged some steel. Unusual in a gel your age. Your Althea is doubtless a lovely young woman, but tender lambs like that give me a headache. They can always be depended on to say the right thing and to suffer for the stupidity of others."

"It wasn't stupidity that killed her fiancé."

"How do you know? War is stupid, anyway. Do you know we lost ten times as many men to disease as wounds? Ten times, and a regiment of women with sense could have saved most of 'em. Enough of that. I want to have things clear. We're to find her a good husband, are we?"

Clarissa imagined that Wellington's troops must have felt like this before battle, and yet there was a starchy comfort in it. Miss Hurstman, despite her unlikely appearance, radiated competence and confidence.

"Yes."

"Any dowry at all?"

"A very small amount."

Miss Hurstman *humphed.* "The right man will find that romantic. What's her family?"

"Her father is the vicar of Saint Stephen's in Bucklestead St. Stephens. He's brother to Sir Clarence Trist there. Her mother is from a good family, too. But there's no money and seven other children."

"Where did the fine clothes come from, then?"

"I gave them to her."

"Why?"

Clarissa considered her answer. "Do you know Messrs. Euston, Layton, and Keele, ma'am?"

"Only by repute and a letter."

"Thorough," said Clarissa. "Conscientious. Determined to pass over my fortune when I'm twenty-one with scarcely a nibble out of it."

"Very right and proper."

"Carried to ridiculous lengths. I can buy what I want and they will pay the bills, but they allow me virtually no money to spend on my own. They would never have let me hire Althea to be my companion—and you have to admit that having her here will be much more pleasant than being here alone."

"You have me," said Miss Hurstman with a wicked smirk.

Clarissa swallowed a laugh, and suspected it showed.

The truth was that she was beginning to like Miss Hurstman. There was no need to pretend with her. With Althea, dear though she was, Clarissa always felt she had to watch herself so as not to bruise her friend's tender feelings. With Miss Hurstman, she could probably damn the king, pick a fight, or use scandalous language and stir no more than a blink.

"Clothes," Miss Hurstman prompted.

"Oh, yes. The ELK didn't object to my bringing Althea as a friend, but she needed fashionable clothing. They'd not pay for that, but they'd pay for new clothes for me."

"Shady dealings, gel." Miss Hurstman waggled her finger, but the twinkle might be admiration.

Clarissa was surprised to feel that Miss Hurstman's admiration might be worth something. "It wasn't a noble sacrifice. I would never have worn those gowns again. They were bought for me to parade before Lord Deveril."

"Ah. And that shade of blue wouldn't have suited you any better than the one you're wearing now. Hope you chose better this time."

Clarissa looked down at the tiny sprigged pattern that had been the best material Miss Mallory's seamstress had to hand. "So do I. I chose rather bold colors."

"Bold seems suitable," said Miss Hurstman dryly. "If they don't suit, we'll choose again. Won't make a dent in your fortune. So, Miss Trist needs to marry money. And generous money, at that."

"What she needs is a man who loves her."

Miss Hurstman's brows rose. "When she can't love him back? She'd go into a decline under the guilt of it. And if she doesn't marry money, she'll feel she's let down her family."

Clarissa wanted to object, but the blasted woman had clearly taken Althea's measure to the inch. She needed to be of service to all.

"I want her to be happy."

Miss Hurstman nodded. "She'll be content with a good man and children, and plenty of worthwhile work to do. You, on the other hand, need a man who loves you."

Major Hawkinville, Clarissa thought, and reacted by stating, "I don't need a man at all. I'm rich."

"You're obsessed by your money. Guineas are uncomfortable bedfellows."

"They can buy comfort."

Miss Hurstman's brows shot up. "Planning to buy yourself a lover?"

"Of course not!" Clarissa knew she was red. "You, ma'am, are obsessed with . . . with bed! My trustees cannot have known your true colors."

Despite that, she could see the wicked twinkle in Miss Hurstman's eyes, and felt its reflection in herself. She'd never known anyone so willing to say outrageous things.

"Why are you my chaperon?" she demanded. "You are clearly a most unusual choice, even if you are well connected."

"Nepotism," said Miss Hurstman, but that twinkle told Clarissa that there was more to the word than there seemed to be. "And you come into your money at twenty-one," Miss Hurstman carried on. "Unusual situation all around. Unusual that Deveril leave you anything. Even more unusual that he arrange for you to be free of control at such a tender age."

"I know, and sometimes I wish he hadn't." After a moment, Clarissa admitted something she'd never told anyone before. "It frightens me. I've tried to learn something about management, but I don't feel able to deal with such wealth."

Miss Hurstman nodded. "You can hire Euston, Layton, and Keele to manage your affairs, but it will still be a tricky road. It's not just a matter of management. A woman is not supposed to live without male supervision, especially a young unmarried lady of fortune. The world will watch every move you make, and scoundrels will hover with a thousand clever ways to filch your money from you."

Major Hawkinville, she thought, though she couldn't see him as a scoundrel. "Fortune hunters. I know."

"At the end of a few weeks with me," Miss Hurstman stated, "you'll be more ready, and in ways other than administrative. But don't put the thought of a husband out of your mind entirely. There are good men in the world, and one of them would make your life a great deal easier. I don't see you as content with celibate living."

Put like that, Clarissa wasn't sure she would be content, either, and she knew part of that feeling was because of the heroic major, even though he hadn't touched her in any meaningful way. She wasn't ready to expose such sensitive uncertainties to Miss Hurstman's astringent eye, however.

Her companion rose in a sharp, smooth motion. "There's a lot about you that I don't understand. I won't pry. As long as it doesn't affect what we're doing here, it's no business of mine. But I'll listen if you want to talk, and I can keep secrets. You probably won't believe it, but I can be trusted, too."

Clarissa did believe it. She was tempted to lay all her burdens on the older woman's shoulders—Lord Deveril and his death; Lord Arden's cruelty to Beth; even the Company of Rogues, Lord Arden's friends, who had helped her, whose burden of secrets she carried, who frightened her in vague, elusive ways.

That the idea tempted her was alarming in itself.

Chapter Six

Hawk rode into Brighton at half past eight, before the fashionable part of town was stirring. He turned into the Red Lion Inn and arranged to stable Centaur there. He had a standing invitation to stay with Van and his wife, who'd taken a house on the Marine Parade, but he wouldn't disturb them at this hour.

He wasn't sure why he was here so uselessly early except that he'd wanted to get on with his pursuit of Miss Greystone. Time was shortening before Slade's deadline, but more than that, like a novice before battle, he feared losing his nerve.

Miss Greystone might seem innocent, but he couldn't imagine how she could not have been involved in Deveril's death and that forged will. She was, as far as he could see, the sole beneficiary. Anything he discovered was likely to lead to her destruction, and quite simply, he balked at that. He'd spent the past weeks seeking some other way of claiming the Deveril money.

He'd failed.

If he'd failed, he doubted it was possible. He'd used every angle and connection to try to find the forger, or a hint of the killer. Nothing, which meant he was up against a clever mind and that line of inquiry was dead, especially given his shortage of time. One day, however, he hoped to know who had constructed the deceit, and how.

And why. That in particular puzzled him. The heiress had the money. Why had a clever mind gone to such illegal lengths for no obvious profit?

A lover? He didn't want to think he'd been as deeply fooled by her as that.

From servants and gossips, he'd compiled a list of people Clarissa had been seen with during her time in London, but it was short and unhelpful. The

Greystones and Deveril had only been tolerated, so her social circle had not been wide. The highest-born connection was Lady Gorgros, a vastly stupid woman who couldn't be the genius behind anything.

Viscount Starke had hung around Deveril, but he'd shake hands with anyone for another bottle of brandy, and his hands perpetually shook on their own, anyway. There'd been others of his sort, and a couple of upstart families who had wined and dined the Greystones under the illusion that it was a step toward the *haut ton*.

After Deveril's death, however, she'd been taken up by the Marchioness of Arden. That had struck him as strange enough to be interesting until he'd discovered that Lady Arden had been a teacher at Miss Mallory's School. Obviously, in time of need Clarissa had turned to her. Hawk would have spoken to the marchioness to see if she had anything to tell, but the lady was living in the country, expecting to be confined with her first child at any moment.

It was perhaps as well. Poking in such high-flowing waters was likely to be dangerous. That explained, however, why the heiress's guardian was the Duke of Belcraven, Arden's father. Her own father had been persuaded to sign away all his rights for five thousand pounds. With the Greystones, it would appear, everything was for sale.

So, after weeks of work, he had facts but no clue about Clarissa Greystone's mysterious partner in crime. Thus his only key was Clarissa herself. Perhaps her honesty and innocence were a deep disguise, and she was a thorough villain. Perhaps she was the puppet of some undiscovered manipulator.

Whatever the truth, Hawk was going to uncover it, and he would do whatever it took.

As soon as the post office opened he went to speak to his obliging informant there. Since Hawk was from a well-known local family, Mr. Crawford had made no difficulty over accepting a crown to send word when Miss Clarissa Greystone arrived in town.

"Came to register with me yesterday, Major Hawkinville," the rotund man said with a wink. "Miss Greystone, a pretty friend, and their chaperon."

"Any other notable arrivals?" Hawk asked, attempting to mask his interest a little.

Crawford consulted his book. "The Earl and Countess of Gresham, sir. Mrs. and Miss Nutworth-Hulme . . ."

When the man had run down the list, Hawk thanked him again and left, pausing to allow a couple to enter the room. An arresting couple.

The woman was a silver-haired beauty in pure white, from the plumes on her bonnet to her kid slippers. Somehow she tweaked at his memory, though he didn't know her. Certainly no man would forget her. Her companion was a tall, darkly handsome man with an empty sleeve tucked between the buttons of his jacket. Military, Hawk guessed, but again, no one he knew.

"Mrs. Hardcastle!" Mr. Crawford exclaimed, coming around his counter to bow to the lady.

Ah, he remembered her now. She was the actress they called the White Dove of Drury Lane. She'd been playing Titania when he'd tracked Van down in the theater a while ago. His mind had been entirely on Van's danger, but even so, her grace and charm had made an impression.

She was irrelevant to his current concerns, however.

As he continued on his way he heard Crawford greet the man as Major Beaumont, confirming that he was military and a stranger. All the same, that irrelevant name would now have slotted into his mind.

He found it tiresome to have nearly every detail stick, even something like a chance-met actress and her escort, but he'd learned to live with it, and it was the basis of his skill. He still had time to kill, so he walked over to the seafront, hoping the brisk breeze would clear his mind.

He wasn't used to having a tangled mind, but Clarissa Greystone had achieved it. Looked at from the angle of the evidence, she could not be an innocent. Hell, she was a *Greystone,* and even if she had spent most of the recent years at Miss Mallory's School, that had to carry a taint.

As well, he knew better than most that appearances could be completely deceptive. He remembered a wide-eyed child in Lisbon who had mutilated the soldiers he had murdered and robbed.

The ethereal White Dove was probably a foulmouthed wanton, and wholesome Clarissa Greystone was neck-deep in slime. He need have no qualms about pleasing her and wooing her until she let something slip that would open the puzzle-box of Deveril's affairs.

If only he felt that way.

He watched the dippers lead their horses down to the beach and harness them to the bathing machines, getting ready for the first bathers of the day. Business might be light, given the clouds graying the sky. Even so, perhaps he should sea-bathe despite the weather, and try to be washed clean of the stink he felt creeping over him.

Maudlin thought, but he'd never used lovemaking as a weapon before.

He suddenly remembered recruiting someone to do just that, however—

if coupling with a notorious whore could be called lovemaking. It had been two years ago, just after the taking of Paris. Napoleon had abdicated, and Richard Anstable, an inoffensive British diplomat, had been found stabbed to death.

The man who'd found him had been Nicholas Delaney, and Hawk had recognized the name. Delaney had been the creator and leader of the Company of Rogues, Con's group of friends at Harrow School.

Hawk, curious about a person he'd heard so much about, had immediately wondered what Delaney was doing at the liberation of Paris. He'd sought Delaney out, and there'd been an instant liking, though Hawk had instinctively blocked the man's charisma.

That charisma, however, had landed Delaney with the very devil of a job, and because of their acquaintance, Hawk had been given the task of putting it to him.

The Foreign Office, the Horse Guards, and the military command all had files on a woman called Thérèse Bellaire. A daughter of the minor nobility, she had risen in wealth and power as mistress and procuress to Napoleon's most important men. In 1814, with Napoleon abdicating, she had turned to Colonel Coldstrop of the Guards, and begged his help in fleeing to England. No one thought her purpose innocent.

It had been decided to support her plan so as to find out what she was up to and whom she contacted. The files showed that a few years before, Delaney had been her resident lover for months. The files also said that he'd left her, not the other way around, and that she still cared.

Hawk's orders had been blunt. "She's up to something," General Featheringham had said, "and we need to know what. Only idiots think Boney's going to sit on Elba growing violets, and there are Bonapartist sympathizers everywhere, including Britain. Tell Delaney to get back into the woman's good graces and rut the truth out of her."

Hawk had put it more politely, but Nicholas Delaney's eyes had turned steady and cool. All he'd said, however, was, "And to think I felt guilty about not fighting in the Peninsula."

Hawk had tried to sugar the pill. "I hear she's a very beautiful woman, and skilled at the erotic arts."

Delaney had stood up at that. "Then you do it," he'd said, and left.

It hadn't been a rejection. Hawk had known that, and within days he'd heard that Delaney was part of a wild circle including Thérèse Bellaire. Soon after that, he'd left for England with the woman, presumably doing his noble service.

Hawk had heard no more of it, and hadn't cared to, but when Napoleon, as predicted, had returned to France and power, the Bellaire woman had reappeared in the inner circle. She'd disappeared around the time of Waterloo, and now, surely, her goose must be cooked.

It had all come back to him because he'd met Delaney again recently—in Devon, at Con's place there. Delaney's country estate lay not far away, and he'd come to look over the strange collection left by Con's predecessor and to help Con with a dilemma to do with Susan.

Delaney and Hawk had both pretended not to have met before, and it hadn't seemed that Delaney held a grudge. All the same, Hawk wondered how many thorns from his past would turn up to jab him.

Thorns from his present, as well.

He returned to the Red Lion and ate a mediocre breakfast, waiting for fashionable Brighton to emerge. Waiting for Clarissa Greystone to become vulnerable to his Hawk's eye and talons.

The fashionable throng kept earlier hours at Brighton, so by eleven he could go out to stroll among them. He circled the open grassy area called the Steyne, chatting to the occasional acquaintance, many of them military, casually keeping an eye out for his quarry.

He recognized Miss Trist first. Or rather, he was alerted by a swirl of attention around a lovely lady in a white dress trimmed with periwinkle blue, and then saw who it was. It took him a moment to recognize the lively creature beside her as Clarissa Greystone.

No sign of the unsophisticated schoolgirl now. What an excellent actress she was.

She wasn't wearing a bonnet. Instead, a daringly elegant hat with a small curved brim revealed all of her face and quite a lot of her stylishly dressed curls. It didn't make her a beauty, but it gave a vibrancy to her features. To protect her complexion, she carried the latest thing, a pagoda-style parasol. Or, to be precise, she twirled it. Even at a distance she looked confident, full of the zest of life—and dangerous.

Her gown was an off-white color strongly trimmed with rust-colored braid and edged around the hem with a deep fringe. As she walked, that fringe swung, giving tantalizing glimpses of shapely ankles emphasized by cream-and-rust-striped stockings.

Every man on the Steyne was doubtless looking at those ankles.

He jerked his own eyes up, steadied himself, and planned his intercept. He saw others making a direct line, including a number of military men. The last thing he wanted was the heiress in the protection of another man. Disguising his urgency, he moved in swiftly for the kill.

"I say, Aunt Arabella, fancy seeing you here! And in such charming company!"

Clarissa started. She'd been so intent on looking carefree and confident despite feeling sick with nerves that she hadn't noticed the dark-haired, dark-eyed young officer until he was upon them.

Miss Hurstman stopped and looked him up and down. "Afraid the mold'll rub off on them, Trevor? You were a big-eared gawk when I saw you last. Heard you did well at Waterloo, though. Good boy. You don't want to chatter to me, I'm sure. I know what you want. Miss Trist and Miss Greystone. Consider yourself introduced. Lieutenant Lord Trevor Ffyfe. He'll be a safe flirt for you because he knows I'll cut his nose off if he ain't."

The young man laughed. "Remarkable woman, my aunt. Are you new to Brighton, ladies? You must be. I couldn't possibly have missed two such beauties . . ."

After a few moments of his flattering, chattering company, Clarissa's nerves began to settle, and tentative joy crept in. Was it really going to work? Was Miss Hurstman going to perform the miracle and gain her entrance to society? This was what she'd dreamed of—becoming clothes, a fashionable throng, and a gallant, even titled, flirt.

She and Althea had lived in seclusion for two days while Mrs. Howell and her assistants rushed backward and forward doing final fittings on the gowns. They hadn't been bored, because there had been the hairdresser, the dancing master, and Miss Hurstman's own drill in perfect, confident behavior.

"Never fluster!" she commanded Clarissa. "Althea can be as demure and uncertain as she pleases, but if you are, they'll eat you alive. Look them in the eye, remember your fortune, and dare them to turn their backs."

Now she was being hatched, and in very fine feathers. She loved the bold colors of this one, and the deep, daring fringe. Perhaps in fine feathers she became a little bit of a fine bird?

She kept her chin up, her smile in place, and prepared to look anyone and everyone in the eye.

"Do say that you'll give me a dance at the assembly on Friday, Miss Greystone."

Clarissa focused on handsome Lord Trevor, and her smile became genuine. "I'd be delighted to, my lord."

"I consider myself the most fortunate of men, Miss Greystone!" He was attempting to sound sincere, but she could tell that his dazed attention was more on Althea than herself. She didn't mind. That was the true purpose of this adventure.

More or less.

She couldn't resist glancing around in search of Major Hawkinville. There was no reason under the sun for him to be here today, but she couldn't help but look.

Imagine being able to talk with him at leisure.

Imagine him asking her to reserve a dance.

But then, perhaps the dazzling appeal had been a figment of the moment and here, among so many fine military men, he would be ordinary.

There was only one way to find out.

Another survey showed no sign of him. Patience, she told herself, and concentrated on the increasing number of fine military men. It was as if Lord Trevor had breached the walls—they were surrounded by uniforms, all seeking introductions.

Only one said to Clarissa, "Oh, I say, aren't you—?" and then shut up, turning red.

"Dunce," said Lord Trevor with a reassuring smile at Clarissa.

But her nerves started to churn again. She was still the Devil's Heiress. It was all very well to be swarmed by young officers. Would other parts of society accept her?

The officers all had excellent manners, at least, and shared their attention between Althea and herself. Since all she wanted from them was the lightest flirtation, it was heavenly.

But what about the major? She glanced around again, searching the clusters of people dotting the fashionable gathering place. She was sure that if he was here he would stand out for her . . .

And he did!

After just one glimpse, her heart started a nervous patter.

She instantly turned back to the group, smiling brightly at a lieutenant whose name had flown right out of her head, chattering to him in what was probably a stream of nonsense.

Remember, he is a fortune hunter. This is only for amusement, not for life.

"Miss Greystone. Miss Trist. How delightful to see you here."

Clarissa turned, putting on what she hoped was a merely warm smile. "Major Hawkinville. What a lovely surprise."

His smiling eyes held a distinct hint of wickedness. "Not entirely a surprise, Miss Greystone. We did speak of it."

A little shocked by that betrayal, Clarissa was still seeking the right response when a poke in her side alerted her to Miss Hurstman, expecting to be introduced. She grasped the escape, and her chaperon asked a few pointed questions before giving him the nod. Clarissa was surprised to detect something negative in her dragon. Wariness? Concern? Was there something wrong with his family? His reputation?

But then she had it. Probably Miss Hurstman knew him to be a man in need of marrying a fortune. Sad to have that confirmed, but not a shock. She could still enjoy him. In fact, it could be seen as educational. Once word escaped, she was bound to be swarmed by fortune hunters. She would learn from the major what to expect, and how to handle it.

"Major Hawkinville!" Lord Trevor said. "I say, sir, how good to see you again. And now you meet my redoubtable Aunt Arabella."

Miss Hurstman's eyes narrowed. "Been gossiping about me in the mess, Trevor?"

Lord Trevor went red and stammered a denial.

"He was singing your praises," said the major, "about some work you did helping young workhouse girls."

Miss Hurstman looked between them. "Strange topic for officers."

"We try to be eclectic. Educate the subalterns, you know." Hawk turned to Clarissa. "Are you enjoying Brighton, Miss Greystone?"

"Perfectly," she said, adding a silent *now*.

She'd wondered whether he would seem as special away from riot and adventure, but if anything, he was more so, even when surrounded by other eligible men. He was remarkably elegant, without being foppish. She wasn't sure how that came about, but she would be happy to study the question.

What was her fortune hunter going to do next?

He chatted to the other men for a moment or two, then he held out his arm to her. Concealing a smile, she put her hand on it, and let him cut her out of the group to stroll about the Steyne.

A simple and direct first step. She approved.

How would he open his wooing?

"You've acquired a formidable dragon, Miss Greystone."

She looked at him in surprise. "Miss Hurstman? She was hired by my trustees, Major."

"Ffyfe's aunt?"

"Is that so extraordinary?"

"Ffyfe's aunt, I believe, is actually cousin to his father, the Marquess of Mayne, rather than sister. However, she's sister to one viscount, aunt to another, and granddaughter of a duke. Hardly the type to hire herself out for the season."

"You're surprisingly well informed, Major." She supposed a fortune hunter needed to gather information about his quarry, but such blatant evidence of it dismayed her. And where was the amusing flattery and charm she had anticipated?

But then he smiled rather wryly. "I'm blessed—or cursed—with a retentive memory, Miss Greystone. Facts stick. You may wish to be a little on your guard."

"Against your retentive memory?"

It came out rather snappishly, and he looked startled. "Against Ffyfe's aunt." But then he added, "Ignore me, please. Someone who's been in battle often jumps at loud noises. My active service had more to do with puzzles than cannon fire, but I'm left with a sharp reaction to things and people that seem amiss."

"You see Miss Hurstman as amiss?" Clarissa asked, beginning to be intrigued by the puzzle. "I'd think her eminent background would put her beyond reproach."

"High rank doesn't always go hand in hand with virtue, Miss Greystone. I would think you would know that."

"I?" she asked, a nervous tremor starting. Was he referring to her family?

"I could not help but be curious about you, Miss Greystone, and I learned that you were betrothed to Lord Deveril."

Despite the sun, Clarissa felt as if a chill wind blew around her. Something must have shown on her face, for he said, "Have I offended you by mentioning it?"

She looked at him. He did not seem repentant. Only watchful. Was this really how fortune hunters behaved? And, she suddenly thought, if he was honest about his curiosity, had he not known in Cheltenham that she was rich?

"It is common knowledge, Major."

"As was Lord Deveril's vice. I confess to being curious as to how you came to be committed to him. It cannot have been by choice."

She silently thanked him for that, but could not, would not, talk about it. It made her almost physically sick. "My parents compelled me, Major. But it is a matter I prefer not to discuss. I must thank you for the name you gave me, though it was not required. My trustees have found me a pleasant house in Broad Street."

"A good address. Close enough to the Steyne for convenience, but not so close as to be affected by rowdiness. What with bands, parades, and donkey races, this is often not a restful place."

She glanced at him. "But do I want to rest?"

He returned her look, and it was suddenly like the time when they had been watching the parade, when he'd silently challenged her. Had he not known then who she was? It seemed crucial, but she had no way to be sure.

"I see," he said. "You enjoy riot and mayhem?"

She twirled her parasol, sending the fringe dancing at the edge of her vision. "Not precisely that, but some little adventures . . ."

"You could creep out of your house tonight to explore Brighton with me in the dark."

"Major!"

But he was teasing, and she loved it.

His smile crinkled his eyes and dug deep brackets beside his mouth. "Too extreme? Or simply too early?" Before she could find a reply, he added, "We must establish boundaries, Miss Greystone. Could I tempt you to stroll beyond this treeless space and find more privacy?"

"To do what?" she asked, glancing away, but as if she might consider something so outrageous.

"Part of the adventure, Miss Greystone, is the mystery involved."

She looked back. "But a mystery, Major, might prove to be pleasant, or very unpleasant."

"There would be no excitement otherwise, would there?"

She met his eyes. "No danger, you mean."

His only response was a slight deepening of his tantalizing smile.

Suddenly she wanted to say yes. To go off with him and discover just how dangerous he could be. If this was a fortune hunter's trick, then she could begin to understand why some ladies fell victim to them!

Time to be wise. She looked back toward Miss Hurstman, Althea, and the group of red coats around them. "I think we had best return, Major. I cannot afford to endanger my reputation, for Althea's sake. I hope she will make a good connection here."

He turned back without complaint. "You do not seek a husband yourself?"

It pleased her to be able to say, "No." How would he deal with that?

"That is unusual in a young woman, Miss Greystone."

"I am an unusual woman, Major Hawkinville."

She meant merely that she was—or soon would be—independently wealthy, but when he said, "Yes, you are," it seemed to mean a great deal more.

Despite reason, warmth stirred within her, and it was caused by the admiration in his eyes. She tried to dismiss it as a fortune hunter's trick, but she could not.

"Your good sense and courage during the riot made a strong impression upon me, Miss Greystone. It also cannot have been easy to be put into such a situation with Lord Deveril, and yet you have survived unscathed."

She wished he would stop referring to that, but said, "Thank you."

"You are free of your parents' cruelty now, I hope?"

"I am under the guardianship of the Duke of Belcraven." Then she remembered his curiosity, and her wits sharpened. "You did not find that out, Major?"

A quirk of his lips seemed to be acknowledgment of a hit. "Yes, but not why. Or how."

"Then that puzzle can lend excitement to your life, Major."

His brows rose. "I am newly back from war, Miss Greystone. I am in no need of excitement."

She stopped to face him. "That was an unfair blow, sir!"

"Are we duelists, then? I thought us conspirators against your dull world."

"My world is not at all dull." *Especially not with you in it!*

"Ah, of course. You are new to Brighton. Perhaps I should return in a week or two when the novelty has worn off."

A second too late she knew she had let her dismay at that show. She had forgotten that he didn't live here. When would she see him again, enjoy his sparring again?

From inside a posy of scarlet coats, Althea flashed Clarissa a speculative look. Clarissa realized that she and the major were standing face-to-face in a way that must look particular. What now? She didn't know how to do this any more than she knew how to swim. Was she being wooed, or simply toyed with? How should she react? How far could she go without endangering her liberty?

She fell back on frankness. "When you do return, Major, I hope you'll call. Broad Street. Number eight."

He bowed, and by accord they moved on to join her party. "When in

Brighton, I am based at number twenty-two, Marine Parade. It has been taken by my friend Lord Vandeimen and his bride." He glanced past her. "Ah, and here they are, lured by curiosity. Or," he added softly, "your delectable fringe-veiled ankles."

Stupidly, she looked down at her fringe as if she wasn't aware that it effectively made her skirt three inches shorter. By the time she looked up again to greet his friends, she was thoroughly off-balance.

Delectable? He thought her ankles delectable?

Chapter Seven

Major Hawkinville's friends were an elegant couple, though Lord Vandeimen's skin was darker than Hawk's, and a jagged scar marred his right cheek. Another officer, she was sure. Lady Vandeimen's complexion was perfect, her eyes heavy-lidded and fine, and her smile warm.

Clarissa thought that the lady must be older than her husband, but little smiles seemed to speak of the warmest feelings.

"Maria!" Miss Hurstman marched over. "Good to see you. This must be the scamp you just married." She gave Lord Vandeimen a swift perusal. "Good for you."

"Jealous?" murmured Lady Vandeimen, breaking a laugh from her husband, who captured Miss Hurstman's hand and kissed it.

"The redoubtable Miss Hurstman. Honored, ma'am."

Astonishingly, Miss Hurstman might be blushing. "Scamp," she repeated. "But twenty years ago you might have deprived me of my wits, too. At least you're safely chained and one less rascal I have to guard these flighty creatures from."

She seemed to emphasize that with a sharp glance at Major Hawkinville. After a little more chat, Miss Hurstman turned to Clarissa. "We'd best be off. We have things to do."

We do? wondered Clarissa, but Miss Hurstman was in command of this expedition, so she said farewells attended by promises of meeting at the assembly. It was frustratingly unclear whether they included the major or not.

As she, Althea, and Miss Hurstman headed out of the Steyne, the younger officers trailed along. "Not good enough," complained Lord Trevor to

Clarissa. "Letting yourself get stolen by a staff officer, Miss Greystone. What are we poor fellows to do about that?"

"Fight?" Clarissa teased.

"Hawk Hawkinville? I think not."

Hawk Hawkinville. Yes, it suits him.

"He has a formidable reputation?" She knew she was showing her interest, but was unable to resist. Folly blowing on the wind in Brighton, Miss Hurstman had said. It was more as if it shone down with the emerging sun, melting will and wits to a soggy mess.

"Right-hand man to Colonel De Lancey, Wellington's quartermaster general. Crucial work. But he enjoyed some action too. Saved one battalion at St. Pierre single-handed, they say, when all the officers were killed."

"Really?" prompted Clarissa. Of course, a military hero could still be a scoundrel in other areas. A fortune hunter. Insidiously, it was ceasing to be so appalling a notion.

"I heard his main work was in investigations, Miss Greystone."

"Of crimes?"

"Yes, but also problems. When we were sent cartloads of shoes when we needed meat, or meat when the horses needed hay. When boots turned out to have paper soles, and rifles were off. No shifty supplier wanted to come under the Hawk's scrutiny, I assure you. It's said that he rarely misses or forgets a detail."

So finding out about her engagement to Lord Deveril and her guardian would have been child's play. With sudden unease, Clarissa wondered what Hawk Hawkinville might find out if he began to look more closely. He had no reason to look into the details of Lord Deveril's death, but it seemed as if danger brushed against her.

"He did immediately know all Miss Hurstman's connections," she said.

"Did he?" Miss Hurstman's question was rather sharp. "Was he right, though?"

"I confess, I've forgotten exactly what he said, ma'am. I think that Lord Trevor is the son of your cousin rather than being a nephew, and that you are the granddaughter of a duke."

Was she silly to think that Miss Hurstman also looked worried? Did she have something to hide, too? Why *was* she employed as a chaperon?

But Miss Hurstman only said, "Ha! Not infallible, then. I'm the great-granddaughter of a duke. Trevor, take yourself and your friends off. You'll have another chance tomorrow."

Miss Hurstman swept Althea and Clarissa away with suspicious urgency. "You want to watch a man with a name like Hawk Hawkinville."

"Why?" Dirty laundry in Miss Hurstman's cupboard? Out of sheer, mischievous curiosity, Clarissa wanted to know what it was.

"A hawk's eye for detail and a close-to-infallible memory? A woman would never be able to wear the same gown twice."

"As if I cared. And you certainly don't."

Miss Hurstman didn't respond directly. "You'd be wiser to avoid him. Come along."

They were already out of the Steyne and heading back to Broad Street. Miss Hurstman was upset, and Clarissa found herself feeling more protective than curious. She understood what it was not to want a hawkish eye on one's past.

But Miss Hurstman? Her overactive imagination began to play. A scandalous affair when young? Cheating at whist? Time in the Fleet for debt? All seemed highly unlikely.

But then her own involvement in violence probably seemed that way too—a thought that wiped all whimsy and humor from her mind. Major Hawkinville was, in effect, a professional hunter of criminals. He was the last person she should encourage to take an interest in her affairs.

The immediate resistance she felt to the idea of giving him up was warning that her feelings were stronger than she thought. For the first time she let herself seriously contemplate being caught by her fortune hunter. Merely needing to marry money did not make a person a villain. Althea needed to marry a man with at least a comfortable income.

But Clarissa knew she shouldn't indulge in this particular predator.

She arrived home queasy with worry. Mr. Delaney, leader of the Company of Rogues, had stressed that she mustn't let out a hint about Deveril's death, or those who had helped her could hang. She might hang for her involvement.

Beth Arden, who had been so kind, would be involved too, just when she was expecting her child. And Blanche Hardcastle.

She needed a quiet place to think, but Miss Hurstman ordered her and Althea into the parlor. Once there, she fixed Clarissa with her gimlet gaze. "How do you know Hawkinville?"

Clarissa had not expected this attack. She knew her color was flaring, though she had nothing really to be ashamed of.

"We met in Cheltenham. He rescued me and some of the schoolgirls from a riot."

"Cheltenham?" The woman's eyes narrowed. "What was he doing in Cheltenham?"

"Why shouldn't he be in Cheltenham?"

"His home lies near here, unless I'm mistaken. So why Cheltenham?"

"He was en route to some property his father had recently acquired."

"Ah." Miss Hurstman suddenly seemed thoughtful.

"Ah?" Clarissa echoed. "What does that mean? Miss Hurstman, if you know something to the major's detriment, I wish to know it too."

Of course Miss Hurstman knew he was a fortune hunter. Clarissa wanted that minor problem out in the open and dealt with.

But Miss Hurstman said, "To his detriment? No. According to Trevor, a fine officer. One of the oldest families, too. They go back to the Conquest." She waved a bony hand. "Off you go and do something."

Clarissa stayed put. "Why were you sounding so suspicious?"

"Why? I was told that you'd lived in almost nunlike seclusion, and then a buck of the first stare with no connection to Cheltenham claims acquaintance. Of course I wonder. And from the way the two of you were looking into one another's eyes, you were up to more than you're telling me!"

Clarissa knew she'd turned red, but she said, "It was exactly as I have told you." She couldn't help but add, "So you don't know anything shameful about him?"

"No."

But Clarissa heard a frustrating shadow of doubt. She changed tack. "Do you know anything about Lord and Lady Vandeimen?"

"Another gallant rescue in Cheltenham?" Miss Hurstman asked caustically. "If so, he's escaped your net. Married a few weeks back. She was Mrs. Celestin, wealthy widow of a foreigner. She's older than he, of course, but there's nothing wrong with that, and she's of the best blood. A Dunpott-Ffyfe. We're cousins of the more distant sort. His family's quite new here. Dutch originally, but his mother was a Grenville. Why are you so curious?"

Clarissa felt as if she'd turned on a tap and been drenched in information, all of it irrelevant. "Major Hawkinville gave me their direction as a place to contact him."

"And why, pray, would you be contacting him?"

An excellent question. Clarissa had felt that she'd dealt with the major's risqué behavior well, but he had still pushed her into impropriety. "I don't know why. I did say he would be welcome to call here."

"Nothing wrong with that. But neither of you will receive a gentleman here alone, do you understand?"

"Of course," said Clarissa for both of them. Althea looked as if another headache was coming on.

"No clandestine meetings, and no clandestine marriages. And if either of you ends up expecting a bastard child, I'll be disgusted at your folly."

Althea squeaked and stuttered something about *never* and *shock*.

Clarissa, however, dropped a meek, schoolgirl curtsy. "Yes, Miss Hurstman."

The woman's snort of amusement said she'd deflected suspicion, but inside she was a churning mass of confusion and anxiety. Hawk Hawkinville was a danger to both her virtue and her secrets, but the only safety lay in cutting herself off from him entirely.

She wasn't sure she was strong enough to do that.

When the young women had left, Arabella Hurstman stood frowning in thought. Then she walked to the small desk, sat, and pulled out a sheet of writing paper. In dark, neat script, she told the man who'd sent her here what was happening.

> *You warned of possible danger from the new Lord Deveril, and here is John Gaspard's son, as wickedly handsome as his father, dancing attendance and clearly having already made inroads. What's more, Major Hawkinville is not a man to be taken lightly. I sense a great deal more going on than I was led to expect. I require full and complete details immediately. Preferably in person.*
>
> *And bring my goddaughter with you. It's too long since I saw her.*

She folded it, sealed it, and addressed it to The Honorable Nicholas Delaney, Red Oaks, Near Yeovil, Somerset.

In the sanctuary of their room, Althea pressed her hands to her cheeks. "That woman says the most outrageous things!"

"She does, doesn't she? I rather like it."

"You would." Althea blew out a breath and began to remove her elaborate bonnet. "So, are you still pleased with the major?"

Clarissa suppressed a sigh. Still no peace. She was going to have to discuss beaux.

"He will serve to pass the time," she said lightly, dropping her hat on a chair.

"Is that fair?"

"I doubt that his heart is engaged, Thea. So, are you smitten by Lord Trevor?"

Althea gave her a look. "He's far too young. Stop trying to change the subject." She put her bonnet carefully into its box. "You must not become a flirt, Clarissa."

"But I want to flirt! And as I don't intend to marry, that is all it can be. I have warned the major of that."

Althea's eyes widened. "What did he say?"

Clarissa grinned. "I think he took it as a challenge." Her humor faded. It would be perfectly delightful if he hadn't turned out to be a Hawk.

"What is it, Clarissa?"

She couldn't explain, because that would involve explaining about Deveril's death. "This is all very new to me. I want to enjoy it, but without creating a scandal."

"Simply behave properly."

"But that would be so boring!" Irresistibly, Clarissa thought of slipping out at night to explore Brighton.

Impossible, of course, but oh, so tempting.

At school she had often slipped out into the garden at night. A minor wickedness, but she'd loved it. If she had not discovered that Major Hawkinville was so dangerous, she might perhaps have been tempted eventually into that adventure.

Althea was shaking her head. "I heard that you were not the best-behaved girl at Miss Mallory's, and now I'm coming to believe it."

Clarissa had to chuckle. "Guilty, I'm afraid. But I never created a scandal, and I won't now, Thea. So don't worry."

Then, to Clarissa's relief, Althea sat down to write her daily letter to her family. She pretended to read a book so as to have time to think.

The only sensible course was to rebuff Major Hawkinville and get him out of her life. But would it do any good? If he wanted her fortune, he would pursue, and besides that, his interest in Lord Deveril's death might already have been stirred.

Perhaps it would be better to continue the acquaintance and watch what he was doing. That was pure sophistry, of course, for if he was investigating her past, what could she do about it?

Kill him?

She'd intended the thought to be humorous, but it sparked a new fear.

The Rogues had been kind to her, but she didn't underestimate their ruthlessness. What might they do when it came to defending those they loved?

She suddenly felt as if she were a Jonah, bringing ruin to whoever she touched—Beth, the Rogues, even Lord Deveril. And now innocent Major Hawkinville. Perhaps she should lock herself away in a convent to keep the world safe!

Hawk returned with the Vandeimens to their house, though he'd decided not to stay the night. His encounter with Clarissa Greystone had left him damnably unbalanced. Was she innocent or wicked, honest or false? He needed time and distance to regroup.

Every instinct reported that she was the same gallant, unsophisticated young woman he had met in Cheltenham. Every fact pointed to the opposite.

What was she? He had no idea except that she was surprisingly dangerous to him on a personal level. He enjoyed bandying words with her. He was feeling peculiarly protective. He was even beginning to find her pretty in the way the French referred to as *une jolie laide*, a woman who is not beautiful but almost becomes so through vitality.

"Do you like this design of porte cochere, Hawk?"

Maria's voice snapped him out of his thoughts, and he looked at the drawing spread on the parlor table. Maria and Van—mostly Maria—were engaged in refurbishing Van's neglected home. That was why they were in Brighton for the summer. To be away from dust and noise but close enough to supervise.

"It would serve the purpose." He glanced at Van. "You're adding a porte cochere?"

Van shrugged. "Maria wants one."

"Of course I do! What if we return home one night in the pouring rain?"

"Umbrellas?" Van suggested.

Maria simply gave him a look, but it sizzled.

Hawk sighed. Newlyweds. Another reason not to stay. He felt intrusive, and also a touch envious. And where had that come from? He stood, putting down his half-drunk cup of tea. "I should set off back to Hawkinville."

Maria rose, too. "Wait just a moment, Hawk. I have something for you to take, if you would be so kind. Special nails." She hurried out of the room.

"Rushing away?" Van said. "You would be welcome to stay. I saw you gazing soulfully into Miss Greystone's eyes."

Hawk threw him a scathing look, though he'd created that moment of contact for precisely that effect. To alert others, especially other men. To put his mark on her.

"Perhaps I'm fleeing soulfulness," he said.

"She seems charming."

"She's a minx."

"A charming minx, then. There's nothing wrong with marriage, Hawk. I recommend it. And Miss Greystone would be an excellent choice. I hear she's quite an heiress."

"You think I need to marry for money, too?"

The "too" made it a jab at his friend, who had married a very rich woman. It was deliberate. Hawk didn't want Van digging into these matters.

Van leaned against the table, completely unruffled. "Running scared?"

"Running cautiously. I hardly know the chit, so why the talk of marriage?"

"I'm like a convert. Ardent to recruit new disciples."

Hawk laughed. "I'm delighted to see you happy, Van, but it isn't my path at the moment. Can you imagine me bringing a bride home to Hawkinville Manor, to live among the incessant skirmishing between me and my father?"

"Tricky, I grant you."

"And I must stay there until the squire recovers strength enough to run the estate."

He hadn't told anyone about the squire's title, or about the threat to Hawk in the Vale. The title was an absurdity, and he hoped to block the threat. At the back of his mind was the thought that if desperate he could apply to Van and Maria for a loan to pay off Slade.

Twenty thousand pounds?

When on earth could he repay a sum like that? And he doubted Maria now had much money to spare.

Hawk knew that she'd been returning money to people her first husband had cheated, and giving generously to charities for veterans because Maurice Celestin had made profits from shoddy military supplies. With the extensive renovations to Steynings, cash was probably in short supply.

More than that, however, he didn't want to admit what he was doing to try to get the Deveril money. Though he could justify it, he didn't want anyone to know what he was up to with the heiress.

"I hope you can take time for frequent visits here, at least," Van said equably. "Con and Susan are speaking of joining us for a few days."

"Of course."

Hawk was spared more conversation when Maria came in with a satchel over one shoulder and a leather bag in her arms. "The nails are rather heavy, I'm afraid."

He took the bag, pretending that his knees buckled under the weight. "Centaur will never make it home."

She chuckled. "If I can importune, the carpenter is waiting for them. The decorative heads are part of the design."

"I'll get them there this evening."

"And you'll be back soon, I hope," she said with a wide, friendly smile. Remarkable, when he'd done his best at one point to turn Van away from her.

"In pursuit of Miss Greystone, perhaps?" she teased.

"After a fashion," said Hawk, and escaped.

Chapter Eight

Miss Hurstman was everything she claimed. Despite her unfashionable appearance and brusque manner, she led Clarissa and Althea neatly into the very heart of Brighton's fashionable world. Clarissa went with delight, savoring her dreamed-for season like a fine wine. She would have been in heaven if not for her secrets and the worry about Major Hawkinville. He had returned to his home, but he had promised to ask for a dance at the next assembly at the Old Ship.

She knew she should hope never to see him again, but the thought of another encounter was like the last cream cake on the plate.

She couldn't resist.

He couldn't really be a danger, she rationalized. He wanted her fortune. Why would he spend time poking around in stale matters of a year ago?

And, she realized, if he wanted her fortune, he would do nothing to upset the situation. Nicholas Delaney had also said that the truth about Deveril's death could make her ineligible to inherit.

Relieved, she flung herself into every day, her circle of acquaintance constantly growing. Word was out that she was the Devil's Heiress, but this did not seem to have reduced her appeal. Instead she found herself something of a curiosity, and a lodestone for nearly every unmarried man, along with his mother and sisters.

As common wisdom said, Money will always buy friends.

There were also true friends, however. Althea, of course, but also Miriam Mosely, and Florence Babbington of the famous brother. Unfortunately he was now married and fixed in Hertfordshire, so she couldn't find out whether his manly orbs still stirred her to poetry.

Even Lord and Lady Vandeimen were friends of a sort, for they always came over to speak to her, and Clarissa and her party had been invited to take tea with Lady Vandeimen one day.

Clarissa understood that this was probably because their friend would like to marry her money, but she didn't mind.

Now, however, with the night of the assembly here at last, she teetered on the brink of something thrilling. As Elsie assisted her with her lovely *eau de nil* silk evening dress, Clarissa tried to disguise the shivers of excitement and nerves that seemed to be skittering over her skin.

It was very strange. Perhaps she was addicted to Major Hawkinville as people were said to become addicted to opium. Miss Mallory had arranged lectures for the girls from Doctor Carlisle on the dangers of the overuse of laudanum. He had described in awful detail the progression of the dependency, so that in the end the addict could not resist the drug, even knowing that it held destruction, in part because of the terrible physical suffering of withdrawal.

But after two—no, three—meetings?

The addict also, according to Doctor Carlisle, lost interest in all other aspects of life. A mother would neglect her child. A father would neglect his work. Even nourishing food and drink were unimportant to the person ruled by opium.

Clarissa bit her lip on a laugh. She wasn't so far gone as that. She had taken a second helping of Mrs. Taddy's jam pudding this evening, and she was enjoying all aspects of this stay in Brighton. Her unsteadiness now was simply that this would be her first grand affair here, her first trial before society en masse.

London didn't count. In London, Lord Deveril had not wanted her to go to any event unless he was with her.

Her dress, at least, was perfect. The subtly colored silk skimmed her curves and exposed just enough of her bosom to be interesting. The delicate gold-thread embroidery shimmered in the evening light. It would be magical under candles. Her hair looked as pretty as possible, and the bandeau of gold and pearls set it off very well.

Thank heavens for Miss Hurstman.

There had been no jewelry in Lord Deveril's possession, and Clarissa owned only a few valueless pieces. It was not a matter she had thought of. Miss Hurstman had, however, and had sent an urgent message to the Duke of Belcraven. A messenger had soon arrived with a selection of items.

None of them were precious, which was a great relief. Clarissa would have hated to risk losing an heirloom. They were all lovely, however. The gold filigree set with seed pearls went perfectly with her gown. She'd offered Althea her pick, but Althea had insisted on wearing only her own very simple pearl pendant and earrings.

Clarissa looked at her friend and sighed with satisfaction. In a pure white dress, stripped down to simple lines, and adorned only by her beauty, Althea would outshine every other woman present tonight and have every available man on his knees by tomorrow. She was sure of it.

She held out her gloved hand to her friend. "Onward to our adventure!"

Their hackney coach rolled up to the Old Ship Inn, which stretched along the seafront, every window illuminated to welcome the guests. The stream of people was continuous, the men in dark evening wear or uniforms, the ladies a rainbow of silk, lace, and jewels. All of fashionable Brighton would be here, and excitement danced in the air on a drifting mélange of perfume.

Clarissa pulled up the hood of her cloak to protect her coiffure from the brisk wind and stepped down from the coach. She worked hard to keep her smile at a suitably subdued level, but excitement was bubbling up in her like water in a hot pot. Her first true ball, and already she had promised dances to five men! Althea would never sit one out unless from exhaustion. It would be a splendid evening.

She caught Miss Hurstman's eye on her and tried to rein in her smile even more, but her dragon said, "Enjoy yourself. Though everyone puts on an air of boredom, it's a pleasure to be with people prepared to admit to a little excitement."

Clarissa set her smile free, this time at Miss Hurstman. Her liking and admiration for the woman grew day by day. It was so typical that her dress for this grand event was only slightly more festive than her daywear—a maroon gown and a very plain matching turban. Clarissa was reveling in fine clothes, but she relished the fact that Miss Hurstman did not care, and did not care what anyone else thought about that.

Quite possibly, she thought, as she entered the brilliantly lit hotel, she would be like Miss Hurstman one day. A crusty spinster who did and said exactly as she wished. But not yet, not yet. Tonight was for youth, and excitement, and even, perhaps, a little judicious folly.

Major Hawkinville had asked her to go apart with him on the Steyne. What would she do if he made the same invitation tonight, at the assembly?

If he was here.

He'd said he would be, but until she saw him . . .

She tried not to show it, but as she looked around, enjoying the company and acknowledging acquaintances, she was looking, looking, looking for Major Hawkinville.

Then she saw him enter, smiling at something said by one of his companions—the Vandeimens and another couple. He wore perfect dark evening clothes, but a blue cravat the color of his eyes was a playful touch that made her want to run over to him to tease. Then he laughed and raised the second woman's hand to his lips for a hotly flirtatious kiss.

A surge of pure fury hit Clarissa, but then the woman laughed too, rapping his arm hard with her fan, and it was clear that she was with the other man and no threat.

Clarissa realized that she'd been staring and looked hastily away, praying that no one had noticed. But, oh, she hoped he would kiss her hand that way.

She couldn't help it. She had to glance back. He and his party were approaching!

They were all still in the spacious entry area, for Miss Hurstman had paused to speak to someone, but all around, guests were flowing toward the ballroom. The major and his friends had to navigate the stream.

It was only when they arrived that Clarissa realized that she had watched him all the way. Immediately she decided she didn't care. She didn't know how to play sophisticated games, and she didn't enjoy them, so she wouldn't.

Hawk approached Clarissa Greystone with increasing concern. It was no good. Time away had not altered anything. He could not see her as a disguised villainess.

Look at her now! Beneath the Ship's chandeliers, she sparkled and shone, but it wasn't light on gold and embroidery, it was unabashed excitement. She was innocently, honestly delighted to be here and anticipated a magical evening.

That, surely, couldn't be faked.

As he crossed the lobby smiling, he was rapidly rearranging the pieces in his mind.

She was someone's innocent dupe, and that someone would plan to get the money back somehow.

How?

By marriage, or by inheritance.

Theft was a possibility, but as dangerous as the original crimes. Gaming was another, but not until she left her minority and was in independent control of her money.

He almost paused in his step. That would explain that strange provision of the will that put a fortune in her hands at twenty-one. An unpredictable device, however. Who was to say she would become a rash gambler? And who could say that she wouldn't marry before she reached twenty-one and have a husband to control her? In fact, it was highly likely.

Marriage? Illogical to put the money in her hands, then plan to marry it, especially as no one seemed to have made any attempt to secure her affections during the past year.

Inheritance, then. But Deveril's will stated that if Clarissa died before her majority her family should have no right to the money and it should go to the Middlesex Yule Club.

That was an absurdity, out of keeping with what he'd learned of Deveril, unless it was a cover for some depraved enterprise. In his week in London, he'd failed to find any trace of such an organization.

His main emotion, however, was a chill fear.

Inheritance necessitated death.

It was only as he introduced Con and his wife to Clarissa's party that he remembered there was another way to get the money from her—by proving the will false and being Deveril's default heir.

The course he was pursuing.

It didn't threaten her life, but seeing her here, shining with the pleasure of this wealthy, privileged life, he suspected that it was close.

Hawk in the Vale, he reminded himself. All the people of Hawk in the Vale, not to mention his own dreams, hinged upon this. He would take care of her, though. She would not be abandoned to the cruelty of the world, or of her family.

As they moved to follow the crowd toward the ballroom, he offered an arm to Clarissa and Miss Hurstman.

The latter immediately said, "You spend much time in Brighton, Major?"

He recognized an attack, though he had no idea why she was hostile. "When the company pleases me, Miss Hurstman."

At her narrow look, he went on. "My friends the Vandeimens are fixed here at the moment, and the Amleighs have joined them for a week or so."

"Thought he'd inherited the earldom of Wyvern," Miss Hurstman said, as if Con's title was suspicious too.

"It's under dispute, so he has reverted to the viscountcy. He'll be happy to have it stay that way."

"The old earl was certainly a dirty dish. Bad blood." But it was said with an eye on him. He came to the alert. What did she know? It would be disastrous if Clarissa discovered his connection to Deveril.

"There's bad blood in every family, Miss Hurstman," Hawk replied, meeting that look. "Wasn't it your paternal grandfather who tried to stake his daughter in a game of hazard?"

Clarissa was astonished and alarmed to see Miss Hurstman silenced, and she leaped into the conversation. "So are you fixed here for a few days, Major?"

He turned to her, his expression warming. "I am, Miss Greystone. I anticipate a great deal of pleasure from it."

Clarissa didn't think she mistook his meaning, and she turned away to hide a smile. He was here to hunt her. She still wasn't sure if she should let herself be caught, but the pursuit promised extraordinary pleasure.

She had promised the first dance to dashing Captain Ralstone, and forbade herself to regret it. She couldn't dance every dance with the major. She had to confess to being relieved, however, when he led out Lord Amleigh's wife rather than some other unmarried woman.

Jealousy? That was ridiculous.

She made herself pay full attention to Captain Ralstone during their dance, but this had the unfortunate effect of increasing his confidence. By the end of the set, his comments were becoming a little warm, and his manner almost proprietary. She was delighted in more ways than one to move off with Major Hawkinville in preparation for the next set.

"Ralstone is a gazetted fortune hunter, you know," he said, as they strolled around the room.

"And you are not?" It popped out, and she immediately wished it back.

His brows rose, but he didn't immediately answer. Eventually he said, "My father owns a modest property, and I am his only son."

She knew she was red. "I do beg your pardon, Major. I had decided to put off affectation and behave naturally, but I see now why it is unwise."

She was rewarded with his smile. "Not at all. I would be delighted if you would be natural with me, Miss Greystone. After all, as we see, it dispels misunderstandings before they can root."

"Yes," she said, but she didn't think his talk of natural behavior related entirely to dispelling misunderstandings.

He covered her gloved hand on his arm. "Perhaps we can begin by using first names with each other, just between ourselves."

She glanced down at their hands for a moment. He wore a signet ring with a carved black stone, and his fingers were long, with neatly oblong nails.

She smiled up at him. "I would like that. My name is Clarissa."

"I know. And mine is George, but no one uses it. You may if you wish, or you may call me Hawk, as most do."

"Hawk? A somewhat frightening name."

"Is it? You are no pigeon to be afraid of a hawk."

"But I am told that you investigate everything, and forget nothing."

He laughed. "That sounds tiresome rather than frightening."

"Then what about the fortune hunting? Are you hunting me, Hawk?" She longed to have everything honest between them.

He touched her necklace where it lay against her throat, sliding a finger slowly beneath it. "What do you think?"

Clarissa wasn't sure whether to swoon or be outraged.

"And be assured," he murmured, lowering his hand, "if I capture you, my little pigeon, you will enjoy it."

She escaped by looking around at the company and fanning herself. "It is not pleasant, you know, to be prey, no matter how benign the hunter."

"Bravo," he said softly. "Well, then, you will have to be a predator, too. I think I will call you Falcon."

She looked back at him. "Ah, I like that."

"I thought you might."

But then she realized that he had brought them to a halt and was gazing into her eyes. Fortune hunting, she realized, could take many subtle forms. He was trying to mark her as his. She probably should not allow it, but it was too exciting to decline.

"Electricity," she said.

"Definitely. You have experienced that mysterious force?"

"At school. We had a demonstration."

"Education is wonderful, is it not?"

It was perhaps as well that the warning chords sounded then for the next dance, for Clarissa wasn't sure what she might have done. The simplest fortune-hunting technique, she realized, would be to compromise her.

She must certainly guard against that, but she could certainly enjoy this.

It was only a dance.

Clarissa tried to remind herself of that, but she had danced with a man so rarely. The dancing master at the school hardly counted. Last year in London, she had attended two balls, but on both occasions she had been on Lord Deveril's arm and had danced only with him. She wasn't sure if her lack of partners had been because of her own lack of charms or because of Deveril.

And here she was, dancing with a man who seemed able to generate electricity without any machine at all!

It was a lively country dance that gave little opportunity for talk, but that didn't matter. It would be an effort to be coherent. The movements allowed her to look at him, to smile at him, and to receive looks and smiles in return. They held hands, linked arms, and even came closer in some of the moves. She began to feel that she was losing contact with the wooden floor entirely . . .

When it came to an end, she fanned herself, trying to think of something lightly coherent to say. Suddenly she found herself in a cooler spot, and realized that he had moved them into the corridor outside the ballroom.

She half opened her mouth to object, to say that she would be looked for by other partners, or by Miss Hurstman, for that matter, but then she closed it again.

What next?

She couldn't wait to find out.

The corridor—alas?—was not completely deserted, but as they strolled along it he captured her fan, sliding the ribbon off her wrist, and began to ply it for her. The cool breeze was not adequate competition for the additional heat swirling inside her.

"What are you doing, Hawk?"

His lips twitched. "Hunting?"

"Pray, for politeness' sake, call it courting, sir."

"Courting? I have much practice at the hunt, but little at courtship. How should we go on?"

She put on a mock flirtatious air. "Poetry would be welcome, sir. To my eyes. To my lips . . ."

"Ah." He ceased fanning, but only to capture her gloved hand and raise it to his lips. *"Sweet maid, your lips I long to kiss / To seal to mine in endless bliss / Let but your eyes send welcome here / And I, your swain, will soon be near."*

His lips pressed, and she resented her silk gloves, which muted the effect. "A sweet rhyme, but it comes rather easily to you, sir."

His eyes lit with laughter. "Alas, it is commonly used. Written on a scrap of paper and slipped to a lady."

"Not always with proper intentions? Tut, tut! Let me think what I can contribute."

Her hand still in his, she recited, *"O noble man, tall, chaste, and bold / So like a gallant knight of old / Turn on me once, lest I expire / Those sapphire orbs filled with manly fire."*

He laughed, covering his face for a moment with his free hand. "Manly fire?"

"And sapphire orbs," she agreed. "Though I feel obliged to confess that the original was obsidian."

"Ah. That probably explains the 'chaste' too."

Clarissa blushed, though heaven knows she'd not expected him to be inexperienced. "He was one of my friend's brothers, and I was twelve. It's a very romantic age, twelve."

"And you're so old and shriveled now."

She looked into his teasing eyes and quickly, before she lost courage, drew his hand to her lips for a kiss. Warm skin, firm flesh and bone. A hint of cologne and . . . him.

Remembering that they were not alone, she hastily dropped his hand, grabbed her fan, and fanned herself frantically.

"It is hot, isn't it?" He put a hand at her elbow and moved her sideways. Into a room.

She stopped fanning, though she was certainly no cooler. It was a small withdrawing room set with armchairs, and with copies of magazines and newspapers available. At the moment it was deserted.

He made no attempt to shut the door. If he had, she thought she would have objected despite her riveted fascination.

To be compromised would be disastrous, she tried to remind herself, but a part of her simply didn't care.

That part seemed to be the one in control. And the door, after all, was wide open.

"Major?" she said as a light query.

"Hawk," he reminded her.

"Hawk." But she blushed. The word seemed wicked, here, alone.

He touched her lips. "You only have to fly away, my dear."

She met his eyes, her heart thundering. "I know."

He took her hand and drew her across the room. When he stopped, she realized that they were no longer visible to anyone in the corridor.

But the door was still open . . .

Then he raised her chin with his knuckles, and kissed her.

It was a light kiss—a mere pressure of his lips against hers—and yet it sent a shiver of delight through her.

Her first kiss!

But then she stiffened. Not her first. Deveril had been her first. A memory of vomit made her pull back.

He stood absolutely still. "You do not like to be kissed?" Then, perceptively, he added, "Deveril?"

Her silence was all the answer he needed. "What a shame he is already dead."

"You would have killed him for me?"

"With pleasure."

He was serious. And he was a soldier. The idea of having a champion, a man ready to defend her with his life, was even more seductive than kisses. It was too soon, ridiculously too soon, but she wanted this man.

"Lord Deveril was murdered, I understand," he said. "I don't suppose it was you, was it?"

The seductive mist froze into horror. "No!"

He caught her arm before she could run away. "It was a joke, Falcon, but I see it's no matter for humor." The touch turned into a caress. "You must forgive a soldier still rough from the war."

She was struck dumb by fear of saying the wrong thing, and by the tender pleasure of his hand against her arm, her shoulder, her neck . . .

"If I were persuaded into marriage with a person I disliked," he said, "and had unpleasant kisses forced upon me, I would do away with the offender."

"But you're a man."

"Women are capable of violence too, you know."

Lulled, relaxed, she said, "Yes. Yes, they are."

As soon as the words escaped, she knew she had finally said too much. It shouldn't matter. It was of no significance to him. But she had said too much.

Making herself be calm, she moved away from his touch, wondering whether to spill more words to cover what she'd said. No. "We must return to the dance. As I said, Major, I do not plan to create a scandal."

Even to her own ears it sounded brittle.

He merely said, "Of course." But as they moved toward the door, he put his hand on the small of her back. She felt it there through silk—possession and promise.

She had overreacted. He'd been joking, teasing.

And, as she'd decided before, her future husband would not want the truth about Deveril's death to come out. Perhaps it was her sacred duty to marry him!

As they moved into the corridor, he linked their arms again. "You mustn't let one man have such a victory over you, Falcon. You are entitled to enjoy kisses, and kisses are not so very wicked." He waited until she looked at him, then added, "I hope you will soon let me show you how pleasant they can be."

She was tempted to move back out of sight for an immediate demonstration, but she made herself be sensible and return to the ballroom. For one thing, she had another partner waiting. For another, she needed time and peace to think this all through.

A hollowness ached in her, however. Harmless as it had been, she should not have said that about a woman and violence. Nor should she have panicked at a joke about her killing Deveril.

Could she not engage in simple conversation without perilous shards of truth slipping out?

She danced one later set with the major, and it was the supper dance, but she made sure that afterward they stayed with a group. He didn't seem to mind. He was, she was sure, a very patient hunter, and if he felt confident, it was hardly surprising.

As they returned home, Miss Hurstman said, "I warned you, Clarissa, about slipping off into anterooms."

Foolish to hope that the dragon had not noticed. "It was hot in the ballroom."

"That is the usual excuse. If you'd been gone any longer I would have found you."

Clarissa sighed. "I'm sorry, Miss Hurstman, but Major Hawkinville was a perfect gentleman."

It wasn't really a lie.

"So I would hope, but have a care. I have no doubt he has an eye on your fortune."

"Nor do I." The coach drew up in Broad Street and they climbed down. "But tell me, Miss Hurstman, which of my partners tonight did not?"

Althea exclaimed, "Clarissa!" but Miss Hurstman, consistently honest, made no rebuttal.

Althea would have liked to chatter about the evening, but for once

Clarissa claimed a headache and even accepted a little laudanum in the hope that it would still the whirling doubts and questions in her head.

It worked, but in the morning all the doubts and questions were still there, along with the acceptance of a simple fact. Hawk Hawkinville was winning. She was beginning to fall in love with him.

Chapter Nine

As they sat at a late breakfast the next morning, a note came from Lady Vandeimen inviting Clarissa and Althea to walk with her. Miss Hurstman made no objection and remarked that Maria Vandeimen would be a strict chaperon. "She was spun off her feet by a handsome opportunist once."

"A fortune hunter?" Clarissa asked.

"There are different types of fortunes."

"What was hers?"

"Her blood. Celestin had money and wanted the entrée. But it wasn't her, you see. It could have been anyone of high enough birth."

Clarissa nodded, understanding the warning. "Yes, I see."

As expected, when Lady Vandeimen arrived, she was accompanied by her husband, the Amleighs, and Major Hawkinville.

Hawk.

And the question was, Did he simply want money, or was there something of her about it?

Clarissa was not at all surprised when Althea ended up walking with the Amleighs, leaving her to Hawk's escort. Nor could she regret it. One thing was certain—she could not make any kind of decision without learning more about Hawk Hawkinville, and the lessons were perfectly delightful.

It was not a delightful day, being overcast and somewhat chilly. But as Lady Vandeimen had remarked when she'd arrived, in this unsettled summer, overcast was a pleasant alternative to rain. The weather had given Clarissa the opportunity to wear a very stylish Prussian blue spencer with bronze braid and frogs, so that was a silver lining.

As they paused to look at the unused bathing machines, however, she said, "I wish the weather would turn warmer. I might brave the water."

"Do you swim?"

She looked at him. "Not at all. But the dippers take care of the bathers, don't they?"

"And keep to the shallows."

He turned to lean back against the wooden railing. A deliberate ploy, surely, to make her breathless at the long, lean length of him, and the strength that was clear, even when he was at rest.

A ploy did not mean that any of it was false. She'd met any number of men in the past days, many of them handsome, but none had the power over her that this man seemed to have.

"We have a river back home," he said. "The Eden. Perhaps I will take you there to swim one day."

"Perhaps." She tried for the same light manner but feared her feelings must show. "But can I trust you not to lead me into deep water?"

His slight smile acknowledged the double entendre. "You can't really swim in the shallows."

"I can't really swim at all."

"I could teach you."

"Or drown me."

His brows rose. "O ye of little faith."

"O me of great caution, Major." Lord above, but this verbal play alone could seduce her into folly, never mind all his other charms.

"Hawk," he reminded her.

"Very well, Hawk. I wonder where the others are," she asked, looking back.

"Nervous?" he murmured.

"Of course not." Yet the mere suggestion had stirred nerves within her. The others were only a few yards away, speaking to another party. There were people all around. There was nothing to fear, except the reactions inside herself, which seemed to be rapidly spinning out of control.

"Perhaps you should be nervous."

She swiveled back to face him. "Why?"

"Because we are already in deep water. Can't you tell?"

Oh, yes. "We are in public on the Marine Parade in Brighton."

"Even so . . ."

The others joined them then, and Clarissa could only be glad. She wasn't sure she had a coherent response to make.

"The Pytchleys were just speaking of the fair," Maria Vandeimen said. "They say it is very amusing. Lord Vandeimen and I are thinking of driving out there this afternoon. Perhaps you would care to come if you are free, Miss Greystone, Miss Trist."

"The fair?" Clarissa asked, trying to surface from deep waters.

"Out on the Downs," Lord Vandeimen said. "A little wild, but perfectly safe with good escorts."

She couldn't help but look at Hawk.

What if the escorts were a little wild?

"I will have to ask Miss Hurstman," she said.

When asked, Miss Hurstman again made no objection, though to Clarissa she did not seem entirely happy.

"Be sure to stay with your party," she said to both of them, though it seemed to be directed particularly at Clarissa.

The sun broke through the clouds as the two open carriages rolled up to the sprawling fairground set up on the Downs. Clarissa looked back toward the town spread out before them, with the silvery sea beyond, then turned to the gaudy, hurly-burly jumble of the fair.

"Your eyes are sparkling, Miss Greystone," said Hawk from his seat opposite her.

"I've never been to a fair before."

He smiled. "Then I'm particularly glad Maria had this fancy."

They were sharing the vehicle with Lord and Lady Vandeimen, while Althea came behind with the Amleighs and Lord Amleigh's secretary, Mr. de Vere. Clarissa hoped he wouldn't catch Althea's fancy. He could hardly have a fortune, and seemed mischievous.

They descended from the carriages and headed for the first tents, but they had to pick their way, for the ground was soft after the wet weather and much trampled. This meant that Clarissa must keep a firm hold on Hawk's arm, which did not displease her at all.

"What fairground pleasure most appeals?" he asked her.

"I don't know. Everything!"

He laughed, and they paused at a miniature model of Paris, complete with a glassy River Seine.

"Is it true to life?" Clarissa asked.

"Yes, it seems to be," he said, dropping a coin in the box there, "except that Versailles is not so close."

She looked at him. "You must have seen many countries."

"Not so many. My service was confined to Europe."

She looked at another model, which claimed to be Rome. "I would like to travel. I would like to see Spain, and Italy, and the ruins of Greece."

"When you have your fortune and your independence, there will be nothing to stop you."

"True." But she knew she was not brave enough to wander the world alone. A weakness, but it must be faced. Coming to Brighton was enough of an adventure for her so far.

There was a more popular display, but their party wandered past it without a close look. Clarissa peered and saw that it was a representation of the Battle of Waterloo.

No wonder. But it amazed her to think that their urbane escorts had, not long ago, been part of that dire and desperate affair.

Had killed.

She glanced at Lord Vandeimen of the smooth and silky blond hair—though there was that scar.

Lord Amleigh was more saturnine, but when he smiled, dimples showed.

No one would think that smiling de Vere had been to war. As for Hawk, he looked as if he would hate to have his clothes disarranged, and yet he had been a hero at least once, according to Lord Trevor. And even if he hadn't raised a sword at Waterloo, he'd been there, among the carnage.

She realized how little she really knew of him. She must be careful.

For the moment, however, she was reveling in innocent fun. They all progressed merrily from sideshows to trials of skill to prizewinning animals. The men teasingly encouraged the ladies to try their hands at everything, applauding successes and commiserating with failures. Lady Amleigh proved to have a very good throwing arm at the coconut shy, and Lady Vandeimen was skilled at archery. Clarissa had no such skills, but she managed a lucky roll at dice, which doubled her sixpence to a shilling, and Althea hooked a cork fish with a little fishing pole to win a carved fan.

They paused outside a black tent spangled with golden stars. "Madame Mystique," said Lord Vandeimen. "She's the latest sensation here in Brighton. Would any of you ladies like to have your fortune told?"

Althea said an emphatic no, and the other ladies both made a laughing comment about already having their excellent fortune. Clarissa was tempted, but she didn't want to be the only one, so she said no as well, and they moved on to the next stall, where sticky buns were for sale. The men hailed this as if they were starving, and soon they all had a bun in their hands, though the ladies had to remove their gloves first.

"This feels wonderfully wicked," Clarissa declared, licking sweetness from around her lips.

"Wicked?" Hawk asked.

"Standing in a public place eating, and eating so messily! Miss Mallory would definitely not approve."

He smiled. "We can be a great deal more wicked than this, I assure you, Falcon. But perhaps just as sweetly."

The others were laughing together and trying to clean sticky fingers. Clarissa savored her last mouthful, looking at him, thinking about the tantalizingly light kiss they'd enjoyed.

"Perhaps you are a devil that tempts rather than a hawk that hunts."

"Any good hunter knows to lure his prey. And the devil hunts souls, that's for sure."

"To their destruction."

"True."

Then he grasped her wrist and inspected her hand. For a heart-stopping moment, she thought he would start to lick her fingers clean, but instead he drew her toward some enterprising children who were offering a hand-washing service next to the bun stall.

She staggered. His warm, firm fingers were light against her skin, but they were there, sending her nerves jumping.

He let her go, and Clarissa found herself clasping the wrist his fingers had circled, aware of her own frantically pounding pulse.

One smiling girl took his penny, and a second poured cool water over Clarissa's hands into a bowl. A third offered soap, and Clarissa rubbed away the stickiness, but was careful not to wash her wrist. She wanted the memory of his touch.

A fourth child, a pretty red-haired urchin, offered a towel, and Clarissa dried her hands while watching the other members of the party follow. This was all innocent fun, but something stronger beat beneath it. She knew it, and knew it to be dangerous, but she couldn't resist.

Then she was snapped out of her dreamy thoughts by a spot of rain.

She realized that the sun had disappeared again, and a heavier layer of dark clouds was sliding in. The rain was only a hint on the air at the moment, but Lord Vandeimen said, "Back to the carriages, I think."

No one protested, though Clarissa wanted to. What would have happened next?

Lady Amleigh said, "I do wish that volcano had kept its head!"

To which her husband responded, "Perhaps it was in love."

The look in his eye and the lady's blush said it had special meaning for them. Clarissa wondered what it would be like to have that sort of private connection, that sort of love.

It was beginning to seem a prize worth more than a mere fortune.

A number of people had the same idea of leaving the fair, but then, as the rain held off, some turned back. Suddenly there was a swirling crowd that reminded her of the riot in Cheltenham.

Hawk put his arm around her and held her close. "Don't worry. There's limitless space here, so it can't become a deadly crush."

All the same, they were jostled a little, and he eased them between two stalls and into more open space. Clarissa couldn't help noticing that the other couples had gone in another direction.

Accident, or design?

She glanced at him, not at all nervous. He'd mentioned her going apart with him. She was ready to find out what it involved. She glanced at the darkening sky, praying that the storm would hold off for a while.

Then the wind squalled, almost flinging her skirts up. She fought to hold them down. "I think the storm's about to hit!" she called, in case his wicked purposes had blinded him to nature.

"I know." He glanced around, then said, "Come on!" His arm around her, he ran toward a large tent. The rain hit like a gray sheet just as they made it to safety.

It was a rough stable with lines of tethered horses, many of them moving restively with the storm. They became even more agitated as people rushed and staggered in in various states of wetness.

A couple of grooms tried to stop the invasion, but it was no good. The rain was coming down in torrents, driven hard by the wind, and the ground outside was already a swamp.

They ended up with only about twenty people in the tent, but with everyone squeezing away from the nervous horses, it was a crush. The stink of dung, horse, wet clothing, and unwashed bodies made Clarissa almost wish that she was out in the torrent.

Hawk eased them into a corner, but said, "I apologize."

"It's not your fault, but I do wish there was some fresh air."

Suddenly he had a knife in his hand, a slender knife that, all the same, cut a slit in the canvas wall as if it were muslin. When it was clear that the rain was coming from the other direction, he made the cut into a rectangular flap.

"Do you have a pin?" he asked.

"What lady would be without one?" Clarissa said, shocked by that efficient blade. She had never imagined a gentleman carrying such a thing and had no idea what to do with the information.

She gave him a pin. "You are very resourceful, Hawk. And very well equipped."

He was pinning up the flap. The knife had somehow disappeared. He looked at her for a moment, then held out his hand. Pushing back his cuff, he slid the dagger out again.

"An interesting fashion accessory," she said.

"More of a bad habit."

"I thought soldiers went more normally armed."

"Wise soldiers go armed in any way that will keep them alive. I've been in places where a secret weapon was almost expected, however." His lips quirked. "Don't think me a hero. It was generally a matter of dealing with shady merchants, thieves, and even pirates. And there being little difference between the three."

She smiled, content now that she had fresh air to breathe. They were hardly alone, but the people all around seemed to be country folk or fair workers. No one to care what she and Hawk did or said.

"You have to know that I find that exciting," she remarked.

Hawk almost had her where he wanted her, where he had to want her, but as usual her disarming frankness was like a shield, turning away all weapons.

He made himself smile teasingly. "Is it? Most ladies find killing knives frightening."

She tried. She tried very hard. But he saw the flicker of muscles that registered a hit.

"Killing?" she said, in the way of a person who knows they have to say it.

He handled his stiletto, carefully out of the way of nearby people. "A knife like this is not for mending pens, Falcon. Though it does that job very well." He turned the handle toward her. "Here."

She stared at it, all guard shattered. "What? I don't want it!"

"You said it excited you."

"No, I didn't!" She was fixed on the knife like a rabbit on the snake that will kill it. He saw her swallow. It was like a knife in his own gut. A knife he had to push in deeper rather than draw out.

"What did you mean, then?"

She looked up. Tried to step back, but a tent support blocked her from behind. She was pale, her eyes stark, but she managed a kind of lightness. "I meant pirates and such. Romantic things."

"If you think pirates romantic, I should definitely equip you with a knife, and teach you how to use it."

"No, thank you."

"No?" He moved the knife again. *Did you kill Deveril? If not, who used a knife on him?* "I call this my talon. A Falcon should have a talon, too." When she didn't respond, he pushed. "Why does it bother you? Something else to do with Lord Deveril?"

For a moment she looked shockingly like a man who realizes that his guts are hanging out, that he's dying. "No!"

People nearby turned to look. Damn. He slipped the knife back in its sheath and took her gloved hands. "Have I upset you? I'm sorry."

She stayed silent, though her chest was rising and falling.

"It's Deveril's death, isn't it?" he said softly, sympathetically. "These things heal when they're spoken of."

It was usually a surprisingly successful ploy. He'd had men talking their way to the gallows this way. No words spilled, so he asked a simple, factual question. Often once people started to talk, they couldn't stop.

"When did he die?"

She blinked at him. "June the eighteenth. When so many others were dying . . ."

Against reason, he pulled her into his arms. "Hush, I don't mean to upset you. Don't talk about it if you don't want to."

But the words he'd wanted were like lead in his heart.

June 18. The day of Waterloo, when, indeed, so many others had been dying. But Deveril's body hadn't been found until the twentieth, and the date of his death had never been certain.

To be so sure, Clarissa had to know all about the murder, and he knew now that he'd been stupidly hoping that she didn't, that she was the innocent she seemed.

How had it been? Had she killed Deveril to stop him from raping her? And was he going to send her to the gallows for it?

That or Hawkinville, he reminded himself.

He knew, abruptly and with astonishing relief, that he could not do it. Not even Hawkinville was worth that.

Perhaps his father had had the right idea after all. Persuade her to marry him. He would not be like his father, after all, courting callously for gain. He truly admired his gallant Falcon. He would protect her, cherish her. A picture began to unfold of them together at Hawkinville. Children . . .

But then a dark curtain fell. He wasn't simply Hawk Hawkinville, fortune hunter. He was heir to Lord Deveril!

It was hard not to burst out laughing at the farce of it. When did he tell her she was going to have to live her life with the name she loathed? Not before the wedding, for sure. She would run away. Right after the ceremony? No, he'd better make sure of her and wait until it was consummated.

Damnable.

And how did he expect to marry her? If she'd killed Deveril, she hadn't done it alone. And there was that forged will, and someone after her money. Announce their betrothal and the other parties would have to act.

Elope, then. But the other objection still stood. Could he really persuade a woman into a clandestine marriage knowing she would loathe him once she knew the truth?

For once, he was totally adrift.

He gently eased her away. "It's stopped raining. It's a sea of mud out there, but we should try to find the others."

She looked up, a little pale but much restored, perhaps even with a hint of stars in her eyes. Stars he'd been working so hard to put there. Pointed stars, that could do nothing but hurt her, one way or another.

People were moving out of the tent, but slowly. Suddenly needing to be free of the place, he pulled out his knife and extended the hole, stepped through, then helped her out. They emerged into a field, so they escaped the trodden mud, but she still had to teeter over a deep puddle. That seemed to drive the clouds away entirely. She laughed, looking up at him, clinging to his hand.

He put his hands at her waist and swept her over the puddle, wishing he could sweep her away entirely. Wishing he were someone other than the Hawk, and heir to John Gaspard, Viscount Deveril.

They picked their way down the back of the tents toward the carriages as the fair slowly came back to life around them.

"How optimistic people are," she said, looking at the sky.

"Another torrent on the way," he agreed. "But optimism is good. *Carpe diem.*"

She glanced at him, seeming almost completely restored now. "Is that optimism? Surely optimism should say that tomorrow will be as pleasant as today?"

"Whereas Horace advised us to put no trust in tomorrow."

They were apart from the crowds, but he wasn't sure he cared about proprieties anyway. He felt as if this might be his last moment. He drew her into his arms, and she came willingly, a trusting pigeon.

"This is most improper," he murmured against her lips.

"Improper, yes. But most?"

It broke a full smile from him, which he gave her in the kiss, then lost as he tasted her fully for the first time. Soft, sweet. With wondrous amusement he found he could actually taste her delighted curiosity as he teased her mouth open to him.

Her hands clutched, holding him tighter. He could feel all the promising, firm curves of her body and a faint tremor that might even be partly his own.

When had he last kissed for the kiss alone? When had he last lost himself in a kiss so that when their mouths slid free he felt dazed, as if from too much hot sun—which there certainly wasn't today on the rainy downs.

Her eyes were wide, but not with horror. After a moment she said, "I don't think I need to worry about the memory of Deveril's kiss anymore."

He pulled her close and held her. "Then I'm glad of that." Did it mean Deveril was no longer such a power in her mind? If he told her the truth now, would she shrug it off?

If she didn't, he would have burned every conceivable bridge.

She pushed slightly free. "You are not glad of other things?"

What could he say? Hardly surprising that she expected more after a kiss like that. Hardly surprising if she expected a proposal.

"I am glad that the rain has stopped, and for the tip of your nose." He kissed it.

She chuckled, blushing.

"I'm glad to be out of the tent, and for your elegant ankles."

Her eyes shone.

"I'm glad that I might, one day, discover other elegant parts . . ."

He was saved from pursuing that insane course when something hurtled through the air and hit her.

Clarissa screamed, but he grabbed the thing and discovered that it was a muddy, raggedy cat, hissing, squirming, and doing its damn best to sink in its claws.

"Don't!" Clarissa screamed.

"I'm not going to break its neck." He usually had a way with animals. He held it close to his body and started murmuring to it. In moments it calmed.

She staggered closer. "Is it all right? Where did it come from?"

"Hush." He worked at shrugging out of his coat one sleeve at a time without letting the cat free, murmuring to keep it calm as he gradually swathed it. Then a purr started and quickly grew in volume.

Chapter Ten

Clarissa watched him with astonishment. She never would have thought that her hawk of elegant plumage would go to such trouble for a scrawny cat.

Now that the cat seemed calm, she looked around. A man came out of the back of a nearby tent and chucked a handful of dead rats into a sack, then ducked inside again. She heard squeals, yowls, and shouting from inside.

She marched over to yank back the canvas curtain. As she thought, it was a ratter's tent, where cats and dogs were set to kill rats. People were packed onto ranks of rough benches cheering on the hunters and calling out bets. Assaulted by noise, stink, and pure violence, she staggered back.

Then a burly man blocked her view. "If yer want to come in, go round the front and pay."

Clarissa remembered her purpose. "Who threw that cat?"

"What frigging business is it of yours?"

"It hit me! What's more, it's wounded and needs care."

"I didn't wring its neck. What more does it need? Useless piece of scrag."

"You may not have heard," said a calm voice behind her. "The cat hit the lady."

The ratter whipped off his hat. "Hit the lady, sir? Well, I never! Are you all right, miss?"

How infuriating not to be taken seriously without a man at her back! This was an active lesson on the points Mary Wollstonecraft had been making in her writings.

"What about the cat?" she demanded, though she was beginning to realize that the last thing the poor creature needed was to be returned to the ratters. People nearby were turning to look, too, their avid faces suggesting that they expected another juicy battle.

The ratter put on an apologetic expression. "Didn't turn out to be much of a ratter, you see, miss. If you'd like the dear creature, please, take her."

The purring vibrated the air by her side. Clarissa glanced once at Hawk, almost distracted by the fact that he was in shirtsleeves, but hoping he would take over. He had his arms full of purring cat, however, and his look seemed to say, This is your game. You play it.

"Very well. I will take her. Does she have a name?"

"Fanny Laycock," said the man with a very false smile.

Someone nearby sniggered.

"Take her," Hawk said.

Clarissa found herself with her arms full of coat and cat. The purring stopped, and a slight shivering began. She tried murmuring to it, and it calmed a little. Her attention was all on Hawk, however, as he walked toward the ratter. The man's eyes suddenly widened. Whatever it was Hawk did to impress people, he was doing it again.

"You can't go around throwing cats," he said, almost lazily. "I'm sure that when my companion gets into clear light, she will find that her gown is snagged and stained with blood. I doubt you can afford the cost of a replacement, but a guinea will serve as penance."

"A guinea—!"

He stopped and swallowed. Slowly, he dug into a pocket, but Clarissa caught a movement and saw the two other men moving closer. They were all so big!

"Hawk!" she said sharply in warning, just as the first man ran for him.

"You really shouldn't," Hawk said. But his fist had already shot out, hurtling the first man back into the stands, causing a yelling commotion among the people sitting there. He'd somehow avoided the other two.

But then men leaped out of the stands and fists flew. Rats escaped and were darting underfoot, pursued by ferocious dogs and cats. Women screamed and wood shattered.

It was the riot all over again!

Trying to protect the frantic cat, Clarissa was forced back, right out of the riotous tent into a gathering crowd.

What was happening?

Hawk!

What if he was dead?

She tried to soothe the poor cat, tried to soothe herself, but tears trickled down her face. Another disaster, and entirely her fault. She truly was a Jonah . . .

But then she heard chattering and realized the tumult had calmed. The flap opened, and Hawk appeared in the midst of a group of cheerful, admiring men.

Hard to imagine him so disordered and muddy, but he seemed unharmed. A giggle escaped. He'd lost his hat again! Then someone hurried after and gave it to him.

He thanked all the men, who presumably had been on his side, then looked around for her. "Are you all right?"

"Yes, but what of you?"

"Nothing serious." He brushed a tear off her cheek. "I'm sorry if you were frightened."

"It wasn't your fault."

"It's an escort's duty to protect against all affront. I clearly need practice." He took the cat, and the ungrateful beast immediately started purring again. "Let's find the others before they call out the army."

As they walked away, navigating to avoid puddles, she glanced back. "What of the ratters?"

"They decided not to be any more trouble. Oh, that reminds me," he said, stopping. "One of them relieved his master of a guinea for you. It's in my right pocket."

She glanced at his tight-fitting breeches. "I'm sure you can give it to me later."

"Are you encouraging me to be in debt?"

She met his eyes and hid a smile. "I am rich enough to ignore a guinea. Please, consider it yours."

"Falcon, I'm disappointed in you. Think of it as storming a spiked wall under enemy fire."

Fresh from violence, it made her shiver. "Have you done that?"

"Yes."

Despite what he said about his military life, he must have risked death so many times. "Then I can hardly retreat, can I?"

"I didn't think so." It was almost a purr of his own.

She wanted to laugh, but found a frown instead. "I'm perfectly aware of what you're doing. You think I can't resist a challenge."

"I seem to be right. Perhaps you need lessons. Sometimes it is wise to retreat."

"In this case?"

"Probably."

"It's only a pocket," she said.

She glanced around. They were still off to one side of the fair, with no one else nearby. They were in sight of the dozens of waiting carriages, but she couldn't make out the rest of their party, so she doubted they could see her.

Truth to tell, she didn't care. She wanted this excuse to touch him. Perhaps it was something to do with the violence, the danger, the thought of his perilous past . . .

She moved behind him and slid her hand into his pocket.

Of course it meant standing close. It meant sliding her hand against his hip as if there was scarcely anything between her and his naked body. Well, there *was* scarcely anything between her and his naked body, his warm naked body, but she would do it anyway.

In fact, since it was a challenge, she would raise the stakes. She pulled her hand out and stripped off her glove, then slid her hand in again.

She heard a choked laugh, and grinned. "Feeling for a small coin with gloves on would be so awkward," she said, spreading her fingers and exploring with them, hoping it tickled. What she discovered through two layers of cotton was strong, hard bone and warm muscle.

And pleasure in the firmness of it beneath her hand.

He was still, but she could feel tension. He'd invited this, however, challenged her to it. If it embarrassed him, it was his fault. She supposed she should be embarrassed, but she wasn't. Truly, she felt as if she was blossoming into someone very unlike Clarissa Greystone!

She moved slightly closer, curling her left arm around his torso, and pressing her cheek against his hot back. How firm he was. Muscle everywhere. Used to being close only with female bodies, she found this to be a magic all its own.

An image flashed into her mind—the groom's naked chest, rippling with well-defined muscles. The major wasn't as big a man, but would his naked chest look like that?

Would she ever find out?

Suddenly, so closely and hotly entwined, it seemed a moment for bald truth. "You're a fortune hunter, aren't you, Hawk?"

She felt his instant tension.

"Why else were you in Cheltenham? You knew about me and came to steal a march on the others. You tempted me into coming to Brighton, and you've been stalking me ever since. I'd rather there were truth between us."

She felt him breathe, three steady breaths. "And if I am?"

"I don't mind." Then she felt that went too far too soon. "But I make no promises, either."

"I see. But you won't blame a man for trying?"

"No," she said, smiling against his back. "I won't blame a man for trying." *And truth is, I can't wait until he wins.*

Smiling at her golden future, she angled her hand down and forward, following the deep pocket of the man who would one day be her husband. Whose body would be intimate with hers. She sucked in a deep, steadying breath and wriggled her fingers in search of the coin. She felt him suddenly stiffen.

"Am I tickling you?" she said unrepentantly.

"After a fashion."

Her fingers touched a bone, but then she realized there couldn't be a bone in the middle of his belly. Her little finger caught the edge of the coin as her mind grasped what she had to be touching.

A girls' school is not a haven of innocence. There had been many discussions, much sharing of knowledge, and not a few books stolen from fathers and brothers and smuggled into school.

According to a slim, alliterative volume called *The Annals of Aphrodite,* she was brushing against the Rod of Rapture. But didn't men only Mount to Magnificence just prior to Carnal Conquest?

She seized her coin, pulled her hand out, and retreated a few steps, pulling on the armor of her sensible glove.

He turned, not changed in any drastic way. A quick glance, however, showed that he was still Mounted to Magnificence. She knew her face had to be bright red.

"So," he said, "the raw recruit has scaled the walls but is defeated by the sight of fire within."

"Not defeated. Just not willing to be burned."

"Even if duty calls?"

"Duty, I think, calls in another direction entirely." She set off briskly for the carriages.

He soon caught up. "I'm not planning a rape."

"Good. I don't want to talk about it."

"How disappointing."

She fired a mock glare at him. "No, you are not going to challenge me into it." But she was loving, loving, loving this. To be able to talk this way with a man!

He laughed. "Another time, then."

But then Hawk sickeningly remembered that there were not going to be other times. Now that he was certain his Falcon had been involved with Deveril's death, he had hard choices to make—and he could see none that would lead to a happy ending.

For him or for her.

When they arrived back at the carriages, Van gave him a rather steely look. Since Maria was the chaperon for this excursion, Van would feel responsible, and he wasn't liking what he saw. Hawk wondered exactly what he saw.

The short version of their story satisfied Maria, but Hawk thought Van was still watchful. Not surprising. Despite long periods of separation, they knew each other very well.

"But what are we to do with the cat?" Maria asked, clearly not taken with the creature.

Hawk looked at the sleepy animal, which was filthy, scrawny, and missing part of an ear. "I'll keep it."

"Your father's dogs will eat it," Van predicted.

"I shall have to stand protector." Hawk climbed into the carriage, cat still bundled in his coat, feeling a maudlin need to protect something.

Clarissa needed advice, and Althea did not seem likely to help with this. Instead, once she'd changed from her soiled dress, she sought out her chaperon. Miss Hurstman, as usual, was in the front parlor reading what looked like a very scholarly book.

"Miss Hurstman, may I talk to you? About Major Hawkinville."

The woman's brows rose, but she put her book aside. "What has he done?"

"Nothing!" Clarissa roamed the small room. "Well, he's wooing me. He's a fortune hunter, I'm sure, even though he says he will inherit his father's estate. He admitted that it isn't very large, and he's as good as admitted that he does want to marry me. For my money—" She stopped for a breath.

Miss Hurstman studied her. "I assume there is no need for this panic?"

Clarissa, suddenly bereft of words, shook her head.

"Then what has caused it?"

The woman's calm was infectious. Clarissa sat down. "I didn't plan to marry. I saw no need to. But now, it is beginning to be appealing. You did warn me. I don't know if this all shows a flexible mind, or a weak one."

Miss Hurstman's lips twitched. "Clever girl. The difference between the two can be hard to judge. The main question—the only question, really—is, Will he make you a good husband for the next twenty, forty, sixty years?"

Clarissa could feel her eyes widen at the idea. "I don't know."

"Precisely. He is a handsome man, and I assume he knows how to please and interest a woman. His father certainly did."

"His father?"

"I knew him when I was young. A dashing military man with an eye to bettering himself."

A fortune hunter. Like father, like son? And yet the father had clearly settled for his modest estate.

Miss Hurstman was looking at her as if she could read every thought. "You cannot know enough about Major Hawkinville yet to make a rational decision, Clarissa. Time will solve that. Take your time."

"I know, but . . ." Clarissa looked at the older woman. "You speak of when you were young. Don't you remember? Just now, reason has nothing to do with it!"

Miss Hurstman's eyes twinkled. "That, my dear, is why young women have chaperons. Did Lady Vandeimen not play her part?"

Clarissa bit her lip, then said, "We were separated for a little while by a squall of bad weather."

"For a sufficiently little while, I hope?"

"Oh, yes. Nothing . . . nothing *truly* happened."

Miss Hurstman gave one of her snorts, whether of disapproval or amusement was hard to tell. "I do enjoy an enterprising scoundrel." Amusement, then. "Panic over?" she asked.

Surprisingly, it was. Perhaps it was simply being away from Hawk, or perhaps it was Miss Hurstman's dry practicality, but Clarissa didn't feel so caught in swirling madness anymore.

Time. That was the answer to her dilemma over Hawk Hawkinville, and she had no shortage of it other than that created by impatience. She would make herself wait a week or two without commitment. And without being compromised.

She did not fool herself that it would be easy.

She wished she could discuss her other problem with Miss Hurstman— the matter of Deveril's death, the way she kept speaking of it, the disastrous effects she seemed to have on other people's lives—but her trust did not go so deep as that.

Chapter Eleven

awk entered the Marine Parade house with his friends, but he went straight up to his room with the cat. He hoped to avoid Van, but wasn't surprised when he walked in not long after.

Hawk had taken the cat out of his jacket and was gently checking it for serious injuries.

"What are you going to do with it?" Van asked.

They might as well get to the topic at once. "I suspect Miss Greystone will wish me to care for it."

"And what Miss Greystone wishes is of importance to you?"

"Yes." The damnable thing was that he didn't want to lie to his friend, not even by implication, but he couldn't tell the truth. Above all, he needed time to think.

Surely there had to be some way to save Hawkinville from Slade, and Clarissa from the gallows.

The cat squawked as he touched a sore spot, but it was a polite complaint without claws attached.

"Quite the lady, aren't you?" he murmured.

Van came over. "Is it? Female, I mean."

"Yes, and not in bad shape, considering."

He finished his examination and put the cat down on the carpet. After a body-shaking shudder, it picked its way around the room like a tattered lady bountiful inspecting a lowly cottage.

"No problem with movement at all," Hawk said. "In fact, quite a dainty piece. Tolerable quarters for you, your ladyship?"

The cat gave him an inscrutable look.

Hawk picked up his jacket and contemplated its sorry state. He hadn't bothered to hire a valet since returning home, but he needed one now.

Van took it and went to the door. "Noons!" he shouted, and in moments his valet appeared, complained about the jacket, and went off to put it right.

The cat had sat to clean itself with dogged persistence.

"Tidiness above all. That's the spirit," Hawk said, scooping it up and carrying it to his washstand. There was a slight chance that if he was busy enough Van would put off the talk to another time.

"What you are about to get," he told the cat as he gingerly sat it in the wide china bowl, "is some assistance in the cleaning department. Do not be so rude as to scratch me."

He heard Van laugh and wondered if he was going to get away with it.

The cat had stiffened, but it wasn't frightened.

"Bear up like a good soldier," he said soothingly, and poured a little warm water over the side where blood was thick and sticky. The animal gave a yowl of complaint, but turned its head to lick. "No, no," he said blocking its head. "Let me. You can clean up the remains later."

He gently rubbed the blood till it softened, then washed it away under a new dribble of water. He was careful of the gash above it, and to soothe the cat, he kept talking.

"Not all of this blood is yours, is it? You must have done a fair bit of damage. It's my guess you could take on any rat you wanted. Beneath your dignity, was it, duchess? Risked having your neck broken over it, though, didn't you?"

As he started on a patch on one shoulder, Van interrupted his monologue. "What exactly are your plans in regard to Miss Greystone?"

Hawk hadn't really expected to get away with it.

"*In loco parentis* are you?"

"After a fashion, yes."

Hawk tried a mild deflection. "Marriage is making you damn dull."

Watching, Hawk could see Van control his temper. Damn. When they were boys a comment like that would have led either to a fight or to Van slamming out to work his temper off elsewhere. Either would have cut short the discussion.

They weren't boys anymore.

The cat licked his hand. It was probably a command for more water, so he supplied it, working on another spot.

"Maria thinks she is assisting a courtship," Van said. "A courtship very much to your advantage. Generous of her, wouldn't you say?"

Hawk winced at that one. "I do not necessarily need assistance."

"You are likely to get it anyway, women being women. The question is, Do you deserve it?"

Hawk lifted the cat from the muddy, bloody water and wrapped it in a towel for a quick dry. Though not scratching, it wasn't purring either.

He had to say something. "I'm not sure what you mean by that, Van."

Van rubbed a hand over his face. "I'm not either. Damn it all, Hawk, Maria likes Miss Greystone. She's playing at matchmaking. I don't want her hurt."

Ah, that Hawk could understand.

He put the cat down, and it stalked to a corner and began furiously cleaning itself.

"I don't want anyone hurt, Van. Not even a damn cat. A fine state of affairs for a veteran, isn't it?"

"A pretty natural state, I'd say. What's going on?"

Hawk realized that it was no good. Van wouldn't be deflected, or satisfied with a denial, and a good part of it was probably concern for him. The past was a strange beast. It lay dormant, appearing to be harmless, but it had claws and fangs and leaped up to take another bite at unexpected moments.

A poor analogy. He would embrace the past and the future it promised, if he could.

He would have to tell Van part of it, at least.

He emptied the dirty water into the slop bucket and washed his hands in fresh. "My father has mortgaged Hawkinville to Josiah Slade."

"That damned ironmonger? Why?" After a moment, Van asked, "How much?"

Hawk turned to him, drying his hands. "More than you can afford."

Van smiled. "Come on. I'm not ashamed to use my wife's money in a good cause."

"How much of it is left? Maria returned the money that her husband cheated your family out of. She's been doing that elsewhere, too, hasn't she? She has her dependents to take care of and Steynings to restore."

"You think patching the plaster at Steynings is more important than keeping Slade out of Hawkinville? Perdition, he'd be squire too, wouldn't he? Intolerable! How much?"

"Twenty thousand."

Van stared, struck silent.

"Even if you could lend me that much, when could I pay it back? Even squeezing the tenants for every penny, it would take decades."

"But what option do you have?" Van asked. "You can't let Slade . . ." But then he answered himself. "Ah. Miss Greystone."

Lying by implication, Hawk said, "Ah, indeed. Miss Greystone."

Van was frowning over it. "Do you love her?"

"How does one know love?"

"Believe me, Hawk, you know. Do you at least care for her?"

"Yes, of course. But will she marry me without protestations of love?"

Will she elope with you, you mean.

Van grimaced. "Probably not."

"With my father's example before me, I am naturally reluctant to woo an heiress under false pretenses."

But wasn't that exactly what he was doing?

The cat came to rub against his leg, miaowing. He scooped it up.

"The ratter told Clarissa the cat was called Fanny Laycock."

"I see why you had to thrash him."

It was cant for a low whore.

"But I'd better find another name before she remembers it." He looked into the cat's slitted green eyes. "Care to give me a hint? No, I don't think 'Your Highness' acceptable. I will call you Jetta. You are jet black, and you were *jeter'd,* as the French would say. *Getare* in Italian, but I'm afraid in Spanish it would merely mean 'snout.' "

He looked at Van, who was grinning at this byplay. At least he'd managed to change the subject. "I'd better go down to the kitchen and beg some scraps for her. I never thought to ask if you minded a cat in the house."

"No, of course not. But your father's dogs are going to eat her when you take her home."

Hawk looked at the cat again. "Somehow I doubt it."

He didn't escape scot-free. Van left the room with him and said quietly, "I need your word, Hawk, that you won't go beyond the line with Miss Greystone."

Hawk bit back anger. He had no right to it anyway.

"You have it, of course," he said and left, wondering if his friendships, too, were going to die in this bloody mess.

He got milk and bits of chicken for Jetta, then since the cook didn't seem to mind the intruder, he escaped out through the kitchen door. There was no thinking room there, however, so he went round to the street, to the seafront.

He was coatless and hatless, but he didn't care. The rough weather had driven nearly everyone off the seafront anyway, even though it wasn't raining at this moment. The wind still whipped, carrying damp air and even spray off the churning waves. He saw the packet from France bucking its way in and could imagine the state of the poor passengers.

It was good weather for hard thinking, though. Rough and clean.

Did he love Clarissa? He had no experience of love, so how could he know? But Van said he'd know, so it couldn't be love. Or not that kind of love. His feelings were close to those that he had for Van and Con, and that he'd had for some other friends in the army.

Friends, then. He and Clarissa were, in a fragile way, friends. He groaned into the wind. That made it worse. Betrayal in love was a theoretical evil. Betrayal of friendship . . .

And damn it, now Maria and thus Van—a deep and necessary friend— were tangled up in the affair.

He reined in his panicked mind. When had his mind last been panicked?

Fact one. Clarissa had at the least been present at Deveril's murder. It was the only rational explanation for her reaction to the knife and her knowing the exact date.

Hypothesis. She might have killed him herself, but it would have been in self-defense, not to get his money.

Was he besotted to think that? No. He hadn't known her long, but he knew her well enough to know she couldn't be a coldhearted, greedy villain. A crime of passion was much more in keeping.

Fact two. If it came out that she had killed a peer of the realm under any provocation, she might hang for it. Or at least be transported. At best, she would have to await trial in prison among the scum of the world.

Therefore, her crime could never be made public.

It settled Hawk to realize that as an absolute certainty.

He would tear down Hawk in the Vale himself before it came to that.

Having reached that bleak point, he found he could think properly again.

What if she had only been witness to the killing? Perhaps someone else had killed Deveril to save her. Did that really fit better, or did he just want it to be so? It was no great improvement. She would still be an accessory to the murder and liable to the same punishment, and he could hardly send a man to trial for defending her.

However, if he could not prosecute anyone for murder, he was unlikely to break the will.

He leaned against a wooden railing, cursing softly into the snarling sea.

Always, always, always was the fact that the will had been forged and planted in Deveril's house. It shattered any illusion of noble deeds. A cunning rogue was behind that, and Hawk couldn't believe that he intended to leave Clarissa in peaceful possession of a fortune.

So, even walking away from Clarissa and leaving her in peace was not an option.

He circled and circled it, and came down to the heart of the matter. He could persuade her to elope.

No question of marrying her in the normal way. As soon as he applied to the Duke of Belcraven his family would be investigated. The most casual search would uncover that his father was a Gaspard, and probably that he was within days of being pronounced Viscount Deveril. Even if Belcraven was willing to permit the marriage, he would tell Clarissa, and that would be that. He wasn't sure she would be able to bear the thought of being Lady Deveril one day, but he knew she wouldn't forgive the deception.

Elope, then. He would have to pretend love, but he was at least very fond of her. He would not be like his father. She would not have cause to complain of neglect. With luck she wouldn't have to be Lady Deveril for a long time, so perhaps it wouldn't be a terrible blow.

But what if it was? What if the blow, in particular the deception behind it, was enough to kill all affection? Would he end up in a marriage as bitter as that of his parents', with one lost wedding-night child to show for it?

He could do that to himself for Hawkinville, but not to her. Not to his Falcon, who was in such fledgling flight in search of life.

And anyway, he thought with a wry laugh, he'd promised Van. He was sure Van would see an elopement as going far beyond the line.

Which brought him, via a sharp sense of loss, back to the killer. Was there, perhaps, another way . . . ?

Clarissa and Althea were promised to a birthday party being given that evening by Lady Babbington for Florence. Clarissa didn't really want to go, but Florence was an old school friend, and it would do no good to stay home drowning in longing, doubts, and questions. It was to be an event for young ladies only, so at least she wouldn't have to deal with Hawk again.

She found that the Babbingtons' small drawing room felt almost like the senior girls' parlor at Miss Mallory's and slid with relief into the uncomplicated past. Soon she was chattering and giggling, and the high spirits continued over dinner since, unlike at school, wine was served with the meal.

Perhaps that was why the after-dinner chatter turned naughty, especially when it was revealed that Florence had made a transcription of *The Annals of Aphrodite*. As those new to the book huddled to read it, whispering aloud the more exciting phrases, Clarissa wondered how many of them had acquired a little practical experience of the Risen Rod of Rapture.

Then Florence placed letter cards in a bag and invited everyone to pick two to find the initials of their future husband. Clarissa was interested to note how many of the ten young women clearly hoped for a particular set of initials.

Clarissa's heart pounded when her first letter was a *G*, but then she lost all faith when the second turned out to be a *B*.

Suggestions were called out.

"Gregory Beeston."

"Lord Godfrey Breem."

"Florence," said one, "isn't your brother called Giles?"

"But he's married," Florence pointed out.

"Is he still as handsome?" Clarissa asked, and recited her poem. It received great applause, and they all began to put together admiring doggerel.

"George Brummel," Lady Violet Stavering suggested. She had been at Miss Mallory's too, but had considered Clarissa beneath her notice. She still liked to cloak herself in an air of bored sophistication and was not taking part in the versification.

"He could certainly use your fortune, Clarissa," she added.

Clarissa might sometimes feel at sea in society, but she could swim like a fish in schoolgirl malice. "So could nearly everyone," she said, dropping her letters back into the bag. "Including your brother, Violet. But I am hardly likely to bestow my riches on an elderly and broken dandy like Brummel. If I enter into trade, I will buy the highest quality."

"Such as Major George Hawkinville?" purred Lady Violet.

So their meetings had been observed. Clarissa willed herself not to blush. "Perhaps." But she added, "Or some other young, honorable man."

Florence leaped in with suggestions, and Clarissa regretted the spark of unpleasantness at her friend's party. Soon every eligible man of Brighton was being assessed with startling frankness.

Mr. Haig-Porter's legs were too thin, Lord Simon Rutherford's fingers too short and fat. Sir Rupert Grange laughed like a donkey, and Viscount Laverley had a chest so narrow it was surprising he could breathe.

"But a viscount," said Cecilia Porteous tentatively. "It is a consideration."

Nearly everyone agreed that a peer of the realm might be excused some flaws.

"Even Lord Deveril," murmured Lady Violet.

"Don't be a cat, Vi," snapped Florence. "We all know poor Clarissa didn't want to marry him."

"And we thanked heavens for his timely death," agreed Lady Violet sweetly.

Clarissa stiffened, wondering if Lady Violet suspected.

But that was ridiculous. She was simply scratching for the fun of it.

She was saved by an interruption from Miriam Mosely. "I don't know how it is that men like Lord Vandeimen and Lord Amleigh, who have both title and physique, are snapped up before they properly appear on the market. I think it vastly unfair!"

"But remember," said Lady Violet, "Lord Vandeimen was thought to be as rolled up as Brummel, and drowning in gaming and drink as well, before he married the Golden Lily."

This was news to Clarissa, and she recognized that Lady Violet had raised it because the Vandeimens were friends of Clarissa's. She would very much like to put snails in Violet's bed. Again.

She hoped the comment would be ignored, but some others demanded details. Lady Violet chose a sugarplum and bit into it. "Oh, Vandeimen came home from the war to find his father dead and the estates quite ruined."

"Hardly like Brummel, then," said Clarissa.

Lady Violet was not silenced. "He consoled himself with drink and the tables, but then had the good fortune to snare the rich Mrs. Celestin. Trade, you know."

"That's not true!" objected Dottie Ffyfe. "She married a merchant, but she was born into a good family. She's a connection of mine!"

Lady Violet's lips tightened, but she shrugged. "A woman moves to her husband's level upon marriage. First trade. And a foreigner. Then a demon." She allowed a pause for effect before continuing, "According to my brother, in the army he was known as Demon Vandeimen."

Everyone was now leaning forward avidly, and Clarissa felt wretched for having started this. Lord and Lady Vandeimen were both properly behaved and kind, and obviously in love. Someone else who was being tarnished by association with her.

"My brother says that they've been close friends forever," Violet continued, lapping up being the center of attention. "Vandeimen and Amleigh. And," she added with a sly look at Clarissa, "Major Hawkinville."

Clarissa smiled back in a way that she hoped said she was politely bored to death.

"All born and raised near here," Violet continued. "Reggie said that they each have a tattoo on their chest." Someone gasped. "Said he'd seen Lord Amleigh's in the army, and been told about the others."

She looked around, licking sugar off her fingers. "A hawk for Major Hawkinville, a dragon for Lord Amleigh." Then she added, pink tongue circling her lips, "And a demon for Lord Vandeimen."

The synchronous inhalation made a kind of *oooh* around the room.

"What a pity," said Miriam, "that we are unlikely to ever see that."

But Clarissa was thinking how wonderful it would be to see that, because it would mean she was seeing Hawk's naked chest. Impossible, of course, short of marriage.

Marriage.

It was all very well for Miss Hurstman to talk about reason, and waiting, and thinking of the years of marriage, but could she bear *not* to do it? Wouldn't she regret it all her life, wondering what it might have been? Whether it might have been true heaven . . .

". . . Hawkinville."

With a start, she realized that they were talking about Hawk—as if he were a piece of meat on a butcher's slab.

"Handsome."

"Perhaps a little lightly built."

"But wide shoulders."

"And excellent thighs!"

Thighs! Sally Highcroft had been looking at Hawk's thighs?

"Delicious blue eyes."

"I prefer brown myself," said Violet.

Clarissa was astonished to find that her fingers were trying to make claws.

It was Althea, however, who spoke up. "I don't think it at all seemly to talk about a gentleman in this way."

Violet laughed. Her practiced laugh that said that others were silly, unsophisticated ninnies. "They do it about us all the time, according to my brother."

"Ladies," said Althea, "should set a higher standard. And we should be more respectful of those who fought for us in the war."

This did subdue everyone, and Clarissa flashed Althea a grateful smile.

"But did he fight?" asked Violet, who never stayed subdued for long. "Quartermastering, I believe."

Again Althea was there first. "Such administrative matters are extremely important, Lady Violet. My late fiancé was in the army, and he often said so."

"You cannot deny that an officer who was often in battle is more dashing."

"No. But I can deny that dash is the most important thing about any gentleman!"

Althea was in her Early Christian Martyr mood, and clearly ready to throw herself to the lions. Or turn into one. Poor Florence was looking close to tears, so Clarissa rushed in. "There are any number of eligible names being discussed here who never went to war at all. We can surely assess each gentleman as to his qualities." Remembering Miss Hurstman's words, she added, "Their qualities as husbands over the next twenty, forty, sixty years."

"Lud!" exclaimed Florence, but with a grateful look, "what a dismal thought. They'll all be boring, bulging, and bald by then."

"So will most of us," said Althea, still looking militant.

"Not bald," Clarissa pointed out.

"Gray, then," said Althea, but she relaxed.

"Thank heavens for the dye pot—"

Violet was interrupted by a maid, and Florence leaped up with obvious relief. "Speaking of futures, I have a special treat for us. The fortune-teller Madame Mystique has been engaged to give us each a reading. I'm sure one of the things she will be able to predict will be our marital fate. Now, who would like to go first?"

Everyone politely urged Florence to be first, and when she left, Clarissa led a determined foray into talk about fashion. Violet would still be a cat, but it was unlikely to become quite so personal.

Florence returned blushing, and Violet leaped up to go next.

"Well," Sally asked, "what did she say? Are you allowed to tell?"

"It's not like a wish, Sally." Florence sat down among them. "She spoke of a man of honor and good family. And she mentioned his high brow." She looked around, blushing. "That does sound rather like Lord Arthur Carlyon, doesn't it?"

So, that was where Florence's interest lay. A pleasant man who was showing signs of losing his hair. A high brow. Madame Mystique was clearly tactful, and clever as well.

They had played at fortune-telling at school, so she understood how it was done. If possible, the fortune-teller learned about her clients beforehand, and, of course, certain things could please almost everyone. Promises of happiness in love and of good fortune. Flattering comments about strength and wisdom. In addition, and most important, a fortune-teller watched to see what random comments triggered a response.

Having been engaged for this event, Madame Mystique would have learned about Florence, at the very least. She might even have been given the guest list. Clarissa assumed she would be told about Hawk. Handsome, honorable, and a war hero, and perhaps something cryptic about a bird.

Violet returned not so pleased, having been told that the ideal husband for her was not highborn, but wealthy. "The woman is a charlatan!"

But Miriam returned with high hopes of Sir Ralph Willoughby. "But Queen Cleopatra said I must be bolder with him!"

"Queen Cleopatra?" Florence asked.

"Apparently sometimes Queen Cleopatra speaks through Madame to give a special message. She said that if I want Sir Ralph to show the depth of his feelings, I . . . must not be so nervous of being alone with him."

She looked around for advice.

Clarissa, thinking of her time at the fair with Hawk, knew that Queen Cleopatra had the right idea, but she wouldn't say so with Violet listening.

Althea said, "She is right, after a fashion, Miriam. I have, after all, been engaged to marry. Some men find it hard to show their feeling when constantly under the eye of others. This does not mean that you should go far apart with him, or put yourself in danger."

"Oh," said Miriam, her thoughts obviously churning. Her eyes flickered around the group. "She also said . . ."

"Yes?"

"That touch could encourage a gentleman."

Touch! Clarissa couldn't imagine Miriam sliding her hand into Sir Ralph's pocket.

"She said that when most touches are improper, they can have great power. That since ladies are generally gloved, our naked hands have"—she looked at her own pale hand—"sensual power."

"Naked!" exclaimed Florence, looking at her own hand. "I suppose we are gloved when out of the house. So we make an excuse to take off our gloves—"

"And then touch his skin," said Miriam, who looked as if she didn't quite believe what she was saying.

Clarissa thought about the fair, about sticky buns, and Hawk's hand on her wrist. A naked wrist . . .

"Lud!" said Lady Violet. "You're all talking like Haymarket whores. The woman is depraved."

Miriam flushed. "We're only talking about touching hands, Violet!"

"Or faces, I suppose," said Florence, eyes bright with mischief. "Hands and faces are the only naked spots available, aren't they? No wonder men go around so wrapped up. It's probably like armor."

They fell into a laughing view of a world where men were terrified of attacking female hands, but then it was Clarissa's turn to visit Madame Mystique.

Chapter Twelve

She was smiling as she followed the maid to the room set aside and hoping that she, too, would be advised by the naughty Queen Cleopatra. The dispensing of such titillating advice doubtless explained the woman's popularity.

The maid opened the door to reveal a curtain. Clarissa pushed it aside and entered the room.

Gloom halted her. If this room had windows, the curtains were drawn, for there seemed to be no natural light.

There was some light, however. Hanging oil lamps with dark, jewel-colored glass turned the room into a mysterious cave of swaying shadows. The oil must be perfumed, for a sweet, exotic tang wafted through the air, making this place like an otherworld, nothing to do with fashionable Brighton at all. Clarissa shivered, then reminded herself that this was all theatrics.

Madame Mystique sat behind a table covered with a pale, shimmering cloth. She wore some kind of dark silken robe and a veil over the lower half of her face. Her hair was covered by a helmet of silver coins that hung down to her shoulders in back and to her eyebrows in front. Her large eyes were heavily outlined in black.

"Sit," she said in a soft foreign voice, "and I will reveal the secrets of your heart."

Clarissa knew that running away now would make her look the fool, so despite a flash of irrational panic, she took the few steps and sat down across the table from the woman.

There was nothing to fear here, and yet wariness was tightening her shoulders and causing her heart to pound. Perhaps it was simply the intent look in the woman's eyes, but, of course, she would only be studying her for things to use in her "predictions."

There was no crystal ball. Instead, the table was scattered with an assortment of items—well-used cards with strange designs, carved sticks, disks with markings, unpolished stones in many shapes and colors, and ornate ribbons, some of them knotted.

"Surely I know the secrets of my own heart," she said as lightly as she could. "I would rather you tell me something I do not know."

"Indeed? Then consider the items on the table," the fortune-teller said with an elegant sweep of a beringed hand, "and pick the three that interest you most."

Clarissa stared at the objects, wondering what each meant. She didn't believe in fortune-telling, but even so she was suddenly nervous of letting this woman probe. She picked ordinary, unrevealing things—one stick, a plain length of ribbon, and a clear chunk of crystal.

Madame Mystique took them, holding them. "You have secrets. Many secrets. And they trouble you greatly."

Clarissa stiffened with annoyance. Of course someone who picked the plainest items was trying to hide things. "Everyone has secrets."

"Not at all." The large eyes smiled. "Have you not noticed how many people long to tell their secrets if they can only find an excuse? You, however, have true secrets. You would be afraid to whisper them into the ground for fear that the growing grass would speak of them."

Clarissa almost rose to leave, but she remembered in time that any sharp reaction would tell Madame Mystique that her guess was correct. She produced a shrug. "Then I am managing to keep them secret from myself as well."

But why was the woman touching on such matters? Was it possible she truly did have powers? That could be disastrous!

Cradling the items, the woman asked, "What did you come here to learn?"

"I didn't. You are simply a party favor." She intended it to be a slight.

The woman was as impassive as the Sphinx, however, and Clarissa realized that her eye decoration was in the Egyptian style. "But you came. What brought you here? What do you wish to learn?"

After a moment, Clarissa said the obvious. "Something about my future husband." That should not lead to dangerous matters.

"Very well." The fortune-teller let the objects fall on the table and picked up the three cards they landed on. She laid them in front of Clarissa, each with a sharp snap. "He will be handsome. He will be brave . . ."

Snap. "He will be poorer than you."

Clarissa stared, her heart thundering now. Few young ladies married poorer men. But then she almost sagged with relief. Madame Mystique had done her preparatory work and knew Clarissa was the Devil's Heiress.

"How tedious," she drawled. "Can you tell me nothing more?"

"What do you truly wish to know?"

Will Hawk offer marriage? Should I accept? Will he stir the issue of Deveril's death to our destruction? Whom can I trust?

Unable to ask the questions that mattered, Clarissa stared at Madame Mystique.

The woman exclaimed with exasperation. "Ah! You are so guarded. Knotted. You will strangle yourself!"

She seized Clarissa's right hand to peer at the lines. Clarissa thought of fighting free, but part of her had to know what the woman would say next.

"Ah," said Madame Mystique again, but softly this time. "Now I see. I see blood. I see a knife."

Clarissa began to drag her hand away, but then she remembered. The woman was fishing for a reaction. That was how fortune-tellers worked. That and prior knowledge.

But a chill swept over her, as if the cold wind outside was whistling through the curtains. What strange waters to fish in.

She calmly pulled her hand free. On the slight chance that Madame Mystique might have the true sight, she must get away from her.

"You have nothing to fear from me," said the woman, "but you are right to be afraid. Your secrets are dangerous." In a very soft voice she added, "A murder, yes?"

Clarissa was nailed in place, not knowing whether to stay or flee.

"A murder linked to money. Much money. But it is poisoned, my dear. It comes from evil and will always carry evil. You must escape its toils."

"I don't know what you're talking about." Clarissa instantly knew she shouldn't have spoken, because all the willpower in the world couldn't make her voice sound convincing. But her silence must have been eloquent, too.

Sweat was sending chills down her spine, and she didn't know what to do. It was as if the woman were forcing open a door into the past, into secrets and places that must stay in the dark forever.

"Listen to me." The fortune-teller leaned forward, capturing Clarissa with her large, dark eyes. "The money will bring you nothing but pain. You must tell the truth about it or it will cause you agony and death. Guard yourself, guard yourself! There are rogues around you who will cause your ruin."

Rogues? Clarissa felt her heart rise up to choke her.

The Company of Rogues?

But then she shivered with relief. "Rogues" was just a word. A word for scoundrels. Of course a person should avoid scoundrels. This woman couldn't possibly know about the Company of Rogues.

And all she had said could come from common knowledge. She was the Devil's Heiress. Lord Deveril had been stabbed to death, and she'd ended up with his undoubtedly dirty money. She couldn't imagine why Madame Mystique was making such high drama out of it except for effect.

Perhaps having at least one guest totter out of the room white and shaking was good for business.

"I inherited a great deal of money from a man who was murdered," she said flatly. "The whole world knows that. I thought you were going to tell me something new."

The flash of annoyance in the woman's eyes was satisfying, but Clarissa wanted to leave. Would it hint at guilt?

"You refuse to recognize your danger," the woman said. "I will ask Queen Cleopatra to advise you."

Ah, the sensual advice. That she could deal with. But then the clear chime of a bell almost shocked her out of her chair.

"I am Cleopatra, Queen of the Nile," said Madame Mystique in a high-pitched, ethereal voice. "My handmaiden speaks for me."

Despite herself, Clarissa couldn't help a shiver.

"Beware," the voice sang out. "Beware all rogues!"

It's just a word.

"Beware a man with the initials *N.D.*"

Clarissa stopped breathing.

Nicholas Delaney?

Could Madame Mystique have found out the name of the leader of the Rogues? Impossible!

Could she have the true gift?

If so, how much had the woman seen in her hand? Had she seen whose blood, whose knife? And what was this danger that surrounded her, connected to the money?

"N.D. does not want you to tell the truth," the eerie voice continued, "but you must. Only then will you be free. Heed my words. Heed them, or you will die within the year."

Die? Clarissa felt as if she were fighting for breath. Tell the truth? She couldn't! She couldn't possibly.

The dark-lined eyes opened. "Queen Cleopatra does not speak to everyone," Madame Mystique said in her ordinary voice. "I hope what she said was useful."

"You don't know?"

"I am merely the vessel for her words." The dark eyes studied her. "You are upset. I am sorry. She usually brings good advice."

Clarissa somehow dragged herself out of her trance. The woman must never know how close her words had come to dangerous matters. "Everything I've heard here was nonsense," she said. "In fact, you didn't really predict my future at all."

Madame Mystique did not seem upset. She picked up the plain crystal and placed it in Clarissa's hand, closing her fingers over it. "You do not believe, but keep this stone. It will help you when your troubles begin."

Clarissa could only think how Hawk's touch had made her shiver, and this one made her shudder. She wanted to leave the woman convinced that her predictions and warnings had been meaningless, but hunt as she might she could not find the right words. In the end she simply turned and walked out of the room.

She took a moment to steady herself, slapping her cheeks a little since she was sure she was pale. Then she returned to the drawing room, trying for a light smile.

Someone else left to see Madame Mystique, and the others began questioning Clarissa.

"What did she say?"

"Whom are you to marry?"

"Was it frightening?" Althea asked. "You look a little pale."

Clarissa found a shrug. "Terrifying! She said I would marry a man poorer than myself."

"But a truth," said Violet.

"Yes, of course. Clearly she has the gift. Althea, do you have one of your headaches?"

Althea, bless her, took her cue. "I'm afraid so, Clarissa. I don't wish to spoil your enjoyment . . ."

"Not at all. It is late." She thanked Florence for the party, and soon they were out in the fresh air with their footman for escort on the short walk home.

"You seem upset," Althea said as they walked.

"Not really, but it was a silly event."

Althea glanced at her. "Because they were discussing Major Hawkinville?"

That was a much safer speculation than any other, so Clarissa smiled and admitted it.

In bed, however, anxiety defeated sleep.

Madame Mystique had clearly seen more than could be guessed or discovered. What if she talked? She might even go to the magistrates to tell them about a young woman involved with blood and murder. When people realized the young woman was the murdered Lord Deveril's betrothed and heir, might that not start speculation?

The Rogues had clearly covered up the events of that night very skillfully, but was it skillful enough to resist an intense investigation?

She tried to tell herself that Madame Mystique would see no profit in going to the authorities. Magistrates tended to look sourly on such fairground tricks, and the woman had no proof.

Clarissa couldn't be sure, though. She couldn't be sure!

And the woman had predicted her *death* if she didn't somehow get rid of the money.

No, if she didn't tell the truth about the money.

What truth? The will, at least, was honest.

"Truth" must refer to the fact that a person involved in a death could not benefit from it. That had been explained to her. Mr. Delaney had not been crude about it, but she'd understood. If she let slip the truth about Lord Deveril's death, many people would suffer, including her. She was ashamed to think that at the time she'd appeared to be the sort of ninny who would gabble, but she hadn't been at her best.

And perhaps she was that sort of ninny. She knew she'd said a few things to Hawk that she shouldn't have.

She couldn't tell the truth, though. That was completely impossible.

What should she do?

She chewed on her knuckle. The Rogues should be warned about this danger. She didn't want to contact Mr. Delaney. She would have to confess to being less than reliable, but on top of that, they all made her uneasy. They seemed to be good men, honorable men. Except perhaps the brutish Marquess of Arden. But they were also ruthless. Only think how coolly they'd re-acted to bloody murder! Mr. Delaney had seemed almost amused.

Perhaps, behind their superficial gloss, they were too like Arden, given to violence when crossed.

But she had to tell them. They had risked much for her, so she must guard them. She slipped out of bed and lit a candle from her night-light. When Althea did not stir, she wrote a very carefully phrased warning to Nicholas Delaney. She folded it, sealed it, and returned to bed to plot how to get it into the post without anyone knowing. She might be going to extremes, but Miss Hurstman was bound to question her about the connection, and she didn't want to tangle in any more deceit.

Madame Mystique collected the items from the table and left her assistant, Samuel, to clear away the lamps and curtains. She left the room, hearing the last of the guests taking an excited farewell, and dispatched a maid to tell Lady Babbington that she was ready to leave.

The plump and amiable lady bustled into view, beaming. "Thank you so much, Madame Mystique! The girls are thrilled with your prognostications."

Thérèse smiled. Young women were always excited by ways to entice and entrance men.

Lady Babbington extended the guineas, then tittered. "They talk of cross-ing a gypsy's palm with gold, don't they?"

Older women, too.

"But I am not a gypsy, madame. My art is an older one than theirs." She held out her hand, and when the flustered woman put the money into it, she added, "But sometimes visions come to me. You are a very fortunate woman, madame, blessed by the fates with a healthy family and a loving husband."

"Oh, yes. Yes indeed!"

"But the fires perhaps only smolder?" She reached into her bag of items and pulled out a ribbon at random. A blue one. "Blue," she said, "is your color of power. Take this ribbon, Lady Babbington, and wear it on your per-son at all times. It reminds you of your younger days, yes? When you and your husband first fell in love?"

Lady Babbington looked a little blank, but then said, "I'm sure I had rib-bons of all kinds then."

"You will recall. You will recall much about those times. Then you will look at your husband and see that man who thrilled you so, and it will be so again."

The woman was pink but fascinated. She even looked younger.

Madame Mystique patted her on the hand. "You and your husband are really no different, are you, now? Good night, my lady, and thank you for engaging me."

"Oh. Good night, I'm sure."

Madame Mystique made her way out of the back of the house. Or rather, Thérèse Bellaire did, not totally disappointed by her night's work. A number of women might lead more interesting lives because of it—and she had met Deveril's heiress.

Not what she had expected. More brain and steel. But she'd confirmed by her reactions that the Rogues were involved.

That Nicholas was involved.

She waited in the basement for Samuel, telling fortunes for free for the servants, promising them windfalls, handsome admirers, and appreciation for their talent.

For so many people, that was all they wanted, to be appreciated, though often for talents they did not possess. The cook was not the finest, but a simple compliment about her cake and she preened. When she was told she was appreciated, she doubtless saw herself the talk of Brighton for her culinary skills.

The lanky footman in the overlarge livery, Adam's apple bobbing, probably saw himself as the object of every housemaid's lust. The shy, dough-faced maid envisioned being snatched up by a solid tradesman because of her unpretentious goodness.

This fortune-telling was such an easy business that she could no doubt make her living at it forever. But she would have her fortune.

If Deveril had not already been dead, she would have killed him for stealing it from her two years ago. Now her sole purpose was to get it back. It was hers, earned in the sweetest ploy ever imagined, and Deveril would not have been able to steal it if not for Nicholas Delaney and his Company of Rogues.

Samuel arrived, the curtains in a bundle and the empty lamps dangling from his big right hand.

A strapping lad for seventeen, and of course he was devoted to her.

She adored him, as she adored all handsome young men . . .

As a tiger adores goats.

She rose and took her leave of the dazzled servants, who would spread the word. No, Madame Mystique would never lack work here in Brighton. But her main concern was her plan.

Would the heiress heed her warning? Would she confide in someone that the Rogues had killed Deveril and forged that will? Alas, it was unlikely, and she hadn't spilled any information.

Too much brain and spine.

As she walked to her Ship Street establishment, she mourned her pretty, elegant plan. Prove the will false—and entangle the Rogues in a murder charge at the same time—and the new Lord Deveril would have the money.

Mrs. Rowland's invalid husband would die, and after a short interval, the widow would become Lady Deveril. A little while longer and she would be a widow again, possessed of all that money. The son could have the paltry estate.

So delightfully devious. Whatever suspicions people might have, she would leave for the Americas legally possessed of the wealth. But she had failed to find evidence. Her only hope now was the Hawk.

If he did the job for her, the plan could still work. She had Squire Hawkinville in the palm of her hand. It had added spice to this rather tedious work to dance beneath the Hawk's nose and be overlooked. Perhaps it would be even more delicious if he squeezed the heiress dry for her.

She climbed the steps to her house and unlocked the door, sending Samuel off to put the things away, but with a look he recognized, that made him blush.

Ah, seventeen.

She went to her room and stripped off Madame Mystique, slipping into a silk robe that had been appreciated by Napoleon himself. Tomorrow, alas, she would have to return to Hawk in the Vale for a while, to be that dreary Mrs. Rowland. Her excuse for absence was that she was pursuing an elusive inheritance. But it would not do to be away too long.

All the more reason to enjoy tonight.

She rang her bell and summoned her dinner—and her goat.

Hawk slept that night. If he'd not learned to sleep through external and internal turmoil, he wouldn't have survived a month in his army work. He'd formed his plan anyway. He'd found the way out, but it would be stronger if he could squeeze a bit more information out of Clarissa.

It was a way out that would mean that she would never speak to him again. He preferred to think of it as freeing her from him.

Over breakfast he felt Van observing him, but the talk was all gossip and chatter. Maria had received a letter with a new view on Caroline Lamb's novel, *Glenarvon.* It kept her interested, as she'd witnessed several of the scandalous incidents between the lady and Byron.

Con, Susan, and de Vere were to leave today, claiming that a little Brighton was enough for them. Everyone rose to see them on their way.

Then Maria said, "The sun's shining! We must go out immediately before it rains again."

Van laughed. "It's not quite that dire, my dear."

"Is it not?"

"I'll send a note to see if Miss Greystone and Miss Trist wish to join us."

Hawk met Van's look blandly and received a distinctly warning look in return.

"Don't worry," he said as they left the room. "I have absolutely no intention of seducing Miss Greystone today."

It was, alas, damnably true.

Chapter Thirteen

By the time breakfast was over, Clarissa had come up with and discarded any number of cunning plans for posting her letter. In the end, she chose the simplest. While Miss Hurstman was reading the newspaper, and Althea was writing her daily letter home, she slipped out of the house and hurried through the few streets to the post office.

If Mr. Crawford thought it strange to see a young lady alone, he made no comment.

Clarissa gave him the letter. "Can you tell me how soon it will be there, please?"

He studied the address. "Near Yeovil? Tomorrow, dear lady. I will make sure it leaves on the earliest and best mail."

His benign smile said he thought it was a love missive. But then he looked at the letter again. "Mr. Delaney of Red Oaks? Why, I am almost certain that your companion, Miss Hurstman, sent a letter to exactly that address not many days ago."

It hadn't occurred to her that a man like Mr. Crawford would keep track of letters passing through his hands. Lord help her, had she just done something else stupid?

But then the full meaning struck her.

Miss Hurstman!

Miss Hurstman in league with the Rogues?

She hadn't time to analyze it now, with Mr. Crawford smiling at her. She took the letter out of his fingers. "If Miss Hurstman has already written to Mr. Delaney, then this is old news, I'm afraid." She pasted on a carefree smile. "Thank you, Mr. Crawford."

She hurried away, going two streets before she let herself pause to think. It was absurd, but she felt as if someone was watching her, looking for signs of guilt.

It was still early, so only the most hardy were out for brisk walks, but she couldn't stand here like a statue. And if she didn't get home, she would be missed. She felt like tearing up the letter and throwing the scraps into the sea, but she immediately thought of someone chasing after them and piecing them together.

Ridiculous. She was going mad.

At the very least, she was thoroughly rattled and needed someone to talk to. Someone to trust. First Madame Mystique, now Miss Hurstman.

She pushed the letter to the bottom of her pocket and hurried back to Broad Street, trying to make sense of things.

Crawford could be wrong, but that was outlandish.

So, Miss Hurstman knew Mr. Delaney.

There was no getting around it. It was likely that Mr. Delaney had arranged for Miss Hurstman to be Clarissa's chaperon here in Brighton. And she could see why. It must have worried him that she was moving out into the world, so he had installed what amounted to a warder. Miss Hurstman hadn't been a very good one or she'd have stuck with Clarissa at all times, but perhaps the lady didn't understand all that was at stake.

The huge question was, What was Miss Hurstman supposed to do if Clarissa posed a threat?

What could the Rogues do—except kill her?

She couldn't believe it, but she forced herself to be logical about it. They would have no other way of keeping themselves and their loved ones safe. It wasn't just the Rogues and herself. Beth Arden was at risk. Blanche Hardcastle was at greatest risk of all.

Madame Mystique had warned of death . . .

She came to a sudden stop, then stepped hastily into Manchester Street. After a moment, she carefully peered around the corner. On the opposite side of the Marine Parade, the distinctively straight and drab figure of Miss Hurstman was talking to a blond man.

To Nicholas Delaney!

He was already here, because Miss Hurstman had summoned him. And it must have been at least two days ago, perhaps because Hawk was courting her. The Hawk. Miss Hurstman had been alarmed to hear that he was a skilled investigator.

Clarissa headed up Manchester Street to come down Broad Street from the other end.

Mr. Delaney was here, so she could go to him and tell him about Madame Mystique. If she trusted him. She could also assure him that she was no danger to him. Would he believe her?

He'd been kind to her once. He'd been the only one to realize that night that she had been ignored. Beth was being comforted by the marquess, Blanche by Major Beaumont, but she had been left shivering alone. He'd taken her in his arms and somehow given her the feeling that it wasn't so bad and that everything would be all right.

But still, what was she to expect of a man who entered a bloody scene of murder and complained that he'd "missed the action"?

She paused outside the door to her house, vaguely understanding people who threw themselves into the ocean to escape a dilemma. She would not be so weak, though. She had to do the right thing—the right thing for Beth and Blanche, and also for herself. She did not want to die over this.

She slipped in but did not make it upstairs undetected. Althea came out of the front parlor. "Have you been out? I thought it must be Miss Hurstman. She received a note and went out. There's a message here from Lady Vandeimen."

At least Althea didn't ask where Clarissa had been. Clarissa took the note and opened it. "We're invited to walk with them again."

"And Major Hawkinville?" teased Althea.

Everything stopped for Clarissa, then moved again in new patterns. "And Major Hawkinville. I will send an acceptance and then change into a prettier dress."

As she went to the desk she asked, "Where did Miss Hurstman go?"

"She didn't say. Where did you go?"

"I wanted a bit of fresh air before the crowds."

Clarissa dashed off the note and summoned the footman to take it. Then she called for Elsie and went to change. She chose the rust-and-cream dress she'd worn on the first day, and took her parasol as well. It had so little chance to be useful.

Hawk. The one person she could trust was Hawk. Well, she trusted Althea, but Althea was of no use in this predicament. In fact, she was another burden for Clarissa. Althea must not become embroiled in this.

With Hawk, Clarissa knew exactly where she was. He was a fortune hunter. Other than that, he was as honorable as could be. And he was the Hawk. He would protect her.

Especially, she thought suddenly, if they were married. Once they were married his interests would entirely match hers. She would have to tell him the truth, of course—but not until they were married. For Beth, and Blanche, and the Rogues, she could not tell him the truth before.

She grieved for that, for she would like to marry him with full honesty between them, but it was the only way. And she couldn't believe that it would be a terrible blow to him. After all, he'd said he wished he could kill Deveril for her. No one could look on Deveril's death as a wrongful act. Except perhaps a court of law.

So. Enough of playful games. She must bring Hawk to the point of offering for her hand, which surely could not be so very hard. Then she would have to insist on a rapid marriage. The thought of marrying Hawk, of capturing him for her own, was enough to put a golden glow around all the darkness. If she could persuade everyone, it could happen within the week!

Miss Hurstman returned and made no objection to the outing, though she declined to go herself. "Mindless gallivanting," she said, but she looked a little grim.

"Was there something in your message to distress you, Miss Hurstman?" Clarissa asked.

"No." But that was all she said, and since the Vandeimens and Hawk arrived at that point, Clarissa could not probe. She doubted it would do any good anyway, though she'd love to know exactly what Miss Hurstman and King Rogue—as Nicholas Delaney was called— had discussed.

Soon Clarissa was alone with the man she needed to marry, but found herself alarmingly tongue-tied. Hawk could fluster her with a look, but she was generally able to keep her wits. Now, knowing she was hunting him, she couldn't think what to say.

She found a safe subject. "How is the cat, Major Hawkinville?"

He offered his arm as they went down the shallow steps. "Thriving on a diet of liver and cream. It caught three mice last night, and has become the cook's pet."

"Then why didn't it please the ratters?" They turned to stroll down toward the seafront.

"Pure pride. Would you have worked for them?"

She returned his smile. "Oh, I approve!"

"I have called it Jetta from its color, and because it was thrown."

"Jettisoned. I hope it has a better future."

"Do you want the cat?"

"I? I have no place to keep a cat just now."

"You have more of a place than I do."

Clarissa realized that they'd slipped into their usual easy exchange, which was not likely to take them to marriage. A conversation about homes might, however.

"But you have a home in Hawk in the Vale, do you not?" she asked.

"That is my father's."

A strange thing to say. "A father's home is generally thought of as his son's home. Especially his heir's."

"Perhaps my years away have made it less homelike to me."

"Then where will you live, when you settle down?" There. That was a hint.

He didn't seem to notice it. "I have to live there for a while. My father is not well and needs help in managing his affairs. Jetta can return with me to Hawkinville when I go."

They crossed the road to the seafront, where the bathing machines were still doing poor business. Clarissa, however, was fixed on other matters. "Do you plan to return soon?"

If her concern showed, all the better.

He glanced at her. "I cannot stay away for long periods. What of your home, Falcon? When the season ends here, will you go to live with your guardian?"

When the season ended—she hoped to be married to him. "I don't think so. I don't know what I'll do."

How exactly did a woman edge a man into proposing?

"Will Miss Hurstman stay with you?"

Not if I have anything to do with it. "I don't know that, either. I haven't been looking very far ahead. After all," she said with a twirl of her parasol, "something might occur . . ." *Like marriage,* she thought at him.

As usual, Althea was being swarmed by suitors, and the Vandeimens had stayed with her. Clarissa wondered if she should go back, but she couldn't do much to help decide which gentleman should have the honor.

"Perhaps you will stay with Lady Arden," Hawk said.

Clarissa stared at him. Surely she'd never spoken of Beth to him.

"Why do you suggest that?"

But of course. He was the Hawk. And that was part of the reason she must marry him. If only he'd get around to asking her! He was doubtless acting the proper fortune hunter, but here she was, like a deer in his sights with a label on saying, Shoot me, and nothing was happening!

"She was a teacher at Miss Mallory's," he said. "It was a simple assumption that she asked her father-in-law to oversee your affairs."

"I suppose I could stay with her for a little while," she said. "By then her baby should be born and past its first weeks."

"But you do not want to? She is still the harsh schoolmistress?"

Clarissa laughed at that. "She never was."

"But . . . ?"

She looked at him. "You're very persistent, Hawk. What is this to you?"

He smiled. "It pleases me to see you challenging."

"Does it please you to answer?" Something about his manner unsettled her.

"But of course. I would not want you moving to, for example, County Durham."

His manner was flirtatious, which was promising at least.

Clarissa turned away, as if fascinated by the sea. "I have no relatives in County Durham, as best I know."

"It's surprising what you can find on the family tree," he said in a tone that made her wonder what it meant. Before she could ask, he added, "But you ease my heart."

Aha! She turned back. "*Heart*, Hawk?"

But the moment was shattered by a sharp yapping and a tug at her skirt. A ball of white fur had its teeth in her dangling fringe.

"*Stop!*" She tried to drag her skirt free, and Hawk swooped to capture the dog. But when he picked it up, the skirt came with it.

"*Hawk!*" Clarissa shrieked, trying to hold her hem down.

He laughed and went to his knees, grabbing the growling dog's jaws to force them open. Clarissa was laughing at the absurd scene, but burningly aware of being the focus of all eyes and still showing too much leg.

"Button, no!" a woman cried, running over and leaning to slap the dog's muzzle. "Let go! Let go!"

And the dog obeyed, wriggling frantically in Hawk's hands toward its mistress.

It was Blanche Hardcastle, dressed as always in white, but stunningly flushed pink with annoyance and exertion.

She held the small dog close, and she and Clarissa stared at each other.

Major Beaumont and another couple were nearby, but everything was, for a moment, frozen and silent.

For a panicked moment Clarissa felt that Hawk would immediately know all the truth about Deveril's death. But then sanity returned, and her only concern was scandal. Blanche was an actress, and though she was highly regarded in her profession, the world knew that her past was not unblemished. She'd been Lord Arden's acknowledged mistress, for a start.

However, it revolted Clarissa to think of snubbing the woman who had been so kind—more than kind. "Blanche," she said with a smile. "Is that monster yours?"

Blanche looked a little worried too, but she smiled back. "Alas, I found him abandoned, and he is white, but I cannot teach him manners."

"That's because you're not firm enough with him," said Major Beaumont.

Blanche retorted, "You'd doubtless like to thrash the poor mite."

But the smile they shared took any sting out of it. Clarissa was genuinely delighted to see the two of them so relaxed and happy. She certainly couldn't let anything destroy that.

Major Beaumont turned to her. "Miss Greystone, you have to take some blame. That fringe of yours is designed to provoke madness in males."

It made her laugh, even though she was frantically thinking, *He was involved too! Would there be anything in that for Hawk to weave the truth from?*

"I confess it," she said as lightly as she could. "Do you know Major Hawkinville?" She performed the introductions, noting that the other couple had wandered off. Probably other actors being discreet.

Hawk and Major Beaumont exchanged some comments about the military, which seemed to establish each other in a few words. There was time for Blanche to say, "You're looking splendid, Clarissa, and your 'Hawk' is very handsome."

Clarissa blushed to think that she'd shrieked that in front of half the world, but she agreed. And here was someone she could go to for advice. Blanche knew all the secrets, and she had worldly wisdom for ten.

"Could I come to see you?" Clarissa asked.

Blanche's eyebrows rose, but she said, "If it won't get you into trouble. I'm in Prospect Row. Number two. I'm performing here at the New Theater." With a watchful look, she added, "In *Macbeth*."

Clarissa knew she gaped for a moment, but covered it. She smiled at something Major Beaumont said, but inside she was wondering whether she could even depend on Blanche.

Madness to play Lady Macbeth!

She was sinking into the past, to Blanche saying, "I have always wanted to do *Macbeth*." Even Lord Arden had been shocked by that after hearing her quote from the play earlier. *Who would have thought the old man to have had so much blood in him?*

A squeeze on the hand pulled her back. It was Blanche. "I hope my little pet didn't frighten you, Clarissa."

She laughed. "No, of course not!" And she told the story of the ratters the day before.

"So that was you," said Major Beaumont. "There's an account in today's *Herald,* but the names of the lady and gentleman are not given."

"Not known, we hope," said Hawk, and after a little more chat, Blanche and her major walked on.

"May I be curious?" Hawk asked. "A famous London actress is an unusual friend for a Cheltenham schoolgirl."

Clarissa had expected it, and had prepared a response. "It is a strange connection, and slightly scandalous. Can I trust you with it?"

To her concern, he seemed to think about it, but then said, "Of course. I'm no gossip."

They strolled back toward the Vandeimens and the well-attended Althea. "Blanche was the mistress of the Marquess of Arden until just before his marriage. You might think that this would create a rift between her and the marquess's wife—"

"I'd think it would make any meeting impossible."

"Ah, but you don't know Lady Arden."

"And how do you know of these things?"

How did she explain that? She hadn't thought this through.

"It slipped out." It wasn't entirely a lie. She looked at him. "I'm not an innocent, Hawk, and I won't pretend to be with you."

His lips twitched. "I hope not. So, how did these two unlikely ladies meet?"

"Beth heard about Blanche and contrived a meeting."

"Strange. Mrs. Hardcastle seemed unscratched."

Clarissa frowned at him. "You would of course think that two ladies would fight over a man. In fact, they discovered they shared an interest in the rights of women and the works of Mary Wollstonecraft, and became firm friends. The marquess," she added, "was somewhat disconcerted."

Hawk laughed. "An understatement, I'd think."

"Definitely." Clarissa's smile widened and she lost herself in thinking how very handsome he was when he laughed . . .

"And Lady Arden introduced you?"

She collected her wits. "Yes. Though I went to Blanche's house only once." She prayed not to show how that once had changed her life.

He was studying her. Why? "Are you a follower of Mary Wollstonecraft?"

She almost laughed with relief at such a prosaic concern. "Would you mind?"

"I would have to study the lady's writings to be sure. But the proof is in the product, I think."

He was looking at her, surely, with warm approval. She stopped, waiting, hoping . . .

"And Major Beaumont?" he asked. "How does he come into the picture?"

Clarissa was hard-pressed not to scowl. "He's a close friend of the marquess's from their school days. And as you see, he now has a special relationship with Blanche. According to Beth, he wants to marry her, but Blanche thinks it unsuitable. She clearly thought speaking to me unsuitable, too. Sometimes our world does not please me."

Especially having to play these silly games!

His brows rose at her sharp tone, but he said, "I see you as too much of a free spirit, Falcon, to be severely constrained by society."

That could almost be an opening for *her* to propose to *him*, but Clarissa's nerve failed her. What if he said no? What then? Perhaps he would say no on principle if she broke the rules so thoroughly.

She took a cowardly escape. "I'm trying to be good for Althea's sake. We should rescue her."

"From admirers? Will she thank you?"

"Definitely. She becomes flustered by too much flattery, and men will insist on saying the most absurd things."

Unlike you. She'd felt so certain that he was at least pursuing her fortune, but now sickening doubt invaded. Was he slow to capture her because he didn't find her appealing after all? Was she completely fooling herself?

"Perhaps men say absurd things because women like it?" he commented. "Would you be offended to be told you are like a golden rose?"

She stared at him. "Skeptical, perhaps," she said with a dry mouth and a racing heart.

"You would accuse me of lying?"

"Of flattering."

"In fact," he said almost prosaically, "you do remind me of a golden rose. Not red, which is too deep and dark, nor white, which is too calm. Nor even pink, which is too coy and blushing, but golden, like warm sunshine, brightening what you touch."

She had to lick her lips, and she knew she was blushing. She should protest again that it was not true, but she wanted it to be. She wanted him for any number of reasons, but she wanted to be loved by him more than anything in the world.

Because she loved him.

Breath-stealing, panic-building, but true. She loved him. She could not bear to lose him.

In the end, she simply said, "Thank you," and prayed for more.

Hawk wondered what demented demon had taken control of his tongue. He'd come out today to learn more about Clarissa and the Ardens, and had succeeded beyond his hopes because of that chance encounter.

He had not come out to break her heart even more. He feared he could read the glowing expression in her eyes.

"Miss Trist," he reminded her, turning toward her friend.

He sensed her disappointment, but after a moment she spoke calmly enough. "With such eligible men around her, you'd think Althea would be developing a preference."

Strong Clarissa. If only . . . "Do you think that perhaps she dislikes the fuss of it?" he asked.

She looked at him in surprise, in control. "Dislikes being the toast of Brighton?"

"It is possible."

"How else is she to find a grand husband?"

"Perhaps she doesn't want one."

"She does, Hawk. If she doesn't find something better, she'll have to go home and marry a stuffy widower with children nearly as old as she is."

He couldn't help but smile. "You are charmingly ardent in her cause. And kind."

"It's not kindness. It's friendship. You understand that, surely. I hear that you and Lord Vandeimen are old friends."

Yes, he understood that. "From the cradle."

"Althea and I have been friends for less than a year, but true friendships can happen quickly."

It was said with meaning, as a challenge to him. She was right. Over and above any emotions, they had discovered friendship. Friendship in marriage. It had been his ideal once.

Ah, well. Ideals often drowned in war.

She turned to study her friend. "You think she is not finding what she wants?"

"I don't think she seems happy," he said honestly, "but as you say, somewhere in Brighton the perfect man must exist."

They moved in, and Miss Trist clearly was relieved to be rescued.

"Are you not happy here, Thea?" Clarissa asked quietly, studying Althea.

"Of course I am." But she added, "I do miss the country a little, though."

It was said quietly, but Lady Vandeimen heard. "We could drive out to visit Hawk in the Vale."

"Why?" Hawk asked.

To Clarissa, that sounded rather sharp, and Lady Vandeimen was looking at him with surprise. "Why not? Trips to the nearby country are all the rage, and I would enjoy a chance to check on the work at Steynings. If we set off early tomorrow, we can enjoy a whole day."

"It will probably rain."

"Hawk, if we stayed at home for fear of rain, none of us would do anything this summer!"

Clarissa watched this exchange, wondering why the project displeased him. She longed to see his home. The home she hoped would be hers. Did he think it wouldn't appeal?

She wished she could reassure him. It could be a hovel and she wouldn't care. After all, with her money they could build a better place, and it was Hawk she wanted.

Hawk.

Perhaps on a trip to the country, to his home, there'd be more opportunity to progress. Queen Cleopatra had given her very strange messages, but her advice to Miriam had been promising. Get the man apart, take off her gloves, and touch.

Perhaps, in the country, she could do that.

And now, with Hawk's attention drawn to Blanche, she must succeed. She must bind him to their cause.

Chapter Fourteen

As they strolled back, Van said to Hawk, "Wasn't that the White Dove you were talking to? Not done to introduce her to a proper young lady, you know."

"What proper young lady? Clarissa introduced her to me."

Van laughed, but didn't look as if he entirely believed it.

"The White Dove?" Maria said. "Oh, the actress. We saw her play Titania, Van. Do you remember? She's very good. In fact, she's playing Lady Macbeth here."

"A violent change of roles," Hawk said. "And it's hard to see her as the bloodstained power behind the rotten throne."

Maria gave him a look. "Are you saying that a beautiful woman cannot also be dangerous?"

He blew her a kiss. "No man of sense would."

"Especially armed with a pistol," Van said, which seemed to be a private joke.

Hawk, on the other hand, was thinking that classical beauty had little to do with it either.

It would be so damn easy to take the beckoning path. Marry. No, elope. He suspected he could get her to do it.

Roses. Hades.

Think of the three-day journey to the border, surrounded by her glowing enthusiasm, knowing he was leading her to the slaughter. Imagine a wedding night. Her innocent, trusting surrender.

God, no, don't. Don't even think of that.

Better by far that she simply hate him and be free.

Carpe diem, whispered the devil in his mind.

He could probably steal one more day before the morrow.

And he might as well be Hawkishly practical. He still didn't know quite enough about her and the Ardens. If he played his cards right, he might learn the details he needed.

Tomorrow.

In Hawk in the Vale.

The next day, Clarissa looked excitedly out of the Vandeimen coach windows as it rolled over the humpbacked bridge into the village of Hawk in the Vale. She was full of curiosity, but also primed to take any opportunity to pursue her cause. If Hawk didn't propose, she vowed she would do it before they left.

The ladies were in the coach, and the gentlemen—Hawk, Lord Vandeimen, and Lord Trevor—rode alongside. Althea had muttered that she did not need a partner, but Clarissa thought she was relieved it was Lord Trevor, who was excellent company without showing any sign of wanting to be a suitor.

Miss Hurstman was not with them, since today was her weekly meeting of the Ladies' Scholarly Society, which she declared to be "an oasis of sanity in Bedlam." She did not seem particularly different in her manner, and there had been no sign of Mr. Delaney. Clarissa was relieved, however, to be out of Brighton and safe.

The gentlemen were all superb riders, but Clarissa couldn't help but smile at the cat riding proudly erect in front of Hawk. Jetta had refused to ride in the carriage, clearly thinking the company of other females inferior.

Hawk stroked her occasionally, and her eyes slitted with pleasure. Clarissa could rather imagine reveling in his touch in just the same way. She wondered if men ever stroked women the way they stroked cats.

During the journey, Lady Vandeimen had insisted that they all be on first-name terms. Clarissa had happily agreed, thinking that soon they would be true friends. The lady shared what she knew of Hawk in the Vale, and Clarissa savored every morsel, especially as it felt as if she was being welcomed into the community.

She now knew that Hawk's family was the most ancient, and in many ways the most important, in the area, though there was no title except squire, which went with the manor house. If someone else were to buy the manor, he would become squire.

The other principal families were the Vandeimens and the Somerfords, headed by Lord Amleigh. Both families had estates outside of the village, but Hawkinville Manor was in Hawk in the Vale in the old style.

Maria had shared some interesting gossip along the way. "Lord Amleigh recently inherited the title of Earl of Wyvern. The seat is in Devonshire. However, it appears that the late earl might have had a legitimate son who has a prior claim. Quite a strange story. The earl and the woman—a member of a good local family—married in secret. They were both so displeased with each other, however, that they kept the matter secret, and she took up with a local tavern keeper, who is reputed to also be a smuggler!"

"And now the secret heir emerges?" Clarissa inquired. "It's like a play. Or a Gothic novel."

"Except that in this case the 'wicked earl' is Lord Amleigh, and he doesn't want the inheritance at all."

"That's an interesting idea, however," Clarissa said. "A trial marriage. I imagine any number of disasters could be averted."

"Clarissa!" Althea objected, but she was laughing.

"Well, it's true."

"Indeed," said Maria, and seemed to mean it.

It made Clarissa wonder about her first marriage, for there could surely be no disillusion with her second. "However, there is the matter of offspring," Maria continued. "What if the trial has consequences?"

What, wondered Clarissa, if the trial was discovered?

Could *she* compromise *Hawk*?

"I have sent a message inviting the Amleighs to take lunch with us at Steynings," Maria said. "If, that is, the dining room plasterwork is finally finished."

Clarissa then learned more than she really cared to know about the trials of repairing a decade's neglect of a house that had not been well built in the first place.

Hawk's home was older. Was it in even worse repair? She, like Maria, had the money to repair it.

He'd ridden ahead to make sure all was ready for them. Already she was longing to see him.

The coach was lurching along a rough road around the central village green, past a row of ancient stone cottages that looked in need of as much care as the road.

Perhaps this was why Hawk was hunting a fortune.

A swarm of piglets suddenly dashed out between two cottages, chased by three barefoot children. It was fortunate that it was after the coach had passed, not before. Clarissa watched with amusement as the urchins tried to herd the piglets back home.

Maria directed her attention to the church. "Anglo-Saxon, of course."

Yes, it looked it, complete to the square stone tower. Age made the village picturesque, but it was something more subtle that made it feel . . . right. Clarissa had never visited a place where the varied bits and pieces fit together so well, like the assorted flowers in a country garden.

Her eye was caught—hooked, more like—by a discordant piece, a monstrous stuccoed house with Corinthian pillars flanking its glossy doorway. There were other new buildings, buildings from every period over hundreds of years, but only that one seemed so appallingly out of place.

"What is that white house?" Clarissa asked.

"Ah. That belongs to a newcomer. A wealthy industrialist called Slade." Maria pulled a face. "It doesn't fit, does it? But he's very proud of it."

"Couldn't he be stopped?"

"Apparently not. He seems to have ingratiated himself with the squire. Hawk's father."

The carriage halted, and the footman leaped down to assist the ladies out. Lord Trevor and Lord Vandeimen dismounted, and a groom trotted out through open gates to take the horses. Through those gates Clarissa could see an ancient building.

Hawkinville Manor. It must be.

She was astonished that she hadn't spotted it more easily, but it did blend in with the row of cottages and other nearby buildings, and was surrounded by a high wall covered by a rampant miscellany of plants. Ivy cloaked the tower, too.

Wall and tower had doubtless been necessary for defense in the past, but now the double gates stood open, and Clarissa could glimpse a garden courtyard and part of the house—thatched roof and old diamond-pane windows. Roses and other climbing plants ran up the wall, making it seem more a work of landscape than architecture.

She vaguely heard the carriage crunch on its way to the inn, but she was moving forward, through the gates.

"How charming," Althea said in a polite way.

"Yes," Clarissa agreed, though the word seemed completely inadequate. Only a poet could do justice to the sheer magic of Hawkinville Manor.

The courtyard was sensibly graveled, but that was the only modern touch. In the center, an island full of heavy roses held in its very heart an ancient sundial. It was tilted in a way that surely meant that it couldn't tell the time, but then she doubted that sundials had ever been accurate.

This place had formed before the counting of minutes or even precise hours had any meaning.

Both courtyard and house were bathed in sunlight. Warm sunlight, for a miracle, and it gave the illusion that the sun always shone here. Many windows stood open, as did the iron-mounted oak door. The view through the doorway gave a tantalizing glimpse of a tiled hall that seemed to run, uneven as the river surface and worn in the middle by many feet, to another open door and a beckoning garden beyond. *

She took a step forward.

A dog growled. She blinked, seeing four large hounds sprawled near the threshold in the sun. One was looking at her lazily, but with a warning eye.

"Daffy."

At the word, the dog subsided. Hawk walked past, out of the house, Jetta still in his arms.

He stroked the purring cat, but his eyes were on Clarissa. "Welcome to Hawkinville."

Now why, thought Hawk, did he feel almost shocked to see Clarissa here when she was fully expected? It was as if the air had thinned, or as if he'd been riding and working to the point of wavering exhaustion.

He pulled himself together and answered questions. Yes, the sundial was very old and had come from the monastery at Hawks Monkton when it had been destroyed in the sixteenth century. Yes, the tower did date back to before the Conquest but had been fixed and improved a number of times.

Clarissa's dress was a simple one for this day in the country. It had not seemed special before. Now the color reminded him of the richest cream in the cool dairy and made him want to lick something.

Yes, he said to Lord Trevor, there was a home farm, and this was it. The manor house also served as a modest farmhouse. There were more buildings beyond the wall to the right.

That dress was doubtless the simplicity of a very expensive modiste, but the effect was charming and comfortable and fit here like the roses. Her wide straw hat was caught down at either side with golden ribbons.

Why hadn't he noticed before that it would prevent kisses?

She turned to look more closely at the sundial, leaning in but laughingly trying to protect her flimsy skirts from the rose thorns. He stepped forward to help, and she smiled up at him.

The buzz of insects among the flowers turned into a buzz in his head. Her hat shaded her face from the sun, but cast a golden glow and a hint of mystery. Her smiling lips were pink and parted, and he could almost taste their warmth.

What was beauty if not this?

With frightening clarity he could imagine her here as his wife. He would sweep her laughing into his arms and carry her upstairs to a bed covered with smooth sheets fresh from hanging in the sun. And there he would slowly, perfectly, ravish her.

He remembered to breathe, and when his hand was steady, he pulled out his penknife. "Let me cut you each a rose, ladies."

He cut a pink one for Miss Trist, and carefully stripped the thorns before giving it to her. He cut a white one for Maria. But then he looked for a golden one, a perfect golden rose, just beginning to unfurl from bud, and gave it to Clarissa.

She remembered. He could tell by the way she blushed within the golden mysteries of her hat and raised the rose to inhale its perfume. He remembered his foolish, thoughtless words about roses . . .

And that she wasn't for him.

Carpe diem.

The morrow was not for them.

He ached to reach out and touch her, simply touch her cheek. He wanted to tell her that this moment, at least, was true. He wanted to lock her in a safe and private place where she would never be in danger again.

The church clock began to chime, pulling him back to reality.

By the time it had struck the full ten, he could speak normally and invite his guests into the house. He steered them to the right, into the front parlor, then escaped, his excuse being having to tell his father they were here.

Clarissa looked around the modest but lovely room. The ceilings were low, and she'd noticed that Hawk had to duck slightly to get through the door, but it all created a coziness that wrapped itself around her. She could imagine sitting here on a stormy winter night, a huge fire burning in the hearth, curtains tightly drawn. A person would always feel safe here.

Even the Devil's Heiress.

She knew without doubt that she would be safe in Hawk's arms, and in his home.

She raised the golden rose to her nose. The scent was light, almost elusive, but it was sweet and seemed to carry the charm of sunlight. A golden rose. That had to mean that his fondness was real, and her plan was good. Whatever the reason for his hesitation, it was not from reluctance.

Perhaps he simply felt it wrong to hurry her. Though it seemed like a lifetime, she had been in Brighton for only a week. Perhaps he'd set himself a restraint—that he not propose inside a fortnight, for example.

She inhaled the rose again, smiling. She was sure that restraint could be broken.

Maria sat in one of the old wooden chairs with crewelwork cushions. "Do you like the manor, Clarissa?"

Clarissa pulled her wits together. "It's lovely."

"Perhaps it's as well you think so. But at the least it needs new carpets."

"Maria," said her husband, "don't start doing over someone else's home."

They shared a teasing smile, and Maria said, "That will be for Hawk's wife to do."

"Not until his father's dead," said Lord Vandeimen, and Clarissa saw a slight reserve touch his face. At thought of wife, or thought of father? Maria Vandeimen was discreet, but there might have been coolness in her mention of Squire Hawkinville during the journey here.

That was a small cloud on the horizon, she had to admit. She adored this house, but what would it be like sharing it with Hawk's father, especially if he was an unpleasant man?

A small price for heaven.

"So," said Maria, "what do you think on the subject of carpets, Clarissa?"

Clarissa looked at the faded and worn Turkish carpet that covered the rippling dark oak floor and felt that any change would disturb something as natural and perfect as the roses in the garden. When she looked carefully, she could see that the cushions on the old chairs sagged and the embroidery was faded and worn with time.

"I think they suit the house," she replied with a smile, and Maria laughed.

"It's as well we have different tastes, isn't it?"

Clarissa glanced at Lord Vandeimen, a fine-looking man and pleasant, who stirred her not at all. "Yes, indeed."

Maria chuckled.

A huge fireplace took up most of one wall, and an old oak settle sat to one side of it. The front wall was a bank of small-paned windows that stood open to the sunny courtyard. Clarissa wandered over. Soft perfume drifted in— rose, lavender, and many other plants she could not even name. Sparrows chirped in the eaves, doves cooed nearby, and all around, birds sang.

Oh, but she wanted Hawkinville Manor!

It seemed almost wrong to feel that way. It was Hawk she should want, and she did, desperately, but she was tumbling into mad love with his home as well.

More than love. It was as if the place was her setting, where she fit perfectly. She felt as if she were putting down roots now, tendrils winding through faded carpet and old oak floor into the earth beneath, determined to stay.

A gig rattled by outside the gates, startling her out of her impatient thoughts. Two women hurried past, chattering, laughing. Clarissa stepped back as if they might look and see her there, might see her yearning, but all the same she loved the way the house was part of the village, not stuck far away in a huge park.

Then Hawk returned, making her heart do a dizzying dance. The cat was still in his arms. "Let me show you around this floor. I'm afraid the manor isn't a showplace, just a simple home."

Clarissa went forward into the flagstoned hall.

The walls were wainscoted in blackened oak and painted white above, hung with the occasional painting. A small table against one wall held a bowl of mixed garden flowers. It wasn't a formal arrangement, any more than this was a formal house, but it was pretty and entirely right for the setting.

A faint purr hummed from Jetta. Clarissa knew she would purr too if Hawk was stroking her in that absentminded but continuous way.

"It's lovely," she said.

"I think so. It is doubtless impractical of me, but I don't want to see it change."

"Who would?"

He flashed her a smile. "Most people, especially if they had to actually live here. And are tall." He ducked slightly to lead her into a dark-paneled dining room with another huge fireplace, ancient oak sideboards, and a thick table. That table had been polished so long and lovingly that the glossy top seemed to have the depth of a dark pool.

A mobcapped, aproned woman came in bearing plates. She bobbed a curtsy and went on with her business.

"Aren't you tempted to have the doorways made higher?" she asked.

"It would be a serious structural challenge. I'm learning by painful experience."

He led the way through an adjoining door into another parlor.

Another bank of windows almost filled the wall, and a window seat ran the width of it. Beyond lay a simple garden with lawn, rockery, and beds of flowers. And beyond that flowed the river. Two swans glided past as if completing the picture for her particular delight.

How wonderful to spend long summer evenings on this seat, by this river. With Hawk.

It was not just wishful thinking.

Clarissa was determined that it would be so.

Chapter Fifteen

They walked over, as if in perfect accord, to look out at the view. Beyond the river lay peaceful fields, some with crops and some with cows. The land rose in the distance to the downs that lay between here and Brighton.

"What is the big white house up there?" she asked. "Steynings?"

"Yes."

"Why is the village only on this side of the river?"

"The Eden's deep here and tricky to cross, and the bridge is quite recent. Before that a person needed a boat or to go downstream a mile to Tretford to cross."

She saw an old boathouse off to one side, unused now, wrapped around and split by wisteria.

"So Lord Vandeimen's house wouldn't have been built over there before the bridge."

"Not unless he wanted to keep his inferior neighbors at bay."

She sat on the seat and smiled up at him, simply happy. Happy with everything. "And did he?"

His hand continued to stroke the blissful cat. "When the first Baron Vandeimen settled here, he was inclined to look down on our simple ways, they say. Foreign, you see. Over the generations, they are beginning to fit in."

Clarissa heard a laughing comment from Lord Vandeimen, but her attention was all on Hawk. His eyes were warm and full of humor. And something else?

He was very hard to read.

He looked out at the view again. "My bedroom is directly above here. We experimented with flashing candlelight messages in the night. Van and I could see each other's lights, then Van and Con could send messages clear across the vale."

"I'm surprised that isn't done more often."

"It is used—especially by smugglers—but, of course, it's subject to bad weather. Come on, I'll show you something else."

He guided her back across the hall and up a short flight of stairs into another room as if she were the only one on this tour.

"But this is too big," Clarissa said, looking around at a space that seemed as big again as the house.

"We call it the great hall, which is a little grandiose, but it serves the function. My mother held the occasional small ball here." He led her further in. "Now you're in the old tower."

Then she understood where the extra space had come from. Most of the room was inside the hexagonal tower. To her right were the arrow slits she'd seen from the courtyard. Now she could see that they were glazed. There were more at regular intervals, but in the side of the tower opposite the door, another bank of windows had been cut. Since the tower walls were deep, the window seat was in an alcove of its own.

She went to kneel on the cushions to look out. This view was on a diagonal, looking out at a kitchen garden and an orchard, the trees already laden with small fruit. To the right she glimpsed the farm buildings he'd mentioned, and beyond, the river wound on through yet more fertile countryside.

"The kitchens and such are below, which is why this is raised." He had come over to stand close behind her, so Jetta's purr almost vibrated through her. If she turned, how close? "And that, I'm afraid, is all I can show you today. My father does not want to be disturbed."

She swiveled and found that her knees almost touched his. "He is very unwell?"

"He's partly paralyzed. He's improving, but it's slow and he prefers not to show himself to strangers. He's also often out of temper." He took her hand and gently tugged her off the cushioned seat. "Let me take you out into the garden."

It was a surprise to find the others in the large alcove with them, and frankly she wished they weren't. According to Queen Cleopatra, she needed to be apart with him.

Then she realized that Hawk held on to her hand. She still wore her gloves, but they were cotton lace and it was almost skin to skin. Queen Cleopatra had been right about the potency of that.

His other arm still cradled the cat, who was eyeing Clarissa suspiciously through slit eyes, but at least wasn't hissing as yet. She liked the thought that the cat was jealous. Animals were supposed to have good instincts.

As they followed a stone-paved path down to the riverbank, she felt as if she and Hawk blended at palms and fingers to become one, but when they reached the riverbank he abruptly disentangled them. Almost as if he'd only just noticed the joining.

She was lost without a map in a wilderness of emotions and touches.

A family of ducks paddled busily around, bobbing for food, ducklings quacking and dashing. Jetta leaped down from Hawk's arms to lie in the sun watching the ducklings, as if she hoped one would come close.

"Don't you dare," Clarissa warned.

The cat only blinked.

Clarissa decided to stay close, just in case, but she turned back to look at the house. It seemed contentedly slumberous in the sun, wrapped in its blanket of climbing plants and thatch. The sun was warm on her skin and gave a glow to everything.

This was one of life's perfect moments. She hadn't had many, but she recognized it. It was a moment she would never forget, but she hoped there would be many more like it.

"Penny for your thoughts?" he said.

Now that was an invitation, but she wouldn't rush in until he had been given his chance. She could wait.

"My thoughts are that this is a lovely home, and you are very fortunate to have grown up here."

"Ah."

At the tone she glanced at him.

"True fortune is to grow up surrounded by love, wouldn't you say, despite the circumstances? If this had been your family home, would it have made your youth happy?"

"If this had been my family home, it would not be in nearly such good repair. And anything of value would have been stripped from it years ago."

"I see. You think I should count my blessings?"

She met his eyes. "I think we all should. And the main blessing is a future. Whatever the past has been, the future is always ours to make."

He was clearly listening and thinking.

"A future without the tendrils of the past?" He looked at the manor. "A house like this says otherwise. The future is not a road stretching cleanly in front of us. It is a layer built on the foundation of the past."

She thought of her family, her childhood, Deveril, Deveril's death. "Does no one ever get to start building anew?"

His smile was wry. "Perhaps. But not someone who belongs to a place like Hawkinville Manor."

"Belongs to," she said. "I like that."

But a movement on the ground caught her eye. Jetta had risen to a hunting crouch, and one little duckling was paddling close to the bank.

Clarissa stepped forward and shooed it away.

"She wouldn't, would she?" she asked Hawk.

"She's an excellent mouser."

"That's different."

"Not to the mouse. The cat is a predator, Clarissa. It is its nature to hunt."

She turned back to watch the ducklings. "It is a hawk's nature too."

"And a falcon's."

She glanced at him. Was that a hint? Did he want her to ask him? Why? "I assure you, I won't bring you gifts of small victims."

He reached out and lightly touched her cheek. "Whereas I would like to bring you your enemies, headless."

"Enemies?" His touch and the word had her dazed.

"People who wish you ill. People you fear."

She laughed, though to her own ears it sounded shaky. "Alas, I have no enemies worthy of a hawk."

"Alas, indeed. But lacking a true enemy, I will make do with a petty one. No one has spoken to you unkindly? No carriage has splashed mud on your gown? No servant has served your soup cold?"

He was teasing, but he hadn't been teasing before. Why should he suspect enemies? How much of the picture had he put together?

"I wouldn't demand anyone's head for that," she said. "In fact, I want no more violence in my life."

"More?"

She was stuck, but then Lord Trevor said, "Someone's waving, sir."

They both looked around to see an aproned figure waving from the manor door.

"Ah," Hawk said. "The carriage must have returned to take us up to Steynings."

As the others went ahead, he scooped up the cat, then put his free hand on Clarissa's back to direct her toward the house. As he had in that room in the Old Ship . . .

Her dress was fine, and she was wearing the lightest of corsets. She felt the heat, and a thread of excited pleasure up and down her spine as she retraced her steps to the house.

Hawk and Hawkinville.

She would have both. She must have both!

Steynings was certainly a complete contrast to the manor—all clean, modern lines and symmetry. Inside, however, the place was a hive of mending, hammering, painting, and cleaning. The smell of wet plaster, sawdust, and linseed oil stole any sense of comfort for Clarissa. She followed Maria's guided tour, wondering if her husband minded his family home being taken over in this way by his new wife.

She didn't think Lord Vandeimen minded much that his wife did, just as she would find it hard to mind much that Hawk did. He wasn't by her side now—the men had disappeared, probably to find a quiet corner and drink ale—and every moment of this tour seemed a waste of time.

Since there was no escaping, however, she tried to pay attention and make intelligent comments. One day soon, she hoped, the Vandeimens would be neighbors.

When she studied things, it did seem to her that most of the work was an improvement. Some doors had been moved, and two rooms had been opened up into one. The pale paintwork was fresh and airy and suited this building. It was easy to comment approvingly.

As they all returned to the marble-floored entrance hall, the men emerged.

Hawk came over to her. "More to your taste, I gather?"

Clarissa checked that her hostess was out of earshot before answering, "Not at all, I'm afraid. It's too cool and big."

He looked skeptical. Did he really think everyone preferred the modern style?

"Truly, Hawk. I think the manor house is lovely."

Frustratingly, he seemed to take her comment as mere good manners. What else could she say? That she loved his house so much that she would marry Lord Deveril for it? Well, not quite that, for sure.

Then Lord Amleigh and his wife strode in in riding dress and high spirits. Clarissa did not think she imagined their sharp looks, as if she was being assessed. That was a very hopeful sign, if both of Hawk's friends thought her of interest.

They all sat down in the dining room for a cold luncheon. Though the room was in a state for guests, Clarissa could see that work had been left half done in various spots. The food was excellent, however, and a general peace suggested that the workmen were also taking their meal.

She began to take in a sense of the house as it would be, and amid the relaxed conversation, indulged herself in imagining dinners here with these couples as her good friends. Her mind sped ahead to children growing up together as the three men had, but all in completely happy homes.

Not in a home like hers, or like Hawk's.

In some things, at least, a new beginning was possible.

She heard about the Vandeimens' wedding feast. It would be wonderful to be married like that, to be introduced to the village like that.

"You'll have to choose a bride soon, Hawk," teased Lady Amleigh, "so we can have another party before the summer is out."

"Greedy, aren't you, Susan? Wouldn't it be better to wait a summer or two? There aren't likely to be any more of that sort for a generation."

"Speaking of generations," Lady Amleigh responded, "we can celebrate christenings!" She blushed and grinned. "And yes, that does mean that I think there's going to be a christening in February."

Everyone congratulated the Amleighs, but Hawk said, "Hardly the time for a village fête, I'm afraid."

Clarissa detected a touch of wistfulness in Maria Vandeimen's expression, and wondered. The lady had been married and had no children. Could that happen to her? She supposed it could happen to any woman.

With talk of fêtes and babies, everyone was lazy about rising from the table, but eventually Maria said that the workmen needed to get back to their tasks and they'd been told to be quiet while the guests were here.

They all walked out into the hall, and the Amleighs took their departure. The Vandeimens, however, were approached by an aproned man holding rolls of plans, and soon they were embroiled in an intent discussion.

Lord Trevor and Althea wandered to study some painted panels, leaving Clarissa and Hawk alone. It was not a good enough separation, however. The day here was almost done. Soon they would be in the carriage home, all chances gone. And she'd vowed to propose before they left.

Here?

The acoustics of the hall were such that she could almost catch what everyone else was saying. She needed to be outside with him. For quite a long time.

"After a lunch like that," she said, "I would love a walk. Could we walk back to the village, perhaps?"

Hawk looked at her, but then said, "Maria will probably be some time, and would be relieved not to have us hovering. There's a pleasant footpath that should take only a half hour or so."

Anticipation and pure nerves tied Clarissa's insides in a knot, but she said, "That sounds perfect!"

But then he said, "I'll ask Lord Trevor and Miss Trist."

Clarissa fiercely projected a message to Althea to refuse, but the other couple came over while Hawk went to speak to the Vandeimens. Clarissa looked for an opportunity to whisper to Althea, but none presented itself and in moments they were leaving the house by the back terrace, any hopes and plans in ruins.

She tried to imagine Althea lingering behind with Lord Trevor, but couldn't. Althea, after all, was a stickler for the proprieties.

Halfway across the lawn toward the woodland, however, Althea stopped. "Oh, dear. I'm terribly sorry. My ankle has begun to ache. I twisted it slightly in the mud at the fair."

They all stood there for a moment, then Hawk said, "We will go back."

"Oh, no! Please don't," Althea protested. "I'm sure you were looking forward to the walk." She turned to Lord Trevor. "But if you could give me your arm back to the house, my lord . . ."

Of course he agreed. Clarissa glanced at Hawk, wondering if he would insist on returning as well, but he said nothing.

"Well, then," she said to Althea, "if you will be all right . . ."

"Perfectly." And Althea winked.

Clarissa had to fight not to laugh as she turned again, alone with Hawk at last.

Instinct told her that this could be the most important half hour of her life.

Chapter Sixteen

Hawk linked arms with Clarissa and led her toward the woods and wilderness. He looked down at her, but her golden straw hat shielded her face and made her a woman of mystery—as if she wasn't enough of a mystery already.

He'd not planned this unchaperoned walk, but now that it sat in his hands he could not reject the gift. He could use it to seek details about Deveril's death, but he knew he simply wanted to enjoy this time with the woman he could not have.

It was perilous. He recognized that. Strange magic was weaving through this day, and he felt as if he were walking into a fairy circle, being slowly deprived of logic and purpose.

He would do no wrong, however. He had promised Van, and a promise like that was sacred. All the same, a stern chaperon would have been safer.

A yowl made him look back to see Jetta running after them like a thoroughbred. "Ah. A chaperon after all."

"Do we need one?"

He glanced at Clarissa, catching a wickedly demure look that made him want to groan. What was he going to do if *she* had wicked designs upon *him*?

The cat arrived with a final yowl of protest. He picked it up, saying to Clarissa, "If you don't think we do, Falcon, you are being naive."

She blushed, but it only created a more devastating glow. "I am capable of saying no to anything I do not want, Hawk. Are you saying you would force me?"

"You have a mistaken idea of the role of the chaperon, my girl." They strolled on, the cat now limply content. "Her role is not to prevent wolves from attacking, but to prevent maidens from throwing themselves into the jaws of the wolves."

She turned her head so he could see her whole face, and her expression was decidedly wicked. "I have always disliked having a chaperon."

He stroked the cat. "Jetta, I think you are truly needed here."

Clarissa laughed, a charming gurgle of laughter that was new. A few weeks ago in Cheltenham she hadn't laughed like that—relaxed and happy. Seductive.

He could vividly imagine her laughing like that in bed. Naked in a well-used bed . . .

He'd seen men bewitched by wicked women, often to the extent of besmirching their honor, once or twice to their complete destruction. Had they, too, felt careless as they fell, as if a few magical moments were worth any fate?

If he had any sense, he would return to the house now.

Instead, he went on with her, out of the sunshine and into the cool mystery of the woodland. Jetta leaped down to explore, and Hawk searched for something innocuous to say. "We played here a great deal as boys."

"Knights and dragons?" she asked.

"And crusaders and infidels. Pirates and the navy—but we were always the pirates."

The hat tilted, showing a glimpse of nose. "A criminal inclination, I see."

An opening. He could not fail to take it. "Of course. Have you never played the criminal?"

He watched carefully, but since he could still see only her nose, it was hard to judge her reaction.

"Have you?" she said.

Yes, now.

How peaceful it seemed in this other world under the green shade, busy birdsong all around them. Jetta pounced into some ferns, then out again, thankfully without a trophy.

Hawk looked at the siren walking so demurely by his side and wished this was the innocent, unshadowed stroll it seemed.

"Not here. None of us wanted to play the true villains. We didn't consider pirates villains, of course. The dragons, infidels, and navy had to be imaginary."

She turned so he could see her complete smile. "But villains often have the best lines. I always asked to play the villain in school plays."

"A villainous inclination, I see."

"Perhaps." There was laughter in it, however, not dark meaning. "I certainly preferred it to being the heroine. There are so few good roles for a heroine."

"Shakespeare has some."

"True. Portia. Beatrice. I played Lady Macbeth once—"

He could imagine that a hand tightened on her throat, sealing off any more words. Why? What was it about Lady Macbeth that could not be spoken? Like the distant rumble of cannons, speaking of death, he remembered the bloody dagger in the play.

"But is she a heroine?" he asked, watching. "She incites a murder . . ."

He was almost certain that Lord Arden had killed Deveril, but had Clarissa incited him to it? Pressed the dagger into his hands? It was not a picture he wanted to envision.

"She suffers for it," Clarissa said.

"But some murderers benefit from their crimes."

"Only if they're not caught."

She was getting better and better at tossing words around without showing her feeling. He admired it, but he wished for a little more transparency.

Exactly how had it gone? Planned assassination, or crime of the moment? It mattered. It mattered to him because he did not want her to be guilty in the tiniest degree, and it would matter if it ever, God forbid, came to the courts.

He knew he was dicing with that. By stirring this pot, he risked everything pouring out to destroy.

"It's a difficult role for a schoolgirl," he remarked, "but playing Macbeth would be harder still."

"Oh, not really." Her voice seemed normal again. "He's caught up in circumstances, isn't he? And anyway, schoolgirls love dark drama and tragedy. Every fifteen-year-old girl longs to die a martyr. We used to enact the story of Joan of Arc for amusement."

She'd slid deftly away from the edge.

"You played Joan of Arc, while we played Robin Hood. Saint and thief. That probably reflects the difference between girls and boys."

"Militant saint and honorable thief. We girls weren't attracted to the kind of saint who spent her life in prayer and peace, just as none of you wanted to play the true villains."

"We conscripted some." He lifted a trailing branch out of her way. "The head groundsman here was unknowingly our sheriff of Nottingham. Avoiding him was a challenge, especially as he didn't always approve of what we were doing and carried a sturdy stick."

"And what about Maid Marian?" she asked with a look.

"Not until we were *much* older."

She laughed again, that charming chuckle.

He suddenly stopped, and without question or apology loosened her bonnet ribbons so the hat flattened and hung down her back.

She looked up at him, unresisting.

Tempting. Demanding, even.

With difficulty he remembered his promise to Van. A kiss, perhaps?

No, even a kiss was too dangerous now.

"We did a play about Robin Hood once," she said.

"Who were you? Robin? Maid Marian? The wicked sheriff?"

"Alan-a-dale."

"The minstrel? Do you sing, then?"

It shocked him that there might be something significant about her that he didn't know.

She smiled, a lovely picture of freckled innocence under the green-and-gold filtered light of the summer woods. Then she began to sing.

> *Under the greenwood tree*
> *Who loves to lie with me,*
> *And turn a merry note*
> *Unto the sweet bird's throat.*

She began to back away, still singing:

> *Come hither, come hither, come hither.*
> *Here shall you see*
> *No enemy but winter and rough weather.*
> *Come hither, come hither, come hither.*

Hawk stood, almost breathless, caught by her sweet, strong voice and the invitation in her eyes.

No enemy but winter and rough weather . . .

If only that were true.

He walked slowly forward. "Shakespeare? I didn't know he wrote about Robin Hood."

"As You Like It. It's mostly set in the forest, so we stole bits."

"You have a lovely voice. And," he added, "you issue a lovely invitation."

" 'All the world's a stage,' " she quoted lightly, " 'and all the men and women merely players . . .' "

He wanted to shoo her away, as she'd shooed away the duckling. *You are in the company of predators. Flee, flee back to safety.* Instead, his will crushed, he held out a hand.

A kiss. Just a kiss.

Her eyes still and thoughtful, she loosened the fingers of one lacy white glove and slowly pulled it off. Then she began on the other. He watched her unveil creamy, silken skin, a shiver passing through him.

Hands touched, hers cool and soft, and he drew her close, drew her hands to curl behind him. Dappled light turned her hair to a deep, burnished gold, and he loved the rioting wildfire of it. In every way, it suited her. The curve of her full lips and the look in her steady eyes were pure perfection.

She moved a little closer and raised her face expectantly for the kiss. The very boldness was a warning, but he couldn't heed it now. He took the offered kiss that he needed.

Clarissa took the kiss that she needed.

As their lips blended and sweet satisfaction rippled through her, she didn't regret anything, past or future. She sank into the spicy pleasure of his mouth and gladly drowned. She held back nothing, holding him tight to her so every possible inch joined with him, absorbed him.

When the kiss ended, she shivered. It was partly pleasure, but more the ache of drawing apart and the hunger for more. For eternity.

She waited for the words that would speak the message in his darkened eyes, in his hands that played gently against her cheeks, but then he stepped carefully away. "I wonder where Jetta is."

She caught his hand. "Do we care?"

His fingers tightened on hers, but he said, "Yes, I think we must."

He was right. If they wanted to be honorable, they could not keep kissing like that. But why would he not speak? She felt she might die of this restraint, but she would give him till they were almost back in the village. She would give him that much.

She was the one who turned to follow the path, he the one to be drawn along by their interwoven fingers. "Tell me more about yourself, Hawk. Tell me about your work in the army." She hungered for everything about him, and there was so much she did not know.

She thought he might resist, but after a moment he led her onward and answered. "I started out in the cavalry, but I was seconded to the Quartermaster General's Department. It's a separate administrative unit. There is also the Commissariat, and the duties often overlap.

"The main purpose is the management of the army. It's no easy matter to move tens of thousands of men and all the hangers-on around efficiently and bring them to battle in good order. In addition, an army is like a city. Everything that happens in a city happens there. Brawls, theft, crimes of passion. Most matters are sorted out by the officers—think of them as magistrates." He helped her over a spot where a crumbling hole spanned the path. "Sometimes there are more complex problems. Organized thievery, forgery, murder."

"Murder?" She hoped she sounded merely curious. She'd reacted to the word like a spooked horse.

He gave her one of his sharp glances. She told herself it didn't matter. Soon they would be bound, and then she would tell him everything.

"Murder," he agreed, "but rarely of any cleverness. It was usually a case of following the bloody footprints."

She hoped she didn't shiver at that.

"We mostly looked into crimes involving officers or civilians, and of course there were always spies, some of them traitors."

"Men in the army who turned traitor?" she asked, genuinely shocked.

"Sometimes."

"Why would anyone do that?"

"For money. There's no limit to what some people will do for money."

There seemed a dark tone to that. Was it because he was thinking of himself as a fortune hunter? Was it simple guilt over that which made him hesitate?

They were talking of crimes, however. It was an excellent opportunity to see just how strictly he kept to the letter of the law.

"Did you always enforce the law?" she asked. "Sometimes there must be excuses. Should a starving person hang for stealing a loaf of bread?"

"No one should hang for stealing a loaf of bread. Our punishment system is barbaric and irrational. But those with wealth live in fear of those who are poor."

She made herself ask the next question. "What of those who steal life? Should a person always hang for murder?"

He glanced at her, and she could glean nothing from his expression. "You think there should be clemency?"

"Why not? The Bible says an eye for an eye. What if it's a crime of revenge?"

"The Bible also says, 'He that smiteth a man so that he die, shall surely be put to death.' "

That wasn't what she wanted to hear. "What of a duel? Should the victor who kills his opponent be executed?"

"That is the law. It's generally ignored if the affair is handled according to the rules."

She took a risk and referred to the heart of the matter. "Yet you said you would have liked to kill Lord Deveril for me."

He was looking at her intently. She met his eyes, waiting for his answer.

"Some people deserve death," he agreed.

"So in such a case, you wouldn't want the law to run its course?" She was being too direct, too bold, but she must know.

He didn't instantly agree. "Who are we to play the angel of death or the angel of mercy? Who are we to subvert justice?"

"Subvert justice?"

"Isn't that what you're suggesting? Shielding a criminal from the wrath of the law?"

It was precisely what she was suggesting, and she didn't like his answers.

"I was thinking more of a jury," she said quickly. "Often they let people go rather than expose them to harsh penalties."

"Ah, true, and why our system does not work." They had stopped, and he rubbed a knuckle softly in the dip beneath her lips. "We are being very serious for a summer afternoon. You think often and deeply about justice and the law?"

"We had to discuss such matters at Miss Mallory's," she said, beginning to melt again—and at such a slight touch. "Do you mind a thoughtful, educated w . . . woman?"

She'd almost said *wife*!

His eyes crinkled with laughter. "Not at all. So," he added, soberly, "what is it you want to know about my views on the law?"

She thought for a moment, then asked a direct question. "Did you ever let a guilty person go because you thought it just, even though the law would have punished them?"

His hand stilled. After a thoughtful moment, he said, "Yes."

She took what felt like the first deep breath in minutes. "I'm glad."

"I thought you might be. In at least one case, I was wrong and thus responsible for another death."

"But—"

Jetta leaped out of the undergrowth just then, and Clarissa started with shock. She put a hand to her chest and Hawk laughed. "That cat will be the death of me. Come on. We are commanded onward by our chaperon."

Jetta was walking haughtily ahead.

Chaperon or not, Hawk put his arm around her as he had that day at the fair. Here, however, there was no need to protect her from a crowd.

She relaxed into the gentle protectiveness of it, but dared another question. "Did you ever have to investigate a friend?"

"Once. I had no choice. He was guilty of repeated cowardice, and a danger to all around him."

"What happened to him?"

"Nothing dramatic. He was allowed to resign his commission on the grounds of ill health. Last I heard, he goes around recounting his brave deeds and regretting that his weak body forced him to leave the scene of battle." After a moment, he looked at her and added, "Sometimes we do not know our friends."

Was that a warning?

"Can we know people at all?" she asked. "Can we ever know another person too well to be surprised?"

"Can we ever know ourselves too well to be surprised?"

She frowned over that. "I feel I know myself fairly well, faults and all."

"But—forgive me, Falcon—you have flown in circumscribed territory. If you were plunged into the extraordinary, you would doubtless surprise yourself. One way or another."

She looked up at him. "If we are uncertain of everything, even ourselves, how do we go on?"

"Ultimately, blind faith and trust."

Trust. That was the key. "I trust you, Hawk."

His eyes shifted away. "Ah," he said. "Perhaps you shouldn't."

Chapter Seventeen

S
he looked ahead, to find that the path wound around a large boulder. Jetta, following it, glanced back, then disappeared.

"What's the matter?" she asked.

He took her hand and pulled her along. "Come."

Beyond the boulder the path tumbled down long, rough steps. It didn't go very far before it divided, seeming to wander through shrubs and rocky outcroppings. She could hear splashing water somewhere.

"I have led you," he said, "like the children of Israel, into the wilderness."

Then she realized what this was. A wilderness garden. "So you have. But surely that isn't such a terrible thing."

"It has not, I fear, received Maria's efficient care as yet, and thus is rather more realistically wild than it should be. Yet it stands between us and our goal." He looked at her. "Do we go on, or back?"

A wilderness was designed to look wild but to also provide safe, smooth paths for civilized enjoyment. She could see that some paths here were almost overgrown, and there might be other hazards.

She smiled at him. "We go on, of course."

His smile suddenly matched hers. "So be it."

He helped her down the rough, rocky steps. "This is all completely artificial, of course. Dig here and you'll hit chalk, not granite. Careful."

The final rock was covered in tangling ivy. He stepped on it in his riding boots, grasped her at the waist and swung her completely over to the path beyond.

She landed feeling as if she'd left her stomach and her wits behind her entirely. When he stepped down beside her, she curled a hand around his neck.

"A hero deserves a kiss," she said, and rewarded him, rejoicing in the first kiss she had taken for herself.

When they drew apart, she dared to caress his lean cheek with her fingers, her delighted fingers. "Knight errant and princess."

"Or," he said, "dragon and princess . . . ?"

"With sharp teeth?"

He turned and nipped at her fingers, and she snatched them away. "But you are Saint George! Georgina West said so that first day."

He captured her hand and drew it to his mouth, to his teeth. "I'm no saint, Clarissa." He pressed teeth softly into her knuckle. "Remember that."

Astonishingly, she wanted him to bite harder.

But then he lowered her hand and tugged her along a path. "Come on."

She laughed and went, their bare hands clasped as if it were the most natural thing in the world. And it was. They were friends. They were joined. He was hers, and she was his, and before they returned to the civilized world she would be sure of it.

He often had to hold back invading branches. At one point, Clarissa raised her skirts to work past a brambly spot. It was necessary, but she didn't mind showing an extra bit of leg.

"Daisies," he said, admiring her stockings with a grin. "Are all your stockings fancied in some way?"

She deliberately fluttered her lashes at him. "Why, sir, that is for you to find out!"

When he reached for her, she ducked under a drooping branch and evaded him. Something snagged at her, and she realized that her hat was still down her back. She didn't mind, but waited for him to unhook her. Then froze at the tender touch at her nape . . .

They seemed magically transported out of the real world and real cares, to a place where wild rules reigned. She turned slowly to look at him, but he shook his head and drew her onward.

Then they came to the water, a little stream trickling out of a rock to splash into a moss-covered dip and flow away into a weedy pond. Clarissa put her hand under the cool stream.

"Piped, of course," he said.

She flicked a handful of spray at him. "Just because you have a house that looks as if it's grown where it stands! That's no reason to sneer because others have to construct their little bit of heaven."

"Minx." Laughing, he brushed away the sparkling trail from his hair. "Nature is beautiful enough. Why try to turn it into something it isn't? But we did have fun here as boys."

He looked around. "I remember we knotted a rope onto a branch up there," he said, pointing at a tall elm that overhung them. "We were planning to swing from one side to the other, like pirates boarding a Spanish treasure ship. Van broke his collarbone."

"Your parents must have been terrified."

"We hid the rope and said Van had fallen on the path. We were going to try another time, but never did. Perhaps we did have some sense."

He put his hand under the water, letting it stream out between his fingers like diamonds in a shaft of bright sun. She watched him carefully, expecting retaliation.

He turned to her, and with his wet hand he gently traced a cool line across her brows, down her cheek, and to her lips. Then he kissed her, hot against the cool, so she hummed with pleasure.

He drew back, frowning. "This is no good. Maria will send out a search party."

She grasped his jacket and pulled him back. "Can't we hide here and never be found?"

"Hide in the wilderness?" He freed himself, gripping her hands to prevent further attack. "No, fair nymph, I'm afraid we cannot. The world is a demanding mistress and will recapture us." He looked around. "The paths wind all over, but we can cut through by going that way."

She looked where he pointed. "That's the pond."

"It's about six inches deep." He suddenly swept her into his arms.

She shrieked, but then wrapped one arm around his neck and kissed his jaw. "My hero!"

"You may want to wait and see if I can do this without dropping you. I suspect the bottom is pure slime."

As soon as he put his boots into the water she felt them slip. "Hawk . . ."

"What is life without risk?"

"This is a brand-new gown!"

"O little mind, tied down in mundane cares."

The pond was only about ten feet wide, but he was having to take each step with exquisite care. Clarissa began to laugh.

"Stop that, woman. You'll have us drowning in duckweed!"

She stopped it by sucking lightly at his jaw.

"Is that supposed to help?"

"Promise of reward?" she whispered.

He halted. "Stop that, or I drop you."

She looked into his smiling eyes. "Do I believe you?"

"Do you think I wouldn't?"

"Yes," she said, and nibbled him.

He groaned and stepped quickly, rashly, the rest of the way across, then set her on her feet. He kept one arm around her, however, and swung her hard against him for a kiss that made their others seem lukewarm.

Clarissa sagged, her knees weakening under that assault. The next she knew she was sprawled back against a rock, a sun-warmed rock, grit and heat clear even through cloth. It was only slightly inclined. Perhaps if his legs weren't so pressed to hers she would slide down.

All she could think of, however, was his passionate eyes, on her. On her. Everything she wanted in life was here.

"Your gown is probably becoming stained with moss," he whispered, leaning closer, supported by one arm. The other hand rose to play on her cheek, her neck . . .

"Is it?" Her own voice astonished her with its husky mystery.

"Your new gown," he reminded her.

"Am I supposed to care?"

"Yes," he said. "I rather think you are."

"But I'm rich, Major Hawkinville. Very rich. What is one dress here or there?"

His lips twitched. "Then what about the evidence of moss on a lady's back?"

"Ah. But isn't the damage done? And I can always claim that you were a poor escort and let me tumble in the wilderness."

" 'Tumble,' " he said, brushing his lips over hers. "That has two meanings, you know."

"Like 'rod'?" she dared.

Those creases dug deep beside his mouth. "Very like 'rod,' yes. You frighten me, Clarissa."

"Do I? How?"

"Don't look so pleased. You frighten me because you have no true sense of caution. Aren't you at all afraid?"

"I'm not afraid of you, Hawk."

"You should be afraid of all men here, alone in the wilderness."

"Should I? Show me why."

With a laugh that sounded partly like a groan, he looked down, down at her bodice. Her gown's waist was very high and the bodice very skimpy, though made demure by a fine cotton fichu that tucked into it.

He pulled that out.

Clarissa lay there, heart pounding, as he softly kissed the upper curves of her breasts, a feather-stroke of lips across skin that had never known a man's touch before. A wise and cautious woman would stop him at this point. She raised a hand and let her fingers play with his hair as his lips teased at her.

Then his hand slid up to cup her breast. A new, strange feeling, but she liked it. His thumb began to rub and she caught her breath. Ah, she liked that even more!

She realized her hand had stilled and was clutching at the back of his neck. Her eyes half-focused on sunlight on his hair . . .

A sudden coolness made her start and look down. His thumb had worked both gown and corset off her nipple! She watched numbly as his mouth moved over and settled . . .

She let her head fall back and closed her eyes, the sun a warm haze behind her lids as he stirred magic in first one breast, then the other.

No, not just in her breasts.

Everywhere. Perhaps because his hand was beneath her skirt, up on her naked thigh. At some time her legs had parted and he pressed between them. She moved her body against his, holding him closer.

So, this was lovemaking.

Ruin.

How very, very sweet.

A deep beat started between her thighs, teaching her what wanting truly was. Wanting a specific man, in a specific way, at a specific moment.

Now.

She wriggled to press closer.

"Good God!"

He pushed away, jerking her up straight. Clarissa opened dazzled eyes to see him in a shimmering halo of light. He pulled up her bodice and searched around for her discarded fichu.

She put a hand on the rock to stay upright, but she was laughing. "That was astonishing! Can we do it again?"

He straightened, fichu in hand. "You're an unrepentant wanton!" But he was flushed and half laughing too. "You've bewitched me completely out of my senses. Heaven knows how long we've been here." He flung the soft cotton around her neck and began to tuck it in with unsteady fingers.

Then he stood back. "You do that. Maria will want my head. And Van will want—"

He stopped what he was saying, and she fixed the fichu over her breasts, fighting back her laughter. She was incapable of anything except total delight. That kiss, that encounter, had wiped away the last trace of doubt about his feelings. He'd gone further than he'd intended. He'd lost track of time.

He, the Hawk, had been lost in his senses with her.

She knew he was appalled, and that spoke of the power of their love.

Their love . . .

"We need only say we were lost in the wilderness, Hawk."

"We need to get out of here. Where's our damned inadequate chaperon?"

He took her hand and virtually dragged her up some more steps and around another boulder out into an open grassy space. There sat Jetta in front of a gate in the estate wall, waiting.

"Don't ask how she knew where we were going," he said. "She's never been here before." He strode forward and grasped the iron bolt, then swore. "It's stuck. My apologies."

"For language or gate?" But Clarissa knew laughter was in her tone. She couldn't help it. She'd laugh at rain at the moment, at thunder, or at hurricane. He was anxious to get through the gate for fear of her! Of what more they might do here.

She rather hoped the latch was fused shut.

He struggled with it for a moment more, then suddenly stood back and kicked at the rusty bolt. The gate sprang open, the bolt flying off the shattered rotten wood.

She caught her breath.

Crude, effective violence.

A side of Hawk Hawkinville that she had not seen before, suddenly reminding her of handsome, civilized Lord Arden lost in rage, hitting his wife . . .

He shook himself and turned, the elegant man again. "Come."

Chapter Eighteen

Clarissa went through the splintered gate. All the beautiful certainty she'd floated in had gone, and she was jolted to dubious earth. Would his next violent outburst be against her? When she told him the truth?

Beyond the gate lay civilization. The English countryside. A well-trodden pathway ran along the edge of a field of barley, winding up the hill behind them, and down toward the village in front.

The path to where? She had vowed to ask him to marry her if he didn't propose first. Now she faltered before uncertain flames.

"The path rises up to Hawks Monkton," he said in a very normal voice. "It's about three miles."

Jetta rubbed past their legs and headed down. What was there to do but follow?

"Perhaps you would care to visit it one day," he said as if giving a guided tour. "We have the remains of a monastery there. Very remaining remains. The stones were too useful to be left untouched."

"We?" she asked. "Does the manor hold this land?"

"No, this is Van's. The only manor land on this side of the river is around Hawks Monkton. On the other side, we own the village, and land nearly all the way to Somerford Court up there."

From this height Clarissa could see more of Lord Amleigh's home—a solid stone block with a lot of chimneys. "Jacobean?" she guessed.

"Early Charles I, but close enough. It doesn't have the elegance of Van's house, or the age of mine, and the Somerfords haven't been wealthy since the Civil War, so it's shabby in places. But it was always my favorite place to be."

He'd come to a halt considering it. "It was always a place of love and kindness and tranquil days."

"What happened to them?"

More violence?

He looked at her as if coming out of memories. "Was I speaking in the past tense? That comes out of my mind rather than reality. But Con's father and brother died while we were in the army. It was his father's heart. His brother drowned. Fred was boating mad. His mother and younger sister still live there, however, and he has two older sisters who are married with families of their own."

Clarissa gave thanks for what sounded like a normal family. She was beginning to think such things a matter only for fable!

"And Lord Vandeimen? He doesn't mention any family."

He gestured for them to walk on, and she obeyed. She noted, however, that he didn't touch her this time as he had so many times before. Had that burst of violence indicated a change of mind in him, as well as for her?

What was she to do about that?

"Sadly, Van has none left. It's hard to believe. Steynings was always so full of life. His mother and one sister died in the influenza that swept through here. His other sister died in childbirth a year ago, on the exact day of Waterloo. God alone knows, death was not short of business that day." He collected himself. "It's not surprising that his father went downhill. He shot himself."

"And Lord Vandeimen came home from battle to all that? How terrible."

"But his marriage has begun to heal the wounds."

Marriage. Capable of healing, capable of wounding. She suddenly saw it not as a device, as a comfortable matter of orange blossoms and beds, but as an elemental force.

"My parents were not like that," she said, half to herself. "I'm sure their marriage was always . . . arid."

"Perhaps not. Many marriages begin with dreams and ideals."

She looked at him, realizing that they were talking about marriage—now, when she had become dreadfully uncertain.

"What of your parents, Hawk?"

"Mine?" His laugh was short and bitter. "My father tricked my mother into marriage to gain her estate. Once he had it, he gave her no further thought other than to push her out of his way."

She stared at him, thinking perhaps she at last understood his lack of action. "You fear to be like your father?" she asked softly.

They had stopped again. "Perhaps," he said.

She grasped her courage. "If we were to marry, would you give me no further thought other than to push me out of your way?"

Humor, true humor, sparked in his eyes. "If I found you in my way, I'd likely ravish you on the spot."

She laughed, feeling her face burn with hot pleasure. "Then marry me, Hawk!"

And thus Hawk found himself frozen, pinned to an impossible spot by the words that had escaped him. If he said no, she would shrivel. If he said yes, it would be the direst betrayal.

He could not trap her without telling her the truth. If he told the truth, she would flee.

He'd been silent too long. Mortification rushed into her cheeks, and she turned to stumble away down the path.

He caught her round the waist, stopping her, pulling her against him. "Clarissa, I'm sorry! You are being very generous, and I . . . Dazzled by sunshine and wilderness adventures with you, I'm in no state to make a logical decision."

She fought him. He felt tears splash on his hands. In fear of hurting her, he let her go.

She whirled on him, brushing angrily at her eyes with both hands. "Logical! Do you deny that you went to Cheltenham in search of the Devil's Heiress?"

"No."

"Then why, for heaven's sake, when the rabbit wants to leap into the wolf's jaws, are you stepping back?"

"Perhaps, dammit, because rabbits are not supposed to leap into jaws!"

She planted her fists on her hips. "So! You will hold my boldness against me and cling to conventional ways!" Her look up and down was magnificently annihilating. "I thought better of you, sir."

With that salvo, she turned and marched away, and this time he did not try to stop her. He watched for a moment, transfixed with admiration and pure, raging lust.

My God, but he wanted this treasure of a woman in every possible way. He forced his feet into action to follow, plunging madly back into thought to find an answer, a solution. And it was as much for her as for him. He could not bear to see her suffer like this.

He could accept her offer of marriage. He recognized it for the worm it was, but he could make a clear case in favor.

She loved him. Perhaps she would forgive. Perhaps she would accept a future as Lady Deveril. If not, she would be the offended party, and could march off, banners flying. He'd keep not a penny more of her money than he absolutely needed, and would never try to restrict her freedom. He'd give her a divorce if she wanted it.

But divorce always shamed the woman. She would never be restored to the promise of life that she had now. He would be stealing that from her.

And it would have to be an elopement, with all the problems he'd already considered. All the problems that had made him reject that course. He had always prided himself on courage and an iron will, but now he'd found his weakness. He seemed able to stick to nothing where Clarissa was concerned.

Van.

He had made his friend a promise. He'd already gone further than he ought. Elopement, though—that would be an outright violation. Van might even feel obliged to call him out.

God Almighty! That would be the hellish nadir, to risk killing or being killed by one of his closest friends.

The path separated from the high stone wall, and Clarissa took the branch heading toward the river and the humpbacked bridge. He watched her straight back and high-held head.

Such courage, though he was sure she was still fighting tears. She hurt. He knew that. She wouldn't agree now, but it was a minor hurt that time would heal.

He must stick to his other plan and let her fly free.

Clarissa watched a crow flap up from the field in front of her and wished she could simply fly away from this excruciating situation. All she could do, however, was hurry to rejoin her party and return to Brighton.

Empty, purposeless Brighton.

No more Hawk.

Why had he pursued her if he did not want her? Why had he kissed her like that in the wilderness if he did not want her? Was it true what they said, that a man would kiss and ravish any woman, given the chance?

It hadn't felt like that, but what did she know of the reality between men and women?

But, oh, it hurt to think that all her money was not sweetening enough to make her palatable.

She was sure that he was still coming along behind her, and she longed to turn and scream stupid, pride-salving things at him. That she didn't want him. Didn't need him. That she thought his kisses horrid.

She bit her lip. As if anyone would believe that.

All she could do was escape with the shreds of her dignity intact.

And then what?

No more Hawk.

No Hawk in the Vale.

No heaven for her. Ever.

She came to a stile, and for a stupid moment the wooden structure seemed like an insurmountable obstacle, especially with tears blurring her vision. She gathered her skirts in order to climb it.

Hawk suddenly stepped past her to climb over and offer her a hand. She had to face him again. Was she fooling herself that his eyes seemed to mirror her pain?

She put her hand in his, realizing by sight that it was gloveless. Somewhere in the wilderness she had mislaid that symbol of the well-bred lady.

As she stepped up on her side, he said, "I'm sorry. You know how to turn a man topsy-turvy, Clarissa."

"It's entirely an accident, I assure you. I know nothing."

"I shouldn't have criticized you for making that proposal." He was blocking her way, but at a point where she was nearly a foot taller. Deliberately giving her that superiority?

"I meant what I said," he went on. "I'm dazzled. This has been an unexpected and remarkable day, and our adventures in the wilderness were enough to turn any man crazed. You must see that."

The splinters of ice in her heart started to melt, but he wasn't really explaining. Or accepting her offer.

"I can't answer you now," he said. "I told you about my parents. My mother flung herself into marriage with my father in a state of blind adoration, then clung to her disappointment for the rest of her life. Marriage is not a matter to be decided in emotion."

She stared down at him. "You're likening me to your father? You, sir, are the fortune hunter here!"

"Then why did you ask me to marry you?"

She knew she was turning red again. "Very well. I, like your father, lust after Hawk in the Vale. At least I'm honest about it. And I won't push you aside if you get in my way."

There was something to be said for anger, she realized, and for an additional foot of height!

"And," she added, "*you* went to Cheltenham looking for *me*."

"Yes."

"Checking me out before making a commitment?"

A smile twitched his lips. "I liked what I found."

"And you suggested that I come to Brighton."

"Yes."

"And kissed me at the fair."

"Yes."

"And took me into the wilderness."

He looked rather as if she were raining blows on him. That didn't stop her. She would not play coy games anymore.

She stepped over the middle of the stile to loom over him even more. "So, Major Hawkinville, what happens next?"

"You fly like the falcon you are." He put his hands at her waist and lifted her, spinning her in a circle twice, then down to the grass beyond.

She landed, laughing despite herself. "No one but you has ever done that to me, Hawk. Made me fly." She meant it in many more ways than a spin through the air, and she knew he'd know that.

What now? Should she risk devastation by asking him again . . . ?

A scream severed the moment.

A young child's shriek.

After a dazed moment, Clarissa realized that a splash had gone with the scream. Hawk was already running, already halfway across a field to the river—the river so deep it had kept the village on one side until the bridge was built. She picked up her skirts and raced after him, dodging around slightly startled cows.

The child was still screaming, but she couldn't see the riverbank for bullrushes. Screaming was good, but then she realized that there might be more than one child. One screaming, one drowning.

Hawk could swim. She remembered that and thanked God.

The screaming stopped, and she saw that Hawk was there, and a small child was pointing. Then he waded through the rushes.

She ran the last little way, gasping, and took the girl's hand. She could see a boy flailing, but in quite shallow water near the edge. Hawk grabbed the boy's arm and hauled him close.

Safe.

Safe.

Clarissa sucked in some needed air, collapsing onto the grass with the little girl in her lap. "There, there, sweetheart. It's all right. Major Hawkinville has your friend."

The dark-haired child was very young to be out without an adult, and the lad didn't look much older. No wonder they'd fallen into such trouble.

Wondering at the silence, she turned the girl's face toward her and found tears pouring from huge blue eyes, but eerily without a sound. "Oh, poppet, cry if you want." She raised her cream skirt to wipe the tears.

A hiccup escaped, but that was all. But then suddenly the child buried her face in Clarissa's shoulder and clung, shivering like Jetta that first day. Clarissa held her tight and crooned to her.

She thought to look around for the forgotten cat and found it there, lying in the grass, eyes on the child in Clarissa's lap. Clarissa made a little room, and Jetta leaped up.

The child flinched, but Jetta pushed closer, purring, and the little girl put out a grubby hand to touch her. Then shivering little arms encircled, and tears fell onto the silky fur.

Hawk had the other child out of the water and was hugging him too. He and she were both going to be muddy, but Hawk didn't seem to mind, and she certainly didn't. She was glad that he wasn't wasting breath yelling at the frightened boy.

Clarissa hid her face in the girl's curls. She was besotted by everything about Major Hawk Hawkinville. She could even, in a way, admire him for not snatching the prize she'd dangled in front of him.

He would be a wonderful father, though. She'd never thought that way before, but she wanted him as father to her children.

He carried the boy over. "He seems to mostly speak French, and be of a taciturn disposition, but he's one of Mrs. Rowland's children, so this must be the other."

"Who's Mrs. Rowland?"

"A Belgian woman married to an invalid English officer. She has rooms in the village."

"Her children shouldn't be out alone."

"No, but there's little money. She has to go away sometimes, seeking an inheritance. People have offered to help, but she's proud. We'll take them home as we go."

Clarissa separated reluctant child and cat, then held out a hand. He helped her up with the little girl still clutching.

"At least," he said, looking her over, "no one is going to be commenting about stains on your dress now."

Clarissa chuckled. "I'm definitely not still tied down by mundane cares."

She didn't want to think back to all that had happened, however, and she had no idea how to go forward. She focused instead on the fact that the little girl was barefoot, and the boy too.

"Where are your shoes, little one?" she asked the girl in French.

The dark curls shook, no.

The boy said, "We were not wearing any."

"That's not uncommon in the country," Hawk said, "and even less so on the continent. But I suspect that these two slipped out of the cottage without permission. Their mother is probably frantic."

They crossed the bridge into the village, passing a sinewy woman with a basket who clucked her tongue. "Those little imps. Do you want me to take them, sir?"

Hawk thanked her but refused, and led the way behind the clanging smithy to a door in the back of another building.

"Bert Fagg lets out these rooms," he said.

"A rough place for an officer and his wife," Clarissa said.

"I know, but she's living on my father's charity. She claims to be a connection of his. He certainly enjoys her company. He said he invited her to live in the manor house, but she refused. She's a strange, difficult woman."

He knocked on the door of the very silent building. Rough cloths covered the windows, so Clarissa couldn't see inside.

"Perhaps she's out looking for the children," she said.

But then the door swung open and a dark-clothed woman stepped out. The only brightness about her was a stark white cap that covered her graying hair and tied under her chin with narrow laces. She did not look well. Her skin was sallow, and dark rings circled her eyes.

"*Oh, mon dieu!*" she exclaimed, snatching the little girl from Clarissa's arms. "Delphie!" Then she went off into a rapid tirade of French that Clarissa could not follow.

She heard a noise and looked down to see Jetta, back arched, hissing at the woman. She hastily picked up the cat. "Hush."

Jetta relaxed, but still looked at Mrs. Rowland with a fixed stare. Clarissa could almost hear a silent hiss, and knew just how the cat felt. Yes, any mother might berate a child who had fallen into danger, but there was something coldly furious rather than panicked about Mrs. Rowland.

Clarissa glanced at the boy, whom Hawk had put down. He looked suitably afraid. Any child could be afraid after being caught in such naughtiness, and he had taken his baby sister into danger with him. All the same, there was something *old* about his fear. She desperately wanted to stand between the woman and her children, as she'd stood between Jetta and the duckling.

Mrs. Rowland suddenly put the girl down and said in clear French, "Come, Pierre. Take Delphie inside."

Pierre walked over to his sister, head held high, and led her into the cottage.

"Thank you, Major Hawkinville," said Mrs. Rowland in heavily accented English. She sounded as if she'd rather be eating glass.

"Anyone would have helped. May I ask that you not be too harsh on them, Mrs. Rowland? I think they have learned their lesson through their fright."

The woman did not thaw. "They must learn not to slip away." She went back into her house and shut the door.

Clarissa blinked, startled by such lack of gratitude, and also by a flash of recognition. Who? Where? She was certain she'd never met Mrs. Rowland before.

Hawk drew her away. "There's nothing we can do. Any family in the village would spank the pair of them for that."

"I know. But I don't like that woman." She stroked the cat in her arms. "Jetta hissed at her."

"Understandable. That's only the second time we've spoken, and she makes the hair on the back of my neck stand on end. I'd think she was avoiding me except that she avoids everyone except my father."

They walked back around the smithy onto the green.

"She visits your father?"

"Yes, and surprisingly he frets if she stays away too long."

"You don't like it?"

He glanced at her. "I told you once, I'm inclined to be suspicious of every little thing."

"I suspect your instincts are finely tuned."

His look turned intent. "At the time, as I remember, I was speaking of Miss Hurstman. You have reason to worry about her?"

Clarissa almost told him. But no. At this point she wasn't at all sure that he could be trusted with her secrets.

"Surely Hawk Hawkinville can find out about a Belgian woman married to a British officer called Rowland."

"Hawk Hawkinville has been somewhat busy. But certainly the next time I'm in London I'll check on them both at the Horse Guards. She rubs me the wrong way, but she's probably simply a poor woman in a very difficult situation and with a prickly nature."

Then he said, "Gads, Maria is probably already at the Peregrine, steaming! Come on!"

He took her hand and they hurried across the green. This was the moment when Clarissa had promised herself that she would propose.

But she had, and she'd been rejected. It was so painful that she couldn't imagine how men plucked up the courage to do it, especially the second time.

She'd spiraled up to heaven in his arms, then plunged into fear at his violence, and then to hurt and furious shame at his rejection. But she still loved him. Silly, besotted fool that she was, she still loved, still hoped.

They were almost at the inn. She said, "That is a horrid house," meaning the stuccoed one next door.

"Thoroughly."

"If your father owns the village, didn't the builder need permission?"

He stopped and turned her toward him. "Clarissa, I need to tell you something."

"Yes?" Her heart speeded. She sensed this was something crucial.

"My father is deep in debt to Slade, the man who owns that house. That's why he couldn't stop it. My father has mortgaged Hawkinville Manor and all its estates to Slade. If we don't get a lot of money soon, Slade will be squire here. And the first thing he plans to do is to rip down the manor and the cottages to build an even more monstrous house on the river."

She stared at him, struck by an almost physical sense of loss. "You can't permit that! My money. It's my money that you need, isn't it? Then why . . . ?"

He winced. "I can't explain everything now, Clarissa. But I wanted you to know the truth. So you'd understand."

"But I *don't* understand."

"Major Hawkinville! Good day to you, sir."

They both turned to the man who had come out of the white monster. He was middle-aged, fit, and well dressed. If Clarissa had been a cat, she would have hissed.

Hawk put an arm around her as if in protection and moved to avoid the man.

"A lovely day, is it not?" Slade persisted.

"It is becoming less so." Clarissa could feel tension in Hawk—the leashed desire for violence. The wretched Slade must know it and was deliberately tormenting him.

"You and your lovely lady have had an accident, Major?" the man asked, narrow eyes flicking over them.

Clarissa realized that in addition to being a mess she still had her hat hanging down her back, and her hair was doubtless rioting. A glance showed her that Hawk for once was almost as disordered.

"Only in meeting you, sir," said Hawk.

"So I suspect," said Slade in a voice full of innuendo.

Clarissa felt Hawk inhale, and hastily stepped between the men. "You must be Mr. Slade. Major Hawkinville has told me how kind you have been to his poor father."

Slade froze, and his narrowed gaze flicked between her and Hawk.

"Clarissa . . ." Hawk put his hand on her again to move her away.

"How happy you will be," she said, evading him again, "to know that soon your generosity will be repaid. I am a very wealthy woman."

It was delicious to see the odious Slade turn pale with shock and fury, but Clarissa didn't dare look at Hawk. He was probably pale with shock and fury too, but she hadn't been able to stand seeing him baited.

"My congratulations, Major," Slade spat out.

"Thank you, Slade." Hawk's voice sounded flat. "It must be a great relief to know that your generous loans will be repaid in full, with interest, before the due date."

"A hasty marriage, eh? Doubtless wise."

Clarissa blocked Hawk again, facing the iron founder. "Not at all, sir." She wanted to knock the man down herself! "It will take time to arrange a suitably grand affair. On the village green, no doubt, since Major Hawkinville's family is so important here."

Oh, lord. She could feel Hawk's anger blistering her back.

"The loans come due on the first of August, young lady."

She assumed what she hoped was a look of astonished distaste. "If you insist on payment on the dot, sir, it will be arranged by my trustees. Under no circumstances will I permit Hawkinville Manor to change hands."

Hawk's arm came around her then, pulling her to his rigid, angry side. "As you see, Slade, there is no point in your further residence here."

The man's face was still pale, but now splotches of angry color marked his cheeks. "I believe I will wait to dance at your grand wedding, Major."

"If you insist."

Hawk turned Clarissa toward the inn, but Slade said, "Is the name of the bride a dreadful secret?"

Clarissa twisted back to say, "Not at all, Mr. Slade. I am Miss Greystone. You might have heard of me. Some call me the Devil's Heiress."

She was then swept away by an arm as strong as iron. Lord, that had been thoroughly wicked, but also thoroughly satisfying. Slade was probably drooling with fury.

So was someone else. Not drooling, but furious.

Chapter Nineteen

Hawk dragged her not to the main door of the inn, but through the arch into the inn yard. Ignoring, or perhaps oblivious to, the various servants there, he thrust her against the rough wall. "What exactly do you think you are doing?"

"Trouncing the odious Slade!" she declared, grinning even though her knees were turning to jelly with fear. Glory in the battle warred with memories of Beth's bruised face. "Don't tell me you didn't enjoy that."

"Enjoy being taken by the scruff and dragged through a bramble patch?"

"Enjoy watching him drink bile."

Suddenly his furious eyes closed, and then he laughed, leaning his forehead against hers. "Zeus, yes. It was worth a thousand torments."

Clarissa knew she should feel hurt by that, but she didn't. She was suddenly certain that all was right in her world. She didn't understand his reluctance, but she was sure it could be blasted into dust. Above all, she was sure that she wanted him, and that he would be all she wanted and more.

She poked him hard in the belly. "If you're rude again about the prospect of marrying me, I'll go right back and tell Slade he can have Hawkinville, every last post and stone."

He straightened to look at her, eyes still wild with laughter. "Clarissa, there is nothing I want more than to marry you."

"Well, then—"

His kiss silenced her, a hot, enthralling kiss that sent fire into every part of her, though she couldn't help thinking of the watching servants.

With glee.

He'd certainly have to marry her after this.

"Hawk! Clarissa! Stop that!"

Clarissa emerged from a daze to find Maria hitting Hawk's back with a piece of wood. Fortunately it was rotted, and was flying into pieces with each blow.

Hawk turned to her laughing, hands raised, and she threw the remaining fragments away in disgust. "What do you think you're doing?" she demanded. Then she stared at Clarissa. "Or more to the point, what *have* you done?"

"I ravished her in the wilderness, of course."

"*What?*"

"Don't be a goose, Maria. That wilderness of yours, by the way, is too damn wild. But most of the damage to our appearance was done by our gallant rescue of two children from the river."

"Rescue?" Maria collected herself. "That doesn't explain such a shocking kiss in front of the servants."

"A certain madness comes upon us all after battle."

"Battle?"

Clarissa was threatened by incapacitating giggles, for a hundred reasons. She simply leaned against the wall and enjoyed the show.

"Clarissa just routed Slade by telling him we are engaged to be married. I thought I had better compromise her thoroughly before she changed her mind."

She'd won! She didn't know how, but she'd won. She lovingly brushed some fragments of rotted wood off her future husband's shoulders.

He turned, and the look in his eyes turned her delight to cold stone. The laughter had gone, and was replaced by something dark and almost lost. A movement beyond him caught her eye, and she saw Lord Vandeimen emerge from one of the stable buildings, suddenly deadly.

Why on earth would she think that?

As if alerted, Hawk swung around. "Nothing happened."

"Nothing!" exclaimed Lady Vandeimen, but then she seemed silenced by the crackling tension.

"Nothing of any great significance," Hawk said with precision.

Clarissa wanted to protest that, but she too was frozen by something ready to burst out of this ordinary place into the world of claw and fang.

Lord Vandeimen said, "A word with you, Hawk." His head indicated the stable behind him.

Clarissa put her hand on Hawk's arm as if to hold him back, but Maria pulled her away. "Come into the inn and tidy up, Clarissa."

"But—"

"You can't possibly return to Brighton looking like that." She ruthlessly steered Clarissa into the building, chattering.

"Lord Vandeimen is not my guardian!" Clarissa broke in, forcing a halt. "What's going on out there?"

Maria looked at her. "More to the point, what went on during your walk?"

"Nothing," said Clarissa, "of any great significance." Then the whole tumultuous half hour burst out of her in tears, and Maria gathered her into her arms, hurrying her along to a private room.

"Hush, dear. Hush. Whatever went on, we'll arrange matters. I know Hawk loves you."

Clarissa looked at her and blew into her handkerchief. "You do?"

"Yes, of course."

"Then why doesn't he want to marry me?"

Maria's smile was close to a laugh. "Of course he does!"

Clarissa shook her head. "Men are very hard to understand, aren't they?"

Maria hugged her again. "There you have a universal truth, my dear."

Hawk followed Van into the pleasantly pungent stable thinking that the day couldn't get much worse, but knowing that in fact it could.

Van turned and merely waited.

"That kiss probably did go beyond the line," Hawk said. "But nothing worse happened." Then he remembered the wilderness. "More or less. That bloody wilderness of yours is a disgrace."

He saw Van fight it, then laugh. "It's almost worth it to see you in this state, Hawk. What the devil are you up to?"

"I'm trying to save Hawkinville."

"I assume you have decided to woo Miss Greystone. Is it necessary to be so crude about it?"

"She told Slade we were engaged to marry."

Van visibly relaxed. "Why the devil didn't you say so? Congratulations!"

"I'm not going to marry her, Van."

Van leaned back against a wooden post, frowning in perplexity. "Would you care to start at the beginning? Or at some point that makes sense?"

Hawk said, "My father is the new Viscount Deveril."

Van frowned even more. "You're the son of Lord Devil? The one Miss Greystone inherited from? And I've never heard of it?"

"The new Lord Deveril. You know my father changed his name as a price of marrying my mother. He was born a Gaspard, and that's the Deveril name. When Lord Devil died last year, he chased back up and down the family tree and discovered that he's the heir. It's taken him the best part of a year to settle it, but it's just about done."

"Congratulations. You'll outrank me one day."

"Bugger that. The name's fit to be spat upon."

"A name's a name. The first Lord Vandeimen was a spineless lickspittle. Is this where the debt comes from?"

"More or less. The squire's been obsessed by the Deveril money. He thinks he should get it along with the title, that the will was a forgery." Hawk looked around and spotted a room with a door. "Come in here."

Van followed, and Hawk shut the door. The room was small and seemed mostly to hold nostrums for treating horses.

"Unfortunately," Hawk said, "my father is probably right." He didn't want to say it, but he had no choice. "I've been dangling after Miss Greystone not to woo her but to entice her to spill something about the will."

"You're a damn fine actor, then."

"I've learned to be. Van, for God's sake, there's no question of marriage! Once Clarissa discovers what I've been up to, and that I'm a future Lord Deveril, it'll all be over."

"Hawk, this doesn't sound like you."

"What, underhanded trickery and sneaky investigation? It's my stock-in-trade. I've softened up plenty of villains for the gutting."

"But not an innocent young woman."

"If she was innocent, there wouldn't be any gutting to be done."

Van frowned. "All right, let's talk about this. What exactly do you think her guilty of?"

"Murder, or conspiracy to murder."

"*Murder?*" Van managed to keep it soft. "If I'm any judge, Miss Greystone would run from killing a mouse."

"The mouse wouldn't be forcing vile kisses on her, and threatening worse."

"You think she killed Deveril when he tried to rape her? You'd send her to the gallows for that?"

"No, dammit. But remember, she ended up with the dead man's money." It was a detail he tended to willfully ignore.

"All right," said Van, "do you have any reason other than wishful thinking to believe that Lord Deveril's will was forged?"

"When have you ever known me to indulge in wishful thinking?"

But his thinking about Clarissa came perilously close.

"It was handwritten," he said crisply, "witnessed by servants who have conveniently disappeared, and it left everything not entailed to a young woman, to come to her completely and without control at age twenty-one."

Van's expression lost its indulgence. "Hell."

"Hell, indeed. I can add, from Clarissa's own lips, that she was sold to Deveril and hated him, which he must have known. She threw up over him when he tried to kiss her."

"It does look damned bad. How did Deveril die?"

"Knifed. Viciously."

But then Van shook his head. "It still doesn't fit. I know I don't have your acute sense for truth and lies, but Clarissa Greystone makes an unlikely thief and an impossible murderer."

"Appearances can be deceptive. Did I ever tell you about an innocent-looking, big-eyed child in Lisbon? Never mind. You don't want to know."

Van's brows rose. "Are you protecting Demon Vandeimen from sordid details, Hawk?"

Hawk sighed. "I would if I could. We none of us need more darkness in our lives. But I have to save Hawkinville. You must see that, Van."

"Yes, of course. Perhaps I'll simply cut Slade's scrawny throat."

It was a joke. Hawk hoped, but he shook his head. "No more blood if I can help it."

"So, let's sort it out."

Hawk put up a hand. "Maria will be waiting. We can talk later if you want."

"No, let's deal with this now. If necessary we can stay the night and get Con in on it. You really think Clarissa Greystone committed a vicious murder and planted a forged will?"

"No, dammit, but that could be willful delusion."

Van smiled slightly at the implied admission. "I'm not willfully deluded. Let's consider this. If someone else was the murderer and thief last year, who could it have been? From what I've heard, she left school and went to London. She can't have known many people who would kill and forge for her—" He broke off. "Talk about teaching a grandmother to suck eggs. You must have been through this."

Hawk resisted for a moment, but he knew Van wouldn't let it go. "Arden," he said.

"Arden?"

"The Marquess of Arden was the killer. Last year he married a teacher at Clarissa's Cheltenham school."

Van's jaw dropped. "The heir to Belcraven? Are you mad?"

"High rank means honor? You know better than that, Van."

"It means hell's fires if you meddle there and can't prove it beyond doubt. And what motive could he have?"

"Maria has that pretty niece, Natalie. What if she were in the power of a man like Deveril? Couldn't Maria persuade you into doing something illegal to rescue her?"

"I'd knife him in public if necessary."

Hawk knew Van was speaking the literal truth. He himself would do it too. And so would a man like Arden, he was sure.

"If that was the way it was," Van said, "give the man a medal."

"Then how do I get the money?"

"How do you get the money this way?"

Hawk put it into plain words. "I blackmail him for it."

Van braced himself against a worktable. "You'd destroy essentially honorable people?"

"Don't get too misty-eyed. Disposing of Deveril was a virtuous act, but misappropriating his money was straight-out, deliberate theft."

"How in God's name do you think to go about this? Men like Arden and his father can destroy with a word."

"Ah, yes, the Duke of Belcraven. He's Clarissa's guardian, by the way."

"Zeus! They're all in it? But why?"

"Simply protecting her, I assume. Which has my sympathy. But I must save Hawkinville, and I see no reason not to have enough of that money to also rebuild Gaspard Hall and get my father off my back. And do something for the poor Deveril tenants."

Van was looking slightly alarmed. It took a lot to alarm Demon Vandeimen. "You'll have to convince the duke that you would make it public. And," he added, "watch your back."

"I'm good at that. Van, I'm depending upon the fact that these are essentially honorable people. Deveril was thought to be without an heir. Surely they'll see that it's wrong to divert all that money."

"And Clarissa?"

"She'll hardly be left penniless."

"She's an innocent party."

"Innocent! She shows no guilty conscience over enjoying the ill-gotten gains." Then another piece clicked into place. "Devil take it, the fortune is *payment*. She was present at the murder, so Arden arranged the forgery to pay her off. No wonder she's as closemouthed as a tomb about it."

"Hawk, this is wrong."

"No, dammit, forgery is wrong. My father, damn his eyes, is right. The money belongs to Hawkinville, and I won't see Slade destroy it because I was too squeamish to hurt Clarissa's feelings!"

"You can't do it."

Hawk was about to wring Van's neck when he saw the expression on his friend's face. As if he'd suddenly seen an unpleasant vision.

Van straightened. "Arden will call your bluff."

"He daren't risk it."

"Why not? If you prove anything, you will destroy Clarissa as well as him."

"With any luck, he won't know that's a factor."

"More to the point," said Van slowly. "Arden is a Rogue."

"What?"

"One of Con's Company of Rogues. I can't believe that slipped by your brain. Roger, Nick, Francis, Hal, Luce . . ." Van recited. "We heard enough about them. And Luce is Lucien de Vaux, Marquess of Arden."

It had slipped by him. Devil in flames. Something about Arden had been niggling him, but Con had always talked about the Rogues by first names—unusual enough. Luce.

"And Hal Beaumont," he said. "The man with Mrs. Hardcastle. Clarissa said he was an old friend of Arden's. But being a Rogue doesn't give Arden immunity."

"No, but he has to know who you are. I'm sure Con spoke of us to them as much as he spoke of them to us. And there's only two of us. Unless he has the brain of a sheep and the spine of a rabbit, he'll have to know that you could not possibly attempt to destroy one of Con's Rogues. However, perhaps Con can act as go-between."

"No!" Hawk's rejection was instinctive, but reason followed. "That's an intolerable position to put him in. 'Admit to murder and forgery of your free will and quietly move half of Clarissa's fortune to my friend Hawk.' No," he repeated, standing among ruins. "I'll come up with something else."

"You don't have much time. Why not simply tell Clarissa the truth? Perhaps she will be able to forgive your deception and overlook a future as Lady Deveril."

"But how will Arden and his father feel about it? She still needs her guardian's permission."

"Damn."

"Strange, isn't it? I have all the cards in my hand, and yet it still seems possible that I might lose."

"We have to tell Con. He can't be left out of this."

"Haven't you thought that he might know? The Rogues don't keep secrets from each other."

"You think he knows that they set up a will that defrauded you?"

Hawk shook his head. "I haven't told him anything about the debt or the Deveril title. Someone in the Rogues has to know, though, with my father chasing it through the courts."

"I can't believe Con would do nothing about a situation like that."

"He'd be caught in the middle."

"No," Van said. "It's more likely that they're protecting him from it. He's only recently started to recover from Waterloo and Dare."

Hawk considered it and knew it might be true. "All the more reason not to tell him yet." He went toward the door. "I need a little more time, Van. Perhaps if I shuffle the cards again. At the least I need to go down to the manor to get clean clothes."

They emerged from the room and separated, but as Hawk walked to the manor, he couldn't seem to shuffle the cards into anything but disastrous patterns.

Who should suffer? Himself, for certain, but he was choosing the pain.

What of Con, or Clarissa?

What of the Dadswells, the Manktelows, and the Ashbees? Was Granny Muggridge to have the roof torn down around her head?

But at what point did the price of Hawkinville become too high?

Cut the loss.

It was a process he'd done often in the war, even when it meant choosing between one set of soldiers or another. Perhaps if he thought of everyone as troops of soldiers.

The option with the least loss was to elope with Clarissa. He would have the money, or at least the expectation of it. He knew the will, and the money came to her at her majority, regardless of what she did or whom she married. As her husband, he could easily borrow against it.

Hawkinville would be safe.

There would be a fighting chance of happiness for them. There was something deep and true between them, and he would work to gain her forgiveness for the deception.

Van might never forgive him for breaking his word, but he could hope that time would heal that, especially if he could make Clarissa happy.

Con. At the moment, Con was an unknown. If he saw this as a betrayal of the Rogues, it could lead to a rift. The Rogues certainly weren't going to like it. They were going to have to damn well trust him not to expose their criminal acts.

But it was the only way.

Gathering the detached purposefulness that had carried him through scenes of carnage, he went swiftly to his room to change, then gathered the money available in the house. He thought about leaving a note for the squire, but then knocked and entered his father's room.

The squire was lying on his daybed fondling—there was no other word—some papers. "They have come," he said, with shining eyes. "The documents. You may now officially call me Lord Deveril!"

Hawk had to stop himself from seizing the papers and ripping them to shreds. Pointless. Pointless.

This settled things, however. In moments his father could begin spreading the word. Since Clarissa was in the village, she would hear about it, and that would be the end of that.

"Congratulations, my lord. You may congratulate me, also. I am about to marry Miss Greystone."

His father beamed. "There, you see. All's well that ends well. And her money will pay to refurbish Gaspard Hall."

"Not a penny of her money will go on Gaspard Hall, my lord. We will pay off Slade, but the rest will remain under her control."

If he had to do this, it had to be that way.

"What? Are you mad? Leave a fortune in the grasp of a chit like that? I will not allow it."

"You will have no say in it." He turned toward the door. "I merely came to say that I will be gone a few days."

"Gone? Gone where? We must arrange a grand fête to announce my elevation to the village! I outrank Vandeimen now, and I'll see him recognize it."

The fury boiling inside Hawk threatened to burst out of control, but he'd not struck his father yet. Now was definitely not the time to start.

"It will have to wait, my lord. I am off to Gretna Green."

He closed the door on his father's protests—not about the elopement but about delay in his fête—and ran down the stairs. Somehow he had to get Clarissa out of the Peregrine and on the road north before his father set the news spreading.

He fretted even over the time it took a groom to saddle up Centaur, imagining his father leaning out of his window above to shout the news. He wouldn't do that, but he would tell his valet—might already have told his valet. His valet would tell the other servants and . . .

Perhaps a servant had already hurried home to spread the word.

He led Centaur up to the inn, considering how to steal Clarissa. Perhaps he'd have to snatch her on the way to the coach, like Lochinvar snatching his beloved from her wedding.

> So light to the croup the fair lady he swung.
> So light to the saddle before her he sprung!
> "She is won! We are gone, over bank, bush, and scaur;
> They'll have fleet steeds that follow," quoth young Lochinvar.

And that, of course, was the problem. He was dubious about young Lochinvar riding so rashly with a lady at his back, and he'd no intention of attempting it with Van and Con—especially Van, an incredible horseman now equipped by his rich bride with the finest horses—in hot pursuit.

He would have to go in and try to lure her out.

Then he saw Clarissa—beloved, unconventional, impetuous Clarissa—in the arch to the inn yard. Alone. Her hat shaded her face again, and some order had been brought to her curls, but her dress was irredeemably stained.

When he reached her, she stepped forward. "I've told them all what I did with Slade and that I kissed you, not the other way around."

If he hadn't adored her already, he'd have crumpled then. He held out his gloved hand. "Elope with me."

Her eyes widened, but she only said, "Why?"

"So that this can't be snatched from us."

She looked down and away, obviously flustered, but then back at him. "Do you love me, Hawk? Don't lie. Please don't lie."

"I adore you, Clarissa. And that is no lie."

Then she smiled and put her hand in his. "Then, of course. It's a mad, impetuous notion, but that probably suits us both."

He laughed as he swung his fair lady to the crupper and settled in front of her. "I used to be a very sane, thoughtful man," he said. "Hold tight. We're going over bank, bush, and scaur."

And he set off, past a few startled villagers, along the road that would eventually take them north to Scotland, where minors could still legally marry without the permission of parents, guardians, or Rogues.

But he soon turned off, going west instead of north. He couldn't outride Van. But, by heaven, he could probably still outthink him.

Chapter Twenty

The rest of the party was in the entrance hall of the Peregrine, waiting with some impatience for Clarissa to return from the privy. Eventually, Maria asked Althea to find her, but Althea returned frowning. "She's not there. I don't know where she can have gone to. Perhaps she's returned to the room upstairs."

But then one of the Misses Weatherby trotted in, cheeks flushed. "My dear Lady Vandeimen!" she gasped. "Oh, my lords." She curtsied around, clearly breathless with excitement. "Are you by any chance looking for your companion? We saw you earlier. My sister and I. Saw you on the green, and returning. And the handsome major returning with the lady."

"Miss Weatherby," Maria interrupted ruthlessly. "Do you know where Miss Greystone is?"

"Why, yes," said the lady, not well concealing her glee. "She's just ridden off behind Major Hawkinville."

Maria looked at her husband. "Van?"

He'd turned pale with anger in a way she'd never seen before.

He was actually moving when she grasped his sleeve. "Wait! Talk." She smiled back at Miss Weatherby. "Thank you so much. I know I can trust you not to spread this around."

Unlikely hope, but it might stop the news for a minute or two. She didn't think there'd been any inn servants nearby to hear. She dragged her husband into the adjoining parlor, the rest following, and shut the door. She couldn't have done it if he'd resisted, so she knew she was right.

"I think he truly loves her," she said. "And I know she loves him."

But Miss Trist wrung her hands. "Why run off together? She's refused him, and he's abducted her!"

"Nonsense," Maria snapped. "Abduction is completely illegal these days. He can hardly drag her against her will to Scotland."

Van said, "I have to stop this, Maria. For everyone's sake. I'm sending a note up to Con."

He left before she could stop him again, and indeed, she wasn't sure she should. But he'd looked for a moment as if he would kill his friend.

Demon Vandeimen. Did she know what he was really capable of?

Van returned with a letter in his hand. "I've sent for Con. When he arrives, give him this."

Maria took it, but she knew he was setting off in pursuit. "Don't kill him, Van. For your own sake, don't."

He relaxed slightly. "I won't. I might beat him to a pulp, but I won't kill him." He kissed her quickly, tenderly, then rubbed at what must be lines in her brow. "Don't worry. This is a mess, but I'll find a way to bring it all out right."

"He hasn't abducted her," she said. "Clarissa's besotted with him, and I'd say he feels the same way about her. What's going on?"

"It's complicated." He kissed her again quickly, then left.

Maria could have screamed with frustration. Complicated! She'd give him complicated. She considered snapping the seal on the letter in hopes that it explained, but long training in proper behavior would not permit it.

Instead she called for tea and settled to soothing Althea. Poor Lord Trevor was looking as if he wished himself elsewhere, but he was bearing up like the well-trained officer he was.

It took remarkably little time for Con to turn up, though it had felt like an hour. He strode in, another man behind him.

"Mr. Nicholas Delaney," he said. "My guest at the moment, but he's probably involved." He took the letter, opened it, and read.

Then he passed it to his friend.

"Con," said Maria, "if you don't tell me what is going on, I am going to do someone serious injury."

He laughed, but sobered, looking around the room. "Ffyfe, I'm sure you're as curious as any human would have to be, but it would simplify things if you weren't here. And Miss Trist, you could help Miss Greystone as well by strolling on the green."

Lord Trevor accepted his orders remarkably well, but Althea looked around. "What's going on? Is Clarissa in danger?"

Lord Trevor took her arm. "Truly, Miss Trist, it would be simplest if we left. I trust Lord Amleigh to take care of everything."

Maria watched him coax Althea out of the room, and said, "He'll go far."

"Doubtless. Listen, Maria. The squire has mortgaged Hawkinville to Slade. More than mortgaged. He's deep in debt to the man, and Slade plans to tear down most of the village to build a preposterous villa on the river. Of course Hawk has to stop him."

"Of course, but— Ah, I see. Clarissa's fortune. But why elope?"

"Because, according to Van's letter, the squire is about to become Lord Deveril. Sorry," he said, passing over the letter. "Read it yourself."

Maria took it and read quickly. "He really thought she would reject him for the name?"

"And for the deceit of it all. It was more a case, I assume, of him not being willing to risk everything on the chance that she might. It's the way Hawk's mind has learned to work. Pinpoint the one thing that must or must not happen and work toward it, damn the incidentals."

"Incidentals," Maria muttered, scanning through the letter again. "Some of this is so cryptic!"

"Judiciously so," said Mr. Delaney, whom she'd forgotten entirely, which was surprising, since he was a good-looking man with presence. "Con," he said, "you should follow to assist Vandeimen. I'll hold the fort here. Talking of things that must not happen, Clarissa must not marry Hawkinville without knowing the truth."

Con nodded and strode out, and he must have narrowly missed colliding with Althea rushing in. "That Miss Weatherby says that Major Hawkinville's father is now Lord Deveril! *Lord Deveril!*"

"We know," said Maria with a sigh. "Sit down, Althea, and have some more tea."

Thérèse Bellaire stood by the smithy, observing confusion on the village green and seething.

She'd been uneasy about that encounter with the heiress, though the girl had shown no sign of recognition. Her main concern, however, had been the relationship between the two. To her experienced eye it hadn't looked like a man bewitching a silly young woman, but like a man bewitched.

By love. The greatest traitor of all the emotions.

The Hawk was supposed to remove the heiress and leave the old man in possession of the money! If he married the heiress there would be three lives between her and victory. Two accidental deaths could be arranged. Three, however, would be perilously suspicious, especially if she survived as Squire Hawkinville's wealthy widow.

And now what was going on? One of the silly, nosy Weatherby sisters was flitting around in an ugly, over-ornamented bonnet. People were appearing from buildings like worms from bad apples.

Surely she'd seen Lord Vandeimen ride north out of the village. Not at a dangerous gallop, but with some urgency, and yet his wife's carriage had not left.

Then two men rode to the inn at speed.

Lord Amleigh, she thought, and . . .

Nicholas?

Danger skittered down her spine, but excitement too. Ah, if he was here it would become a great game. And perhaps she would have the chance of true revenge. There was his dull wife. And a child now, as well. She'd checked on him, and he rarely left their sides. What if they were here too?

She licked her lips. This was almost as good as a tender goat in her bed.

It would be so deliciously dangerous to go over to the other side of the green, to be close to the inn, where Nicholas might see her.

Would even Nicholas know her in this disguise?

She began to walk across the green, wondering whether she dared to go into the inn and seek a meeting to see if he would know her like this. If anyone would, he would. They had been so spicily intimate six years ago, when he had been so young, so tender. None other of her young conquests had been like him.

They had been so wickedly intimate two years ago, as well. Compelling him had added a delightful twist. If she held his child captive, would he surrender again?

Fatally tempting, but too much so. It was time to be sensible if she was to have the life she wanted. She would have her fortune back, or as much as she could get, and escape.

As she neared the groups of people, she heard the name Deveril.

"Why, Miss Rowland," said one of the Misses Weatherby. "Have you heard? Our dear squire has become Viscount Deveril! He has just received the news!"

"Amazing!" she said. "I must go and congratulate my cousin."

Miss Weatherby's scrawny face pinched. She and her sister had never quite believed the supposed connection. But then, both sisters were enamored of Squire Hawkinville in their pathetic, spinsterish way. What would they think to know that Thérèse could have him at a snap of her fingers because she provided flattery, a clever mouth, and opium?

One of the inn's grooms was out here, and he smiled his crooked-tooth grin. He was proof that she could still enslave men in this ugly guise. It was never entirely a matter of looks. So few women realized that.

Probably the poor man was bemused and guilty about the lustful urges he felt toward the drab foreign woman with the sick husband.

He sidled over. "Grand news, ain't it, ma'am?"

"Wonderful."

"And such a coming and going." He was almost bursting with news.

"Yes?" she asked, as if he were clever and important.

"Here's Lord and Lady Vandeimen at the inn with a party, visiting the village. And one of the young ladies has disappeared! Miss Weatherby"—he tipped his head in the lady's direction—"she says she saw the lass off with Major Hawkinville on a horse! And," he added in a whisper, "now Lord Vandeimen's hurried off in a fine old mood. Known him since he was a lad, I have, and there'll be blows before the night's out, even if it is another George."

Sometimes the English idioms escaped her. She ignored the last comment, but inside she was cursing.

Eloped. She'd feared as much.

"And here's the other one arrived with a friend."

Since the groom clearly had no more to say, she thanked him and hurried down to the manor. The new Lord Deveril was of no use to her anymore, but it was best not to drop a part. And he would be good for a few guineas.

When she left, it was with guineas, and confirmation that the Hawk was off to Scotland with the heiress.

She paused to look at the bucolic setting and the robust English peasantry still gossiping. Thank God she could escape this place. If only she could set fire to its smug prettiness before she went.

She might try if not for the wet weather. It had doubtless left the thatch too sodden to catch.

She had survived a perilous life by recognizing when to drop one plan and pick up another. She headed briskly for her home here.

She still had Lieutenant Rowland, and there was a chance of Nicholas's child. All was not lost. Possibly, just possibly, she could have her money and Nicky on his knees begging before it ended.

Once Althea was calmed, Maria looked at Mr. Delaney. "You're the leader of the Company of Rogues, aren't you? I heard of you from Sarah Yeovil, and of course some more from Van."

"Leader?" he said, looking strangely both relaxed and poised for action. "That was at Harrow. Now we're simply a group of friends."

Maria glanced at Althea, wishing she could send her away again. Sensible Lord Trevor had not reappeared.

"But what connection is there between a group of school friends and Clarissa that leads to you giving Con a command? Ah, no, I'm sure you'd call it some friendly advice."

His eyes sparkled with amusement. "The connection is Lord Arden," he said, and it was fencing for the hell of it. "He's a Rogue. His wife was one of Clarissa's schoolteachers and is by way of being a friend and mentor now."

"You Rogues are very willing to put yourselves out for each other, aren't you?"

"Of course. Is that not the root of friendship?"

They were interrupted by Lord Trevor, carrying Hawk's cat. "Lady Vandeimen? This cat's hanging around and making a nuisance of itself. Someone said it was the major's."

"It belongs at the manor, I suppose . . ." But Maria remembered Van saying the squire's dogs would eat it.

The cat leaped out of Lord Trevor's arms and up onto the table to look around with what could only be described as severe annoyance. Maria sketched the rescue story for Delaney, and he laughed. "I'll take her up to the Court and try to keep her there until Hawkinville returns. One certainty in all this is that he will return."

He picked up the cat, and though still radiating grievance, she stayed in his arms. "What do you wish to do now, Lady Vandeimen? There is nothing you can accomplish here, I think."

Maria sympathized with the cat's feelings. "I am not one of your Rogues, Mr. Delaney." Even so, she rose. "I see that I get the task of explaining to Clarissa's chaperon that I have allowed her to be carried off to a clandestine marriage."

He put on a look of mild alarm. "Definitely. I'm not going to take that news to Arabella Hurstman."

"You know the lady, I see," she said, pulling on her gloves.

"Oh, yes. I asked her to take care of Clarissa."

"Nepotism!" gasped Althea, who was looking dazed.

He glanced at her. "Did she say that? She would. As it happens, she's god-mother to my daughter. Tell her that Arabel is nearby and will come to visit when this is straightened out—if she doesn't eat anyone in the meantime."

"Your child has cannibalistic tendencies, Mr. Delaney?"

He grinned. "More than likely. But I was referring to Miss Hurtsman. Don't worry. This all seems high drama at the moment, but it will sort out readily enough with a little attention."

"Indeed! What a shame you weren't involved in the war."

Though he scarcely twitched, it hit home, and she shepherded Althea out of the room regretting her sharp words. She was irritated at being excluded from the inside circle, however, and deeply worried about Van.

All had been delightful since their marriage, but it wasn't that long since he'd tried to blow his brains out. His estates were in no danger, and he had many reasons to live, but some of those reasons were rooted in Hawk in the Vale and the Georges.

What would happen if this caused a deep breach with Hawk?

They climbed into the waiting carriage, and Lord Trevor appeared, leading his horse, ready to escort them. Such an excellent young man, and thank heavens he'd been spared both physically and mentally by the war.

Unlike Con. Con had left to follow Van, but she suddenly realized that Con could be put in a position of having to choose between two groups of friends.

She almost left the carriage, driven to stay here. But why? There was nothing she could do. Whatever happened would happen far from here, presumably on the road north. Could Hawk really outrace Van? What would happen when Van caught them?

Van said that Con was the steady one, the one who had anchored them to prevent extremes. But the Con Somerford she had known in the past weeks did not strike her as rock solid, even with Susan and his new happiness.

Van said it was Waterloo, and the loss of his fellow Rogue, Dare Deben-ham, there.

Maria had known Dare. His mother, the Duchess of Yeovil, was a distant cousin. Dare had been a young man put on earth to make others smile, and Sarah Yeovil had not even begun to recover from his loss, especially as there had been no body to bury. It had taken months for her to accept that he was gone.

Con Somerford hadn't deceived himself that way, but apparently, despite all reason, he blamed himself, as if he could have nursemaided Dare through the battle and kept him safe.

He couldn't afford to lose another friend.

Chapter Twenty-one

Tollgates, thought Van, were a very useful institution. Not only did they provide the funding for decent roads, they marked the passage of travelers, especially unusual ones such as a man with a lady up behind him.

When he joined the London road, the keeper of the first tollbooth north told him that no such couple had gone that way, on horse, by carriage, or on foot. Of course. Hawk would hardly try to outrace him on the direct route, double-laden.

He had to turn back toward Brighton to check the side roads, but there were dozens of them weaving off into a complex network linking village to village. Damn Hawk. He was going to have to waste hours, and he didn't have the patient nature for this kind of work.

Con might follow, so he left a quick note with the tollkeeper explaining his actions, and saying that he would leave a clue on the signposts of the roads he went down. It would be one of their old boyhood signs. A twist of wheat. The fields were full of it.

Then he turned back, stopping to ask anyone he passed if they'd seen the couple, and also to cut a handful of wheat from the edge of a field. He turned off onto the first side road after sticking a crude wheat dolly in a crack on the top of the signpost.

Damn Hawk! He'd throttle him when he caught him. And yet a part of him hoped his friend would get away, marry Clarissa, and that it would all somehow work out for the best.

*   *   *

Hawk followed side roads and did some cross-country work, though he couldn't jump hedges with Clarissa at his back. They didn't talk and he was glad of it. He didn't know what to say.

Speed wasn't important at this point; concealment was. At an out-of-the-way village he stopped at a small inn and asked if anyone in the area would have a gig to hire out. Luck was with him, and Mr. Idler, the squint-eyed innkeeper, admitted to having one available himself. "Mostly used to go to market day, sir."

Despite the squint, Hawk assessed the man as honest, and the type to hold his own counsel. "May I hire your gig, sir, for a week or more?"

The man pursed his lips. "A week or more, sir? That'd be a bit of an inconvenience."

"I'd pay very well. And I'd leave my horse as security."

The man's eyes sharpened, and he went over to give Centaur an expert scrutiny. "Nice beast," he said, but he still looked suspicious. "Where you and the lady be going, then, sir?"

Hawk gave him the true answer. "Gretna Green. But I'll only take the gig as far as London. Perhaps not even so far as that. I won't be able to return it until we come back, though."

The man looked between them, then fixed his eyes—more or less—on Clarissa. "You going willingly, miss?"

Hawk watched her response. She smiled brilliantly. "Oh, yes. And I'm not being duped by a worthless rascal, either. My companion is an army officer who served well with the Duke of Wellington."

Mr. Idler was not impressed. "There's many a gallant soldier no sane woman would want to husband, miss, but that's your affair." He turned to Hawk. "Right, then, sir."

They settled terms quickly, then Idler added, "Your lady might want a cloak, sir. I could sell you one my daughter left behind for a shilling."

The deal was struck, and Clarissa climbed into the gig wearing a typical hooded country cloak of bright-red wool over the shambles of her fashionable gown. She smiled down at the innkeeper and said, "Thank you. You've been very kind."

"Aye, well, I hope so."

Hawk extended his hand to the man, and after a surprised moment, Idler shook it. "I'll take good care of your horse, sir. But if you're not back here in a few weeks with my gig, I'll sell it."

"Of course. I make no demands on you, but if my lady's brothers should happen by, we would appreciate it if you didn't tell them of our business."

But Idler didn't make any promises. "Depends on what they say, sir, and what I make of them."

Hawk laughed. "As is your right. My thanks for your help."

He climbed up, accepted Clarissa's bright smile wishing he were worthy of it, and set a rough course east to pick up the Worthing road north of Horsham and work his way to London by that roundabout route.

They went four hours on the Worthing-to-London road, able to make only a steady pace because of the one horse. He wanted to push closer to London, but the sun set and then darkness crept in, with rain threatening. Hawk turned off into a narrow road to a village called Mayfield, which he hoped would have some sort of inn.

He halted the gig partway, however. "We'll have to stop here for the night. Any regrets?"

She looked at him with a calm, direct gaze. "None, except that you can't tell me why."

He was tempted, but he said, "No, I can't. But we'll stay here as brother and sister."

She smiled as if she was hiding laughter. "No one will believe it. We look completely unalike. We might as well stay as husband and wife. It is what we will be, isn't it?"

His heart began to thump, but she was right. "Yes, it is." He dug in his pocket and took out the rings he'd brought—a plain gold band, and the one with the smooth ruby between two hearts.

"It's been the betrothal ring in my family since Elizabethan times," he said, taking her left hand and sliding the ring onto her finger. "A perfect fit. We do seem to be fated."

"I think so." She blinked away tears. "I didn't know I could be so happy as this. And the other?"

He held it in his fingers. "My mother's wedding ring. I'm not sure we want to use it. She wore it all her life, but apparently refused to be buried with it."

She closed his hand around the ring. "You are not your father, Hawk, and neither am I. We are marrying because we love each other. Nothing else matters." She opened his hand again to look at the ring. "I wish I could wait until we say our vows, but I suppose I should wear it."

Her complete trust was undermining him, but he'd known how it would be. Rather as a man facing amputation knows how it will be. Knows it has to be.

He slid the ruby ring back off her finger and put the gold band on. "With this ring," he said to her, "I promise that I will always cherish you, Clarissa, and will do everything in my power to make your life happy."

He meant every word, but even so they were tainted by what was really going on.

She shone without reservation. He put the ruby ring above the other and clicked the tired horse into motion again. "We'll wait until the real vows are said before we go any further with this, of course."

She didn't say anything, but when he glanced at her she was smiling in a damned mysterious manner.

The Dog and Partridge was small, but the buxom landlady admitted to a room for the night. He didn't think she believed for a moment that they were married, even with the rings, but she was willing to mind her own business.

He saw Clarissa blush as they were led upstairs and into a clean, surprisingly spacious bedroom, but she showed no sign of doubt or hesitation. What would he do if she did begin to get cold feet? Compel her to go through with it?

Impossible.

The woman lit a lamp and went to arrange their washing water and their dinner. Then they were alone.

As well as the bed, the room contained a table and chairs, and two good-sized armchairs with cushions on the seats. A washstand occupied one corner and a chamber pot another, both with screens, thank heavens, though he would use the outside convenience.

Clarissa hung up her cloak, then sat in a chair. "I'm astonishingly happy. But, then, you know I have an impatient nature. Waiting weeks for a church wedding would have been torture. I only wish it were possible to fly to Gretna Green."

Hawk laughed, wondering if it sounded like a groan. "I wish that too."

He meant that he'd not have to worry about pursuit anymore, and would be sooner done with deception, but he saw her take it as a longing for her delightful body naked in a bed with him.

Another groan threatened. He did long, and from her slight, totally wicked smile, he feared his bride longed too.

How the devil had it come to this? And yet this was the only option that would save the village and give at least a fragile chance of winning Clarissa too. But if he didn't win her . . .

He could shoot himself. Hawk in the Vale would be saved.

But then it would end up sold when the squire died with no heir. Damnation. He had to get her with child to see this through?

After a knock, the door opened to admit two maids with their meal and jugs of washing water. He gave them their vails and they curtsied out.

Hawk pulled himself together. He'd never been one to do things halfheartedly. These moody silences didn't serve at all. He smiled at Clarissa. "Do you want to wash first, or eat?"

"Eat," she said with a grin. "But I'll wash my face and hands at least. I am starving, though. I was in too much of a tizzy to eat much at lunch." She looked at him, rosy with some kind of humorous guilt. "I'd vowed to propose to you, you see, if you didn't get around to it. I wasn't leaving Hawkinville without trying to capture you."

He could not resist. He went over and kissed her. "I am certainly thoroughly snared."

"No regrets?" she said to him, direct and sober.

He couldn't flat-out lie. "Given a different world, Falcon, I would rather have married you in a church before your friends. But I do not regret the marriage."

It was enough to make her smile. Soon they sat to their meal, divided by large amounts of very welcome food.

It seemed almost inappropriate to be so hungry at such a time, but life marched on in the midst of even the most extraordinary events.

Clarissa considered it unfortunate that the chairs had been placed at either end of the table. It put five feet between them. All the same, they were alone, and in a more steadily intimate situation than they'd ever been.

And, by some miracle, on their way to their wedding.

With only one bed for the night.

Her heartbeat was already fast, but she was willing to wait for the first seductive moves.

Hawk poured wine into her glass and indicated the plates. "It's probably best if we help ourselves."

Though she'd honestly claimed hunger, now she wasn't sure she could eat, but she took a chicken breast and some vegetables, then sipped her wine, watching him in the pool of lamplight.

It touched gold in his hair and picked out the handsome lines of his face and the elegance of his hands. Was it kind to her? A flutter of uncertainty at her appearance started inside. The small mirror had told her that neatness, as usual, had totally escaped her. Perhaps she should have asked to borrow his comb. He'd used it to restore his usual elegance.

Then he looked up, and something heated danced in his eyes that smoothed the flutter away. He raised his glass to her. "To our future. May it be all you deserve."

She raised her own. "And all you deserve, too."

As she sipped, she saw a twitch of expression.

"Hawk! Don't you think you deserve happiness?"

"You forget. Any future is built on the past."

It was as if Deveril were trying to bully his way into the room. She should tell him before he committed himself . . .

But she thrust it away. "Tonight, can't we forget about the past?"

"The past is always beneath our feet. Without it, we walk on nothing."

"Perhaps without it, we fly."

And he smiled as if the shadows fled. "Perhaps we do, wise Falcon. Perhaps we do. Eat. You'll regret it later if you don't."

"Advice from experience?" she asked, but she cut into the tender chicken and made herself eat a mouthful. Then she discovered that she was hungry, and she ate a few more forkfuls of food in silence.

"See?" he said, his lips twitching.

Lamentably, she flicked a piece of bean at him.

He caught it in his mouth. "Army tricks. Never waste food."

They laughed together and she thought, *friend.*

She'd had friends at school, some of whom she'd felt close to, but she'd never felt as she did about Hawk. She didn't know how to say it—it seemed almost childish—but it was a warm glow near her heart. Something steady and dependable. Unlike the rather frantic burning of her love.

She talked a bit about Miss Mallory's and he shared some of his time at his school, Abingdon.

"Van, Con, and I went to different schools," he said. "Different family traditions. And I think our families thought a little variety would be good for us. Part of the purpose of schooling is to make useful connections, after all."

"Did you enjoy it?"

"Time away from the manor was always pleasant."

She sensed a hard truth being delivered. "We won't let your father destroy our happiness, Hawk."

"I pray not." But he didn't seem to believe it.

She chattered for a while about Brighton matters, but something was disturbing that warm glow of friendship like a chill draft playing on a candle flame.

They might as well talk of serious matters. "How long will it take us to get to Scotland?"

"Three days, with good speed."

"Can we elude pursuit?"

He pushed away his plate still half full. He hadn't touched it for some time. "I hope so. Van doubtless has murder on his mind." He picked up the decanter of claret. "More wine?"

She wasn't used to a lot of wine and had already drunk two glasses, but she accepted more. "He'll never catch us on this route."

"It will be luck if he does. He does, however, have amazing luck." He shrugged and filled his own glass. "We'll be in London tomorrow and can arrange some disguise and then speed north."

She looked down at her stained and muddy dress. "I'll treasure this dress, though. It has very special memories." That flicked her mind to something else. "Do you know, during the journey I've been thinking about the horrible Mrs. Rowland. I know her from somewhere."

"Where?" he asked, eyes suddenly alert. "Is there anything else to the feeling? Any connection?"

She laughed. "Always the Hawk! It wasn't anything dire or suspicious. Just curious. I wish I could pin it down."

He relaxed again, but she thought his eyes still seemed intent. He'd told her he couldn't resist a mystery, and it seemed to be true. She was definitely right to be binding him.

"Well, then," he said, "where might you have met her?"

"That's it. I have no idea. You have to understand, Hawk, I haven't led a very adventurous life."

He laughed, and she protested, "I haven't! Things have happened to me recently, but most of my life has been positively boring. The only place I might have met her was last year in London."

"More or less at the time of Waterloo, when Lieutenant Rowland was in Belgium fighting and being wounded. It would be strange if his wife and children were in London then."

"And I'm sure I never encountered a Belgianwoman. I was restricted to fashionable circles, and rarely escaped my mother's eye." She shook her head. "It's probably a mistake. Some people look like others."

"But you aren't confusing her with someone else, are you?"

She could only shrug. That faint sense of recognition was becoming less substantial by the minute. The talk had passed some time, but she was no longer interested.

"Never mind," he said, one finger stroking the long stem of his glass. It reminded her of his stroking of Jetta, and of how very much she wanted him to be stroking her.

She couldn't bear it. She stood and carried her wineglass around to his side of the table.

Their eyes locked for a moment, and then he pushed back his chair, inviting her to sit on his lap. An invitation she took, heart racing, heat surging through her.

It must be the wine, but it was magical.

"Another adventure," she said, adjusting herself and looping her free hand around his neck. "I've never sat on a man's lap before."

"As usual, you get the idea very quickly." He accepted her daring kiss, then one hand rose to cradle the back of her head. His lips opened and she settled, melted, into a deep joining.

After a languorous time, their mouths parted and he whispered, "Do I want to know what other adventures you have planned?"

"Plan?" she said, exploring his jaw, his ear with her lips. "I'm a creature of impulse."

"Heaven protect me. What impulse drives you?"

"I think you know."

He moved her apart a little. "Clarissa, I promised Van that I wouldn't seduce you."

"I didn't promise anything."

She swooped in for another kiss, but he held her away. His face was flushed, his breathing unsteady. "I think perhaps you're unaccustomed to wine . . ."

"Not that unaccustomed." She cradled his face, feeling the roughness of a day's beard on his cheeks. "Why wait? What if they do manage to stop us?"

"Then it would be better."

"Or our marriage would be essential."

He captured her hands and held them away. "Clarissa—"

"There's only one bed. Where are you going to sleep?"

"On the floor. I've done it before."

"You've *eloped* before?" she teased.

The look in his eyes filled her with a sense of extraordinary power. She could hardly believe that she was doing this—trying to seduce a man. She, Clarissa, the plain one that no man ever looked twice at.

But she was, and she was winning, and it didn't seem so extraordinary, so ridiculous. She could feel it in his hands, still controlling her wrists, and see it in his eyes. She could sense it in the very air around them.

His scarce-checked desire.

For her.

For her.

"What would you do if I started to undress here, in front of you?"

His eyes closed with what looked like pain.

"You'd like it?" she asked, astonished to hear it come out in an almost Jetta-like purr.

"Would I like to be burned to a cinder?"

"Well, would you?"

His lids lifted, heavily. "It's every man's deepest longing."

That might be teasing, but she knew it went deeper than that. It was hunger.

She leaned forward, letting him keep control of her hands, to brush her lips across his. "Make love to me tonight, Hawk. It is my deepest longing."

His lips moved beneath hers for a moment, then slid away. "What if you change your mind, if you decide you don't want to marry me?"

"You think I will be so disappointed?" she teased.

He avoided her lips again. "Clarissa, I'm trying to be noble, dammit. If anything prevents our marriage, you'd be ruined."

"Are you saying you won't marry me?"

"No. But you may change your mind."

"You forget. I'm in love with your house."

He laughed, and rolled his head back, eyes closed. "Think. You might get with child."

She nibbled down his neck. "So, I'll be the even more scandalous Devil's Heiress. I don't care."

"The child might."

"Then I'll buy it a father. But, Hawk, I want you. Nothing is going to change my mind. I love you."

His lids lifted, heavily. "You said you loved my home."

"And you. If Slade tears down Hawkinville Manor, I will still love you. But he won't do that. We are on our way to our wedding to prevent it."

He swallowed. She felt it.

"Do you feel your feet sliding, Falcon?" he said softly. "Love only greases the path. It doesn't promise a safe landing."

"Some paths lead to heaven."

"Downward?"

She chuckled and moved her lips downward, nuzzling at the edge of his collar. "It would seem so . . ."

Dimly, somewhere far away in the house, a clock began to chime. She decided to kiss his neck and jaw for each chime, and ended at ten. "Ten fathoms deep," she breathed against his skin.

He released her hand to hold her off at the shoulders. "I surrender to the depths."

Triumphant, sizzling, she relaxed away from him, and he raised her left hand to his mouth. "I give you my love and allegiance, Falcon. I swear that if this falls apart, it will be at your desire, not mine."

"Then it will never fall apart."

He slid her from his knee to lead her to the bed.

"Electricity," she said.

"Lightning."

"Yes." She knew she was blushing, but she didn't mind. Despite *The Annals of Aphrodite,* she was unclear about what was going to happen here, but she didn't mind that either.

She simply waited, for Hawk.

He raised his hands to her hair, which she knew was a mess. "I suppose your maid arranged this carefully this morning. Does that seem a very long time ago?"

"A mere century or two."

"And the destruction is considerable." Pins fell to the floor, and his fingers threaded into her curls. "But it is rioting, tempestuous hair, like its owner." His eyes met hers. "And as lovely."

"You like storm and riot?"

"Very much." He raised her hair and let it fall. "It catches the lamplight in a net of fire."

He lowered his hands and turned her to the bed. It was set high, and steps stood ready for them to climb into it. Should she take off her clothes yet, or would he do that for her?

He dropped her hand to pull off the buttercup-yellow coverlet. Meticulously, he folded it and put it on the chest that sat at the base of the bed. Then he folded down the other covers, exposing a large expanse of pure white sheet.

The precise preparations stirred a pang of panic. "Won't I bleed?"

"The people here must suspect what is going on. If it bothers you, we can stop now."

"Oh, no." Then she plunged into honesty. "It's just that this suddenly frightens me, but in the spiciest way. Does that make sense?"

He put his hands on her waist and lifted her to sit on the high bed. "Of course. It frightens me, too. Because I want it too much."

He was looking into her eyes as if searching for doubts, for retreat. She smiled and leaned forward to kiss him.

He laughed, broke free. "Stay there."

He went to pile the remains of their meal on the tray, then put it outside the door.

"You think of everything," she said, and heard a touch of a pout in it.

He came back toward her. "That is my reputation." He went to his knees and began to unlace her right half boot.

Clarissa sat there, feeling slightly like a child, but at his touch, intensely woman. Keen anticipation suddenly swirled inside her.

And impatience.

"I feel," she said, looking down at his bent head, "that at a moment like this I should be wearing satin slippers, not muddy shoes."

"At least they're leather." He put the right one on the floor and began on the left. "The mud and water don't seem to have soaked through to your stockings."

She flexed the toes of her liberated right foot. Her daisy-embroidered stockings were pretty, but sturdy. "I should be wearing silk stockings, too."

He glanced up, smiling. "For a day in the country? I'd think you a flighty piece."

"You don't think me a flighty piece?"

He discarded her left boot. "Hmmmm. Now that you come to speak of it . . ."

He began to slide his hands up her leg beneath her skirts, making her stir and catch her breath.

"Is this . . . is this the way it's usually done?"

"What?" He met her eyes, but his hands continued to move up.

"Is the gentleman supposed to remove a lady's shoes and stockings? Is that part of it?"

His lips twitched. "Are you going to analyze every step?"

"This is a very important experience for me, you know."

"Yes, I think I know that."

His hands found her garter, and undid the knot by feel, sending the most extraordinary feelings up the inside of her thigh.

"There are a thousand ways to make love, Clarissa. Doubtless more. If this was our wedding night, I might have left you with your maid to undress and get into bed, then joined you later." He looked down again, and pushing her skirts up to her knee, rolled down her stocking.

"I bought those yesterday," she said softly. "With you in mind."

"And they are much appreciated." His voice seemed suddenly husky, and she couldn't contain a smile, even though her heart was beating so deeply she wondered if she might faint.

Dazedly, she watched her pale leg reveal itself. Doubts stirred. It was a very ordinary leg.

He stroked his fingers up and down her shin, then raised her foot to kiss her instep. "This is definitely an argument for anticipating marriage."

"What? Oh, no maid et cetera . . ."

"Precisely."

"So many places to kiss."

"And I intend to kiss every one."

So many places on him to kiss, she thought. Would she be brave enough to kiss every one?

Then he explored for the garter of the left stocking. Clarissa leaned back on her elbows, closing her eyes in order to concentrate on the feel of his hands. She felt unsteady. Quivery. She wasn't sure she wasn't actually quivering.

When he kissed her left instep, his hand cradled her foot warmly to raise it, fingers brushing against the side of her heel. Then his hands slid slowly back up her legs, opening the way for cool air. He was pushing her skirts up now.

She truly did quiver, for he must be close to her naked privacy.

Lips hot on the top of each knee in turn, hands stroking the length of her thighs.

Then he pulled her up and lifted her off the bed to stand.

Chapter Twenty-two

She opened dazzled eyes to see him framed in a halo from the lamp. "This is remarkable."

He laughed, and it seemed to be with unshadowed pleasure. "I hope it becomes even more so." He pulled her suddenly close for a kiss. "You're not at all afraid, are you?"

"Is there anything to be afraid of?"

"A little pain?"

She shrugged. "I'm sure it hurt to swing on ropes across the wilderness."

"That was Van, not me."

"But you'd have been next, wouldn't you?"

He grinned. "We'd already argued over it. And you're right. I wouldn't have counted the scrapes and bruises." He raised a hand and brushed some hair off her cheek, back behind her ear.

"But lovemaking is dangerous, Falcon. Be warned. At its best or its worst it takes us to places beyond the ordinary. Beyond swinging ropes, beyond battle, even. The French call it the little death. They believe that for a moment the heart stops and all bodily sensations cease, so that return to life is both exquisite delight and exquisite agony."

She quivered again, deep inside, with hunger. "Can it be like that the first time?"

He laughed, or it might have been a groan. "If I can possibly make it so. Which at the moment," he added, turning her to unfasten her dress, "might come down to a question of how long I can stand this torture."

"Torture?" she asked, shrugging out of the dress.

"Only moderate so far. Corsets, however, are the very devil."

She giggled, but could only wait as he unknotted and loosened her laces. She turned then. "I can get out of this and my shift while you undress. Or do you need me to help you?"

"That would probably be my undoing." He began to rip off his clothes, as she struggled out of the corset. He was watching her in a way that brought back every scrap of that sense of female power, and she was clumsy with humming excitement.

He pulled off his shirt, and she froze, corset dangling from her failing fingers. Not so massive as the groom in Brownbutton's stableyard, but the stuff of maidens' dreams all the same, with ridged muscles down his belly and curved ones in his arms.

There was a dark mark above his right breast. She let the corset fall and walked over to him.

"The tattoo," she said. "I see it at last."

"Didn't you always know you would?"

She smiled up at him. "Yes. This was inevitable from the first day, wasn't it?" She raised her left hand to trace the purple lines. "A *G* and a hawk?"

"Van was a demon. Con a dragon."

"Why?"

"Why do sixteen-year-old boys do most of the things they do? Because one of them suggests it, and it seems like a good idea at the time. We wanted to be able to recognize one another's mangled bodies."

She shuddered and with her left hand on the tattoo, she ran her right down a jagged scar in his side. "You could have died before we met."

"True, though I didn't have a very dangerous war."

"What was this, then?" she asked, still touching the scar.

"A chance to swing over the wilderness. If staff duties were light, we were sometimes given permission to join the fighting forces."

She looked up. "And I suppose you leaped at it."

He seemed surprised by her tone. "Of course. Can't you imagine how frustrating it is to be surrounded by the fever of battle—the electricity—and not be caught up in it?" He ran a hand up her side to stroke the curve of her breast. "Rather as if we were to be suspended like this for the rest of our lives, never to fall fully into the madness of desire."

At the look in his eyes, and the tantalizing touch, a shudder passed through her, a shudder of pleasure and pain such as she had never even imagined. She felt as if she contained seething power between her two hands. His heat, his breathing, his controlled patience . . .

She leaned closer to press her cheek against his hot, smooth skin. He sucked in a deep breath, moving against her like a wave, and she let her hands slide around him, encircle him, pressing to him so only the fine cotton of her shift lay between their bodies.

"What would I have done if you had died?" she murmured.

His arms came around her. "Found some other man to love."

"It doesn't seem possible."

"It doesn't, does it?" His head rested against hers. "When I watched you at the manor house today, standing near the sundial, surrounded by roses, it was as if a missing piece had fallen into my life. I give you fair warning, Falcon. You will have to fight to be free of my hood and jesses."

She smiled into his skin. "As will you. And a falcon, remember, is a superior bird to a hawk."

She heard a hum, presumably of pleasure. "The thought of you hunting me down," he said, "almost tempts me to fly."

"I have claws to catch you with." She lightly pressed her nails into his back.

His inhaled breath swayed her again. "Have you any idea," he said, "how perfectly happy I am at this moment? Or, come to think of it, it's more a state of perfectly happy anticipation."

Understanding, she moved back, though she would willingly have stood like that, so intimately close, for hours longer.

He sat on the bed and urgently pulled off his boots. She went to help, tossing first one, then the other aside. She put hands to his right stocking, but he seized her, swinging her onto the bed, and falling on her with a ravishing kiss.

At last!

She wrapped her arms and legs around him, kissing him back, pressing a burning, aching need against him. Then he broke contact, freed himself to pull off her shift.

Thus, finally, she was naked, and fear hit her. Not fear of joining, but fear of disappointing.

He put a hand to her breast, slid it down over her ribs, her hip, her thigh, then back up again. "You are so beautiful," he murmured.

"You don't have to lie to me."

He looked up at her. "I'm not lying, love. Don't you know? Your legs, your hips, your breasts . . . You're cream and gold and honey. A perfect, delicious sweetmeat."

He suddenly swooped down and licked, licked up her belly, around her breast.

She had a beautiful *body*? She'd never thought beyond her plain face, but the way he was cherishing her with touch and gaze, the hunger she sensed in every touch, tempted her to believe. The perfect jewel in a perfect day. He was taking pleasure, true pleasure, in her body.

He tongued her nipple, making her catch her breath, mostly in anticipation. This she already knew, and she remembered the way he'd been swept beyond sense in the wilderness.

She wanted to do that to him again.

Again and again.

Forever . . .

He suckled her, first gently, then more deeply, and she arched. "Hurry," she said. "Hurry."

"Patience," he murmured. "Patience."

"I don't want to be patient!"

"Trust me."

He slipped away from her breast and began to lick slowly toward the other one.

She punched at his shoulders with both fists.

He laughed.

Loving the feel of his broad shoulders, she began to knead them. She loved the feel of his tongue, too, though not as much as the suckling.

He hummed again, approvingly, so she kneaded him some more, more deeply as he suckled, kneading her need into his deep muscles again and again.

Her leg was rubbing against his and his breeches bothered her. "Undress," she commanded.

He pushed away from her, and she grabbed for him. "No, don't stop."

"Patience," he said, laughing and escaping. "A little waiting will definitely do you good."

She sat up, hands on hips, pretending annoyance, not having to pretend frustration at their separation. But it was almost worth it to watch as he stripped off his remaining clothes.

He stepped out of his drawers and looked at her, and suddenly his jutting manly part grew larger, rising.

"Oh, my," she said. "I thought the pictures exaggerated."

"Pictures?" He climbed back on the bed and gently pushed her down.

"Men have books, and women steal them." She was still looking at his Rod of Rapture, wondering if the book was right, and he would like her Felicitous Fingers. "Some of the girls brought interesting treasures back to school."

"But you didn't quite believe them? From what I've seen of such books, you were very wise." He captured her face and looked into her eyes. "Are you frightened, love?"

She thought about it. Something was beating in her, but she didn't think it was fear. She certainly didn't want to stop. "What I'm feeling is nothing I've ever experienced before."

He kissed her, laughing. "Still analyzing."

Despite the fluttering inside and outside of her skin, she chuckled. "Of course. I don't want to miss or forget any of this. Perhaps I should keep a diary."

"Now that would shock our grandchildren." His hand had found her breast again.

Grandchildren. An astonishingly beautiful thought.

Grandchildren at Hawkinville.

"I'd write it in code," she murmured, dazed by his touch. "The first sight of you. The first feel of your skin. The special smell of your body. My own strange state. Your every touch . . ."

His hand stilled. "It is somewhat disconcerting, you know, to think of you taking notes."

She looked at him. "Hawk, are you nervous?"

"You think I'm not?" When she just looked at him, he said, "I want this to be perfect for you, my heart. But perfection really isn't possible."

She smiled and ran her hand through his hair. "Whatever it is, it will be perfect."

He kissed her quickly. "Continue to take notes, then," he said, and turned his attention to her breasts.

"I like that," she said. "Oh! I feel as if I'm coming down with a fever. But not at all ill. Uncomfortable, though. Inside."

His hand slid down. "Perhaps I can heal that." He paused to circle her navel; then his fingers pushed into the hair between her thighs, close to the tingling ache.

She followed every touch and sensation in her mind, marveling.

"Open for me, sweetheart."

When had she pushed her thighs so tightly together? She hastily spread them, breath held, and his fingers slid deeper.

Slid. She could feel moisture there. "The Delectable Dew of Deliquescent Desire . . ."

"What?"

She hadn't realized that she'd spoken aloud. "A book called it that."

"A bedazzling book of bridal bemusement?"

Laughing, she said, *The Annals of Aphrodite.* It was rather alliterative."

"So I hear. You are Definitely Delectable."

"Impossibly Impatient?"

"Dauntingly Demanding."

They collapsed into laughter, but he looked at her. "Don't you think perhaps we could take this seriously?"

"Why?"

"Because I'm becoming Desperately Desirous."

He was ruffled and rosy. She laughed again at all the *r*'s, but said, "Then I am Wonderfully Willing."

He pressed his hand back between her thighs. "But not Rapturously Ready, my Pulchritudinous Pleasure."

Beautiful pleasure. She didn't know if she was truly beautiful, but he was, and this was, made more so by the blessing of laughter. She would never have imagined being in a bed with a naked man entwined in laughter.

Her hips rose of their own accord to greet his fingers, and an ache intensified. Passion's Penultimate Pang. They were near the end?

It was deep, deep inside her. Where he would go.

Soon, she prayed. Soon.

"Does that feel good?" he asked.

"Oh, yes. But . . ."

He began to circle his hand. "Better?"

All the feelings seemed to rush to the place he pressed on, and her hips pushed up again. "Oh! The Precious Pearl of Eden's Ecstasy."

"Probably." He laughed into her dazed eyes. "By all means, tell me what else you recognize as we go."

"The Wanton Wave of Womanly Welcome," she gasped as her body rose up and fell of its own accord. "I tried it. Stroking the Precious Pearl . . . It was pleasant, but not like this!"

Her body seemed to clench itself painfully, but she wanted more.

"Books for men tend to emphasize the delicacy of the pearl," he murmured into her ear. "Those for women should doubtless emphasize firmness. Tell me if I hurt you."

His hand pressed harder, and his mouth settled hot against her breast. Something shot between his mouth and his hand, and Clarissa let out a little shriek. "The Searing Spear of Sensual Sublimation!"

Her senses were firing off into sparks and sparkles, but she tried to comment as he'd asked, "And . . . the Final Fragrant Fragmentation. Oh, my! Don't stop!"

"I won't."

She wanted to push back, so she did, again and again, desperately seeking something that wasn't alliterative at all.

And then she died.

She felt it. That sudden, perfect stop, then the torrent of sensation that left her shaking and breathless.

Then he moved over her, and as her mind came together she realized that it wasn't his hand anymore.

It was him against her.

She was still quivering and aching, and she caught back a cry, not sure if it was of need or protest. Her body seethed with sensitivity, but he was forcing her hips wide, forcing her open in a way his fingers had not. She felt impaled—

She stifled the shriek, but then said, "That hurt!" and was shocked back to the real and awkward world.

He stilled. "Are you all right?"

She wanted to say no, that she needed time to get used to this, that perhaps they should try again another day. But she could sense his tense desperation, and could imagine what he might be feeling.

"Of course," she said, trying for laughter again. "The . . . Perfumed Portal has been Pierced." Oh, but she was invaded. "So it's time for the . . . Masculine Mastery of Maidenly Mysteries."

"Not maidenly anymore," he said, but she was rewarded by his abrupt surrender to his needs.

The Fearful Phallic Ferocity. She knew just what the *Annals* had meant.

Again, and again, and again.

She could bear it, she could bear it, she could bear it.

But then pain faded and other feelings flowed back. Fierce, thunderous feelings, shared with him. She found she was meeting his movements, harder and harder, thrust for thrust.

The Joyous Joust!

Then he froze. She could feel the rigid tension in every inch of his muscular body. She opened her eyes to revel in the sight of him, beautiful in the light and shadow of this perfect room, lost in the little death.

Oh, yes, making love was a very dangerous thing. They were more than naked here. They were naked to the soul.

He relaxed as if the Wave of Womanly Welcome had rolled over him, and collapsed to kiss her in the way she needed to be kissed. In the way that expressed the shattering experienced.

Then he rolled to the side, still tangled with her, to hold her close. They were plastered together at every possible point, sealed by sweat, and she found it impossible to imagine ever being separated again, even by clothes.

They were one. Forever. Indivisible.

She kissed his chest, then wriggled up to kiss his mouth, then looked into his sated eyes. "That was perfect."

"Perfectly Perfect? That's as close to alliteration as I can come at the moment."

His eyes were amused, but above all they were deeply content and centered on her. "Perfection will come, and we'll enjoy the practice." He closed his eyes and laughed. "Is it possible to say a sentence without two words starting with the same sound? After this, I'm going to embarrass myself every time I open my mouth."

She sprawled on his chest, looking at him. "Persistent Practice?"

His eyes opened. "You want to fly higher and higher?"

"Why not? Why stay close to ground?"

"For safety?"

"Do we care about safety?"

"Yes," he said, smile fading, "I rather think we do. I intend to keep you safe, love, even if it does mean staying in the nest."

She snuggled even closer. "That won't be too bad if the nest has a bed. When can we do it again?"

He looked at her. "I had the impression it hurt you quite a bit."

When she thought about it, she could feel soreness. "The design of the female body is very inconvenient."

"Most parts of it are thoroughly delightful," he said, cradling a breast and kissing it. "Especially yours."

She dared to ask. "Do you like my breasts?"

"I adore your breasts."

"More than other women's breasts?"

He looked up. "Don't. That's a game that no one wins. You are you. I love you. I have never loved a woman as I love you. As it happens, you have very beautiful breasts, full and pale, with generous, rosy nipples. But it wouldn't matter if they were otherwise. They would still be the breasts of the woman I love."

She put wondering hands to her body, to her breasts. "It's hard for me to think of myself that way."

"As beautiful?"

"And loved." She felt tears threaten, and she didn't want to spoil this with tears. She smiled and put one hand on his chest. "You have a beautiful body, too."

"Is that all I am to you? A beautiful body?"

He spoke teasingly, but she sensed that the same need pulsed through him as her.

"No, you're the man I love. If you went back to war and came home scarred and maimed, you would still be the man I love."

"Why?" But then he put up a hand to stop her answer. "God, no. That's another game that no one wins."

She wanted to laugh. "Why wouldn't any woman fall in love with you? You're handsome, honorable, brave, strong . . ." But she moved down to kiss the hawk on his chest. "For me, though, the most wonderful thing is the way I've been able to talk to you from the first. You are my deepest, lifelong friend. I know you have other friends—"

He sealed her lips with his fingers. "None closer. Now."

"Truly?"

His eyes were steady and deep. "Truly. For as long as you wish."

She began to cry. She couldn't help it. This was the most perfect moment of her life, but she was sobbing as if she'd lost everything that mattered. He gathered her close, rocking her and murmuring for her to stop. She tried, but she couldn't.

"It's all right," she managed. "I'm happy, not sad!"

"Lord save me from you sad, then, love. Do stop, please."

She laughed and wiped her face on the sheet. "I look a mess when I cry, too."

He helped her dry her eyes and didn't deny her statement. For some reason, that put the perfect finish on perfection.

This was all completely honest.

She ran a hand across Hawk's wide shoulders, then down the center of his chest, just wanting to touch. She traced the scar again, chilled by how close it must have been to fatal.

"It was a mere glancing blow."

"I'm surprised it didn't break your ribs."

"Cracked them. Hurt like the devil."

She stroked along the scar. "I'm glad you're not at war anymore."

"I was rarely in much danger. Unlike others."

She looked up. "Why do you blame yourself? Your work was important."

"I know."

"But you still felt as if you were shirking," she risked, sliding down and holding him, his head on her shoulder.

She thought he wouldn't speak of it, and she didn't dare to press him further. But then he began to talk, about his army life, but especially about others, including Lord Vandeimen and Lord Amleigh.

She listened, stroking his hair, blending deeper with him at every word. She kept feeling she'd found perfect happiness, only to rise up to more, and more. She truly felt she might fly away, but it would be to heaven.

Heaven. Ah, yes. No purgatory for her. Certainly no hell. Instead, miraculously, she had heaven.

Except for the small worm of her involvement in Deveril's death.

It was time to tell her story. But not quite yet. This time was for him. He was talking about Hawkinville now.

"I went into the army to escape it. When I returned a few weeks ago, I planned to deal with whatever problems my father had and ride away. I didn't intend to cut myself off from Van and Con, but I didn't think I could live there.

"But when I rode in, people recognized me. God knows how, since most of them hadn't seen me since I was sixteen. And I recognized them. Not always immediately, but within minutes it was as if the passing years had disappeared. Even my old nurse . . ."

He moved his head restlessly against her. "Nanny Briggs saved my life. She was my mother in all true senses of the word. Even after she left my father's service, I spent more time in her house than at the manor. I sent her letters and gifts. But I hadn't thought she really mattered to me anymore until I saw her.

"In ten years she'd gone from a robust woman to a frail one, shrunken, crooked, and in pain. And in ten years, I'd hardly given her a thought apart from casually sent packages. Of course, she'd treasured every one."

He suddenly shifted, moving up to look at her. "Why am I boring you with all this? Come and be kissed for being such a good listener."

The kiss was Hawk's kiss, as skillful and delightful as ever, and yet afterward, cuddled against him, Clarissa pined for the links that might have been forged with the words he had left unsaid.

"I wasn't bored," she said. "I don't think you should blame yourself for not thinking of them. When a person grows, he will often leave his home and start anew. And I'm sure war demands a man's attention. You would not have wanted to be distracted."

His hand was stroking her back again, and she remembered him stroking Jetta, remembered wanting to be stroked that way. And now she had it. For as long as they both should live . . .

He nuzzled her hair. "I've never embarrassed myself with so much chatter before."

She smiled against his skin. "You've never been married before."

"We're not now."

"As good as. In the eyes of heaven. I've never felt like this, either, Hawk. I've never truly had someone to be with like this. It's like catching sunlight and finding it can be held in the hands forever."

"Or having heaven here on earth."

"Perfect Perpetual Paradise," she murmured on a laugh. This would be the moment to tell him. So at peace, so relaxed, so inextricably bound.

And yet, it would change things. They'd have to talk, to make sense, to leave the soft clouds. Better surely to sleep now, and do the telling in the morning.

Chapter Twenty-three

Clarissa awoke to sunshine and warm, musky smells, to strangeness inside and around. And then to memory.

She turned her head slowly, but he was there, beside her, still trustingly asleep, turned away. He'd thrown the covers off down to his waist, so she could indulge in luxuriant study of the lines of his back, of his muscular arm bent close to her. She longed to ease forward and kiss it, taste his warmth and skin, but she wouldn't wake him yet.

When he awoke she would have to tell him, and it pricked at her. It wasn't precisely wrong not to have told him. It couldn't make any particular difference to him. It wasn't as if she was in danger of being arrested.

But she wished this moment was enshrined in perfect honesty.

On that thought, she reached out to touch his arm.

He stirred, rolled, then his eyes opened sharply. She saw that second of disorientation before he relaxed and smiled. But guardedly. Such shadows behind his smile. Why?

Ah.

She smiled for him. "I have no regrets. I love you, and this was the first night of our life together."

He took her hand, the one wearing the rings, and pressed it to his lips. "I love you, too, Clarissa. This will be as perfect as I can possibly make it."

She almost let go of why she'd awakened him, but she would not weaken now. "Almost no regrets," she amended. As he became suddenly watchful, she added, "I have something to tell you, Hawk, and I think it requires clothing and cool heads."

He kept hold of her hand. "You're already married?"

606 ∞   Jo Beverley

"Of course not!"

"You're not Clarissa Greystone, but her maid in disguise."

"You've been reading too many novels, sir."

He pulled her closer. "You eloped only because you were consumed with carnal lust for my luscious body."

She resisted. "You're beginning to sound like *The Annals of Aphrodite*," she said severely, "and of course I lust. But I also love."

"Then nothing troubles us."

"I could have lost all my money on wild investments in fur cloaks for Africa."

His smile deepened. "You're a minor."

"I gammoned my trustees."

"I'm not at all surprised." He gently tugged her closer. "Would you care to gammon me?"

She went, let herself be drawn to his lips, but in a moment she tugged free and clambered out of the bed. "Later," she said, but then froze, suddenly aware of her total nakedness.

Then she laughed and faced him brazenly.

He sat up equally brazenly, completely splendid, tousled, smiling.

"Carnal lust," she murmured, and made herself turn away to search for her shift, her corset, and her lamentably muddy stockings.

When she looked back he was already into his drawers. "I wish I had a clean dress to wear."

"We'll find you one in London. Much though I'd like to linger here, beloved, we'd best have breakfast and be on our way."

Awareness of the world, of pursuit, drained delight. She hurried into her shift and corset, then went to him to have the strings tied. A sweet and simple task, and yet to have a man tie her laces seemed a mark of the complete change in her life.

As he tied the bow, she turned in his hands and started what must be done. "I was present when Lord Deveril died," she said, intent on his expression.

It hardly seemed to change at all. "I guessed."

"How? Why?"

"Perhaps because I'm the Hawk." But his lashes lowered as if that might not be the whole truth.

She put that aside. "I need to tell you about it. I should have before, but I couldn't until now. You'll see why."

His eyes were steady on her again. "Very well. But you wanted clothing and cool?"

She hurried to put on her dress and stockings, though she had to hunt for her second garter. He was dressed by then, and she went to him to have her buttons fastened. As he did the last one, he brushed her hair aside and she felt heat, wet heat, up the back of her neck.

"When I saw you in this dress, Falcon, you made me think of dairy cream, and I wanted to lick you."

She laughed and turned, pushing him playfully away. Something she could do when she knew there would be tomorrow and tomorrow and to-morrow.

Even, perhaps, later. They'd clearly eluded any pursuit. There was no real need to rush on to London.

Once her conscience was clear.

She sat on the rather hard chair at one end of the table and indicated that he should sit on the other, at a safe distance. His brows rose, but he obeyed.

"You were present at Deveril's death," he said obligingly. "I assume he was doing something vile and his death was deserved. I also assume that you did not kill him, but if you did it would only make me admire you more."

She bit her lip on tears at his understanding.

"You don't have to tell me any more, Falcon. It really doesn't matter."

She smiled. "But I want to. I have many failings, and one is an incurable urge toward honesty."

"I don't see that as a failing, beloved." And yet something somber touched him.

Beloved. She plunged into it. "I don't need to tell you that Deveril was an evil man. After he kissed me, I ran away from him."

"When you threw up over him."

"Yes. Perhaps I should have been able to control myself better . . ."

"Not at all. We use what weapons we have to hand."

She laughed. "I see what you mean. It certainly stopped him! Well, then, I escaped through the window in my brother's clothes, but Deveril hunted me down and caught me at . . . at a friend's house." Even now she faltered about telling him everything. "He had two men with him, so we couldn't do anything, and he threatened . . . He was going to do horrible things to us both, but he was going to kill my friend. So . . . he was killed."

She paused for breath and pulled a face. "That wasn't much of a tale, was it?"

"It does rather skip the who, the where, and especially the how—which I admit fascinates me. But I understand, and you bear no guilt."

"You won't feel obliged to pursue justice about it?"

He reached a hand across the table. "What is justice here? I award your noble defender the medal."

She put her hand in his, knots untangling that she'd hardly been aware of. "I knew you would think like that. I'm sorry, Hawk, deeply sorry, that I didn't tell you everything before."

"Before?"

"Before we committed ourselves."

He tugged, and she understood and went to sit in his lap, to be in his arms. "There is no shame in this, Falcon. But I confess to Hawkish curiosity. About the how, and how it was concealed."

"The how comes mostly from Deveril's being taken by surprise. And from reinforcements." She reached out to touch a silver button on his jacket. "I'm not sure how much else I can tell, even to you." She looked up. "There are secrets we are bound not to share. Does that apply to husband and wife?"

"Not if it affects both husband and wife. But take time, love. Our only urgency now is to eat and be on our way."

"I long for complete honesty between us," she said. "On all things. But would you tell me something truly secret that Lord Vandeimen shared with you?"

He thought for a moment. "I might not." He touched her cheek. "Do what you think is best, love. I trust you."

Trust. It was like a perfect golden rose. She sat up slightly and faced him. "Then I have to tell you one thing, Hawk. I did not behave at all like a Falcon last year. I was frozen with fear. Paralyzed. I did nothing. And afterward . . . Afterward, afterward I was heartless to the one who saved me. Shocked because others weren't shocked—"

He put his fingers over her lips. "Hush. It was your first battle. Few of us are heroes the first time out. I threw up after mine."

His understanding was so perfect. She took his face between her hands and kissed him, without words to express the wholeness that she felt.

She drew back at a tumultuous pealing of church bells. "Is it Sunday and I didn't notice?" she asked.

"Not unless we've spent days in heaven instead of just one night. And it's very early for a wedding."

*   *   *

Hawk eased Clarissa off his lap and went to open the door. There were many innocent explanations for the bells, but his instinct for danger was at the alert.

It could be nothing to do with Van, surely.

A sparkle-eyed maidservant was just running up the stairs and paused to gasp, "Not to worry, sir! It's the duke's heir born at last and all safe! And free ale to be served in the tap in celebration!"

"Duke?" Hawk asked, alarm subsiding, but trying to think what ducal estate was in the vicinity.

"Belcraven, sir! Not the duke's heir, of course, but his heir's heir. His estate is here. A fine, handsome boy born to be duke one day, God willing, just as his father was born here twenty-six years ago!"

"A true cause for celebration," Hawk said, amazed that his voice sounded normal.

Arden here? What strange star had brought this about?

He'd discovered that the marquess had a Surrey estate called Hartwell, his principal country residence. He'd not troubled to find out precisely where. Details, details. It was always in the details.

"The marquess's estate is very close?" he asked in faint hope.

"Not a mile out of the village, sir! And he and his lovely wife as easy as can be with everyone here." She gave him a sly look. "Not like in the old days, when the company was very different, let me tell you."

"Marriage reforms many a man."

"And many a man it don't!" she flashed back with a grin, and hurried off on her errand. An increasing babble could be heard below.

Hawk turned slowly back into the room, rapidly absorbing the situation and the implications. Could they get away undetected? From what he knew about the Marquess of Arden, his displeasure was likely to be expressed physically and effectively.

Clarissa, however, did not seem to realize their danger. Her eyes were shining. "Beth's had the baby and all is well! She'll be somewhat put out at it being a boy, of course."

"Put out that it is a boy?" he asked, swiftly gathering their few possessions.

"She doesn't approve of the aristocracy's obsession with male heirs."

It was sufficiently startling to make Hawk pause.

"She's a firm believer in the equal rights of women, you see, and of a rather republican turn of mind."

"The Marchioness of Arden?"

"She wrote that it would be bad enough having a son born to be duke without him being the eldest, too. She hoped for a few older females to keep him in line. Apparently Lord Arden was the youngest and has two older sisters, and she said that might have been the saving of him."

Hawk laughed. "Very likely. I'm sorry about breakfast, but we should be away from here. I doubt there'll be much service here soon, anyway."

"Oh, I suppose so." She unhooked her cloak, but said wistfully, "It does seem a shame not to be able to visit Beth, being so close."

"No," he said firmly and guided her out of the room.

"I know. I know. And she's doubtless resting. But it does seem . . . A note? No," she said for him.

"No," he said again as they went downstairs, wishing he could give her this small indulgence.

In the plain hall, he grabbed an excited potboy and asked him to find the landlady. People were streaming toward the inn from all directions.

"It's a bit like the Duke of Wellington, isn't it?" she said.

"I hope not." *Come on. Come on.*

She turned suddenly, the scarlet cloak clasped to her. "You said Deveril's death was justified," she said quietly. "So I want to tell you who killed Deveril."

Trust and honesty. Hawk wished that he could tell her now. But she could still back away. "Arden," he said, looking around for the landlady. "It doesn't matter except that we don't want to be caught by him here."

"Why . . . ? But no, it wasn't the marquess."

He turned to look at her. He had given up the plan of blackmailing the marquess and duke, but even so, it was as if solid ground disappeared from beneath his feet. Had he been wrong about everything?

"It was Blanche Hardcastle," she whispered.

"The actress?" It was probably the stupidest response he'd ever been guilty of.

"Yes. I know why you're so shocked. A woman, and one who seems so delicate. But she was a butcher's daughter, apparently. And now, of course, she's playing Lady Macbeth."

"Zeus!" He wasn't actually shocked that a woman had ripped Deveril open. A man has to be dense indeed to preserve illusions about the gentler sex during wartime. For some reason, however, the image of the killer going on to play the part of the woman with the bloody knife did outrage him.

Clarissa was looking at him slightly anxiously, and he was relieved to be able to say with honesty, "Mrs. Hardcastle is in no danger from me, Falcon. I salute her."

Wryly he acknowledged, however, that he'd held a sharper weapon than he'd known. Belcraven and Arden might well have called his bluff, secure that if he did seek a Pyrrhic victory, they stood behind high walls of power and privilege. An actress, however, was another matter entirely. An actress with a somewhat dubious past would hang for the bloody murder of a peer.

"You see, don't you," she said slightly anxiously, "that Blanche must never suffer for her gallantry. She took him . . . she took him up to her bed to get him away from his guards. . . . She was so brave."

"I see. Don't worry about this."

She smiled, a hint of tears in it again. "I'm so glad I told you. I feel truly free now. Free to be happy."

" 'And ye shall know the truth,' " said Hawk, " 'and the truth shall set you free.' "

He teetered on the edge of taking the great gamble, of trusting to her love, to the magic they'd shared.

She did love Hawkinville.

She did love him. If that survived the strain.

But years of caution tied his tongue. What if he was wrong?

He'd heard of men sentenced to death spinning out the moments with one slim excuse or another, against all reason delaying the inevitable. Now, at last, he understood.

Another moment of her untarnished admiration and trust . . .

Then a tall, athletic blond man strode into the inn smiling, gloves and crop in hand. Hawk knew instantly, fatally, who it must be. Pre-ducal arrogance radiated from every pore.

People rushed forward to bow, to congratulate. Then the smiling gaze hit Clarissa, moved to Hawk, and changed.

No chance of escape. Hawk put Clarissa behind him as the marquess smiled again, escaped his well-wishers, and came over to them, cold murder in his eyes.

Clarissa, however, slipped around him. "Congratulations on the baby, Lord Arden."

Damnation, she was trying to protect him, and he could hear the fear in her voice. Arden would never hit a woman, but Hawk pulled her back to his side.

Arden, however, softened to concern when he looked at her. "Thank you. Clarissa—"

"I do hope Beth is well," she interrupted, a tone too high.

"Beth is a great deal weller than is seemly." The marquess's voice took on an exasperated edge. "The baby was born at four in the morning, but the mother is already out of her bed and well enough to fight the midwife about the need to lie down, and me about the appropriate establishment for a future Duke of Belcraven. Having lost a night's sleep and years of my life, I wouldn't mind even a few hours in bed, never mind a week of rest and loving attention, but how can I even sit down and try to recover when Beth is bustling about? And now I find this!"

At the return of fury, Hawk expected Clarissa to falter, but her chin went up. "Are you planning to hit someone again?"

Color flared in Arden's cheeks. "Probably."

"Typical!"

Hawk forced Clarissa behind him. "Did he hit you before?"

By Hades, he'd take Arden apart!

"No!" Her hands clamped around his right arm, and he realized his hands were fists. And so were Arden's, though he looked more startled than enraged.

Then Arden looked at Clarissa, eyes narrowing. "Stop trying to deflect the conversation."

And he was right. Clever Clarissa.

"Don't you think we should move this into privacy?"

A new voice. Hawk looked behind Arden and saw that Con had come into the inn. And that a bunch of villagers were sucking in every word.

Con was standing at the door to a small room. Hawk took Clarissa in there, feeling something sizzle and die.

Con had come in pursuit and somehow managed to be close. Being in the area, he'd sought a bed with his friend, which must have been interesting when it turned out to be a night of *accouchement*. Now they were discovered, and surely Con's steady eyes were disappointed.

Perhaps worried, too. About the role he'd have to play?

Second at a duel? He wouldn't let it come to that.

If only, though, he'd seized the moment to tell Clarissa the truth.

Arden strode in, and Con closed the door. "Want to explain, Hawk?" He stayed close to Arden. A show of support, or readiness to control violent impulses?

Clarissa replied before Hawk could. "We're eloping, Lord Amleigh. What need of explanation?"

"Why would be a start," Arden said.

Silence fell, and then Clarissa looked at Hawk. "Tell him why." She was clearly confident that he could.

Hawk smiled wryly, and looked at Con rather than Arden, seeing the firm resolve of an executioner. It wasn't a matter of Rogues versus the Georges for Con. It was simply the right thing to do.

Slippery slopes. From right to wrong as well as from virtue to sin.

"Why, Hawk?" Con asked. It wasn't a repetitive demand for an answer, but an opening offered so that he could tell Clarissa rather than have someone else do it.

So he turned to her and put the noose around his own neck.

Chapter Twenty-four

B ecause," he said, "if I try to marry you in the ordinary way, you won't do it."

She blinked at him. "I won't?"

"You won't." It was Arden's voice, cold and relentless.

Her eyes flicked to him, then back to Hawk, and she smiled slightly, as if any impediment was a laughing matter. "Tell me, then. It can't be as bad as you think."

"It is, Falcon." He took a last breath and kicked away the stool. "My father was born a Gaspard. You may not know, but that was Lord Deveril's family name. After much effort, he has managed to establish his claim to be the next Lord Deveril. And I, of course, am his heir."

In a way it sounded silly put into words. No hanging matter at all. Just a name, as Van had said.

But it was more than a name.

And just at the name, she paled. *"Deveril!"*

"Which means," said Arden moving to her side, as if protecting her from him, damn it, "you would have one day been Lady Deveril."

The tense he used neatly put an end to all hope, and when Arden put his arm around her, she did not resist. She did, however, stammer, "But . . ." confusion in her eyes.

"As you see," the marquess continued, his eyes suggesting that he was talking to a slug, "this raises questions about Major Hawkinville's attentions all along."

"Luce," said Con quietly, moving between them. "There's more to this than that."

"Is there?" Arden asked, his eyes still on Hawk.

"Yes." Everyone else in the room spoke at once, and the shock of it broke the tension. Clarissa laughed, then bit her lip, eyes still shadowed by shock and uncertainty. She pulled free of Arden, but made no move closer to Hawk.

This had snatched away her elusive beauty. All he wanted in life was to make Clarissa beautiful, each and every day, and yet by his actions he had doubtless thrown away the chance.

He spoke to her alone, without hope. "My father thought he should have inherited Deveril's wealth along with the title, and he spent in expectation of it. That's where the debt came from. I sought you out looking for evidence that you were involved in Deveril's murder because then the will would be overturned and the new viscount—my father—would inherit the money."

"You thought me a murderer! I suppose in some ways I should be flattered."

"Clarissa . . ."

But her hand covered her mouth. "I've just given you the evidence."

"You have?" Arden asked, sharply.

"I told him everything. Just as he planned."

"No!" Hawk exclaimed, but there seemed nothing left to pin hopes to except honesty. "At the beginning, yes."

"Do I have to slap you with my gloves?" Arden asked coldly. "I'd have to burn them afterward."

"Not now!" Hawk commanded, aware of Clarissa's sudden pallor. "Con—"

He put his hand on her arm to push her toward Con, but she twitched away. "Don't try and get rid of me! Don't you dare! Any of you. I'm not a child." She whirled on Arden. "You are not to fight over me."

"You have no say in this."

"I demand a say. I insist on it." When Arden stayed tight-lipped and resolute, she said, "If you duel him, I'll shoot you."

"Clarissa," said Hawk, wanting to laugh and cry at once. "I'm sure you don't know how."

"It can't be so hard as all that." She stared at him, eyes brimming with tears. "You said it was an honorable act for someone to kill Deveril. How could you even think of destroying people over it? Even for Hawkinville."

"I didn't."

"Then what drove you?"

"The will," he snapped. "Forgery is hardly cloaked with honor, Clarissa, no matter how you care to deceive yourself."

She stared at him and the elusive truth dawned even as she whirled to face Arden.

"It was a *forgery?*" She laughed. "Of course it was. How very stupid I've been. Deveril—Deveril!—leaving me all his money. He'd have rather left it to the Crown, or scattered it in the streets if it comes to that." She suddenly struck out at the marquess with both fists, pummeling him.

Arden stepped back, and before Hawk could reach her, he grasped her wrists and spun her to face him. "Hit him if you're feeling violent. He's the villain of the piece."

She staggered forward, weeping, and Hawk caught her, held her for a precious moment. "*I* have committed no crime."

Except breaking a heart.

"Abduction, for a start," Arden said.

"Stop." Con took Clarissa from Hawk, keeping an arm around her. She wasn't crying, but she seemed ready to collapse. "There'll be no duel," Con said, in an officer's unquestionable voice, "and no violence." Then he looked at Arden with a frown. "I gather criminal acts are not to be shared among the Rogues these days."

The marquess looked to be at the end of his tether. "Not lightly, no. And you came back from Waterloo in a bad way. We weren't about to add to your burdens."

Con pulled a face and sat Clarissa in a chair. He went to his haunches in front of her. "What do you want to do?"

She looked at him, pallid, then up at Hawk. "I want to arrange to give the money to the new Lord Deveril."

Arden took a step toward her. "Don't be foolish."

Without looking, Con put a hand out to stop him. "It will be as Clarissa wishes."

"On Hawkinville's side, I see," said Arden coldly.

Con was steady as a rock. "It is Clarissa's choice. That has been decided."

It seemed to stop Arden's fight, but he said, "Perhaps she'll see sense when the shock's worn off."

"Do I have any say?" Hawk interrupted.

They all looked at him, but he spoke to Clarissa. "Hawkinville only needs some of the money—"

"Damn your eyes!" Arden exploded. "How much filthy money do you need?"

Hawk faced him. "Legally, the money belongs to my father. But twenty thousand pounds will suffice."

The arrogant disdain was designed to annihilate. "I will provide it for you on agreement that you leave Clarissa in peace."

There was nothing left but icy invulnerability. "Within the week?" Hawk inquired.

"Within the week."

Clarissa started to say something, but Arden overrode her. "We can discuss your situation later. Come along now. Beth will want to take care of you."

"But the baby . . ."

"Is not enough to tax my Amazon." He turned to Con, acting as if Hawk was not there. "Coming?"

"No. I'll deal with Hawk."

"He can't be allowed to harm Blanche."

"He won't."

"Of course I won't," Hawk snapped. Arden had drawn Clarissa to her feet, but she looked stricken still. "Clarissa, you don't have to go."

It was a faint hope, and her blankness denied it. She made no protest as the marquess took her out of the room, but then she suddenly stopped.

Hawk watched in faint beating hope as she turned back. She pulled off the two rings and put them on a table against the wall. And then she was gone.

Hawk was left with Con and could collapse into a chair and put his head in his hands. "I've known battles that have been easier."

"I'm sure you have."

"She was innocent," Hawk said, to himself as much as to Con. "All along, she was completely innocent."

And thus his treatment of her had been atrocious from first moment to now. He'd hunted down a sheltered young woman who'd been forced into an engagement with a depraved man. She'd been abused, terrified, threatened, and then witness to his bloody murder.

Arden was right. He deserved to be shot.

"You're not totally the villain, you know," Con said in a steadying voice.

Hawk looked up. "Oh, please, explain why not."

"You can't let Slade rape Hawk in the Vale."

"So I rape Clarissa instead."

"I am sure you did not."

Hawk sighed. "No, but I've used her shamefully."

"Last night was unwise, but understandable. And you planned to marry her." Con smiled a little. "If you wish, you can lay most of it at the Rogues' door. We came up with the forgery."

"You weren't even there."

"All the same."

"Ah," said Hawk, suddenly wracked by a weariness he hadn't felt since Waterloo, since after Waterloo with the chaos and the wounded and the mounds and sweeps of bodies and body parts so that victory, for the moment, was valueless. So one only wanted to turn back time for a few brief days to restore life and joy to the thousands of dead, and to their families still to hear the news, and then change history so that such battles never happened again.

Events, however, are written in ink the moment they occur, and cannot be erased.

"In that case," Hawk said, standing and beginning to pull together what was left of his life, "can I ask you to deal with Arden about this? A duel, though I can understand his feelings, would serve no one. You can assure him that I will do nothing to endanger Mrs. Hardcastle or anyone else involved in Deveril's death. For the sake of Hawk in the Vale, however, I must take his money. In strict honor, I should not let the matter of the forgery go."

Con rubbed his chin thoughtfully. "Nicholas arrived at Somerford Court yesterday. You know who I mean? Nicholas Delaney? Apparently his Aunt Arabella summoned him to Brighton."

"Arabella Hurstman? Good God, a Rogue dragon as well. I was doomed."

"I'm afraid so, but since she was largely kept in the dark, I think the doom will fall on us. But when Van explained about the Deveril title, we agreed immediately that the money had been improperly redirected."

A crack of laughter escaped Hawk. "Now that's a way to describe forgery. And a damn good forgery, too."

"But of course," said Con with a smile. "You have to understand that everyone, including Deveril himself, thought he was heirless. The money was going to buy the Regent another gold plate or two, and without money, Clarissa's situation was desperate. You may not know, but Nicholas has an interest in that money. It was originally gathered by a woman called Thérèse Bellaire—" Con must have caught a reaction. "That name means something?"

"Oh, yes," said Hawk with another laugh. The debacle was beginning to take on an absurd humor. "I recruited Delaney for that job. He must be enjoying this turn of the wheel."

"Not particularly. But at least I don't need to dance around the details. The Bellaire woman gathered the money from Bonapartist supporters. She was supposed to take it to France to be ready for Napoleon's return. Instead she planned a new life in America. Nicholas distracted her sufficiently that Deveril was able to steal it."

"Gad. And she didn't kill him then and there?"

"She was, as I said, distracted. And by then, England was not safe for her. But Nicholas could hardly be happy leaving that money with a man like Deveril. When Clarissa's affair erupted, it was simply too good a chance to pass up."

Still swimming in lunatic humor, Hawk asked, "I wonder what happened to Thérèse Bellaire? She managed to work her way back into Napoleon's inner circle, you know, but Waterloo must have ended her hopes."

"I pray that's true. I'm sure she's never forgotten or forgiven any of this. I remember her. Honeyed poison. But the forgery was done under the assumption that no one had a better claim. Right is on your father's side and the money should be his. We agree on that, but Clarissa's situation makes matters difficult."

Hawk sighed. "I don't want all the money, Con."

"Fifty fifty," Con suggested.

Hawk laughed. "I see. You were sent here with power to negotiate, were you? How does Delaney plan to get around her guardian and trustees?"

"The Rogues can raise that much money until Clarissa comes of age. If she insists on having it all, so be it."

Hawk pressed his hands to his face. "On what's left of my honor, I'd not take a penny if it weren't for the people of Hawk in the Vale."

"I know that."

He pulled himself together. "I need the twenty, and I have to take a bit more for Gaspard Hall. Not for the place itself, and certainly not for my father, but for the people there. Something needs to be done to correct the decades of neglect. The Deveril tenants are probably the most innocent victims of all. But I want Clarissa to have the rest. Try to persuade her of that."

Con nodded. "She may not be willing to take anything now."

"I wish to heaven I'd never let that slip, but I didn't know— I should have known. She should have the money, but if she's difficult, point out that if the Devil's Heiress turns suddenly poor it would raise awkward questions."

They were talking so calmly of the future. The future with Hawkinville, perhaps even with his father at Gaspard Hall.

But a future without Clarissa.

Unendurable, except that like a soldier with a shattered leg, he had no choice but to endure the amputation and then—if that was God's choice—limp on.

"Are you all right?" Con asked.

With Con he could let the exasperation show. "No, of course not! I'm stuck in hell. Some of it is my own fault, but most of it isn't. It's my father's, and Slade's, and Deveril's, and your damned Rogues'. It's like being under the control of an insane and inept commanding officer who sends his men marching straight into a battery of enemy guns. And there's nothing, absolutely nothing, one can do but march."

Con, who had doubtless been in that situation, pulled a face. "What will you do now?"

"March back to Hawk in the Vale and arrange to pay off Slade. What else?"

Con nodded. "Nicholas would probably like to talk to you about this."

Hawk wanted nothing to do with the man, but he would go where the insanity sent him. "We didn't part on good terms back in '14, and I'm not sure I'm in the mood to be conciliating."

"He'll cope."

Hawk looked around and picked up the rings. "I knew my mother's ring was a bad omen." He put them in his pocket, then turned to go. But he stopped. "Dammit. I need to write to her."

He had to hunt down the innkeeper to get paper, pen, and ink—a slightly bosky innkeeper, who gave him a very suspicious look. Then he went back to the bedroom, out of Con's sight, though he didn't suppose his friend would be able to tell anything from simply looking at him as he wrote.

A wounded animal seeking a hole in which to lick its wounds.

There was no lasting privacy in any of this, however. It was going to have to be acted out on an open stage. Could he mitigate things for her?

Writing was part of his expertise. Writing clearly, precisely, and succinctly so the recipient would understand the information or instruction without delay. Now, the blank sheet of paper was as daunting as a well-armed garrison, impossible to conquer.

He shrugged and dipped the rather unpromising pen. No words were going to create a miracle here, but he could not ride away without at least expressing himself clearly.

Honestly.

Yes, at this point at least he had honesty, with all its sharp tangs.

My dear Clarissa . . .

Then he wished he'd said "Falcon." No, it was better as it was. Or perhaps he should have written "Miss Greystone."

Perhaps he had better be more careful, or less particular. He'd been able to acquire only one sheet of paper, and he could hardly keep Con waiting for hours as he tried to form a miracle. He must also phrase this so it would not cause disaster if it fell into the wrong hands.

> *My dear Clarissa,*
>
> *Please read this letter to the end. I understand how you must feel, but you will not, I believe, find anything maudlin or embarrassing here.*
>
> *I wish to outline first what I have proposed to deal with our situation. Please believe that I sincerely wish only the best for you, but that I also have others to consider. You said that you had fallen in love with Hawk in the Vale, and I hope therefore that you will not mind providing money to dispose of the odious Slade.*
>
> *In addition, there will be a small sum to begin the restoration of the Deveril estate, which has suffered greatly, through no fault of the people there.*
>
> *The rest is yours. At your majority, you will be able to dispose of it as you will, but I hope you will feel able to enjoy it.*
>
> *As for our personal affairs, I cannot apologize for everything, since I was striving to protect the innocents who would be harmed by Slade, but I do truly regret ever thinking less than the best of you. I should have known, as soon as I knew you, that you were always beyond reproach.*

He paused, knowing he should sign it there, but unable to forgo a little gesture toward hope. And also, maybe, to salve her hurts. He knew, like a deep wound, that her fragile confidence would be cracked. Pray God, not shattered.

> *Perhaps I will sound maudlin here, so by all means cease to read if you wish. The necessary part is over. I give you my word, my dear Falcon, that as I once promised, I have never flattered you. My delight in you—*

Hawk halted to contemplate a tense. Whoever would have thought that tenses could be so crucial?

> *My delight in you has been real, my admiration of you deep and true. I am, alas, cursed with a future as Lord Deveril, but perhaps that fate will not arrive for many years, and perhaps it will seem less appalling by that time. Perhaps, too, you will one day be able to forgive my many deceptions and trust me enough to venture into the wilderness again with me.*

He paused again, wanting to write "I will wait," but he knew that might place a burden on her, and above all, he wanted to preserve her precious, hard-won freedom. And so, in the end, he merely signed it, "Hawk."

He resisted the urge to reread it, which would lead him to want to rewrite it, he was sure. He folded it with his usual precise edges, then realized he had no means to seal it. It didn't matter. Con wouldn't read it—and what matter if he did?

He looked once at the room, at the disordered bed with the slight, telltale splash of blood, and a lifetime's worth of memories. Constantly, constantly, like a manic millstone, his mind ground round and round, seeking things he could have changed, paths he could have logically taken.

He shrugged and went back downstairs to where his friend patiently waited.

Perhaps still his friend, though he wasn't sure he deserved it.

"You always were the steadiest of us," he said as he passed over the letter.

"Someone had to try to steer us away from disaster. But I'm not doing very well by my friends, am I? Dare, Van, you—"

"Dare was not your fault. War is a temperamental bitch who gives no care to good or bad, justice or injustice. Look at De Lancey, killed by a ricocheting cannonball by my side, almost at the end of the battle. There was no point to it. And it could have hit me, or even Wellington, as easily."

"I know. But I've been too wrapped up in myself."

Hawk gripped his arm. "Perhaps none of us came out of Waterloo with anything in reserve for the other. We just chose different ways of hiding it."

Con's gray eyes searched him. "Will you be all right?"

"Of course. I certainly have plenty of work to do."

"Including saving Clarissa's reputation. You were seen racing out of the village."

Hawk grimaced. "Damn. I'll come up with something."

After a moment, Con clasped hands. "I'll take care of Clarissa for you. I have a horse in the stables here. Take it. I'll see you in Hawk in the Vale."

Con left, and Hawk took a moment to steady himself. The mill was still grinding, and probably would do so for the rest of his life, but even if it came up with the most brilliant solution, it was too damn late.

Chapter Twenty-five

Lord Arden had apparently ridden to the village—simply to accept the congratulations of the people gathered at the inn. To return, he commandeered Hawk and Clarissa's gig. She was slightly amused by seeing his lordly magnificence in such a lowly vehicle pulled by the placid cob. Only slightly, however, for she did not have the heart for humor of any kind.

She was trying very hard not to think about all that had happened, all she had learned, but it surrounded her like a chill wind, or an overcast day.

Hartwell. Thank God there was somewhere to go now, some haven. It had been a haven before. Beth had taken her there a few days after Deveril's death, and it was there she had made decisions about the future. If they could be called decisions. All she had wanted then was a place to hide.

She did not let the bitter laugh escape. She'd thought that she'd grown so strong, so brave, so able to deal with life, but here she was, rushing back to a safe place, and she could no more stay here this time than last.

Last year Beth had invited her to live with her, at Hartwell and elsewhere. Clarissa would have been safe inside the de Vaux family, but she had not wanted to be anywhere near the marquess, who had blacked Beth's eye.

As they rolled along the country lane, she glanced at him, realizing that she felt differently now. Though she'd been stupid, gullible, and weak about Hawk, she had changed over the past year. She understood more about emotions, about control, and about how easily strong emotions could explode control.

She had hit Arden. A feeble hit, but only because she was feeble. If she'd been able she might have knocked him to the ground.

In an uncontrolled moment Hawk had shattered a gate, and he had not believed that his beloved had been with another man.

"I'm sorry for what I said back there, Lord Arden. As you guessed, I was deflecting the conversation."

"Next time choose another weapon."

She pulled a face. They had never been on good terms. She had indirectly caused his violent moment, and guilty people blame others if they can. Even so, he'd worked hard and taken risks for her, and she knew he would continue to do so. It was nothing to do with her, but all to do with Beth, whom he loved.

That was the point.

She understood now what Beth had been trying to tell her last year, that the love was true and deep, and that therefore he would make sure that such lack of control never, ever happened again.

"Beth won't be happy if we're at odds, my lord," she said. "And even if she's weller than she should be, I'm sure tranquility is good for a new mother."

He did glance at her then. "Her tranquility would be undisturbed if you'd behaved properly."

She swallowed an instinctive retort. "Yes, you're right. I was foolish. But . . . I didn't want to lose heaven, you see."

She bit her lip, determined not to cry. Now she certainly had lost heaven in all its aspects—both Hawk and Hawkinville. It had probably all been an imaginary heaven, anyway, but for a little while it had felt astonishingly real, as if it could, truly, be for her.

Lord Arden reached over and gently squeezed her hand. He was gloved, but still it was the most human contact she remembered with him. "My instinct is to tear Hawkinville limb from limb, but it's not so long since I did questionable things. I have some sympathy for him, pressured by the needs of his family and his land."

"So do I."

He glanced at her again, clearly expecting more, but she couldn't speak it. Deep inside she felt raw, where trust had been uprooted from her. Did Hawk want her now that he could have the money regardless? Last night she would have laughed at doubt, but now, swirling in the awareness of deception, it ate at her.

If he protested on his knees that he loved her, would it be pity, or obligation?

And then there was the problem of Lord Deveril. It should be a little thing, but it simply wasn't.

Deveril!

It was as if a ghoul had risen from the grave to drool all over her.

Lord Arden turned the gig between open gates and into the short drive through lovely gardens to the house. Hartwell was what people called a cottage ornée. It looked like a thatched village cottage, only grown to three times the size. Clarissa couldn't help comparing its pretty perfection unfavorably with Hawkinville Manor, which was real even to its warped beams and uneven floors.

Beth had joked that Hartwell was a bucolic toy for the wealthy aristrocracy rather like Queen Marie Antoinette's "farm" at Le Petit Triannon, but Clarissa knew Beth loved it, probably because it was home to her and the man she loved.

She'd told Hawk that she would live with him in love anywhere. And it had been true.

As Lord Arden turned the gig down a side drive toward the stables at the side, she swallowed tears. She was not going to turn into a wailing fool over this. She'd lost her virtue, her beloved, her heavenly home, and her fortune all in one day, but crying wouldn't bring any of it back.

She went into the house with the marquess somewhat nervously, however. She was not so strong as to ignore what Beth would think of her adventures. They were still more teacher and student, and she had always been awed by Beth's intelligence and strong will.

When they found that Beth was asleep, she was as relieved as the marquess.

"And thank heavens for that," Lord Arden muttered. He looked at Clarissa, and she saw that he hadn't a notion what to do with her. Beneath the gloss and the highly trained ability to be the Heir to the Dukedom under the most trying circumstances, he was, quite simply, exhausted.

She was astonished to feel a need to pat him on the shoulder and tell him to go and have a nice rest. She settled for saying, "I know the house, my lord, so you may feel easy leaving me to my own devices for a while."

His look was, if anything, kind. "I'm sorry, Clarissa. I can say he's not worth it, but at this moment you won't believe that."

"This certainly isn't how I want things to be." But she looked him in the eye. "I wouldn't give up the past few weeks, Lord Arden, even had I known it would bring me here."

He reached out and touched her cheek. "I know that feeling. You have friends, Clarissa. You will be happy again soon."

"I'm ruined, you know," she said, wondering if he didn't quite understand.

"No, you're not," he said with a smile. "Just a little more experienced. You know Beth wouldn't disapprove of experience. Ask the servants for anything you need. Amleigh will be here soon, I have no doubt."

He'd made her laugh, and she watched him go upstairs, astonished by a touch of affection. Truly her experience seemed to have stretched her mind in some way, giving her glimpses of subtleties and, more important, understanding.

What to do?

She should be hungry, but she was sure food would choke her. She probably should ask to borrow a dress of Beth's. They were, or had been, much of a size.

Perhaps she should write to Miss Hurstman, or even to the duke. Would the duke have to know about this?

In the end, aimlessly, she drifted out into the garden, wandering down to the river, where ducks busily paddled and dipped under the surface for food.

In her mind she was immediately back at another house on another river. With Hawk in Hawkinville.

She sat down on the grass to think, to try to see what had really happened.

Hawk had gone to Cheltenham to find a criminal. She thought back over that day, tried to see it through his eyes. He must have been telling the truth when he said he changed his mind then. She'd been the most unlikely villain.

He'd drawn her to Brighton so he could dig for more evidence. She remembered wryly the number of times their talk had turned to London and Deveril, and the things she'd let slip.

The knife in the tent.

He was good. Very good.

But had the connection, the friendship, the passion, all been artifice?

What about the wilderness? That she would swear was real.

Ah. She remembered the splintered gate, and was suddenly sure that yes, it had all been real. Hawk would not lose control like that as a stratagem.

And last night. Surely there had been nothing false about last night.

But what did she really know about these things? He'd planned to marry her for her money and so he would have wanted her bound by passion.

And love.

And trust.

She grimaced at the way she'd babbled about perfection and honesty and trust. And told him everything.

She could only pray that he'd told the truth, that he had what he wanted. That Blanche would be safe.

She watched the river, thinking stupidly that it must be much easier to be a duck.

She heard footsteps and turned, thinking it would be the marquess, hoping against hope that it would be Hawk.

It was Lord Amleigh.

"There are suddenly a lot of titled gentlemen in my life," she said, and it was silly.

He smiled and dropped to the grass by her side, dark-haired, square-chinned, and steady-eyed. "Just me and Arden, isn't it?"

"And Lord Vandeimen."

"And, indirectly, Lord Deveril." He was still smiling, but there was something in his eyes that made demands of her. "Perhaps if you called me Con it would simplify your life."

"You're his friend. Have you come to ask me to forget it all?"

"I'm a Rogue, too, remember, and you are the one person who least deserves to suffer. Everything will be exactly as you wish."

She laughed, hiding her face against her skirt, into the deceptively simple cream muslin gown that she had chosen yesterday morning with such hopes and dreams, and that now held only stains, and memories.

"That does assume that I know my own wishes."

"You will, but perhaps not now. I know that at the moment it probably seems urgent, but it will all wait."

She turned her head sideways to look at him, this virtual stranger who was so intimately linked with her affairs. "But will the world wait—before condemning me?"

"The world won't know. Who's to tell them?"

Strange to think about that. Not the Rogues. Not Hawk, or Lord Vandeimen or Lord Amleigh. Althea? Hardly. Lord Trevor? Miss Hurstman would cut his nose off.

"The village of Hawk in the Vale?" she asked.

"Hawk will deal with them. He's gone back there."

She studied him. "You trust him."

"With my life and all I hold dear." After a moment he added, "That doesn't mean he's without faults."

She looked forward at the river. "So I can return to Brighton, and assemblies, and parties. It seems completely impossible, you know."

"I know. But life goes on. He sent a letter and asked that you read it."

She sat up and took the folded paper, but she wasn't sure she wanted to read it.

"It doesn't have to be now, if you don't want. But I think you should, when you're ready to."

Clarissa looked at the folded sheet. There was nothing on the outside, not even her name. There'd been no need of name or direction, of course, but it struck her as very Hawkish to be so precise about the necessities.

It was also, she realized, folded in half and then in three with impressive precision. Every angle was exact, every edge in line. How distressing it must be to a man of such discipline and order to be thrown into such discord.

She looked at his friend. "Is he all right?"

"No more than you."

"I'm in love with him, so even more than I want him, I want to make everything perfect for him. But I'm not sure what that perfect would be, and I am sure that I mustn't .... melt myself into him for his comfort and pleasure."

"An extraordinary way of putting it, but I know what you mean. I don't have any wisdom to offer." After a moment he said, "I'm not even sure there is any wisdom when it comes to the heart, except the old nostrum that time heals. It heals, but healing is not always without scars, or even deformities."

She stared at him. "I'm certainly not being treated as a silly child, am I?"

"Do you wish to be?"

"Doesn't everyone wish to be, sometimes?"

"There you have an excellent point." He opened his arms, and she went into them. It was fatherly, or perhaps brotherly. She, who had never had father or brother interested in holding her.

She remembered that after Deveril's death, Nicholas Delaney had held her in the same way. But none of these men, even if full to brimming with goodwill, could solve her dilemmas for her.

"I suppose I have to return," she said. "To Brighton."

"Certainly Miss Hurstman will want to see you safe."

"Miss Hurstman is a Rogue." She said it firmly but without resentment.

"No, she's not. She's a Rogue's aunt. Lord Middlethorpe's aunt, to be precise. If you think she's on our side against you, you don't know her very well.

She's a fierce defender of women in any practical way. There'll be skin lost over our mismanagement of this."

She pulled free of his arms to look at him. "She didn't know any of this?"

"Not unless she's a fortune-teller. Nicholas asked her to take you on because he thought you needed special help to win your place in society. That's all."

"But she wrote to him. Reporting, I assume."

"Ah, that. She wrote demanding his presence. She has an encyclopedic knowledge of society that exceeds Hawk's. As soon as he appeared she remembered that his father had been born a Gaspard, and that Gaspard was the Deveril family name. It rang enough of an alarm bell for her to send for him, but not enough of one to take any action. She had no idea—probably still doesn't—that Hawk's father has the title now."

"Then I'd like to go back there." She stood up and brushed off her hopeless skirt. "Life goes on, but it hardly seems possible."

Like a claw scratching at the back of her mind, she wondered what she would do if she was with child. All very well for Lord Arden to brush off her ruin, but a swelling belly would be a very obvious sign of experience.

Would that mean that she'd have to marry Hawk?

He'd argued with her about just this. About her changing her mind, being with child.

Had he really tried to resist? Or had that simply been more cunning on his part?

She wanted him too much to make sense. Wanting was not the guide.

A child can want to grasp the fire, an adult want to throw away a fortune on cards.

Something popped up from the jumble of her mind. "You mentioned fortune-telling. . . . It's tugging at something . . . oh, Mrs. Rowland!"

He frowned slightly. "The woman in the village with the invalid husband?"

"Yes, I felt as if I knew her, but now I see she reminds me of that fortune-teller in Brighton. Madame Mystique."

Who had talked about the money not really being hers, and death if she did not tell the truth. She'd told the truth, but she still felt half dead.

"What is it? Are you faint?"

"No." She couldn't deal with another stir of the pot. "I think I need to eat something. And probably borrow a clean gown. Con," she added as a mark of appreciation for his kindness.

He smiled. "Come along, then." They began to walk back to the peaceful house.

Most people would prefer Hartwell, with its picturesque charms around a thoroughly modern and convenient interior.

But Clarissa knew that Hawkinville still held her heart.

Chapter Twenty-six

Hawk rode south almost by compass, driven by duty alone. It might be pleasant, in fact, to become lost. He'd looked into some cases of people who simply disappeared. Perhaps they too found themselves in a dead spot of life and went away. Went anywhere so long as it was not here.

He might collide with Van by pure accident on this journey, but that encounter could not be avoided. It really didn't matter when. It mattered whether Van, like Con, could hold on to old bonds in spite of present insanity, but he couldn't affect that.

He could affect Clarissa's reputation, and he put his mind to that.

He made Hawk in the Vale without incident, and saw everyone in the village turn to stare.

The Misses Weatherby popped out of their house, agape. Good.

Grimly amused, Hawk touched his hat. "Good evening, ladies."

They gaped even more, and he waited for them to frame a question.

But Slade marched out between his ridiculous pillars right up to his saddle. "Where's your impetuous bride, Major? Fled to warmer arms?"

Rage surged. Barely resisting the urge to kick the man's teeth in, Hawk put his crop beneath Slade's wattly chin and raised it. "One more word, and I will thrash you. My father's folly is to blame more than your greed, but you are very unwelcome here, sir. And your comments about a lady can only be attributed to a vulgar mind."

As if breaking a spell, Slade dashed away the crop and stepped back, puce with choler. "Lady?" he spat, then stopped. "May we know where the charming Miss Greystone is, Major?"

Very well. Slade would do, and the Weatherbys were all ears.

"It's none of your business, Slade, but she heard that her dear friend the Marchioness of Arden was in childbed and wished to be with her. As you said, she is somewhat impetuous."

Slade opened, then shut, his mouth. "And the happy event?" he inquired with a disbelieving sneer.

"A son. The heir to Belcraven, born just before dawn."

He heard the Misses Weatherby twittering, as women always did at these events, and of course at the slight vicarious connection to the birth of such an august child.

The birth was just the kind of incontrovertible fact that could glue together almost any lie.

Slade was certainly believing it.

"And the money?" he asked stiffly.

Hawk permitted himself a disdainful sneer. "Will be yours, sir, before the due date. I must thank you for being so obliging to my family."

With that, he turned his horse toward the manor, which apparently would survive, along with the heart of Hawk in the Vale. At the moment, he felt no satisfaction. He did not dismiss the value of preserving the village, but he did not dismiss the cost, either.

As he dismounted in the courtyard the scent of roses met him—sickeningly. He left the horse to the groom and strode swiftly inside.

"George? Where's your bride?"

His father stood in the doorway to the back parlor, leaning on a stick.

"Isn't it more a case of where's the money?"

"Definitely, definitely. You have it? If so, we can start planning the celebration."

"Go to the devil," Hawk snapped, then quickly reined in his temper before it drove him into something else to be ashamed of. "I have the money to pay off Slade, but there is no extra, my lord."

"There is always more money, my boy! I thought a fête similar to that one Vandeimen threw for his wedding. But more regal. Full dress. A procession—"

Hawk turned to go up the stairs. "You will, of course, do exactly as you wish, sir. I have no interest in it."

"Damn your eyes! And where is your bride, eh? Lost her already?"

Hawk paused on the landing. "Precisely, sir."

He entered his room tempted to sink into the darkness, but he had done this for a cause, and the cause went on. He opened his campaign desk. The familiar paper and pens swept him back to his other life. He thought there might even be a trace of smoke and powder trapped in the wood.

Why had the skills that had carried him through challenging and even torturous tasks in the army failed him here?

He picked up the flattened pistol ball that had been his constant reminder that blind luck played a huge part in fate. Perhaps this time his luck had run out.

But, no, that wasn't it. In the army he'd usually worked toward a single imperative. He'd had no personal stake, and a good part of his skill had been in blocking out all distractions of fact or sentiment.

In fact, this campaign was a resounding success.

Hawkinville was safe.

He deserved a medal.

He wrote a Spartan letter to Arden thanking him for his assistance and requesting that he arrange for the money to be available at his Brighton bank before the end of the month. Then, with distaste, he wrote a note to Slade requesting the name of the institution where his money should be deposited.

He went downstairs and sent a servant off with it.

And that, pretty well, was that.

All that was left was the rest of his life.

He walked out of the house at the back, and down to the river, but the ducks must have been enjoying some other part of the water, and heavy clouds were drifting between the earth and the sun. It seemed symbolic, but he knew the sun would shine another day and the ducks would return.

Only Clarissa would be perpetually absent.

Was there any chance that she would relent once the shock wore off? He couldn't bear to hope. If he did, he thought he would be frozen in time, waiting.

He heard a footstep and turned.

Van's fist caught him hard on the jaw and flung him backward into the river.

He sat up spluttering, hand to his throbbing jaw, tasting blood from the inside of his cheek. Van waited, icy.

"If you hit me again," Hawk said, "I'll have to fight back."

"You think you can win?"

"Would anyone win?"

Van glared at him, but the ice was cracking a little. "What's this claptrap about Clarissa going to Lady Arden's lying-in?"

Hawk decided he could probably stand up without having to kill Van and did so. "As a story it can hold if not challenged too strongly."

That was a hint, and he saw Van take it.

"What did happen?"

His boots were full of water. "I tried to elope. I evaded pursuit, but made the mistake of staying the night in Arden's home village."

A crack of laughter escaped Van. "Wellington would have your guts!"

"The thought has occurred to me. I forgot, I assume, that I was at war."

The ducks chose that moment to scoot quacking along the river, perhaps drawn by the splash. One duckling scuttled over to peck at his boots.

Hawk looked down contemplatively. "It seems to be my day for being attacked by animals."

"Are you referring to me?"

Hawk smiled slightly. "Is a demon an animal?"

With a shake of his head, Van stuck out his hand. Hawk took it and climbed out of the river to drip on the bank.

"What happened?" Van demanded. "The whole truth."

"I'm not going to add pneumonia to my other follies. Come inside and I'll tell you as I change."

Hawk discarded his boots by the back door and left wet prints as he padded along the flagstoned corridor and up the stairs. "Mind your head," he said as he went into his room.

Van ducked just in time, then flung himself into the big leather chair with old familiarity. The three of them had rarely chosen the manor over Steynings or the Court, but they had spent some time here, mostly in this room.

"You gave me your word that you wouldn't ruin Clarissa."

Hawk stripped, piling his sodden clothes in his washbasin to spare the wooden floors. "I said, if I remember, that I would not ruin her that day." He kept a careful eye on Van's fists. "I did not mean to be specious, but as it happens, I kept to the letter of my promise."

"And yesterday?"

"And yesterday, I did not." He toweled himself dry. "We were, however, on our way to our wedding. Except that we were stopped."

"By Arden. You don't seem to have been bruised before now."

"My golden tongue."

"Against *Arden*, when he found you bedding a woman he has to regard as being within his protection?"

"We weren't bedding at that moment," Hawk pointed out, pulling clean clothes out of drawers. "And," he added, "Con was there. And Clarissa."

"Didn't want to create a fuss in front of her?"

"Couldn't get through her would be more exact. This was before she realized the truth, of course." He pulled on his breeches, fastened them, and sat down. "She had no idea the will was a forgery, Van. No idea at all."

Van looked at him for a moment, unusually thoughtful. "What now?"

"Now I pay off Slade with Arden's money. It must be pleasant to be able to afford such lordly gestures, and it seems the Rogues wish to arrange to cover it." He explained the arrangements.

"But what of your father? He accosted me in the hall, chortling about outranking me. And going on about a grand fête to beat my wedding celebration."

Hawk sighed. "I deserve a penance, and I certainly have one."

After a moment, Van said, "At least you're free of that Mrs. Rowland. She packed her household into Old Matt's cart yesterday and headed away."

The part of him that was still the Hawk stirred at that. "Do we know why?"

"Not that I know. The general feeling is, good riddance."

"I agree, but I meant to visit her poor husband in case something could be done for him."

"I tried a few weeks back. I forced it as far as a glimpse into his room. I think he's done for. Haggard and frail. I gather there was a dreadful blow to the head."

"Poor man." But at the moment Hawk couldn't feel strongly about it. He couldn't feel very much of anything except loss and pain.

"Do you love her?" Van asked.

Instinctive defense almost had him denying it. "Yes, but it's completely impossible. Apart from my behavior, can you imagine her here with my father insisting on being Lord Deveriled at every turn, and complaining endlessly of not enjoying his true splendor at Gaspard Hall?"

"But her money . . . ?"

"The clear impression is that she would rather eat glass than take a penny of stolen money, and knowing Clarissa, I'm sure she'll stick to her guns."

Hawk couldn't speak of her without becoming maudlin. He surged to his feet and put on his shirt. He couldn't be bothered to go further than that. "Convey my apologies to Maria. What of Miss Trist?"

"Maria and Lord Trevor returned her to Brighton, I understand. Doubtless not looking forward to explaining the situation to Miss Hurstman." Van rose too. "Nicholas Delaney is here, by the way. Staying at the Court with his wife and child. I suspect he'll want a word with you, too."

"So Con said. I'm sure I have enough unmarked skin to go around. Are you off for Brighton, since Maria's there?"

"Yes. Will you be coming in?"

"What for?"

Van grimaced, gripped his arm for a moment, then left.

Hawk went to his window to contemplate ducklings.

Clarissa, dressed in one of Beth's simpler gowns, was attempting to consume a bowl of soup in a spare bedroom while waiting for Con to return with a carriage. She'd suggested that they use the gig, but he'd insisted that she have something better for the journey to Brighton.

The soup was a tasty mix of chicken broth and vegetables, and doubtless nourishing, but she was having trouble finishing it. Tears prickled around her eyes almost constantly, and Hawk's letter was a sharp-edged presence in her pocket.

After a rap, the door opened and Beth came in.

Clarissa leaped to her feet. "Beth, you shouldn't be up!"

"Don't you start pestering me," Beth said, sitting at the table. "Sit down. Eat."

"You look very well," Clarissa said, and Beth did. She was in a loose dressing gown with her hair in one long plait, but she looked much the same as always.

"I am well. It went easily, and I have done considerable research. There is no reason for women to lie around for days or even weeks after a healthy birth. Such a practice quite likely encourages debility. That and lack of fresh air and exercise during pregnancy. I walked at least a mile every day."

Clarissa chuckled, and some of the sodden sadness lifted. "And the baby?"

Beth's face lit up. "Perfect, of course. You must come and see him when you're finished."

Clarissa had no reluctance about abandoning the soup. "I'm finished. I can't wait."

Beth beamed and led the way down the corridor to the nursery. "This is next door to our bedchamber," she said softly, as a maid rose from a chair by the cradle to curtsy.

She led the way over to the grand gilded cradle swathed in blue satin. Inside, a tiny swaddled baby slept. To Clarissa he looked rather grumpy, but she whispered that he was beautiful.

Beth picked him up, and the tiny mouth opened and shut a few times, but then the baby stilled again. She carried him into the bedroom and shut the door. "It's ridiculous, but I feel as if I am stealing him," she said to Clarissa. "He has a staff of three, and that was only after a battle royal. Lucien can't imagine why he shouldn't have his own liveried footman! I have had to be very firm to have time to myself with him."

Clarissa smiled. "He's only eight hours old and you're already at war."

"I've been establishing the rules for months, but they still must be implemented." She grinned, however, as she sat down in a rocking chair, her baby in her arms.

Once settled, she gave Clarissa a clear look. "Now, tell me everything."

"Won't we wake the baby?"

"Not unless you plan to shriek. Anyway," she said, looking down at her child, "I won't mind if he wakes. He has the most beautiful huge blue eyes. I'm feeding him, you know. It's a bit sore at the moment, but it's wonderful." She touched the baby's cheek, and he made little sucking movements but didn't wake.

Clarissa was sure Beth didn't really want to hear about the distressing debacle. But then Beth looked up, all schoolteacher. "Out with it, Clarissa. What have you been up to?"

By the end of the story the baby had awakened, squawked a little, and been put to the breast, with some winces. Beth had told her to keep telling her tale.

Now she asked, "What is your intention now?"

"Not to take any of that money. I'm resolved on that. I still can't believe the Rogues would steal."

She thought that Beth was wincing at the suckling, but then she said, "It was my idea, actually. Forging the will."

"Yours!" Clarissa exclaimed, close enough to a shriek for the baby to jerk off the breast and cry. By the time Beth had him soothed and on the other breast, Clarissa was calm again. Astonished, but calm.

"Why?"

"Why not? Everyone said Deveril had no heir. You needed money. I was afraid even Lucien wouldn't be able to stop your parents from selling you in some way or another."

"But it's a crime."

Beth pulled a laughing face. "I must be of a criminal inclination, then. I even took part in the planting of the will at Deveril's house. Blanche and I acted the part of whores."

Clarissa gaped, and Beth chuckled. "Lucien was dumbfounded too. I wore a black wig, lashings of crude face paint, and a bodice that just barely covered the essentials."

"Dumbfounded" summed it up, especially since Beth seemed to be recalling a delightful memory.

"Do you think I should keep the money, then?"

Beth sobered. "It is more complicated now, isn't it? There is a new Lord Deveril, and without our interference he would have inherited it all." She considered Clarissa. "I am not clear how you regard Major Hawkinville at this time."

"Probably because I'm not clear either. My heart says one thing. My mind shouts warnings. We were warned often enough at school about the seductive wiles of rascals and the susceptible female heart."

"True," said Beth, but with a rather mysterious smile. "But it's as much a mistake to expect perfection from a man as it is to tumble into the power of a rake. After all, can we offer perfection? Do we want to have to try?"

"Heaven forbid. He wrote me a letter."

"What did it say?"

"I haven't read it yet."

"There's no need to make a hasty decision, my dear, but reading the letter might be a good start."

The door opened then and Lord Arden walked in. He halted, and looked almost embarrassed, perhaps because he was in an open-necked shirt and pantaloons and nothing else. Not even stockings and shoes.

But then he looked at his wife and the baby, and Clarissa saw that nothing else mattered.

As he went over to Beth, she slipped out of the room, certain of one thing. She wanted that one day. To be a new mother with the miracle of a child and a husband who looked at her and the child as Lord Arden had looked.

And she wanted it to be Hawk.

She went back to her cold soup to read his letter, then cooled the soup some more with tears. Neat, crisp folds and neat, crisp phrases, but then those poignant perhapses.

Or were they simply the pragmatic analysis of the Hawk's mind?

If only she had some mystical gift that would detect the truth in another person's heart.

Chapter Twenty-seven

The trip by carriage took a lot less time than the wandering journey that had carried Clarissa and Hawk to the fateful village. Con, wonderful man, did not attempt conversation, but eventually she weakened and asked him about Hawk.

His look was thoughtful, but he talked. She saw their childhood from another angle. The bond was still there, and the fun, but they were shaded by Con's exasperation with his wilder friends. Lord Vandeimen, it was clear, had always been given to extremes, inclined to act first, think second. Hawk, on the other hand, had thought too much, but relished challenges. He had also lacked a happy home.

She learned more about his parents. Though Con was moderate in his expressions, it was clear that he despised Squire Hawkinville and merely pitied his wife.

"She was hard done to," he said, "but it was her own folly. Everyone in the village agrees that she was a plain woman past any blush of youth. Would the sudden appearance of a handsome gallant protesting adoration not stir a warning?"

He clearly had no idea how his words hit home to her.

"He must have been very convincing," she said.

"Such men usually are. When the truth dawned, she would have been wiser to make the best of it."

"Why? To make it easier for him?"

He looked at her. "That was her attitude, I'm sure. But she only made matters bitter for herself, her child, and everyone around her. There was no changing it."

"And she couldn't even leave," Clarissa said. "It was her home." And perhaps she, too, had loved Hawkinville.

Con said, "It's made Hawk somewhat cold. Not truly cold, but guarded in his emotions. And he's never had a high opinion of marriage."

Clarissa was aware of the letter in her pocket. Guarded, perhaps, but not well. And not cold. And he wanted marriage.

Could it all be false?

She didn't think so.

Con called for the carriage to stop, and she saw they were at a crossroads. "We can turn off here for Hawk in the Vale," he said.

"No."

She wasn't ready yet. She was determined to be thoughtful about this.

"I was thinking more that we could go to my home, to Somerford Court. We don't even have to go through the village to get to it from here. Nicholas Delaney is there, and I'm sure he'd like to speak to you. We can send a note to Miss Hurstman and go on to Brighton tomorrow."

Clarissa was certainly in no rush to return to Brighton. "Why not? I wouldn't mind a word with him, either."

The Court was almost as charming as Hawkinville Manor, though centuries younger, but Clarissa was past caring about such things. Con's wife, mother, and sister were welcoming—Con's wife insisted on being Susan—but it couldn't touch her distraction. Nothing in the world seemed real except her and Hawk and her dilemma.

And stopping where he was mere minutes away had not been a good idea.

Nicholas Delaney took one look at her and suggested that they talk, but ordered a wine posset for her. As she went with him into a small sitting room, she said, "I'm not hungry."

"You need to eat. You can't fight well on an empty stomach."

"I'm likely to fight you. This is all your fault."

"If you wish, but I think the blame can be well spread around. There's nothing so weak as 'I meant well,' but in this everyone meant well, Clarissa."

"Not Hawk. Hawk wanted my money. I'm not touching it." That should shake his complacency.

"As you wish, of course," he said. "I'm sure Miss Hurstman can find you a position pandering to a not-too-tyrannical old lady."

She picked up a china figurine and hurled it at him.

He caught it. "It would be foolish to be wantonly poor, Clarissa, and no one has a greater right to that money than you."

"What about Hawk's father?" She made herself say it. "The new Lord Deveril."

"Only by the most precise letter of the law." He put the figurine on a small table. "Sit down, and I'll tell you where that money came from."

She sat, her revivifying anger sagging like a pricked bladder. "From Lord Deveril's unpleasant businesses, I assume."

"He might have increased it a bit that way, but even vice is not quite so profitable in a short time."

Clarissa listened in amazement to a story of treason, embezzlement, and pure theft.

"Then the money belongs to the people this woman got it from. Except," she added thoughtfully, "they would hardly want to claim it, would they?"

"They could be found. Thérèse happily gave up a list of their names once she had no more use for them. In the end the government settled for letting them know that they were known. Many of them fled the country, and I don't think those that remain would want to be reminded of their folly."

"The Crown, then."

"The Regent would love it. It would buy him some trinket or other. But by what excuse can the money be given to the Crown?"

She was arguing for the sake of arguing, because she was angry with them all. "When I'm twenty-one, I can do with it as I wish."

"Of course. I arranged it that way. In retrospect, that was an indulgence. It apparently gave Hawkinville reason to doubt the will." He smiled. "It does seem unfair that women at twenty-one are considered infantile, when men at the same age are given control of their affairs."

"That sounds like Mary Wollstonecraft."

"She made some good points."

There was a knock on the door, and a maid came in with the steaming posset. When she'd left, Clarissa decided not to be infantile. She sat at a small table and dipped in her spoon.

Cream, eggs, sugar, and wine. After a few mouthfuls she did begin to feel less miserable. "This will have me drunk."

He sat across the table from her. "Probably why it's excellent for the suffering invalid. There are times when a little inebriation helps."

She looked at him. "What do you want me to do?"

He shook his head. "I have put you in charge of your own destiny."

She took more of the posset, and the wine untangled some of her sorest knots.

"I'm afraid of making a fool of myself."

"We all are, most of the time."

She glanced up. "For life? How does anyone make choices?"

"Of marriage partners? If people worried too much about making the perfect choice, the human race would die out."

"Not necessarily," she pointed out, and he laughed.

"True, but it would be a chaotic system. Marriage brings order to the most disorderly of human affairs."

"But there are many bitter, corroding marriages. Hawk's parents, for example. And mine."

"True fondness, goodwill, and common sense can get us over most hurdles."

She spooned up the last of the sweet liquid, and the wine probably gave her courage to ask a personal question. "Is that what your marriage is like?"

He laughed. "Oh, no. My marriage is one of complete insanity. But I recommend it to you, too. It's called love."

Love.

"Perhaps I should see Hawk," she said, a warm spiral beginning to envelop her in betraying delight.

But Delaney shook his head. "I think we'll wait an hour or so to see if that's only the wine talking." He rose. "Meanwhile, come and meet my insanity. Eleanor, and my daughter, Arabel."

As they went to the door he said, "Would you be able to call me Nicholas?"

"In what circumstances?" she teased.

"Damned tenses. I would like it if you would call me Nicholas. I think you are by way of being an honorary Rogue."

Con, and Nicholas. New friends. And her acceptance of it was something to do with Hawk, and with Lord Arden.

"Nicholas," she said, but she added with a giggle, "I'm not sure I can call Lord Arden Lucien, though."

"Definitely the wine," he said, guiding her out of the room. "The number of people to call Arden Lucien is small. If not for the Rogues it might be down to one—his mother."

"And Beth, surely."

"Perhaps."

She understood. Without the Rogues, Lord Arden might not be the sort of husband Beth would call by his first name. He might be the sort who expressed every sour emotion with his fists.

"Perhaps I should call Hawk George," she said. "Less predatory. But then he wouldn't call me Falcon."

Nicholas shook his head. "We must definitely wait an hour."

Eleanor Delaney was a handsome woman with a rooted tranquility that Clarissa admired. Of course, it must be easy to be tranquil with a husband such as Nicholas. Clarissa was sure he had given her no trouble, told her no lies.

Arabel was a charming toddler in a short pink dress showing lace-trimmed pantalettes. Her chestnut curls were cut short, and she was playing with a cat that Clarissa recognized.

"Jetta!"

The cat reacted to the name, or perhaps to her. Whichever, Clarissa certainly received a cold stare. Lord above, was a cat capable of fixing blame for the loss of its hero?

"It was thought to be in danger from the manor dogs, so I brought it up here." Nicholas swooped up his daughter and carried her, laughing, over to be introduced. Clarissa saw identical sherry-gold eyes.

Arabel smiled with unhesitating acceptance. " 'Lo!"

"Not the beginning of an ode," said Nicholas, "but her greeting."

The child turned to him, beaming, to say, " 'Lo! 'Lo! 'Lo!" But then she said, "Papa. Love Papa."

Clarissa almost felt she should look away as Nicholas kissed his daughter's nose and said, "I love you too, cherub."

Insanity.

Love.

Heaven.

But then Arabel turned to her and stretched out. Astonished, Clarissa took the child and duly admired the wooden doll clutched in one fist. Nicholas went to talk to Eleanor, and the child didn't turn to look.

What blithe confidence in love that was, that never doubted, or feared the loss of it. Would she ever feel that way?

Then Arabel squirmed to get down and led the way back to the cat and some other toys. Clarissa sat on the carpet and played, discovering one certainty.

She wanted a child.

She wanted to be married to Hawk and have Hawk's children, but if that didn't happen, she wanted to be a mother. A married mother.

She tried to imagine being married to someone else. It didn't seem possible, but time must have an effect on that. What was the difference between a wild passion and an eternal love?

Easier by far to play with the child than to tussle with adult problems.

But then Mrs. Delaney insisted that it was bedtime. When she came to pick up her daughter, she said, "I understand that you are a Rogue now. I hope you will call me Eleanor."

Clarissa scrambled to her feet, not quite so comfortable with this informality, but she agreed.

"And if you want a woman to talk to," Eleanor Delaney said, "I am a good listener. No hand at good advice, you understand, but we can often work these things out for ourselves once we start, can't we?"

She carried the child away, and Clarissa glanced at the clock.

"Still half an hour to go," Nicholas said.

She pulled a face, but said, "Then I think I'll walk in the garden and talk to myself."

She expected a comment, but he only said, "By all means—if you promise not to sneak down to the village."

She glared, but the thought hadn't occurred to her. It was a very little time to wait, and she knew it was wise to see if her forgiveness seeped away with the effects of the posset.

When she left the room, the cat came with her. She looked down. "I thought I was the enemy."

The cat merely waited. Perhaps the clever animal had decided she was the key to Hawk. It would be nice if true.

The Somerford Court gardens were pleasant, though rather formal. She crossed a lawn and wandered down a yew-lined path, greeted by a gardener busy keeping the hedges trim. It was a warm but heavy evening. Even the birds were quiet. Apart from the *snick, snick, snick* of the gardener's shears, it was soundless.

She came to a round fishpond dotted with water lilies and sat on the stone edge to trail her hand in the water. A fat carp came to nibble, then swam away, disappointed. Jetta crouched on the rim, also disappointed.

No food.

No fortune.

Her slightly inebriated mind didn't want to focus, not even on talking over her problem with herself.

She looked around, but nothing offered wisdom or inspiration. The pond sat in the middle of a hedge-lined square, with four neat flower beds set with bushes in the center and lined with low white flowers. It struck her as amusing that Hawk of the neatly folded note had the lush, willful garden, while Con owned such precision.

Both had been formed by previous generations, however.

Each side of the square hedge had an opening leading to another path. None of them invited.

Then a figure crossed over one of those paths. A maid in dark clothing with a large bundle. And Jetta rose to hiss.

Clarissa looked at the cat. "Another rival for Hawk's affections?" But the cat was simply twitching its tail restlessly.

Clarissa frowned at it. "Now you have me twitchy." She scooped it up and went down the path to catch another glimpse. The woman was far ahead, going briskly about her business, which was probably to take laundry to the village. Jetta gave another, almost huffy, hiss; the woman turned right and was out of sight.

Clarissa turned back toward the house, but something about the woman was on her mind now. She hurried in a direction that should provide another view, giving thanks for the straight lines of the garden. She came to the abrupt end of the garden, with countryside before her.

The woman was already across a pasture and climbing a stile, bundle under her arm, to follow a footpath along the edge of a harvested field toward the village. It wasn't a servant. It was that Mrs. Rowland.

"Still don't approve?" she muttered to the tense cat. "Misfortune turns some people miserable, you know. And see, she has to take in laundry to put food on the table."

Or she might be stealing. An unfair thought about the poor woman, who'd shown no sign of furtiveness, but Clarissa decided she had to tell someone. She turned back to the now rather distant house.

Somerford Court was a rambling place, and when she eventually entered, she found herself near the kitchens. She stopped in there, faced by half a dozen female servants who didn't know who she was, and feeling very foolish.

"I'm Miss Greystone. A guest."

Then Jetta leaped down and was immediately the center of attention. "Wonderful mouser, it is," said the woman who was probably the cook, smiling. "Can we help you, miss?"

Clarissa felt that she had been properly introduced. She almost didn't want to spoil it by saying anything, but she made herself speak.

"I just saw someone in the garden. I think it was Mrs. Rowland, from the village. Does she take in laundry, or mending, perhaps?"

And what business is it of yours? she could imagine the servants saying.

"Her?" said the cook. "Not likely. She has been here now and then, to speak to her ladyship—the Dowager Lady Amleigh, that is. Begging, if you ask me, for all her airs. But not today, miss."

Protesting that would do no good. Perhaps she should speak to the dowager.

She left the kitchen and headed toward the front of the house. The Court, however, was the sort of rambling place built in stages, where no corridor went in a straight line. She was beginning to think she'd have to call for help, but then she tentatively opened a door and found herself in the front hall.

Now what? Her alarm about Mrs. Rowland was beginning to seem very silly, but she decided she would find the dowager.

At the moment the house was as sleepy as the gardens, but she'd seen a bellpull in the small room where she'd talked with Nicholas. She was heading there when Nicholas came out of another room. "Ah, your hour's up," he said, smiling.

If she'd wanted to block her decisions from her mind, she'd certainly succeeded. For the past little while she hadn't thought of Hawk at all. Perhaps that was why her mind had eagerly clutched the little mystery.

Now that the idea was back, it pushed out all others. "I still want to see him," she said.

"Very well—"

"Nicholas!" They both turned to see Eleanor racing down the stairs, white-faced. "I can't find Arabel!"

Nicholas caught her in his arms. "She likes to hide—"

"We've searched her room. The ones nearby. I've called." She turned, searching the hall. "Arabel! Arabel!"

He pulled her back into his arms. "Hush. She can't have come down here. We'll get everyone to search."

Con and Susan had emerged from the room where Nicholas had been. They immediately went off to set all the servants to the search, inside and out, and a message was sent to the village for extra people.

The Delaneys hurried upstairs, calling their daughter's name. Clarissa raced after them, caught up in the alarm at the thought of that sweet child perhaps stuck in a chest, or having tumbled down some stairs.

It was only upstairs, wondering helplessly where to look, that the thought struck. It was too ridiculous to bother Nicholas with, so she ran in search of Con, finding him in the front hall marshaling affairs. Quickly, she told him about Mrs. Rowland.

"You're sure it was she?"

"Mostly," she said, less sure by the moment. She almost said, "Jetta hissed," but that would make her seem a complete idiot.

"But she was carrying something?"

"I thought it was laundry. Or mending."

But then his eyes sharpened. "Didn't you mention her earlier? That she reminded you of someone?"

"Of the fortune-teller." But then she inhaled with shock. "She talked about Rogues. And she gave me Nicholas's initials!" She quickly sketched that encounter.

"Who could be interested in Clarissa's money and in the Rogues?"

Clarissa turned to see Hawk there, hat, crop, and gloves in hand. Their eyes met in a sudden collision of need and problems.

Con said, "Madame Thérèse Bellaire." But then he added, "It's insanity. Why would she even be in England?" He was already turning to run upstairs, however. "We have to tell Nicholas. Dear God . . ."

Clarissa and Hawk ran after him.

They found the Delaneys opening and shutting drawers and armoires that had to have been searched before.

Con told them, and they both turned impossibly paler.

"Thérèse," Nicholas said. "Please, God, no."

Eleanor clutched his arm, and then they were wrapped with each other. Clarissa remembered that Madame Bellaire was the woman who had gathered the money, then lost it to Deveril. She'd thought when Nicholas told her that there was more to the story.

If only she had pursued. Or done *something*.

"We have to follow it up," said Nicholas, coming back to life. To Clarissa he said, "Which way did you see her go?"

"Down to the village." She described it exactly.

Before she could say she was sorry, Hawk said, "That path splits three ways. And I doubt she took the village one. She moved her whole household out at crack of dawn."

"Where?" Nicholas asked.

"No one knows, and we won't until Old Matt returns to say where he took his cartload. Madame Mystique must have some base in Brighton, but there's no saying she's returned there. If it is she." He added, looking at Clarissa, "Fortune-tellers can be uncanny."

"I know! I'm not sure of anything."

Clarissa could almost feel Nicholas's need to rush off, but he looked at Hawk. "I'm in no state to think, Hawkinville. I gather this is your forte. Will you take command?"

Clarissa saw a touch of color on Hawk's cheeks. She remembered then that he and Nicholas could be seen as on opposite sides in respect to her. All that was unimportant now.

"Of course," Hawk, said. "I'm sure you want to do something, however. Why not follow the route Clarissa described? Look for clues or people who saw the woman. Take a couple of Con's grooms to follow other routes when it splits."

Nicholas hugged his wife and left. Susan went to hold Eleanor's hand.

Hawk turned to Con. "I'd like you to head for Brighton by the most direct route, looking for the Frenchwoman or Old Matt. If you get there without a trace, find Madame Mystique's establishment and check it out. Take a couple of armed grooms—and be careful."

"Aye-aye, sir," said Con ironically, but without resentment, and hurried out.

The salute brought a slight smile to Hawk's lips.

"Shouldn't someone check Mrs. Rowland's place here?" Clarissa asked.

"Yes, I'll do that. It won't take long, and it needs a careful eye. I'll see if my father knows anything about the woman, too. He was mightily upset to hear of her leaving."

He turned to go, but Clarissa grabbed his sleeve. She wasn't sure what to say except that she had to say something. "Find her."

He looked at her with deep darkness, then touched her cheek. "If it is humanly possible—"

Then in a black streak, Jetta leaped in to sit on his boots, as if trying to pin him down. Clarissa wondered for a mad moment whether the cat knew he was going into danger. He picked it up and moved it, and strode out. After a shake, Jetta strode after him. There was no other word for it. Clarissa felt as if he had a guard.

But then she turned back and saw Eleanor's face. "I'm sorry. I should have gone after her."

But Eleanor shook her head. "She would have killed you. Or taken you with her if she could."

"Then I should have raised the alarm! Immediately."

"Why?" Eleanor had lost all that placid calm, but she came to take Clarissa's hands. "Why should you imagine anything so extreme? Life would be impossible if we all jumped to such conclusions every time we saw something out of the ordinary."

"But," Clarissa said bitterly, "I should have learned from experience. Everyone who has anything to do with me ends up in disaster."

Eleanor gathered her into her arms. "No, no, my dear. Everyone who has anything to do with Thérèse Bellaire ends up in disaster. Really," she added, with a touch of unsteady humor, "Napoleon would have been well advised to wring her neck."

Chapter Twenty-eight

The women continued the search for a while—Clarissa even ran out to the fishpond in case the child had escaped the house and drowned—but no one's heart was in it. They were all sure that Arabel had been stolen away.

Clarissa took a moment in the garden to let out her tears, and she felt better for it, if drained. But, oh, the thought of that sweet, trusting infant, who seemed innocent of anything but adoring kindness, in the hands of "Mrs. Rowland"! If only she'd not acted sensibly for once. If only she'd been impetuous, and pursued. Perhaps she might at least be with the child and able to protect and comfort her.

The only "if only" that mattered now, however, was if only she could do something to speed up the child's safe return.

She returned to the house and discovered that Hawk also had returned and taken over Con's study for what could only be called a command post. She entered to find that he'd set the women to work, even the dowager and Con's sister.

A map was spread on the desk, and Hawk was studying paths and roads under the eye of a watchful cat. Eleanor was taking notes and seemed much steadier. Everyone else seemed to be drawing. Clarissa soon gathered that they were drawing rough sketches of routes, with churches, houses, streams, and such as markers.

She was given a piece of paper, and Eleanor read off some details for her.

"We're going to send out riders along all these routes," Eleanor said. "It will cover everything from here to a five-mile radius." She glanced at Hawk. "He is very meticulous, isn't he?"

Clarissa looked at him too. "He has that reputation." She couldn't help adoring him for his control and discipline. Knowing him, she realized that inside he was probably as achingly worried and anxious as they all were, but he was intent on his goal. Rescue.

He said something to Eleanor, looking up, and his eyes found Clarissa. Something flashed there—a need, she hoped—but immediately it was controlled. "The Henfield road goes through two tollgates," he said to Eleanor. "The second should be far enough. The river blocks any roundabout route. Who has that one?"

Eleanor looked at her list. "Susan." She went to relay the instructions to Susan, who was using the deep windowsill to work on.

Then Nicholas returned, looking exhausted but better somehow for racing around. She realized that Hawk had sent him for exactly that reason, and had probably put Eleanor to work to help her, too. So many threads in his fingers, each one to be done perfectly, because failure was impossible.

Then the maps were finished, the waiting grooms summoned, instructed with crisp precision, and sent off.

"They can be back within the hour," said Hawk, but he glanced out of the window at the overcast sky. "If the weather holds." He looked at Nicholas. "The woman may have gone to Brighton, but it might be too obvious. What do you want to do?"

"Ride hell-bent for Brighton, of course," said Nicholas. "Or to London. Or to the Styx to bargain with Charon—" He stopped himself. "We will wait until the riders return, and hope there's a clear path. It would be worse, after all, to go in the wrong direction entirely."

"Then we must eat," Hawk said. "Susan?"

Susan left, and everyone moved restlessly, waiting for something that could not come for a while.

"If Con finds anything along the road," Hawk said, "he'll send back word. What's the woman like? From all I've heard of her, devious but not stupid."

Nicholas rubbed his hands over his face. "No, not stupid. But she can be foolish. She prides herself on her arcane plans, but then gets lost in them. Certainly following a straight line is unlikely to find her. You're going about it the right way. Spin a web."

Now that the immediate work was done, Eleanor Delaney had sunk into a chair, staring into nowhere. Nicholas went to her.

Clarissa turned to look out of the window. Evening was beginning to mute the day. Realistically speaking, it was no more terrible for the child to be in the hands of a madwoman at night, but it felt as though it was.

Hawk came to stand nearby. She knew it even before she looked.

"Is she mad?" she asked.

"Probably not. But there's a kind of madness that thinks only of itself. All controls to do with decency or humanity are lost, and only the desires and pleasures of the person matter. I suspect she is that sort of woman. What do you think?"

"I think of her with her children."

He put out a hand to her, then stopped it, lowered it. She did not protest. There was no place in this for them, for the tangles and dilemmas still to be sorted out.

Susan returned, followed by maids with trays holding tea, wine, and plates of hastily made sandwiches. Certainly, thought Clarissa, sitting down to dinner would be macabre. The maids left, and everyone was busy for a moment, pouring, passing, taking plates. But then stillness settled.

"Eat," Hawk said. "You can get it down if you try, and strength is needed. And don't get drunk."

After a moment, Nicholas put down his wineglass and picked up a sandwich. Eleanor was drinking tea, but she started to eat too.

Hawk ate two sandwiches, but he seemed to be thinking throughout the meal. Then he said, "The most likely situation is that the Bellaire woman has taken the child to hold for ransom. I gather she has reason of sorts to think that Clarissa's money is hers. My father was under the illusion that she was going to marry him as soon as she was widowed. No illusion, actually. That doubtless was her plan once he had the money. I suspect I was her hunting dog, sent to sniff out the villains. An interesting mind. I assume that my elopement told her the plan was dead—so we have this."

Nicholas put down his food. "But we only arrived yesterday. This has to have been an impulse. Had she no other device? It is unlike her."

"She prefers multiple plans?"

"She adores them."

"Mrs. Rowland had two children," Hawk said, "a boy and a girl. Are they hers?"

Nicholas laughed. "Thérèse? Impossible to imagine, and two years ago she boasted of the perfection of her body, unmarked by birth. Good God, has she kidnapped others?"

"Or adopted, to be fair. She's been here for months with them. A strange ploy if she took them for money. No," Hawk said.

He picked up Jetta and stroked the cat as if it helped him think. "I suspect the children were simply disguise. Perhaps poor Rowland was too. Intriguing, really. She must have been left in a very difficult situation after Waterloo. Stranded in Belgium, without her powerful protectors, and thinking of her money in England. If she found a wounded officer and persuaded him to claim her as his common-law wife—perhaps in exchange for nursing him— and acquired a couple of the stray orphans that always wander after battle, she would have an excellent cover for a Frenchwoman to enter England."

"You sound as if you're falling under her spell."

Hawk looked at Nicholas. "I'll wring her neck if need be. It's often necessary to enter into the mind of villains to decide what they will do. And villains rarely see themselves that way. They see themselves as clever, as entitled to what they seize, as justified in the evil that they do. You're right about her having some other plan. Knowing what it is would be useful, but the main point is that she will demand money. A great deal of money and in short order. Can you raise it?"

Clarissa stood. "I wish I could give her all of mine! I don't want it. She was right when she said it was poisoned."

"But you can't get it in a day or two," Hawk said, as if the money was of no importance to him. "Arden offered me twenty thousand, so I assume he can put his hands on that quickly."

"The Rogues," said Nicholas, suddenly alert.

But then pounding feet had them all turning to the door. It burst open, and a panting groom raced in. He looked around the crowded room in confusion. "Sirs, letter from his lordship!"

Hawk took it and opened it. It contained another sealed paper. "She went through the Preston toll," he said, reading. "A woman fitting her description in a fast carriage. Bold. And, even bolder," he added. He looked at Nicholas. "The woman paid the tollkeeper to give this letter to anyone who asked." He held it out. "It's addressed to you, but of course Con read it."

Nicholas was already reading. "She wants a hundred thousand pounds before eight o'clock tomorrow evening." He gave it to Eleanor.

"Impossible," gasped the dowager Lady Amleigh.

"And she has her other string," Nicholas carried on, looking strangely stunned. "She claims to have Dare."

Clarissa looked around in confusion. Hawk said, "It's not possible—" But then he breathed, "Lieutenant Rowland." He cursed, which, given the presence of ladies, showed how deeply shocked he was.

"She wouldn't lie," Nicholas said. "It has to be true. Pray God it doesn't make Con do something wild. We have to go."

"Yes, of course." But Hawk held up a hand. "What of the money? We have to think now how to raise it." But then he looked at Nicholas. "If it's Dare, he's in bad shape. Van saw him briefly. He thought he was dying."

"We get him and Arabel back," said Nicholas flatly. "By all means, let's think how to get the money. If Thérèse can be easily found in Brighton, Con and Vandeimen will do it."

Hawk sat at the desk and put a clean sheet of paper in front of him. "You have all I can raise, but it's precious little, even with jewels included. Arden's twenty thousand, of course."

Clarissa bit her lip, thinking what that meant for Hawk in the Vale, but there was no choice.

The dowager suddenly stood and took off her rings and a brooch, putting them on the desk. "I'll go and get my jewel box."

Con's wife and sister did the same. Eleanor said, "Everything I have with me, of course. But most is back in Somerset. There's not time, is there?"

Nicholas took her hand. "We can try. But there are those closer. Arden," he said to Hawk. "He's good for more. Beth has diamonds worth a good part of the amount."

Clarissa had seen Beth's diamonds. They were part of the ducal estate and not really Lord Arden's to give, but she knew he would.

"Leander's probably in Somerset, but we'll send to his Sussex estate in case. Francis. Hal's in Brighton, but he has little. I think Stephen's in London. If there are ways of raising money, he'll find it. We have to contact the Yeovils too."

"Dare's parents?" Hawk said. "Yes, of course. Though he may not be a pretty sight."

"If he's alive, do you think that matters?"

"No." Hawk added the name.

The two Lady Amleighs and Helen Somerford returned and put jewel boxes on the table. Clarissa didn't think the contents would be worth a vast sum, but they would be treasured pieces given up in this cause.

"I have some jewelry in Brighton lent me by the Duke of Belcraven," she said. "You can have that. When I come of age," she added firmly, "Deveril's money will go to repay all these debts. I am determined on it."

She said it looking at Hawk, afraid of objection, but he nodded. "I hope to get through this without paying a penny, and with the woman locked up for her crimes."

"Not wise."

They all looked at Nicholas. "We really don't want Thérèse on trial. She knows or guesses far too much. I'm sure she's counting on that. Of course, if she harms Arabel in any way, I will kill her. I hope she's counting on that, too."

The first grooms began to return with their pointless reports on their routes. They were sent to eat while Nicholas wrote letters to the Rogues and the Yeovils, asking for the money and jewels, and a message to his home in Somerset instructing a trusted servant to bring the contents of his safe.

Clarissa couldn't help thinking that some lucky highwaymen might make the strike of their lives.

"Where shall we ask that it be sent?" Nicholas asked.

After a moment, Hawk said, "Van's house in Brighton," and gave the address. Once the letters were on their way, he said, "And now we can go. She's gone to ground in Brighton, but by God, there has to be a way to find her."

Clarissa, Eleanor, and Susan jammed into the Amleigh phaeton, Eleanor driving, the gentlemen on horseback. Again Jetta insisted on riding with Hawk, sitting upright in front of him.

"She'll fall off at speed," Clarissa said.

"I doubt it," said Nicholas, his horse sidling impatiently, doubtless a reflection of the rider. "The Chinese trained cats to ride into war exactly like that. They would leap at opponents and blind them."

Clarissa shivered at the thought, but all in all, the more protectors Hawk had, the better.

Then they were off. Five grooms not needed for other duties rode with them. Heads turned as the speeding cavalcade whipped past. Clarissa could only think of all the people with small problems, all the parents whose children were safe.

In a short while Nicholas drew alongside to tell Eleanor he was riding ahead, and she gave him her blessing.

"If I were any rider at all, I'd go with him. It is so *intolerable* not to be racing to do something, no matter how futile." She cracked her whip, and the horses picked up pace as the sun set sulkily behind heavy clouds.

Chapter Twenty-nine

Brighton. Clarissa remembered entering Brighton a short while before, full of nerves and hope. How different now, with so much at stake. How trivial all her earlier anxieties seemed. The past hours of stress had scoured away her uncertainties about Hawk. In this uncertain world, what did twenty, forty, sixty years matter?

Carpe diem, for indeed, one could not know what the morrow would bring.

The sunlight had almost gone by the time they entered Lord Vandeimen's house, finding the Vandeimens there, along with Con and Nicholas. Con seemed afire with new purpose, and it was all to do with Lord Darius.

"Madame Mystique has a house on Ship Street," he said, "but it seems deserted. I hesitated to break in."

"Good," Hawk said. "We can't be precipitous. We risk triggering her to do something undesirable. No sign of Old Matt?"

Clarissa had to think who that was. Oh, the carter who had transported Lieutenant Rowland and the children.

No, she corrected. He'd transported Lord Darius Debenham and the poor waifs picked up from who-knew-where and subjected to Thérèse Bellaire's cold heart for a year. She desperately regretted returning the children, but couldn't see how she and Hawk could have done anything else.

"Not on the road," Con said. "I've sent the grooms to check on all the inns and taverns. He likes a drink. But how do we search all Brighton?"

"Meticulously," said Hawk with a hint of a self-mocking smile.

"We don't have enough people to comb thousands of households!"

There was a rap on the door and they all turned. They were all, Clarissa realized, still standing in the narrow hall.

The nearest person opened the door—Susan.

Blanche and Major Beaumont came in. Blanche went straight to Eleanor and put a bundle in her hands. "Lucien's necklace is the most valuable piece, but I've put in some stage trumpery too. Perhaps she won't have time to study it."

"Good idea," said Nicholas. "Maria, which jewelers here are most likely to keep paste for people to wear?"

Everyone flowed into the front parlor and soon Maria had a list, but it was too late to visit jewelers today.

"We have to do something," said Eleanor fiercely, desperately. "Dear heaven, if she's awake, she will be so frightened!" Nicholas went to her, but he was haggard with the same need.

"We try to find her," Hawk said steadily. "Maria, may I have some of your servants?"

"Of course! Which ones?"

"A few who are Brighton born and bred."

She hurried out and soon returned with a maid, a sturdy young man, and a frightened-looking boy, whose eyes seemed to be trying to go all ways at once.

"Listen carefully," Hawk said in a clipped, military voice. "We need to find a woman in Brighton. The main thing is that she is French. She was last seen looking sallow and dressed in black, but she may have changed. She's slim, dark-eyed, and about thirty. She will probably have one or three young children with her. We're also looking for a very sick officer, who might go by the name Lieutenant Rowland. The last person is a carter called Old Matt. Old Matt Fagg. He might simply be drunk in one of the taverns. All three people are somewhere in Brighton. You are to alert as many people as possible—children too—that anyone who brings me news of where any of these people are will receive ten guineas."

The maid and groom came to sharp attention. The lad gaped. That was probably his yearly wage.

"What's more, if any of these people are found by anyone, you three will each receive ten guineas for yourself. Mind, though, everyone is to be careful. We only want to know where she is. We do not want her disturbed. Do you understand?"

All three nodded, though "dazzled" might have better described their state than "comprehending."

"Do you have any questions?"

The lad said, "Ten guineas, sir?"

"Yes."

The three servants backed out, but then Clarissa heard one set of running footsteps. She was sure they were the boy's.

"I do hope no one will get hurt," she said.

"You wouldn't make a general, love."

It slipped out and they looked at one another.

"I have this constant urge," said Nicholas, pacing the room, "to go and search the streets. It's irrational."

"But perfectly reasonable," Hawk said. "Waiting—and watching—are always the hardest parts."

Clarissa guessed that he referred to his army career.

"What about Madame Mystique's house?" she asked.

"She might try to hide in open view?" Hawk asked. "I doubt it. It would be a trap. But it certainly should be checked. Who's best at housebreaking?"

"I've done it," said Nicholas with a wry smile, "but I wouldn't say it's a skill of mine."

"I'll do it, then," said Hawk, picking up a satchel he'd brought and taking out a ring of strange-looking keys.

"You must have had an interesting war," Nicholas remarked.

"That's one way of looking at it. As I pointed out recently, however, it was nothing so dramatic as chasing down spies. More a question of checking out warehouses."

Clarissa remembered, and knew he'd said it deliberately, as a kind of connection.

He took Nicholas with him, as a kindness, she was sure, and Jetta by necessity, but they were soon back to say that the house was deserted and no clue could be found there. "Except traces of opium," Hawk said. "So she probably does have Lord Darius and the children drugged."

"It can be so dangerous," Eleanor whispered. "I've never given her it. Not even for teething."

The door suddenly opened and Miss Hurstman stood there. "Ha!" she exclaimed, fixing Clarissa with a dragon's eye. "Maria, I told you to tell me if she turned up." But then she looked around. "What's the matter?"

Nicholas went and took her hands. "Thérèse Bellaire has kidnapped Arabel."

Miss Hurstman, who Clarissa had thought was made of pure steel, went sickly sallow and sat down with a thump. "Oh, heaven help the poor angel!"

Clarissa thought the woman might cry, but then she stiffened. "I assume you men are dealing with it?"

"As best we can," said Hawk dryly.

A knock on the door brought the maidservant who'd been sent out to search. "I found the carter, sir!" she declared, flushed with excitement as if this was a treasure hunt. For her, Clarissa supposed, it was. "At Mrs. Purbeck's lodging house, sir, but dead drunk. Really drunk. She thinks he's drunk uncut brandy, sir, for there was a half-anker nearby."

Maria gave the woman her ten guineas and told her to go and find a way to bring the unconscious man here.

"Uncut brandy?" she asked when the maid was gone.

"Smugglers ship it double strength in small casks," Susan said. "It saves space. Then it's watered to the right proof over here. There's many a man drunk himself to death sneaking a bit from a smuggler's cask."

Clarissa had learned that Susan was from the coast of Devon. Did all people there know such details?

After that, it was merely a question of waiting. Old Matt was trundled over in a handcart and put to bed in the kitchen, but it was clear he would not wake soon—and perhaps not at all.

The Delaneys left to go up to the room prepared for them.

Clarissa realized that she would have to return to Broad Street. Foolishly, she didn't want to leave Hawk, and she didn't want to leave the center of the action in case some miracle should occur.

But then, after a short interval, the other two servants straggled in to say that no one seemed to have seen a trace of the Frenchwoman, or the invalid officer. Hawk gave the lad and the man their ten guineas anyway, and rubbed a hand over his face.

"She can't have hidden that thoroughly. It's not possible."

"Unless it's a blind," Con said, "and she's not in Brighton at all."

Hawk considered it, but then shook his head. "She wants her money, and this is the place she appointed. I'm missing something. We all need sleep."

Clarissa couldn't imagine how anyone could sleep, but Miss Hurstman rose, a very subdued Miss Hurstman. Clarissa realized that there hadn't been a word about her elopement. It was a very minor thing.

She turned to Hawk. Minor or not, it seemed strange to leave without something meaningful between them. "Can you sleep?" she asked. Good heavens, it had been only last night that they'd slept together.

It was Lord Vandeimen who answered. "He can sleep through anything when he decides he needs it. We thought it would be a nice nostalgic touch to share quarters before Waterloo. We didn't realize then what kind of work Hawk really did. Con, Dare, and I couldn't get a moment's rest for the coming and going. Hawk, on the other hand, would suddenly stop, lie down, and go to sleep, telling whoever was there to take messages."

Hawk winced. "Was it as bad as that?"

"Yes." But then Lord Vandeimen added, "We wouldn't have missed it, all the same. I hope to God it is Dare, and we can save him."

Hawk picked up a pen from the table, turning it restlessly in his fingers. "He came to speak to me that last night. He was leaving for the Duchess of Richmond's ball. You two had already gone to your regiments, and I was busy, but Wellington wanted as many officers as possible there to keep up appearances.

"He came into my room and said he wanted to thank me. I asked what for, of course. Probably rather shortly. I was busy, and his gadfly antics in the past weeks hadn't endeared him to me. He gestured at all the papers in that way he had that made it seem that he took nothing seriously. 'Oh, for all this, I suppose,' he said. 'An excellent education in the complexities of military affairs.' Then he said that if he lived, he planned to take a seat in Parliament and work to improve army administration.

"I suddenly took him more seriously, and I worried. Men do get a premonition of death. I asked him, but he shrugged and said something about it being reasonable to consider death on the eve of battle. Flippantly, in his usual way. Then he asked me to take care of you, Con, and I realized that most of his gadfly japes had been a deliberate attempt to carry you through the waiting time."

Con's mouth was tight with suppressed tears. "But he's alive. And we'll find him and make him well again."

"Yes, we will. I didn't look after you, Con, but we'll get Dare back, so he can berate me about it."

Clarissa couldn't be cautious or discreet. She went over to Hawk and pulled his head down for a gentle kiss. "Tomorrow is the battle, but I will be by your side."

He cradled her head for a moment, his eyes telling her what she knew, that there was a great deal to be said but that this was not the time. Then he kissed her back and said, "Sleep well."

She nodded and left with Miss Hurstman.

She arrived back at Broad Street exhausted from an astonishing few days, but not ready for sleep. She wandered into the front parlor.

To find Althea in the arms of a dashing gentleman.

"Althea!" Clarissa gasped, absurdly shocked.

Althea and the man broke apart, both red-faced and appalled.

Miss Hurstman let out a crack of laughter. "It's as well I don't plan a career as a chaperon. I'm clearly a total loss at it. You, sir—who are you, and what are you doing? Oh, forget that. It's clear what you're doing."

The man had struggled to his feet and was pulling his waistcoat down. He was not a young gallant, but he was a fine figure of a man, with short, curly hair, a handsome face, and good broad shoulders. Althea leaped up and stood beside him in a protective posture that Clarissa recognized.

How on earth had Althea got to this point with this man with her none the wiser? She'd never seen him before.

The man tugged on his cravat, then said, "I am extremely sorry. Carried away, you see. But Miss Trist and I have just agreed to marry."

"Very nice," said Miss Hurstman. "But who are you?"

"The name's Verrall," he said, swallowing. "I do have Miss Trist's father's permission."

Clarissa gaped. This was Althea's hoary widower?

He stood straighter, chin set. "I thought I was prepared to wait while Althea had her holiday here, but her letters began to worry me." He turned to Althea. "I hope you don't mind your father sharing them with me, my dear?"

Althea shook her head, blushing beautifully.

"I did not like to push my suit too strongly, but I became convinced that it would be folly to delay with so many handsome gallants around. So here I am."

"So here you are," Miss Hurstman said. "Excellent, but there's no bed for you here, Mr. Verrall, so off you go. You can return in the morning."

Mr. Verrall took his leave, not even daring to take a final kiss under Miss Hurstman's eye. Despite everything that had happened, Clarissa felt like giggling, and she was truly delighted for her friend's happiness. Incidentals like age didn't matter. Only trust and love.

But then Althea obviously gathered her wits. "But you, Clarissa. We heard . . . Maria Vandeimen said . . ."

Clarissa made a decision. "Oh, that was all a misunderstanding." She used the excuse Hawk had apparently spread around. "I went to attend Beth Arden's lying-in."

"You, an unmarried lady!" Althea gasped.

"I was always somewhat rash, Althea, you know that. Come up to bed."

She glanced at Miss Hurstman and saw that the woman understood. There was no point in disturbing Althea's happiness with a crisis she could not help with.

It was dark in the small space, and windowless, but a tight grille in the door let in glimmers from a lamp some distance away. A swaying lamp.

Lord Darius Debenham lay propped up on the narrow bed, watching the two older children play with their food. Exactly that. There was bread here. They'd eaten some, then molded bits into little animals with practiced skill. So few proper toys they'd had.

They spoke in whispers. They always spoke in whispers, probably because Thérèse Bellaire had punished them if they didn't.

Thérèse Bellaire. The whore who had tormented Nicholas for fun. She would have no sweet ending planned. They were to die here, and he couldn't do a damn thing about it except pray.

And keep the children at peace as long as he could.

He gently touched the hair of the one cuddled against him. Thérèse had said she was Arabel, Nicholas's child. He'd last seen her as a baby, but in the uncertain light he thought she had Nicholas's eyes. Dear God, what he must be suffering.

And there wasn't a damn thing he could do to help.

Little Arabel had awakened crying and had called for her mama and papa, but she'd calmed. Lord knows why. He couldn't think he was a sight to soothe a child. Perhaps it was Delphie and Pierre, who'd hovered, whispering their comforts and their admonitions to be quiet.

So she was quiet, but she stayed close by his side, and the trust pierced him when it was so misplaced. The child might well be stronger than he was. He'd made himself eat some of the food left here, but when had he eaten before that? Food had no savor for him, no importance.

His recent life seemed like pictures glimpsed in darkness. She'd said it had been a year. A year! That he'd been close to death.

He remembered the battle, but not whatever disaster had ended it for him. A bullet in the side and a hoof in the head, she'd said. Certainly he had headaches. He could remember the pain so fierce that he'd welcomed the drug, begged for it.

But had it been a year?

And had he really believed he was another man? He couldn't think clearly

about it all, but he remembered a time when everything had been blank.
He'd welcomed the facts she put in his memory, meaningless though they
had been. When he'd begun to doubt, there had been the children. If he
wasn't Rowland, they weren't his. So they weren't his.

How could he save them?

Did he want to be saved?

He looked at his bony, quivering hand.

He thought of his parents, his friends. He thought of them finding him
like this, a weak husk of a man, already shaking with the need of the stuff in
the bottle she'd left.

Perhaps he'd be better dead. But he had to stay alive to take care of the
children.

He ached for the laudanum, but she'd left only a spoonful, maybe less. A
calculated torment. He didn't need it badly enough yet. She'd given him a lot
before she moved him here. Enough for deep dreams, enough for thought.
But all he had was in that bottle. Once that was gone, it was gone, and the
need would tear him apart. He couldn't let the children see that.

He would kill himself first. It would be kinder.

If he had the strength.

He looked at the bottle again, could almost smell the bitter liquid through
the glass. He started to sweat, belly aching.

No. Not yet.

They needed to escape.

He would have laughed if he'd had the energy. He could hardly walk. He'd
checked the space, crawling, sweating, and aching every inch of the way.
When he'd tried to stand, his legs had buckled under him. Delphie and Pierre
had helped him back to the bed.

The door was solid and locked. If he could smash out the tiny grille, not
even Delphie could escape through it. And he'd be hard-pressed to gather the
strength to pick up the damn bottle and pull out the stopper!

Delphie scrambled to her feet and came over to him, holding the rough
doll he'd made for her one day. It was just sticks and rags, but it had been the
best he could do. It was their secret, always carefully hidden.

"Mariette's arm is broken, Papa," she whispered in French.

He looked at it as she climbed up beside him. "I can't fix it now, sweetheart. There's no need to whisper. She's gone."

Delphie looked up at him with huge eyes. "I like to whisper."

He held her close as weak tears escaped.

Delphie looked at Arabel, then put the doll into her hand. "You can have her for a little while."

Arabel doubtless didn't understand French, but she clutched Mariette as if the doll could take her back to her loving home.

Dare leaned his head back and did the only thing he still could. He prayed.

When Clarissa woke the next morning she was thrust abruptly back into the horrific situation. She sat up, wondering where the poor children had spent the night. She looked at the window and realized it was raining. That seemed suitable. This was the day of battle. Presumably at some point Thérèse Bellaire would tell them where to send the money. The money Clarissa prayed had been coming in through the night.

Then she would tell them where the prisoners were.

If Hawk hadn't found them beforehand.

Althea stirred and smiled, clearly full of more pleasant thoughts. "Clarissa," she said, turning sober and sitting up, "would you mind very much if I returned with Mr. Verrall to Bucklestead St. Stephens? He can't be away long, you see, because of the children. And . . . and I want to go home. I'm very sorry, but I don't like Brighton very much."

Clarissa took her hands. "Of course you must go. But all the way with only Mr. Verrall?"

She was teasing somewhat, but Althea flushed. "I'm sure he can be trusted."

"Ah," said Clarissa, "but a chaperon is not to keep the wolves away. It's to keep the ladies from leaping into the jaws of the wolves."

"Clarissa!" gasped Althea. But then she colored even more. "I know what you mean. But," she added, "it's not like that with Mr. Verrall and me yet, and I'm sure I can trust him to be a gentleman."

Clarissa smiled and kissed her. "I'm sure you'll be very happy, no matter what happens."

They both climbed out of bed, and Althea asked, "What of you and the major? It all seemed so strange."

Clarissa didn't want to lie. She looked at Althea and said, "I'm not sure you want to know."

Althea blushed again. "Perhaps I don't. But are you going to marry him?"

"Oh, yes," Clarissa said. "I'm sure I am."

As soon as she was dressed, she hurried downstairs and told Miss Hurstman about Althea's plans, and that she herself was going over to the Vandeimens' house. She was braced for battle, but Miss Hurstman nodded. "I'll come over myself when Althea's on her way. Take the footman, though. Just in case."

So Clarissa was escorted all the way, astonished that she had never considered that she might be in danger. After all, she was the one who was technically in possession of Thérèse Bellaire's money.

She arrived without incident, however, to find that wealth had poured in, but that nothing new had turned up to tell them where the hostages were.

There was a heavy sack of jewels. Some were Blanche's theatrical pieces, but most were real. A great deal of it had come from Lord Arden, including, originally, what Blanche had referred to as Lucien's necklace, which was a ridiculously gaudy piece with huge stones in many colors; it had to be worth thousands.

Clarissa smiled at the friendly, understanding love that had given the White Dove something she would never wear but something that would amuse her, and keep her if she ever fell into need.

A strongbox had come from someone in London, and more from Lord Middlethorpe in Hampshire. Clarissa looked at it all, remembering with some satisfaction that all these people would be paid back from her money.

But then she realized that would mean that Hawk would lose Hawkinville. She could bear that, but she ached for the poor people there, and she knew the pain must be ten times worse for him. Ignoring the presence of all the others, she went to where he sat, clearly furious at himself for not being able to solve the problems single-handedly. Jetta was curled at his feet. Tentatively, Clarissa put her hand on his shoulder.

He started and looked up, then covered her hand with his. "Where do we stand?"

She smiled. She too wanted this clear. "On our own two feet? I suppose that should be four. I meant what I said about using my money to pay everyone back. Even if they resist."

He turned to face her. "I know. It's all right."

"What about Hawkinville?"

"That's not all right, but if it's the price, I'll pay it."

She raised his hand and kissed it. "If you happen to have a ring, I'd be proud to wear it."

He stood, smiling, and produced it, slid it on her finger.

She smiled back at him, not teary at all, but firmly happy that things were right. About this, at least.

"And now," she said, "please solve all our problems, sir."

He groaned, but said, "I don't expect always to do miracles, but in this case I feel that I've missed something."

She sat down beside him. "What if I go over it? She snatched the baby from the Court and brought it to Brighton. Lord Darius and the children had already been brought here by Old Matt. I assume he hasn't said anything?"

"He's dead, love. The alcohol killed him."

It sent a chill through her. One death could so easily be followed by more. He took her hand. "She might not have meant to kill him."

"But she didn't care, did she?"

"No," he admitted. "She didn't care."

She pulled her mind straight and tried to help him again. "She sent a note . . ."

But he said, "Wait! Smuggler's brandy! Smugglers," he said to the room at large. "Of course! She's linked up with smugglers. She's on a boat."

The room suddenly buzzed, and Susan said, "I know smuggling."

"Do you know any smugglers here?" Hawk asked.

She pulled a face. "No, but my father's name will count."

Even more interesting, thought Clarissa. But she was fizzing with excitement, too.

"Go out and see what you can learn. Con—"

"Of course I'm going with her."

The two men shared a look, then laughed.

The Amleighs left and Hawk paced. "She's on a boat, ready to take off for the Continent as soon as she has the money. I'll go odds she has her hostages on the boat too. No, not on the same boat—on another boat. We need to check the fishermen as well as the smugglers. They're not always the same thing. Van? And see what there is that we can hire. We need to be on the water."

Lord Vandeimen left, and Hawk looked around the room. "I wonder if anyone but Susan knows how to handle a boat."

"She's a smuggler?" Clarissa asked tentatively.

"Just closely connected," said Hawk with a smile that was partly excitement. "We've cut through her lines at last. We'll have this all tight by evening."

Time returned to creeping in halting steps. Clarissa kept thinking of the children, wondering if they were still drugged—which would be dangerous—or frightened, or hungry. If they were on a boat, were they safe or could they fall overboard and drown? Were there rats?

She knew it must be much worse for the Delaneys, but they seemed to have found a stoic calm as they waited.

Con and Susan returned first. "I made contact eventually," Susan said. "I had to persuade Con to go away. He has far too much of a military look about him. I put the word out and offered a reward, but no one would say anything directly. They'll send word here if there's anything."

"Can you sail a fishing boat?" Hawk asked.

"Of course," she said, as if it were the most common thing.

"We weren't all raised by the sea, you know. With any luck, Van has found us a boat. We need to be on the water this evening when the payment is made." He looked out of the window at the sea, choppy and gray on this miserable day. There were plenty of boats bobbing at anchor. Clarissa wondered which ones held the villain and the hostages, and what would happen if they searched them all.

Disaster, probably.

Then Lord Vandeimen returned. "The *Pretty Anna*," he said, eyes bright. "I can point it out."

"We've hired it?" Hawk asked.

"No. We've hired the *Seahorse*. The *Pretty Anna* is probably where Dare and the children are. The young man who owns it has been acting strange recently. Not going out fishing on good days, disappearing now and then. Talking about traveling. Yesterday he talked to one man about selling the *Pretty Anna* to him."

"Show us."

Everyone crowded to the window, and Lord Vandeimen pointed out one small boat among many, but that one had the dull glimmer of a lantern, showing that someone must be on board.

"Can we go?" Eleanor asked. "Now?"

But there was a new knock on the door. There seemed to be a confusion of footsteps, then the door opened. "A message for Mr. Delaney," the footman announced, the paper on a silver tray.

Nicholas strode over to take it.

"And," intoned the footman, "there's a man at the back door asking after Lady Amleigh."

Susan rushed out, pushing the footman out of the way. Someone shut the door on him. Everyone looked at Nicholas.

"She must have caught wind of our tack. It's the *Pretty Anna*, now, with whatever valuables we have. No promise of telling us where the hostages are."

He looked at Clarissa. "You and I are to take the ransom, dressed in only the lightest clothes."

"Clarissa?" said Hawk. "That's not acceptable."

"I agree," said Nicholas. "I'll go alone."

"No. If she wants me, I have to go. We can't risk the children."

"She probably has no intention of telling us where they are," Hawk said. "And with luck, we can find them with the other boat."

"Luck is not acceptable."

"Use some sense! She'll probably take you as a new hostage."

"I'd die first," said Nicholas.

"So you'd be dead. What good would that be?"

Silence crackled.

Clarissa put her hands on his arm. "Hawk, I have to go. With or without your blessing."

He glared at her, but then brought himself under control. "All right. I go with Susan. I'm a strong swimmer. If we can close, I can swim over."

"You'll need weapons," Nicholas said.

Hawk's knife appeared in his hand.

Nicholas said, "I have something similar upstairs. But Clarissa could do with one too."

Clarissa shook her head. "I can't use a knife on someone."

"You can if you have to."

"I'll get something from the kitchen," Maria said and hurried away.

Susan came in, bright with excitement. "We've got her! She's paying Sam Pilcher to take her to France. He has a fast cutter he claims can outrun the navy. He was taken with her charms, but he's beginning to wonder."

"Is she on the boat now?" Nicholas asked.

"No. He's just been sent word that she'll be there in the hour. But," she added, "he swears there's no one else on the boat now. He'll take someone of ours out there to capture her."

"I'll go," said Lord Vandeimen, clearly itching for action.

"And I," said Major Beaumont.

Susan went out with them to introduce them. Clarissa heard her instructing them not to act like military men.

"So," said Hawk, "she has them on the *Pretty Anna*. She'll plan to take the money there, then probably be rowed over to the other ship. Susan can block that as soon as we have the hostages. I don't think it will be so easy."

"She'll take Arabel with her," Nicholas suggested.

"It's possible. You have to kill her, you know. She's a viper. You can't take her to court, and if she gets away you'll never know when she'll be back, more vengeful than before."

"You can't doubt I will if necessary."

Maria came back with a handful of knives. "Cook's in tears."

The note specified that Clarissa was to wear only a dress—no spencer or cloak. Nicholas was to be in breeches and shirt. Few places to hide weapons. No place to hide a pistol.

Soon Clarissa had a narrow knife tucked down her gown in front of her corset, carefully pinned in place in a kind of sheath. The heavy linen protected her from the blade, but she could feel it, hard and unnatural.

"I still don't think I could use it," she said to Hawk, who had put it there without a hint that he found it arousing.

He looked at her, all officer. "Don't let her hurt you without a fight. Go for the face. She's vain. For the eyes with your fingers and nails. If this works properly, however, I'll be there to take care of you."

He kissed her fiercely and left with Con and Susan for the *Seahorse*. Clarissa saw Jetta streak to catch up and hoped the cat truly was descended from an ancient Chinese warrior line.

Nicholas had two knives tucked away. They gathered the money and jewels into a heavy leather bag.

"We'll delay a little," he said to Clarissa. "Give the others time. But we can't wait too long. All right?"

Clarissa felt the electricity of fear, and wasn't sure if it was bad or good. "Yes. I suffer terribly from impatience, though. I want to get on with it."

"Let's go, then." He went to kiss his wife.

As he swept Clarissa out of the room, however, she saw the expression on Eleanor Delaney's face. She looked as if she feared that she would never see her husband again.

Chapter Thirty

The rain was a weary drizzle, soft but chill. They crossed the deserted Parade to the seafront, then headed right. "Now that we're out here there's no need to hurry. She's probably watching through a telescope, and if she sees we're doing the right things, it will be all right."

Clarissa scanned the choppy gray sea for Hawk and Susan, but there were so many boats, and she couldn't even tell if most of them were moving or not.

"Why did Eleanor look so very frightened?" she asked. "Did she think we're to be murdered?" She was proud of her level tone.

Nicholas looked at her. "It's old history. I got on a boat with Thérèse Bellaire once before and she didn't see me for six months. She thought I was dead. We're on a basis of truth, aren't we? The truth is that Thérèse might want me dead, but she certainly wants to taunt me, to finally prove that she can win. I don't think she wishes you harm. I think she wants a witness, and she'll be as unpleasant, as lewd, as she can be. I'm sorry."

"It's not your fault."

"Who can say? If I'd had the sense not to dally with her so many years ago . . . Hawk was right, though. If necessary, don't hesitate to hurt her."

He stopped and looked out to sea. "That's the *Pretty Anna,* and there's our boat." He pointed to a dinghy tied up at a wooden jetty.

"All details taken care of," she said, and they hurried in that direction.

Clarissa shivered. In part it was because the rain had soaked her light dress, and the breeze was cold. It was also because of that waiting boat, because they were walking a path created by the evil Madame Bellaire.

She scanned the water again and saw no other boat swooping in. Of course it was too soon.

Their footsteps rattled on the uneven planks of the jetty, and then they were above the boat, a rough wooden ladder leading down.

"Can you manage it?" Nicholas asked.

"I'll have to, won't I?"

"I'll go first," he said, and climbed nimbly down with the bag of loot.

Clarissa took a deep breath and eased herself over onto the ladder. "Give thanks," she said, "that Miss Mallory's School for Ladies believes in physical exercise and womanly strength."

The ladder was rough beneath her hands, and the wind swirled, seeming to snatch at her, making her skirts snag on rough edges. She went steadily down, letting the fine cotton rip if it had to. Another dress ruined.

At the bottom, Nicholas gripped her waist and eased her into the swaying, bouncing boat. He settled her on one bench, then took the other and swung the oars over the water.

She clung to the sides, feeling sure it would tip with the next wave. "I've never been in a boat before."

"There are worse things," he said with a smile, and started to pull.

"I can't swim, either." The boat bucked, and she held on tighter, determined not to scream. Were they making any progress against this rough water? And how was everyone else? The children. Lord Darius. Hawk.

From above, the sea had seemed choppy. From down here, the waves seemed huge.

"Hawk said he would *swim* in this?"

"He'll be all right," Nicholas said, rowing in an easy rhythm. "He said he is a strong swimmer, and I don't think he's the boastful type."

A wave slapped and drenched her hand. They were getting nearer to the *Pretty Anna,* but not quickly enough for her. A viper waited, and perhaps a test of courage, but it looked so much more solid than this swaying, bouncing little boat.

Nicholas's drenched shirt clung to his body, a body, she noted, as well made as Hawk's. It pleased her, but it didn't excite her. Please, God, let Hawk be safe. Please, God, let them save the children and Lord Darius.

Please, if that's what it takes, let the Frenchwoman have the jewels and money, and go. Go far, far away. She knew Hawk wanted her stopped, but Clarissa was with Nicholas in simply wanting this over.

"Do you see anything?" Nicholas asked.

Clarissa snapped out of her thoughts and looked at the boat, twenty feet away. "No sign of anyone."

"Keep looking."

She scanned the simple boat with the small shedlike room and a tall mast. A lantern bobbed, but the vessel looked completely empty. If Nicholas was right that Thérèse Bellaire wanted to gloat, she had to be there somewhere.

Their boat jarred against the *Anna,* and Nicholas tied it up close to a ladder. "I'd better go first," he said.

"No," said a familiar French voice. "The girl first, with the ransom."

Clarissa started to shake and tried desperately not to. After a shared look with Nicholas, she put the satchel across her chest and gripped the ladder. It was harder going up than down. She felt heavy, and her hands were aching with cold. She made it, though, and scrambled over the top to tumble awkwardly onto the deck.

She struggled to her feet. "I'm here," she said, wishing her voice didn't shake. "With the money."

She heard a sound and whirled, but it was only Nicholas beside her.

"Thérèse?" he said, sounding completely at ease. "At your service, as always."

A woman ducked out of the small covered area. She wore an encompassing cloak, but Clarissa could hardly believe it was Mrs. Rowland. The skin was clear, and even glowing in the chilly air. The eyes seemed huge, the lips full and red. In a chilling way, she was very beautiful.

"Nicky, darling," she said. And he'd been right. She was gloating. Clarissa fought a desperate battle not to look around for the *Seahorse,* which carried Susan and Hawk.

The woman stepped a little closer, and a man emerged behind her. A handsome man. Young, but tall and strong, and with a pistol in his hand.

"These the ones, then?" he said in a local accent. "The ones who stole your money?"

"Yes," she purred. "But they have returned part of it, so we need not be too harsh. Come forward, my dear, and give me the bag."

Clarissa shrugged it off so it was in her hands, then walked forward. She suspected what was going to happen here. When she got close, the man would grab her and Nicholas would be at the woman's mercy.

She dropped the bag on the deck a few feet from the Frenchwoman's feet.

The dark eyes narrowed. "Bring it to me."

"Why? That's it. Take it and go."

"If you don't bring it to me, I will not tell you where the children are, where Lord Darius Debenham is."

"Do I care?" Clarissa asked, drawing on experience of the most silly, heartless schoolgirls she'd ever known. "You're taking my money. You say it's yours, but it's mine, and you're stealing it."

The young man started to speak, and Thérèse hissed at him to be silent. "It is *mine*. I worked hard for that money, and you did nothing. Nothing! You didn't even kill Deveril. Now pick up that bag and bring it to me."

"Make me."

Thérèse smiled. "Samuel, shoot the man."

The young man blanched, but his pistol rose.

Clarissa snatched up the bag from the deck.

"That's better," said Thérèse. "You see, it does not pay to fight me. You cannot win. Bring it here."

Clarissa walked forward as slowly as she dared, willing Hawk to appear. She was about to put the bag into the Frenchwoman's hand, when the man said, "Here! What're you doing?"

Clarissa turned to see that Nicholas had unfastened the flap in his breeches and was undoing the drawers beneath. "This is what you want, Thérèse, isn't it?"

The Frenchwoman seemed transfixed. Not by the sight—Clarissa could tell that—but by satisfaction. "Yes. Strip."

Nicholas continued to unfasten his clothing, slowly, seductively. Clarissa realized she was gaping and looked quickly at the young man. He was red-faced. He suddenly jerked the pistol up and aimed it.

Clarissa swung the heavy bag and knocked the weapon flying into the sea.

Samuel howled and rushed at her. She dodged, fell, and quite by accident slipped behind Madame Bellaire so he ran into her.

He howled again, staggering back. Clarissa saw blood.

"Oaf!" the Frenchwoman spat, a bloodstained knife in her hand.

Nicholas had a knife out too, and Clarissa saw a boat sweeping close, sails full. It looked as if it was going to crash into them. Not with the children surely here!

She scrambled up and ran for the shed, but she was grabbed and hauled back. She saw the knife in Madame Bellaire's hand and knew she should be terrified. She thought she heard someone bellow, "Clarissa!"

Hawk.

Go for the eyes. She scratched the woman's face as hard as she could.

The Frenchwoman shrieked and Clarissa was free. She ran, but tripped over the bag of treasure.

Then Madame Bellaire was coming at her again, livid scratches on her face, a face ugly with furious hate.

Nicholas was running forward, but the man Samuel, blood still streaming down his side, threw himself at him.

It all seemed slow, but Clarissa did the only thing she could. She threw the bag.

It hit the woman, staggering her, then fell, spilling gold and jewels.

Madame Bellaire froze for a moment, staring at it. Clarissa fumbled for her knife, catching it on every edge, it seemed, as she struggled to get it free.

Then something jarred the boat, and Hawk landed on the deck. He grabbed the woman's arm, but she twisted, knife lunging. A black shape flew through the air at her face, and she screamed.

Hawk tore the spitting cat away, trapped the woman in his arms, turned her . . .

And threw her, suddenly limp, over the side.

When he turned back, the knife was gone.

It wasn't quiet. The wind rattled the assorted bits of the boat, and the waves slapped hard at the sides. But the people were silent, even the young man, Samuel, who'd been fighting Nicholas in the cause of the woman who had stabbed him.

"What have you done with her?" he cried, and staggered over to look out at the sea.

Hawk and Nicholas looked at each other.

"She was beautiful to me once," Nicholas said, fastening his clothing. "But thank you."

Samuel was weeping.

But then a faint voice cried, "Papa!" and Nicholas ran for the shed that must contain the steps.

Clarissa watched in a daze as the Amleighs climbed over the side of the boat. They must have rowed over. Susan began to do things to the boat, but her husband raced below.

Clarissa looked at Hawk.

He said, "Yes, I killed her. I'm sorry if that upsets you."

"I'll grow accustomed."

He pulled her into his arms. "God, love, I pray not!"

They clung together as things happened around them, and then Nicholas was on deck, a wan child clinging to him, and the boat was under one sail and moving carefully toward the jetty.

Con brought the other two children up, and they huddled close to each other, but Clarissa separated from Hawk and sat down to hold out her arms. After a moment they came forward. Hawk sat beside her, and soon Delphie was in her lap, Pierre in Hawk's.

"Mrs. Rowland," Hawk said gently to them in French, and their eyes dilated. "She is dead. She will not return."

The two children looked at each other, and the boy said, "Papa?"

Clarissa bit her lip.

"Your papa will be fine," Hawk said, but he gave Clarissa a helpless look. She mouthed, "Perhaps we can take care of them?"

He smiled and nodded.

The boat bumped gently against the dock, and Hawk and Clarissa scrambled off, each with a child. She, for one, was deeply grateful for a solid surface beneath her feet. Eleanor was already there, and Nicholas put Arabel into her shaking arms, then held her close. Blanche wrapped a cloak around them both.

Major Beaumont and Lord Vandeimen ran up and helped carry Lord Darius gently off the boat. Though it took three men, it was clear that he weighed little.

The children pulled away from Clarissa and Hawk's arms and pressed close, whispering, "Papa, Papa," and he touched them with his trembling hands, telling them in French that it would be all right. That all these people were their friends. That he would make sure they were all right.

A black cat wound around from Hawk to child to child to child . . .

And Clarissa wept. She wept for love, and courage, and trust, and hope. She wept for weariness, cold, and death. She wept in Hawk's arms as he led her away from horror, back to the Vandeimens' house.

And the Duke and Duchess of Yeovil were there.

At the sight of her son, the duchess half fainted, and then crawled to him. The duke was pale and trembling, but he helped her to sit up, and gripped his son's hand. Delphie and Pierre were tucked close to Lord Darius, as if they'd never leave. Clarissa didn't think they would accept any other home, or that Lord Darius would easily let them go.

She heard him struggle to say, "It's opium, Mama. I'm addicted to opium," and his mother say that it was all right, that he was home now, and she would make sure it was all right.

Clarissa turned to Hawk. "We're home now," she said. "And I believe it will be all right."

"You have my solemn vow on it, my love. Marry me, Falcon."

"Of course."

Heaven suddenly seemed possible, but it was rather alarming, even so, when a knock on the door produced the Duke and Duchess of Belcraven. Slim, cool, and elegant, the duke raised his quizzing glass and looked at her. "I hear alarming things of you, young lady."

Clarissa couldn't help it. She curtsied and said, "Probably all true. I'm delighted you're here, your grace. You'll make it easy for me to marry Major Hawkinville as soon as possible."

"I gather that is a necessity."

"Completely," she said. The duchess laughed and came over to hug her.

The duke's lips twitched, and he looked around. "From the general tone, I assume the valuable items I've brought are not necessary. The Rogues rule the day again?"

"And the Georges," said Hawk, stepping forward to bow. "You doubtless have misgivings, your grace, but I hope you will consent to our marriage. I will do my best to make her happy."

"As I will do my best to ensure that you do, sir. And my best is very formidable indeed. In moments, I wish to see you to discuss the marriage contract." He then went over to talk to the Yeovils and congratulate them on the return of their son.

The legal discussion did not take place in moments. A doctor was summoned for Lord Darius, and rooms were arranged for the Yeovils at the Old Ship. Once the doctor assured the duke and duchess that it was safe, they all left, Lord Darius on a stretcher, two waifs attached. Clarissa recognized that Delphie and Pierre had chosen their own home. Surprisingly, Jetta had too. She leaped onto the stretcher but eyed the children, as if they were her new charges.

All who had been on the water were damp and went to change. Clarissa hated to leave, even for a moment, but Hawk escorted her back to Broad Street for a dry dress, and then brought her and a relieved Miss Hurstman back. Althea and Mr. Verrall had apparently only just left. Clarissa chose to wear the cream-and-rust dress she had worn that first day on the Steyne, the one with the deep fringe. She grinned at Hawk, and raised the skirt a little to show more of her striped stockings.

He shook his head, but his eyes sent another message.

She could wait. Now all was certain, she could wait to lie again with him naked in bed.

Back at the Vandeimens' they found everyone in the riotous high spirits of relief. The ladies were adorning themselves with the jewelry, real and fake. Clarissa acquired a tiara, and Miss Hurstman didn't complain when Nicholas pinned a gaudy brooch onto her plain gown. She had Arabel in her arms by then, and the child, beginning to blossom again, reached for it with delight.

Nicholas laughed and gave his daughter Blanche's necklace, which met with her rapturous approval. Clarissa noted a shadow on him at times, however, and remembered him saying, "She was beautiful to me, once."

She knew the death would not rest easily upon Hawk, either, though it could not be the first time he had killed. It was his way, she was sure, to deal with such problems by himself, but in time it would be her blessing to share them with him.

Then they all sat at the dinner table, with candlelight shooting fire from thousands of pounds' worth of jewelry. Hawk rose again, however, and raised his glass. "To friends," he said, "old and new. May we never fail."

Everyone drank the toast, and then Nicholas stood to propose one. "To the Rogues, who in the end, at least, never fail. Dare will be whole again."

Con rose to add to it. "With the help of the Georges." He grinned. "An interesting alliance, wouldn't you say?"

"The world is doubtless tipping on its axis," murmured the Duke of Belcraven, but with a smile, and he drank the toast along with everyone else. He even proposed one himself—a slightly naughty one about marriage, which made his duchess blush.

By the time the dinner was over, the duke remarked that no one was in a state to draw up legal agreements, and made an appointment the next day at the Old Ship, where he, too, had rooms. Clarissa insisted on being present. He gave in in the end, but insisted on seeing Clarissa and Miss Hurstman back to Broad Street.

"We'll have no more impropriety, Clarissa," he said on leaving her there.

She just smiled. "I will try, your grace, though I'm not sure it is in my nature."

She slept deeply and late, awakening to an extraordinary sense of calm—like the calm of the sea on a perfect day, all the power of the oceans still beneath it. She breakfasted with Miss Hurstman and told her the details she'd missed. Miss Hurstman was astonished to find that she'd been regarded as a warder, but rather amused that she'd been thought to be part of a wicked plot.

Hawk came to escort Clarissa to the Old Ship. They strolled along the Marine Parade, by a calm sea touched to blue by the sky and sunshine.

"Do you think summer is here at last?" she asked.

"Carpe diem," he replied with a grin.

She smiled back. "I promised the duke to try to behave. We can marry soon, can't we?"

"Today would not be too soon for me, love."

"Or me. But, Hawk, I would like a village wedding like Maria had. Is it possible?"

He took her hand and kissed it. "I would give you the stars if I could. A village wedding is surely possible."

They entered the hotel in perfect harmony, but Clarissa found that she had to fight to give him enough for his father to fully restore Gaspard Hall.

"Think of it from my point of view," she said. "I want our home to ourselves. If we give your father enough money, perhaps he'll leave immediately to take up the work."

"An excellent point. Hawkinville," said the duke, "consider it settled. In strict legality, all the money should go to your father. If you present difficulties, I may make it so."

Hawk rolled his eyes, but surrendered. "The rest of the money is Clarissa's, however. I want it retained under her control. Once free of debt, the manor will provide for us."

Clarissa didn't argue except to say, "You know I will spend some on our comforts and pleasures. But I do want to use most of it for charity. It has a dark history. I thought perhaps a charity school in Slade's house."

Hawk laughed. "A wonderful idea! He'll doubtless have to sell it to us cheap as well."

"So?" Clarissa asked Hawk. "When do we marry? I am ready to fly."

"It is for the lady to say, but the license will take a few days."

"A week, then, if all can be arranged."

He stood, bringing her to her feet. "It will all be arranged with Hawkish perfection. To do it, though, and to retain my sanity, I'm going to leave." Ignoring the duke, he kissed her. "We have no need to seize the day, love. We have the promise of perfect tomorrows."

"Alliteration?" she murmured, and he winced.

Hawk walked out of the dark church into sunshine, and into a shower of grain and flowers thrown by his boisterous villagers. Everyone smiled at a wedding, but he could see that these smiles reflected delight of an extraordinary degree. Not only was the Young Squire—as they'd decided to call him—married, but the Old Squire had already gone. His father had leased a house near to Gaspard Hall and left without a hint of regret.

The village was free of Slade, too, and the threat they'd all sensed from him. His house would soon be Clarissa's to do with as she wished. The most important repairs to the cottages were already in hand, which was also providing necessary work.

He looked at his bride, glowing with her own perfect happiness as the villagers welcomed her as one of their own. He said a prayer to be worthy, to be able to create the happiness neither of them had ever truly known. It should be easy. She'd had her modiste re-create the simple cream dress that had marked their adventures, and she was wearing a similar hat and fichu. He could hardly wait to strip it off her, in the manor, which sat contentedly waiting, open-windowed in the sun.

He turned from that—it would wait—to accept the congratulations of Van and Con. Susan was definitely with child, and now Maria had hope. It was possible that Clarissa would also have a child in nine months. A new threesome to run wild around the area.

Unable to bear to be apart, he retrieved his bride from among beaming villagers and drew her in for a kiss.

"Give thanks," he said, wondering how soon he could sweep her laughing into his arms and carry her upstairs to a bed covered with smooth sheets fresh from hanging in the sun. "We have hope of heaven."

"Alliteration!" Clarissa pointed out, with a twinkle in her eye that told him her thoughts were perfectly in accord with his.

Enough! He picked her up and spun her around and around. Then, "Enjoy the feast!" he called, and ran for their home.